LITTLE MEN
&
JO'S BOYS

Little Men

Life at Plumfield with Jo's Boys

&

Jo's Boys

And How They Turned Out

LOUISA MAY ALCOTT

WORDSWORTH CLASSICS

For my husband
ANTHONY JOHN RANSON
with love from your wife, the publisher.
Eternally grateful for your unconditional love.

Readers who are interested in other titles from
Wordsworth Editions are invited to visit our website at
www.wordsworth-editions.com

This edition first published in 2009 by
Wordsworth Editions Limited
8B East Street, Ware, Hertfordshire SG12 9HJ

ISBN   978 1 84022 176 3

Text © Wordsworth Editions Limited 2009

Wordsworth® is a registered trade mark of
Wordsworth Editions Limited

Wordsworth Editions
is the company founded in 1987 by
MICHAEL TRAYLER

Typeset in Great Britain by Antony Gray
Printed and bound by Clays Ltd, St Ives plc

Little Men

Life at Plumfield with Jo's Boys

CONTENTS

CHAPTER I

Nat

'Please, sir, is this Plumfield?' asked a ragged boy of the man who opened the great gate at which the omnibus left him.

'Yes. Who sent you?'

'Mr Laurence. I have got a letter for the lady.'

'All right; go up to the house, and give it to her; she'll see to you, little chap.'

The man spoke pleasantly, and the boy went on, feeling much cheered by the words. Through the soft spring rain that fell on sprouting grass and budding trees, Nat saw a large square house before him – a hospitable-looking house, with an old-fashioned porch, wide steps, and lights shining in many windows. Neither curtains nor shutters hid the cheerful glimmer; and, pausing a moment before he rang, Nat saw many little shadows dancing on the walls, heard the pleasant hum of young voices, and felt that it was hardly possible that the light and warmth and comfort within could be for a homeless 'little chap' like him.

'I hope the lady will see to me,' he thought, and gave a timid rap with the great bronze knocker, which was a jovial griffin's head.

A rosy-faced servant-maid opened the door, and smiled as she took the letter which he silently offered. She seemed used to receiving strange boys, for she pointed to a seat in the hall, and said, with a nod: 'Sit there and drip on the mat a bit, while I take this in to missis.'

Nat found plenty to amuse him while he waited, and stared about him curiously, enjoying the view, yet glad to do so unobserved in the dusky recess by the door.

The house seemed swarming with boys, who were beguiling the rainy twilight with all sorts of amusements. There were boys everywhere, 'upstairs and downstairs and in the lady's chamber', apparently, for various open doors showed pleasant groups of big boys, little boys, and middle-sized boys in all stages of evening relaxation, not to say effervescence. Two large rooms on the right were evidently school-rooms, for desks, maps, blackboards, and books were scattered about. An open fire burned on the hearth, and several indolent lads lay on their backs before it, discussing a new cricket-ground, with such animation that their boots waved in the air. A tall youth was practising on the flute in one corner, quite undisturbed by the racket all about him. Two or three others were jumping over the desks, pausing, now and then, to get their breath and laugh at the droll sketches of a little wag who was caricaturing the whole household on a blackboard.

In the room on the left a long supper-table was seen, set forth with great pitchers of new milk, piles of brown and white bread, and perfect stacks of the shiny gingerbread so dear to boyish souls. A flavour of toast was in the air, also suggestions of baked apples, very tantalising to one hungry little nose and stomach.

The hall, however, presented the most inviting prospect of all, for a brisk game of tag was going on in the upper entry. One landing was devoted to marbles, the other to checkers, while the stairs were occupied by a boy reading, a girl singing a lullaby to her doll, two puppies, a kitten, and a constant succession of small boys sliding down the banisters, to the great detriment of their clothes and danger to their limbs.

So absorbed did Nat become in this exciting race, that he ventured farther and farther out of his corner; and when one very lively boy came down so swiftly that he could not stop himself, but fell off the banisters, with a crash that would have broken any head but one rendered nearly as hard as a cannonball by eleven years of constant bumping, Nat forgot himself, and ran up to the fallen rider, expecting to find him half-dead. The boy, however, only winked rapidly for a second, then lay calmly looking up at the new face with a surprised, 'Hello!'

'Hello!' returned Nat, not knowing what else to say, and thinking that form of reply both brief and easy.

'Are you a new boy?' asked the recumbent youth, without stirring.

'Don't know yet.'

'What's your name?'

'Nat Blake.'

'Mine's Tommy Bangs. Come up and have a go, will you?' and

Tommy got upon his legs like one suddenly remembering the duties of hospitality.

'Guess I won't, till I see whether I'm going to stay or not,' returned Nat, feeling the desire to stay increase every moment.

'I say, Demi, here's a new one. Come and see to him,' and the lively Thomas returned to his sport with unabated relish.

At his call, the boy reading on the stairs looked up with a pair of big brown eyes, and after an instant's pause, as if a little shy, he put the book under his arm, and came soberly down to greet the newcomer, who found something very attractive in the pleasant face of this slender, mild-eyed boy.

'Have you seen Aunt Jo?' he asked, as if that was some sort of important ceremony.

'I haven't seen anybody yet but you boys; I'm waiting,' answered Nat.

'Did Uncle Laurie send you?' proceeded Demi, politely, but gravely.

'Mr Laurence did.'

'He is Uncle Laurie; and he always sends nice boys.'

Nat looked gratified at the remark, and smiled, in a way that made his thin face very pleasant. He did not know what to say next, so the two stood staring at one another in friendly silence, till the little girl came up with her doll in her arms. She was very like Demi, only not so tall, and had a rounder, rosier face, and blue eyes.

'This is my sister, Daisy,' announced Demi, as if presenting a rare and precious creature.

The children nodded to one another; and the little girl's face dimpled with pleasure, as she said affably: 'I hope you'll stay. We have such good times here; don't we, Demi?'

'Of course, we do: that's what Aunt Jo has Plumfield for.'

'It seems a very nice place indeed,' observed Nat, feeling that he must respond to these amiable young persons.

'It's the nicest place in the world, isn't it, Demi?' said Daisy, who evidently regarded her brother as authority on all subjects.

'No, I think Greenland, where the icebergs and seals are, is more interesting. But I'm fond of Plumfield, and it *is* a very nice place to be in,' returned Demi, who was interested just now in a book on Greenland. He was about to offer to show Nat the

pictures and explain them, when the servant returned, saying
with a nod toward the parlour door: 'All right; you are to stop.'

'I'm glad; now come to Aunt Jo.' And Daisy took him by the hand
with a pretty protecting air, which made Nat feel at home at once.

Demi returned to his beloved book, while his sister led the newcomer into a back room, where a stout gentleman was frolicking
with two little boys on the sofa, and a thin lady was just finishing
the letter which she seemed to have been re-reading.

'Here he is, Aunty!' cried Daisy.

'So this is my new boy? I am glad to see you, my dear, and
hope you'll be happy here,' said the lady, drawing him to her,
and stroking back the hair from his forehead with a kind hand
and a motherly look, which made Nat's lonely little heart yearn
toward her.

She was not at all handsome, but she had a merry sort of face
that never seemed to have forgotten certain childish ways and
looks, any more than her voice and manner had; and these things,
hard to describe but very plain to see and feel, made her a genial,
comfortable kind of person, easy to get on with, and generally
'jolly', as boys would say. She saw the little tremble of Nat's lips as
she smoothed his hair, and her keen eyes grew softer, but she only
drew the shabby figure nearer and said, laughing, 'I am Mother
Bhaer, that gentleman is Father Bhaer, and these are the two little
Bhaers. Come here, boys, and see Nat.'

The three wrestlers obeyed at once; and the stout man, with a
chubby child on each shoulder, came up to welcome the new boy.
Rob and Teddy merely grinned at him, but Mr Bhaer shook
hands, and pointing to a low chair near the fire, said in a cordial
voice, 'There is a place all ready for thee, my son; sit down and
dry thy wet feet at once.'

'Wet? So they are! My dear, off with your shoes this minute, and
I'll have some dry things ready for you in a jiffy,' cried Mrs Bhaer,
bustling about so energetically that Nat found himself in the cosy
little chair, with dry socks and warm slippers on his feet, before he
would have had time to say Jack Robinson, if he had wanted to try.
He said 'Thank you, ma'am,' instead; and said it so gratefully that
Mrs Bhaer's eyes grew soft again, and she said something merry,
because she felt so tender, which was a way she had.

'These are Tommy Bangs' slippers; but he never will remember to put them on in the house; so he shall not have them. They are too big; but that's all the better; you can't run away from us so fast as if they fitted.'

'I don't want to run away, ma'am.' And Nat spread his grimy little hands before the comfortable blaze, with a long sigh of satisfaction.

'That's good! Now I am going to toast you well, and try to get rid of that ugly cough. How long have you had it, dear?' asked Mrs Bhaer, as she rummaged in her big basket for a strip of flannel.

'All winter. I got cold, and it wouldn't get better, somehow.'

'No wonder, living in that damp cellar with hardly a rag to his poor dear back!' said Mrs Bhaer, in a low tone to her husband, who was looking at the boy with a skilful pair of eyes that marked the thin temples and feverish lips, as well as the hoarse voice and frequent fits of coughing that shook the bent shoulders under the patched jacket.

'Robin, my man, trot up to Nursey, and tell her to give thee the cough-bottle and the liniment,' said Mr Bhaer, after his eyes had exchanged telegrams with his wife's.

Nat looked a little anxious at the preparations, but forgot his fears in a hearty laugh, when Mrs Bhaer whispered to him, with a droll look, 'Hear my rogue Teddy try to cough. The syrup I'm going to give you has honey in it, and he wants some.'

Little Ted was red in the face with his exertions by the time the bottle came, and was allowed to suck the spoon after Nat had manfully taken a dose and had the bit of flannel put about his throat.

These first steps toward a cure were hardly completed when a great bell rang, and a loud tramping through the hall announced supper. Bashful Nat quaked at the thought of meeting many strange boys, but Mrs Bhaer held out her hand to him, and Rob said, patronisingly, 'Don't be 'fraid; I'll take care of you.'

Twelve boys, six on a side, stood behind their chairs, prancing with impatience to begin, while the tall flute-playing youth was trying to curb their ardour. But no one sat down till Mrs Bhaer was in her place behind the teapot, with Teddy on her left, and Nat on her right.

'This is our new boy, Nat Blake. After supper you can say how do you do? Gently, boys, gently.'

As she spoke everyone stared at Nat, and then whisked into their seats, trying to be orderly and failing utterly. The Bhaers did their best to have the lads behave well at meal times, and generally succeeded pretty well, for their rules were few and sensible, and the boys, knowing that they tried to make things easy and happy, did their best to obey. But there are times when hungry boys cannot be repressed without real cruelty, and Saturday evening, after a half-holiday, was one of those times.

'Dear little souls, do let them have one day in which they can howl and racket and frolic to their hearts' content. A holiday isn't a holiday without plenty of freedom and fun; and they shall have full swing once a week,' Mrs Bhaer used to say, when prim people wondered why banister sliding, pillow fights, and all manner of jovial games were allowed under the once decorous roof of Plumfield.

It did seem at times as if the aforesaid roof was in danger of flying off, but it never did, for a word from Father Bhaer could at any time produce a lull, and the lads had learned that liberty must not be abused. So, in spite of many dark predictions, the school flourished, and manners and morals were insinuated, without the pupils exactly knowing how it was done.

Nat found himself very well off behind the tall pitchers, with Tommy Bangs just around the corner, and Mrs Bhaer close by to fill up plate and mug as fast as he could empty them.

'Who is that boy next the girl down at the other end?' whispered Nat to his young neighbour under cover of a general laugh.

'That's Demi Brooke. Mr Bhaer is his uncle.'

'What a queer name!'

'His real name is John, but they call him Demi-John, because his father is John too. That's a joke, don't you see?' said Tommy, kindly explaining. Nat did not see, but politely smiled, and asked, with interest, 'Isn't he a very nice boy?'

'I bet you he is; knows lots and reads like anything.'

'Who is the fat one next him?'

'Oh, that's Stuffy Cole. His name is George, but we call him Stuffy 'cause he eats so much. The little fellow next Father Bhaer is his boy Rob, and then there's big Franz his nephew; he teaches some, and kind of sees to us.'

'He plays the flute, doesn't he?' asked Nat as Tommy rendered himself speechless by putting a whole baked apple into his mouth at one blow.

Tommy nodded, and said, sooner than one would have imagined possible under the circumstances, 'Oh, don't he, though? And we dance sometimes, and do gymnastics to music. I like a drum myself, and mean to learn as soon as ever I can.'

'I like a fiddle best; I can play one too,' said Nat, getting confidential on this attractive subject.

'Can you?' and Tommy stared over the rim of his mug with round eyes, full of interest. 'Mr Bhaer's got an old fiddle, and he'll let you play on it if you want to.'

'Could I? Oh, I would like it ever so much. You see, I used to go round fiddling with my father, and another man, till he died.'

'Wasn't that fun?' cried Tommy, much impressed.

'No, it was horrid; so cold in winter, and hot in summer. And I got tired; and they were cross sometimes; and I didn't get enough to eat.' Nat paused to take a generous bite of gingerbread, as if to assure himself that the hard times were over; and then he added regretfully, 'But I did love my little fiddle, and I miss it. Nicolo took it away when father died, and wouldn't have me any longer, 'cause I was sick.'

'You'll belong to the band if you play good. See if you don't.'

'Do you have a band here?' Nat's eyes sparkled.

'Guess we do; a jolly band, all boys; and they have concerts and things. You just see what happens tomorrow night.'

After this pleasantly exciting remark, Tommy returned to his supper, and Nat sank into a blissful reverie over his full plate.

Mrs Bhaer had heard all they said, while apparently absorbed in filling mugs, and overseeing little Ted, who was so sleepy that he put his spoon in his eye, nodded like a rosy poppy, and finally fell fast asleep, with his cheek pillowed on a soft bun. Mrs Bhaer had put Nat next to Tommy, because that roly-poly boy had a frank and social way with him, very attractive to shy persons. Nat felt this, and had made several small confidences during supper, which gave Mrs Bhaer the key to the new boy's character, better than if she had talked to him herself.

In the letter which Mr Laurence had sent with Nat, he had said:

DEAR JO – Here is a case after your own heart. This poor lad is an orphan now, sick and friendless. He has been a street musician; and I found him in a cellar, mourning for his dead father, and his lost violin. I think there is something in him, and have a fancy that between us we may give this little man a lift. You cure his over-tasked body, Fritz help his neglected mind, and when he is ready I'll see if he is a genius or only a boy with a talent which may earn his bread for him. Give him a trial, for the sake of your own boy,

TEDDY

'Of course we will!' cried Mrs Bhaer, as she read the letter; and when she saw Nat she felt at once that, whether he was a genius or not, here was a lonely, sick boy who needed just what she loved to give, a home and motherly care. Both she and Mr Bhaer observed him quietly; and in spite of ragged clothes, awkward manners, and a dirty face, they saw much about Nat that pleased them. He was a thin, pale boy, of twelve, with blue eyes, and a good forehead under the rough, neglected hair; an anxious, scared face at times, as if he expected hard words, or blows; and a sensitive mouth that trembled when a kind glance fell on him; while a gentle speech called up a look of gratitude, very sweet to see. 'Bless the poor dear, he shall fiddle all day long if he likes,' said Mrs Bhaer to herself, as she saw the eager, happy expression on his face when Tommy talked of the band.

So, after supper, when the lads flocked into the school-room for more 'high jinks', Mrs Jo appeared with a violin in her hand, and after a word with her husband, went to Nat, who sat in a corner watching the scene with intense interest.

'Now, my lad, give us a little tune. We want a violin in our band, and I think you will do it nicely.'

She expected that he would hesitate; but he seized the old fiddle at once, and handled it with such loving care it was plain to see that music was his passion.

'I'll do the best I can, ma'am,' was all he said; and then drew the bow across the strings, as if eager to hear the dear notes again.

There was a great clatter in the room, but as if deaf to any sounds but those he made, Nat played softly to himself, forgetting everything in his delight. It was only a simple melody, such as street musicians play, but it caught the ears of the boys at once, and silenced them, till they stood listening with surprise and pleasure. Gradually they got nearer and nearer, and Mr Bhaer came up to watch the boy; for, as if he was in his element now, Nat played away and never minded anyone, while his eyes shone, his cheeks reddened, and his thin fingers flew, as he hugged the old fiddle and made it speak to all their hearts the language that he loved.

A hearty round of applause rewarded him better than a shower of pennies, when he stopped and glanced about him, as if to say, 'I've done my best; please like it.'

'I say, you do that first-rate,' cried Tommy, who considered Nat his protégé.

'You shall be the first fiddle in my band,' added Franz, with an approving smile.

Mrs Bhaer whispered to her husband, 'Teddy is right: there's something in the child.' And Mr Bhaer nodded his head emphatically, as he clapped Nat on the shoulder, saying heartily, 'You play well, my son. Come now and play something which we can sing.'

It was the proudest, happiest minute of the poor boy's life when he was led to the place of honour by the piano, and the lads gathered round, never heeding his poor clothes, but eying him respectfully and waiting eagerly to hear him play again.

They chose a song he knew; and after one or two false starts they got going, and violin, flute, and piano led a chorus of boyish voices that made the old roof ring again. It was too much for Nat, more feeble than he knew; and as the final shout died away, his face began to work, he dropped the fiddle, and turning to the wall sobbed like a little child.

'My dear, what is it?' asked Mrs Bhaer, who had been singing with all her might, and trying to keep little Rob from beating time with his boots.

'You are all so kind and it's so beautiful I can't help it,' sobbed Nat, coughing till he was breathless.

'Come with me, dear; you must go to bed and rest; you are worn out, and this is too noisy a place for you,' whispered Mrs Bhaer; and took him away to her own parlour, where she let him cry himself quiet.

Then she won him to tell her all his troubles, and listened to the little story with tears in her own eyes, though it was not a new one to her.

'My child, you *have* got a father and a mother now, and this is home. Don't think of those sad times any more, but get well and happy; and be sure you shall never suffer again, if we can help it. This place is made for all sorts of boys to have a good time in, and to learn how to help themselves and be useful men, I hope. You shall have as much music as you want, only you must get strong first. Now come up to Nursey and have a bath, and then go to bed, and tomorrow we will lay some nice little plans together.'

Nat held her hand fast in his, but had not a word to say, and let his grateful eyes speak for him, as Mrs Bhaer led him up to a big room, where they found a stout German woman with a face so round and cheery that it looked like a sort of sun, with the wide frill of her cap for rays.

'This is Nursey Hummel, and she will give you a nice bath, and cut your hair, and make you all "comfy", as Rob says. That's the bathroom in there; and on Saturday nights we scrub all the little lads first, and pack them away in bed before the big ones get through singing. Now then, Rob, in with you.'

As she talked, Mrs Bhaer had whipped off Rob's clothes and popped him into a long bathtub in the little room opening into the nursery.

There were two tubs, besides footbaths, basins, douche-pipes, and all manner of contrivances for cleanliness. Nat was soon luxuriating in the other bath; and while simmering there, he watched the performances of the two women, who scrubbed, clean night-gowned, and bundled into bed four or five small boys, who, of course, cut up all sorts of capers during the operation, and kept everyone in a gale of merriment till they were extinguished in their beds.

By the time Nat was washed and done up in a blanket by the fire, while Nursey cut his hair, a new detachment of boys arrived and were shut into the bathroom, where they made as much splashing and noise as a school of young whales at play.

'Nat had better sleep here, so that if his cough troubles him in the night you can see that he takes a good draught of flaxseed tea,' said Mrs Bhaer, who was flying about like a distracted hen with a large brood of lively ducklings.

Nursey approved the plan, finished Nat off with a flannel night-gown, a drink of something warm and sweet, and then tucked him into one of the three little beds standing in the room, where he lay looking like a contented mummy and feeling that nothing more in the way of luxury could be offered him. Cleanliness in itself was a new and delightful sensation; flannel gowns were unknown comforts in his world; sips of 'good stuff' soothed his cough as pleasantly as kind words did his lonely heart; and the feeling that somebody cared for him made that plain room seem a sort of heaven to the homeless child. It was like a cosy dream; and he often shut his eyes to see if it would not vanish when he opened them again. It was too pleasant to let him sleep, and he could not have done so if he had tried, for in a few minutes one of the peculiar institutions of Plumfield was revealed to his astonished but appreciative eyes.

A momentary lull in the aquatic exercises was followed by the sudden appearance of pillows flying in all directions, hurled by white goblins, who came rioting out of their beds. The battle raged in several rooms, all down the upper hall, and even surged at intervals into the nursery, when some hard-pressed warrior took refuge there. No one seemed to mind this explosion in the least; no one forbade it, or even looked surprised. Nursey went on hanging up towels, and Mrs Bhaer laid out clean clothes, as calmly as if the most perfect order reigned. Nay, she even chased one daring boy out of the room, and fired after him the pillow he had slyly thrown at her.

'Won't they hurt 'em?' asked Nat, who lay laughing with all his might.

'Oh dear, no! We always allow one pillow fight Saturday night. The cases are changed tomorrow; and it gets up a glow after the boys' baths; so I rather like it myself,' said Mrs Bhaer, busy again among her dozen pairs of socks.

'What a very nice school this is!' observed Nat, in a burst of admiration.

'It's an odd one,' laughed Mrs Bhaer, 'but you see we don't believe in making children miserable by too many rules, and too much study. I forbade nightgown parties at first; but, bless you, it

was of no use. I could no more keep those boys in their beds than
so many jacks in the box. So I made an agreement with them: I
was to allow a fifteen-minute pillow fight every Saturday night;
and they promised to go properly to bed every other night. I tried
it, and it worked well. If they don't keep their word, no frolic; if
they do, I just turn the glasses round, put the lamps in safe places,
and let them rampage as much as they like.'

'It's a beautiful plan,' said Nat, feeling that he should like to join
in the fray, but not venturing to propose it the first night. So he
lay enjoying the spectacle, which certainly was a lively one.

Tommy Bangs led the assailing party, and Demi defended his
own room with a dogged courage fine to see, collecting pillows
behind him as fast as they were thrown, till the besiegers were out
of ammunition, when they would charge upon him in a body, and
recover their arms. A few slight accidents occurred, but nobody
minded, and gave and took sounding thwacks with perfect good
humour, while pillows flew like big snowflakes, till Mrs Bhaer
looked at her watch, and called out: 'Time is up, boys. Into bed,
every man jack, or pay the forfeit!'

'What is the forfeit?' asked Nat, sitting up in his eagerness to
know what happened to those wretches who disobeyed this most
peculiar, but public-spirited schoolma'am.

'Lose their fun next time,' answered Mrs Bhaer. 'I give them
five minutes to settle down, then put out the lights, and expect
order. They are honourable lads, and they keep their word.'

That was evident, for the battle ended as abruptly as it began – a
parting shot or two, a final cheer, as Demi fired the seventh pillow
at the retiring foe, a few challenges for next time, then order
prevailed. And nothing but an occasional giggle or a suppressed
whisper broke the quiet which followed the Saturday-night frolic,
as Mother Bhaer kissed her new boy and left him to happy dreams
of life at Plumfield.

CHAPTER 2

The Boys

While Nat takes a good long sleep, I will tell my little readers something about the boys, among whom he found himself when he woke up.

To begin with our old friends. Franz was a tall lad, of sixteen now, a regular German, big, blond, and bookish, also very domestic, amiable, and musical. His uncle was fitting him for college, and his aunt for a happy home of his own hereafter, because she carefully fostered in him gentle manners, love of children, respect for women, old and young, and helpful ways about the house. He was her right-hand man on all occasions, steady, kind, and patient; and he loved his merry aunt like a mother, for such she had tried to be to him.

Emil was quite different, being quick-tempered, restless, and enterprising, bent on going to sea, for the blood of the old Vikings stirred in his veins, and could not be tamed. His uncle promised that he should go when he was sixteen, and set him to studying navigation, gave him stories of good and famous admirals and heroes to read, and let him lead the life of a frog in river, pond, and brook, when lessons were done. His room looked like the cabin of a man-of-war, for everything was nautical, military, and shipshape. Captain Kyd was his delight, and his favourite amusement was to rig up like that piratical gentleman, and roar out sanguinary sea-songs at the top of his voice. He would dance nothing but sailors' hornpipes, rolled in his gait, and was as nautical in conversation as his uncle would permit. The boys called him 'Commodore', and took great pride in his fleet, which whitened the pond and suffered disasters that would have daunted any commander but a sea-struck boy.

Demi was one of the children who show plainly the effect of intelligent love and care, for soul and body worked harmoniously together. The natural refinement which nothing but home

influence can teach, gave him sweet and simple manners: his
mother had cherished an innocent and loving heart in him; his
father had watched over the physical growth of his boy, and kept
the little body straight and strong on wholesome food and
exercise and sleep, while Grandpa March cultivated the little mind
with the tender wisdom of a modern Pythagoras, not tasking it
with long, hard lessons, parrot-learned, but helping it to unfold as
naturally and beautifully as sun and dew help roses bloom. He was
not a perfect child, by any means, but his faults were of the better
sort; and being early taught the secret of self-control, he was not
left at the mercy of appetites and passions, as some poor little
mortals are, and then punished for yielding to the temptations
against which they have no armour. A quiet, quaint boy was Demi,
serious, yet cheery, quite unconscious that he was unusually bright
and beautiful, yet quick to see and love intelligence or beauty in
other children. Very fond of books, and full of lively fancies, born
of a strong imagination and a spiritual nature, these traits made
his parents anxious to balance them with useful knowledge and
healthful society, lest they should make him one of those pale
precocious children who amaze and delight a family sometimes,
and fade away like hothouse flowers, because the young soul
blooms too soon, and has not a hearty body to root it firmly in the
wholesome soil of this world.

So Demi was transplanted to Plumfield, and took so kindly to the
life there, that Meg and John and Grandpa felt satisfied that they
had done well. Mixing with other boys brought out the practical
side of him, roused his spirit, and brushed away the pretty cobwebs
he was so fond of spinning in that little brain of his. To be sure, he
rather shocked his mother when he came home, by banging doors,
saying 'by George' emphatically, and demanding tall thick boots
'that clumped like papa's'. But John rejoiced over him, laughed at
his explosive remarks, got the boots, and said contentedly, 'He is
doing well, so let him clump. I want my son to be a manly boy,
and this temporary roughness won't hurt him. We can polish him
up by and by; and as for learning, he will pick that up as pigeons
do peas. So don't hurry him.'

Daisy was as sunshiny and charming as ever, with all sorts of
womanlinesses budding in her, for she was like her gentle mother,
and delighted in domestic things. She had a family of dolls, whom

she brought up in the most exemplary manner; she could not get on without her little work-basket and bits of sewing, which she did so nicely, that Demi frequently pulled out his handkerchief to display her neat stitches, and Baby Josy had a flannel petticoat beautifully made by Sister Daisy. She liked to quiddle about the china closet, prepare the salt cellars, put the spoons straight on the table; and every day went round the parlour with her brush, dusting chairs and tables. Demi called her a 'Betty', but was very glad to have her keep his things in order, lend him her nimble fingers in all sorts of work, and help him with his lessons, for they kept abreast there, and had no thought of rivalry.

The love between them was as strong as ever; and no one could laugh Demi out of his affectionate ways with Daisy. He fought her battles valiantly, and never could understand why boys should be ashamed to say 'right out' that they loved their sisters. Daisy adored her twin, thought 'my brother' the most remarkable boy in the world, and every morning, in her little wrapper, trotted to tap at his door with a motherly 'Get up, my dear, it's 'most breakfast time; and here's your clean collar.'

Rob was an energetic morsel of a boy, who seemed to have discovered the secret of perpetual motion, for he never was still. Fortunately, he was not mischievous, nor very brave; so he kept out of trouble pretty well, and vibrated between father and mother like an affectionate little pendulum with a lively tick, for Rob was a chatterbox.

Teddy was too young to play a very important part in the affairs of Plumfield, yet he had his little sphere, and filled it beautifully. Everyone felt the need of a pet at times, and Baby was always ready to accommodate, for kissing and cuddling suited him excellently. Mrs Jo seldom stirred without him; so he had his little finger in all the domestic pies, and everyone found them all the better for it, for they believed in babies at Plumfield.

Dick Brown, and Adolphus or Dolly Pettingill, were two eight year-olds. Dolly stuttered badly, but was gradually getting over it, for no one was allowed to mock him and Mr Bhaer tried to cure it, by making him talk slowly. Dolly was a good little lad, quite uninteresting and ordinary, but he flourished here, and went through his daily duties and pleasures with placid content and propriety.

Dick Brown's affliction was a crooked back, yet he bore his burden so cheerfully, that Demi once asked in his queer way, 'Do humps make people good-natured? I'd like one if they do.' Dick was always merry, and did his best to be like other boys, for a plucky spirit lived in the feeble little body. When he first came, he was very sensitive about his misfortune, but soon learned to forget it, for no one dared remind him of it, after Mr Bhaer had punished one boy for laughing at him.

'God don't care; for my soul is straight if my back isn't,' sobbed Dick to his tormentor on that occasion; and, by cherishing this idea, the Bhaers soon led him to believe that people also loved his soul, and did not mind his body, except to pity and help him to bear it.

Playing menagerie once with the others, someone said, 'What animal will you be, Dick?'

'Oh, I'm the dromedary; don't you see the hump on my back?' was the laughing answer.

'So you are, my nice little one that don't carry loads, but marches by the elephant first in the procession,' said Demi, who was arranging the spectacle.

'I hope others will be as kind to the poor dear as my boys have learned to be,' said Mrs Jo, quite satisfied with the success of her teaching, as Dick ambled past her, looking like a very happy, but a very feeble little dromedary, beside stout Stuffy, who did the elephant with ponderous propriety.

Jack Ford was a sharp, rather a sly lad, who was sent to this school because it was cheap. Many men would have thought him a smart boy, but Mr Bhaer did not like his way of illustrating that Yankee word, and thought his unboyish keenness and money-loving as much of an affliction as Dolly's stutter, or Dick's hump.

Ned Barker was like a thousand other boys of fourteen, all legs, blunder, and bluster. Indeed the family called him the 'Blunder-buss', and always expected to see him tumble over the chairs, bump against the tables, and knock down any small articles near him. He bragged a good deal about what he could do, but seldom did anything to prove it, was not brave, and a little given to tale-telling. He was apt to bully the small boys, and flatter the big ones, and without being at all bad, was just the sort of fellow who could very easily be led astray.

George Cole had been spoilt by an over-indulgent mother, who stuffed him with sweetmeats till he was sick, and then thought him too delicate to study, so that at twelve years old, he was a pale, puffy boy, dull, fretful, and lazy. A friend persuaded her to send him to Plumfield, and there he soon got waked up, for sweet things were seldom allowed, much exercise required, and study made so pleasant, that Stuffy was gently lured along, till he quite amazed his anxious mamma by his improvement, and convinced her that there was really something remarkable in Plumfield air.

Billy Ward was what the Scotch tenderly call an 'innocent', for though thirteen years old, he was like a child of six. He had been an unusually intelligent boy, and his father had hurried him on too fast, giving him all sorts of hard lessons, keeping at his books six hours a day, and expecting him to absorb knowledge as a Strasburg goose does the food crammed down its throat. He thought he was doing his duty, but he nearly killed the boy, for a fever gave the poor child a sad holiday, and when he recovered, the overtasked brain gave out, and Billy's mind was like a slate over which a sponge has passed, leaving it blank.

It was a terrible lesson to his ambitious father; he could not bear the sight of his promising child changed to a feeble idiot, and he sent him away to Plumfield, scarcely hoping that he could be helped, but sure that he would be kindly treated. Quite docile and harmless was Billy, and it was pitiful to see how hard he tried to learn, as if groping dimly after the lost knowledge which had cost him so much.

Day after day, he pored over the alphabet, proudly said A and B, and thought that he knew them, but on the morrow they were gone, and all the work was to be done over again. Mr Bhaer had infinite patience with him, and kept on in spite of the apparent hopelessness of the task, not caring for book lessons, but trying gently to clear away the mists from the darkened mind, and give it back intelligence enough to make the boy less a burden and an affliction.

Mrs Bhaer strengthened his health by every aid she could invent, and the boys all pitied and were kind to him. He did not like their active plays, but would sit for hours watching the doves, would dig holes for Teddy till even that ardent grubber was satisfied, or follow Silas, the man, from place to place seeing him work, for honest Si was very good to him, and though he forgot his letters Billy remembered friendly faces.

Tommy Bangs was the scapegrace of the school, and the most trying scapegrace that ever lived. As full of mischief as a monkey, yet so good-hearted that one could not help forgiving his tricks; so scatterbrained that words went by him like the wind, yet so penitent for every misdeed, that it was impossible to keep sober when he vowed tremendous vows of reformation, or proposed all sorts of queer punishments to be inflicted upon himself. Mr and Mrs Bhaer lived in a state of preparation for any mishap, from the breaking of Tommy's own neck, to the blowing up of the entire family with gunpowder; and Nursey had a particular drawer in which she kept bandages, plasters, and salves for his especial use, for Tommy was always being brought in half-dead; but nothing ever killed him, and he arose from every downfall with redoubled vigour.

The first day he came, he chopped the top off one finger in the hay-cutter, and during the week, fell from the shed roof, was chased by an angry hen who tried to pick his eyes out because he examined her chickens, got run away with, and had his ears boxed violently by Asia, who caught him luxuriously skimming a pan of cream with half a stolen pie. Undaunted, however, by any failures or rebuffs, this indomitable youth went on amusing himself with all sorts of tricks till no one felt safe. If he did not know his lessons, he always had some droll excuse to offer, and as he was usually clever at his books, and as bright as a button in composing answers when he did not know them, he go on pretty well at school. But out of school – Ye gods and little fishes! how Tommy did carouse!

He wound fat Asia up in her own clothes line against the post, and left her there to fume and scold for half an hour one busy Monday morning. He dropped a hot cent down Mary Ann's back as that pretty maid was waiting at table one day when there were gentlemen to dinner, whereat the poor girl upset the soup and rushed out of the room in dismay, leaving the family to think that she had gone mad. He fixed a pail of water up in a tree, with a bit of ribbon fastened to the handle, and when Daisy, attracted by the gay streamer, tried to pull it down, she got a douche bath that spoiled her clean frock and hurt her little feelings very much. He put rough white pebbles in the sugar bowl when his grandmother came to tea, and the poor old lady wondered why they didn't melt in her cup, but was too polite to say anything. He passed around snuff in church so that five of the boys sneezed with such violence they had to go out. He dug paths in winter time, and then privately watered them so that people should tumble down. He drove poor Silas nearly wild by hanging his big boots in conspicuous places, for his feet were enormous, and he was very much ashamed of them. He persuaded confiding little Dolly to tie a thread to one of his loose teeth, and leave the string hanging from his mouth when he went to sleep, so that Tommy could pull it out without his feeling the dreaded operation. But the tooth wouldn't come at the first tweak, and poor Dolly woke up in great anguish of spirit, and lost all faith in Tommy from that day forth.

The last prank had been to give the hens bread soaked in rum, which made them tipsy and scandalised all the other fowls, for the respectable old biddies went staggering about, pecking and clucking in the most maudlin manner, while the family were convulsed with laughter at their antics, till Daisy took pity on them and shut them up in the henhouse to sleep off their intoxication.

These were the boys and they lived together as happy as twelve lads could, studying and playing, working and squabbling, fighting faults and cultivating virtues in the good old-fashioned way. Boys at other schools probably learned more from books, but less of that better wisdom which makes good men. Latin, Greek, and mathematics were all very well, but in Professor Bhaer's opinion, self-knowledge, self-help, and self-control were more important, and he tried to teach them carefully. People shook their heads sometimes at his ideas, even while they owned that the boys improved wonderfully in manners and morals. But then, as Mrs Jo said to Nat, it was an 'odd school'.

CHAPTER 3

Sunday

The moment the bell rang next morning Nat flew out of bed, and dressed himself with great satisfaction in the suit of clothes he found on the chair. They were not new, being half-worn garments of one of the well-to-do boys; but Mrs Bhaer kept all such cast-off feathers for the picked robins who strayed into her nest. They were hardly on when Tommy appeared in a high state of clean collar, and escorted Nat down to breakfast.

The sun was shining into the dining-room on the well-spread table, and the flock of hungry, hearty lads who gathered round it. Nat observed that they were much more orderly than they had been the night before, and everyone stood silently behind his chair while little Rob, standing beside his father at the head of the table, folded his hands, reverently bent his curly head, and softly repeated a short grace in the devout German fashion, which Mr Bhaer loved and taught his little son to honour. Then they all sat down to enjoy the Sunday morning breakfast of coffee, steak, and baked potatoes, instead of the bread and milk fare with which they usually satisfied their young appetites. There was much pleasant talk while the knives and forks rattled briskly, for certain Sunday lessons were to be learned, the Sunday walk settled, and plans for the week discussed. As he listened, Nat thought it seemed as if this day must be a very pleasant one, for he loved quiet, and there was a cheerful sort of hush over everything that pleased him very much; because, in spite of his rough life, the boy possessed the sensitive nerves which belong to a music-loving nature.

'Now, my lads, get your morning jobs done, and let me find you ready for church when the 'bus comes round,' said Father Bhaer, and set the example by going into the school-room to get books ready for the morrow.

Everyone scattered to his or her task, for each had some little daily duty, and was expected to perform it faithfully. Some brought wood and water, brushed the steps, or ran errands for Mrs Bhaer. Others fed the pet animals, and did chores about the barn with Franz. Daisy washed the cups, and Demi wiped them, for the twins liked to work together, and Demi had been taught to make himself useful in the little house at home. Even baby Teddy had his small job to do, and trotted to and fro, putting napkins away, and pushing chairs into their places. For half an hour the lads buzzed about like a hive of bees, then the 'bus drove round, Father Bhaer and Franz with the eight older boys piled in, and away they went for a three-mile drive to church in town.

Because of the troublesome cough Nat preferred to stay at home with the four small boys, and spent a happy morning in Mrs Bhaer's room, listening to the stories she read them, learning the hymns she taught them, and then quietly employing himself pasting pictures into an old ledger.

'This is my Sunday closet,' she said, showing him shelves filled with picture books, paintboxes, architectural blocks, little diaries, and materials for letter-writing. 'I want my boys to love Sunday, to find it a peaceful, pleasant day, when they can rest from common study and play, yet enjoy quiet pleasures, and learn, in simple ways, lessons more important than any taught in school. Do you understand me?' she asked, watching Nat's attentive face.

'You mean to be good?' he said, after hesitating a minute.

'Yes; to be good, and to love to be good. It is hard work sometimes, I know very well; but we all help one another, and so we get on. This is one of the ways in which I try to help my boys,' and she took down a thick book, which seemed half-full of writing, and opened at a page on which there was one word at the top.

'Why, that's my name!' cried Nat, looking both surprised and interested.

'Yes; I have a page for each boy. I keep a little account of how he gets on through the week, and Sunday night I show him the record. If it is bad I am sorry and disappointed, if it is good I am glad and proud; but, whichever it is, the boys know I want to help them, and they try to do their best for love of me and Father Bhaer.'

'I should think they would,' said Nat, catching a glimpse of Tommy's name opposite his own, and wondering what was written under it.

Mrs Bhaer saw his eye on the words, and shook her head, saying, as she turned a leaf

'No, I don't show my records to any but the one to whom each belongs. I call this my conscience book; and only you and I will ever know what is to be written on the page below your name. Whether you will be pleased or ashamed to read it next Sunday depends on yourself. I think it will be a good report; at any rate, I shall try to make things easy for you in this new place, and shall be quite contented if you keep our few rules, live happily with the boys, and learn something.'

'I'll try, ma'am;' and Nat's thin face flushed up with the earnestness of his desire to make Mrs Bhaer 'glad and proud', not 'sorry and disappointed'. 'It must be a great deal of trouble to write about so many,' he added, as she shut her book with an encouraging pat on the shoulder.

'Not to me, for I really don't know which I like best, writing or boys,' she said, laughing to see Nat stare with astonishment at the last item. 'Yes, I know many people think boys are a nuisance, but that is because they don't understand them. I do; and I never saw the boy yet whom I could not get on capitally with after I had once found the soft spot in his heart. Bless me, I couldn't get on at all without my flock of dear, noisy, naughty, harum-scarum little lads, could I, my Teddy?' and Mrs Bhaer hugged the young rogue, just in time to save the big inkstand from going into his pocket.

Nat, who had never heard anything like this before, really did not know whether Mother Bhaer was a trifle crazy, or the most delightful woman he had ever met. He rather inclined to the latter opinion, in spite of her peculiar tastes, for she had a way of filling up a fellow's plate before he asked, of laughing at his jokes, gently tweaking him by the ear, or clapping him on the shoulder, that Nat found very engaging.

'Now, I think you would like to go into the school-room and practise some of the hymns we are to sing tonight,' she said, rightly guessing the thing of all others that he wanted to do.

Alone with the beloved violin and the music book propped up before him in the sunny window, while Spring beauty filled the world outside, and Sabbath silence reigned within, Nat enjoyed an hour or two of genuine happiness, learning the sweet old tunes, and forgetting the hard past in the cheerful present.

When the church-goers came back and dinner was over, everyone read, wrote letters home, said their Sunday lessons, or talked quietly to one another, sitting here and there about the house. At three o'clock the entire family turned out to walk, for all the active young bodies must have exercise; and in these walks the active young minds were taught to see and love the providence of God in the beautiful miracles which Nature was working before their eyes. Mr Bhaer always went with them, and in his simple, fatherly way, found for his flock, 'Sermons in stones, books in the running brooks, and good in everything.'

Mrs Bhaer with Daisy and her own two boys drove into town, to pay the weekly visit to Grandma, which was busy Mother Bhaer's one holiday and greatest pleasure. Nat was not strong enough for the long walk, and asked to stay at home with Tommy, who kindly offered to do the honours of Plumfield. 'You've seen the house, so come out and have a look at the garden, and the barn, and the menagerie,' said Tommy, when they were left alone with Asia, to see that they didn't get into mischief; for, though Tommy was one of the best-meaning boys who ever adorned knickerbockers, accidents of the most direful nature were always happening to him, no one could exactly tell how.

'What is your menagerie?' asked Nat, as they trotted along the drive that encircled the house.

'We all have pets, you see, and we keep 'em in the corn-barn, and call it the menagerie. Here you are. Isn't my guinea-pig a beauty?' and Tommy proudly presented one of the ugliest specimens of that pleasing animal that Nat ever saw.

'I know a boy with a dozen of 'em, and he said he'd give me one, only I hadn't any place to keep it, so I couldn't have it. It was white, with black spots, a regular rouser, and maybe I could get it for you if you'd like it,' said Nat, feeling it would be a delicate return for Tommy's attentions.

'I'd like it ever so much, and I'll give you this one, and they can live together if they don't fight. Those white mice are Rob's, Franz gave 'em to him. The rabbits are Ned's, and the bantams outside are Stuffy's. That box thing is Demi's turtle-tank, only he hasn't begun to get 'em yet. Last year he had sixty-two, whackers some of 'em. He stamped one of 'em with his name and the year, and let it go; and he says maybe he will find it ever so long after and know it. He read about a turtle being found that had a mark on it that showed it must be hundreds of years old. Demi's such a funny chap.'

'What is in this box?' asked Nat, stopping before a large deep one, half-full of earth.

'Oh, that's Jack Ford's worm-shop. He digs heaps of 'em and keeps 'em here, and when we want any to go a-fishing with, we buy some of him. It saves lots of trouble, only he charged too much for 'em. Why, last time we traded I had to pay two cents a dozen, and then got little ones. Jack's mean sometimes, and I told him I'd dig for myself if he didn't lower his prices. Now, I own two hens, those grey ones with top knots, first-rate ones they are too, and I sell Mrs Bhaer the eggs, but I never ask her more than twenty-five cents a dozen, never! I'd be ashamed to do it,' cried Tommy, with a glance of scorn at the worm-shop.

'Who owns the dogs?' asked Nat, much interested in these commercial transactions, and feeling that T. Bangs was a man whom it would be a privilege and a pleasure to patronise.

'The big dog is Emil's. His name is Christopher Columbus. Mrs Bhaer named him because she likes to say Christopher Columbus, and no one minds it if she means the dog,' answered Tommy, in the tone of a showman displaying his menagerie. 'The white pup is Rob's, and the yellow one is Teddy's. A man was going to drown them in our pond, and Pa Bhaer wouldn't let him. They do well enough for the little chaps, I don't think much of 'em myself. Their names are Castor and Pollux.'

'I'd like Toby the donkey best, if I could have anything, it's so nice to ride, and he's so little and good,' said Nat, remembering the weary tramps he had taken on his own tired feet.

'Mr Laurie sent him out to Mrs Bhaer, so she shouldn't carry Teddy on her back when we go to walk. We're all fond of Toby, and he's a first-rate donkey, sir. Those pigeons belong to the whole lot of us, we each have our pet one, and go shares in all the little ones as they come along. Squabs are great fun; there ain't any now, but you can go up and take a look at the old fellows, while I see if Cockletop and Granny have laid any eggs.'

Nat climbed up a ladder, put his head through a trapdoor and took a long look at the pretty doves billing and cooing in their spacious loft. Some on their nests, some bustling in and out, and some sitting at their doors, while many went flying from the sunny housetop to the straw-strewn farmyard, where six sleek cows were placidly ruminating.

'Everybody has got something but me. I wish I had a dove, or a hen, or even a turtle, all my own,' thought Nat, feeling very poor as he saw the interesting treasures of the other boys. 'How do you get these things?' he asked, when he joined Tommy in the barn.

'We find 'em or buy 'em, or folks give 'em to us. My father sends me mine; but as soon as I get egg money enough, I'm going to buy a pair of ducks. There's a nice little pond for 'em behind the barn, and people pay well for duck eggs, and the little duckies are pretty, and it's fun to see 'em swim,' said Tommy, with the air of a millionaire.

Nat sighed, for he had neither father nor money, nothing in the wide world but an old empty pocketbook, and the skill that lay in his ten fingertips. Tommy seemed to understand the question and the sigh which followed his answer, for after a moment of deep thought, he suddenly broke out, 'Look here, I'll tell you what I'll do. If you will hunt eggs for me, I hate it, I'll give you one egg out of every dozen. You keep account, and when you've had twelve, Mother Bhaer will give you twenty-five cents for 'em, and then you can buy what you like, don't you see?'

'I'll do it! What a kind feller you are, Tommy!' cried Nat, quite dazzled by this brilliant offer.

'Pooh! that is not anything. You begin now and rummage the barn, and I'll wait here for you. Granny is cackling, so you're sure to find one somewhere,' and Tommy threw himself down on the hay with a luxurious sense of having made a good bargain, and done a friendly thing.

Nat joyfully began his search, and went rustling from loft to loft till he found two fine eggs, one hidden under a beam, and the other in an old peck measure, which Mrs Cockletop had appropriated.

'You may have one and I'll have the other, that will just make up my last dozen, and tomorrow we'll start fresh. Here, you chalk your accounts up near mine, and then we'll be all straight,' said Tommy, showing a row of mysterious figures on the side of an old winnowing machine.

With a delightful sense of importance, the proud possessor of one egg opened his account with his friend, who laughingly wrote above the figures these imposing words, 'T. Bangs & Co.'

Poor Nat found them so fascinating that he was with difficulty persuaded to go and deposit his first piece of portable property in Asia's storeroom. Then they went on again, and having made the acquaintance of the two horses, six cows, three pigs, and one Alderney 'Bossy', as calves are called in New England, Tommy took Nat to a certain old willow tree that overhung a noisy little brook. From the fence it was an easy scramble into a wide niche between the three big branches, which had been cut off to send out from year to year a crowd of slender twigs, till a green canopy rustled overhead. Here little seats had been fixed, and in a hollow place a closet made big enough to hold a book or two, a dismantled boat, and several half-finished whistles.

'This is Demi's and my private place; we made it, and nobody can come up unless we let 'em, except Daisy, we don't mind her,' said Tommy, as Nat looked with delight from the babbling brown water below to the green arch above, where bees were making a musical murmur as they feasted on the long yellow blossoms that filled the air with sweetness.

'Oh, it's just beautiful!' cried Nat. 'I do hope you'll let me up sometimes. I never saw such a nice place in all my life. I'd like to be a bird, and live here always.'

'It is pretty nice. You can come if Demi don't mind, and I guess he won't, because he said last night that he liked you.'

'Did he?' and Nat smiled with pleasure, for Demi's regard seemed to be valued by all the boys, partly because he was Father Bhaer's nephew, and partly because he was such a sober, conscientious little fellow.

'Yes; Demi likes quiet chaps, and I guess he and you will get on if you care about reading as he does.'

Poor Nat's flush of pleasure deepened to a painful scarlet at those last words, and he stammered out, 'I can't read very well; I never had any time; I was always fiddling round, you know.'

'I don't love it myself, but I can do it well enough when I want to,' said Tommy, after a surprised look, which said as plainly as words, 'A boy twelve years old and can't read!'

'I can read music, anyway,' added Nat, rather ruffled at having to confess his ignorance.

'I can't;' and Tommy spoke in a respectful tone, which emboldened Nat to say firmly, 'I mean to study real hard and learn everything I can, for I never had a chance before. Does Mr Bhaer give hard lessons?'

'No; he isn't a bit cross; he sort of explains and gives you a boost over the hard places. Some folks don't; my other master didn't. If we missed a word, didn't we get raps on the head!' and Tommy rubbed his own pate as if it tingled yet with the liberal supply of raps, the memory of which was the only thing he brought away after a year with his 'other master'.

'I think I could read this,' said Nat, who had been examining the books.

'Read a bit, then; I'll help you,' Tommy said patronisingly.

So Nat did his best, and floundered through a page with many friendly 'boosts' from Tommy, who told him he would soon 'go it' as well as anybody. Then they sat and talked boy-fashion about all sorts of things, among others, gardening; for Nat, looking down from his perch, asked what was planted in the many little patches lying below them on the other side of the brook.

'These are our farms,' said Tommy. 'We each have our own patch, and raise what we like in it, only have to choose different things, and can't change till the crop is in, and we must keep it in order all summer.'

'What are you going to raise this year?'

'Wal, I *cattle*ated to hev beans, as they are about the easiest crop a-goin'.'

Nat could not help laughing, for Tommy had pushed back his hat, put his hands in his pockets, and drawled out his words in unconscious imitation of Silas, the man who managed the place for Mr Bhaer.

'Come, you needn't laugh; beans are ever so much easier than corn or potatoes. I tried melons last year, but the bugs were a bother, and the old things wouldn't get ripe before the frost, so I didn't have but one good water and two little "mush mellions",' said Tommy, relapsing into a 'Silasism' with the last word.

'Corn looks pretty growing,' said Nat, politely, to atone for his laugh.

'Yes, but you have to hoe it over and over again. Now, six weeks' beans only have to be done once or so, and they get ripe soon. I'm going to try 'em, for I spoke first. Stuffy wanted 'em, but he's got to take peas; they only have to be picked, and he ought to do it, he eats such a lot.'

'I wonder if I shall have a garden?' said Nat, thinking that even corn-hoeing must be pleasant work.

'Of course you will,' said a voice from below, and there was Mr Bhaer returned from his walk, and come to find them, for he managed to have a little talk with every one of the lads some time during the day, and found that these chats gave them a good start for the coming week.

Sympathy is a sweet thing, and it worked wonders here, for each boy knew that Father Bhaer was interested in him, and some were readier to open their hearts to him than to a woman, especially the older ones, who liked to talk over their hopes and plans, man to man. When sick or in trouble they instinctively turned to Mrs Jo, while the little ones made her their mother-confessor on all occasions.

In descending from their nest, Tommy fell into the brook; being used to it, he calmly picked himself out and retired to the house to be dried. This left Nat to Mr Bhaer, which was just what he wished, and, during the stroll they took among the garden plots, he won the lad's heart by giving him a little 'farm', and discussing crops with him as gravely as if the food for the family depended on the harvest. From this pleasant topic they went to others, and Nat had many new and helpful thoughts put into a mind that received them as gratefully as the thirsty earth had received the warm spring rain. All supper-time he brooded over them, often fixing his eyes on Mr Bhaer with an enquiring look, that seemed to say, 'I like that, do it again, sir.' I don't know whether the man understood the child's mute language or not, but when the boys were all gathered together in Mrs Bhaer's parlour for the Sunday evening talk, he chose a subject which might have been suggested by the walk in the garden.

As he looked about him Nat thought it seemed more like a great family than a school, for the lads were sitting in a wide half-circle round the fire, some on chairs, some on the rug, Daisy and Demi on the knees of Uncle Fritz, and Rob snugly stowed away in the back of his mother's easy chair, where he could nod unseen if the talk got beyond his depth.

Everyone looked quite comfortable, and listened attentively, for the long walk made rest agreeable, and as every boy there knew that he would be called upon for his views, he kept his wits awake to be ready with an answer.

'Once upon a time,' began Mr Bhaer, in the dear old-fashioned way, 'there was a great and wise gardener who had the largest garden ever seen. A wonderful and lovely place it was, and he watched over it with the greatest skill and care, and raised all manner of excellent and useful things. But weeds would grow even in this fine garden; often the ground was bad and the good seeds sown in it would not spring up. He had many under-gardeners to help him. Some did their duty and earned the rich wages he gave them; but others neglected their parts and let them run to waste, which displeased him very much. But he was very patient, and for thousands and thousands of years he worked and waited for his great harvest.'

'He must have been pretty old,' said Demi, who was looking straight into Uncle Fritz's face, as if to catch every word.

'Hush, Demi, it's a fairy story,' whispered Daisy.

'No, I think it's an arrygory,' said Demi.

'What is a arrygory?' called out Tommy, who was of an enquiring turn.

'Tell him, Demi, if you can, and don't use words unless you are quite sure you know what they mean,' said Mr Bhaer.

'I do know, Grandpa told me! A fable is a arrygory; it's a story that means something. My "Story without an end" is one, because the child in it means a soul; don't it, Aunty?' cried Demi, eager to prove himself right.

'That's it, dear; and Uncle's story is an allegory, I am quite sure; so listen and see what it means,' returned Mrs Jo, who always took part in whatever was going on, and enjoyed it as much as any boy among them.

Demi composed himself, and Mr Bhaer went on in his best English, for he had improved much in the last five years, and said the boys did it.

'This great gardener gave a dozen or so of little plots to one of his servants, and told him to do his best and see what he could raise. Now this servant was not rich, nor wise, nor very good, but he wanted to help because the gardener had been very kind to him in many ways. So he gladly took the little plots and fell to work. They were all sorts of shapes and sizes, and some were very good soil, some rather stony, and all of them needed much care, for in the rich soil the weeds grew fast, and in the poor soil there were many stones.'

'What was growing in them besides the weeds, and stones?' asked Nat; so interested, he forgot his shyness and spoke before them all.

'Flowers,' said Mr Bhaer, with a kind look. 'Even the roughest, most neglected little bed had a bit of heartsease or a sprig of mignonette in it. One had roses, sweet peas, and daisies in it,' here he pinched the plump cheek of the little girl leaning on his arm. 'Another had all sorts of curious plants in it, bright pebbles, a vine that went climbing up like Jack's beanstalk, and many good seeds just beginning to sprout; for, you see, this bed had been taken fine care of by a wise old man, who had worked in gardens of this sort all his life.'

At this part of the 'arrygory', Demi put his head on one side like an inquisitive bird, and fixed his bright eye on his uncle's face, as if he suspected something and was on the watch. But Mr Bhaer looked perfectly innocent, and went on glancing from one young face to another, with a grave, wistful look, that said much to his wife, who knew how earnestly he desired to do his duty in these little garden plots.

'As I tell you, some of these beds were easy to cultivate – that means to take care of, Daisy – and others were very hard. There was one particularly sunshiny little bed that might have been full of fruits and vegetables as well as flowers, only it wouldn't take any pains, and when the man sowed, well, we'll say melons in this bed, they came to nothing, because the little bed neglected them. The man was sorry, and kept on trying, though every time the crop failed, all the bed said, was, "I forgot".'

Here a general laugh broke out, and everyone looked at Tommy, who had pricked up his ears at the word 'melons', and hung down his head at the sound of his favourite excuse.

'I knew he meant us!' cried Demi, clapping his hands. 'You are the man, and we are the little gardens; aren't we, Uncle Fritz?'

'You have guessed it. Now each of you tell me what crop I shall try to sow in you this spring, so that next autumn I may get a good harvest out of my twelve, no, thirteen, plots,' said Mr Bhaer, nodding at Nat as he corrected himself.

'You can't sow corn and beans and peas in us. Unless you mean we are to eat a great many and get fat,' said Stuffy, with a sudden brightening of his round, dull face as the pleasing idea occurred to him.

'He don't mean that kind of seeds. He means things to make us good; and the weeds are faults,' cried Demi, who usually took the lead in these talks, because he was used to this sort of thing, and liked it very much.

'Yes, each of you think what you need most, and tell me, and I will help you to grow it; only you must do your best, or you will turn out like Tommy's melons, all leaves and no fruit. I will begin with the oldest, and ask the mother what she will have in her plot, for we are all parts of the beautiful garden, and may have rich harvests for our Master if we love Him enough,' said Father Bhaer.

'I shall devote the whole of *my* plot to the largest crop of patience I can get, for that is what I need most,' said Mrs Jo, so soberly that the lads fell to thinking in good earnest what they should say when their turns came, and some among them felt a twinge of remorse, that they had helped to use up Mother Bhaer's stock of patience so fast.

Franz wanted perseverance, Tommy steadiness, Ned went in for good temper, Daisy for industry, Demi for 'as much wiseness as Grandpa', and Nat timidly said he wanted so many things he would let Mr Bhaer choose for him. The others chose much the same things, and patience, good temper, and generosity seemed the favourite crops. One boy wished to like to get up early, but did not know what name to give that sort of seed; and poor Stuffy sighed out, 'I wish I loved my lessons as much as I do my dinner, but I can't.'

'We will plant self-denial, and hoe it and water it, and make it grow so well that next Christmas no one will get ill by eating too much dinner. If you exercise your mind, George, it will get hungry just as your body does, and you will love books almost as much as my philosopher here,' said Mr Bhaer, adding, as he stroked the hair off Demi's fine forehead, 'You are greedy also, my son, and you like to stuff your little mind full of fairy-tales and fancies, as well as George likes to fill his little stomach with cake and candy. Both are bad, and I want you to try something better. Arithmetic is not half so pleasant as *The Arabian Nights*, I know, but it is a very useful thing, and now is the time to learn it, else you will be ashamed and sorry by and by.'

'But, "Harry and Lucy", and "Frank", are not fairy books, and they are all full of barometers, and bricks, and shoeing horses, and useful things, and I'm fond of them; ain't I, Daisy?' said Demi, anxious to defend himself.

'So they are; but I find you reading "Roland and Maybird", a great deal oftener than "Harry and Lucy", and I think you are not half so fond of "Frank" as you are of "Sinbad". Come, I shall make a little bargain with you both, George shall eat but three times a day, and you shall read but one story book a week, and I will give you the new cricket-ground; only, you must promise to play in it,' said Uncle Fritz, in his persuasive way, for Stuffy hated to run about, and Demi was always reading in play hours.

'But we don't like cricket,' said Demi.

'Perhaps not *now*, but you will when you know it. Besides, you do like to be generous, and the other boys want to play, and you can give them the new ground if you choose.'

This was taking them both on the right side, and they agreed to the bargain, to the great satisfaction of the rest.

There was a little more talk about the gardens, and then they all sang together. The band delighted Nat, for Mrs Bhaer played the piano, Franz the flute, Mr Bhaer a bass viol, and he himself the violin. A very simple little concert, but all seemed to enjoy it, and old Asia, sitting in the corner, joined in at times with the sweetest voice of any, for in this family, master and servant, old and young, black and white, shared in the Sunday song, which went up to the Father of them all. After this they each shook hands with Father Bhaer; Mother Bhaer kissed them every one from sixteen-year-old Franz to little Rob, who kept the tip of her nose for his own particular kisses, and then they trooped up to bed.

The light of the shaded lamp that burned in the nursery shone softly on a picture hanging at the foot of Nat's bed. There were several others on the walls, but the boy thought there must be something peculiar about this one, for it had a graceful frame of moss and cones about it, and on a little bracket underneath stood a vase of wild flowers freshly gathered from the spring woods. It was the most beautiful picture of them all, and Nat lay looking at it, dimly feeling what it meant, and wishing he knew all about it.

'That's my picture,' said a little voice in the room. Nat popped up his head, and there was Demi in his nightgown pausing on his way back from Aunt Jo's chamber, whither he had gone to get a cot for a cut finger.

'What is he doing to the children?' asked Nat.

'That is Christ, the Good Man, and He is blessing the children. Don't you know about Him?' said Demi, wondering.

'Not much, but I'd like to, He looks so kind,' answered Nat, whose chief knowledge of the Good Man consisted in hearing His name taken in vain.

'I know all about it, and I like it very much, because it is true,' said Demi.

'Who told you?'

'My Grandpa, he knows *everything*, and tells the best stories in the world. I used to play with his big books, and make bridges, and railroads, and houses, when I was a little boy,' began Demi.

'How old are you now?' asked Nat, respectfully.

' 'Most ten.'

'You know a lot of things, don't you?'

'Yes; you see my head is pretty big, and Grandpa says it will take a good deal to fill it, so I keep putting pieces of wisdom into it as fast as I can,' returned Demi, in his quaint way.

Nat laughed, and then said soberly, 'Tell on, please.'

And Demi gladly told on without pause or punctuation. 'I found a very pretty book one day and wanted to play with it, but Grandpa said I mustn't, and showed me the pictures, and told me about them, and I liked the stories very much, all about Joseph and his bad brothers, and the frogs that came up out of the sea, and dear little Moses in the water, and ever so many more lovely ones, but I liked about the Good Man best of all, and Grandpa told it to me so many times that I learned it by heart, and he gave me this picture so I shouldn't forget, and it was put up here once when I was sick, and I left it for other sick boys to see.'

'What makes Him bless the children?' asked Nat, who found something very attractive in the chief figure of the group.

'Because He loved them.'

'Were they poor children?' asked Nat, wistfully.

'Yes, I think so; you see some haven't got hardly any clothes on, and the mothers don't look like rich ladies. He liked poor people, and was very good to them. He made them well, and helped them, and told rich people they must not be cross to them, and they loved Him dearly, dearly,' cried Demi, with enthusiasm.

'Was He rich?'

'Oh no! He was born in a barn, and was so poor He hadn't any house to live in when He grew up, and nothing to eat sometimes, but what people gave Him, and He went round preaching to everybody, and trying to make them good, till the bad men killed Him.'

'What for?' and Nat sat up in his bed to look and listen, so interested was he in this man who cared for the poor so much.

'I'll tell you all about it; Aunt Jo won't mind;' and Demi settled himself on the opposite bed, glad to tell his favourite story to so good a listener.

Nursey peeped in to see if Nat was asleep, but when she saw what was going on, she slipped away again, and went to Mrs Bhaer, saying with her kind face full of motherly emotion, 'Will the dear lady come and see a pretty sight? It's Nat listening with all his heart to Demi telling the story of the Christ-child, like a little white angel as he is.'

Mrs Bhaer had meant to go and talk with Nat a moment before he slept, for she had found that a serious word spoken at this time often did much good. But when she stole to the nursery door, and saw Nat eagerly drinking in the words of his little friend, while Demi told the sweet and solemn story as it had been taught him, speaking softly as he sat with his beautiful eyes fixed on the tender face above them, her own filled with tears, and she went silently away, thinking to herself, 'Demi is unconsciously helping the poor boy better than I can; I will not spoil it by a single word.'

The murmur of the childish voice went on for a long time, as one innocent heart preached that great sermon to another, and no one hushed it. When it ceased at last, and Mrs Bhaer went to take away the lamp, Demi was gone and Nat fast asleep, lying with his face toward the picture, as if he had already learned to love the Good Man who loved little children, and was a faithful friend to the poor. The boy's face was very placid, and as she looked at it she felt that if a single day of care and kindness had done so much, a year of patient cultivation would surely bring a grateful harvest from this neglected garden, which was already sown with the best of all seed by the little missionary in the nightgown.

CHAPTER 4

Stepping Stones

When Nat went into school on Monday morning, he quaked inwardly, for now he thought he should have to display his ignorance before them all. But Mr Bhaer gave him a seat in the deep window, where he could turn his back on the others, and Franz heard him say his lessons there, so no one could hear his blunders or see how he blotted his copybook. He was truly grateful for this, and toiled away so diligently that Mr Bhaer said, smiling, when he saw his hot face and inky fingers: 'Don't work so hard, my boy; you will tire yourself out, and there is time enough.'

'But I *must* work hard, or I can't catch up with the others. They know heaps, and I don't know anything,' said Nat, who had been reduced to a state of despair by hearing the boys recite their grammar, history, and geography with what he thought amazing ease and accuracy.

'You know a good many things which they don't,' said Mr Bhaer, sitting down beside him, while Franz led a class of small students through the intricacies of the multiplication table.

'Do I?' and Nat looked utterly incredulous.

'Yes; for one thing, you can keep your temper, and Jack, who is quick at numbers, cannot; that is an excellent lesson, and I think you have learned it well. Then, you can play the violin, and not one of the lads can, though they want to do it very much. But, best of all, Nat, you really care to learn something, and that is half the battle. It seems hard at first, and you will feel discouraged, but plod away, and things will get easier and easier as you go on.'

Nat's face had brightened more and more as he listened, for, small as the list of his learning was, it cheered him immensely to feel that he had anything to fall back upon. 'Yes, I can keep my temper – father's beating taught me that; and I can fiddle, though I don't know where the Bay of Biscay is,' he thought, with a sense of comfort impossible to express. Then he said aloud, and so earnestly that Demi heard him: 'I *do* want to learn, and I *will* try. I never went to school, but I couldn't help it; and if the fellows don't laugh at me, I guess I'll get on first-rate – you and the lady are so good to me.'

'They shan't laugh at you; if they do, I'll – I'll tell them not to,' cried Demi, quite forgetting where he was.

The class stopped in the middle of 7 times 9, and everyone looked up to see what was going on.

Thinking that a lesson in learning to help one another was better than arithmetic just then, Mr Bhaer told them about Nat, making such an interesting and touching little story out of it that the good-hearted lads all promised to lend him a hand, and felt quite honoured to be called upon to impart their stores of wisdom to the chap who fiddled so capitally. This appeal established the right feeling among them, and Nat had few hindrances to struggle against, for everyone was glad to give him a 'boost' up the ladder of learning.

Till he was stronger, much study was not good for him, however, and Mrs Jo found various amusements in the house for him while others were at their books. But his garden was his best medicine, and he worked away like a beaver, preparing his little farm, sowing his beans, watching eagerly to see them grow, and rejoicing over each green leaf and slender stock that shot up and flourished in the warm spring weather. Never was a garden more faithfully hoed; Mr Bhaer really feared that nothing would find time to grow, Nat kept up such a stirring of the soil; so he gave him easy jobs in the flower garden or among the strawberries, where he worked and hummed as busily as the bees booming all about him.

'This is the crop I like best,' Mrs Bhaer used to say, as she pinched the once thin cheeks, now getting plump and ruddy, or stroked the bent shoulders that were slowly straightening up with healthful work, good food, and the absence of that heavy burden, poverty.

Demi was his little friend, Tommy his patron, and Daisy the comforter of all his woes; for, though the children were younger than he, his timid spirit found a pleasure in their innocent society, and rather shrunk from the rough sports of the elder lads. Mr Laurence did not forget him, but sent clothes and books, music and kind messages, and now and then came out to see how his boy was getting on, or took him into town to a concert; on which occasions Nat felt himself translated into the seventh heaven of bliss, for he went to Mr Laurence's great house, saw his pretty wife and little fairy of a daughter, had a good dinner, and was made so comfortable, that he talked and dreamed of it for days and nights afterwards.

It takes so little to make a child happy that it is a pity, in a world so full of sunshine and pleasant things, that there should be any wistful faces, empty hands, or lonely little hearts. Feeling this, the Bhaers gathered up all the crumbs they could find to feed their flock of hungry sparrows, for they were not rich, except in charity. Many of Mrs Jo's friends who had nurseries sent her the toys of which their children so soon tired, and in mending these Nat found an employment that just suited him. He was very neat and skilful with those slender fingers of his, and passed many a rainy afternoon with his gum-bottle, paintbox, and knife, repairing furniture, animals, and games, while Daisy was dressmaker to the dilapidated dolls. As fast as the toys were mended, they were put carefully away in a certain drawer which was to furnish forth a Christmas tree for all the poor children of the neighbourhood, that being the way the Plumfield boys celebrated the birthday of Him who loved the poor and blessed the little ones.

Demi was never tired of reading and explaining his favourite books, and many a pleasant hour did they spend in the old willow, revelling over *Robinson Crusoe*, *Arabian Nights*, Edgeworth's *Tales*, and the other dear immortal stories that will delight children for centuries to come. This opened a new world to Nat, and his eagerness to see what came next in the story helped him on till he could read as well as anybody, and felt so rich and proud with his new accomplishment, that there was danger of his being as much of a bookworm as Demi.

Another helpful thing happened in a most unexpected and agreeable manner. Several of the boys were 'in business', as they called it, for most of them were poor, and knowing that they would have their own way to make by and by, the Bhaers encouraged any efforts at independence. Tommy sold his eggs; Jack speculated in livestock; Franz helped in the teaching, and was paid for it; Ned had a taste for carpentry, and a turning-lathe was set up for him in which he turned all sorts of useful or pretty things, and sold them; while Demi constructed water-mills, whirligigs, and unknown machines of an intricate and useless nature, and disposed of them to the boys.

'Let him be a mechanic if he likes,' said Mr Bhaer. 'Give a boy a trade, and he is independent. Work is wholesome, and whatever talent these lads possess, be it for poetry or ploughing, it shall be cultivated and made useful to them if possible.'

So, when Nat came running to him one day to ask with an excited face: 'Can I go and fiddle for some people who are to have a picnic in our woods? They will pay me, and I'd like to earn some money as the other boys do, and fiddling is the only way I know how to do it.'

Mr Bhaer answered readily: 'Go, and welcome. It is an easy and a pleasant way to work, and I am glad it is offered you.'

Nat went, and did so well that when he came home he had two dollars in his pocket, which he displayed with intense satisfaction, as he told how much he had enjoyed the afternoon, how kind the young people were, and how they had praised his dance music, and promised to have him again.

'It is so much nicer than fiddling in the street, for then I got none of the money, and now I have it all, and a good time besides. I'm in business now as well as Tommy and Jack, and I like it ever so much,' said Nat, proudly patting the old pocketbook, and feeling like a millionaire already.

He was in business truly, for picnics were plenty as summer opened, and Nat's skill was in great demand. He was always at liberty to go if lessons were not neglected, and if the picnickers were respectable young people. For Mr Bhaer explained to him that a good plain education is necessary for everyone, and that no amount of money should hire him to go where he might be tempted to do wrong. Nat quite agreed to this, and it was a pleasant sight to see the innocent-hearted lad go driving away in the gay wagons that stopped at the gate for him, or to hear him come fiddling home tired but happy, with his well-earned money in one pocket, and some 'goodies' from the feast for Daisy or little Ted, whom he never forgot.

'I'm going to save up till I get enough to buy a violin for myself, and then I can earn my own living, can't I?' he used to say, as he brought his dollars to Mr Bhaer to keep.

'I hope so, Nat; but we must get you strong and hearty first, and put a little more knowledge into this musical head of yours. Then Mr Laurie will find you a place somewhere, and in a few years we will all come to hear you play in public.'

With much congenial work, encouragement, and hope, Nat found life getting easier and happier every day, and made such progress in his music lessons that his teacher forgave his slowness in some other things, knowing very well that where the heart is the mind works best. The only punishment the boy ever needed for neglect of more important lessons was to hang up the fiddle and the bow for a day. The fear of losing his bosom friend entirely made him go at his books with a will; and having proved that *he could* master the lessons, what was the use of saying 'I can't?'

Daisy had a great love of music, and a great reverence for anyone who could make it, and she was often found sitting on the stairs outside Nat's door while he was practising. This pleased him very much, and he played his best for that one quiet little listener; for she never would come in, but preferred to sit sewing her gay patchwork, or tending one of her many dolls, with an expression of dreamy pleasure on her face that made Aunt Jo say, with tears in her eyes: 'So like my Beth,' and go softly by, lest even her familiar presence mar the child's sweet satisfaction.

Nat was very fond of Mrs Bhaer, but found something even more attractive in the good professor, who took fatherly care of the shy feeble boy, who had barely escaped with his life from the rough sea on which his little boat had been tossing rudderless for twelve years. Some good angel must have been watching over him, for, though his body had suffered, his soul seemed to have taken little harm, and came ashore as innocent as a shipwrecked baby. Perhaps his love of music kept it sweet in spite of the discord all about him; Mr Laurie said so, and he ought to know. However that might be, Father Bhaer took pleasure in fostering poor Nat's virtues, and in curing his faults, finding his new pupil as docile and affectionate as a girl. He often called Nat his 'daughter' when speaking of him to Mrs Jo, and she used to laugh at his fancy, for Madame liked manly boys, and thought Nat amiable but weak, though you never would have guessed it, for she petted him as she did Daisy, and he thought her a very delightful woman.

One fault of Nat's gave the Bhaers much anxiety, although they saw how it had been strengthened by fear and ignorance. I regret to say that Nat sometimes told lies. Not very black ones, seldom getting deeper than grey, and often the mildest of white fibs; but that did not matter, a lie is a lie, and though we all tell many polite untruths in this queer world of ours, it is not right, and everybody knows it.

'You cannot be too careful; watch your tongue, and eyes, and hands, for it is easy to tell, and look, and act untruth,' said Mr Bhaer, in one of the talks he had with Nat about his chief temptation.

'I know it, and I don't mean to, but it's so much easier to get along if you ain't very fussy about being exactly true. I used to tell 'em because I was afraid of father and Nicolo, and now I do sometimes because the boys laugh at me. I know it's bad, but I forget,' and Nat looked much depressed by his sins.

'When I was a little lad I used to tell lies! Ach! what fibs they were, and my old grandmother cured me of it how, do you think? My parents had talked, and cried, and punished, but still did I forget as you. Then said the dear old grandmother, "I shall help you to remember, and put a check on this unruly part," with that she drew out my tongue and snipped the end with her scissors till the blood ran. That was terrible, you may believe, but it did me much good, because it was sore for days, and every word I said came so slowly that I had time to think. After that I was more careful, and got on better, for I feared the big scissors. Yet the dear grandmother was most kind to me in all things, and when she lay dying far away in Nuremberg, she prayed that little Fritz might love God and tell the truth.'

'I never had any grandmothers, but if you think it will cure me, I'll let you snip my tongue,' said Nat, heroically, for he dreaded pain, yet did wish to stop fibbing.

Mr Bhaer smiled, but shook his head.

'I have a better way than that, I tried it once before and it worked well. See now, when you tell a lie I will not punish you, but you shall punish me.'

'How?' asked Nat, startled at the idea.

'You shall ferrule me in the good old-fashioned way; I seldom do it myself, but it may make you remember better to give me pain than to feel it yourself.'

'Strike you? Oh, I couldn't!' cried Nat.

'Then mind that tripping tongue of thine. I have no wish to be hurt, but I would gladly bear much pain to cure this fault.'

This suggestion made such an impression on Nat, that for a long time he set a watch upon his lips, and was desperately accurate, for Mr Bhaer judged rightly, that love of him would be more powerful with Nat than fear for himself. But alas! one sad day Nat was off his guard, and when peppery Emil threatened to thrash him, if it was he who had run over his garden and broken down his best hills of corn, Nat declared he didn't, and then was ashamed to own up that he did do it, when Jack was chasing him the night before.

He thought no one would find it out, but Tommy happened to see him, and when Emil spoke of it a day or two later, Tommy gave his evidence, and Mr Bhaer heard it. School was over, and they were all standing about in the hall, and Mr Bhaer had just set down on the straw settee to enjoy his frolic with Teddy; but when he heard Tommy and saw Nat turn scarlet, and look at him with a frightened face, he put the little boy down, saying, 'Go to thy mother, bübchen, I will come soon,' and taking Nat by the hand led him into the school and shut the door.

The boys looked at one another in silence for a minute, then Tommy slipped out and peeping in at the half-closed blinds, beheld a sight that quite bewildered him. Mr Bhaer had just taken down the long rule that hung over his desk, so seldom used that it was covered with dust.

'My eye! He's going to come down heavy on Nat this time. Wish I hadn't told,' thought good-natured Tommy, for to be ferruled was the deepest disgrace at this school.

'You remember what I told you last time?' said Mr Bhaer, sorrowfully, not angrily.

'Yes; but please don't make me, I can't bear it,' cried Nat, backing up against the door with both hands behind him, and a face full of distress.

'Why don't he up and take it like a man? I would,' thought Tommy, though his heart beat fast at the sight.

'I shall keep my word, and you must remember to tell the truth. Obey me, Nat, take this and give me six good strokes.'

Tommy was so staggered by this last speech that he nearly tumbled down the bank, but saved himself, and hung on to the window ledge, staring in with eyes as round as the stuffed owl's on the chimney piece.

Nat took the rule, for when Mr Bhaer spoke in that tone everyone obeyed him, and, looking as scared and guilty as if about to stab his master, he gave two feeble blows on the broad hand held out to him. Then he stopped and looked up half-blind with tears, but Mr Bhaer said steadily: 'Go on, and strike harder.'

As if seeing that it must be done, and eager to have the hard task soon over, Nat drew his sleeve across his eyes and gave two more quick hard strokes that reddened the hand, yet hurt the giver more.

'Isn't that enough?' he asked in a breathless sort of tone.

'Two more,' was all the answer, and he gave them, hardly seeing where they fell, then threw the rule all across the room, and hugging the kind hand in both his own, laid his face down on it sobbing out in a passion of love, and shame, and penitence: 'I will remember! Oh! I will!'

Then Mr Bhaer put an arm about him, and said in a tone as compassionate as it had just now been firm: 'I think you will. Ask the dear God to help you, and try to spare us both another scene like this.'

Tommy saw no more, for he crept back to the hall, looking so excited and sober that the boys crowded round him to ask what was being done to Nat.

In a most impressive whisper Tommy told them, and they looked as if the sky was about to fall, for this reversing the order of things almost took their breath away.

'He made me do the same thing once,' said Emil, as if confessing a crime of the deepest dye.

'And you hit him? dear old Father Bhaer? By thunder, I'd just like to see you do it now!' said Ned, collaring Emil in a fit of righteous wrath.

'It was ever so long ago. I'd rather have my head cut off than do it now,' and Emil mildly laid Ned on his back instead of cuffing him, as he would have felt it his duty to do on any less solemn occasion.

'How could you?' said Demi, appalled at the idea.

'I was hopping mad at the time, and thought I shouldn't mind a bit, rather like it perhaps. But when I'd hit uncle one good crack, everything he had ever done for me came into my head all at once somehow, and I couldn't go on. No sir! If he'd laid me down and walked on me, I wouldn't have minded, I felt so mean,' and Emil gave himself a good thump in the chest to express his sense of remorse for the past.

'Nat's crying like anything, and feels no end sorry, so don't let's say a word about it; will we?' said tender-hearted Tommy.

'Of course we won't, but it's awful to tell lies,' and Demi looked as if he found the awfulness much increased when the punishment fell not upon the sinner, but his best Uncle Fritz.

'Suppose we all clear out, so Nat can cut upstairs if he wants to,' proposed Franz, and led the way to the barn, their refuge in troublous times.

Nat did not come to dinner, but Mrs Jo took some up to him, and said a tender word, which did him good, though he could not look at her. By and by the lads playing outside heard the violin, and said among themselves: 'He's all right now.' He was all right, but felt shy about going down, till opening his door to slip away into the woods, he found Daisy sitting on the stairs with neither work nor doll, only her little handkerchief in her hand, as if she had been mourning for her captive friend.

'I'm going to walk; want to come?' asked Nat, trying to look as if nothing was the matter, yet feeling very grateful for her silent sympathy, because he fancied everyone must look upon him as a wretch.

'Oh yes!' and Daisy ran for her hat, proud to be chosen as a companion by one of the big boys.

The others saw them go, but no one followed, for boys have a great deal more delicacy than they get credit for, and the lads instinctively felt that, when in disgrace, gentle little Daisy was their most congenial friend.

The walk did Nat good, and he came home quieter than usual, but looking cheerful again, and hung all over with daisy-chains made by his little playmate while he lay on the grass and told her stories.

No one said a word about the scene of the morning, but its effect was all the more lasting for that reason, perhaps. Nat tried his very best, and found much help, not only from the earnest little prayers he prayed to his Friend in heaven, but also in the patient care of the earthly friend whose kind hand he never touched without remembering that it had willingly borne pain for his sake.

CHAPTER 5

Patty Pans

'What's the matter, Daisy?'

'The boys won't let me play with them.'

'Why not?'

'They say girls can't play football.'

'They can, for I've done it!' and Mrs Bhaer laughed at the remembrance of certain youthful frolics.

'I know I can play; Demi and I used to, and have nice times, but he won't let me now because the other boys laugh at him,' and Daisy looked deeply grieved at her brother's hardness of heart.

'On the whole, I think he is right, deary. It's all very well when you two are alone, but it is too rough a game for you with a dozen boys; so I'd find some nice little play for myself.'

'I'm tired of playing alone!' and Daisy's tone was very mournful.

'I'll play with you by and by, but just now I must fly about and get things ready for a trip into town. You shall go with me and see Mamma, and if you like you can stay with her.'

'I should like to go and see her and Baby Josy, but I'd rather come back, please. Demi would miss me, and I love to be here, Aunty.'

'You can't get on without your Demi, can you?' and Aunt Jo looked as if she quite understood the love of the little girl for her only brother.

' 'Course I can't; we're twins, and so we love each other more than other people,' answered Daisy, with a brightening face, for she considered being a twin one of the highest honours she could ever receive.

'Now, what will you do with your little self while I fly around?' asked Mrs Bhaer, who was whisking piles of linen into a wardrobe with great rapidity.

'I don't know, I'm tired of dolls and things; I wish you'd make up a new play for me, Aunty Jo,' said Daisy, swinging listlessly on the door.

'I shall have to think of a brand new one, and it will take me some time; so suppose you go down and see what Asia has got for your lunch,' suggested Mrs Bhaer, thinking that would be a good way in which to dispose of the little hindrance for a time.

'Yes, I think I'd like that, if she isn't cross,' and Daisy slowly departed to the kitchen, where Asia, the black cook, reigned undisturbed.

In five minutes, Daisy was back again, with a wide-awake face, a bit of dough in her hand and a dab of flour on her little nose.

'Oh Aunty! Please could I go and make gingersnaps and things? Asia isn't cross, and she says I may, and it would be such fun, please do,' cried Daisy, all in one breath.

'Just the thing, go and welcome, make what you like, and stay as long as you please,' answered Mrs Bhaer, much relieved, for sometimes the one little girl was harder to amuse than the dozen boys.

Daisy ran off, and while she worked, Aunt Jo racked her brain for a new play. All of a sudden she seemed to have an idea, for she smiled to herself, slammed the doors of the wardrobe, and walked briskly away, saying, 'I'll do it, if it's a possible thing!'

What it was no one found out that day, but Aunt Jo's eyes twinkled so when she told Daisy she had thought of a new play, and was going to buy it, that Daisy was much excited and asked questions all the way into town, without getting answers that told her anything. She was left at home to play with the new baby, and delight her mother's eyes, while Aunt Jo went off shopping. When she came back with all sorts of queer parcels in corners of the carryall, Daisy was so full of curiosity that she wanted to go back to Plumfield at once. But her aunt would not be hurried, and made a long call in mamma's room, sitting on the floor with baby in her lap, making Mrs Brooke laugh at the pranks of the boys, and all sorts of droll nonsense.

How her aunt told the secret Daisy could not imagine, but her mother evidently knew it, for she said, as she tied on the little bonnet and kissed the rosy little face inside, 'Be a good child, my Daisy, and learn the nice new play Aunty has got for you. It's a most useful and interesting one, and it is very kind of her to play it with you, because she does not like it very well herself.'

This last speech made the two ladies laugh heartily, and increased Daisy's bewilderment. As they drove away something rattled in the back of the carriage.

'What's that?' asked Daisy, pricking up her ears.

'The new play,' answered Mrs Jo, solemnly.

'What is it made of?' cried Daisy.

'Iron, tin, wood, brass, sugar, salt, coal, and a hundred other things.'

'How strange! What colour is it?'

'All sorts of colours.'

'Is it large?'

'Part of it is, and a part isn't.'

'Did I ever see one?'

'Ever so many, but never one so nice as this.'

'Oh! what can it be? I can't wait. When shall I see it?' and Daisy bounced up and down with impatience.

'Tomorrow morning, after lessons.'

'Is it for the boys, too?'

'No, all for you and Bess. The boys will like to see it, and want to play one part of it. But you can do as you like about letting them.'

'I'll let Demi, if he wants to.'

'No fear that they won't all want to, especially Stuffy,' and Mrs Bhaer's eyes twinkled more than ever as she patted a queer knobby bundle in her lap.

'Let me feel just once,' prayed Daisy.

'Not a feel; you'd guess in a minute and spoil the fun.'

Daisy groaned and then smiled all over her face, for through a little hole in the paper she caught a glimpse of something bright.

'How *can* I wait so long? Couldn't I see it today?'

'Oh dear, no! It has got to be arranged, and ever so many parts fixed in their places. I promised Uncle Teddy that you shouldn't see it till it was all in apple-pie order.'

'If Uncle knows about it then it must be splendid!' cried Daisy, clapping her hands; for this kind, rich, jolly uncle of hers was as good as a fairy godmother to the children, and was always planning merry surprises, pretty gifts, and droll amusements for them.

'Yes; Teddy went and bought it with me, and we had such fun in the shop choosing the different parts. He would have everything fine and large, and my little plan got regularly splendid when he took hold. You must give him your very best kiss when he comes, for he is the kindest uncle that ever went and bought a charming little coo – Bless me! I nearly told you what it was!' and Mrs Bhaer cut that most interesting word short off in the middle, and began to look over her bills, as if afraid she would let the cat out of the bag if she talked any more. Daisy folded her hands with an air of resignation, and sat quite still trying to think what play had a 'coo' in it.

When they got home she eyed every bundle that was taken out, and one large heavy one, which Franz took straight upstairs and hid in the nursery, filled her with amazement and curiosity. Something very mysterious went on up there that afternoon, for Franz was hammering, and Asia trotting up and down, and Aunt Jo flying around like a will-o'-the-wisp, with all sort of things under her apron, while little Ted, who was the only child admitted, because he couldn't talk plain, babbled and laughed, and tried to tell what the 'sumpin pitty' was.

All this made Daisy half-wild, and her excitement spread among the boys, who quite overwhelmed Mother Bhaer with offers of assistance, which she declined by quoting their own words to Daisy: 'Girls can't play with boys. This is for Daisy, and Bess, and me, so we don't want you.' Whereupon the young gentlemen meekly retired, and invited Daisy to a game of marbles, horse, football, anything she liked, with a sudden warmth and politeness which astonished her innocent little soul.

Thanks to these attentions, she got through the afternoon, went early to bed, and next morning did her lessons with an energy which made Uncle Fritz wish that a new game could be invented every day. Quite a thrill pervaded the school-room when Daisy was dismissed at eleven o'clock, for everyone knew that now she was going to have the new and mysterious play.

Many eyes followed her as she ran away, and Demi's mind was

so distracted by this event that when Franz asked him where the desert of Sahara was, he mournfully replied, 'In the nursery,' and the whole school laughed at him.

'Aunt Jo, I've done all my lessons, and I can't wait one single minute more!' cried Daisy, flying into Mrs Bhaer's room.

'It's all ready, come on;' and tucking Ted under one arm, and her work-basket under the other, Aunt Jo promptly led the way upstairs.

'I don't see anything,' said Daisy, staring about her as she got inside the nursery door.

'Do you hear anything?' asked Aunt Jo, catching Ted back by his little frock as he was making straight for one side of the room.

Daisy did hear an odd crackling, and then a purry little sound as of a kettle singing. These noises came from behind a curtain drawn before a deep bay window. Daisy snatched it back, gave one joyful, 'Oh!' and then stood gazing with delight at – what do you think?

A wide seat ran round the three sides of the window; on one side hung and stood all sorts of little pots and pans, gridirons and skillets; on the other side a small dinner and tea set; and on the middle part a cooking-stove. Not a tin one, that was of no use, but a real iron stove, big enough to cook for a large family of very hungry dolls. But the best of it was that a real fire burned in it, real steam came out of the nose of the little tea-kettle, and the lid of the little boiler actually danced a jig, the water inside bubbled so hard. A pane of glass had been taken out and replaced by a sheet of tin, with a hole for the small funnel, and real smoke went sailing away outside so naturally, that it did one's heart good to see it. The box of wood with a hod of charcoal stood near by; just above hung dustpan, brush and broom; a little market basket was on the low table at which Daisy used to play, and over the back of her little chair hung a white apron with a bib, and a droll mob cap. The sun shone in as if he enjoyed the fun, the little stove roared beautifully, the kettle steamed, the new tins sparkled on the walls, the pretty china stood in tempting rows, and it was altogether as cheery and complete a kitchen as any child could desire.

Daisy stood quite still after the first glad 'Oh!' but her eyes went quickly from one charming object to another, brightening as they looked, till they came to Aunt Jo's merry face; there they stopped as the happy little girl hugged her, saying gratefully: 'Oh Aunty, it's a splendid new play! Can I really cook at the dear stove, and have parties and mess, and sweep, and make fires that truly burn? I like it *so* much! What made you think of it?'

'Your liking to make gingersnaps with Asia made me think of it,' said Mrs Bhaer, holding Daisy, who frisked as if she would fly. 'I knew Asia wouldn't let you mess in her kitchen very often, and it wouldn't be safe at this fire up here, so I thought I'd see if I could find a little stove for you, and teach you to cook; that would be fun, and useful too. So I travelled round among the toy shops, but everything large cost too much and I was thinking I should have to give it up, when I met Uncle Teddy. As soon as he knew what I was about, he said he wanted to help, and insisted on buying the biggest toy stove we could find. I scolded, but he only laughed, and teased me about my cooking when we were young, and said I must teach Bess as well as you, and went on buying all sorts of nice little things for my "cooking class" as he called it.'

'I'm so glad you met him!' said Daisy, as Mrs Jo stopped to laugh at the memory of the funny time she had with Uncle Teddy.

'You must study hard and learn to make all kinds of things, for he says he shall come out to tea very often, and expects something uncommonly nice.'

'It's the sweetest, dearest kitchen in the world, and I'd rather study with it than do anything else. Can't I learn pies, and cake, and macaroni, and everything?' cried Daisy, dancing round the room with a new saucepan in one hand and the tiny poker in the other.

'All in good time. This is to be a useful play, I am to help you, and you are to be my cook, so I shall tell you what to do, and show you how. Then we shall have things fit to eat, and you will be really learning how to cook on a small scale. I'll call you Sally, and say you are a new girl just come,' added Mrs Jo, settling down to work, while Teddy sat on the floor sucking his thumb, and staring at the stove as if it was a live thing, whose appearance deeply interested him.

'That will be so lovely! What shall I do first?' asked Sally, with such a happy face and willing air that Aunt Jo wished all new cooks were half as pretty and pleasant.

'First of all, put on this clean cap and apron. I am rather old-fashioned, and I like my cook to be very tidy.'

Sally tucked her curly hair into the round cap, and put on the apron without a murmur, though usually she rebelled against bibs.

'Now, you can put things in order, and wash up the new china. The old set needs washing also, for my last girl was apt to leave it in a sad state after a party.'

Aunt Jo spoke quite soberly, but Sally laughed, for she knew who the untidy girl was who had left the cups sticky. Then she turned up her cuffs, and with a sigh of satisfaction began to stir about her kitchen, having little raptures now and then over the 'sweet rolling pin', the 'darling dish-tub', or the 'cunning pepper pot'.

'Now, Sally, take your basket and go to market; here is the list of things I want for dinner,' said Mrs Jo, giving her a bit of paper when the dishes were all in order.

'Where is the market?' asked Daisy, thinking that the new play got more and more interesting every minute.

'Asia is the market.'

Away went Sally, causing another stir in the school-room as she passed the door in her new costume, and whispered to Demi, with a face full of delight, 'It's a perfectly splendid play!'

Old Asia enjoyed the joke as much as Daisy, and laughed jollily as the little girl came flying into the room with her cap all on one side, the lids of her basket rattling like castanets and looking like a very crazy little cook.

'Mrs Aunt Jo wants these things, and I must have them right away,' said Daisy, importantly.

'Let's see, honey; here's two pounds of steak, potatoes, squash, apples, bread, and butter. The meat ain't come yet; when it does I'll send it up. The other things are all handy.'

Then Asia packed one potato, one apple, a bit of squash, a little pat of butter, and a roll into the basket, telling Sally to be on the watch for the butcher's boy, because he sometimes played tricks.

'Who is he?' and Daisy hoped it would be Demi.

'You'll see,' was all Asia would say; and Sally went off in great spirits, singing a verse from dear Mary Howitt's sweet story in rhyme:

'Away went little Mabel,
    With the wheaten cake so fine,
The new-made pot of butter,
    And the little flask of wine.'

'Put everything but the apple into the store closet for the present,' said Mrs Jo, when the cook got home.

There was a cupboard under the middle shelf, and on opening the door fresh delights appeared. One half was evidently the cellar, for wood, coal, and kindlings were piled there. The other half was full of little jars, boxes, and all sorts of droll contrivances for holding small quantities of flour, meal, sugar, salt, and other household stores. A pot of jam was there, a little tin box of gingerbread, a cologne bottle full of currant wine, and a tiny canister of tea. But the crowning charm was two doll's pans of new milk, with cream actually rising on it, and a wee skimmer all ready to skim it with. Daisy clasped her hands at this delicious spectacle, and wanted to skim it immediately. But Aunt Jo said: 'Not yet; you will want the cream to eat on your apple pie at dinner, and must not disturb it till then.'

'Am I going to have pie?' cried Daisy, hardly believing that such bliss could be in store for her.

'Yes; if your oven does well we will have two pies, one apple and one strawberry,' said Mrs Jo, who was nearly as much interested in the new play as Daisy herself.

'Oh, what next?' asked Sally, all impatience to begin.

'Shut the lower draught of the stove, so that the oven may heat. Then wash your hands and get out the flour, sugar, salt, butter, and cinnamon. See if the pie board is clean, and pare your apple ready to put in.'

Daisy got things together with as little noise and spilling as could be expected, from so young a cook.

'I really don't know how to measure for such tiny pies; I must guess at it, and if these don't succeed, we must try again,' said Mrs Jo, looking rather perplexed, and very much amused with the small concern before her. 'Take that little pan full of flour, put in a pinch of salt, and then rub in as much butter as will go on that plate. Always remember to put your dry things together first, and then the wet. It mixes better so.'

'I know how; I saw Asia do it. Don't I butter the pie plates too? She did, the first thing,' said Daisy, whisking the flour about at a great rate.

'Quite right! I do believe you have a gift for cooking, you take to it so cleverly,' said Aunt Jo, approvingly. 'Now a dash of cold water, just enough to wet it; then scatter some flour on the board, work in a little, and roll the paste out; yes, that's the way. Now put dabs of butter all over it, and roll it out again. We won't have our pastry very rich, or the dolls will get dyspeptic.'

Daisy laughed at the idea, and scattered the dabs with a liberal hand. Then she rolled and rolled with her delightful little pin, and having got her paste ready proceeded to cover the plates with it. Next the apple was sliced in, sugar and cinnamon lavishly sprinkled over it, and then the top crust put on with breathless care.

'I always wanted to cut them round, and Asia never would let me. How nice it is to do it all my ownty donty self!' said Daisy, as the little knife went clipping round the doll's plate poised on her hand.

All cooks, even the best, meet with mishaps sometimes, and Sally's first one occurred then, for the knife went so fast that the plate slipped, turned a somersault in the air, and landed the dear little pie upside down on the floor. Sally screamed, Mrs Jo laughed, Teddy scrambled to get it, and for a moment confusion reigned in the new kitchen.

'It didn't spill or break, because I pinched the edges together so hard; it isn't hurt a bit, so I'll prick holes in it, and then it will be ready,' said Sally, picking up the capsized treasure and putting it into shape with a childlike disregard of the dust it had gathered in its fall.

'My new cook has a good temper, I see, and that is such a comfort,' said Mrs Jo. 'Now open the jar of strawberry jam, fill the uncovered pie, and put some strips of paste over the top as Asia does.'

'I'll make a D in the middle, and have zigzags all round, that will be so interesting when I come to eat it,' said Sally, loading the pie with squirls and flourishes that would have driven a real pastry cook wild. 'Now I put them in!' she exclaimed; when the last grimy knob had been carefully planted in the red field of jam, and with an air of triumph she shut them into the little oven.

'Clear up your things; a good cook never lets her utensils collect. Then pare your squash and potatoes.'

'There is only one potato,' giggled Sally.

'Cut it in four pieces, so it will go into the little kettle, and put the bits into cold water till it is time to cook them.'

'Do I soak the squash too?'

'No, indeed! Just pare it and cut it up, and put in into the steamer over the pot. It is drier so, though it takes longer to cook.'

Here a scratching at the door caused Sally to run and open it, when Kit appeared with a covered basket in his mouth.

'Here's the butcher boy!' cried Daisy, much tickled at the idea, as she relieved him of his load, whereat he licked his lips and began to beg, evidently thinking that it was his own dinner, for he often carried it to his master in that way. Being undeceived, he departed in great wrath and barked all the way downstairs, to ease his wounded feelings.

In the basket were two bits of steak (doll's pounds), a baked pear, a small cake, and paper with them on which Asia had scrawled, 'For Missy's lunch, if her cookin' don't turn out well.'

'I don't want any of her old pears and things; my cooking *will* turn out well, and I'll have a splendid dinner; see if I don't!' cried Daisy, indignantly.

'We may like them if company should come. It is always well to have something in the storeroom,' said Aunt Jo, who had been taught this valuable fact by a series of domestic panics.

'Me is hundry,' announced Teddy, who began to think what with so much cooking going on it was about time for somebody to eat something. His mother gave him her work-basket to rummage, hoping to keep him quiet till dinner was ready, and returned to her housekeeping.

'Put on your vegetables, set the table, and then have some coals kindling ready for the steak.'

What a thing it was to see the potatoes bobbing about in the little pot; to peep at the squash getting soft so fast in the tiny steamer; to whisk open the oven door every five minutes to see how the pies got on, and at last when the coals were red and glowing, to put two real steaks on a finger-long gridiron and proudly turn them with a fork. The potatoes were done first, and no wonder, for they had boiled frantically all the while. They were pounded up with a little pestle, had much butter and no salt put in (cook forgot it in the excitement of the moment), then it was made into a mound in a gay red dish, smoothed over with a knife dipped in milk, and put in the oven to brown.

So absorbed in these last performances had Sally been, that she forgot her pastry till she opened the door to put in the potato, then a wail arose, for alas! alas! the little pies were burnt black!

'Oh, my pies! My darling pies! They are all spoilt!' cried poor Sally, wringing her dirty little hands as she surveyed the ruin of her work. The tart was especially pathetic, for the quirls and zigzags stuck up in all directions from the blackened jelly, like the walls and chimney of a house after a fire.

'Dear, dear, I forgot to remind you to take them out; it's just my luck,' said Aunt Jo, remorsefully. 'Don't cry, darling, it was my fault; we'll try again after dinner,' she added, as a great tear dropped from Sally's eyes and sizzled on the hot ruins of the tart.

More would have followed, if the steak had not blazed up just then, and so occupied the attention of cook, that she quickly forgot the lost pastry.

'Put the meat dish and your own plates down to warm, while you mash the squash with butter, salt, and a little pepper on the top,' said Mrs Jo, devoutly hoping that the dinner would meet with no further disasters.

The 'cunning pepper pot' soothed Sally's feelings, and she dished up her squash in fine style. The dinner was safely put upon the table; the six dolls were seated three on a side; Teddy took the bottom, and Sally the top. When all were settled, it was a most imposing spectacle, for one doll was in full ball costume, another in her nightgown; Jerry, the worsted boy, wore his red winter suit, while Annabella, the noseless darling, was airily attired in nothing but her own kid skin. Teddy, as father of the family, behaved with great propriety, for he smilingly devoured everything offered him, and did not find a single fault. Daisy beamed upon her company like the weary, warm, but hospitable hostess so often to be seen at larger tables than this, and did the honours with an air of innocent satisfaction, which we do *not* often see elsewhere.

The steak was so tough that the little carving knife would not cut it; the potato did not go round, and the squash was very lumpy; but the guests appeared politely unconscious of these trifles; and the master and mistress of the house cleared the table with appetites that anyone might envy them. The joy of skimming a jugful of cream mitigated the anguish felt for the loss of the pies, and Asia's despised cake proved a treasure in the way of dessert.

'That is the nicest lunch I ever had; can't I do it every day?' asked Daisy as she scraped up and ate the leavings all round.

'You can cook things every day after lessons, but I prefer that you should eat your dishes at your regular meals, and only have a bit of gingerbread for lunch. Today, being the first time, I don't mind, but we must keep our rules. This afternoon you can make something for tea if you like,' said Mrs Jo, who had enjoyed the dinner party very much, though no one had invited her to partake.

'Do let me make flapjacks for Demi, he loves them so, and it's such fun to turn them and put sugar in between,' cried Daisy, tenderly wiping a yellow stain off Annabella's broken nose, for Bella had refused to eat squash when it was pressed upon her as good for 'lumatism', a complaint which it is no wonder she suffered from, considering the lightness of her attire.

'But if you give Demi goodies, all the others will expect some also, and then you will have your hands full.'

'Couldn't I have Demi come up to tea alone just this one time? And after that I could cook things for the others if they were good,' proposed Daisy, with a sudden inspiration.

'That is a capital idea, Posy! We will make your little messes rewards for the good boys, and I don't know one among them who would not like something nice to eat more than almost anything else. If little men are like big ones, good cooking will touch their hearts and soothe their tempers delightfully,' added Aunt Jo, with a merry nod toward the door, where stood Papa Bhaer, surveying the scene with a face full of amusement.

'That last hit was for me, sharp woman. I accept it, for it is true; but if I had married thee for thy cooking, heart's dearest, I should have fared badly all these years,' answered the professor, laughing as he tossed Teddy, who became quite apoplectic in his endeavours to describe the feast he had just enjoyed.

Daisy proudly showed her kitchen, and rashly promised Uncle Fritz as many flapjacks as he could eat. She was just telling about the new rewards when the boys, headed by Demi, burst into the room snuffing the air like a pack of hungry hounds, for school was out, dinner was not ready, and the fragrance of Daisy's steak led them straight to the spot.

A prouder little damsel was never seen than Sally as she displayed her treasures and told the lads what was in store for them. Several rather scoffed at the idea of her cooking anything fit to eat, but Stuffy's heart was won at once. Nat and Demi had firm faith in her skill, and the others said they would wait and see. All admired the kitchen, however, and examined the stove with deep interest. Demi offered to buy the boiler on the spot, to be used in a steam engine which he was constructing; and Ned declared that the best and biggest saucepan was just the thing to melt his lead in when he ran bullets, hatchets, and such trifles.

Daisy looked so alarmed at these proposals, that Mrs Jo then and there made and proclaimed a law that no boy should touch, use, or even approach the sacred stove without a special permit from the owner thereof. This increased its value immensely in the eyes of the gentlemen, especially as any infringement of the law would be punished by forfeiture of all right to partake of the delicacies promised to the virtuous.

At this point the bell rang, and the entire population went down to dinner, which meal was enlivened by each of the boys giving Daisy a list of things he would like to have cooked for him as fast as he earned them. Daisy, whose faith in her stove was unlimited, promised everything, if Aunt Jo would tell her how to make them. This suggestion rather alarmed Mrs Jo, for some of the dishes were quite beyond her skill – wedding cake, for instance, bull's-eye candy; and cabbage soup with herrings and cherries in it, which Mr Bhaer proposed as his favourite, and immediately reduced his wife to despair, for German cookery was beyond her.

Daisy wanted to begin again the minute dinner was done, but she was only allowed to clear up, fill the kettle ready for tea, and wash out her apron, which looked as if she had a Christmas feast. She was then sent out to play till five o'clock, for Uncle Fritz said that too much study, even at cooking stoves, was bad for little minds and bodies, and Aunt Jo knew by long experience how soon new toys lose their charm if they are not prudently used.

Everyone was very kind to Daisy that afternoon. Tommy promised her the first fruits of his garden, though the only visible crop just then was pig weed; Nat offered to supply her with wood, free of charge; Stuffy quite worshipped her; Ned immediately fell to work on a little refrigerator for her kitchen; and Demi, with a punctuality beautiful to see in one so young, escorted her to the nursery just as the clock struck five. It was not time for the party to begin, but he begged so hard to come in and help that he was allowed privileges few visitors enjoy, for he kindled the fire, ran errands, and watched the progress of his supper with intense interest. Mrs Jo directed the affair as she came and went, being very busy putting up clean curtains all over the house.

'Ask Asia for a cup of sour cream, then your cakes will be light without much soda, which I don't like,' was the first order.

Demi tore downstairs, and returned with the cream, also a puckered-up face, for he had tasted it on his way, and found it so sour that he predicted the cakes would be uneatable. Mrs Jo took this occasion to deliver a short lecture from the stepladder on the chemical properties of soda, to which Daisy did not listen, but Demi did, and understood it, as he proved by the brief but comprehensive reply: 'Yes, I see, soda turns sour things sweet, and the fizzling up makes them light. Let's see you do it, Daisy.'

'Fill that bowl nearly full of flour and add a little salt to it,' continued Mrs Jo.

'Oh dear, everything has to have salt in it, seems to me,' said Sally, who was tired of opening the pill-box in which it was kept.

'Salt is like good humour, and nearly everything is better for a pinch of it, Posy,' and Uncle Fritz stopped as he passed, hammer in hand, to drive up two or three nails for Sally's little pans to hang on.

'You are not invited to tea, but I'll give you some cakes, and I won't be cross,' said Daisy, putting up her floury little face to thank him with a kiss.

'Fritz, you must not interrupt my cooking class, or I'll come in and moralise when you are teaching Latin. How would you like that?' said Mrs Jo, throwing a great chintz curtain down on his head.

'Very much, try it and see,' and the amiable Father Bhaer went singing and tapping about the house like a mammoth woodpecker.

'Put the soda into the cream, and when it "fizzles", as Demi says, stir it into the flour, and beat it up as hard as ever you can. Have your griddle hot, butter it well, and then fry away till I come back,' and Aunt Jo vanished also.

Such a clatter as the little spoon made, and such a beating as the batter got, it quite foamed, I assure you; and when Daisy poured some on to the griddle, it rose like magic into a puffy flapjack that made Demi's mouth water. To be sure, the first one stuck and scorched, because she forgot the butter, but after that first failure all went well, and six capital little cakes were safely landed in a dish.

'I think I like maple syrup better than sugar,' said Demi, from his armchair where he had settled himself after setting the table in a new and peculiar manner.

'Then go and ask Asia for some,' answered Daisy, going into the bathroom to wash her hands.

While the nursery was empty something dreadful happened. You see, Kit had been feeling hurt all day because he had carried meat safely and yet got none to pay him. He was not a bad dog, but he had his little faults like the rest of us, and could not always resist temptation. Happening to stroll into the nursery at that moment, he smelt the cakes, saw them unguarded on the low table, and never stopping to think of consequences, swallowed all six at one mouthful. I am glad to say that they were very hot, and burned him so badly that he could not repress a surprised yelp. Daisy heard it, ran in, saw the empty dish, also the end of a yellow tail disappearing under the bed. Without a word she seized that tail, pulled out the thief, and shook him till his ears flapped wildly, then bundled him downstairs to the shed, where he spent a lonely evening in the coal bin.

Cheered by the sympathy which Demi gave her, Daisy made another bowlful of batter, and fried a dozen cakes, which were even better than the others. Indeed, Uncle Fritz after eating two sent up word that he had never tasted any so nice, and every boy at the table below envied Demi at the flapjack party above.

It was a truly delightful supper, for the little teapot lid only fell off three times and the milk jug upset but once; the cakes floated in syrup, and the toast had a delicious beef-steak flavour, owing to cook's using the gridiron to make it on. Demi forgot philosophy, and stuffed like any carnal boy, while Daisy planned sumptuous banquets, and the dolls looked on smiling affably.

'Well, dearies, have you had a good time?' asked Mrs Jo, coming up with Teddy on her shoulder.

'A very good time. I shall come again soon,' answered Demi, with emphasis.

'I'm afraid you have eaten too much, by the look of that table.'

'No, I haven't; I only ate fifteen cakes, and they were very little ones,' protested Demi, who had kept his sister busy supplying his plate.

'They won't hurt him, they are so nice,' said Daisy, with such a funny mixture of maternal fondness and housewifely pride that Aunt Jo could only smile and say, 'Well, on the whole, the new game is a success then?'

'I like it,' said Demi, as if his approval was all that was necessary.

'It is the dearest play ever made!' cried Daisy, hugging her little dish-tub as she proposed to wash up the cups. 'I just wish everybody had a sweet cooking stove like mine,' she added, regarding it with affection.

'This play ought to have a name,' said Demi, gravely removing the syrup from his countenance with his tongue.

'It has.'

'Oh, what?' asked both children eagerly.

'Well, I think we will call it patty pans,' and Aunt Jo retired, satisfied with the success of her last trap to catch a sunbeam.

CHAPTER 6

A Firebrand

'Please, ma'am, could I speak to you? It is something very important,' said Nat, popping his head in at the door of Mrs Bhaer's room.

It was the fifth head which had popped in during the last half-hour; but Mrs Jo was used to it, so she looked up, and said, briskly, 'What is it, my lad?'

Nat came in, shut the door carefully behind him, and said in an eager, anxious tone, 'Dan has come.'

'Who is Dan?'

'He's a boy I used to know when I fiddled round the streets. He sold papers, and he was kind to me, and I saw him the other day in town, and told him how nice it was here, and he's come.'

'But, my dear boy, that is rather a sudden way to pay a visit.'

'Oh, it isn't a visit; he wants to stay if you will let him!' said Nat innocently.

'Well, I don't know about that,' began Mrs Bhaer, rather startled by the coolness of the proposition.

'Why, I thought you liked to have poor boys come and live with you, and be kind to 'em as you were to me,' said Nat, looking surprised and alarmed.

'So I do, but I like to know something about them first. I have to choose them, because there are so many. I have not room for all. I wish I had.'

'I told him to come because I thought you'd like it, but if there isn't room he can go away again,' said Nat, sorrowfully.

The boy's confidence in her hospitality touched Mrs Bhaer, and she could not find the heart to disappoint his hope, and spoil his kind little plan, so she said, 'Tell me about this Dan.'

'I don't know anything, only he's got no folks, and he's poor, and he was good to me, so I'd like to be good to him if I could.'

'Excellent reasons every one; but really, Nat, the house is full, and I don't know where I could put him,' said Mrs Bhaer, more and more inclined to prove herself the haven of refuge he seemed to think her.

'He could have my bed, and I could sleep in the barn. It isn't cold now, and I don't mind, I used to sleep anywhere with Father,' said Nat, eagerly.

Something in his speech and face made Mrs Jo put her hand on his shoulder, and say in her kindest tone: 'Bring in your friend, Nat; I think we must find room for him without giving him your place.'

Nat joyfully ran off, and soon returned followed by a most unprepossessing boy, who slouched in and stood looking about him, with a half bold, half sullen look, which made Mrs Bhaer say to herself, after one glance, 'A bad specimen, I am afraid.'

'This is Dan,' said Nat, presenting him as if sure of his welcome.

'Nat tells me you would like to come and stay with us,' began Mrs Jo, in a friendly tone.

'Yes,' was the gruff reply.

'Have you no friends to take care of you?'

'No.'

'Say, "No, ma'am",' whispered Nat.

'Shan't neither,' muttered Dan.

'How old are you?'

'About fourteen.'

'You look older. What can you do?'

' 'Most anything.'

'If you stay here we shall want you to do as the others do, work and study as well as play. Are you willing to agree to that?'

'Don't mind trying.'

'Well, you can stay a few days, and we will see how we get on together. Take him out, Nat, and amuse him till Mr Bhaer comes home, when we will settle about the matter,' said Mrs Jo, finding it rather difficult to get on with this cool young person, who fixed his big black eyes on her with a hard, suspicious expression, sorrowfully unboyish.

'Come on, Nat,' he said, and slouched out again.

'Thank you, ma'am,' added Nat, as he followed him, feeling without quite understanding the difference in the welcome given to him and to his ungracious friend.

'The fellows are having a circus out in the barn; don't you want to come and see it?' he asked, as they came down the wide steps on to the lawn.

'Are they big fellows?' said Dan.

'No; the big ones are gone fishing.'

'Fire away, then,' said Dan.

Nat led him to the great barn and introduced him to his set, who were disporting themselves among the half-empty lofts. A large circle was marked out with hay on the wide floor, and in the middle stood Demi with a long whip, while Tommy, mounted on the much-enduring Toby, pranced about the circle playing being a monkey.

'You must pay a pin apiece, or you can't see the show,' said Stuffy, who stood by the wheelbarrow in which sat the band, consisting of a pocket-comb blown upon by Ned, and a toy drum beaten spasmodically by Rob.

'He's company, so I'll pay for both,' said Nat, handsomely, as he stuck two crooked pins in the dried mushroom which served as moneybox.

With a nod to the company they seated themselves on a couple of boards, and the performance went on. After the monkey act, Ned gave them a fine specimen of his agility by jumping over an old chair, and running up and down ladders, sailor fashion. Then Demi danced a jig with a gravity beautiful to behold. Nat was called upon to wrestle with Stuffy, and speedily laid that stout youth upon the ground. After this, Tommy proudly advanced to turn a somersault, an accomplishment which he had acquired by painful perseverance, practising in private till every joint of his little frame was black and blue. His feats were received with great applause, and he was about to retire, flushed with pride and a rush of blood to the head, when a scornful voice in the audience was heard to say, 'Ho! that ain't anything!'

'Say that again, will you?' and Tommy bristled up like an angry turkeycock.

'Do you want to fight?' said Dan, promptly descending from the barrel and doubling up his fists in a businesslike manner.

'No, I don't;' and the candid Thomas retired a step, rather taken aback by the proposition.

'Fighting isn't allowed!' cried the others, much excited.

'You're a nice lot,' sneered Dan.

'Come, if you don't behave, you shan't stay,' said Nat, firing up at that insult to his friends.

'I'd like to see him do better than I did, that's all,' observed Tommy, with a swagger.

'Clear the way, then,' and without the slightest preparation Dan turned three somersaults one after the other and came up on his feet.

'You can't beat that, Tom; you always hit your head and tumble flat,' said Nat, pleased at his friend's success.

Before he could say any more the audience were electrified by three more somersaults backwards, and a short promenade on the hands, head down, feet up. This brought down the house, and Tommy joined in the admiring cries which greeted the accomplished gymnast as he righted himself, and looked at them with an air of calm superiority.

'Do you think I could learn to do it without its hurting me very much?' Tom meekly asked, as he rubbed the elbows which still smarted after the last attempt.

'What will you give me if I'll teach you?' said Dan.

'My new jackknife; it's got five blades, and only one is broken.'

'Give it here, then.'

Tommy handed it over with an affectionate look at its smooth handle. Dan examined it carefully, then putting it into his pocket, walked off, saying with a wink, 'Keep it up till you learn, that's all.'

A howl of wrath from Tommy was followed by a general uproar, which did not subside till Dan, finding himself in a minority, proposed that they should play stick-knife, and whichever won should have the treasure. Tommy agreed, and the game was played in a circle of excited faces, which all wore an expression of satisfaction, when Tommy won and secured the knife in the depth of his safest pocket.

'You come off with me, and I'll show you round,' said Nat, feeling that he must have a little serious conversation with his friend in private.

What passed between them no one knew, but when they appeared again, Dan was more respectful to everyone, though still gruff in his speech, and rough in his manner; and what else could be expected of the poor lad who had been knocking about the world all his short life with no one to teach him any better?

The boys had decided that they did not like him, and so they left him to Nat, who soon felt rather oppressed by the responsibility, but too kind-hearted to desert him.

Tommy, however, felt that in spite of the jackknife transaction, there was a bond of sympathy between them, and longed to return to the interesting subject of somersaults. He soon found an opportunity, for Dan, seeing how much he admired him, grew more amiable, and by the end of the first week was quite intimate with the lively Tom.

Mr Bhaer, when he heard the story and saw Dan, shook his head, but only said quietly, 'The experiment may cost us something, but we will try it.'

If Dan felt any gratitude for his protection, he did not show it, and took without thanks all that was give him. He was ignorant, but very quick to learn when he chose; had sharp eyes to watch what went on about him; a saucy tongue, rough manners, and a temper that was fierce and sullen by turns. He played with all his might, and played well at almost all the games. He was silent and gruff before grown people, and only now and then was thoroughly sociable among the lads. Few of them really liked him, but few could help admiring his courage and strength, for nothing daunted him, and he knocked tall Franz flat on one occasion with an ease that caused all the others to keep at a respectful distance from his fists. Mr Bhaer watched him silently, and did his best to tame the 'Wild Boy', as they called him, but in private the worthy man shook his head, and said soberly, 'I hope the experiment will turn out well, but I am a little afraid it may cost too much.'

Mrs Bhaer lost her patience with him half a dozen times a day, yet never gave him up, and always insisted that there was something good in the lad, after all; for he was kinder to animals than to people, he liked to rove about in the woods, and, best of all, little Ted was fond of him. What the secret was no one could discover, but Baby took to him at once – gabbled and crowed whenever he saw him – preferred his strong back to ride on to any of the others and called him 'My Danny' out of his own little head. Teddy was the only creature to whom Dan showed an affection, and this was only manifested when he thought no one else would see it; but mothers' eyes are quick, and motherly hearts instinctively divine who love their babies. So Mrs Jo soon saw and felt that there was a soft spot in rough Dan, and bided her time to touch and win him.

But an unexpected and decidedly alarming event upset all their plans, and banished Dan from Plumfield.

Tommy, Nat, and Demi began by patronising Dan, because the other lads rather slighted him; but soon they each felt there was a certain fascination about the bad boy, and from looking down upon him they came to looking up, each for a different reason. Tommy admired his skill and courage; Nat was grateful for past kindness; and Demi regarded him as a sort of animated story book, for when he chose Dan could tell his adventures in a most interesting way. It pleased Dan to have the three favourites like him, and he exerted himself to be agreeable, which was the secret of his success.

The Bhaers were surprised, but hoped the lads would have a good influence over Dan, and waited with some anxiety, trusting that no harm would come of it.

Dan felt they did not quite trust him, and never showed them his best side, but took a wilful pleasure in trying their patience and thwarting their hopes as far as he dared.

Mr Bhaer did not approve of fighting, and did not think it a proof of either manliness or courage for two lads to pommel one another for the amusement of the rest. All sorts of hardy games and exercises were encouraged, and the boys were expected to take hard knocks and tumbles without whining; but black eyes and bloody noses given for the fun of it were forbidden as a foolish and a brutal play.

Dan laughed at this rule, and told such exciting tales of his own valour, and the many frays that he had been in, that some of the lads were fired with a desire to have a regular good 'mill'.

'Don't tell, and I'll show you how,' said Dan; and, getting half a dozen of the lads together behind the barn, he gave them a lesson in boxing, which quite satisfied the ardour of most of them. Emil, however, could not submit to be beaten by a fellow younger than himself, for Emil was past fourteen and a plucky fellow, so he challenged Dan to a fight. Dan accepted at once, and the others looked on with intense interest.

What little bird carried the news to headquarters no one ever knew, but, in the very hottest of the fray, when Dan and Emil were fighting like a pair of young bulldogs, and the others with fierce, excited faces were cheering them on, Mr Bhaer walked into the ring, plucked the combatants apart with a strong hand, and said, in the voice they seldom heard, 'I can't allow this, boys! Stop it at once; and never let me see it again. I keep a school for boys, not for wild beasts. Look at each other and be ashamed of yourselves.'

'You let me go, and I'll knock him down again,' shouted Dan, sparring away in spite of the grip on his collar.

'Come on, come on, I ain't thrashed yet!' cried Emil, who had been down five times, but did not know when he was beaten.

'They are playing at gladdy – what-you-call-'ems, like the Romans, Uncle Fritz,' called out Demi, whose eyes were bigger than ever with the excitement of this new pastime.

'They were a fine set of brutes; but we have learned something since then, I hope, and I cannot have you make my barn a Colosseum. Who proposed this?' asked Mr Bhaer.

'Dan,' answered several voices.

'Don't you know that it is forbidden?'

'Yes,' growled Dan, sullenly.

'Then why break the rule?'

'They'll all be mollycoddles, if they don't know how to fight.'

'Have you found Emil a mollycoddle? He doesn't look much like one,' and Mr Bhaer brought the two face to face. Dan had a black eye, and his jacket was torn to rags, but Emil's face was covered with blood from a cut lip and a bruised nose, while a bump on his forehead was already as purple as a plum. In spite of his wounds however, he still glared upon his foe, and evidently panted to renew the fight.

'He'd make a first-rater if he was taught,' said Dan, unable to withhold the praise from the boy who made it necessary for him to do his best.

'He'll be taught to fence and box by and by, and till then I think he will do very well without any lessons in mauling. Go and wash your faces; and remember, Dan, if you break any more of the rules again, you will be sent away. That was the bargain; do your part and we will do ours.'

The lads went off, and after a few more words to the spectators, Mr Bhaer followed to bind up the wounds of the young gladiators. Emil went to bed sick, and Dan was an unpleasant spectacle for a week.

But the lawless lad had no thought of obeying, and soon transgressed again.

One Saturday afternoon as a party of the boys went out to play, Tommy said, 'Let's go down to the river, and cut a lot of new fish-poles.'

'Take Toby to drag them back, and one of us can ride him down,' proposed Stuffy, who hated to walk.

'That means *you*, I suppose; well, hurry up, lazybones,' said Dan.

Away they went, and having got the poles were about to go home, when Demi unluckily said to Tommy, who was on Toby with a long rod in his hand, 'You look like the picture of the man in the bullfight, only you haven't got a red cloth, or pretty clothes on.'

'I'd like to see one; there's old Buttercup in the big meadow, ride at her, Tom, and see her run,' proposed Dan, bent on mischief.

'No, you mustn't,' began Demi, who was learning to distrust Dan's propositions.

'Why not, little fuss-button?' demanded Dan.

'I don't think Uncle Fritz would like it.'

'Did he ever say we must not have a bullfight?'

'No, I don't think he ever did,' admitted Demi.

'Then hold your tongue. Drive on, Tom, and here's a red rag to flap at the old thing. I'll help you to stir her up,' and over the wall went Dan, full of the new game, and the rest followed like a flock of sheep; even Demi, who sat upon the bars, and watched the fun with interest.

Poor Buttercup was not in a very good mood, for she had been lately bereft of her calf, and mourned for the little thing most dismally. Just now she regarded all mankind as her enemies (and I do not blame her), so when the matador came prancing towards her with the red handkerchief flying at the end of his long lance, she threw up her head, and gave a most appropriate 'Moo!' Tommy rode gallantly at her, and Toby recognising an old friend, was quite willing to approach; but when the lance came down on her back with a loud whack, both cow and donkey were surprised and disgusted. Toby backed with a bray of remonstrance, and Buttercup lowered her horns angrily.

'At her again, Tom; she's jolly cross, and will do it capitally!' called Dan, coming up behind with another rod, while Jack and Ned followed his example.

Seeing herself thus beset, and treated with such disrespect, Buttercup trotted round the field, getting more and more bewildered and excited every moment, for whichever way she turned, there was a dreadful boy, yelling and brandishing a new and very disagreeable sort of whip. It was great fun for them, but real misery for her, till she lost patience and turned the tables in the most unexpected manner. All at once she wheeled short round, and charged full at her old friend Toby, whose conduct cut her to the heart. Poor slow Toby backed so precipitately that he tripped over a stone, and down went horse, matador, and all, in one ignominious heap, while distracted Buttercup took a surprising leap over the wall, and galloped wildly out of sight down the road.

'Catch her, stop her, head her off! run, boys, run!' shouted Dan, tearing after her at his best pace, for she was Mr Bhaer's pet Alderney, and if anything happened to her, Dan feared it would be all over with him. Such a running and racing and bawling and puffing as there was before she was caught! The fish-poles were left behind; Toby was trotted nearly off his legs in the chase; and every boy was red, breathless, and scared. They found poor Buttercup at last in a flower garden, where she had taken refuge, worn out with the long run. Borrowing a rope for a halter, Dan led her home, followed by a party of very sober young gentlemen, for the cow was in a sad state, having strained her shoulder jumping, so that she limped, her eyes looked wild, and her glossy coat was wet and muddy.

'You'll catch it this time, Dan,' said Tommy, as he led the wheezing donkey beside the maltreated cow.

'So will you, for you helped.'

'We all did, but Demi,' added Jack.

'He put it into our heads,' said Ned.

'I told you not to do it,' cried Demi, who was most broken-hearted at poor Buttercup's state.

'Old Bhaer will send me off, I guess. Don't care if he does,' muttered Dan, looking worried in spite of his words.

'We'll ask him not to, all of us,' said Demi, and the others assented with the exception of Stuffy, who cherished the hope that all the punishment might fall on one guilty head. Dan only said, 'Don't bother about me;' but he never forgot it, even though he led the lads astray again, as soon as the temptation came.

When Mr Bhaer saw the animal, and heard the story, he said very little, evidently fearing that he should say too much in the first moments of impatience. Buttercup was made comfortable in her stall, and the boys sent to their rooms till supper-time. This brief respite gave them time to think the matter over, to wonder what the penalty would be, and to try to imagine where Dan would be sent. He whistled briskly in his room, so that no one should think he cared a bit; but while he waited to know his fate, the longing to stay grew stronger and stronger, the more he recalled the comfort and kindness he had known here, the hardship and neglect he had felt elsewhere. He knew they tried to help him, and at the bottom of his heart he was grateful, but his rough life had made him hard and careless, suspicious and wilful. He hated restraint of any sort, and fought against it like an untamed creature, even while he knew it was kindly meant, and

The matador came prancing towards Buttercup with the red
handkerchief flying at the end of his long lance

dimly felt that he would be the better for it. He made up his mind to be turned adrift again, to knock about the city as he had done nearly all his life; a prospect that made him knit his black brows, and look about the cosy little room with a wistful expression that would have touched a much harder heart than Mr Bhaer's if he had seen it. It vanished instantly, however, when the good man came in, and said in his accustomed grave way, 'I have heard all about it, Dan, and though you have broken the rules again, I am going to give you one more trial, to please Mother Bhaer.'

Dan flushed up to his forehead at this unexpected reprieve, but he only said in his gruff way, 'I didn't know there was any rule about bullfighting.'

'As I never expected to have any at Plumfield, I never did make such a rule,' answered Mr Bhaer, smiling in spite of himself at the boy's excuse. Then he added gravely, 'But one of the first and most important of our few laws is the law of kindness to every dumb creature on the place. I want everybody and everything to be happy here, to love and trust, and serve us, as we try to love and trust and serve them faithfully and willingly. I have often said that you were kinder to the animals than any of the other boys, and Mrs Bhaer liked that trait in you very much, because she thought it showed a good heart. But you have disappointed us in that, and we are sorry, for we hoped to make you quite one of us. Shall we try again?'

Dan's eyes had been on the floor, and his hands nervously picking at the bit of wood he had been whittling as Mr Bhaer came in, but when he heard the kind voice ask that question, he looked up quickly, and said in a more respectful tone than he had ever used before, 'Yes, please.'

'Very well, then, we will say no more, only you will stay at home from the walk tomorrow, as the other boys will and all of you must wait on poor Buttercup till she is well again.'

'I will.'

'Now, go down to supper, and do your best, my boy, more for your own sake than for ours.' Then Mr Bhaer shook hands with him, and Dan went down more tamed by kindness than he would have been by the good whipping which Asia had strongly recommended.

Dan did try for a day or two, but not being used to it, he soon tired and relapsed into his old wilful ways. Mr Bhaer was called from home on business one day, and the boys had no lessons. They liked this, and played hard till bedtime, when most of them turned in and slept like dormice. Dan, however, had a plan in his head, and when he and Nat were alone, he unfolded it.

'Look here!' he said, taking from under his bed a bottle, a cigar, and a pack of cards, 'I'm going to have some fun, and do as I used to with the fellows in town. Here's some beer, I got it off the old man at the station, and this cigar; you can pay for 'em or Tommy will, he's got heaps of money and I haven't a cent. I'm going to ask him in; no, you go, they won't mind you.'

'The folks won't like it,' began Nat.

'They won't know. Daddy Bhaer is away, and Mrs Bhaer's busy with Ted; he's got croup or something, and she can't leave him. We shan't sit up late or make any noise, so where's the harm?'

'Asia will know if we burn the lamp long, she always does.'

'No, she won't, I've got the dark lantern on purpose; it don't give much light, and we can shut it quick if we hear anyone coming,' said Dan.

This idea struck Nat as a fine one, and lent an air of romance to the thing. He started off to tell Tommy, but put his head in again to say, 'You want Demi, too, don't you?'

'No, I don't; the Deacon will roll up eyes and preach if you tell him. He will be asleep, so just tip the wink to Tom and cut back again.'

Nat obeyed, and returned in a minute with Tommy half dressed, rather tousled about the head and very sleepy, but quite ready for fun as usual.

'Now, keep quiet, and I'll show you how to play a first-rate game called "poker",' said Dan, as the three revellers gathered round the table, on which were set forth the bottle, the cigar, and the cards. 'First we'll all have a drink, then we'll take a go at the "weed", and then we'll play. That's the way men do, and it's jolly fun.'

The beer circulated in a mug, and all three smacked their lips over it, though Nat and Tommy did not like the bitter stuff. The cigar was worse still, but they dared not say so, and each puffed away till he was dizzy or choked, when he passed the 'weed' on to his neighbour. Dan liked it, for it seemed like old times when he now and then had a chance to imitate the low men who surrounded him. He drank, and smoked, and swaggered as much like them as he could, and, getting into the spirit of the part he assumed, he soon began to swear under his breath for fear someone should hear him. 'You mustn't; it's wicked to say "Damn!"' cried Tommy, who had followed his leader so far.

'Oh, hang! don't you preach, but play away; it's part of the fun to swear.'

'I'd rather say "thunder-turtles",' said Tommy, who had composed this interesting exclamation and was very proud of it.

'And I'll say "the Devil"; that sounds well,' added Nat, much impressed by Dan's manly ways.

Dan scoffed at their 'nonsense', and swore stoutly as he tried to teach them the new game.

But Tommy was very sleepy, and Nat's head began to ache with the beer and the smoke, so neither of them was very quick to learn, and the game dragged. The room was nearly dark, for the lantern burned badly; they could not laugh loud nor move about much, for Silas slept next door in the shed-chamber, and altogether the party was dull. In the middle of a deal Dan stopped suddenly, and called out, 'Who's that?' in a startled tone, and at the same moment drew the slide over the light. A voice in the darkness said tremulously, 'I can't find Tommy,' and then there was the quick patter of bare feet running away down the entry that led from the wing to the main house.

'It's Demi! he's gone to call someone; cut into bed, Tom, and don't tell!' cried Dan, whisking all signs of the revel out of sight, and beginning to tear off his clothes, while Nat did the same.

Tommy flew to his room and dived into bed, where he lay, laughing till something burned his hand, when he discovered that he was still clutching the stump of the festive cigar, which he happened to be smoking when the revel broke up.

It was nearly out, and he was about to extinguish it carefully when Nursey's voice was heard, and fearing it would betray him if he hid it in the bed, he threw it underneath, after a final pinch which he thought finished it.

Nursey came in with Demi, who looked much amazed to see the red face of Tommy reposing peacefully upon his pillow.

'He wasn't there just now, because I woke up and could not find him anywhere,' said Demi, pouncing on him.

'What mischief are you at now, bad child?' asked Nursey, with a good-natured shake, which made the sleeper open his eyes to say meekly, 'I only ran into Nat's room to see him about something. Go away, and let me alone; I'm awful sleepy.'

Nursey tucked Demi in, and went off to reconnoitre, but only found two boys slumbering peacefully in Dan's room. 'Some little frolic,' she thought, and as there was no harm done she said nothing to Mrs Bhaer, who was busy and worried over little Teddy.

Tommy was sleepy, and telling Demi to mind his own business and not ask questions, he was snoring in ten minutes, little dreaming what was going on under his bed. The cigar did not go out, but smouldered away on the straw carpet till it was nicely on fire, and a hungry little flame went creeping along till the dimity bedcover caught, then the sheets, and then the bed itself. The beer made Tommy sleep heavily, and the smoke stupified Demi, so they slept on till the fire began to scorch them, and they were in danger of being burned to death.

Franz was sitting up to study, and as he left the school-room he smelt the smoke, dashed upstairs and saw it coming in a cloud from the left wing of the house. Without stopping to call anyone, he ran into the room, dragged the boys from the blazing bed, and splashed all the water he could find at hand on to the flames. It checked but did not quench the fire, and the children wakened on being tumbled topsy-turvy into a cold hall, began to roar at the top of their voices. Mrs Bhaer instantly appeared, and a minute after Silas burst out of his room shouting, 'Fire!' in a tone that raised the whole house. A flock of white goblins with scared faces crowded into the hall, and for a minute everyone was panic-stricken.

Then Mrs Bhaer found her wits, bade Nursey see to the burnt boys, and sent Franz and Silas downstairs for some tubs of wet clothes which she flung on the bed, over the carpet, and up against the curtains, now burning finely, and threatening to kindle the walls.

Most of the boys stood dumbly looking on, but Dan and Emil worked bravely, running to and fro with water from the bath-room, and helping to pull down the dangerous curtains.

The peril was soon over, and ordering the boys all back to bed, and leaving Silas to watch lest the fire broke out again, Mrs Bhaer and Franz went to see how the poor boys got on. Demi had escaped with one burn and a grand scare, but Tommy had not only most of his hair scorched off his head, but a great burn on his arm, that made him half crazy with the pain. Demi was soon made cosy, and Franz took him away to his own bed, where the kind lad soothed his fright and hummed him to sleep as cosily as a woman. Nursey watched over poor Tommy all night, trying to ease his misery, and Mrs Bhaer vibrated between him and little Teddy with oil and cotton, paregoric and squills, saying to herself from time to time, as if she found great amusement in the thought, 'I always *knew* Tommy would set the house on fire, and now he has done it!'

When Mr Bhaer got home next morning he found a nice state of things. Tommy in bed, Teddy wheezing like a little grampus, Mrs Jo quite used up, and the whole flock of boys so excited that they all talked at once, and almost dragged him by main force to view the ruins. Under his quiet management things soon fell into order, for everyone felt that he was equal to a dozen conflagrations, and worked with a will at whatever task he gave them.

There was no school that morning, but by afternoon the damaged room was put to rights, the invalids were better, and there was time to hear and judge the little culprits quietly. Nat and Tommy told their parts in the mischief, and were honestly sorry for the danger they had brought to the dear old house and all in it. But Dan put on his devil-may-care look, and would not own that there was much harm done.

Now, of all things, Mr Bhaer hated drinking, gambling, and swearing; smoking he had given up that the lads might not be tempted to try it, and it grieved and angered him deeply to find that the boy, with whom he had tried to be most forbearing, should take advantage of his absence to introduce these forbidden vices, and teach his innocent little lads to think it manly and pleasant to indulge in them. He talked long and earnestly to the assembled boys, and ended by saying, with an air of mingled firmness and regret, 'I think Tommy is punished enough, and that scar on his arm will remind him for a long time to let these things alone. Nat's fright will do for him, for he is really sorry, and does try to obey me. But you, Dan, have been many times forgiven, and yet it does no good. I cannot have my boys hurt by your bad example, nor my time wasted in talking to deaf ears, so you can say goodbye to them all, and tell Nursey to put up your things in my little black bag.'

'Oh! sir, where is he going?' cried Nat.

'To a pleasant place up in the country, where I sometimes send boys when they don't do well here. Mr Page is a kind man, and Dan will be happy there if he chooses to do his best.'

'Will he ever come back?' asked Demi.

'That will depend on himself; I hope so.'

As he spoke, Mr Bhaer left the room to write his letter to Mr Page, and the boys crowded round Dan very much as people do about a man who is going on a long and perilous journey to unknown regions.

'I wonder if you'll like it,' began Jack.

'Shan't stay if I don't,' said Dan coolly.

'Where will you go?' asked Nat.

'I may go to sea, or out west, or take a look at California,' answered Dan, with a reckless air that quite took away the breath of the little boys.

'Oh, don't! stay with Mr Page awhile and then come back here; do, Dan,' pleaded Nat, much affected at the whole affair.

'I don't care where I go, or how long I stay, and I'll be hanged if I ever come back here,' with which wrathful speech Dan went away to put up his things, every one of which Mr Bhaer had given him.

That was the only goodbye he gave the boys, for they were all talking the matter over in the barn when he came down, and he told Nat not to call them. The wagon stood at the door, and Mrs Bhaer came out to speak to Dan, looking so sad that his heart smote him, and he said in a low tone, 'May I say goodbye to Teddy?'

'Yes, dear; go in and kiss him, he will miss his Danny very much.'

No one saw the look in Dan's eyes as he stooped over the crib, and saw the little face light up at first sight of him, but he heard Mrs Bhaer say pleadingly, 'Can't we give the poor lad one more trial, Fritz?' and Mr Bhaer answer in his steady way, 'My dear, it is not best, so let him go where he can do no harm to others, while they do good to him, and by and by he shall come back, I promise you.'

'He's the only boy we ever failed with, and I am so grieved, for I thought there was the making of a fine man in him, spite of his faults.'

Dan heard Mrs Bhaer sigh, and he wanted to ask for one more trial himself, but his pride would not let him, and he came out with the hard look on his face, shook hands without a word, and drove away with Mr Bhaer, leaving Nat and Mrs Jo to look after him with tears in their eyes.

A few days afterwards they received a letter from Mr Page, saying that Dan was doing well, whereat they all rejoiced. But three weeks later came another letter, saying that Dan had run away, and nothing had been heard of him, whereat they all looked sober, and Mr Bhaer said, 'Perhaps I ought to have given him another chance.'

Mrs Bhaer, however, nodded wisely and answered, 'Don't be troubled, Fritz; the boy will come back to us, I'm sure of it.'

But time went on and no Dan came.

CHAPTER 7

Naughty Nan

'Fritz, I've got a new idea,' cried Mrs Bhaer, as she met her husband one day after school.

'Well, my dear, what is it?' and he waited willingly to hear the new plan, for some of Mrs Jo's ideas were so droll, it was impossible to help laughing at them, though usually they were quite sensible, and he was glad to carry them out.

'Daisy needs a companion, and the boys would be all the better for another girl among them; you know we believe in bringing up little men and women together, and it is high time we acted up to our belief. They pet and tyrannise over Daisy by turns, and she is getting spoilt. Then they must learn gentle ways, and improve their manners, and having girls about will do it better than anything else.'

'You are right, as usual. Now, who shall we have?' asked Mr Bhaer, seeing by the look in her eye that Mrs Jo had someone all ready to propose.

'Little Annie Harding.'

'What! Naughty Nan, as the lads call her?' cried Mr Bhaer, looking very much amused.

'Yes, she is running wild at home since her mother died, and is too bright a child to be spoilt by servants. I have had my eye on her for some time, and when I met her father in town the other day I asked him why he did not send her to school. He said he would gladly if he could find as good a school for girls as ours was for boys. I know he would rejoice to have her come; so suppose we drive over this afternoon and see about it.'

'Have not you cares enough now, my Jo, without this little gypsy to torment you?' asked Mr Bhaer, patting the hand that lay on his arm.

'Oh dear, no,' said Mother Bhaer, briskly. 'I like it, and never was happier than since I had my wilderness of boys. You see, Fritz,

I feel a great sympathy for Nan, because I was such a naughty child myself that I know all about it. She is full of spirits, and only needs to be taught what to do with them to be as nice a little girl as Daisy. Those quick wits of hers would enjoy lessons if they were rightly directed, and what is now a tricksy midget would soon become a busy, happy child. I know how to manage her, for I remember how my blessed mother managed me, and . . . '

'And if you succeed half as well as she did, you will have done a magnificent work,' interrupted Mr Bhaer, who laboured under the delusion that Mrs B. was the best and most charming woman alive.

'Now, if you make fun of my plan I'll give you bad coffee for a week, and then where are you, sir?' cried Mrs Jo, tweaking him by the ear just as if he was one of the boys.

'Won't Daisy's hair stand erect with horror at Nan's wild ways?' asked Mr Bhaer, presently, when Teddy had swarmed up his waist-coat, and Rob up his back, for they always flew at their father the minute school was done.

'At first, perhaps, but it will do Posy good. She is getting prim and Bettyish, and needs stirring up a bit. She always has a good time when Nan comes over to play, and the two will help each other without knowing it. Dear me, half the science of teaching is knowing how much children do for one another, and when to mix them.'

'I only hope she won't turn out another firebrand.'

'My poor Dan! I never can quite forgive myself for letting him go,' sighed Mrs Bhaer.

At the sound of the name, little Teddy, who had never forgotten his friend, struggled down from his father's arms, and trotted to the door, looked out over the sunny lawn with a wistful face, and then trotted back again, saying, as he always did when disappointed of the longed-for sight, 'My Danny's tummin' soon.'

'I really think we ought to have kept him, if only for Teddy's sake, he was so fond of him, and perhaps Baby's love would have done for him what we failed to do.'

'I've sometimes felt that myself; but after keeping the boys in a ferment, and nearly burning up the whole family, I thought it safer to remove the firebrand, for a time at least,' said Mr Bhaer.

'Dinner's ready, let me ring the bell,' and Rob began a solo upon that instrument which made it impossible to hear oneself speak.

'Then I may have Nan, may I?' asked Mrs Jo.

'A dozen Nans if you want them, my dear,' answered Mr Bhaer, who had room in his fatherly heart for all the naughty neglected children in the world.

When Mrs Bhaer returned from her drive that afternoon, before she could unpack the load of little boys, without whom she seldom moved, a small girl of ten skipped out at the back of the carryall and ran into the house, shouting, 'Hi, Daisy! where are you?'

Daisy came, and looked pleased to see her guest, but also a trifle alarmed, when Nan said, still prancing, as if it was impossible to keep still, 'I'm going to stay here always, Papa says I may, and my box is coming tomorrow, all my things had to be washed and mended, and your aunt came and carried me off. Isn't it great fun?'

'Why, yes. Did you bring your big doll?' asked Daisy, hoping she had, for on the last visit Nan had ravaged the baby house, and insisted on washing Blanche Matilda's plaster face, which spoilt the poor dear's complexion for ever.

'Yes, she's somewhere round,' returned Nan, with most unmaternal carelessness. 'I made you a ring coming along, and pulled the hairs out of Dobbin's tail. Don't you want it?' and Nan presented a horsehair ring in token of friendship, as they had both vowed they would never speak to one another again when they last parted.

Won by the beauty of the offering, Daisy grew more cordial, and proposed retiring to the nursery, but Nan said, 'No, I want to see the boys, and the barn,' and ran off, swinging her hat by one string till it broke, when she left it to its fate on the grass.

'Hello! Nan!' cried the boys as she bounced in among them with the announcement, 'I'm going to stay.'

'Hooray!' bawled Tommy from the wall on which he was perched, for Nan was a kindred spirit, and he foresaw 'larks' in the future.

'I can bat; let me play,' said Nan, who could turn her hand to anything, and did not mind hard knocks.

'We ain't playing now, and our side beat without you.'

'I can beat you in running, anyway,' returned Nan, falling back on her strong point.

'Can she?' asked Nat of Jack.

'She runs very well for a girl,' answered Jack, who looked down upon Nan with condescending approval.

'Will you try?' said Nan, longing to display her powers.

'It's too hot,' and Tommy languished against the wall as if quite exhausted.

'What's the matter with Stuffy?' asked Nan, whose quick eyes were roving from face to face.

'Ball hurt his hand; he howls at everything,' answered Jack scornfully.

'I don't, I never cry, no matter how I'm hurt; it's babyish,' said Nan, loftily.

'Pooh! I could make you cry in two minutes,' returned Stuffy, rousing up.

'See if you can.'

'Go and pick that bunch of nettles, then,' and Stuffy pointed to a sturdy specimen of that prickly plant growing by the wall.

Nan instantly 'grasped the nettle', pulled it up, and held it with a defiant gesture, in spite of the almost unbearable sting.

'Good for you,' cried the boys, quick to acknowledge courage even in one of the weaker sex.

More nettled than she was, Stuffy determined to get a cry out of her somehow, and he said tauntingly, 'You are used to poking your hands into everything, so that isn't fair. Now go and bump your head real hard against the barn, and see if you don't howl then.'

'Don't do it,' said Nat, who hated cruelty.

But Nan was off, and running straight at the barn, she gave her head a blow that knocked her flat, and sounded like a battering-ram. Dizzy, but undaunted, she staggered up, saying stoutly, though her face was drawn with pain, 'That hurt, but I don't cry.'

'Do it again,' said Stuffy angrily; and Nan *would* have done it, but Nat held her; and Tommy, forgetting the heat, flew at Stuffy like a little gamecock, roaring out, 'Stop it, or I'll throw you over the barn!' and so shook and hustled poor Stuffy that for a minute he did not know whether he was on his head or his heels.

'She told me to,' was all he could say, when Tommy let him alone.

'Never mind if she did; it is awfully mean to hurt a little girl,' said Demi, reproachfully.

'Ho! I don't mind; I ain't a little girl, I'm older than you and Daisy; so now,' cried Nan, ungratefully.

'Don't preach, Deacon, you bully Posy every day of your life,' called out the Commodore, who just then hove in sight.

'I don't hurt her; do I, Daisy?' and Demi turned to his sister, who was 'pooring' Nan's tingling hands, and recommending water for the purple lump rapidly developing itself on her forehead.

'You are the best boy in the world,' promptly answered Daisy; adding, as truth compelled her to do, 'You hurt me sometimes, but you don't mean to.'

'Put away the bats and things, and mind what you are about, my hearties. No fighting allowed aboard this ship,' said Emil, who rather lorded it over the others.

'How do you do, Madge Wildfire?' said Mr Bhaer, as Nan came in with the rest to supper. 'Give the right hand, little daughter, and mind thy manners,' he added, as Nan offered him her left.

'The other hurts me.'

'The poor little hand! what has it been doing to get those blisters?' he asked, drawing it from behind her back, where she had put it with a look which made him think she had been in mischief.

Before Nan could think of any excuse, Daisy burst out with the whole story, during which Stuffy tried to hide his face in a bowl of bread and milk. When the tale was finished, Mr Bhaer looked down the long table towards his wife, and said with a laugh in his eyes, 'This rather belongs to your side of the house, so I won't meddle with it, my dear.'

Mrs Jo knew what he meant, but she liked her little black sheep all the better for her pluck, though she only said in her soberest way, 'Do you know why I asked Nan to come here?'

'To plague me,' muttered Stuffy, with his mouth full.

'To help make little gentlemen of you, and I think you have shown that some of you need it.'

Here Stuffy retired into his bowl again, and did not emerge till Demi made them all laugh by saying, in his slow wondering way, 'How can she, when she's such a tomboy?'

'That's just it, she needs help as much as you, and I expect you set her an example of good manners.'

'Is she going to be a little gentleman too?' asked Rob.

'She'd like it; wouldn't you, Nan?' added Tommy.

'No, I shouldn't; I hate boys!' said Nan fiercely, for her hand still smarted, and she began to think that she might have shown her courage in some wiser way.

'I am sorry you hate my boys, because they can be well-mannered, and most agreeable when they choose. Kindness in looks and words and ways is true politeness, and anyone can have it if they only try to treat other people as they like to be treated themselves.'

Mrs Bhaer had addressed herself to Nan, but the boys nudged one another, and appeared to take the hint, for that time at least, and passed the butter; said 'please', and 'thank you', 'yes, sir', and 'no, ma'am', with unusual elegance and respect. Nan said nothing, but kept herself quiet and refrained from tickling Demi, though strongly tempted to do so, because of the dignified airs he put on. She also appeared to have forgotten her hatred of boys, and played 'I spy' with them till dark. Stuffy was observed to offer her frequent sucks on his candy-ball during the game, which evidently sweetened her temper, for the last thing she said on going to bed was, 'When my battledore and shuttlecock comes, I'll let you all play with 'em.'

Her first remark in the morning was 'Has my box come?' and when told that it would arrive sometime during the day, she fretted and fumed, and whipped her doll, till Daisy was shocked. She managed to exist, however, till five o'clock, when she disappeared, and was not missed till supper-time, because those at home thought she had gone to the hill with Tommy and Demi.

'I saw her going down the avenue alone as hard as she could pelt,' said Mary Ann, coming in with the hasty-pudding, and finding everyone asking, 'Where is Nan?'

'She has run home, little gypsy!' cried Mrs Bhaer, looking anxious.

'Perhaps she has gone to the station to look after her luggage,' suggested Franz.

'That is impossible, she does not know the way, and if she found it, she could never carry the box a mile,' said Mrs Bhaer, beginning to think that her new idea might be rather a hard one to carry out.

'It would be like her,' and Mr Bhaer caught up his hat to go and find the child, when a shout from Jack, who was at the window, made everyone hurry to the door.

There was Miss Nan, to be sure, tugging along a very large band-box tied up in linen bag. Very hot and dusty and tired did she look, but marched stoutly along, and came puffing up to the steps, where she dropped her load with a sigh of relief, and sat down upon it, observing as she crossed her tired arms, 'I couldn't wait any longer, so I went and got it.'

'But you did not know the way,' said Tommy, while the rest stood round enjoying the joke.

'Oh, I found it, I never get lost.'

'It's a mile, how could you go so far?'

'Well, it was pretty far, but I rested a good deal.'

'Wasn't that thing very heavy?'

'It's so round, I couldn't get hold of it good, and I thought my arms would break right off.'

'I don't see how the stationmaster let you have it,' said Tommy.

'I didn't say anything to him. He was in the little ticket place, and didn't see me, so I just took it off the platform.'

'Run down and tell him it is all right, Franz, or old Dodd will think it is stolen,' said Mr Bhaer, joining in the shout of laughter at Nan's coolness.

'I told you we would send for it if it did not come. Another time you must wait, for you will get into trouble if you run away. Promise me this, or I shall not dare to trust you out of my sight,' said Mrs Bhaer, wiping the dust off Nan's little hot face.

'Well, I won't, only Papa tells me not to put off doing things, so I don't.'

'That is rather a poser; I think you had better give her some supper now, and a private lecture by and by,' said Mr Bhaer, too much amused to be angry at the young lady's exploit.

The boys thought it 'great fun', and Nan entertained them all supper-time with an account of her adventures; for a big dog had barked at her, a man had laughed at her, a woman had given her a doughnut, and her hat had fallen into the brook when she stopped to drink, exhausted with her exertion.

'I fancy you will have your hands full now, my dear; Tommy and Nan are quite enough for one woman,' said Mr Bhaer, half an hour later.

'I know it will take some time to tame the child, but she is such a generous, warm-hearted little thing, I should love her even if she were twice as naughty,' answered Mrs Jo, pointing to the merry group, in the middle of which stood Nan, giving away her things right and left, as lavishly as if the big band-box had no bottom.

It was those good traits that soon made little 'Giddygaddy', as they called her, a favourite with everyone. Daisy never complained of being dull again, for Nan invented the most delightful plays, and her pranks rivalled Tommy's, to the amusement of the whole school. She buried her big doll and forgot it for a week, and found it well mildewed when she dragged it up. Daisy was in despair, but Nan took it to the painter who as at work about the house, got him to paint it brick red, with staring black eyes, then she dressed it up with feathers, and scarlet flannel, and one of Ned's leaden hatchets; and in the character of an Indian chief, the late Poppy-dilla tomahawked all the other dolls, and caused the nursery to run red with imaginary gore. She gave away her new shoes to a beggar child, hoping to be allowed to go barefoot, but found it impossible to combine charity and comfort, and was ordered to ask leave before disposing of her clothes. She delighted the boys by making a fire-ship out of a shingle with two large sails wet with turpentine, which she lighted, and then sent the little vessel floating down the brook at dusk. She harnessed the old turkeycock to a straw wagon, and made him trot round the house at a tremendous pace. She gave her coral necklace for four unhappy kittens, which had been tormented by some heartless lads, and tended them for days as gently as a mother, dressing their wounds with cold cream, feeding them with a doll's spoon, and mourning over them when they died, till she was consoled by one of Demi's best turtles. She made Silas tattoo an anchor on her arm like his, and begged hard to have a blue star on each cheek, but he dared not do it, though she coaxed and scolded till the soft-hearted fellow longed to give in. She rode every animal on the place, from the big horse Andy to the cross pig, from whom she was rescued with difficulty. Whatever the boys dared her to do she instantly attempted, no matter how dangerous it might be, and they were never tired of testing her courage.

Mr Bhaer suggested that they should see who would study best, and Nan found as much pleasure in using her quick wits and fine memory as her active feet and merry tongue, while the lads had to do their best to keep their places, for Nan showed them that girls could do most things as well as boys, and some things better. There were no rewards in school, but Mr Bhaer's 'Well done!' and Mrs Bhaer's good report on the conscience book, taught them to love duty for its own sake, and try to do it faithfully, sure that sooner or later the recompense would come. Little Nan was quick to feel the new atmosphere, to enjoy it, to show that it was what she needed; for this little garden was full of sweet flowers, half hidden by the weeds; and when kind hands gently began to cultivate it, all sorts of green shoots sprung up, promising to blossom beautifully in the warmth of love and care, the best climate for young hearts and souls all the world over.

CHAPTER 8

Pranks and Plays

As there is no particular plan to this story, except to describe a few scenes in the life at Plumfield for the amusement of certain little persons, we will gently ramble along in this chapter and tell some of the pastimes of Mrs Jo's boys. I beg leave to assure my honoured readers that most of the incidents are taken from real life, and that the oddest are the truest; for no person, no matter how vivid an imagination he may have, can invent anything half so droll as the freaks and fancies that originate in the lively brains of little people.

Daisy and Demi were full of these whims, and lived in a world of their own, peopled with lovely or grotesque creatures, to whom they gave the queerest names, and with whom they played the queerest games. One of these nursery inventions was an invisible sprite called 'The Naughty Kitty-mouse,' whom the children had believed in, feared, and served for a long time. They seldom spoke of it to anyone else, kept their rites as private as possible; and, as they never tried to describe it even to themselves, this being had a vague mysterious charm very agreeable to Demi, who delighted in elves and goblins. A most whimsical and tyrannical imp was the Naughty Kitty-mouse, and Daisy found a fearful pleasure in its service, blindly obeying its most absurd demands, which were usually proclaimed from the lips of Demi, whose powers of invention were great. Rob and Teddy sometimes joined in these ceremonies, and considered them excellent fun, although they did not understand half that went on.

One day after school Demi whispered to his sister, with an ominous wag of the head, 'The Kitty-mouse wants us this afternoon.'

'What for?' asked Daisy, anxiously.

'A *sackerryfice*,' answered Demi, solemnly. 'There must be a fire behind the big rock at two o'clock, and we must all bring the things we like best, and burn them!' he added, with an awful emphasis on the last words.

'Oh, dear! I love the new paper dollies Aunt Amy painted for me best of anything; must I burn them up?' cried Daisy, who never thought of denying the unseen tyrant anything it demanded.

'Every one. I shall burn my boat, my best scrapbook, and *all* my soldiers,' said Demi firmly.

'Well, I will; but it's too bad of Kitty-mouse to want our very nicest things,' sighed Daisy.

'A *sackerryfice* means to give up what you are fond of, so we *must*,' explained Demi, to whom the new idea had been suggested by hearing Uncle Fritz describe the customs of the Greeks to the big boys who were reading about them in school.

'Is Rob coming too,' asked Daisy.

'Yes, and he is going to bring his toy village; it is all made of wood, you know, and will burn nicely. We'll have a grand bonfire, and see them blaze up, won't we?'

This brilliant prospect consoled Daisy, and she ate her dinner with a row of paper dolls before her, as a sort of farewell banquet.

At the appointed hour the sacrificial train set forth, each child bearing the treasures demanded by the insatiable Kitty-mouse. Teddy insisted on going also, and seeing that all the others had toys, he tucked a squeaking lamb under one arm, and old Annabella under the other, little dreaming what anguish the latter idol was to give him.

'Where are you going, my chickens?' asked Mrs Jo, as the flock passed her door.

'To play by the big rock; can't we?'

'Yes, only don't do near the pond, and take good care of Baby.'

'I always do,' said Daisy, leading forth her charge with a capable air.

'Now, you must all sit round, and not move till I tell you. This flat stone is an altar, and I am going to make a fire on it.'

Demi then proceeded to kindle up a small blaze, as he had seen the boys do at picnics. When the flame burned well, he ordered the company to march round it three times and then stand in a circle.

'I shall begin, and as fast as my things are burnt, you must bring yours.'

With that he solemnly laid on a little paper book full of pictures, pasted in by himself; this was followed by a dilapidated boat, and then one by one the unhappy leaden soldiers marched to death. Not one faltered or hung back, from the splendid red and yellow captain to the small drummer who had lost his legs; all vanished in the flames and mingled in one common pool of melted lead.

'Now, Daisy!' called the high priest of Kitty-mouse, when his rich offerings had been consumed, to the great satisfaction of the children.

'My dear dollies, how *can* I let them go?' moaned Daisy, hugging the entire dozen with a face full of maternal woe.

'You must,' commanded Demi; and with a farewell kiss to each, Daisy laid her blooming dolls upon the coals.

'Let me keep one, the dear blue thing, she is *so* sweet,' besought the poor little mamma, clutching her last in despair.

'More! more!' growled an awful voice, and Demi cried, 'That's the Kitty-mouse! she must have every one, quick, or she will scratch us.'

In went the precious blue belle, flounces, rosy hat, and all, and nothing but a few black flakes remained of that bright band.

'Stand the houses and trees round, and let them catch themselves; it will be like a real fire then,' said Demi, who liked variety even in his 'sackerryfices'.

Charmed by this suggestion, the children arranged the doomed village, laid a line of coals along the main street, and then sat down to watch the conflagration. It was somewhat slow to kindle owing to the paint, but at last one ambitious little cottage blazed up, fired a tree of the palm species, which fell on to the roof of a large family mansion, and in a few minutes the whole town was burning merrily. The wooden population stood and stared at the destruction like blockheads, as they were, till they also caught and blazed away without a cry. It took some time to reduce the town to ashes, and the lookers-on enjoyed the spectacle immensely, cheering as each house fell, dancing like wild Indians when the steeple flamed aloft, and actually casting one wretched little churn-shaped lady, who had escaped to the suburbs, into the very heart of the fire.

The superb success of this last offering excited Teddy to such a degree, that he first threw his lamb into the conflagration, and before it had time even to roast, he planted poor Annabella on the funeral pyre. Of course she did not like it, and expressed her anguish and resentment in a way that terrified her infant destroyer. Being covered with kid, she did not blaze, but did what was worse, she *squirmed*. First one leg curled up, then the other, in a very awful and lifelike manner; next she flung her arms over her head as if in great agony; her head itself turned on her shoulders, her glass eyes fell out, and with one final writhe of her whole body, she sank down a blackened mass on the ruins of the town. This unexpected demonstration startled everyone and frightened Teddy half out of his little wits. He looked, then screamed and fled toward the house, roaring 'Marmar' at the top of his voice.

Mrs Bhaer heard the outcry and ran to the rescue, but Teddy could only cling to her and pour out in his broken way something about 'poor Bella hurted', 'a dreat fire', and 'all the dollies dorn'. Fearing some dire mishap, his mother caught him up and hurried to the scene of action, where she found the blind worshippers of Kitty-mouse mourning over the charred remains of the lost darling.

'What have you been at? Tell me all about it,' said Mrs Jo, composing herself to listen patiently, for the culprits looked so penitent, she forgave them beforehand.

With some reluctance Demi explained their play, and Aunt Jo laughed till the tears ran down her cheeks, the children were so solemn, and the play was so absurd.

'I thought you were too sensible to play such a silly game as this. If I had any Kitty-mouse I'd have a good one who liked you to play in safe pleasant ways, and not destroy and frighten. Just see what a ruin you have made; all Daisy's pretty dolls, Demi's soldiers, and Rob's new village beside poor Teddy's pet lamb, and dear old Annabella. I shall have to write up in the nursery the verse that used to come in the boxes of toys, "The children of Holland take pleasure in making, What the children of Boston take pleasure in breaking." Only I shall put Plumfield instead of Boston.'

'We never will again, truly, truly!' cried the repentant little sinners, much abashed at this reproof.

'Demi told us to,' said Rob.

'Well, I heard Uncle tell about the Greece people, who had altars and things, and so I wanted to be like them, only I hadn't any live creatures to sackerryfice, so we burnt up our toys.'

'Dear me, that is something like the bean story,' said Aunt Jo, laughing again.

'Tell about it,' suggested Daisy, to change the subject.

'Once there was a poor woman who had three or four little children, and she used to lock them up in her room when she went out to work, to keep them safe. On day when she was going away she said, "Now, my dears, don't let baby fall out of window, don't play with the matches, and don't put beans up your noses." Now the children had never dreamed of doing that last thing, but she put it into their heads, and the minute she was gone, they ran and stuffed their naughty little noses full of beans, just to see how it felt, and she found them all crying when she came home.'

'Did it hurt?' asked Rob, with such intense interest that his mother hastily added a warning sequel, lest a new edition of the bean story should appear in her own family.

'Very much, as I know, for when my mother told me this story, I was so silly that I went and tried it myself. I had no beans, so I took some little pebbles, and poked several into my nose. I did not like it at all, and wanted to take them out again very soon, but one would not come, and I was so ashamed to tell what a goose I been that I went for hours with the stone hurting me very much. At last the pain got so bad I had to tell, and when my mother could not get it out the doctor came. Then I was put in a chair and held tight, Rob, while he used his ugly little pincers till the stone hopped out. Dear me! how my wretched little nose did ache, and how people laughed at me!' and Mrs Jo shook her head in a dismal way, as if the memory of her sufferings was too much for her.

Rob looked deeply impressed and I am glad to say took the

warning to heart. Demi proposed that they should bury poor Annabella, and in the interest of the funeral Teddy forgot his fright. Daisy was soon consoled by another batch of dolls from Aunt Amy, and the Naughty Kitty-mouse seemed to be appeased by the last offerings, for she tormented them no more.

'Brops' was the name of a new and absorbing play, invented by Bangs. As this interesting animal is not to be found in any Zoological Garden, unless Du Chaillu has recently brought one from the wilds of Africa, I will mention a few of its peculiar habits and traits, for the benefit of enquiring minds. The Brop is a winged quadruped, with a human face of a youthful and merry aspect. When it walks the earth it grunts, when it soars it gives a shrill hoot, occasionally it goes erect, and talks good English. Its body is usually covered with a substance much resembling a shawl, sometimes red, sometimes blue, often plaid, and, strange to say, they frequently change skins with one another. On their heads they have a horn very like a stiff brown paper lamp-lighter. Wings of the same substance flap upon their shoulders when they fly; this is never very far from the ground, as they usually fall with violence if they attempt any lofty flights. They browse over the earth, but can sit up and eat like the squirrel. Their favourite nourishment is the seed cake; apples also are freely taken, and sometimes raw carrots are nibbled when food is scarce. They live in dens, where they have a sort of nest, much like a clothes basket, in which the little Brops play till their wings are grown. These singular animals quarrel at times, and it is on these occasions that they burst into human speech, call each other names, cry, scold, and sometimes tear off horns and skin, declaring fiercely that they 'won't play'. The few privileged persons who have studied them are inclined to think them a remarkable mixture of the monkey, the sphinx, the roc, and the queer creatures seen by the famous Peter Wilkins.

This game was a great favourite, and the younger children beguiled many a rainy afternoon flapping or creeping about the nursery, acting like little bedlamites and being as merry as little grigs. To be sure, it was rather hard upon clothes, particularly trouser-knees, and jacket-elbows; but Mrs Bhaer only said, as she patched and darned, 'We do things just as foolish, and not half so harmless. If I could get as much happiness out of it as the little dears do, I'd be a Brop myself.'

Nat's favourite amusements were working in his garden, and sitting in the willow tree with his violin, for that green nest was a fairy world to him, and there he loved to perch, making music like a happy bird. The lads called him 'Old Chirper', because he was always humming, whistling, or fiddling, and they often stopped a minute in their work or play to listen to the soft tones of the violin, which seemed to lead a little orchestra of summer sounds. The birds appeared to regard him as one of themselves, and fearlessly sat on the fence or lit among the boughs to watch him with their quick bright eyes. The robins in the apple tree near by evidently considered him a friend, for the father bird hunted insects close beside him, and the little mother brooded as confidingly over her blue eggs as if the boy was only a new sort of blackbird who cheered her patient watch with his song. The brown brook babbled and sparkled below him, the bees haunted the clover fields on either side, friendly faces peeped at him as they passed, the old house stretched its wide wings hospitably toward him, and with a blessed sense of rest and love and happiness, Nat dreamed for hours in this nook, unconscious what healthful miracles were being wrought upon him.

One listener he had who never tired, and to whom he was more than a mere schoolmate. Poor Billy's chief delight was to lie beside the brook, watching leaves and bits of foam dance by, listening dreamily to the music in the willow tree. He seemed to think Nat a sort of angel who sat aloft and sang, for a few baby memories still lingered in his mind and seemed to grow brighter at these times. Seeing the interest he took in Nat, Mr Bhaer begged him to help them lift the cloud from the feeble brain by this gentle spell. Glad to do anything to show his gratitude, Nat always smiled on Billy when he followed him about, and let him listen undisturbed to the music which seemed to speak a language he could understand. 'Help one another,' was a favourite Plumfield motto, and Nat learned how much sweetness is added to life by trying to live up to it.

Jack Ford's peculiar pastime was buying and selling; and he bid fair to follow in the footsteps of his uncle, a country merchant, who sold a little of everything and made money fast. Jack had seen the sugar sanded, the molasses watered, the butter mixed with lard, and things of that kind, and laboured under the delusion that it was all a proper part of the business. His stock-in-trade was of a different sort, but he made as much as he could out of every worm he sold, and always got the best of the bargain when he traded with the boys for string, knives, fish-hooks, or whatever the article might be. The boys who all had nicknames, called him 'Skinflint', but Jack did not care as long as the old tobacco-pouch in which he kept his money grew heavier and heavier.

He established a sort of auction room, and now and then sold off all the odds and ends he had collected, or helped the lads exchange things with one another. He got bats, balls, hockey-sticks, etc., cheap, from one set of mates, furbished them up, and let them for a few cents a time to another set, often extending his business beyond the gates of Plumfield in spite of the rules. Mr Bhaer put a stop to some of his speculations, and tried to give him a better idea of business talent than mere sharpness in over-reaching his neighbours. Now and then Jack made a bad bargain, and felt worse about it than about any failure in lessons or conduct, and took his revenge on the next innocent customer who came along. His account-book was a curiosity; and his quickness at figures quite remarkable. Mr Bhaer praised him for this, and tried to make his sense of honesty and honour as quick; and, by and by, when Jack found that he could not get on without these virtues, he owned that his teacher was right.

Cricket and football the boys had of course; but, after the stirring accounts of these games in the immortal *Tom Brown at Rugby*, no feeble female pen may venture to do more than respectfully allude to them.

Emil spent his holidays on the river or the pond, and drilled the elder lads for a race with certain town boys, who now and then invaded their territory. The race duly came off, but as it ended in a general shipwreck, it was not mentioned in public; and the Commodore had serious thoughts of retiring to a desert island, so disgusted was he with his kind for a time. No desert island being convenient, he was forced to remain among his friends, and found consolation in building a boathouse.

The little girls indulged in the usual plays of their age, improving upon them somewhat as their lively fancies suggested. The chief and most absorbing play was called 'Mrs Shakespeare Smith'; the name was provided by Aunt Jo, but the trials of the poor lady were quite original. Daisy was Mrs S. S., and Nan by turns her daughter or a neighbour, Mrs Giddygaddy.

No pen can describe the adventures of these ladies, for in one short afternoon their family was the scene of births, marriages, deaths, floods, earthquakes, tea-parties, and balloon ascensions. Millions of miles did these energetic women travel, dressed in hats and habits never seen before by mortal eye, perched on the bed, driving the posts like mettlesome steeds, and bouncing up and down till their heads spun. Fits and fires were the pet afflictions, with a general massacre now and then by way of change. Nan was never tired of inventing fresh combinations, and Daisy followed her leader with blind admiration. Poor Teddy was a frequent victim, and was often rescued from real danger, for the excited ladies were apt to forget that he was not of the same stuff their long-suffering dolls. Once he was shut into the closet for a dungeon, and forgotten by the girls, who ran off to some out-of-door game. Another time he was half drowned in the bathtub, playing be a 'cunning little whale'. And, worst of all, he was cut down just in time after being hung up for a robber.

But the institution most patronised by all was the Club. It had no other name, and it needed none, being the only one in the neighbourhood. The elder lads got it up, and the younger were occasionally admitted if they behaved well. Tommy and Demi were honorary members, but were always obliged to retire un-pleasantly early, owing to circumstances over which they had no control. The proceedings of this club were somewhat peculiar, for it met at all sorts of places and hours, had all manner of queer ceremonies and amusements, and now and then was broken up tempestuously, only to be re-established, however, on a firmer basis.

Rainy evenings the members met in the school-room, and passed the time in games: chess, morris, backgammon, fencing matches, recitations, debates, or dramatic performances of a darkly tragical nature. In summer the barn was the rendezvous, and what went on there no uninitiated mortal knows. On sultry evenings the Club adjourned to the brook for aquatic exercises, and the members sat about in airy attire, froglike and cool. On such occasions the speeches were unusually eloquent, quite flowing, as one might say; and if any orator's remarks displeased the audience, cold water was thrown upon him till his ardour was effectually quenched. Franz was president, and maintained order admirably, considering the unruly nature of the members. Mr Bhaer never interfered with their affairs, and was rewarded for this wise forbearance by being invited now and then to behold the mysteries unveiled, which he appeared to enjoy much.

When Nan came she wished to join the Club, and caused great excitement and division among the gentlemen by presenting endless petitions, both written and spoken, disturbing their solemnities by insulting them through the keyhole, performing vigorous solos on the door, and writing up derisive remarks on walls and fences, for she belonged to the 'Irrepressibles'. Finding these appeals in vain, the girls, by the advice of Mrs Jo, got up an institution of their own, which they called the Cosy Club. To this they magnanimously invited the gentlemen whose youth excluded them from the other one, and entertained these favoured beings so well with little suppers, new games devised by Nan, and other pleasing festivities, that, one by one, the elder boys confessed a desire to partake of these more elegant enjoyments, and, after much consultation, finally decided to propose an interchange of civilities.

The members of the Cosy Club were invited to adorn the rival establishment on certain evenings, and to the surprise of the gentlemen their presence was not found to be a restraint upon the conversation or amusement of the regular frequenters; which could not be said of all Clubs, I fancy. The ladies responded handsomely and hospitably to these overtures of peace, and both institutions flourished long and happily.

CHAPTER 9

Daisy's Ball

Mrs Shakespeare Smith would like to have Mr John Brooke, Mr Thomas Bangs and Mr Nathaniel Blake to come to her ball at three o'clock today.

PS Nat must bring his fiddle, so we can dance, and all the boys must be good, or they cannot have any of the nice things we have cooked.

This elegant invitation would, I fear, have been declined, but for the hint given in the last line of the postscript.

'They have been cooking lots of goodies, I smelt 'em. Let's go,' said Tommy.

'We needn't stay after the feast, you know,' added Demi.

'I never went to a ball. What do you have to do?' asked Nat.

'Oh, we just play be men, and sit round stiff and stupid like grown-up folks, and dance to please the girls. Then we eat up everything, and come away as soon as we can.'

'I think I could do that,' said Nat, after considering Tommy's description for a minute.

'I'll write and say we'll come;' and Demi despatched the following gentlemanly reply, 'We will all come. Please have lots to eat. J. B. Esquire.'

Great was the anxiety of the ladies about their first ball, because if everything went well they intended to give a dinner party to the chosen few.

'Aunt Jo likes to have the boys play with us, if they are not rough; so we must make them like our balls, then they will do them good,' said Daisy, with her maternal air, as she set the table and surveyed the store of refreshments with an anxious eye.

'Demi and Nat will be good, but Tommy will do something bad, I know he will,' replied Nan, shaking her head over the little cake-basket which she was arranging.

'Then I shall send him right home,' said Daisy, with decision.

'People don't do so at parties, it isn't proper.'

'I shall never ask him any more.'

'That would do. He'd be sorry not to come to the dinner-ball, wouldn't he?'

'I guess he would! we'll have the splendidest things ever seen, won't we? Real soup with a ladle and a tureem [she meant *tureen*] and a little bird for turkey, and gravy, and all kinds of nice vegy-tubbles.' Daisy never *could* say vegetables properly, and had given up trying.

'It is 'most three, and we ought to dress,' said Nan, who had arranged a fine costume for the occasion, and was anxious to wear it.

'I am the mother, so I shan't dress up much,' said Daisy, putting on a nightcap ornamented with a red bow, one of her aunt's long skirts, and a shawl; a pair of spectacles and large pocket handker-chief completed her toilette, making a plump, rosy little matron of her.

Nan had a wreath of artificial flowers, a pair of old pink slippers, a yellow scarf, a green muslin skirt, and a fan made of feathers from the duster; also, as a last touch of elegance, a smelling-bottle without any smell in it.

'I am the daughter, so I rig up a good deal, and I must sing and dance, and talk more than you do. The mothers only get the tea and be proper, you know.'

A sudden very loud knock caused Miss Smith to fly into a chair, and fan herself violently, while her mamma sat bolt upright on the sofa, and tried to look quite calm and 'proper'. Little Bess, who was on a visit, acted the part of maid, and opened the door, saying with a smile, 'Wart in, gemplemun; it's all weady.'

In honour of the occasion, the boys wore high paper collars, tall black hats, and gloves of every colour and material, for they were an afterthought, and not a boy among them had a perfect pair.

'Good-day, mum,' said Demi, in a deep voice, which was so hard to keep up that his remarks had to be extremely brief.

Everyone shook hands and then sat down, looking so funny, yet so sober, that the gentlemen forgot their manners, and rolled in their chairs with laughter.

'Oh, don't!' cried Mrs Smith, much distressed.

'You can't ever come again if you act so,' added Miss Smith, rapping Mr Bangs with her bottle because he laughed loudest.

'I can't help it, you look so like fury,' gasped Mr Bangs, with most uncourteous candour.

'So do you, but I shouldn't be so rude as to say so. He shan't come to the dinner-ball, shall he, Daisy?' cried Nan, indignantly.

'I think we had better dance now. Did you bring your fiddle, sir?' asked Mrs Smith, trying to preserve her polite composure.

'It is outside the door,' and Nat went to get it.

'Better have tea first,' proposed the unabashed Tommy, winking openly at Demi to remind him that the sooner the refreshments were secured, the sooner they could escape.

'No, we never have supper first; and if you don't dance well you won't have any supper at all, not one bit, sir,' said Mrs Smith, so sternly that her wild guests saw she was not to be trifled with, and grew overwhelmingly civil all at once.

'*I* will take Mr Bangs and teach him the polka, for he does not know it fit to be seen,' added the hostess, with a reproachful look that sobered Tommy at once.

Nat struck up, and the ball opened with two couples, who went conscientiously through a somewhat varied dance. The ladies did well, because they liked it, but the gentlemen exerted themselves from more selfish motives, for each felt that he must earn his supper, and laboured manfully toward that end. When everyone was out of breath they were allowed to rest; and, indeed, poor Mrs Smith needed it, for her long dress had tripped her up many times. The little maid passed round molasses and water in such small cups that one guest actually emptied nine. I refrain from mentioning his name, because this mild beverage affected him so much that he put cup and all into his mouth at the ninth round, and choked himself publicly.

'You must ask Nan to play and sing now,' said Daisy to her brother, who sat looking very much like an owl, as he gravely regarded the festive scene between his high collars.

'Give us a song, mum,' said the obedient guest, secretly wondering where the piano was.

Miss Smith sailed up to an old secretary which stood in the room, threw back the lid of the writing-desk, and sitting down before it, accompanied herself with a vigour which made the old desk rattle as she sang that new and lovely song, beginning:

> 'Gaily the troubadour
> Touched his guitar,
> As he was hastening
> Home from the war.'

The gentlemen applauded so enthusiastically that she gave them 'Bounding Billows', 'Little Bo-Peep', and other gems of song, till they were obliged to hint that they had had enough. Grateful for the praises bestowed upon her daughter, Mrs Smith graciously announced, 'Now we will have tea. Sit down carefully, and don't grab.'

It was beautiful to see the air of pride with which the good lady did the honours of her table, and the calmness with which she bore the little mishaps that occurred. The best pie flew wildly on the floor when she tried to cut it with a very dull knife; the bread and butter vanished with a rapidity calculated to dismay a housekeeper's soul; and, worst of all, the custards were so soft that they had to be drunk up, instead of being eaten elegantly with the new tin spoons.

I grieve to state that Miss Smith squabbled with the maid for the best jumble, which caused Bess to toss the whole dish into the air, and burst out crying amid a rain of falling cakes. She was comforted by a seat at the table, and the sugar bowl to empty; but during this flurry a large plate of patties was mysteriously lost, and could not be found. They were the chief ornament of the feast, and Mrs Smith was indignant at the loss, for she had made them herself, and they were beautiful to behold. I put it to any lady if it was not hard to have one dozen delicious patties (made of flour, salt, and water, with a large raisin in the middle of each, and much sugar over the whole) swept away at one fell swoop?

'You hid them, Tommy; I know you did!' cried the outraged hostess, threatening her suspected guest with the milk-pot.

'I didn't!'

'You did!'

'It isn't proper to contradict,' said Nan, who was hastily eating up the jelly during the fray.

'Give them back, Demi,' said Tommy.

'That's a fib, you've got them in your own pocket,' bawled Demi, roused by the false accusation.

'Let's take 'em away from him. It's too bad to make Daisy cry,' suggested Nat, who found his first ball more exciting than he expected.

Daisy was already weeping, Bess like a devoted servant mingled her tears with those of her mistress, and Nan denounced the entire race of boys as 'plaguey things'. Meanwhile the battle raged among the gentlemen, for, when the two defenders of innocence fell upon the foe, that hardened youth entrenched himself behind a table and pelted them with the stolen tarts, which were very effective missiles, being nearly as hard as bullets. While his ammunition held out the besieged prospered, but the moment the last patty flew over the parapet, the villain was seized, dragged howling from the room, and cast upon the hall floor in an ignominious heap. The conquerors then returned flushed with victory, and while Demi consoled poor Mrs Smith, Nat and Nan collected the scattered tarts, replaced each raisin in its proper bed, and rearranged the dish so that it really looked almost as well as ever. But their glory had departed, for the sugar was gone, and no one cared to eat them after the insult offered to them.

'I guess we had better go,' said Demi, suddenly, as Aunt Jo's voice was heard on the stairs.

'P'r'aps we had,' and Nat hastily dropped a stray jumble that he had just picked up.

But Mrs Jo was among them before the retreat was accomplished, and into her sympathetic ear the young ladies poured the story of their woes.

'No more balls for these boys till they have atoned for this bad behaviour by doing something kind to you,' said Mrs Jo, shaking her head at the three culprits.

'We were only in fun,' began Demi.

'I don't like fun that makes other people unhappy. I am disappointed in you, Demi, for I hoped you would never learn to tease Daisy. Such a kind little sister as she is to you.'

'Boys always tease their sisters; Tom says so,' muttered Demi.

'I don't intend that *my* boys shall, and I must send Daisy home if you cannot play happily together,' said Aunt Jo, soberly.

At this awful threat, Demi sidled up to his sister, and Daisy hastily dried her tears, for to be separated was the worst misfortune that could happen to the twins.

'Nat was bad, too, and Tommy was baddest of all,' observed Nan, fearing that two of the sinners would not get their fair share of punishment.

'I am sorry,' said Nat, much ashamed.

'I ain't!' bawled Tommy through the keyhole, where he was listening with all his might.

Mrs Jo wanted very much to laugh, but kept her countenance, and said impressively, as she pointed to the door, 'You can go, boys, but remember, you are not to speak to or play with the little girls till I give you leave. You don't deserve the pleasure, so I forbid it.'

The ill-mannered young gentlemen hastily retired, to be received outside with derision and scorn by the unrepentant Bangs, who would not associate with them for at least fifteen minutes. Daisy was soon consoled for the failure of her ball, but lamented the edict that parted her from her brother, and mourned over his short-comings in her tender little heart. Nan rather enjoyed the trouble, and went about turning up her pug nose at the three, especially Tommy, who pretended not to care, and loudly proclaimed his satisfaction at being rid of those 'stupid girls'. But in his secret soul he soon repented of the rash act that caused this banishment from the society he loved, and every hour of separation taught him the value of the 'stupid girls'.

The others gave in very soon, and longed to be friends, for now there was no Daisy to pet and cook for them; no Nan to amuse and doctor them; and, worst of all, no Mrs Jo to make home life pleasant and life easy for them. To their great affliction, Mrs Jo seemed to consider herself one of the offended girls, for she hardly spoke to the outcasts, looked as if she did not see them when she passed, and was always too busy now to attend to their requests. This sudden and entire exile from favour cast a gloom over their souls, for when Mother Bhaer deserted them, their sun had set at noonday, as it were, and they had no refuge left.

This unnatural state of things actually lasted for three days, then they could bear it no longer, and fearing that the eclipse might become total, went to Mr Bhaer for help and counsel.

It is my private opinion that he had received instructions how to behave if the case should be laid before him. But no one suspected it, and he gave the afflicted boys some advice, which they gratefully accepted and carried out in the following manner: secluding themselves in the garret, théy devoted several play-hours to the manufacture of some mysterious machine, which took so much paste that Asia grumbled, and the little girls wondered mightily. Nan nearly got her inquisitive nose pinched in the door, trying to see what was going on, and Daisy sat about, openly lamenting that they could not all play nicely together, and not have any dreadful secrets. Wednesday afternoon was fine, and after a good deal of consultation about wind and weather, Nat and Tommy went off, bearing an immense flat parcel hidden under many newspapers. Nan nearly died with suppressed curiosity, Daisy nearly cried with vexation, and both quite trembled with interest when Demi marched into Mrs Bhaer's room, hat in hand, and said, in the politest tone possible to a mortal boy of his years, 'Please, Aunt Jo, would you and the girls come out to a surprise party we have made for you? Do, it's a *very* nice one.'

'Thank you, we will come with pleasure; only, I must take Teddy with me,' replied Mrs Bhaer, with a smile that cheered Demi like sunshine after rain.

'We'd like to have him. The little wagon is all ready for the girls; you won't mind walking just up to Pennyroyal Hill, will you Aunty?'

'I should like it exceedingly; but are you quite sure I shall not be in the way?'

'Oh, no, indeed! we want you very much; and the party will be spoilt if you don't come,' cried Demi, with great earnestness.

'Thank you kindly, sir;' and Aunt Jo made him a grand curtsey, for she liked frolics as well as any of them.

'Now, young ladies, we must not keep them waiting; on with the hats, and let us be off at once. I'm all impatience to know what the surprise is.'

As Mrs Bhaer spoke everyone bustled about, and in five minutes the three little girls and Teddy were packed into the 'clothes basket', as they called the wicker wagon which Toby drew. Demi walked at the head of the procession, and Mrs Jo brought up the rear, escorted by Kit. It was a most imposing party, I assure you, for Toby had a red feather-duster on his head, two remarkable flags waved over the carriage, Kit had a blue bow on his neck, which nearly drove him wild, Demi wore a nosegay of dandelions in his buttonhole, and Mrs Jo carried the queer Japanese umbrella in honour of the occasion.

The girls had little flutters of excitement all the way; and Teddy was so charmed with the drive that he kept dropping his hat overboard, and when it was taken from him he prepared to tumble out himself, evidently feeling that it behoved him to do something for the amusement of the party.

When they came to the hill 'nothing was to be seen but the grass blowing in the wind', as the fairy books say, and the children looked disappointed. But Demi said, in his most impressive manner, 'Now, you all get out and stand still, and the surprise party will come in;' with which remark he retired behind a rock, over which heads had been bobbing at intervals for the last half-hour.

A short pause of intense suspense, and then Nat, Demi, and Tommy marched forth, each bearing a new kite, which they presented to the three young ladies. Shrieks of delight arose, but were silenced by the boys, who said, with faces brimful of merriment, 'That isn't all the surprise;' and, running behind the rock, again emerged bearing a fourth kite of superb size, on which was printed, in bright yellow letters, 'For Mother Bhaer.'

'We thought you'd like one, too, because you were angry with us, and took the girls' part,' cried all three, shaking with laughter, for this part of the affair evidently *was* a surprise to Mrs Jo.

She clapped her hands, and joined in the laugh, looking thoroughly tickled at the joke.

'Now, boys, that is regularly splendid! Who did think of it?' she asked, receiving the monster kite with as much pleasure as the little girls did theirs.

'Uncle Fritz proposed it when we planned to make the others; he said you'd like it, so we made a bouncer,' answered Demi, beaming with satisfaction at the success of the plot.

'Uncle Fritz knows what I like. Yes, these are magnificent kites, and we were wishing we had some the other day when you were flying yours, weren't we, girls?'

'That's why we made them for you,' cried Tommy, standing on his head as the most appropriate way of expressing his emotions.

'Let us fly them,' said energetic Nan.

'I don't know how,' began Daisy.

'We'll show you, we want to!' cried all the boys in a burst of devotion, as Demi took Daisy's, Tommy Nan's, and Nat, with difficulty, persuaded Bess to let go her little blue one.

'Aunty, if you will wait a minute, we'll pitch yours for you,' said Demi, feeling that Mrs Bhaer's favour must not be lost again by any neglect of theirs.

'Bless your buttons, dear, I know all about it; and here is a boy who will toss up for me,' added Mrs Jo, as the professor peeped over the rock with a face full of fun.

He came out at once, tossed up the big kite, and Mrs Jo ran off with it in fine style, while the children stood and enjoyed the spectacle. One by one all the kites went up, and floated far overhead like gay birds, balancing themselves on the fresh breeze that blew steadily over the hill. Such a merry time as they had! running and shouting, sending up the kites or pulling them down, watching their antics in the air, and feeling them tug at the string like live creatures trying to escape. Nan was quite wild with the fun, Daisy thought the new play nearly as interesting as dolls, and little Bess was so fond of her 'boo tite', that she would only let it go on very short flights, preferring to hold it in her lap and look at the remarkable pictures painted on it by Tommy's dashing brush. Mrs Jo enjoyed hers immensely, and it acted as if it knew who owned it, for it came tumbling down head first when least expected, caught on trees, nearly pitched into the river, and finally darted away to such a height that it looked a mere speck among the clouds.

By and by everyone got tired, and fastening the kite-strings to trees and fences, all sat down to rest, except Mr Bhaer, who went off to look at the cows, with Teddy on his shoulder.

'Did you ever have such a good time as this before?' asked Nat, as they lay about on the grass, nibbling pennyroyal like a flock of sheep.

'Not since I last flew a kite, years ago, when I was a girl,' answered Mrs Jo.

'I'd like to have known you when you were a girl, you must have been so jolly,' said Nat.

'I was a naughty little girl, I am sorry to say.'

'I like naughty little girls,' observed Tommy, looking at Nan, who made a frightful grimace at him in return for the compliment.

'Why don't I remember you then, Aunty? Was I too young?' asked Demi.

'Rather, dear.'

'I suppose my memory hadn't come then. Grandpa says that different parts of the mind unfold as we grow up, and the memory part of my mind hadn't unfolded when you were little, so I can't remember how you looked,' explained Demi.

'Now, little Socrates, you had better keep that question for grandpa, it is beyond me,' said Aunt Jo, putting on the extinguisher.

'Well, I will, *he* knows about those things, and *you* don't,' returned Demi, feeling that on the whole kites were better adapted to the comprehension of the present company.

'Tell about the last time you flew a kite,' said Nat, for Mrs Jo had laughed as she spoke of it, and he thought it might be interesting.

'Oh, it was only rather funny, for I was a great girl of fifteen, and was ashamed to be seen at such a play. So Uncle Teddy and I privately made our kites, and stole away to fly them. We had a capital time, and were resting as we are now, when suddenly we heard voices, and saw a party of young ladies and gentlemen coming back from a picnic. Teddy did not mind, though he was rather a large boy to be playing with a kite, but I was in a great flurry, for I knew I should be sadly laughed at, and never hear the last of it, because my wild ways amused the neighbours as much as Nan's do us.

' "What shall I do?" I whispered to Teddy, as the voices drew nearer and nearer.

' "I'll show you," he said, and whipping out his knife he cut the strings. Away flew the kites, and when the people came up we were picking flowers as properly as you please. They never suspected us, and we had a grand laugh over our narrow escape.'

'Were the kites lost, Aunty?' asked Daisy.

'Quite lost, but I did not care, for I made up my mind that it would be best to wait till I was an old lady before I played with kites again; and you see I have waited,' said Mrs Jo, beginning to pull in the big kite, for it was getting late.

'Must we go now?'

'I must, or you won't have any supper; and that sort of surprise party would not suit you, I think, my chickens.'

'Hasn't our party been a nice one?' asked Tommy, complacently.

'Splendid!' answered everyone.

'Do you know why? It is because your guests have behaved

themselves, and tried to make everything go well. You understand what I mean, don't you?'

'Yes'm,' was all the boys said, but they stole a shamefaced look at one another, as they meekly shouldered their kites and walked home, thinking of another party where the guests had not behaved themselves, and things had gone badly on account of it.

CHAPTER 10

Home Again

July had come, and haying begun; the little gardens were doing finely and the long summer days were full of pleasant hours. The house stood open from morning till night, and the lads lived out of doors, except at school time. The lessons were short, and there were many holidays, for the Bhaers believed in cultivating healthy bodies by much exercise, and our short summers are best used in out-of-door work. Such a rosy, sunburnt, hearty set as the boys became; such appetites as they had; such sturdy arms and legs, as outgrew jackets and trousers; such laughing and racing all over the place; such antics in house and barn; such adventures in the tramps over hill and dale; and such satisfaction in the hearts of the worthy Bhaers, as they saw their flock prospering in mind and body, I cannot begin to describe. Only one thing was needed to make them quite happy, and it came when they least expected it.

One balmy night when the little lads were in bed, the elder ones bathing down at the brook, and Mrs Bhaer undressing Teddy in her parlour, he suddenly cried out, 'Oh, my Danny!' and pointed to the window, where the moon shone brightly.

'No, lovey, he is not there, it was the pretty moon,' said his mother.

'No, no, Danny at a window; Teddy saw him,' persisted baby, much excited.

'It might have been,' and Mrs Bhaer hurried to the window, hoping it would prove true. But the face was gone, and nowhere appeared any signs of a mortal boy; she called his name, ran to the front door with Teddy in his little shirt, and made him call too, thinking the baby voice might have more effect than her own. No one answered, nothing appeared, and they went back much disappointed. Teddy would not be satisfied with the moon, and after he was in his crib kept popping up his head to ask if Danny was not 'tummin' soon'.

By and by he fell asleep, the lads trooped up to bed, the house grew still, and nothing but the chirp of the crickets broke the soft silence of the summer night. Mrs Bhaer sat sewing, for the big basket was always piled with socks, full of portentous holes, and thinking of the lost boy. She had decided that baby had been mistaken, and did not even disturb Mr Bhaer by telling him of the child's fancy, for the poor man got little time to himself till the boys were abed, and he was busy writing letters. It was past ten when she rose to shut up the house. As she paused a minute to enjoy the lovely scene from the steps, something white caught her eye on one of the haycocks scattered over the lawn. The children had been playing there all the afternoon, and, fancying that Nan had left her hat as usual, Mrs Bhaer went out to get it. But as she approached, she saw that it was neither hat nor handkerchief, but a shirt sleeve with a brown hand sticking out of it. She hurried round the haycock, and there lay Dan, fast asleep.

Ragged, dirty, thin, and worn out he looked; one foot was bare, the other tied up in the old gingham jacket which he had taken from his own back to use as a clumsy bandage for some hurt. He seemed to have hidden himself behind the haycock, but in his sleep had thrown out the arm that had betrayed him. He sighed and muttered as if his dreams disturbed him, and once when he moved, he groaned as if in pain, but still slept on quite spent with weariness.

'He must not lie here,' said Mrs Bhaer, and stooping over him she gently called his name. He opened his eyes and looked at her, as if she was a part of his dream, for he smiled and said drowsily, 'Mother Bhaer, I've come home.'

The look, the words, touched her very much, and she put her hand under his head to lift him up, saying in her cordial way, 'I thought you would, and I'm so glad to see you, Dan.' He seemed to wake thoroughly then, and started up looking about him as if he suddenly remembered where he was, and doubted even that kind welcome. His face changed, and he said in his old rough way, 'I was going off in the morning. I only stopped to peek in, as I went by.'

'But why not come in, Dan? Didn't you hear us call you? Teddy saw, and cried for you.'

'Didn't suppose you'd let me in,' he said, fumbling with a little bundle which he had taken up as if going immediately.

'Try and see,' was all Mrs Bhaer answered, holding out her hand and pointing to the door, where the light shone hospitably.

With a long breath, as if a load was off his mind, Dan took up a stout stick, and began to limp towards the house, but stopped suddenly, to say enquiringly, 'Mr Bhaer won't like it. I ran away from Page.'

'He knows it, and was sorry, but it will make no difference. Are you lame?' asked Mrs Jo, as he limped on again.

'Getting over a wall a stone fell on my foot and smashed it. I don't mind,' and he did his best to hide the pain each step cost him.

Mrs Bhaer helped him into her own room, and, once there, he dropped into a chair, and laid his head back, white and faint with weariness and suffering.

'My poor Dan! drink this, and then eat a little; you are at home now, and Mother Bhaer will take good care of you.'

He only looked up at her with eyes full of gratitude, as he drank the wine she held to his lips, and then began slowly to eat the food she brought him. Each mouthful seemed to put heart into him, and presently he began to talk as if anxious to have her know all about him.

'Where have you been, Dan?' she asked, beginning to get out some bandages.

'I ran off more'n a month ago. Page was good enough, but too strict. I didn't like it, so I cut away down the river with a man who was going in his boat. That's why they couldn't tell where I'd gone. When I left the man, I worked for a couple of weeks with a farmer, but I thrashed his boy, and then the old man thrashed me, and I ran off again and walked here.'

'All the way?'

'Yes, the man didn't pay me, and I wouldn't ask for it. Took it out in beating the boy,' and Dan laughed, yet looked ashamed, as he glanced at his ragged clothes and dirty hands.

'How did you live? It was a long, long tramp for a boy like you.'

'Oh, I got on well enough, till I hurt my foot. Folks gave me things to eat, and I slept in barns and tramped by day. I got lost trying to make a short cut, or I'd have been here sooner.'

'But if you did not mean to come in and stay with us, what were you going to do?'

'I thought I'd like to see Teddy again, and you; and then I was going back to my old work in the city, only I was so tired I went to sleep on the hay. I'd have been gone in the morning, if you hadn't found me.'

'Are you sorry I did?' and Mrs Jo looked at him with a half merry, half reproachful look, as she knelt down to look at his wounded foot.

The colour came up into Dan's face, and he kept his eyes fixed on his plate, as he said very low, 'No, ma'am, I'm glad, I wanted to stay, but I was afraid you –'

He did not finish, for Mrs Bhaer interrupted him by an exclamation of pity, as she saw his foot, for it was seriously hurt.

'When did you do it?'

'Three days ago.'

'And you have walked on it in this state?'

'I had a stick, and I washed it at every brook I came to, and one woman gave me a rag to put on it.'

'Mr Bhaer must see and dress it at once,' and Mrs Jo hastened into the next room, leaving the door ajar behind her, so that Dan heard all that passed.

'Fritz, the boy has come back.'

'Who? Dan?'

'Yes, Teddy saw him at the window, and he called to him, but he went away and hid behind the haycocks on the lawn. I found him there just now fast asleep, and half dead with weariness and pain. He ran away from Page a month ago, and has been making his way to us ever since. He pretends that he did not mean to let us see him, but go on to the city, and his old work, after a look at us. It is evident, however, that the hope of being taken in has led him here through everything, and there he is waiting to know if you will forgive and take him back.'

'Did he say so?'

'His eyes did, and when I waked him, he said, like a lost child,

"Mother Bhaer, I've come home." I hadn't the heart to scold him, and just took him in like a poor little black sheep come back to the fold. I may keep him, Fritz?'

'Of course you may! This proves to me that we have a hold on the boy's heart, and I would no more send him away now than I would my own Rob.'

Dan heard a soft little sound, as if Mrs Jo thanked her husband without words, and, in the instant's silence that followed, two great tears that had slowly gathered in the boy's eyes brimmed over and rolled down his dusty cheeks. No one saw them, for he brushed them hastily away; but in that little pause I think Dan's old distrust for these good people vanished for ever, the soft spot in his heart was touched, and he felt an impetuous desire to prove himself worthy of the love and pity that was so patient and forgiving. He said nothing, he only wished the wish with all his might, resolved to try in his blind boyish way, and sealed his resolution with the tears which neither pain, fatigue, nor loneliness could wring from him.

'Come and see his foot. I am afraid it is badly hurt, for he has kept on three days through heat and dust, with nothing but water and an old jacket to bind it up with. I tell you, Fritz, that boy is a brave lad, and will make a fine man yet.'

'I hope so, for your sake, enthusiastic woman, your faith deserves success. Now, I will go and see your little Spartan. Where is he?'

'In my room; but, dear, you'll be very kind to him, no matter how gruff he seems. I am sure that is the way to conquer him. He won't bear sternness nor much restraint, but a soft word and infinite patience will lead him as it used to lead me.'

'As if you ever like this little rascal!' cried Mr Bhaer, laughing, yet half angry at the idea.

'I was in spirit, though I showed it in a different way. I seem to know by instinct how he feels, to understand what will win and touch him, and to sympathise with his temptations and faults. I am glad I do, for it will help me to help him; and if I can make a good man of this wild boy, it will be the best work of my life.'

'God bless the work, and help the worker!'

Mr Bhaer spoke now as earnestly as she had done, and both came in together to find Dan's head down upon his arm, as if he was quite overcome by sleep. But he looked up quickly, and tried to rise as Mr Bhaer said pleasantly, 'So you like Plumfield better than Page's farm. Well, let us see if we can get on more comfortably this time than we did before.'

'Thanky, sir,' said Dan, trying not to be gruff, and finding it easier than he expected.

'Now, the foot! Ach! this is not well. We must have Dr Firth tomorrow. Warm water, Jo, and old linen.'

Mr Bhaer bathed and bound up the wounded foot, while Mrs Jo prepared the only empty bed in the house. It was in the little guest chamber leading from the parlour, and often used when the lads were poorly, for it saved Mrs Jo from running up and down, and the invalids could see what was going on. When it was ready, Mr Bhaer took the boy in his arms, and carried him in, helped him undress, laid him on the little white bed, and left him with another handshake, and a fatherly 'Good-night, my son.'

Dan dropped asleep at once, and slept heavily for several hours; then his foot began to throb and ache, and he awoke to toss about uneasily, trying not to groan lest anyone should hear him, for he *was* a brave lad, and did bear pain like 'a little Spartan', as Mr Bhaer called him.

Mrs Jo had a way of flitting about the house at night, to shut the windows if the wind grew chilly, to draw mosquito curtains over Teddy, or look after Tommy, who occasionally walked in his sleep. The least noise waked her, and as she often heard imaginary robbers, cats, and conflagrations, the doors stood open all about, so her quick ear caught the sound of Dan's little moans, and she was up in a minute. He was just giving his hot pillow a despairing thump when a light came glimmering through the hall, and Mrs Jo crept in, looking like a droll ghost, with her hair in a great knob on the top of her head, and a long grey dressing-gown trailing behind her.

'Are you in pain, Dan?'

'It's pretty bad; but I didn't mean to wake you.'

'I'm a sort of owl, always flying about at night. Yes, your foot is like fire; the bandages must be wet again,' and away flapped the maternal owl for more cooling stuff, and a great mug of ice water.

'Oh, that's *so* nice!' sighed Dan, the wet bandages went on again, and a long draught of water cooled his thirsty throat.

'There, now, sleep your best, and don't be frightened if you see

*Mr Bhaer bathed and bound up the wounded foot, then Mrs Jo
prepared the only empty bed in the house*

me again, for I'll slip down by and by, and give you another sprinkle.'

As she spoke, Mrs Jo stooped to turn the pillow and smooth the bedclothes, when, to her great surprise, Dan put his arm around her neck, drew her face down to his, and kissed her, with a broken, 'Thank you, ma'am,' which said more than the most eloquent speech could have done; for the hasty kiss, the muttered words, meant, 'I'm sorry, I will try.' She understood it, accepted the unspoken confession, and did not spoil it by any token of surprise. She only remembered that he had no mother, kissed the brown cheek half hidden on the pillow, as if ashamed of the little touch of tenderness, and left him, saying, what he long remembered, 'You are my boy now, and if you choose you can make me proud and glad to say so.'

Once again, just at dawn, she stole down to find him so fast asleep that he did not wake, and showed no sign of consciousness as she wet his foot, except that the lines of pain smoothed themselves away, and left his face quite peaceful.

The day was Sunday, and the house so still that he never waked till near noon, and, looking round him, saw an eager little face peering in at the door. He held out his arms, and Teddy tore across the room to cast himself bodily upon the bed, shouting, 'My Danny's tum!' as he hugged and wriggled with delight. Mrs Bhaer appeared next, bringing breakfast, and never seeming to see how shamefaced Dan looked at the memory of the little scene last night. Teddy insisted on giving him his 'betfus', and fed him like a baby, which, as he was not very hungry, Dan enjoyed very much.

Then came the doctor, and the poor Spartan had a bad time of it, for some of the little bones in his foot were injured, and putting them to rights was such a painful job, that Dan's lips were white, and great drops stood on his forehead, though he never cried out, and only held Mrs Jo's hand so tight that it was red long afterwards.

'You must keep this boy quiet, for a week at least, and not let him put his foot to the ground. By that time, I shall know whether he may hop a little with a crutch, or stick to his bed for a while longer,' said Dr Firth, putting up the shining instruments that Dan did not like to see.

'It will get well sometime, won't it?' he asked, looking alarmed at the word 'crutches'.

'I hope so;' and with that the doctor departed, leaving Dan much depressed; for the loss of a foot is a dreadful calamity to an active boy.

'Don't be troubled, I am a famous nurse, and we will have you tramping about as well as ever in a month,' said Mrs Jo, taking a hopeful view of the case.

But the fear of being lame haunted Dan, and even Teddy's caresses did not cheer him; so Mrs Jo proposed that one or two of the boys should come in and pay him a little visit, and asked whom he would like to see.

'Nat and Demi; I'd like my hat too, there's something in it I guess they'd like to see. I suppose you threw away my bundle of plunder?' said Dan, looking rather anxious as he put the question.

'No, I kept it, for I thought they must be treasures of some kind, you took such care of them;' and Mrs Jo brought him his old straw hat stuck full of butterflies and beetles, and a handkerchief containing a collection of odd things picked up on his way: birds' eggs, carefully done up in moss, curious shells and stones, bits of fungus, and several little crabs, in a state of great indignation at their imprisonment.

'Could I have something to put these fellers in? Mr Hyde and I found 'em, and they are first-rate ones, so I'd like to keep and watch 'em; can I?' asked Dan, forgetting his foot, and laughing to see the crabs go sidling and backing over the bed.

'Of course you can; Polly's old cage will be just the thing. Don't let them nip Teddy's toes while I get it;' and away went Mrs Jo, leaving Dan overjoyed to find that his treasures were not considered rubbish, and thrown away.

Nat, Demi, and the cage arrived together, and the crabs were settled in their new house, to the great delight of the boys, who, in the excitement of the performance, forgot any awkwardness they might otherwise have felt in greeting the runaway. To these admiring listeners Dan related his adventures much more fully than he had done to the Bhaers. Then he displayed his 'plunder', and described each article so well, that Mrs Jo, who had retired to the next room to leave them free, was surprised and interested, as well as amused, at their boyish chatter.

'How much the lad knows of these things! how absorbed he is in them! and what a mercy it is just now, for he cares so little for books, it would be hard to amuse him while he is laid up; but the boys can supply him with beetles and stones to any extent, and I am glad to find out this taste of his; it is a good one, and may perhaps prove the making of him. If he should turn out a great naturalist, and Nat a musician, I should have cause to be proud of this year's work;' and Mrs Jo sat smiling over her book as she built castles in the air, just as she used to do when a girl, only then they were for herself, and now they were for other people, which is the reason perhaps that some of them came to pass in reality – for charity is an excellent foundation to build anything upon.

Nat was most interested in the adventures, but Demi enjoyed the beetles and butterflies immensely, drinking in the history of their changeful little lives as if it were a new and lovely sort of fairy-tale for, even in his plain way, Dan told it well, and found great satisfaction in the thought that here at least the small philosopher could learn of him. So interested were they in the account of catching a musk rat, whose skin was among the treasures, that Mr Bhaer had to come himself to tell Nat and Demi it was time for the walk. Dan looked so wistfully after them as they ran off that Father Bhaer proposed carrying him to the sofa in the parlour for a little change of air and scene.

When he was established, and the house quiet, Mrs Jo, who sat near by showing Teddy pictures, said, in an interested tone, as she nodded towards the treasures still in Dan's hands, 'Where did you learn so much about these things?'

'I always liked 'em, but didn't know much till Mr Hyde told me.'

'Who was Mr Hyde?'

'Oh, he was a man who lived round in the woods studying these things – I don't know what you call him – and wrote about frogs, and fishes, and so on. He stayed at Page's, and used to want me to go and help him, and it was great fun, 'cause he told me ever so much, and was uncommon jolly and wise. Hope I'll see him again sometime.'

'I hope you will,' said Mrs Jo, for Dan's face had brightened up, and he was so interested in the matter that he forgot his usual taciturnity.

'Why, he could make birds come to him, and rabbits and

squirrels didn't mind him any more than if he was a tree. Did you ever tickle a lizard with a straw?' asked Dan, eagerly.

'No, but I should like to try it.'

'Well, I've done it, and it's so funny to see 'em turn over and stretch out, they like it so much. Mr Hyde used to do it; and he'd make snakes listen to him while he whistled, and he knew just when certain flowers would blow, and bees wouldn't sting him, and he'd tell the wonderfullest things about fish and flies, and the Indians and the rocks.'

'I think you were so fond of going with Mr Hyde, you rather neglected Mr Page,' said Mrs Jo, slyly.

'Yes, I did; I hated to have to weed and hoe when I might be tramping round with Mr Hyde. Page thought such things silly, and called Mr Hyde crazy because he'd lay hours watching a trout or a bird.'

'Suppose you say *lie* instead of *lay*, it is better grammar,' said Mrs Jo, very gently; and then added, 'Yes, Page is a thorough farmer, and would not understand that a naturalist's work was just as interesting, and perhaps just as important as his own. Now, Dan, if you really love these things, as I think you do, and I am glad to see it, you shall have time to study them and books to help you; but I want you to do something besides, and to do it faithfully, else you will be sorry by and by, and find that you have got to begin again.'

'Yes, ma'am,' said Dan, meekly, and looked a little scared by the serious tone of the last remarks, for he hated books, yet had evidently made up his mind to study anything she proposed.

'Do you see that cabinet with twelve drawers in it?' was the next very unexpected question.

Dan did see two tall old-fashioned ones standing on either side of the piano; he knew them well, and had often seen nice bits of string, nails, brown paper, and such useful matters come out of the various drawers. He nodded and smiled. Mrs Jo went on, 'Well, don't you think those drawers would be good places to put your eggs, and stones, and shells, and lichens?'

'Oh, splendid, but you wouldn't like my things "clutterin' round", as Mr Page used to say, would you?' cried Dan, sitting up to survey the old piece of furniture with sparkling eyes.

'I like litter of that sort; and if I didn't, I should give you the drawers, because I have a regard for children's little treasures, and I think they should be treated respectfully. Now, I am going to make a bargain with you, Dan, and I hope you will keep it honourably. Here are twelve good-sized drawers, one for each month of the year, and they shall be yours as fast as you earn them, by doing the little duties that belong to you. I believe in rewards of a certain kind, especially for young folks; they help us along, and though we may begin by being good for the sake of the reward, if it is rightly used, we shall soon learn to love goodness for itself.'

'Do you have 'em?' asked Dan, looking as if this was new talk for him.

'Yes, indeed! I haven't learnt to get on without them yet. My rewards are not drawers, or presents, or holidays, but they are things which I like as much as you do the others. The good behaviour and success of my boys is one of the rewards I love best, and I work for it as I want you to work for your cabinet. Do what you dislike, and do it well, and you get two rewards, one, the prize you see and hold; the other, the satisfaction of a duty cheerfully performed. Do you understand that?'

'Yes, ma'am.'

'We all need these little helps; so you shall try to do your lessons and your work, play kindly with all the boys, and use your holidays well; and if you bring me a good report, or if I see and know it without words – for I'm quick to spy out the good little efforts of my boys – you shall have a compartment in the drawer for your treasures. See, some are already divided into four parts, and I will have the others made in the same way, a place for each week; and when the drawer is filled with curious and pretty things, I shall be as proud of it as you are; prouder, I think for in the pebbles, mosses, and gay butterflies, I shall see good resolutions carried out, conquered faults, and a promise well kept. Shall we do this, Dan?'

The boys answered with one of the looks which said much, for it showed that he felt and understood her wish and words, although he did not know how to express his interest and gratitude for such care and kindness. She understood the look, and seeing by the colour that flushed up to his forehead that he was touched, as she wished him to be, she said no more about that side of the new plan, but pulled out the upper drawer, dusted it, and set it on two chairs before the sofa, saying briskly, 'Now, let us begin at once by putting those nice beetles in a safe place. These compartments will hold a good deal, you see. I'd pin the butterflies and bugs round the sides; they will be quite safe there, and leave room for the heavy things below. I'll give you some cottonwool, and clean paper and pins, and you can get ready for the week's work.'

'But I can't go out to find any new things,' said Dan, looking piteously at his foot.

'That's true; never mind, we'll let these treasures do for this week, and I dare say the boys will bring you loads of things if you ask them.'

'They don't know the right sort; besides, if I lay, no, *lie* here all the time, I can't work and study, and earn my drawers.'

'There are plenty of lessons you can learn lying there, and several little jobs of work you can do for me.'

'Can I?' and Dan looked both surprised and pleased.

'You can learn to be patient and cheerful in spite of pain and no play. You can amuse Teddy for me, wind cotton, read to me when I sew, and do many things without hurting your foot, which will make the days pass quickly, and not be wasted ones.'

Here Demi ran in with a great butterfly in one hand, and a very ugly little toad in the other.

'See, Dan, I found them, and ran back to give them to you; aren't they beautiful ones?' panted Demi, all out of breath.

Dan laughed at the toad, and said he had no place to put him, but the butterfly was a beauty, and if Mrs Jo would give him a big pin, he would stick it right up in the drawer.

'I don't like to see the poor thing struggle on a pin; if it must be killed, let us put it out of pain at once with a drop of camphor,' said Mrs Jo, getting out the bottle.

'I know how to do it – Mr Hyde always killed 'em that way – but I didn't have any camphor, so I use a pin,' and Dan gently poured a drop on the insect's head, when the pale green wings fluttered an instant, and then grew still.

This dainty little execution was hardly over when Teddy shouted from the bedroom, 'Oh, the little trabs are out, and the big one's eaten 'em all up.' Demi and his aunt ran to the rescue, and found Teddy dancing excitedly in a chair, while two little crabs were scuttling about the floor, having got through the wires of the cage. A third was clinging to the top of the cage, evidently in terror of his life, for below appeared a sad yet funny sight. The big crab had wedged himself into the little recess where Polly's cup used to stand, and there he sat eating one of his relations in the coolest way. All the claws of the poor victim were pulled off, and he was turned upside down, his upper shell held in one claw close under the mouth of the big crab like a dish, while he leisurely ate out of it with the other claw, pausing now and then to turn his queer bulging eyes from side to side, and to put out a slender tongue and lick them in a way that made the children scream with laughter. Mrs Jo carried the cage in for Dan to see the sight, while Demi caught and confined the wanderers under an inverted washbowl.

'I'll have to let these fellers go, for I can't keep 'em in the house,' said Dan, with evident regret.

'I'll take care of them for you, if you will tell me how, and they can live in my turtle-tank just as well as not,' said Demi, who found them more interesting even that his beloved slow turtles. So Dan gave him directions about the wants and habits of the crabs, and Demi bore them away to introduce them to their new home and neighbours. 'What a good boy he is!' said Dan, carefully settling the first butterfly, and remembering that Demi had given up his walk to bring it to him.

'He ought to be, for a great deal has been done to make him so.'

'He's had folks to tell him things, and to help him; I haven't,' said Dan, with a sigh, thinking of his neglected childhood, a thing he seldom did, and feeling as if he had not had fair play somehow.

'I know it, dear, and for that reason I don't expect as much from you as from Demi, though he is younger; you shall have all the help that we can give you now, and I hope to teach you how to help yourself in the best way. Have you forgotten what Father Bhaer told you when you were here before, about wanting to be good, and asking God to help you?'

'No, ma'am,' very low.

'Do you try that way still?'

'No, ma'am,' lower still.

'Will you do it every night to please me?'

'Yes, ma'am,' very soberly.

'I shall depend on it, and I think I shall know if you are faithful to your promise, for these things always show to people who believe in them, though not a word is said. Now here is a pleasant story about a boy who hurt his foot worse than you did yours; read it, and see how bravely he bore his troubles.'

She put that charming little book, *The Crofton Boys*, into his hands, and left him for an hour, passing in and out from time to time that he might not feel lonely. Dan did not love to read, but soon got so interested that he was surprised when the boys came home. Daisy brought him a nosegay of wild flowers, and Nan insisted on helping bring him his supper, as he lay on the sofa with the door open into the dining-room, so that he could see the lads at table, and they could nod socially to him over their bread and butter.

Mr Bhaer carried him away to his bed early, and Teddy came in his nightgown to say good-night, for he went to his little nest with the birds.

'I want to say my prayers to Danny; may I?' he asked; and when his mother said, 'Yes,' the little fellow knelt down by Dan's bed, and folding his chubby hands, said softly, 'Pease Dod bess everybody, and hep me to be dood.'

Then he went away smiling with sleepy sweetness over his mother's shoulder.

But after the evening talk was done, the evening song sung, and the house grew still with beautiful Sunday silence, Dan lay in his pleasant room wide awake, thinking new thoughts, feeling new hopes and desires stirring in his boyish heart, for two good angels had entered in: love and gratitude began the work which time and effort were to finish; and with an earnest wish to keep his first promise, Dan folded his hands together in the darkness, and softly whispered Teddy's little prayer, 'Please God bless everyone, and help me to be good.'

CHAPTER 11

Uncle Teddy

For a week Dan only moved from bed to sofa; a long week and a hard one, for the hurt foot was very painful at times, the quiet days were very wearisome to the active lad, longing to be out enjoying the summer weather, and especially difficult was it to be patient. But Dan did his best, and everyone helped him in their various ways; so the time passed, and he was rewarded at last by hearing the doctor say, on Saturday morning, 'This foot is doing better than I expected. Give the lad the crutch this afternoon, and let him stump about the house a little.'

'Hooray!' shouted Nat, and raced away to tell the other boys the good news.

Everybody was very glad, and after dinner the whole flock assembled to behold Dan crutch himself up and down the hall a few times before he settled in the porch to hold a sort of levee. He was much pleased at the interest and goodwill shown him, and brightened up more and more every minute; for the boys came to pay their respects, the little girls fussed about him with stools and cushions, and Teddy watched over him as if he was a frail creature unable to do anything for himself. They were still sitting and standing about the steps, when a carriage stopped at the gate, a hat was waved from it, and with a shout of 'Uncle Teddy! Uncle Teddy!' Rob scampered down the avenue as fast as his short legs would carry him. All the boys but Dan ran after him to see who should be first to open the gate, and in a moment the carriage drove up with boys swarming all over it, while Uncle Teddy sat laughing in the midst, with his little daughter on his knee.

'Stop the triumphal car and let Jupiter descend,' he said, and jumping out ran up the steps to meet Mrs Bhaer, who stood smiling and clapping her hands like a girl.

'How goes it, Teddy?'

'All right, Jo.'

Then they shook hands, and Mr Laurie put Bess into her aunt's arms, saying, as the child hugged her tight, 'Goldilocks wanted to see you so much that I ran away with her, for I was quite pining for a sight of you myself. We want to play with your boys for an hour or so, and to see how "the old woman who lived in a shoe, and had so many children she did not know what to do", is getting on.'

'I'm so glad! Play away, and don't get into mischief,' answered Mrs Jo, as the lads crowded round the pretty child, admiring her long golden hair, dainty dress, and lofty ways, for the little 'Princess', as they called her, allowed no one to kiss her, but sat smiling down upon them, and graciously patting their heads with her little white hands. They all adored her, especially Rob, who considered her a sort of doll, and dared not touch her lest she should break, but worshipped her at a respectful distance, made happy by an occasional mark of favour from her little highness. As she immediately demanded to see Daisy's kitchen, she was borne off by Mrs Jo, with a train of small boys following. The others, all but Nat and Demi, ran away to the menagerie and gardens to have all in order; for Mr Laurie always took a general survey, and looked disappointed if things were not flourishing.

Standing on the steps, he turned to Dan, saying like an old acquaintance, though he had only seen him once or twice before, 'How is the foot?'

'Better, sir.'

'Rather tired of the house, aren't you?'

'Guess I am!' and Dan's eyes roved away to the green hills and woods where he longed to be.

'Suppose we take a little turn before the others come back? That big, easy carriage will be quite safe and comfortable, and a breath of fresh air will do you good. Get a cushion and a shawl, Demi, and let's carry Dan off.'

The boys thought it a capital joke, and Dan looked delighted, but asked, with an unexpected burst of virtue, 'Will Mrs Bhaer like it?'

'Oh, yes; we settled all that a minute ago.'

'You didn't say anything about it, so I don't see how you could,' said Demi, inquisitively.

'We have a way of sending messages to one another, without any words. It is a great improvement on the telegraph.'

'I know – it's eyes; I saw you lift your eyebrows, and nod toward the carriage, and Mrs Bhaer laughed and nodded back again,' cried Nat, who was quite at his ease with kind Mr Laurie by this time.

'Right. Now then, come on,' and in a minute Dan found himself settled in the carriage, his foot on a cushion on the seat opposite, nicely covered with a shawl, which fell down from the upper regions in a most mysterious manner, just when they wanted it. Demi climbed up to the box beside Peter, the black coachman. Nat sat next Dan in the place of honour, while Uncle Teddy would sit opposite, to take care of the foot, he said, but really that he might study the faces before him, both so happy, yet so different, for Dan's was square, and brown, and strong, while Nat's was long, and fair, and rather weak, but very amiable with its mild eyes and good forehead.

'By the way, I've got a book somewhere here that you may like to see,' said the oldest boy of the party, diving under the seat and producing a book which make Dan exclaim, 'Oh! by George, isn't that a stunner?' as he turned the leaves, and saw fine plates of butterflies, and birds, and every sort of interesting insect, coloured like life. He was so charmed that he forgot his thanks, but Mr Laurie did not mind, and was quite satisfied to see the boy's eager delight, and to hear this exclamations over certain old friends as he came to them. Nat leaned on his shoulder to look, and Demi turned his back to the horses, and let his feet dangle inside the carriage, so that he might join in the conversation.

When they got among the beetles, Mr Laurie took a curious little object out of his vest pocket, and laying it in the palm of his hand, said, 'There's a beetle that is thousands of years old;' and then, while the lads examined the queer stone-bug, that looked so old and grey, he told them how it came out of the wrappings of a mummy, after lying for ages in a famous tomb. Finding them interested, he went on to tell about the Egyptians, and the strange and splendid ruins they have left behind them the Nile, and how he sailed up the mighty river, with the handsome dark men to work his boat; how he shot alligators, saw wonderful beasts and birds; and afterwards crossed the desert on a camel, who pitched him about like a ship in a storm.

'Uncle Teddy tells stories 'most as well as Grandpa,' said Demi, approvingly, when the tale was done, and the boys' eyes asked for more.

'Thank you,' said Mr Laurie, quite soberly, for he considered Demi's praise worth having, for children are good critics in such cases, and to suit them is an accomplishment that anyone may be proud of.

'Here's another trifle or two that I tucked into my pocket as I was turning over my traps to see if I had anything that would amuse Dan,' and Uncle Teddy produced a fine arrowhead and a string of wampum.

'Oh! tell about the Indians,' cried Demi, who was fond of playing wigwam.

'Dan knows lots about them,' added Nat.

'More than I do, I dare say. Tell us something,' and Mr Laurie looked as interested as the other two.

'Mr Hyde told me; he's been among 'em, and can talk their talk, and likes 'em,' began Dan, flattered by their attention, but rather embarrassed by having a grown-up listener.

'What is wampum for?' asked curious Demi, from his perch.

The others asked questions likewise, and, before he knew it, Dan was reeling off all Mr Hyde had told him, as they sailed down the river a few weeks before. Mr Laurie listened well, but found the boy more interesting than the Indians, for Mrs Jo had told him about Dan, and he rather took a fancy to the wild lad, who ran away as he himself had often longed to do, and who was slowly getting tamed by pain and patience.

'I've been thinking that it would be a good plan for you fellows to have a museum of your own; a place in which to collect all the curious and interesting things that you find, and make, and have given you. Mrs Jo is too kind to complain, but it is rather hard for her to have the house littered up with all sorts of rattletraps, half a pint of dor-bugs in one of her best vases, for instance, a couple of dead bats nailed up in the back entry, wasps nests tumbling down on people's heads, and stones lying round everywhere, enough to pave the avenue. There are not many women who would stand that sort of thing, are there, now?'

As Mr Laurie spoke with a merry look in his eyes, the boys laughed and nudged one another, for it was evident that someone told tales out of school, else how could he know of the existence of these inconvenient treasures.

'Where can we put them, then?' said Demi, crossing his legs and leaning down to argue the question.

'In the old carriage-house.'

'But it leaks, and there isn't any window, nor any place to put things, and it's all dust and cobwebs,' began Nat.

'Wait till Gibbs and I have touched it up a bit, and then see how you like it. He is to come over on Monday to get it ready; then next Saturday I shall come out, and we will fix it up, and make the beginning, at least, of a fine little museum. Everyone can bring his things, and have a place for them; and Dan is to be the head man, because he knows most about such matters, and it will be quiet, pleasant work for him now that he can't knock about much.'

'Won't that be jolly?' cried Nat, while Dan smiled all over his face and had not a word to say, but hugged his book, and looked at Mr Laurie as if he thought him one of the greatest public benefactors that ever blessed the world.

'Shall I go round again, sir?' asked Peter, as they came to the gate, after two slow turns about the half-mile triangle.

'No, we must be prudent, else we can't come again. I must go over the premises, take a look at the carriage-house, and have a little talk with Mrs Jo before I go;' and, having deposited Dan on his sofa to rest and enjoy his book, Uncle Teddy went off to have a frolic with the lads who were raging about the place in search of him. Leaving the little girls to mess upstairs, Mrs Bhaer sat down by Dan, and listened to his eager account of the drive till the flock returned, dusty, warm, and much excited about the new museum, which everyone considered the most brilliant idea of the age.

'I always wanted to endow some sort of an institution, and I am going to begin with this,' said Mr Laurie, sitting down on a stool at Mrs Jo's feet.

'You have endowed one already. What do you call this?' and Mrs Jo pointed to the happy-faced lads, who had camped upon the floor about him.

'I call it a very promising Bhaer-garden, and I'm proud to be a member of it. Did you know I was the head boy in this school?' he asked, turning to Dan, and changing the subject skilfully, for he hated to be thanked for the generous things he did.

'I thought Franz was!' answered Dan, wondering what the man meant.

'Oh, dear no! I'm the first boy Mrs Jo ever had to take care of, and I was such a bad one that she isn't done with me yet, though she has been working at me for years and years.'

'How old she must be!' said Nat, innocently.

'She began early, you see. Poor thing! she was only fifteen when she took me, and I led her such a life, it's a wonder she isn't wrinkled and grey, and quite worn out,' and Mr Laurie looked up at her laughing.

'Don't, Teddy; I won't have you abuse yourself so;' and Mrs Jo stroked the curly black head at her knee as affectionately as ever, for, in spite of everything Teddy was her boy still.

'If it hadn't been for you, there never would have been a Plumfield. It was my success with you, sir, that gave me courage to try my pet plan. So the boys may thank you for it, and name the new institution the "Laurence Museum", in honour of its founder, won't we, boys?' she added, looking very like the lively Jo of old times.

'We will! we will!' shouted the boys, throwing up their hats, for though they had taken them off on entering the house, according to rule, they had been in too much of a hurry to hang them up.

'I'm as hungry as a bear, can't I have a cookie?' asked Mr Laurie, when the shout subsided and he had expressed his thanks by a splendid bow.

'Trot out and ask Asia for the gingerbread box, Demi. It isn't in order to eat between meals, but, on this joyful occasion, we won't mind, and have a cookie all round,' said Mrs Jo; and when the box came she dealt them out with a liberal hand, everyone munching away in a social circle.

Suddenly, in the midst of a bite, Mr Laurie cried out, 'Bless my heart, I forgot grandma's bundle!' and running out to the carriage, returned with an interesting white parcel, which, being opened, disclosed a choice collection of beasts, birds, and pretty things cut out of crisp sugary cake, and baked a lovely brown.

'There's one for each, and a letter to tell which is whose. Grandma and Hannah made them, and I tremble to think what would have happened to me if I had forgotten to leave them.'

Then, amid much laughing and fun, the cakes were distributed. A fish for Dan, a fiddle for Nat, a book for Demi, a monkey for

Tommy, a flower for Daisy, a hoop for Nan, who had driven twice round the triangle without stopping, a star for Emil, who put on airs because he studied astronomy, and, best of all, an omnibus for Franz, whose great delight was to drive the family bus. Stuffy got a fat pig, and the little folks had birds, and cats, and rabbits, with black currant eyes.

'Now I must go. Where is my Goldilocks? Mamma will come flying out to get her if I'm not back early,' said Uncle Teddy, when the last crumb had vanished, which it speedily did, you may be sure.

The young ladies had gone into the garden, and while they waited till Franz looked them up, Jo and Laurie stood at the door talking together.

'How does little Giddygaddy come on?' he asked, for Nan's pranks amused him very much, and he was never tired of teasing Jo about her.

'Nicely; she is getting quite mannerly, and begins to see the error of her wild ways.'

'Don't the boys encourage her in them?'

'Yes; but I keep talking, and lately she has improved much. You saw how prettily she shook hands with you, and how gentle she was with Bess. Daisy's example has its effect upon her, and I'm quite sure that a few months will work wonders.'

Here Mrs Jo's remarks were cut short by the appearance of Nan tearing round the corner at a breakneck pace, driving a mettlesome team of four boys, and followed by Daisy trundling Bess in a wheelbarrow. Hat off, hair flying, whip cracking, and barrow bumping, up they came in a cloud of dust, looking as wild a set of little hoydens as one would wish to see.

'So, these are the model children, are they? It's lucky I didn't bring Mrs Curtis out to see your school for the cultivation of morals and manners; she would never have recovered from the shock of this spectacle,' said Mr Laurie, laughing at Mrs Jo's premature rejoicing over Nan's improvement.

'Laugh away; I'll succeed yet. As you used to say at College, quoting some professor, "Though the experiment has failed, the principle remains the same," ' said Mrs Bhaer, joining in the merriment.

'I'm afraid Nan's example is taking effect upon Daisy, instead of the other way. Look at my little princess! she has utterly forgotten her dignity, and is screaming like the rest. Young ladies, what does this mean?' and Mr Laurie rescued his small daughter from impending destruction, for the four horses were champing their bits and curvetting madly all about her, as she sat brandishing a great whip in both hands.

'We're having a race, and I beat,' shouted Nan.

'I could have run faster, only I was afraid of spilling Bess,' screamed Daisy.

'Hi! go long!' cried the princess, giving such a flourish with her whip that the horses ran away, and were seen no more.

'My precious child! come away from this ill-mannered crew before you are quite spoilt. Goodbye, Jo! Next time I come, I shall expect to find the boys making patchwork.'

'It wouldn't hurt them a bit. I don't give in, mind you; for my experiments always fail a few times before they succeed. Love to Amy and my blessed Marmee,' called Mrs Jo, as the carriage drove away; and the last Mr Laurie saw of her, she was consoling Daisy for her failure by a ride in the wheelbarrow, and looking as if she liked it.

Great was the excitement all the week about the repairs in the carriage-house, which went briskly on in spite of the incessant questions, advice, and meddling of the boys. Old Gibbs was nearly driven wild with it all, but managed to do his work nevertheless; and by Friday night the place was all in order – roof mended, shelves up, walls whitewashed, a great window cut at the back, which let in a flood of sunshine, and gave them a fine view of the brook, the meadows, and the distant hills; and over the great door, painted in red letters, was 'The Laurence Museum'.

All Saturday morning the boys were planning how it should be furnished with their spoils, and when Mr Laurie arrived, bringing an aquarium which Mrs Amy said she was tired of, their rapture was great.

The afternoon was spent in arranging things, and when the running and lugging and hammering was over, the ladies were invited to behold the institution.

It certainly was a pleasant place, airy, clean, and bright. A hop-vine shook its green bells round the open window, the pretty aquarium stood in the middle of the room, with some delicate water plants rising above the water, and goldfish showing their brightness as they floated to and fro below. On either side of the window were rows of shelves ready to receive the curiosities yet to be found. Dan's tall cabinet stood before the great door which was fastened up, while the small door was to be used. On the cabinet stood a queer Indian idol, very ugly, but very interesting; old Mr Laurence sent it, as well as a fine Chinese junk in full sail, which had a conspicuous place on the long table in the middle of the room. Above, swinging in a loop, and looking as if she was alive, hung Polly, who died at an advanced age, had been carefully stuffed, and was now presented by Mrs Jo. The walls were decorated with all sorts of things. A snake's skin, a big wasp's nest, a birch-bark canoe, a string of birds' eggs, wreaths of grey moss from the South, and a bunch of cotton-pods. The dead bats had a place, also a large turtle shell, and an ostrich egg proudly presented by Demi, who volunteered to explain these rare curiosities to guests whenever they liked. There were so many stones that it was impossible to accept them all, so only a few of the best were arranged among the shells on the shelves, the rest were piled up in corners, to be examined by Dan at his leisure.

Everyone was eager to give something, even Silas, who sent home for a stuffed wildcat killed in his youth. It was rather moth-eaten and shabby, but on a high bracket and best side foremost the effect was fine, for the yellow glass eyes glared, and the mouth snarled so naturally, that Teddy shook in his little shoes at sight of it, when he came bringing his most cherished treasure, one cocoon, to lay upon the shrine of science.

'Isn't it beautiful? I'd no idea we had so many curious things. I gave that; don't it look well? We might make a lot by charging something for letting folks see it.'

Jack added that last suggestion to the general chatter that went on as the family viewed the room.

'This is a free museum and if there is any speculating on it I'll paint out the name over the door,' said Mr Laurie, turning so quickly that Jack wished he had held his tongue.

'Hear! hear!' cried Mr Bhaer.

'Speech! speech!' added Mrs Jo.

'Can't, I'm too bashful. You give them a lecture yourself – you are used to it,' Mr Laurie answered, retreating towards the window, meaning to escape. But she held him fast, and said, laughing as she looked at the dozen pairs of dirty hands about her, 'If I did lecture, it would on the chemical and cleansing properties of soap. Come now, as the founder of the institution, you really ought to give us a few moral remarks, and we will applaud tremendously.'

Seeing that there was no way of escaping, Mr Laurie looked up at Polly hanging overhead, seemed to find inspiration in the brilliant old bird, and sitting down upon the table, said, in his pleasant way, 'There is one thing I'd like to suggest, boys, and that is, I want you to get some good as well as much pleasure out of this. Just putting curious or pretty things here won't do it; so suppose you read up about them, so that when anybody asks questions you can answer them, and understand the matter. I used to like these things myself, and should enjoy hearing about them now, for I've forgotten all I once knew. It wasn't much, was it, Jo? Here's Dan now, full of stories about birds, and bugs, and so on; let him take care of the museum, and once a week the rest of you take turns to read a composition, or tell about some animal, mineral, or vegetable. We should all like that, and I think it would put considerable useful knowledge into our heads. What do you say, Professor?'

'I like it much, and will give the lads all the help I can. But they will need books to read up these new subjects, and we have not many, I fear,' began Mr Bhaer, looking much pleased, planning many fine lectures on geology, which he liked. 'We should have a library for the special purpose.'

'Is that a useful sort of book, Dan?' asked Mr Laurie, pointing to the volume that lay open by the cabinet.

'Oh, yes! it tells all I want to know about insects. I had it here to see how to fix the butterflies right. I covered it, so it is not hurt;' and Dan caught it up, fearing the lender might think him careless.

'Give it here a minute;' and, pulling out his pencil, Mr Laurie wrote Dan's name in it, saying, as he set the book up on one of the corner shelves, where nothing stood but a stuffed bird without a tail, 'There, that is the beginning of the museum library. I'll hunt up some more books, and Demi shall keep them in order. Where are those jolly little books we used to read, Jo? "Insect Architecture" or some such name, all about ants having battles, and bees having queens, and crickets eating holes in our clothes and stealing milk, and larks of that sort.'

'In the garret at home. I'll have them sent out, and we will plunge into Natural History with a will,' said Mrs Jo, ready for anything.

'Won't it be hard to write about such things?' asked Nat, who hated compositions.

'At first, perhaps; but you will soon like it. If you think that hard, how would you like to have this subject given to you, as it was to a girl of thirteen: A conversation between Themistocles, Aristides, and Pericles on the proposed appropriation of the funds of the confederacy of Delos for the ornamentation of Athens?' said Mrs Jo.

The boys groaned at the mere sound of the long names, and the gentlemen laughed at the absurdity of the lesson.

'Did she write it?' asked Demi, in an awe-stricken tone.

'Yes, but you can imagine what a piece of work she made of it, though she was rather a bright child.'

'I'd like to have seen it,' said Mr Bhaer.

'Perhaps I can find it for you; I went to school with her,' and Mrs Jo looked so wicked that everyone knew who the little girl was.

Hearing of this fearful subject for a composition quite reconciled the boys to the thought of writing about familiar things. Wednesday afternoon was appointed for the lectures, as they preferred to call them, for some chose to talk instead of write. Mr Bhaer promised a portfolio in which the written productions should be kept, and Mrs Bhaer said she would attend the course with great pleasure.

Then the dirty-handed society went off the wash, followed by the Professor, trying to calm the anxiety of Rob, who had been told by Tommy that all water was full of invisible pollywogs.

'I like your plan very much, only don't be too generous, Teddy,' said Mrs Bhaer, when they were left alone. 'You know most of the boys have got to paddle their own canoes when they leave us, and too much sitting in the lap of luxury will unfit them for it.'

'I'll be moderate, but do let me amuse myself. I get desperately tired of business sometimes, and nothing freshens me up like a good frolic with your boys. I like that Dan very much, Jo. He isn't demonstrative; but he has the eye of a hawk, and when you have tamed him a little he will do you credit.'

'I'm so glad you think so. Thank you very much for your kindness to him, especially for this museum affair; it will keep him happy while he is lame, give me a chance to soften and smooth this poor, rough lad, and make him love us. What did inspire you with such a beautiful, helpful idea, Teddy?' asked Mrs Bhaer, glancing back at the pleasant room, as she turned to leave it.

Laurie took both her hands in his, and answered, with a look that made her eyes fill with happy tears, 'Dear Jo! I have known what it is to be a motherless boy, and I never can forget how much you and yours have done for me all these years.'

CHAPTER 12

Huckleberries

There was a great clashing of tin pails, much running to and fro, and frequent demands for something to eat, one August afternoon, for the boys were going huckleberrying, and made as much stir about it as if they were setting out to find the North-West Passage.

'Now, my lads, get off as quietly as you can, for Rob is safely out of the way, and won't see you,' said Mrs Bhaer, as she tied Daisy's broad-brimmed hat, and settled the great blue pinafore in which she had enveloped Nan.

But the plan did not succeed, for Rob had heard the bustle, decided to go, and prepared himself, without a thought of disappointment. The troop was just getting under way when the little man came marching downstairs with his best hat on, a bright tin pail in his hand, and a face beaming with satisfaction.

'Oh, dear! now we shall have a scene,' sighed Mrs Bhaer, who found her eldest son very hard to manage at times.

'I'm all ready,' said Rob, and took his place in the ranks with such perfect unconsciousness of his mistake, that it really was very hard to undeceive him.

'It's too far for you, my love; stay and take care of me, for I shall be all alone,' began his mother.

'You've got Teddy. I'm a big boy, so I can go; you said I might when I was bigger, and I am now,' persisted Rob, with a cloud beginning to dim the brightness of his happy face.

'We are going up to the great pasture, and it's ever so far; we don't want you tagging on,' cried Jack, who did not admire the little boys.

'I won't tag, I'll run and keep up. O Mamma! let me go! I want to fill my new pail, and I'll bring 'em all to you. Please, please, I will be good!' prayed Robby, looking up at his mother, so grieved and disappointed that her heart began to fail her.

'But, my deary, you'll get so tired and hot you won't have a good time. Wait till I go, and then we will stay all day, and pick as many berries as you want.'

'You never do go, you are so busy, and I'm tired of waiting. I'd rather go and get the berries for you all myself. I love to pick 'em, and I want to fill my new pail dreffly,' sobbed Rob.

The pathetic sight of great tears tinkling into the dear new pail, and threatening to fill it with salt water instead of huckleberries, touched all the ladies present. His mother patted the weeper on his back; Daisy offered to stay home with him; and Nan said, in her decided way, 'Let him come; I'll take care of him.'

'If Franz was going I wouldn't mind, for he is very careful; but he is haying with the father, and I'm not sure about the rest of you,' began Mrs Bhaer.

'It's so far,' put in Jack.

'I'd carry him if I was going – wish I was,' said Dan, with a sigh.

'Thank you, dear, but you must take care of your foot. I wish I could go. Stop a minute, I think I can manage it after all;' and Mrs Bhaer ran out to the steps, waving her apron wildly.

Silas was just driving away in the haycart, but turned back, and agreed at once, when Mrs Jo proposed that he should take the whole party to the pasture, and go for them at five o'clock.

'It will delay your work a little, but never mind; we will pay you in huckleberry pies,' said Mrs Jo, knowing Silas's weak point.

His rough, brown face brightened up, and he said, with a cheery 'Haw! haw!' – 'Wal now, Mis' Bhaer, if you go to bribin' of me, I shall give in right away.'

'Now, boys, I have arranged it so that you can all go,' said Mrs Bhaer, running back again, much relieved, for she loved to make them happy, and always felt miserable when she had disturbed the serenity of her little sons; for she believed that the small hopes and plans and pleasures of children should be tenderly respected by grown-up people, and never rudely thwarted or ridiculed.

'Can I go?' said Dan, delighted.

'I thought especially of you. Be careful, and never mind the berries, but sit about and enjoy the lovely things which you know how to find all about you,' answered Mrs Bhaer, who remembered his kind offer to her boy.

'Me too! me too!' sung Rob, dancing with joy, and clapping his precious pail and cover like castanets.

'Yes, and Daisy and Nan must take good care of you. Be at the bars at five o'clock, and Silas will come for you all.'

Robby cast himself upon his mother in a burst of gratitude, promising to bring her every berry he picked, and not eat one. Then they were all packed into the haycart, and went rattling away, the brightest face among the dozen being that of Rob, as he sat between his two temporary little mothers, beaming upon the whole world, and waving his best hat; for his indulgent mamma had not the heart to bereave him of it, since this was a gala-day to him.

Such a happy afternoon as they had, in spite of the mishaps which usually occur on such expeditions! Of course Tommy came to grief, tumbled upon a hornet's nest and got stung; but being used to woe, he bore the smart manfully, till Dan suggested the application of damp earth, which much assuaged the pain. Daisy saw a snake, and flying from it lost half her berries; but Demi helped her to fill up again, and discussed reptiles most learnedly the while. Ned fell out of a tree, and split his jacket down the back, but suffered no other fracture. Emil and Jack established rival claims to a certain thick patch, and while they were squabbling about it, Stuffy quickly and quietly stripped the bushes and fled to the protection of Dan, who was enjoying himself immensely. The crutch was no longer necessary, and he was delighted to see how strong his foot felt as he roamed about the great pasture, full of interesting rocks and stumps, with familiar little creatures in the grass, and well-known insects dancing in the air.

But of all the adventures that happened on this afternoon that which befell Nan and Rob was the most exciting, and it long remained one of the favourite histories of the household. Having explored the country pretty generally, torn three rents in her frock, and scratched her face in a barberry bush, Nan began to pick the berries that shone like big, black beads on the low, green bushes. Her nimble fingers flew, but still her basket did not fill up as rapidly as she desired, so she kept wandering here and there to search for better places, instead of picking contentedly and steadily as Daisy did. Rob followed Nan, for her energy suited him better than his cousin's patience, and he too was anxious to have the biggest and best berries for Marmar.

'I keep putting 'em in, but it don't fill up, and I'm so tired,' said Rob, pausing a moment to rest his short legs, and beginning to think huckleberrying was not all his fancy painted it; for the sun blazed, Nan skipped hither and thither like a grasshopper, and the berries fell out of his pail almost as fast as he put them in, because, in his struggles with the bushes, it was often upside-down.

'Last time we came they were ever so much thicker over that wall – great bouncers; and there is a cave there where the boys made a fire. Let's go and fill our things quick, and then hide in the cave and let the others find us,' proposed Nan, thirsting for adventures.

Rob consented, and away they went, scrambling over the wall and running down the sloping fields on the other side, till they were hidden among the rocks and underbrush. The berries were thick, and at last the pails were actually full. It was shady and cool down there, and a little spring gave the thirsty children a refreshing drink out of its mossy cup.

'Now we will go and rest in the cave, and eat our lunch,' said Nan, well satisfied with her success so far.

'Do you know the way?' asked Rob.

' 'Course I do; I've been once, and I always remember. Didn't I go and get my box all right?'

That convinced Rob, and he followed blindly as Nan led him over stock and stone, and brought him, after much meandering, to a small recess in the rock, where the blackened stones showed that fires had been made.

'Now, isn't it nice?' asked Nan, as she took out a bit of bread and butter, rather damaged by being mixed up with nails, fishhooks, stones and other foreign substances, in the young lady's pocket.

'Yes; do you think they will find us soon?' asked Rob, who found the shadowy glen rather dull, and began to long for more society.

'No, I don't; because if I hear them, I shall hide, and have fun making them find me.'

'P'raps they won't come.'

'Don't care; I can get home myself.'

'Is it a great way?' asked Rob, looking at his little stubby boots, scratched and wet with his long wandering.

'It's six miles, I guess.' Nan's ideas of distance were vague, and her faith in her own powers great.

'I think we better go now,' suggested Rob, presently.

'I shan't till I have picked over my berries;' and Nan began what seemed to Rob an endless task.

'Oh, dear! you said you'd take good care of me,' he sighed, as the sun seemed to drop behind the hill all of a sudden.

'Well, I *am* taking good care of you as hard as I can. Don't be cross, child; I'll go in a minute,' said Nan, who considered five-year-old Robby a mere infant compared to herself.

So little Rob sat looking anxiously about him, and waiting patiently, for, spite of some misgivings, he felt great confidence in Nan.

'I guess it's going to be night pretty soon,' he observed, as if to himself, as a mosquito bit him, and the frogs in a neighbouring marsh began to pipe up for the evening concert.

'My goodness me! so it is. Come right away this minute, or they will be gone,' cried Nan, looking up from her work, and suddenly perceiving that the sun was down.

'I heard a horn about an hour ago; maybe they were blowing for us,' said Rob, trudging after his guide as she scrambled up the steep hill.

'Where was it?' asked Nan, stopping short.

'Over that way;' he pointed with a dirty little finger in an entirely wrong direction.

'Let's go that way and meet them;' and Nan wheeled about, and began to trot through the bushes, feeling a trifle anxious, for there were so many cow-paths all about she could not remember which way they came.

On they went over stock and stone again, pausing now and then to listen for the horn, which did not blow any more, for it was only the moo of a cow on her way home.

'I don't remember seeing that pile of stones do you?' asked Nan, as she sat on a wall to rest a moment and take an observation.

'I don't remember anything, but I want to go home,' and Rob's voice had a little tremble in it that made Nan put her arms round him and lift him gently down, saying, in her most capable way, 'I'm going just as fast as I can, dear. Don't cry, and when we come to the road, I'll carry you.'

'Where is the road?' and Robby wiped his eyes to look for it.

'Over by that big tree. Don't you know that's the one Ned tumbled out of?'

'Are we lost?' quavered Rob, clasping his pail in despair

'So it is. Maybe they waited for us; I'd like to ride home – wouldn't you?' and Robby brightened up as he plodded along toward the end of the great pasture.

'No, I'd rather walk,' answered Nan, feeling quite sure that she would be obliged to do so, and preparing her mind for it.

Another long trudge through the fast-deepening twilight and another disappointment, for when they reached the tree, they found to their dismay that it was not the one Ned climbed, and no road anywhere appeared.

'Are we lost?' quavered Rob, clasping his pail in despair.

'Not much. I don't just see which way to go, and I guess we'd better call.'

So they both shouted till they were hoarse, yet nothing answered but the frogs in full chorus.

'There is another tall tree over there, perhaps that's the one,' said Nan, whose heart sunk within her, though she still spoke bravely.

'I don't think I can go any more; my boots are so heavy I can't pull 'em;' and Robby sat down on a stone quite worn out.

'Then we must stay here all night. *I* don't care much, if snakes don't come.'

'I'm frightened of snakes. I can't stay all night. Oh, dear! I don't like to be lost,' and Rob puckered up his face to cry, when suddenly a thought occurred to him, and he said, in a tone of perfect confidence, 'Marmar will come and find me – she always does; I ain't afraid now.'

'She won't know where we are.'

'She didn't know I was shut up in the ice-house, but she found me. I know she'll come,' returned Robby, so trustfully, that Nan felt relieved, and sat down by him, saying, with a remorseful sigh, 'I wish we hadn't run away.'

'You made me; but I don't mind much – Marmar will love me just the same,' answered Rob, clinging to his sheet anchor when all other hope was gone.

'I'm so hungry. Let's eat our berries,' proposed Nan, after a pause, during which Rob began to nod.

'So am I, but I can't eat mine, 'cause I told Marmar I'd keep them all for her.'

'You'll have to eat them if no one comes for us,' said Nan, who felt like contradicting everything just then. 'If we stay here a great many days, we shall eat up all the berries in the field, and then we shall starve,' she added grimly.

'I shall eat sassafras. I know a big tree of it, and Dan told me how squirrels dig up the roots and eat them, and I love to dig,' returned Rob, undaunted by the prospect of starvation.

'Yes; and we can catch frogs, and cook them. My father ate some once, and he said they were nice,' put in Nan, beginning to find a spice of romance even in being lost in a huckleberry pasture.

'How could we cook frogs? we haven't got any fire.'

'I don't know; next time I'll have matches in my pocket,' said Nan, rather depressed by this obstacle to the experiment in frog-cookery.

'Couldn't we light a fire with a firefly?' asked Rob, hopefully, as he watched them flitting to and fro like winged sparks.

'Let's try;' and several minutes were pleasantly spent in catching the flies, and trying to make them kindle a green twig or two. 'It's a lie to call them fireflies when there isn't a fire in them,' Nan said, throwing one unhappy insect away with scorn, though it shone its best, and obligingly walked up and down the twigs to please the innocent little experimenters.

'Marmar's a good while coming,' said Rob, after another pause, during which they watched the stars overhead, smelt the sweet fern crushed under foot, and listened to the crickets' serenade.

'I don't see why God made any night; day is so much pleasanter,' said Nan, thoughtfully.

'It's to sleep in,' answered Rob, with a yawn.

'Then do go to sleep,' said Nan, pettishly.

'I want my own bed. Oh, I wish I could see Teddy!' cried Rob, painfully reminded of home by the soft chirp of birds safe in their little nests.

'I don't believe your mother will ever find us,' said Nan, who was becoming desperate, for she hated patient waiting of any sort. 'It's so dark she won't see us.'

'It was all black in the ice-house, and I was so scared I didn't call her, but she saw me; and she will see me now, no matter how dark it is,' returned confiding Rob, standing up to peer into the gloom for the help which never failed him.

'I see her! I see her!' he cried, and ran as fast as his tired legs would take him toward a dark figure slowly approaching. Suddenly he stopped, then turned about, and came stumbling back, screaming in a great panic, 'No, it's a bear, a big black one!' and hid his face in Nan's skirts.

For a moment Nan quailed; ever her courage gave out at the thought of a real bear, and she was about to turn and flee in great disorder, when a mild 'Moo!' changed her fear to merriment, as she said, laughing, 'It's a cow, Robby! the nice, black cow we saw this afternoon.'

The cow seemed to feel that it was not just the thing to meet two little people in her pasture after dark, and the amiable beast paused to enquire into the case. She let them stroke her, and stood regarding them with her soft eyes so mildly, that Nan, who feared no animal but a bear, was fired with a desire to milk her.

'Silas taught me how; and berries and milk would be so nice,' she said, emptying the contents of her pail into her hat, and boldly beginning her new task, while Rob stood by and repeated, at her command, the poem from Mother Goose:

> 'Cushy cow, bonny, let down your milk,
> Let down your milk to me,
> And I will give you a gown of silk,
> A gown of silk and a silver tee.'

But the immortal rhyme had little effect, for the benevolent cow had already been milked, and had only half a gill to give the thirsty children.

'Shoo! get away! you are an old crosspatch,' cried Nan, ungratefully, as she gave up the attempt in despair; and poor Molly walked on with a gentle gurgle of surprise and reproof.

'Each can have a sip, and then we must take a walk. We shall go to sleep if we don't; and lost people mustn't sleep. Don't you know how Hannah Lee in the pretty story slept under the snow and died?'

'But there isn't any snow now, and it's nice and warm,' said Rob, who was not blessed with as lively a fancy as Nan.

'No matter, we will poke about a little, and call some more; and then, if nobody comes, we will hide under the bushes, like Hop-'o-my-thumb and his brothers.'

It was a very short walk, however, for Rob was so sleepy he

could not get on, and tumbled down so often that Nan entirely lost patience, being half distracted by the responsibility she had taken upon herself.

'If you tumble down again, I'll shake you,' she said, lifting the poor little man up very kindly as she spoke, for Nan's bark was much worse than her bite.

'Please don't. It's my boots – they keep slipping so;' and Rob manfully checked the sob just ready to break out, adding, with a plaintive patience that touched Nan's heart, 'If the skeeters didn't bite me so, I could go to sleep till Marmar comes.'

'Put your head on my lap, and I'll cover you up with my apron; I'm not afraid of the night,' said Nan, sitting down and trying to persuade herself that she did not mind the shadow nor the mysterious rustlings all about her.

'Wake me up when she comes,' said Rob, and was fast asleep in five minutes with his head in Nan's lap under the pinafore.

The little girl sat for some fifteen minutes, staring about her with anxious eyes, and feeling as if each second was an hour. Then a pale light began to glimmer over the hilltop and she said to herself, 'I guess the night is over and morning is coming. I'd like to see the sun rise, so I'll watch, and when it comes up we can find our way right home.'

But before the moon's round face peeped above the hill to destroy her hope, Nan had fallen asleep, leaning back in a little bower of tall ferns, and was deep in a midsummer night's dream of fireflies and blue aprons, mountains of huckleberries, and Robby wiping away the tears of a black cow, who sobbed, 'I want to go home! I want to go home!'

While the children were sleeping, peacefully lulled by the drowsy hum of many neighbourly mosquitoes, the family at home were in a great state of agitation. The haycart came at five, and all but Jack, Emil, Nan, and Rob were at the bars ready for it. Franz drove instead of Silas, and when the boys told him that the others were going home through the wood, he said, looking ill-pleased, 'They ought to have left Rob to ride, he will be tired out by the long walk.'

'It's shorter that way, and they will carry him,' said Stuffy, who was in a hurry for his supper.

'You are sure Nan and Rob went with them?'

'Of course they did; I saw them getting over the wall, and sung out that it was most five, and Jack called back that they were going the other way,' explained Tommy.

'Very well, pile in then,' and away rattled the haycart with the tired children and the full pails.

Mrs Jo looked sober when she heard of the division of the party, and sent Franz back with Toby to find and bring the little ones home. Supper was over, and the family sitting about in the cool hall as usual, when Franz came trotting back, hot, dusty, and anxious.

'Have they come?' he called out when halfway up the avenue.

'No!' and Mrs Jo flew out of her chair looking so alarmed that everyone jumped up and gathered round Franz.

'I can't find them anywhere,' he began; but the words were hardly spoken when a loud 'Hello!' startled them all, and the next minute Jack and Emil came round the house.

'Where are Nan and Rob?' cried Mrs Jo, clutching Emil in a way that caused him to think his aunt had suddenly lost her wits.

'I don't know. They came home with the others, didn't they?' he answered, quickly.

'No; George and Tommy said they went with you.'

'Well, they didn't. Haven't seen them. We took a swim in the pond, and came by the wood,' said Jack, looking alarmed, as well he might.

'Call Mr Bhaer, get the lanterns, and tell Silas I want him.'

That was all Mrs Jo said, but they knew what she meant, and flew to obey her orders. In ten minutes, Mr Bhaer and Silas were off to the wood, and Franz tearing down the road on old Andy to search the great pasture. Mrs Jo caught up some food from the table, a little bottle of brandy from the medicine closet, took a lantern, and bidding Jack and Emil come with her, and the rest not stir, she trotted away on Toby, never stopping for hat or shawl. She heard someone running after her, but said not a word till, as she paused to call and listen, the light of her lantern shone on Dan's face.

'You here! I told Jack to come,' she said, half-inclined to send him back, much as she needed help.

'I wouldn't let him; he and Emil hadn't had any supper, and I wanted to come more than they did,' he said, taking the lantern from her and smiling up in her face with the steady look in his eyes that made her feel as if, boy though he was, she had someone to depend on.

Off she jumped, and ordered him on to Toby, in spite of his pleading to walk; then they went on again along the dusty, solitary road, stopping every now and then to call and hearken breathlessly for little voices to reply.

When they came to the great pasture, other lights were already flitting to and fro like will-o'-the-wisps, and Mr Bhaer's voice was heard shouting, 'Nan! Rob! Rob! Nan!' in every part of the field. Silas whistled and roared, Dan plunged here and there on Toby, who seemed to understand the case, and went over the roughest places with unusual docility. Often Mrs Jo hushed them all, saying, with a sob in her throat, 'The noise may frighten them, let me call; Robby will know my voice;' and then she would cry out the beloved little name in every tone of tenderness, till the very echoes whispered it softly, and the winds seemed to waft it willingly; but still no answer came.

The sky was overcast now, and only brief glimpses of the moon were seen, heat-lightning darted out of the dark clouds now and then, and a faint far-off rumble as of thunder told that a summer-storm was brewing.

'O my Robby! my Robby!' mourned poor Mrs Jo, wandering up and down like a pale ghost, while Dan kept beside her like a faithful firefly. 'What shall I say to Nan's father if she comes to harm? Why did I ever trust my darling so far away? Fritz, do you hear anything?' and when a mournful, 'No,' came back, she wrung her hands so despairingly that Dan sprang down from Toby's back, tied the bridle to the bars, and said, in his decided way, 'They may have gone down to the spring – I'm going to look.'

He was over the wall and away so fast that she could hardly follow him; but when she reached the spot, he lowered the lantern and showed her with joy the marks of little feet in the soft ground about the spring. She fell down on her knees to examine the tracks, and then sprang up, saying eagerly, 'Yes; that is the mark of my Robby's little boots! Come this way, they must have gone on.'

Such a weary search! But now some inexplicable instinct seemed to lead the anxious mother, for presently Dan uttered a cry, and caught up a little shining object lying in the path. It was the cover of the new tin pail, dropped in the first alarm of being lost. Mrs Jo hugged and kissed it as if it were a living thing; and when Dan was about to utter a glad shout to bring the others to the spot, she stopped him, saying, as she hurried on, 'No, let *me* find them; I let Rob go, and I want to give him back to his father all myself.'

A little farther on Nan's hat appeared, and after passing the place more than once, they came at last upon the babes in the wood, both sound asleep. Dan never forgot the little picture on which the light of his lantern shone that night. He thought Mrs Jo would cry out, but she only whispered, 'Hush!' as she softly lifted away the apron, and saw the little ruddy face below. The berry-stained lips were half-open as the breath came and went, the yellow hair lay damp on the hot forehead, and both the chubby hands held fast the little pail still full.

The sight of the childish harvest, treasured through all the troubles of that night for her, seemed to touch Mrs Jo to the heart, for suddenly she gathered up her boy, and began to cry over him, so tenderly, yet so heartily, that he woke up, and at first seemed bewildered. Then he remembered, and hugged her close, saying with a laugh of triumph, 'I knew you'd come! O Marmar! I did want you so!' For a moment they kissed and clung to one another, quite forgetting all the world; for no matter how lost and soiled and worn out wandering sons may be, mothers can forgive and forget everything as they fold them in their fostering arms. Happy the son whose faith in his mother remains unchanged, and who, through all his wanderings, has kept some filial token to repay her brave and tender love.

Dan meantime picked Nan out of her bush, and, with a gentleness none but Teddy ever saw in him before, he soothed her first alarm at the sudden waking, and wiped away her tears; for Nan also began to cry for joy, it was so good to see a kind face and feel a strong arm round her after what seemed to her ages of loneliness and fear.

'My poor little girl, don't cry! You are all safe now, and no one shall say a word of blame tonight,' said Mrs Jo, taking Nan into her capacious embrace, and cuddling both children as a hen might gather her lost chickens under her motherly wings.

'It was my fault; but I am sorry. I tried to take care of him, and I covered him up and let him sleep, and didn't touch his berries, though I was so hungry; and I never will do it again truly, never, never,' sobbed Nan, quite lost in a sea of penitence and thankfulness.

'Call them now, and let us get home,' said Mrs Jo; and Dan, getting upon the wall, sent a joyful word 'Found!' ringing over the field.

How the wandering lights came dancing from all sides, and gathered round the little group among the sweet fern bushes! Such a hugging, and kissing, and talking, and crying, as went on must have amazed the glowworms, and evidently delighted the mosquitoes, for they hummed frantically, while the little moths came in flocks to the party, and the frogs croaked as if they could not express their satisfaction loudly enough.

Then they set out for home, a queer party, for Franz rode on to tell the news; Dan and Toby led the way; then came Nan in the strong arms of Silas, who considered her 'the smartest little baggage he ever saw', and teased her all the way home about her pranks. Mr Bhaer would let no one carry Rob but himself, and the little fellow, refreshed by sleep, sat up, and chattered gaily, feeling himself a hero, while his mother went beside him holding on to any part of his precious little body that came handy, and never tired of hearing him say, 'I *knew* Marmar would come,' or seeing him lean down to kiss her, and put a plump berry into her mouth, ' 'Cause he picked 'em all for her.'

The moon shone out just as they reached the avenue, and all the boys came shouting to meet them, so the lost lambs were borne in triumph and safety, and landed in the dining-room, where the unromantic little things demanded supper instead of preferring kisses and caresses. They were set down to bread and milk, while the entire household stood round to gaze upon them. Nan soon recovered her spirits, and recounted her perils with a relish now that they were all over. Rob seemed absorbed in his food, but put down his spoon all of a sudden, and set up a doleful roar.

'My precious, why do you cry?' asked his mother, who still hung over him.

'I'm crying 'cause I was lost,' bawled Rob, trying to squeeze out a tear, and failing entirely.

'But you are found now. Nan says you didn't cry out in the field, and I was glad you were such a brave boy.'

'I was so busy being frightened I didn't have any time then. But

I want to cry now, 'cause I don't like to be lost,' explained Rob, struggling with sleep, emotion, and a mouthful of bread and milk.

The boys set up such a laugh at this funny way of making up for lost time, that Rob stopped to look at them, and the merriment was so infectious, that after a surprised stare he burst out into a merry, 'Ha, ha!' and beat his spoon upon the table as if he enjoyed the joke immensely.

'It is ten o'clock; into bed, every man of you,' said Mr Bhaer, looking at his watch.

'And, thank Heaven! there will be no empty ones tonight,' added Mrs Bhaer, watching, with full eyes, Robby going up in his father's arms, and Nan escorted by Daisy and Demi, who considered her the most interesting heroine of their collection.

'Poor Aunt Jo is so tired she ought to be carried up herself,' said gentle Franz, putting his arm round her as she paused at the stair-foot, looking quite exhausted by her fright and long walk.

'Let's make an armchair,' proposed Tommy.

'No, thank you, my lads; but somebody may lend me a shoulder to lean on,' answered Mrs Jo.

'Me! me!' and half a dozen jostled one another, all eager to be chosen, for there was something in the pale motherly face that touched the warm hearts under the round jackets.

Seeing that they considered it an honour, Mrs Jo gave it to the one who had earned it, and nobody grumbled when she put her arm on Dan's broad shoulder, saying, with a look that made him colour up with pride and pleasure, 'He found the children; so I think he must help me up.'

Dan felt richly rewarded for his evening's work, not only that he was chosen from all the rest to go proudly up bearing the lamp, but because Mrs Jo said heartily, 'Good-night, my boy! God bless you!' as he left her at her door.

'I wish I *was* your boy,' said Dan, who felt as if danger and trouble had somehow brought him nearer than ever to her.

'You shall be my oldest son,' and she sealed her promise with a kiss that made Dan hers entirely.

Little Rob was all right next day, but Nan had a headache, and lay on Mother Bhaer's sofa with cold cream upon her scratched face. Her remorse was quite gone, and she evidently thought being lost rather a fine amusement. Mrs Jo was not pleased with this state of things, and had no desire to have her children led from the paths of virtue, or her pupils lying round loose in huckleberry fields. So she talked soberly to Nan, and tried to impress upon her mind the difference between liberty and license, telling several tales to enforce her lecture. She had not decided how to punish Nan, but one of these stories suggested a way, and as Mrs Jo liked odd penalties, she tried it.

'All children run away,' pleaded Nan, as if it was as natural and necessary a thing as measles or whooping cough.

'Not all, and some who do run away don't get found again,' answered Mrs Jo.

'Didn't you do it yourself?' asked Nan, whose keen little eyes saw some traces of a kindred spirit in the serious lady who was sewing so morally before her.

Mrs Jo laughed, and owned that she did.

'Tell about it,' demanded Nan, feeling that she was getting the upper hand in the discussion.

Mrs Jo saw that, and sobered down at once, saying, with a remorseful shake of the head, 'I did it a good many times, and led my poor mother rather a hard life with my pranks, till she cured me.'

'How?' and Nan sat up with a face full of interest.

'I had a new pair of shoes once, and wanted to show them; so, though I was told not to leave the garden, I ran away and was wandering about all day. It was in the city, and why I wasn't killed I don't know. Such a time as I had. I frolicked in the park with dogs, sailed boats in the Back Bay with strange boys, dined with a little Irish beggar girl on salt fish and potatoes, and was found at last fast asleep on a doorstep with my arms round a great dog. It was late in the evening, and I was a dirty as a little pig, and the new shoes were worn out – I had travelled so far.'

'How nice!' cried Nan, looking all ready to go and do it herself.

'It was not nice next day;' and Mrs Jo tried to keep her eyes from betraying how much she enjoyed the memory of her early capers.

'Did your mother whip you?' asked Nan, curiously.

'She never whipped me but once, and then she begged my pardon, or I don't think I ever should have forgiven her, it hurt my feelings so much.'

'Why did she beg your pardon? – my father don't.'

'Because, when she had done it, I turned round and said, "Well, you are mad yourself, and ought to be whipped as much as me." She looked at me a minute, then her anger all died out, and she said, as if ashamed, "You are right, Jo, I *am* angry; and why should I punish you for being in a passion when I set you such a bad example? Forgive me, dear, and let us try to help one another in a better way." I never forgot it, and it did me more good than a dozen rods.'

Nan sat thoughtfully turning the little cold-cream jar for a minute, and Mrs Jo said nothing, but let that idea get well into the busy little mind that was so quick to see and feel what went on about her.

'I like that,' said Nan, presently, and her face looked less elfish, with its sharp eyes, inquisitive nose, and mischievous mouth. 'What did your mother do to you when you ran away that time?'

'She tied me to the bedpost with a long string, so that I could not go out of the room, and there I stayed all day with the little worn-out shoes hanging up before me to remind me of my fault.'

'I should think that would cure anybody,' cried Nan, who loved her liberty above all things.

'It did cure me, and I think it will you, so I am going to try it,' said Mrs Jo, suddenly taking a ball of strong twine out of a drawer in her work-table.

Nan looked as if she was decidedly getting the worst of the argument now, and sat feeling much crestfallen while Mrs Jo tied one end round her waist and the other to the arm of the sofa, saying, as she finished, 'I don't like to tie you up like a naughty little dog, but if you don't remember any better than a dog, I must treat you like one.'

'I'd just as lief be tied up as not – I like to play dog;' and Nan put on a don't-care face, and began to growl and grovel on the floor.

Mrs Jo took no notice, but leaving a book or two and a hand-kerchief to hem, she went away, and left Miss Nan to her own devices. This was not agreeable, and after sitting a moment she tried to untie the cord. But it was fastened in the belt of her apron behind, so she began on the knot at the other end. It soon came loose, and, gathering it up, Nan was about to get out of the window, when she heard Mrs Jo say to somebody as she passed through the hall, 'No, I don't think she will run away now; she is an honourable little girl, and knows that I do it to help her.'

In a minute, Nan whisked back, tied herself up, and began to sew violently. Rob came in a moment after, and was so charmed with the new punishment, that he got a jump-rope and tethered himself to the other arm of the sofa in the most social manner.

'I got lost too, so I ought to be tied up as much as Nan,' he explained to his mother when she saw the new captive.

'I'm not sure that you don't deserve a little punishment, for you knew it was wrong to go far away from the rest.'

'Nan took me,' began Rob, willing to enjoy the novel penalty, but not willing to take the blame.

'You needn't have gone. You have got a conscience, though you are a little boy, and you must learn to mind it.'

'Well, my conscience didn't prick me a bit when she said "Let's get over the wall," ' answered Rob, quoting one of Demi's expressions.

'Did you stop to see if it did?'

'No.'

'Then you cannot tell.'

'I guess it's such a little conscience that it don't prick hard enough for me to feel it,' added Rob, after thinking the matter over for a minute.

'We must sharpen it up. It's bad to have a dull conscience; so you may stay here till dinner-time, and talk about it with Nan. I trust you both not to untie yourselves till I say the word.'

'No, we won't,' said both, feeling a certain sense of virtue in helping to punish themselves.

For an hour they were very good, then they grew tired of one room, and longed to get out. Never had the hall seemed so inviting; even the little bedroom acquired a sudden interest, and they would gladly have gone in and played tent with the curtains of the best bed. The open windows drove them wild because they could not reach them; and the outer world seemed so beautiful, they wondered how they ever found the heart to say it was dull. Nan pined for a race round the lawn, and Rob remembered with dismay that he had not fed his dog that morning, and wondered what poor Pollux would do. They watched the clock, and Nan did some nice calculations in minutes and seconds, while Rob learned to tell all the hours between eight and one so well that he never forgot them. It was maddening to smell the dinner, to know that there was to be succotash and huckleberry pudding, and to feel that they would not be on the spot to secure good helps of both. When Mary Ann began to set the table, they nearly cut themselves in two trying to see what meat there was to be; and Nan offered to help her make the beds, if she would only see that she had 'lots of sauce on her pudding'.

When the boys came bursting out of school, they found the children tugging at their halters like a pair of restive little colts, and were much edified, as well as amused, by the sequel to the exciting adventures of the night.

'Untie me now, Marmar; my conscience will prick like a pin next time, I know it will,' said Rob, as the bell rang, and Teddy came to look at him with sorrowful surprise.

'We shall see,' answered his mother, setting him free. He took a good run down the hall, back through the dining-room, and brought up beside Nan, quite beaming with virtuous satisfaction.

'I'll bring her dinner to her, may I?' he asked, pitying his fellow captive.

'That's my kind little son! Yes, pull out the table, and get a chair;' and Mrs Jo hurried away to quell the ardour of the others, who were always in a raging state of hunger at noon.

Nan ate alone, and spent a long afternoon attached to the sofa. Mrs Bhaer lengthened her bonds so that she could look out of the window; and there she stood watching the boys play, and all the little summer creatures enjoying their liberty. Daisy had a picnic for the dolls on the lawn, so that Nan might see the fun if she could not join in it. Tommy turned his best somersaults to console her; Demi sat on the steps reading aloud to himself, which amused Nan a good deal; and Dan brought a little tree toad to show her as the most delicate attention in his power.

But nothing atoned for the loss of freedom; and a few hours of confinement taught Nan how precious it was. A good many thoughts went through the little head that lay on the window sill during the last quiet hour when all the children went to the brook to see Emil's new ship launched. She was to have christened it, and had depended on smashing a tiny bottle of currant wine over the prow as it was named *Josephine* in honour of Mrs Bhaer. Now she had lost her chance, and Daisy wouldn't do it half so well. Tears rose to her eyes as she remembered that it was all her own fault; and she said aloud, addressing a fat bee who was rolling about in the yellow heart of a rose just under the window, 'If you have run away, you'd better go right home, and tell your mother you are sorry, and never do so any more.'

'I am glad to hear you give him such good advice, and I think he has taken it,' said Mrs Jo, smiling, as the bee spread his dusty wings and flew away.

Nan brushed off a bright drop or two that shone on the window-sill, and nestled against her friend as she took her on her knee, adding kindly – for she had seen the little drops, and knew what they meant, 'Do you think my mother's cure for running away a good one?'

'Yes, ma'am,' answered Nan, quite subdued by her quiet day.

'I hope I shall not have to try it again.'

'I guess not;' and Nan looked up with such an earnest little face that Mrs Jo felt satisfied, and said no more, for she liked to have her penalties do their own work, and did not spoil the effect by too much moralising.

Here Rob appeared, bearing with infinite care what Asia called a 'sarcer pie', meaning one baked in a saucer.

'It's made out of some of my berries, and I'm going to give you half at supper-time,' he announced with a flourish.

'What makes you, when I'm so naughty?' asked Nan, meekly.

'Because we got lost together. You ain't going to be naughty again, are you?'

'Never,' said Nan, with great decision.

'Oh, goody! now let's go and get Mary Ann to cut this for us all ready to eat; it's 'most tea-time;' and Rob beckoned with the delicious little pie.

Nan started to follow, then stopped, and said, 'I forgot, I can't go.'

'Try and see,' said Mrs Bhaer, who had quietly untied the cord sash while she had been talking.

Nan saw that she was free, and with one tempestuous kiss to Mrs Jo, she was off like a hummingbird, followed by Robby, dribbling huckleberry juice as he ran.

CHAPTER 13

Goldilocks

After the last excitement peace descended upon Plumfield and reigned unbroken for several weeks, for the elder boys felt that the loss of Nan and Rob lay at their door, and all became so paternal in their care that they were rather wearying; while the little ones listened to Nan's recital of her perils so many times, that they regarded being lost as the greatest ill humanity was heir to, and hardly dared to put their little noses outside the great gate lest night should suddenly descend upon them, and ghostly black cows come looming through the dusk.

'It is too good to last,' said Mrs Jo; for years of boy-culture had taught her that such lulls were usually followed by outbreaks of some sort, and when less wise women would have thought that the boys had become confirmed saints, she prepared herself for a sudden eruption of the domestic volcano.

One cause of this welcome calm was a visit from little Bess, whose parents lent her for a week while they were away with Grandpa Laurence, who was poorly. The boys regarded Goldilocks as a mixture of child, angel, and fairy, for she was a lovely little creature, and the golden hair which she inherited from her blonde mamma enveloped her like a shining veil, behind which she smiled upon her worshippers when gracious, and hid herself when offended. Her father would not have it cut and it hung below her waist, so soft and fine and bright, that Demi insisted that it was silk spun from a cocoon. Everyone praised the little Princess, but it did not seem to do her harm, only to teach her that her presence brought sunshine, her smiles made answering smiles on other faces, and her baby griefs filled every heart with tenderest sympathy.

Unconsciously, she did her young subjects more good than many a real sovereign, for her rule was very gentle and her power was felt rather than seen. Her natural refinement made her dainty in all things, and had a good effect upon the careless lads about her.

She would let no one touch her roughly or with unclean hands, and more soap was used during her visits than at any other time, because the boys considered it the highest honour to be allowed to carry her highness, and the deepest disgrace to be repulsed with the disdainful command, 'Do away, dirty boy!'

Loud voices displeased her and quarrelling frightened her; so gentler tones came into the boyish voices as they addressed her, and squabbles were promptly suppressed in her presence by lookers-on if the principals could not restrain themselves. She liked to be waited on, and the biggest boys did her little errands without a murmur, while the small lads were her devoted slaves in all things. They begged to be allowed to draw her carriage, bear her berry basket, or pass her plate at table. No service was too humble, and Tommy and Ned came to blows before they could decide which should have the honour of blacking her little boots.

Nan was especially benefited by a week in the society of a well-bred lady, though such a very small one; for Bess would look at her with a mixture of wonder and alarm in her great blue eyes when the hoyden screamed and romped; and she shrunk from her as if she thought her a sort of wild animal. Warm-hearted Nan felt this very much. She said at first, 'Pooh! I don't care!' But she did care, and was so hurt when Bess said, 'I love my tuzzin best, tause she is twiet,' that she shook poor Daisy till her teeth chattered in her head, and then fled to the barn to cry dismally. In that general refuge for perturbed spirits she found comfort and good counsel from some source or other. Perhaps the swallows from their mud-built nests overhead twittered her a little lecture on the beauty of gentleness. However that might have been, she came out quite subdued, and carefully searched the orchard for a certain kind of early apple that Bess liked because it was sweet and small and rosy. Armed with this peace offering, she approached the Princess, and humbly presented it. To her great joy it was graciously accepted, and when Daisy gave Nan a forgiving kiss, Bess did likewise, as if she felt that she had been too severe, and desired to apologise. After this they played pleasantly together, and Nan enjoyed the royal favour for days. To be sure she felt a little like a wild bird in a pretty cage at first, and occasionally had to slip out to stretch her wings in a long flight, or to sing at the top of her voice, where neither would disturb the plump turtledove Daisy, nor the dainty golden canary Bess. But it did her good; for, seeing how everyone loved the little Princess for her small graces and virtues, she began to imitate her, because Nan wanted much love, and tried hard to win it.

Not a boy in the house but felt the pretty child's influence, and was improved by it without exactly knowing how or why, for babies can work miracles in the hearts that love them. Poor Billy found infinite satisfaction in staring at her, and though she did not like it she permitted without a frown, after she had been made to understand that he was not quite like the others, and on that account must be more kindly treated. Dick and Dolly overwhelmed her with willow whistles, the only thing they knew how to make, and she accepted but never used them. Rob served her like a little lover, and Teddy followed her like a pet dog. Jack she did not like, because he was afflicted with warts and had a harsh voice. Stuffy displeased her because he did not eat tidily, and George tried hard not to gobble, that he might not disgust the dainty little lady opposite. Ned was banished from court in utter disgrace when he was discovered tormenting some unhappy field-mice. Goldilocks could never forget the sad spectacle, and retired behind her veil when he approached, waving him away with an imperious little hand, and crying, in a tone of mingled grief and anger, 'No, I tarn't love him; he tut the poor mouses' little tails off, and they queeked!'

Daisy promptly abdicated when Bess came, and took the humble post of chief cook, while Nan was first maid of honour; Emil was chancellor of the exchequer, and spent the public monies lavishly in getting up spectacles that cost whole ninepences. Franz was prime minister, and directed her affairs of state, planned royal progresses through the kingdom, and kept foreign powers in order. Demi was her philosopher, and fared much better than such gentlemen usually do among crowned heads. Dan was her standing army, and defended her territories gallantly; Tommy was court fool, and Nat a tuneful Rizzio to this innocent little Mary.

Uncle Fritz and Aunt Jo enjoyed this peaceful episode, and looked on at the pretty play in which the young folk unconsciously imitated their elders, without adding the tragedy that is so apt to spoil the dramas acted on the larger stage.

'They teach us quite as much as we teach them,' said Mr Bhaer.

'Bless the dears! they never guess how many hints they give us as to the best way of managing them,' answered Mrs Jo.

'I think you were right about the good effect of having girls among the boys. Nan *has* stirred up Daisy, and Bess is teaching the little bears how to behave better than we can. If this reformation goes on as it has begun, I shall soon feel like Dr Blimber with his model young gentlemen,' said Professor, laughing, as he saw Tommy not only remove his own hat, but knock off Ned's also, as they entered the hall where the Princess was taking a ride on the rocking horse, attended by Rob and Teddy astride of chairs, and playing gallant knights to the best of their ability.

'You will never be a Blimber, Fritz, you couldn't do it if you tried; and our boys will never submit to the forcing process of that famous hotbed. No fear that they will be too elegant: American boys like liberty too well. But good manners they cannot fail to have, if we give them the kindly spirit that shines through the simplest demeanour, making it courteous and cordial, like yours, my dear old boy.'

'Tut! tut! we will not compliment; for if I begin you will run away, and I have a wish to enjoy this happy half-hour to the end;' yet Mr Bhaer looked pleased with the compliment, for it was true, and Mrs Jo felt that she had received the best her husband could give her, by saying that he found his truest rest and happiness in her society.

'To return to the children: I have just had another proof of Goldilocks' good influence,' said Mrs Jo, drawing her chair nearer the sofa, where the Professor lay resting after a long day's work in his various gardens. 'Nan hates sewing, but for love of Bess has been toiling half the afternoon over a remarkable bag in which to present a dozen of our love-apples to her idol when she goes. I praised her for it, and she said, in her quick way, "I like to sew for other people; it is stupid sewing for myself." I took the hint, and shall give her some little shirts and aprons for Mrs Carney's children. She is so generous, she will sew her fingers sore for them, and I shall not have to make a task of it.'

'But needlework is not a fashionable accomplishment, my dear.'

'Sorry for it. My girls shall learn all I can teach them about it, even if they give up the Latin, Algebra, and half a dozen ologies it is considered necessary for girls to muddle their poor brains over nowadays. Amy means to make Bess an accomplished woman, but the dear's mite of a forefinger has little pricks on it already, and her mother has several specimens of needlework which she values more than the clay bird without a bill, that filled Laurie with such pride when Bess made it.'

'I also have proof of the Princess's power,' said Mr Bhaer, after he had watched Mrs Jo sew on a button with an air of scorn for the whole system of fashionable education. 'Jack is so unwilling to be classed with Stuffy and Ned, as distasteful to Bess, that he came to me a little while ago, and asked me to touch his warts with caustic. I have often proposed it, and he never would consent; but now he bore the smart manfully, and consoles his present discomfort by hopes of future favour, when he can show her fastidious ladyship a smooth hand.'

Mrs Bhaer laughed at the story, and just then Stuffy came in to ask if he might give Goldilocks some of the bonbons his mother had sent him.

'She is not allowed to eat sweeties; but if you like to give her the pretty box with the pink sugar rose in it, she would like it very much,' said Mrs Jo, unwilling to spoil this unusual piece of self-denial, for the 'fat boy' seldom offered to share his sugarplums.

'Won't she eat it? I shouldn't like to make her sick,' said Stuffy, eyeing the delicate sweetmeat lovingly, yet putting it into the box.

'Oh, no, she won't touch it, if I tell her it is to look at, not to eat. She will keep it for weeks, and never think of tasting it. Can you do as much?'

'I should hope so! I'm ever so much older than she is,' cried Stuffy, indignantly.

'Well, suppose we try. Here, put your bonbons in this bag, and see how long you can keep them. Let me count two hearts, four red fishes, three barley-sugar horses, nine almonds, and a dozen chocolate drops. Do you agree to that?' asked sly Mrs Jo, popping the sweeties into her little spool-bag.

'Yes,' said Stuffy, with a sigh; and pocketing the forbidden fruit, he went away to give Bess the present, that won a smile from her, and permission to escort her round the garden.

'Poor Stuffy's heart has really got the better of his stomach at last, and his efforts will be much encouraged by the rewards Bess gives him,' said Mrs Jo.

'Happy is the man who can put temptation in his pocket and learn self-denial from so sweet a little teacher!' added Mr Bhaer, as the children passed the window, Stuffy's fat face full of placid satisfaction, and Goldilocks surveying her sugar rose with polite interest, though she would have preferred a real flower with a 'pitty smell'.

When her father came to take her home, a universal wail arose, and the parting gifts showered upon her increased her luggage to such an extent that Mr Laurie proposed having out the big wagon to take it into town. Everyone had given her something; and it was found difficult to pack white mice, cake, a parcel of shells, apples, a rabbit kicking violently in a bag, a large cabbage for his refreshment, a bottle of minnows, and a mammoth bouquet. The farewell scene was moving, for the Princess sat upon the hall table, surrounded by her subjects. She kissed her cousins, and held out her hand to the other boys, who shook it gently with various soft speeches, for they were taught not to be ashamed of showing their emotions.

'Come again soon, little dear,' whispered Dan, fastening his best green-and-gold beetle in her hat.

'Don't forget me, Princess, whatever you do,' said the engaging Tommy, taking a last stroke of the pretty hair.

'I am coming to your house next week, and then I shall see you, Bess,' added Nat, as if he found consolation in the thought.

'Do shake hands now,' cried Jack, offering a smooth paw.

'Here are two nice new ones to remember us by,' said Dick and Dolly, presenting fresh whistles, quite unconscious that seven old ones had been privately deposited in the kitchen stove.

'My little precious! I shall work you a bookmark right away, and you must keep it always,' said Nan, with a warm embrace.

But of all the farewells, poor Billy's was the most pathetic, for the thought that she was really going became so unbearable that he cast himself down before her, hugging her little blue boots and blubbering despairingly, 'Don't go away! oh, don't!' Goldilocks was so touched by this burst of feeling, that she leaned over and lifting the poor lad's head, said, in her soft, little voice, 'Don't cry, poor Billy! I will tiss you and tum adain soon.'

This promise consoled Billy, and he fell back beaming with pride at the unusual honour conferred upon him.

'Me too! me too!' clamoured Dick and Dolly, feeling that their devotion deserved some return. The others looked as if they would like to join in the cry; and something in the kind, merry faces about her moved the Princess to stretch out her arms and say, with reckless condescension, 'I will tiss evvybody!'

Like a swarm of bees about a very sweet flower, the affectionate lads surrounded their pretty playmate, and kissed her till she looked like a little rose, not roughly, but so enthusiastically that nothing but the crown of her hat was visible for a moment. Then her father rescued her, and she drove away still smiling and waving her hands, while the boys sat on the fence screaming like a flock of guinea fowls, 'Come back! come back!' till she was out of sight.

They all missed her, and each dimly felt that he was better for having known a creature so lovely, delicate, and sweet; for little Bess appealed to the chivalrous instinct in them as something to love, admire, and protect with a tender sort of reverence. Many a man remembers some pretty child who has made a place in his heart and kept her memory alive by the simple magic of her innocence; these little men were just learning to feel this power, and to love it for its gentle influence, not ashamed to let the small hand lead them, nor to own their loyalty to womankind, even in the bud.

CHAPTER 14

Damon and Pythias

Mrs Bhaer was right; peace was only a temporary lull, a storm was brewing, and two days after Bess left, a moral earthquake shook Plumfield to its centre.

Tommy's hens were at the bottom of the trouble, for if they had not persisted in laying so many eggs, he could not have sold them and made such sums. Money is the root of all evil, and yet it is such a useful root that we cannot get on without it any more than we can without potatoes. Tommy certainly could not, for he spent his income so recklessly, that Mr Bhaer was obliged to insist on a savings bank, and presented him with a private one – an imposing tin edifice, with the name over the door, and a tall chimney, down which the pennies were to go, there to rattle temptingly till leave was given to open a sort of trapdoor in the floor.

The house increased in weight so rapidly, that Tommy soon became satisfied with his investment, and planned to buy unheard-of treasures with his capital. He kept account of the sums deposited, and was promised that he might break the bank as soon as he had five dollars, on condition that he spent the money wisely. Only one dollar was needed, and the day Mrs Jo paid him for four dozen eggs, he was so delighted, that he raced off to the barn to display the bright quarters to Nat, who was also laying by money for the long-desired violin.

'I wish I had 'em to put with my three dollars, then I'd soon get enough to buy my fiddle,' he said, looking wistfully at the money.

'P'raps I'll lend you some. I haven't decided yet what I'll do with mine,' said Tommy, tossing up his quarters and catching them as they fell.

'Hi! boys! come down to the brook and see what a jolly great snake Dan's got!' called a voice from behind the barn.

'Come on,' said Tommy; and, laying his money inside the old winnowing machine, away he ran, followed by Nat.

The snake was very interesting, and then a long chase after a lame crow, and its capture, so absorbed Tommy's mind and time, that he never thought of his money till he was safely in bed that night.

'Never mind, no one but Nat knows where it is,' said the easy-going lad, and fell asleep untroubled by any anxiety about his property.

Next morning, just as the boys assembled for school, Tommy rushed into the room breathlessly, demanding, 'I say, who has got my dollar?'

'What are you talking about?' asked Franz.

Tommy explained, and Nat corroborated his statement.

Everyone else declared they knew nothing about it, and began to look suspiciously at Nat, who got more and more alarmed and confused with each denial.

'Somebody must have taken it,' said Franz, as Tommy shook his fist at the whole party, and wrathfully declared that, 'By thunder-turtles! if I get hold of the thief, I'll give him what he won't forget in a hurry.'

'Keep cool, Tom; we shall find him out; thieves always come to grief,' said Dan, as one who knew something of the matter.

'Maybe some tramp slept in the barn and took it,' suggested Ned.

'No, Silas don't allow that; besides, a tramp wouldn't go looking in that old machine for money,' said Emil, with scorn.

'Wasn't it Silas himself?' said Jack.

'Well, I like that! Old Si is as honest as daylight. You wouldn't catch him touching a penny of ours,' said Tommy, handsomely defending his chief admirer from suspicion.

'Whoever it was had better tell, and not wait to be found out,' said Demi, looking as if an awful misfortune had befallen the family.

'I know you think it's me,' broke out Nat, red and excited.

'You are the only one who knew where it was,' said Franz.

'I can't help it – I didn't take it. I tell you I didn't – I didn't!' cried Nat, in a desperate sort of way.

'Gently, gently, my son! What is all this noise about?' and Mr Bhaer walked in among them.

Tommy repeated the story of his loss, and, as he listened, Mr Bhaer's face grew graver and graver; for, with all their faults and follies, the lads till now had been honest.

'Take your seats,' he said; and, when all were in their places, he added slowly, as his eye went from face to face with a grieved look, that was harder to bear than a storm of words, 'Now, boys, I shall ask each one of you a single question, and I want an honest answer. I am not going to try to frighten, bribe, or surprise the truth out of you, for every one of you has got a conscience, and knows what it is for. Now is the time to undo the wrong done to Tommy, and set yourselves right before us all. I can forgive the yielding to sudden temptation much easier than I can deceit. Don't add a lie to the theft, but confess frankly, and we will all try to help you make us forget and forgive.'

He paused a moment, and one might have heard a pin drop, the room was so still; then slowly and impressively he put the question to each one, receiving the same answer in varying tones from all. Every face was flushed and excited, so that Mr Bhaer could not take colour as a witness, and some of the little boys were so frightened that they stammered over the two short words as if guilty, though it was evident that they could not be. When he came to Nat, his voice softened, for the poor lad looked so wretched, Mr Bhaer felt for him. He believed him to be the culprit, and hoped to save the boy from another lie, by winning him to tell the truth without fear.

'Now, my son, give me an honest answer. Did you take the money?'

'No, sir!' and Nat looked up at him imploringly.

As the words fell from his trembling lips, somebody hissed.

'Stop that!' cried Mr Bhaer, with a sharp rap on his desk, as he looked sternly toward the corner whence the sound came.

Ned, Jack, and Emil sat there, and the first two looked ashamed of themselves, but Emil called out, 'It wasn't me, uncle! I'd be ashamed to hit a fellow when he is down.'

'Good for you!' cried Tommy, who was in a sad state of affliction at the trouble his unlucky dollar had made.

'Silence!' commanded Mr Bhaer; and when it came, he said soberly, 'I am *very* sorry, Nat, but evidences are against you, and your old fault makes us more ready to doubt you than we should be if we could trust you as we do some of the boys, who never fib. But mind, my child, I do not charge you with this theft; I shall not punish you for it till I am *perfectly* sure, nor ask anything more about it. I shall leave it for you to settle with your own conscience. If you are guilty, come to me at any hour of the day or night and confess it, and I will forgive and help you to amend. If you are innocent, the truth will appear sooner or later, and the instant it does, I will be the first to beg your pardon for doubting you, and will so gladly do my best to clear your character before us all.'

'I didn't! I didn't!' sobbed Nat, with his head down upon his arms, for he could not bear the look of distrust and dislike which he read in the many eyes fixed on him.

'I hope not.' Mr Bhaer paused a minute, as if to give the culprit, whoever he might be, one more chance. Nobody spoke, however, and only sniffs of sympathy from some of the little fellows broke the silence. Mr Bhaer shook his head, and added, regretfully, 'There is nothing more to be done, then, and I have but one thing to say: I shall not speak of this again, and I wish you all to follow my example. I cannot expect you to feel as kindly toward anyone whom you suspect as before this happened, but I do expect and desire that you will not torment the suspected person in any way, he will have a hard enough time without that. Now go to your lessons.'

'Father Bhaer let Nat off too easy,' muttered Ned to Emil, as they got out their books.

'Hold your tongue,' growled Emil, who felt that this event was a blot upon the family honour.

Many of the boys agreed with Ned, but Mr Bhaer was right, nevertheless; and Nat would have been wiser to confess on the spot and have the trouble over, for even the hardest whipping he ever received from his father was far easier to bear than the cold looks, the avoidance, and general suspicion that met him on all sides. If ever a boy was sent to Coventry and kept there, it was poor Nat; and he suffered a week of slow torture, though not a hand was raised against him, and hardly a word said.

That was the worst of it; if they would only have talked it out, or even have thrashed him all round, he could have stood it better than the silent distrust that made very face so terrible to meet. Even Mrs Bhaer's showed traces of it, though her manner was nearly as kind as ever; but the sorrowful anxious look in Father Bhaer's eyes cut Nat to the heart, for he loved his teacher dearly, and knew that he had disappointed all his hopes by this double sin.

Only one person in the house entirely believed in him, and stood up for him stoutly against all the rest. This was Daisy. She could not explain why she trusted him against all appearances, she only felt that she could not doubt him, and her warm sympathy made her strong to take his part. She would not hear a word against him from anyone, and actually slapped her beloved Demi when he tried to convince her that it must have been Nat, because no one else knew where the money was.

'Maybe the hens ate it; they are greedy old things,' she said; and when Demi laughed, she lost her temper, slapped the amazed boy, and then burst out crying and ran away, still declaring, 'He didn't! he didn't! he didn't!'

Neither aunt nor uncle tried to shake the child's faith in her friend, but only hoped her innocent instinct might prove sure, and loved her all the better for it. Nat often said, after it was over, that he couldn't have stood it, if it had not been for Daisy. When the others shunned him, she clung to him closer than ever, and turned her back on the rest. She did not sit on the stairs now when he solaced himself with the old fiddle, but went in and sat beside him, listening with a face so full of confidence and affection, that Nat forgot disgrace for a time, and was happy. She asked him to help her with her lessons, she cooked him marvellous messes in her kitchen, which he ate manfully, no matter what they were, for gratitude gave a sweet flavour to the most distasteful. She proposed impossible games of cricket and ball, when she found that he shrank from joining the other boys. She put little nosegays from her garden on his desk, and tried in every way to show that she was not a fair-weather friend, but faithful through evil as well as good repute. Nan soon followed her example, in kindness at least; curbed her sharp tongue, and kept her scornful little nose from any demonstration of doubt or dislike, which was good of Madame Giddygaddy, for she firmly believed that Nat took the money.

Most of the boys let him severely alone, but Dan, though he said he despised him for being a coward, watched over him with a grim sort of protection, and promptly cuffed any lad who dared to molest his mate or make him afraid. His idea of friendship was as high as Daisy's, and, in his own rough way, he lived up to it as loyally.

Sitting by the brook one afternoon, absorbed in the study of the domestic habits of water-spiders, he overheard a bit of conversation on the other side of the wall. Ned, who was intensely inquisitive, had been on tenterhooks to know *certainly* who was the culprit; for of late one or two of the boys had begun to think that they were wrong, Nat was so steadfast in his denials, and so meek in his endurance of their neglect. This doubt had teased Ned past bearing, and he had several times privately beset Nat with questions, regardless of Mr Bhaer's express command. Finding Nat reading alone on the shady side of the wall, Ned could not resist stopping for a nibble at the forbidden subject. He had worried Nat for some ten minutes before Dan arrived, and the first words the spider-student heard were these, in Nat's patient, pleading voice, 'Don't, Ned! oh, don't! I can't tell you because I don't know, and it's mean of you to keep nagging at me on the sly, when Father

Bhaer told you not to plague me. You wouldn't dare to if Dan was round.'

'I ain't afraid of Dan; he's nothing but an old bully. Don't believe but what he took Tom's money, and you know it, and won't tell. Come, now!'

'He didn't, but, if he did, I *would* stand up for him, he has always been so good to me,' said Nat, so earnestly that Dan forgot his spiders, and rose quickly to thank him, but Ned's next words arrested him.

'I *know* Dan did it, and gave the money to you. Shouldn't wonder if he got his living picking pockets before he came here, for nobody knows anything about him but you,' said Ned, not believing his own words, but hoping to get the truth out of Nat by making him angry.

He succeeded in a part of his ungenerous wish, for Nat cried out, fiercely, 'If you say that again I'll go and tell Mr Bhaer all about it. I don't want to tell tales, but, by George! I will, if you don't let Dan alone.'

'Then you'll be a sneak, as well as a liar and a thief,' began Ned, with a jeer, for Nat had borne insult to himself so meekly, the other did not believe he would dare to face the master just to stand up for Dan.

What he might have added I cannot tell, for the words were hardly out of his mouth when a long arm from behind took him by the collar, and, jerking him over the wall in a most promiscuous way, landed him with a splash in the middle of the brook.

'Say that again and I'll duck you till you can't see!' cried Dan, looking like a modern Colossus of Rhodes as he stood, with a foot on either side of the narrow stream, glaring down at the discomfited youth in the water.

'I was only in fun,' said Ned.

'You are a sneak yourself to badger Nat round the corner. Let me catch you at it again, and I'll souse you in the river next time. Get up, and clear out!' thundered Dan, in a rage.

Ned fled, dripping, and his impromptu sitz-bath evidently did him good, for he was very respectful to both the boys after that, and seemed to have left his curiosity in the brook. As he vanished Dan jumped over the wall, and found Nat lying as if quite worn out and bowed down with his troubles.

'He won't pester you again, I guess. If he does, just tell me, and I'll see to him,' said Dan, trying to cool down.

'I don't mind what he says about me so much, I've got used to it,' answered Nat sadly; 'but I hate to have him pitch into you.'

'How do you know he isn't right?' asked Dan, turning his face away.

'What, about the money?' cried Nat, looking up with a startled air.

'Yes.'

'But I don't believe it! *You* don't care for money; all you want is your old bugs and things,' and Nat laughed, incredulously.

'I want a butterfly net as much as you want a fiddle; why shouldn't I steal the money for it as much as you?' said Dan, still turning away, and busily punching holes in the turf with his stick.

'I don't think you would. You like to fight and knock folks round sometimes, but you don't lie, and I don't believe you'd steal,' and Nat shook his head decidedly.

'I've done both. I used to fib like fury; it's too much trouble now; and I stole things to eat out of gardens when I ran away from Page, so you see I *am* a bad lot,' said Dan, speaking in the rough, reckless way which he had been learning to drop lately.

'Oh, Dan! don't say it's you! I'd rather have it any of the other boys,' cried Nat, in such a distressed tone that Dan looked pleased, and showed that he did, by turning round with a queer expression in his face, though he only answered, 'I won't say anything about it. But don't you fret, and we'll pull through somehow, see if we don't.'

Something in his face and manner gave Nat a new idea; and he said, pressing his hands together, in the eagerness of his appeal, 'I think you know who did it. If you do, beg him to tell, Dan. It's so hard to have 'em all hate me for nothing. I don't think I can bear it much longer. If I had any place to go to, I'd run away, though I love Plumfield dearly; but I'm not brave and big like you, so I must stay and wait till someone shows them that I haven't lied.'

As he spoke, Nat looked so broken and despairing, that Dan could not bear it, and, muttered huskily, 'You won't wait long,' and he walked rapidly away, and was seen no more for hours.

'What is the matter with Dan?' asked the boys of one another several times during the Sunday that followed a week which seemed as if it would never end. Dan was often moody, but that day he was so sober and silent that no one could get anything out of him. When they walked he strayed away from the rest, and came home late. He took no part in the evening conversation, but sat in the shadow, so busy with his own thoughts that he scarcely seemed to hear what was going on. When Mrs Jo showed him an unusually good report in the Conscience Book, he looked at it without a smile, and said, wistfully, 'You think I am getting on, don't you?'

'Excellently, Dan! and I am so pleased, because I always thought you only needed a little help to make you a boy to be proud of.'

He looked up at her with a strange expression in his black eyes – an expression of mingled pride and love and sorrow which she could not understand then but remembered afterward.

'I'm afraid you'll be disappointed, but I do try,' he said, shutting the book with no sign of pleasure in the page that he usually liked so much to read over and talk about.

'Are you sick, dear?' asked Mrs Jo, with her hand on his shoulder.

'My foot aches a little; I guess I'll go to bed. Good-night, mother,' he added, and held the hand against his cheek a minute, then went away looking as if he had said goodbye to something dear.

'Poor Dan! he takes Nat's disgrace to heart sadly. He is a strange boy; I wonder if I ever shall understand him thoroughly?' said Mrs Jo to herself, as she thought over Dan's late improvement with real satisfaction, yet felt that there was more in the lad than she had at first suspected.

One of things which cut Nat most deeply was an act of Tommy's, for after his loss Tommy had said to him, kindly, but firmly, 'I don't wish to hurt you, Nat, but you see I can't afford to lose my money, so I guess we won't be partners any longer;' and with that Tommy rubbed out the sign, 'T. Bangs & Co.'

Nat had been very proud of the 'Co.', and had hunted eggs industriously, kept his accounts all straight, and had added a good sum to his income from the sale of his share of stock-in-trade.

'Oh, Tom! must you?' he said, feeling that his good name was gone for ever in the business world if this was done.

'I must,' returned Tommy, firmly. 'Emil says that when one man 'bezzles (believe that's the word – it means to take money and cut away with it) the property of a firm, the other one sues him, or pitches into him somehow, and won't have anything more to do with him. Now you have 'bezzled my property; I shan't sue you, and I shan't pitch into you, but I *must* dissolve the partnership, because I can't trust you, and I don't wish to fail.'

'I can't make you believe me, and you won't take my money, though I'd be thankful to give all my dollars if you'd only say you don't think I took your money. Do let me hunt for you, I won't ask any wages, but do it for nothing. I know all the places, and I like it,' pleaded Nat.

But Tommy shook his head, and his jolly round face looked suspicious and hard as he said, shortly, 'Can't do it; wish you didn't know the places. Mind you don't go hunting on the sly, and speculate in my eggs.'

Poor Nat was so hurt that he could not get over it. He felt that he had lost not only his partner and patron, but that he was bankrupt in honour, and an outlaw from the business community. No one trusted his word, written or spoken, in spite of his efforts to redeem the past falsehood; the sign was down, the firm broken up, and he a ruined man. The barn, which was the boys' Wall Street, knew him no more. Cockletop and her sisters cackled for him in vain, and really seemed to take his misfortune to heart, for eggs were fewer, and some of the biddies retired in disgust to new nests, which Tommy could not find.

'They trust me,' said Nat, when he heard of it; and though the boys shouted at the idea, Nat found comfort in it, for when one is down in the world, the confidence of even a speckled hen is most consoling.

Tommy took no new partner, however, for distrust had entered in, and poisoned the peace of his once confiding soul. Ned offered to join him, but he declined, saying, with a sense of justice that did him honour, 'It might turn out that Nat didn't take my money, and then we could be partners again. I don't think it will happen, but I will give him a chance, and keep the place open a little longer.'

Billy was the only person whom Bangs felt he could trust in his shop, and Billy was trained to hunt eggs, and hand them over unbroken, being quite satisfied with an apple or a sugarplum for wages. The morning after Dan's gloomy Sunday, Billy said to his employer, as he displayed the results of a long hunt, 'Only two.'

'It gets worse and worse; I never saw such provoking old hens,' growled Tommy, thinking of the days when he often had six to rejoice over. 'Well, put 'em in my hat and give me a new bit of chalk; I must mark 'em up, anyway.'

Billy mounted a peck-measure, and looked into the top of the machine, where Tommy kept his writing materials.

'There's lots of money in here,' said Billy.

'No, there isn't. Catch me leaving my cash round again,' returned Tommy.

'I see 'em – one, four, eight, two dollars,' persisted Billy, who had not yet mastered the figures correctly.

'What a jack you are!' and Tommy hopped up to get the chalk for himself, but nearly tumbled down again, for there actually were four bright quarters in a row, with a bit of paper on them directed to 'Tom Bangs', that there might be no mistake.

'Thunder-turtles!' cried Tommy, and seizing them he dashed into the house, bawling wildly, 'It's all right! Got my money! Where's Nat?'

He was soon found, and his surprise and pleasure were so genuine that few doubted his word when he now denied all knowledge of the money.

'How could I put it back when I didn't take it? Do believe me now, and be good to me again,' he said, so imploringly, that Emil slapped him on the back, and declared *he* would for one.

'So will I, and I'm jolly glad it's not you. But who the dickens is it?' said Tommy, after shaking hands heartily with Nat.

'Never mind, as long as it's found,' said Dan with his eyes fixed on Nat's happy face.

'Well, I like that! I'm not going to have my things hooked, and then brought back like the juggling man's tricks,' cried Tommy, looking at his money as if he suspected witchcraft.

'We'll find him out somehow, though he was sly enough to print this to conceal his writing,' said Franz, examining the paper.

'Demi prints tiptop,' put in Rob, who had not a very clear idea what the fuss was all about.

'You can't make me believe it's him, not if you talk till you are blue,' said Tommy, and the others hooted at the mere idea; for the little deacon, as they called him, was above suspicion.

Nat felt the difference in the way they spoke of Demi and himself, and would have given all he had or ever hoped to have to be so trusted; for he had learned how easy it is to lose the confidence of others, how very, very hard to win it back, and truth became to him a precious thing since he had suffered from neglecting it.

Mr Bhaer was very glad one step had been taken in the right direction, and waited hopefully for yet further revelations. They came sooner than he expected, and in a way that surprised and grieved him very much. As they sat at supper that night, a square parcel was handed to Mrs Bhaer from Mrs Bates, a neighbour. A note accompanied the parcel, and, while Mr Bhaer read it, Demi pulled off the wrapper, exclaiming, as he saw its contents, 'Why, it's the book Uncle Teddy gave Dan!'

'The devil!' broke from Dan, for he had not yet quite cured himself of swearing, though he tried very hard.

Mr Bhaer looked up quickly at the sound. Dan tried to meet his eyes, but could not; his own fell, and he sat biting his lips, getting redder and redder till he was the picture of shame.

'What is it?' asked Mrs Bhaer, anxiously.

'I should have preferred to talk about this in private, but Demi has spoilt that plan, so I may as well have it out now,' said Mr Bhaer, looking a little stern, as he always did when any meanness or deceit came up for judgement.

'The note is from Mrs Bates, and she says that her boy Jimmy told her he bought this book of Dan last Saturday. She saw that it was worth much more than a dollar, and thinking there was some mistake, has sent it to me. Did you sell it, Dan?'

'Yes, sir,' was the slow answer.

'Why?'

'Wanted money.'

'For what?'

'To pay somebody.'

'To whom did you owe it?'

'Tommy.'

'Never borrowed a cent of me in his life,' cried Tommy, looked scared, for he guessed what was coming now, and felt that on the whole he would have preferred witchcraft, for he admired Dan immensely.

'Perhaps he took it,' cried Ned, who owed Dan a grudge for the ducking, and, being a mortal boy, liked to pay it off.

'Oh, Dan!' cried Nat, clasping his hands, regardless of the bread and butter in them.

'It is a hard thing to do, but I must have this settled, for I cannot have you watching each other like detectives, and the whole school disturbed in this way. Did you put that dollar in the barn this morning?' asked Mr Bhaer.

Dan looked him straight in the face, and answered steadily, 'Yes, I did.'

A murmur went round the table, Tommy dropped his mug with a crash; Daisy cried out, 'I knew it wasn't Nat;' Nan began to cry, and Mrs Jo left the room, looking so disappointed, sorry, and ashamed that Dan could not bear it. He hid his face in his hands a moment, then threw up his head, squared his shoulders as if settling some load upon them, and said, with the dogged look, and half-resolute, half-reckless tone he had used when he first came, 'I did it; now you may do what you like to me, but I won't say another word about it.'

'Not even that you are sorry?' asked Mr Bhaer, troubled by the change in him.

'I ain't sorry.'

'I'll forgive him without asking,' said Tommy, feeling that it was harder somehow to see brave Dan disgraced than timid Nat.

'Don't want to be forgiven,' returned Dan, gruffly.

'Perhaps you will when you have thought about it quietly by yourself, I won't tell you now how surprised and disappointed I am, but by and by I will come up and talk to you in your room.'

'Won't make any difference,' said Dan, trying to speak defiantly, but failing as he looked at Mr Bhaer's sorrowful face; and, taking his words for a dismissal, Dan left the room as if he found it impossible to stay.

It would have done him good if he had stayed; for the boys talked the matter over with such sincere regret, and pity, and wonder, it might have touched and won him to ask pardon. No one was glad to find that it was he, not even Nat; for, spite of all his faults, and they were many, everyone liked Dan now, because under his rough exterior lay some of the manly virtues which we most admire and love. Mrs Jo had been the chief prop, as well as cultivator, of Dan; and she took it sadly to heart that her last and most interesting boy had turned out so ill. The theft was bad, but the lying about it, and allowing another to suffer so much from an unjust suspicion was worse; and most discouraging of all was the attempt to restore the money in an underhand way, for it showed not only a want of courage, but a power of deceit that boded ill for the future. Still more trying was his steady refusal to talk of the matter, to ask pardon, or express any remorse. Days passed; and he went about his lessons and his work, silent, grim, and unrepentant. As if taking warning by their treatment of Nat, he asked no sympathy of anyone, rejected the advances of the boys, and spent his leisure hours roaming about the fields and woods, trying to find playmates in the birds and beasts, and succeeding better than most boys would have done, because he knew and loved them so well.

'If this goes on much longer, I'm afraid he will run away again, for he is too young to stand a life like this,' said Mr Bhaer, quite dejected at the failure of all his efforts.

'A little while ago I should have been quite sure that nothing would tempt him away, but now I am ready of anything, he is so changed,' answered poor Mrs Jo, who mourned over her boy and could not be comforted, because he shunned her more than anyone else, and only looked at her with the half-fierce, half-imploring eyes of a wild animal caught in a trap, when she tried to talk to him alone.

Nat followed him about like a shadow, and Dan did not repulse him as rudely as he did others, but said, in his blunt way, '*You* are all right; don't worry about me. I can stand it better than you did.'

'But I don't like to have you all alone,' Nat would say, sorrowfully.

'I like it;' and Dan would tramp away, stifling a sigh sometimes, for he *was* lonely.

Passing through the birch grove one day, he came up on several of the boys, who were amusing themselves by climbing up the trees and swinging down again, as the slender elastic stems bent till their tops touched the ground. Dan paused a minute to watch the fun, without offering to join in it, and as he stood there Jack took his turn. He had unfortunately chosen too large a tree; for when he swung off, it only bent a little way, and left him hanging at a dangerous height.

'Go back; you can't do it!' called Ned from below.

Jack tried, but the twigs slipped from his hands, and he could not get his legs round the trunk. He kicked, and squirmed, and clutched in vain, then gave it up, and hung breathless, saying helplessly, 'Catch me! help me! I must drop!'

'You'll be killed if you do,' cried Ned, frightened out of his wits.

'Hold on!' shouted Dan; and up the tree he went, crashing his way along till he nearly reached Jack, whose face looked up at him, full of fear and hope.

'You'll both come down,' said Ned, dancing with excitement on the slope underneath, while Nat held out his arms, in the wild hope of breaking the fall.

'That's what I want; stand from under,' answered Dan, coolly; and, as he spoke, his added weight bent the tree many feet nearer the earth.

Jack dropped safely; but the birch, lightened of half its load, flew up again so suddenly, that Dan, in the act of swinging round to drop feet foremost, lost his hold and fell heavily.

'I'm not hurt, all right in a minute,' he said, sitting up, a little pale and dizzy, as the boys gathered round him, full of admiration and alarm.

'You're a trump, Dan, and I'm ever so much obliged to you,' cried Jack, gratefully.

'It wasn't anything,' muttered Dan, rising slowly.

'I say it was, and I'll shake hands with you, though you are – ' Ned checked the unlucky word on his tongue, and held out his hand, feeling that it was a handsome thing on his part.

'But I won't shake hands with a sneak;' and Dan turned his back with a look of scorn, that caused Ned to remember the brook, and retire with undignified haste.

'Come home, old chap; I'll give you a lift;' and Nat walked away with him leaving the others to talk over the feat together, to wonder when Dan would 'come round', and to wish one and all that Tommy's 'confounded money had been in Jericho before it made such a fuss'.

When Mr Bhaer came into school next morning, he looked so happy, that the boys wondered what had happened to him, and really thought he had lost his mind when they saw him go straight to Dan, and, taking him by both hands, say all in one breath, as he shook them heartily, 'I know all about it, and I beg your pardon. It was like you to do it, and I love you for it, though it's never right to tell lies, even for a friend.'

'What is it?' cried Nat, for Dan said not a word, only lifted up his head, as if a weight of some sort had fallen off his back.

'Dan did not take Tommy's money;' and Mr Bhaer quite shouted it, he was so glad.

'Who did?' cried the boys in a chorus.

Mr Bhaer pointed to one empty seat, and every eye followed his finger, yet no one spoke for a minute, they were so surprised.

'Jack went home early this morning, but he left this behind him;' and in the silence Mr Bhaer read the note which he had found tied to his door handle when he rose.

'I took Tommy's dollar. I was peeking in through a crack and saw him put it there. I was afraid to tell before, though I wanted to. I didn't care so much about Nat, but Dan is a trump, and I can't stand it any longer. I never spent the money; it's under the carpet in my room, right behind the washstand. I'm awful sorry. I am going home, and don't think I shall ever come back, so Dan may have my things.   JACK.'

It was not an elegant confession, being badly written, much blotted, and very short; but it was a precious paper to Dan; and, when Mr Bhaer paused, the boy went to him, saying, in a rather broken voice, but with clear eyes, and the frank, respectful manner they had tried to teach him, 'I'll say I'm sorry now, and ask you to forgive me, sir.'

'It was a kind lie, Dan, and I can't help forgiving it; but you see it did no good,' said Mr Bhaer, with a hand on either shoulder, and a face full of relief and affection.

'It kept the boys from plaguing Nat. That's what I did it for. It made him right down miserable. I didn't care so much,' explained Dan, as if glad to speak out after his hard silence.

'How could you do it? You are always so kind to me,' faltered Nat, feeling a strong desire to hug his friend and cry. Two girlish performances, which would have scandalised Dan to the last degree.

'It's all right now, old fellow, so don't be a fool,' he said, swallowing the lump in his throat, and laughing out as he had not done for weeks. 'Does Mrs Bhaer know?' he asked, eagerly.

'Yes; and she is so happy I don't know what she will do to you,' began Mr Bhaer, but got no farther, for here the boys came crowding about Dan in a tumult of pleasure and curiosity; but before he had answered more than a dozen questions, a voice cried out, 'Three cheers for Dan!' and there was Mrs Jo in the doorway waving her dish-towel, and looking as if she wanted to dance a jig for joy, as she used to do when a girl.

'Now then,' cried Mr Bhaer, and led off a rousing hurrah, which startled Asia in the kitchen, and made old Mr Roberts shake his head as he drove by, saying, 'Schools are not what they were when I was young!'

Dan stood it pretty well for a minute, but the sight of Mrs Jo's delight upset him, and he suddenly bolted across the hall into the parlour, whither she instantly followed, and neither were seen for half an hour.

Mr Bhaer found it very difficult to calm his excited flock; and, seeing that lessons were an impossibility for a time, he caught their attention by telling them the fine old story of the friends whose fidelity to one another has made their names immortal. The lads listened and remembered, for just then their hearts were touched by the loyalty of a humbler pair of friends. The lie was wrong, but the love that prompted it and the courage that bore in silence the disgrace which belonged to another, made Dan a hero in their eyes. Honesty and honour had a new meaning now; a good name was more precious than gold; for once lost money could not buy it back; and faith in one another made life smooth and happy as nothing else could do.

Tommy proudly restored the name of the firm; Nat was devoted to Dan; and all the boys tried to atone to both for former suspicion and neglect. Mrs Jo rejoiced over her flock, and Mr Bhaer was never tired of telling the story of his young Damon and Pythias.

CHAPTER 15

In the Willow

The old tree saw and heard a good many little scenes and confidences that summer, because it became the favourite retreat of all the children, and the willow seemed to enjoy it, for a pleasant welcome always met them, and the quiet hours spent in its arms did them all good. It had a great deal of company one Saturday afternoon, and some little bird reported what went on there.

First came Nan and Daisy with their small tubs and bits of soap, for now and then they were seized with a tidy fit, and washed up all their dolls' clothes in the brook. Asia would not have them 'slopping round' in her kitchen, and the bathroom was forbidden since Nan forgot to turn off the water till it overflowed and came gently dripping down through the ceiling. Daisy went systematically to work, washing first the white and then the coloured things, rinsing them nicely, and hanging them to dry on a cord fastened from one barberry bush to another, and pinning them up with a set of tiny clothes-pins Ned had turned for her. But Nan put all her little things to soak in the same tub, and then forgot them while she collected thistledown to stuff a pillow for Semiramis, Queen of Babylon, as one doll was named. This took some time, and when Mrs Giddygaddy came to take out her clothes, deep green stains appeared on everything, for she had forgotten the green silk lining of a certain cape, and its colour had soaked nicely into the pink and blue gowns, the little chemises, and even the best ruffled petticoat.

'Oh me! what a mess!' sighed Nan.

'Lay them on the grass to bleach,' said Daisy, with an air of experience.

'So I will, and we can sit up in the nest and watch that they don't blow away.'

The Queen of Babylon's wardrobe was spread forth upon the bank, and, turning up their tubs to dry, the little washerwomen

climbed into the nest, and fell to talking, as ladies are apt to do in
the pauses of domestic labour.

'I'm going to have a featherbed to go with my new pillow,' said
Mrs Giddygaddy, as she transferred the thistledown from her
pocket to her handkerchief, losing about half in the process.

'I wouldn't; Aunt Jo says featherbeds aren't healthy. I never
let *my* children sleep on anything but a mattress,' returned Mrs
Shakespeare Smith, decidedly.

'I don't care; my children are so strong they often sleep on the
floor, and don't mind it' (which was quite true). 'I can't afford
nine mattresses, and I like to make beds myself.'

'Won't Tommy charge for the feathers?'

'Maybe he will, but I shan't pay him, and he won't care,' returned
Mrs G., taking a base advantage of the well-known good nature of
T. Bangs.

'I think the pink will fade out of that dress sooner than the green
mark will,' observed Mrs S., looking down from her perch, and
changing the subject, for she and her gossip differed on many
points, and Mrs Smith was a discreet lady.

'Never mind; I'm tired of dolls, and I guess I shall put them all
away and attend to my farm; I like it rather better than playing
house,' said Mrs G., unconsciously expressing the desire of many
older ladies, who cannot dispose of their families so easily however.

'But you mustn't leave them; they will die without their mother,'
cried the tender Mrs Smith.

'Let 'em die then; I'm tired of fussing over babies, and I'm going
to play with the boys; they need me to see to 'em,' returned the
strong-minded lady.

Daisy knew nothing about women's rights; she quietly took all
she wanted, and no one denied her claim, because she did not
undertake what she could not carry out, but unconsciously used
the all-powerful right of her own influence to win from others
any privilege for which she had proved her fitness. Nan
attempted all sorts of things, undaunted by direful failures, and
clamoured fiercely to be allowed to do everything that the boys
did. They laughed at her, hustled her out of the way, and protested against her meddling with their affairs. But she would not
be quenched and she would be heard, for her will was strong, and
she had the spirit of a rampant reformer. Mrs Bhaer sympathised

with her, but tried to curb her frantic desire for entire liberty, showing her that she must wait a little, learn self-control, and be ready to use her freedom before she asked for it. Nan had meek moments when she agreed to this, and the influences at work upon her were gradually taking effect. She no longer declared that she would be engine-driver or a blacksmith, but turned her mind to farming, and found in it a vent for the energy bottled up in her active little body. It did not quite satisfy her, however; for her sage and sweet marjoram were dumb things, and could not thank her for her care. She wanted something human to love, work for, and protect, and was never happier than when the little boys brought their cut fingers, bumped heads, or bruised joints for her to 'mend-up'. Seeing this, Mrs Jo proposed that she should learn how to do it nicely, and Nursey had an apt pupil in bandaging, plastering, and fomenting. The boys began to call her 'Dr Giddygaddy', and she liked it so well that Mrs Jo one day said to the Professor, 'Fritz, I see what we can do for that child. She wants something to live for even now, and will be one of the sharp, strong, discontented women if she does not have it. Don't let us snub her restless little nature, but do our best to give her the work she likes, and by and by persuade her father to let her study medicine. She will make a capital doctor, for she has courage, strong nerves, a tender heart, and an intense love and pity for the weak and suffering.'

Mr Bhaer smiled at first, but agreed to try, and gave Nan a herb garden, teaching her the various healing properties of the plants she tended, and letting her try their virtues on the children in the little illnesses they had from time to time. She learned fast, remembered well, and showed a sense and interest most encouraging to her Professor, who did not shut his door in her face because she was a little woman.

She was thinking of this, as she sat in the willow that day, and when Daisy said in her gentle way, 'I love to keep house, and mean to have a nice one for Demi when we grow up and live together.'

Nan replied with decision, 'Well, I haven't got any brother, and I don't want any house to fuss over. I shall have an office, with lots of bottles and drawers and pestle things in it, and I shall drive round in a horse and chaise and cure sick people. That will be such fun.'

'Ugh! how can you bear the bad-smelling stuff and the nasty little powders and castor oil and senna and hive syrup?' cried Daisy, with a shudder.

'I shan't have to take any, so I don't care. Besides, they make people well, and I like to cure folks. Didn't my sage-tea make Mother Bhaer's headache go away, and my hops stop Ned's tooth-ache in five hours? So now!'

'Shall you put leeches on people, and cut off legs and pull out teeth?' asked Daisy, quaking at the thought.

'Yes, I shall do everything; I don't care if the people are all smashed up, I shall mend them. My grandpa was a doctor, and I saw him sew a great cut in a man's cheek, and I held the sponge, and wasn't frightened a bit, and Grandpa said I was a brave girl.'

'How could you? I'm sorry for sick people, and I like to nurse them, but it makes my legs shake so I have to run away. I'm not a brave girl,' sighed Daisy.

'Well, you can be my nurse, and cuddle my patients when I have given them the physic and cut off their legs,' said Nan, whose practice was evidently to be of the heroic kind.

'Ship ahoy! Where are you, Nan?' called a voice from below.

'Here we are.'

'Ay, ay!' said the voice, and Emil appeared holding one hand in the other, with his face puckered up as if in pain.

'Oh, what's the matter?' cried Daisy, anxiously.

'A confounded splinter in my thumb. Can't get it out. Take a pick at it, will you, Nanny?'

'It's in very deep, and I haven't any needle,' said Nan, examining a tarry thumb with interest.

'Take a pin,' said Emil, in a hurry.

'No, it's too big and hasn't got a sharp point.'

Here Daisy, who had dived into her pocket, presented a neat little housewife with four needles in it.

'You are the Posy who always has what we want,' said Emil; and Nan resolved to have a needle-book in her own pocket hence-forth, for just such cases as this were always occurring in her practice.

Daisy covered her eyes, but Nan probed and picked with a steady hand, while Emil gave directions not down in any medical work or record.

'Starboard now! Steady, boys, steady! Try another tack. Heave ho! there she is!'

'Suck it,' ordered the Doctor, surveying the splinter with an experienced eye.

'Too dirty,' responded the patient, shaking his bleeding hand.

'Wait; I'll tie it up if you have got a handkerchief.'

'Haven't; take one of those rags down there.'

'Gracious! no, indeed; they are doll's clothes,' cried Daisy, indignantly.

'Take one of mine; I'd like to help you,' said Nan; and swinging himself down, Emil caught up the first 'rag' he saw. It happened to be the frilled skirt; but Nan tore it up without a murmur; and when the royal petticoat was turned into a neat little bandage, she dismissed her patient with the command

'Keep it wet, and let it alone; then it will heal right up, and not be sore.'

'What do you charge?' asked the Commodore, laughing.

'Nothing; I keep a 'spensary; that is a place where poor people are doctored free gratis for nothing,' explained Nan, with an air.

'Thank you, Doctor Giddygaddy. I'll always call you in when I come to grief;' and Emil departed, but looked back to say – for one good turn deserves another – 'Your duds are blowing away, Doctor.'

Forgiving the disrespectful word, 'duds', the ladies hastily descended, and, gathering up their wash, retired to the house to fire up the little stove, and go to ironing.

A passing breath of air shook the old willow, as if it laughed softly at the childish chatter which went on in the nest, and it had hardly composed itself when another pair of birds alighted for a confidential twitter.

'Now, I'll tell you the secret,' began Tommy, who was 'swellin' wisibly' with the importance of his news.

'Tell away,' answered Nat, wishing he had brought his fiddle, it was so shady and quiet here.

'Well, we fellows were talking over the late interesting case of circumstantial evidence,' said Tommy, quoting at random from a speech Franz had made at the club, 'and I proposed giving Dan something to make up for our suspecting him, to show our respect, and so on, you know something handsome and useful, that he could keep always and be proud of. What do you think we chose?'

'A butterfly net; he wants one ever so much,' said Nat, looking a little disappointed, for he meant to get it himself.

'No, sir; it's to be a microscope, a real swell one, that we see what-do-you-call-'ems in water with, and stars, and ant eggs, and all sorts of games, you know. Won't it be a jolly good present?' said Tommy, rather confusing microscopes and telescopes in his remarks.

'Tiptop! I'm so glad! Won't it cost a heap, though?' cried Nat, feeling that his friend was beginning to be appreciated.

'Of course it will; but we are all going to give something. I headed the paper with my five dollars; for if it is done at all, it must be done handsome.'

'What! all of it? I never did see such a generous chap as you are;' and Nat beamed upon him with sincere admiration.

'Well, you see, I've been so bothered with my property, that I'm tired of it, and don't mean to save up any more, but give it away as I go along, and then nobody will envy me, or want to steal it, and I shan't be suspecting folks and worrying about my old cash,' replied Tommy, on whom the cares and anxieties of a millionaire weighed heavily.

'Will Mr Bhaer let you do it?'

'He thought it was a first-rate plan, and said that some of the best men he knew preferred to do good with their money instead of laying it up to be squabbled over when they died.'

'Your father is rich; does he do that way?'

'I'm not sure; he gives me all I want; I know that much. I'm going to talk to him about it when I go home. Anyhow, I shall set him a good example;' and Tommy was so serious, that Nat did not dare to laugh, but said, respectfully, 'You will be able to do ever so much with your money, won't you?'

'So Mr Bhaer said, and he promised to advise me about useful ways of spending it. I'm going to begin with Dan; and next time I get a dollar or so, I shall do something for Dick, he's such a good little chap, and only has a cent a week for pocket money. He can't earn much, you know; so I'm going to kind of see to him;' and good-hearted Tommy quite longed to begin.

'I think that's a beautiful plan, and I'm not going to try to buy a fiddle any more; I'm going to get Dan his net all myself, and if there is any money left, I'll do something to please poor Billy. He's fond of me, and though he isn't poor, he'd like some little thing from me, because I can make out what he wants better than the rest of you.' And Nat fell to wondering how much happiness could be got out of his precious three dollars.

'So I would. Now come and ask Mr Bhaer if you can't go in town with me on Monday afternoon, so you can get the net, while I get the microscope. Franz and Emil are going too, and we'll have a jolly time larking round among the shops.'

The lads walked away arm-in-arm, discussing the new plans with droll importance, yet beginning already to feel the sweet satisfaction which comes to those who try, no matter how humbly, to be earthly providences to the poor and helpless, and gild their mite with the gold of charity before it is laid up where thieves cannot break through and steal.

'Come up and rest while we sort the leaves; it's so cool and pleasant here,' said Demi, as he and Dan came sauntering home from a long walk in the woods.

'All right!' answered Dan, who was a boy of few words, and up they went.

'What makes birch leaves shake so much more than the others?' asked enquiring Demi, who was always sure of an answer from Dan.

'They are hung differently. Don't you see the stem where it joins the leaf is sort of pinched one way, and where it joins the twig, it is pinched another. This makes it waggle with the least bit of wind, but the elm leaves hang straight, and keep stiller.'

'How curious! will this do so?' and Demi held up a sprig of acacia, which he had broken from a little tree on the lawn, because it was so pretty.

'No; that belongs to the sort that shuts up when you touch it. Draw your finger down the middle of the stem, and see if the leaves don't curl up,' said Dan, who was examining a bit of mica.

Demi tried it, and presently the little leaves did fold together, till the spray showed a single instead of a double line of leaves.

'I like that; tell me about the others. What do these do?' asked Demi, taking up a new branch.

'Feed silkworms; they live on mulberry leaves, till they begin to spin themselves up. I was in a silk factory once, and there were rooms full of shelves all covered with leaves, and worms eating them so fast that it made a rustle. Sometimes they eat so much they die. Tell that to Stuffy,' and Dan laughed, as he took up another bit of rock with a lichen on it.

'I know one thing about this mullein leaf: the fairies use them for blankets,' said Demi, who had not quite given up his faith in the existence of the little folk in green.

'If I had a microscope, I'd show you something prettier than fairies,' said Dan, wondering if he should ever own that coveted treasure. 'I knew an old woman who used mullein leaves for a nightcap because she had face-ache. She sewed them together, and wore it all the time.'

'How funny! was she your grandmother?'

'Never had any. She was a queer old woman, and lived alone in a little tumbledown house with nineteen cats. Folks called her a witch, but she wasn't, though she looked like an old ragbag. She was real kind to me when I lived in that place, and used to let me get warm at her fire when the folks at the poorhouse were hard on me.'

'Did you live in a poorhouse?'

'A little while. Never mind that – I didn't mean to speak of it;' and Dan stopped short in his unusual fit of communicativeness.

'Tell about the cats, please,' said Demi, feeling that he had asked an unpleasant question, and sorry for it.

'Nothing to tell; only she had a lot of 'em, and kept 'em in a barrel nights; and I used to go and tip over the barrel sometimes, and let 'em out all over the house, and then she'd scold, and chase 'em and put 'em in again, spitting and yowling like fury.'

'Was she good to them?' asked Demi, with a hearty child's laugh, pleasant to hear.

'Guess she was. Poor old soul! she took in all the lost and sick cats in the town; and when anybody wanted one they went to Marm Webber, and she let 'em pick any kind and colour they wanted, and only asked ninepence, she was glad to have her pussies get a good home.'

'I should like to see Marm Webber. Could I, if I went to that place?'

'She's dead. All my folks are,' said Dan, briefly.

'I'm sorry;' and Demi sat silent a minute, wondering what subject would be safe to try next. He felt delicate about speaking of the departed lady, but was very curious about the cats, and could not resist asking softly, 'Did she cure the sick ones?'

'Sometimes. One had a broken leg, and she tied it up to a stick, and it got well; and another had fits, and she doctored it with yarbs till it was cured. But some of 'em died, and she buried 'em; and when they couldn't get well, she killed 'em easy.'

'How?' asked Demi, feeling that there was a peculiar charm about this old woman, and some sort of joke about the cats, because Dan was smiling to himself.

'A kind lady, who was fond of cats, told her how, and gave her some stuff, and sent all her own pussies to be killed that way. Marm used to put a sponge wet with ether, in the bottom of an old boot, then poke puss in head downwards. The ether put her to sleep in a jiffy, and she was drowned in warm water before she woke up.'

'I hope the cats didn't feel it. I shall tell Daisy about that. You have known a great many interesting things, haven't you?' asked Demi, and fell to meditating on the vast experience of a boy who had run away more than once, and taken care of himself in a big city.

'Wish I hadn't sometimes.'

'Why? Don't remembering them feel good?'

'No.'

'It's very singular how hard it is to manage your mind,' said Demi, clasping his hands round his knees, and looking up at the sky as if for information upon his favourite topic.

'Devilish hard – no, I don't mean that;' and Dan bit his lips, for the forbidden word slipped out in spite of him, and he wanted to be more careful with Demi than with any of the other boys.

'I'll play I didn't hear it,' said Demi; 'and you won't do it again, I'm sure.'

'Not if I can help it. That's one of the things I don't want to remember. I keep pegging away, but it don't seem to do much good;' and Dan looked discouraged.

'Yes, it does. You don't say half so many bad words as you used to; and Aunt Jo is pleased, because she said it was a hard habit to break up.'

'Did she?' and Dan cheered up a bit.

'You must put swearing away in your fault-drawer, and lock it up; that's the way I do with my badness.'

'What do you mean?' asked Dan, looking as if he found Demi almost as amusing as a new sort of cockchafer or beetle.

'Well, it's one of my private plays, and I'll tell you, but I think you'll laugh at it,' began Demi, glad to hold forth on this congenial subject. 'I play that my mind is a round room, and my soul is a little sort of creature with wings that lives in it. The walls are full of shelves and drawers, and in them I keep my thoughts, and my goodness and badness, and all sorts of things. The goods I keep where I can see them, and the bads I lock up tight, but they get out, and I have to keep putting them in and squeezing them down, they are so strong. The thoughts I play with when I am alone or in bed, and I make up and do what I like with them. Every Sunday I put my room in order, and talk with the little spirit that lives there, and tell him what to do. He is very bad sometimes, and won't mind me, and I have to scold him, and take him to Grandpa. He always makes him behave, and be sorry for his faults, because Grandpa likes this play, and gives me nice things to put in the drawers, and tells me how to shut up the naughties. Hadn't you better try that way? It's a very good one;' and Demi looked so earnest and full of faith, that Dan did not laugh at his quaint fancy, but said, soberly, 'I don't think there is a lock strong enough to keep my badness shut up. Anyway my room is in such a clutter I don't know how to clear it up.'

'You keep your drawers in the cabinet all spandy nice; why can't you do the others?'

'I ain't used to it. Will you show me how?' and Dan looked as if inclined to try Demi's childish way of keeping a soul in order.

'I'd love to, but I don't know how, except to talk as Grandpa does. I can't do it good like him, but I'll try.'

'Don't tell anyone; only now and then we'll come here and talk things over, and I'll pay you for it by telling all I know about my sort of things. Will that do?' and Dan held out his big, rough hand.

Demi gave his smooth, little hand readily, and the league was made; for in the happy, peaceful world where the younger boy lived, lions and lambs played together, and little children innocently taught their elders.

'Hush!' said Dan, pointing toward the house, as Demi was about to indulge in another discourse on the best way of getting badness down, and keeping it down; and peeping from their perch, they saw Mrs Jo strolling slowly along, reading as she went, while Teddy trotted behind her, dragging a little cart upside down.

'Wait till they see us,' whispered Demi, and both sat still as the pair came nearer, Mrs Jo so absorbed in her book that she would have walked into the brook if Teddy had not stopped her by saying, 'Marmar, I wanter fis.'

Mrs Jo put down the charming book which she had been trying to read for a week, and looked about her for a fishing-pole, being used to making toys out of nothing. Before she had broken one from the hedge, a slender willow bough fell at her feet; and, looking up, she saw the boys laughing in the nest.

'Up! up!' cried Teddy, stretching his arms and flapping his skirts as if about to fly.

'I'll come down and you come up. I must go to Daisy now;' and Demi departed to rehearse the tale of the nineteen cats, with the exciting boot-and-barrel episodes.

Teddy was speedily whisked up; and then Dan said, laughing, 'Come, too; there's plenty of room. I'll lend you a hand.'

Mrs Jo glanced over her shoulder, but no one was in sight; and rather liking the joke of the thing, she laughed back, saying, 'Well, if you won't mention it, I think I will;' and with two nimble steps was in the willow.

'I haven't climbed a tree since I was married. I used to be very fond of it when I was a girl,' she said, looking well-pleased with her shady perch.

'Now, you read if you want to, and I'll take care of Teddy,' proposed Dan, beginning to make a fishing-rod for impatient Baby.

'I don't think I care about it now. What were you and Demi at up here?' asked Mrs Jo, thinking, from the sober look on Dan's face, that he had something on his mind.

'Oh! we were talking. I'd been telling him about leaves and things, and he was telling me some of his queer plays. Now, then, Major, fish away;' and Dan finished off his work by putting a big blue fly on the bent pin which hung at the end of the cord he had tied to the willow-rod.

Teddy leaned down from the tree, and was soon wrapped up in watching for the fish which he felt sure would come. Dan held him by his little petticoats, lest he should take a 'header' into the brook, and Mrs Jo soon won him to talk by doing so herself.

'I am so glad you told Demi about "leaves and things"; it is just what he needs; and I wish you would teach him, and take him to walk with you.'

'I'd like to, he is so bright; but . . . '

'But what?'

'I didn't think you'd trust me.'

'Why not?'

'Well, Demi is so kind of precious, and so good, and I'm such a bad lot, I thought you'd keep him away from me.'

'But you are not a "bad lot", as you say; and I do trust you, Dan, entirely, because you honestly try to improve, and do better and better every week.'

'Really?' and Dan looked up at her with the cloud of despondency lifting from his face.

'Yes; don't you feel it?'

'I hoped so, but I didn't know.'

'I have been waiting and watching quietly, for I thought I'd give you a good trial first; and if you stood it, I would give you the best reward I had. You have stood it well; and now I'm going to trust not only Demi, but my own boy, to you, because you can teach them some things better than any of us.'

'Can I?' and Dan looked amazed at the idea.

'Demi has lived among older people so much that he needs just what you have – knowledge of common things, strength, and courage. He thinks you are the bravest boy he ever saw, and admires your strong way of doing things. Then you know a great deal about natural objects, and can tell him more wonderful tales of birds, and bees, and leaves, and animals, than his story books give him; and, being true, these stories will teach and do him good. Don't you see now how much you can help him, and why I like to have him with you?'

'But I swear sometimes, and might tell him something wrong. I wouldn't mean to, but it might slip out, just as "devil" did a few minutes ago,' said Dan, anxious to do his duty, and let her know his shortcomings.

'I know you try not to say or do anything to harm the little fellow, and here is where I think Demi will help you, because he is so innocent and wise in his small way, and has what I am trying to give you, dear, good principles. It is never too early to try and plant them in a child, and never too late to cultivate them in the most neglected person. You are only boys yet; you can teach one another. Demi will unconsciously strengthen your moral sense, you will strengthen his common sense, and I shall feel as if I had helped you both.'

Words could not express how pleased and touched Dan was by this confidence and praise. No one had ever trusted him before, no one had cared to find out and foster the good in him, and no one had suspected how much there was hidden away in the breast of the neglected boy, going fast to ruin, yet quick to feel and value sympathy and help. No honour that he might earn hereafter would ever be half so precious as the right to teach his few virtues and small store of learning to the child whom he most respected; and no more powerful restraint could have been imposed upon him than the innocent companion confided to his care. He found courage now to tell Mrs Jo of the plan already made with Demi, and she was glad that the first step had been so naturally taken. Everything seemed to be working well for Dan, and she rejoiced over him, because it had seemed a hard task, yet, working on with a firm belief in the possibility of reformation in far older and worse subjects than he, there had come this quick and hopeful change to encourage her. He felt that he had friends now and a place in the world, something to live and work for, and, though he said little, all that was best and bravest in a character made old by a hard experience responded to the love and faith bestowed on him, and Dan's salvation was assured.

Their quiet talk was interrupted by a shout of delight from Teddy, who, to the surprise of everyone, did actually catch a trout where no trout had been seen for years. He was so enchanted with his splendid success that he insisted on showing his prize to the family before Asia cooked it for supper; so the three descended and went happily away together, all satisfied with the work of that half-hour.

Ned was the next visitor to the tree, but he only made a short stay, sitting there at his ease while Dick and Dolly caught a pailful of grasshoppers and crickets for him. He wanted to play a joke on Tommy, and intended to tuck up a few dozen of the

lively creatures in his bed, so that when Bangs got in he would
speedily tumble out again, and pass a portion of the night in
chasing 'hopper-grasses' round the room. The hunt was soon
over, and having paid the hunters with a few peppermints apiece
Ned retired to make Tommy's bed.

For an hour the old willow sighed and sung to itself, talked with
the brook, and watched the lengthening shadows as the sun went
down. The first rosy colour was touching its graceful branches
when a boy came stealing up the avenue, across the lawn, and,
spying Billy by the brook-side, went to him, saying, in a mysterious
tone, 'Go and tell Mr Bhaer I want to see him down here, please.
Don't let anyone hear.'

Billy nodded and ran off, while the boy swung himself up into
the tree, and sat there looking anxious, yet evidently feeling the
charm of the place and hour. In five minutes, Mr Bhaer appeared,
and, stepping up on the fence, leaned into the nest, saying, kindly,
'I am glad to see you, Jack; but why not come in and meet us all at
once?'

'I wanted to see you first, please, sir. Uncle made me come back.
I know I don't deserve anything, but I hope the fellows won't be
hard upon me.'

Poor Jack did not get on very well, but it was evident that he was
sorry and ashamed, and wanted to be received as easily as possible;
for his uncle had thrashed him well and scolded him soundly for
following the example he himself set. Jack had begged not to be
sent back, but the school was cheap, and Mr Ford insisted, so the
boy returned as quietly as possible, and took refuge behind Mr
Bhaer.

'I hope not, but I can't answer for them, though I will see that
they are not unjust. I think, as Dan and Nat have suffered so
much, being innocent, you should suffer something, being guilty.
Don't you?' asked Mr Bhaer, pitying Jack, yet feeling he deserved
punishment for a fault which had so little excuse.

'I suppose so, but I sent Tommy's money back, and I said I was
sorry, isn't that enough?' said Jack, rather sullenly; for the boy
who could do so mean a thing was not brave enough to bear the
consequences well.

'No; I think you should ask pardon of all three boys, openly and
honestly. You cannot expect them to respect and trust you for a

time, but you can live down this disgrace if you try, and I will help you. Stealing and lying are detestable sins, and I hope this will be a lesson to you. I am glad you are ashamed, it is a good sign; bear it patiently, and do your best to earn a better reputation.'

'I'll have an auction, and sell off all my goods dirt cheap,' said Jack, showing his repentance in the most characteristic way.

'I think it would be better to give them away, and begin on a new foundation. Take "Honesty is the best policy" for your motto, and live up to it in act, and word, and thought, and though you don't make a cent of money this summer, you will be a rich boy in the autumn,' said Mr Bhaer, earnestly.

It was hard, but Jack consented, for he really felt that cheating didn't pay, and wanted to win back the friendship of the boys. His heart clung to his possessions, and he groaned inwardly at the thought of actually giving away certain precious things. Asking pardon publicly was easy compared to this; but then he began to discover that certain other things, invisible, but most valuable, were better property than knives, fish-hooks, or even money itself. So he decided to buy up a little integrity, even at a high price, and secure the respect of his playmates, though it was not a saleable article.

'Well, I'll do it,' he said, with a sudden air of resolution, which pleased Mr Bhaer.

'Good! and I'll stand by you. Now come and begin at once.'

And Father Bhaer led the bankrupt boy back into the little world, which received him coldly at first, but slowly warmed to him, when he showed that he had profited by the lesson, and was sincerely anxious to go into a better business with a new stock-in-trade.

CHAPTER 16

Taming the Colt

'What in the world is that boy doing?' said Mrs Jo to herself, as she watched Dan running round the half-mile triangle as if for a wager. He was all alone, and seemed possessed by some strange desire to run himself into a fever, or break his neck; for, after several rounds, he tried leaping walls, and turning somersaults up the avenue, and finally dropped down on the grass before the door as if exhausted.

'Are you training for a race, Dan?' asked Mrs Jo, from the window where she sat.

He looked up quickly, and stopped panting to answer, with a laugh, 'No; I'm only working off my steam.'

'Can't you find a cooler way of doing it? You will be ill if you tear about so in such warm weather,' said Mrs Jo, laughing also, as she threw him out a great palm-leaf fan.

'Can't help it. I *must* run somewhere,' answered Dan, with such an odd expression in his restless eyes, that Mrs Jo was troubled, and asked, quickly, 'Is Plumfield getting too narrow for you?'

'I wouldn't mind if it was a little bigger. I like it though; only the fact is the devil gets into me sometimes, and then I do want to bolt.'

The words seemed to come against his will, for he looked sorry the minute they were spoken, and seemed to think he deserved a reproof for his ingratitude. But Mrs Jo understood the feeling, and though sorry to see it, she could not blame the boy for confessing it. She looked at him anxiously, seeing how tall and strong he had grown, how full of energy his face was, with its eager eyes and resolute mouth; and remembering the utter freedom he had known for years before, she felt how even the gentle restraint of this home would weigh upon him at times when the old lawless spirit stirred in him. 'Yes,' she said to herself, 'my wild hawk needs a larger cage; and yet, if I let him go, I am afraid he will be lost. I must try and find some lure strong enough to keep him safe.'

'I know all about it,' she added, aloud. 'It is not "the devil", as you call it, but the very natural desire of all young people for liberty. I used to feel just so, and once, I really did think for a minute that I would bolt.'

'Why didn't you?' said Dan, coming to lean on the low window ledge, with an evident desire to continue the subject.

'I knew it was foolish, and love for my mother kept me at home.'

'I haven't got any mother,' began Dan.

'I thought you had *now*,' said Mrs Jo, gently stroking the rough hair off his hot forehead.

'You are no end good to me, and I can't ever thank you enough, but it just isn't the same, is it?' and Dan looked up at her with a wistful, hungry look that went to her heart.

'No, dear, it is not the same, and never can be. I think an own mother would have been a great deal to you. But as that cannot be, you must try to let me fill her place. I fear I have not done all I ought, or you would not want to leave me,' she added, sorrowfully.

'Yes, you have!' cried Dan, eagerly. 'I don't want to go, and I won't go, if I can help it; but every now and then I feel as if I must burst out somehow. I want to run straight ahead somewhere, to smash something, or pitch into somebody. Don't know why, but I do, and that's all about it.'

Dan laughed as he spoke, but he meant what he said, for he knit his black brows, and brought down his fist on the ledge with such force, that Mrs Jo's thimble flew off into the grass. He brought it back, and as she took it she held the big, brown hand a minute, saying, with a look that showed the words cost her something, 'Well, Dan, run if you must, but don't run very far; and come back to me soon, for I want you very much.'

He was rather taken aback by this unexpected permission to play truant, and somehow it seemed to lessen his desire to go. He did not understand why, but Mrs Jo did, and, knowing the natural perversity of the human mind, counted on it to help her now. She felt instinctively that the more the boy was restrained the more he would fret against it; but leave him free, and the mere sense of liberty would content him, joined to the knowledge that his presence was dear to those whom he loved best. It was a little experiment, but it succeeded, for Dan stood silent a moment, unconsciously picking the fan to pieces and turning the matter over in his mind. He felt that she appealed to his heart and his honour, and owned that he understood it by saying presently, with a mixture of regret and resolution in his face, 'I won't go yet awhile, and I'll give you fair warning before I bolt. That's fair, isn't it?'

'Yes, we will let it stand so. Now, I want to see if I can't find some way for you to work off your steam better than running about the place like a mad dog, spoiling my fans, or fighting with the boys. What can we invent?' and while Dan tried to repair the mischief he had done, Mrs Jo racked her brain for some new device to keep her truant safe until he had learned to love his lessons better.

'How would you like to be my express-man?' she said, as a sudden thought popped into her head.

'Go into town, and do the errands?' asked Dan, looking interested at once.

'Yes; Franz is tired of it, Silas cannot be spared just now, and Mr Bhaer has no time. Old Andy is a safe horse, you are a good driver, and know your way about the city as well as a postman. Suppose you try it, and see if it won't do most as well to drive away two or three times a week as to run away once a month.'

'I'd like it ever so much, only I must go alone and do it all myself. I don't want any of the other fellows bothering round,' said Dan, taking to the new idea so kindly that he began to put on business airs already.

'If Mr Bhaer does not object you shall have it all your own way. I suppose Emil will growl, but he cannot be trusted with horses, and you can. By the way, tomorrow is market day, and I must make out my list. You had better see that the wagon is in order, and tell Silas to have the fruit and vegetables ready for mother. You will have to be up early and get back in time for school, can you do that?'

'I'm always an early bird, so I don't mind,' and Dan slung on his jacket with despatch.

'The early bird got the worm this time, I'm sure,' said Mrs Jo, merrily.

'And a jolly good worm it is,' answered Dan, as he went laughing away to put a new lash to the whip, wash the wagon, and order Silas about with all the importance of a young express-man.

'Before he is tired of this I will find something else and have it ready when the next restless fit comes on,' said Mrs Jo to herself, as she wrote her list with a deep sense of gratitude that all her boys were not Dans.

Mr Bhaer did not entirely approve of the new plan, but agreed to give it a trial, which put Dan on his mettle, and caused him to give up certain wild plans of his own, in which the new lash and the long hill were to have borne a part. He was up and away very early the next morning, heroically resisting the temptation to race with the milkmen going into town. Once there, he did his errands carefully, to Mr Bhaer's surprise and Mrs Jo's great satisfaction. The Commodore did growl at Dan's promotion, but was pacified by a superior padlock to his new boathouse, and the thought that seamen were meant for higher honours than driving market wagons and doing family errands. So Dan filled his new office well and contentedly for weeks, and said no more about bolting. But one day Mr Bhaer found him pummelling Jack, who was roaring for mercy under his knee.

'Why, Dan, I thought you had given up fighting,' he said, as he went to the rescue.

'We ain't fighting, we are only wrestling,' answered Dan, leaving off reluctantly.

'It looks very much like it, and feels like it, hey, Jack?' said Mr Bhaer, as the defeated gentleman got upon his legs with difficulty.

'Catch me wrestling with him again. He's 'most knocked my head off,' snarled Jack, holding on to that portion of his frame as if it really was loose upon his shoulders.

'The fact is, we began in fun, but when I got him down I couldn't help pounding him. Sorry I hurt you, old fellow,' explained Dan, looking rather ashamed of himself.

'I understand. The longing to pitch into somebody was so strong you couldn't resist. You are a sort of Berserker, Dan, and something to tussle with is as necessary to you as music is to Nat,' said Mr Bhaer, who knew all about the conversation between the boy and Mrs Jo.

'Can't help it. So if you don't want to be pounded you'd better keep out of the way,' answered Dan, with a warning look in his black eyes that made Jack sheer off in haste.

'If you want something to wrestle with, I will give you a tougher specimen than Jack,' said Mr Bhaer; and, leading the way to the woodyard, he pointed out certain roots of trees that had been grubbed up in the spring, and had been lying there waiting to be split.

'There, when you feel inclined to maltreat the boys, just come and work off your energies here, and I'll thank you for it.'

'So I will;' and, seizing the axe that lay near, Dan hauled out a tough root, and went at it so vigorously, that the chips flew far and wide, and Mr Bhaer fled for his life.

To his great amusement, Dan took him at his word, and was often seen wrestling with the ungainly knots, hat and jacket off, red face, and wrathful eyes; for he got into royal rages over some of his adversaries, and swore at them under his breath till he had conquered them, when he exulted, and marched off to the shed with an armful of gnarled oak-wood in triumph. He blistered his hands, tired his back, and dulled the axe, but it did him good, and he got more comfort out of the ugly roots than anyone dreamed, for with each blow he worked off some of the pent-up power that would otherwise have been expended in some less harmless way.

'When this is gone I really don't know what I shall do,' said Mrs Jo to herself, for no inspiration came, and she was at the end of her resources.

But Dan found a new occupation for himself, and enjoyed it some time before anyone discovered the cause of his contentment. A fine young horse of Mr Laurie's was kept at Plumfield that summer, running loose in a large pasture across the brook. The boys were all interested in the handsome, spirited creature, and for a time were fond of watching him gallop and frisk with his plumey tail flying, and his handsome head in the air. But they soon got tired of it, and left Prince Charlie to himself. All but Dan, he never tired of looking at the horse, and seldom failed to visit him each day with a lump of sugar, a bit of bread, or an apple to make him welcome. Charlie was grateful, accepted his friendship, and the two loved one another as if they felt some tie between them, inexplicable but strong. In whatever part of the wide field he might be, Charlie always came at full speed when Dan whistled at the bars, and the boy was never happier than when the beautiful, fleet creature put its head on his shoulder, looking up at him with fine eyes full of intelligent affection.

'We understand one another without any palaver, don't we, old fellow?' Dan would say, proud of the horse's confidence, and so jealous of his regard, that he told no one how well the friendship prospered, and never asked anybody but Teddy to accompany him on these daily visits.

Mr Laurie came now and then to see how Charlie got on, and spoke of having him broken to harness in the autumn.

'He won't need much taming, he is such a gentle, fine-tempered brute. I shall come out and try him with a saddle myself someday,' he said, on one of these visits.

'He lets me put a halter on him, but I don't believe he will bear a saddle even if *you* put it on,' answered Dan, who never failed to be present when Charlie and his master met.

'I shall coax him to bear it, and not mind a few tumbles at first. He has never been harshly treated, so, though he will be surprised at the new performance, I think he won't be frightened, and his antics will do no harm.'

'I wonder what he *would* do,' said Dan to himself, as Mr Laurie went away with the Professor, and Charlie returned to the bars, from which he had retired when the gentlemen came up.

A daring fancy to try the experiment took possession of the boy as he sat on the topmost rail with the glossy back temptingly near him. Never thinking of danger, he obeyed the impulse, and while Charlie unsuspectingly nibbled at the apple he held, Dan quickly and quietly took his seat. He did not keep it long, however, for with an astonished snort, Charlie reared straight up, and deposited Dan on the ground. The fall did not hurt him, for the turf was soft, and he jumped up, saying, with a laugh, 'I did it anyway! Come here, you rascal, and I'll try it again.'

But Charlie declined to approach, and Dan left him resolving to succeed in the end; for a struggle like this suited him exactly. Next time he took a halter, and having got it on, he played with the horse for a while, leading him to and fro, and putting him through various antics till he was a little tired; then Dan sat on the wall and gave him bread, but watched his chance, and getting a good grip of the halter, slipped on to his back. Charlie tried the old trick, but Dan held on, having had practice with Toby, who occasionally had an obstinate fit, and tried to shake off his rider. Charlie was both amazed and indignant; and after prancing for a minute, set off at a gallop, and away went Dan heels over head. If he had not belonged to the class of boys who go through all sorts of dangers unscathed, he would have broken his neck; as it was, he got a heavy fall, and lay still collecting his wits, while Charlie tore round the field tossing his head with every sign of satisfaction at the discomfiture of his rider. Presently it seemed to occur to him that something was wrong with Dan, and, being of a magnanimous nature, he went to see what the matter was. Dan let him sniff about and perplex himself for a few minutes; then he looked up at him, saying, as decidedly as if the horse could understand, 'You think you have beaten, but you are mistaken, old boy; and I'll ride you yet – see if I don't.'

He tried no more that day, but soon after attempted a new method of introducing Charlie to a burden. He strapped a folded blanket on his back, and then let him race, and rear, and roll, and fume as much as he liked. After a few fits of rebellion Charlie submitted, and in a few days permitted Dan to mount him, often stopped short to look round, as if he said, half patiently, half reproachfully, 'I don't understand it, but I suppose you mean no harm, so I permit the liberty.'

Dan patted and praised him, and took a short turn every day, getting frequent falls, but persisting in spite of them, and longing to try a saddle and bridle, but not daring to confess what he had done. He had his wish, however, for there had been a witness of his pranks who said a good word for him.

'Do you know what that chap has ben doin' lately?' asked Silas of his master, one evening, as he received his orders for the next day.

'Which boy?' said Mr Bhaer, with an air of resignation, expecting some sad revelation.

'Dan, he's ben a breaking the colt, sir, and I wish I may die if he ain't done it,' answered Silas, chuckling.

'How do you know?'

'Wal, I kinder keep an eye on the little fellers, and most gen'lly know what they're up to; so when Dan kep going off to the paster, and coming home black and blue, I mistrusted that *suthing* was goin' on. I didn't say nothin', but I creep up into the barn chamber, and from there I see him goin' through all manner of games with Charlie. Blest if he warn't throwed time and agin, and knocked round like a bag o' meal. But the pluck of that boy did beat all, and he 'peared to like it, and kep on as ef bound to beat.'

'But, Silas, you should have stopped it – the boy might have been killed,' said Mr Bhaer, wondering what freak his irrepressibles would take into their heads next.

'S'pose I oughter; but there warn't no real danger, for Charlie ain't no tricks, and is as pretty a tempered horse as ever I see. Fact was, I couldn't bear to spile sport, for ef there's anything I do admire it's grit, and Dan is chock full on 't. But now I know he's hankerin' after a saddle, and yet won't take even the old one on the sly; so I just thought I'd up and tell, and maybe you'd let him try what he can do. Mr Laurie won't mind, and Charlie's all the better for 't.'

'We shall see;' and off went Mr Bhaer to enquire into the matter.

Dan owned up at once, and proudly proved that Silas was right by showing off his power over Charlie; for by dint of much coaxing, many carrots, and infinite perseverance, he really had succeeded in riding the colt with a halter and blanket. Mr Laurie was much amused, and well pleased with Dan's courage and skill, and let him have a hand in all future performances; for he set about Charlie's education at once, saying that he was not going to be outdone by a slip of a boy. Thanks to Dan, Charlie took kindly to the saddle and bridle when he had once reconciled himself to the indignity of the bit; and after Mr Laurie had trained him a little, Dan was permitted to ride him, to the great envy and admiration of the other boys.

'Isn't he handsome? and don't he mind me like a lamb?' said Dan one day as he dismounted and stood with his arm round Charlie's neck.

'Yes, and isn't he a much more useful and agreeable animal than the wild colt who spent his days racing about the field, jumping fences, and running away now and then?' asked Mrs Bhaer from the steps where she always appeared when Dan performed with Charlie.

'Of course he is. See he won't run away now, even if I don't hold him, and he comes to me the minute I whistle; I have tamed him well, haven't I?' and Dan looked both proud and pleased, as well he might, for, in spite of their struggles together, Charlie loved him better than his master.

'Isn't he handsome? and don't he mind me like a lamb?' said Dan

'I am taming a colt too, and I think I shall succeed as well as you if I am as patient and persevering,' said Mrs Jo, smiling so significantly at him, that Dan understood and answered, laughing, yet in earnest, 'We won't jump over the fence and run away, but stay and let them make a handsome, useful span of us, hey, Charlie?'

CHAPTER 17

Composition Day

'Hurry up, boys, it's three o'clock, and Uncle Fritz likes us to be punctual, you know,' said Franz one Wednesday afternoon as a bell rang, and a stream of literary-looking young gentlemen with books and paper in their hands were seen going toward the museum.

Tommy was in the school-room, bending over his desk, much bedaubed with ink, flushed with the ardour of inspiration, and in a great hurry as usual, for easy-going Bangs never was ready till the very last minute. As Franz passed the door looking up laggards, Tommy gave one last blot and flourish, and departed out the window, waving his paper to dry as he went. Nan followed, looking very important, with a large roll in her hand, and Demi escorted Daisy, both evidently brimful of some delightful secret.

The museum was all in order, and the sunshine among the hop-vines made pretty shadows on the floor as it peeped through the great window. On one side sat Mr and Mrs Bhaer, on the other was a little table on which the compositions were laid as soon as read, and in a large semicircle sat the children on camp-stools which occasionally shut up and let the sitter down, thus preventing any stiffness in the assembly. As it took too much time to have all read, they took turns, and on this Wednesday the younger pupils were the chief performers, while the elder ones listened with condescension and criticised freely.

'Ladies first; so Nan may begin,' said Mr Bhaer, when the settling of stools and rustling of papers had subsided.

Nan took her place beside the little table, and, with a preliminary giggle, read the following interesting essay on the sponge.

'THE SPONGE

The sponge, my friends, is a most useful and interesting plant. It grows on rocks under the water, and is a kind of seaweed, I believe. People go and pick it and dry it and wash it, because little fish and insects live in the holes of the sponge; I found shells in my new one, and sand. Some are very fine and soft; babies are washed with them. The sponge has many uses. I will relate some of them, and I hope my friends will remember what I say. One use is to wash the face; I don't like it myself, but I do it because I wish to be clean. Some people *don't*, and they are dirty.'

Here the eye of the reader rested sternly upon Dick and Dolly, who quailed under it, and instantly resolved to scrub themselves virtuously on all occasions.

'Another use is to wake people up; I allude to *boys* par–*tic*–lar–ly.'

Another pause after the long word to enjoy the smothered laugh that went round the room.

'Some boys do not get up when called, and Mary Ann squeezes the water out of a wet sponge on their faces, and it makes them so mad they wake up.'

Here the laugh broke out, and Emil said, as if he had been hit, 'Seems to me you are wandering from the subject.'

'No, I ain't; we are to write about vegetables or animals, and I'm doing both: for boys are animals, aren't they?' cried Nan; and, undaunted by the indignant, 'No!' shouted at her, she calmly proceeded:

'One more interesting thing is done with sponges, and this is when doctors put ether on it, and hold it to people's noses when they have teeth out. *I* shall do this when I am bigger, and give ether to the sick, so they will go to sleep and not feel me cut off their legs and arms.'

'I know somebody who killed cats with it,' called out Demi, but was promptly crushed by Dan, who upset his camp-stool and put a hat over his face.

'I will *not* be interruckted,' said Nan, frowning upon the unseemly scrimmagers. Order was instantly restored, and the young lady closed her remarks as follows:

'My composition has three morals, my friends.'

Somebody groaned, but no notice was taken of the insult.

'First, is keep your faces clean; second, get up early; third, when the ether sponge is put over your nose, breathe hard and don't kick, and your teeth will come out easy. I have no more to say.'

And Miss Nan sat down amid tumultuous applause.

'That is a very remarkable composition; its tone is high, and there is a good deal of humour in it. Very well done, Nan. Now, Daisy,' and Mr Bhaer smiled at one young lady as he beckoned the other.

Daisy coloured prettily as she took her place, and said, in her modest little voice, 'I'm afraid you won't like mine; it isn't nice and funny like Nan's. But I couldn't do any better.'

'We always like yours, Posy,' said Uncle Fritz, and a gentle murmur from the boys seemed to confirm the remark. Thus encouraged, Daisy read her little paper, which was listened to with respectful attention.

'THE CAT

The cat is a sweet animal. I love them very much. They are clean and pretty, and catch rats and mice, and let you pet them, and are fond of you if you are kind. They are very wise, and can find their way anywhere. Little cats are called kittens, and are dear things. I have two, named Huz and Buz, and their mother is Topaz, because she has yellow eyes. Uncle told me a pretty story about a man named Ma–ho–met. He had a nice cat, and when she was asleep on his sleeve, and he wanted to go away, he cut off the sleeve so as not to wake her up. I think he was a kind man. Some cats catch fish.'

'So do I!' cried Teddy, jumping up eager to tell about his trout. 'Hush!' said his mother, setting him down again as quickly as possible, for orderly Daisy hated to be 'interruckted', as Nan expressed it.

'I read about one who used to do it very slyly. I tried to make Topaz, but she did not like the water, and scratched me. She does like tea, and when I play in my kitchen she pats the teapot with her paw, till I give her some. She is a fine cat, she eats apple pudding and molasses. Most cats do not.'

'That's a first-rater,' called out Nat, and Daisy retired, pleased with the praise of her friend.

'Demi looks so impatient we must have him up at once or he won't hold out,' said Uncle Fritz, and Demi skipped up with alacrity.

'Mine is a poem!' he announced in a tone of triumph, and read his first effort in a loud and solemn voice:

> 'I write about the butterfly,
> It is a pretty thing;
> And flies about like the birds,
> But it does not sing.

> 'First it is a little grub,
> And then it is a nice yellow cocoon,
> And then the butterfly
> Eats its way out soon.

> 'They live on dew and honey,
> They do not have any hive,
> They do not sting like wasps, and bees, and hornets,
> And to be as good as they are we should strive.

> 'I should like to be a beautiful butterfly,
> All yellow, and blue, and green, and red;
> But I should not like
> To have Dan put camphor on my poor little head.'

This unusual burst of genius brought down the house, and Demi was obliged to read it again, a somewhat difficult task, as there was no punctuation whatever, and the little poet's breath gave out before he got to the end of some of the long lines.

'He will be a Shakespeare yet,' said Aunt Jo, laughing as if she would die, for this poetic gem reminded her of one of her own, written at the age of ten, and beginning gloomily,

> 'I wish I had a quiet tomb,

Beside a little rill;
Where birds, and bees, and butterflies,
Would sing upon the hill.'

'Come on, Tommy. If there is as much ink inside your paper as there is outside, it will be a long composition,' said Mr Bhaer, when Demi had been induced to tear himself from his poem and sit down.

'It isn't a composition, it's a letter. You see, I forgot all about its being my turn till after school, and then I didn't know what to have, and there wasn't time to read up; so I thought you wouldn't mind my taking a letter that I wrote to my Grandma. It's got something about birds in it, so I thought it would do.'

With this long excuse, Tommy plunged into a sea of ink and floundered through, pausing now and then to decipher one of his own flourishes.

'My dear Grandma – I hope you are well. Uncle James sent me a pocket rifle. It is a beautiful little instrument of killing, shaped like this [Here Tommy displayed a remarkable sketch of what looked like an intricate pump, or the inside of a small steam engine] – 44 are the sights; 6 is a false stock that fits in at A; 3 is the trigger, and 2 is the cock. It loads at the breech, and fires with great force and straightness. I am going out shooting squirrels soon. I shot several fine birds for the museum. They had speckled breasts, and Dan liked them very much. He stuffed them tiptop, and they sit on the tree quite natural, only one looks a little tipsy. We had a Frenchman working here the other day, and Asia called his name so funnily that I will tell you about it. His name was Germain: first she called him Jerry, but we laughed at her, and she changed it to Jeremiah; but ridicule was the result, so it became Mr Germany; but ridicule having been again resumed, it became Garrymon, which it has remained ever since. I do not write often, I am so busy; but I think of you often, and sympathise with you, and sincerely hope you get on as well as can be expected without me. Your affectionate grandson,

Thomas Buckminster Bangs

PS If you come across any postage stamps, remember me.

NB Love to all, and a great deal to Aunt Almira. Does she
     make any nice plum cakes now?
PS Mrs Bhaer sends her respects.
PS And so would Mr B., if he knew I was in act to write.
NB Father is going to give me a watch on my birthday. I am
     glad, as at present I have no means of telling the time, and am
     often late at school.
PS I hope to see you soon. Don't you wish to send for me?
                                                            T. B. B.'

As each postscript was received with a fresh laugh from the
boys, by the time he came to the sixth and last, Tommy was so
exhausted that he was glad to sit down and wipe his ruddy face.

'I hope the dear old lady will live through it,' said Mr Bhaer,
under cover of the noise.

'We won't take any notice of the broad hint given in that last
PS. The letter will be quite as much as she can bear without a visit
from Tommy,' answered Mrs Jo, remembering that the old lady
usually took to her bed after a visitation from her irrepressible
grandson.

'Now, me,' said Teddy, who had learned a bit of poetry, and was
so eager to say it that he had been bobbing up and down during
the reading, and could no longer be restrained.

'I'm afraid he will forget it if he waits; and I have had a deal of
trouble teaching him,' said his mother.

Teddy trotted to the rostrum, dropped a curtsey and nodded his
head at the same time, as if anxious to suit everyone; then, in his
baby voice, and putting the emphasis on the wrong words, he said
his verse all in one breath:

> 'Little drops *of* water,
> Little drains of sand,
> Mate a might okum [ocean],
> *And* a peasant land.
> Little worts *of* kindness,
> Pokin evvy day,
> Make a home a hebbin,
> And hep us *on* a way.'

Clapping his hands at the end, he made another double

salutation, and then ran to hide his head in his mother's lap, quite overcome by the success of his 'piece', for the applause was tremendous.

Dick and Dolly did not write, but were encouraged to observe the habits of animals and insects, and report what they saw. Dick liked this, and always had a great deal to say; so, when his name was called, he marched up, and, looking at the audience with his bright confiding eyes, told his little story so earnestly that no one smiled at his crooked body, because the 'straight soul' shone through it beautifully.

'I've been watching dragonflies, and I read about them in Dan's book, and I'll try and tell you what I remember. There's lots of them flying round on the pond, all blue, with big eyes, and sort of lace wings, very pretty. I caught one, and looked at him, and I think he was the handsomest insect I ever saw. They catch littler creatures than they are to eat, and have a queer kind of hook thing that folds up when they ain't hunting. It likes the sunshine, and dances round all day. Let me see! what else was there to tell about? Oh, I know! The eggs are laid in the water, and go down to the bottom, and are hatched in the mud. Little ugly things come out of 'em; I can't say the name, but they are brown, and keep having new skins, and getting bigger and bigger. Only think! it takes them two years to be a dragonfly! Now *this* is the curious*est* part of it, so you listen tight, for I don't believe you know it. When it is ready it knows somehow, and the ugly, grubby thing climbs up out of the water on a flag or a bulrush, and bursts open its back.'

'Come, I don't believe that,' said Tommy, who was not an observant boy, and really thought Dick was 'making up'.

'It does burst open its back, don't it?' and Dick appealed to Mr Bhaer, who nodded a very decided affirmative, to the little speaker's great satisfaction.

'Well, out comes the dragonfly, all whole, and he sits in the sun – sort of coming alive, you know; and he gets strong, and then he spreads his pretty wings, and flies away up in the air, and never is a grub any more. That's all I know; but I shall watch and try to see him do it, for I think it's splendid to turn into a beautiful dragonfly, don't you?'

Dick had told his story well, and, when he described the flight of the new-born insect, had waved his hands, and looked up as if he saw, and wanted to follow it. Something in his face suggested to the minds of the elder listeners the thought that someday little Dick would have his wish, and after years of helplessness and pain would climb up into the sun some happy day, and, leaving his poor little body behind him, find a new lovely shape in a fairer world than this. Mrs Jo drew him to her side, and said, with a kiss on his thin cheek, 'That is a sweet little story, dear, and you remembered it wonder-fully well. I shall write and tell your mother all about it;' and Dick sat on her knee, contentedly smiling at the praise, and resolving to watch well, and catch the dragonfly in the act of leaving its old body for the new, and see how he did it. Dolly had a few remarks to make upon the 'Duck', and made them in a sing-song tone, for he had learned it by heart, and thought it a great plague to do it at all.

'Wild ducks are hard to kill; men hide and shoot at them, and have tame ducks to quack and make the wild ones come where the men can fire at them. They have wooden ducks made too, and they sail round, and the wild ones come to see them; they are stupid, I think. Our ducks are very tame. They eat a great deal, and go poking round in the mud and water. They don't take good care of their eggs, but let them spoil, and . . .'

'Mine don't!' cried Tommy.

'Well, some people's do; Silas said so. Hens take good care of little ducks, only they don't like to have them go in the water, and make a great fuss. But the little ones don't care a bit. I like to eat ducks with stuffing in them and lots of apple sauce.'

'I have something to say about owls,' began Nat, who had care-fully prepared a paper upon this subject with some help from Dan.

'Owls have big heads, round eyes, hooked bills, and strong claws. Some are grey, some white, some black and yellowish. Their feathers are very soft, and stick out a great deal. They fly very quietly, and hunt bats, mice, little birds, and such things. They build nests in barns, hollow trees, and some take the nests of other birds. The great horned owl has two eggs bigger than a hen's and reddish brown. The tawny owl has five eggs, white and smooth; and this is the kind that hoots at night. Another kind sounds like a child crying. They eat mice and bats whole, and the parts that they cannot digest they make into little balls and spit out.'

'My gracious! how funny!' Nan was heard to observe.

'They cannot see by day; and if they get out into the light, they go flapping round half blind, and the other birds chase and peck at them, as if they were making fun. The horned owl is very big, 'most as big as the eagle. It eats rabbits, rats, snakes, and birds; and lives in rocks and old tumbledown houses. They have a good many cries, and scream like a person being choked, and say, "Waugh O! Waugh O!" and it scares people at night in the woods. The white owl lives by the sea, and in cold places, and looks something like a hawk. There is a kind of owl that makes holes to live in like moles. It is called the burrowing owl, and is very small. The barn owl is the commonest kind; and I have watched one sitting in a hole in a tree, looking like a little grey cat, with one eye shut and the other open. He comes out at dusk, and sits round waiting for the bats. I caught one, and here he is.'

With that Nat suddenly produced from inside his jacket a little downy bird, who blinked and ruffled his feathers, looking very plump and sleepy and scared.

'Don't touch him! He is going to show off,' said Nat, displaying his new pet with great pride. First he put a cocked hat on the bird's head, and the boys laughed at the funny effect; then he added a pair of paper spectacles, and that gave the owl such a wise look that they shouted with merriment. The performance closed with making the bird angry, and seeing him cling to a handkerchief upside down, pecking and 'clucking', as Rob called it. He was allowed to fly after that, and settled himself on the bunch of pine-cones over the door, where he sat staring down at the company with an air of sleepy dignity that amused them very much.

'Have you anything for us, George?' asked Mr Bhaer, when the room was still again.

'Well, I read and learned ever so much about moles, but I declare I've forgotten every bit of it, except that they dig holes to live in, that you catch them by pouring water down, and that they can't possibly live without eating very often;' and Stuffy sat down, wishing he had not been too lazy to write out his valuable observations, for a general smile went round when he mentioned the last of the three facts which lingered in his memory.

'Then we are done for today,' began Mr Bhaer, but Tommy called out in a great hurry, 'No we ain't. Don't you know? We must give the thing;' and he winked violently as he made an eyeglass of his fingers.

'Bless my heart, I forgot! Now is your time, Tom;' and Mr Bhaer dropped into his seat again, while all the boys but Dan looked mightily tickled at something.

Nat, Tommy, and Demi left the room, and speedily returned with a little red morocco box set forth in state on Mrs Jo's best silver salver. Tommy bore it, and, still escorted by Nat and Demi, marched up to unsuspecting Dan, who stared at them as if he thought they were going to make fun of him. Tommy had prepared an elegant and impressive speech for the occasion, but when the minute came, it all went out of his head, and he just said, straight from his kindly boyish heart, 'Here, old fellow, we all wanted to give you something to kind of pay for what happened a while ago, and to show how much we liked you for being such a trump. Please take it, and have a jolly good time with it.'

Dan was so surprised he could only get as red as the little box, and mutter, 'Thanky, boys!' as he fumbled to open it. But when he saw what was inside, his face lighted up, and he seized the long desired treasure, saying so enthusiastically that everyone was satisfied, though his language was anything but polished, 'What a stunner! I say, you fellows are regular bricks to give me this; it's just what I wanted. Give us your paw, Tommy.'

Many paws were given, and heartily shaken, for the boys were charmed with Dan's pleasure, and crowded round him to shake hands and expatiate on the beauties of their gift. In the midst of this pleasant chatter, Dan's eye went to Mrs Jo, who stood outside the group enjoying the scene with all her heart.

'No, I had nothing to do with it. The boys got it up all themselves,' she said, answering the grateful look that seemed to thank her for that happy moment. Dan smiled, and said, in a tone that only she could understand, 'It's you all the same;' and making his way through the boys, he held out his hand first to her and then to the good Professor, who was beaming benevolently on his flock.

He thanked them both with the silent, hearty squeeze he gave the kind hands that had held him up, and led him into the safe refuge of a happy home. Not a word was spoken, but they felt all he would say, and little Teddy expressed his pleasure for them as he leaned from his father's arm to hug the boy, and say, in his baby way, 'My dood Danny! everybody loves him now.'

'Come here, show off your spyglass, Dan, and let us see some of

your magnified pollywogs and annymalcumisms as you call 'em,'
said Jack, who felt so uncomfortable during this scene that he
would have slipped away if Emil had not kept him.

'So I will, take a squint at that and see what you think of it,' said
Dan, glad to show off his precious microscope.

He held it over a beetle that happened to be lying on the table,
and Jack bent down to take his squint, but looked up with an
amazed face, saying, 'My eye! what nippers the old thing has got!
I see now why it hurts so confoundedly when you grab a dor-bug
and he grabs back again.'

'He winked at me,' cried Nan, who had poked her head under
Jack's elbow and got the second peep.

Everyone took a look, and then Dan showed them the lovely
plumage on a moth's wing, the four feathery corners to a hair, the
veins on a leaf, hardly visible to the naked eye, but like a thick net
through the wonderful little glass; the skin on their own fingers,
looking like queer hills and valleys; a cobweb like a bit of coarse
sewing silk, and the sting of a bee.

'It's like the fairy spectacles in my story book, only more curious,'
said Demi, enchanted with the wonders he saw.

'Dan is a magician now, and he can show you many miracles
going on all round you; for he has two things needful – patience
and a love of nature. We live in a beautiful and wonderful world,
Demi, and the more you know about it the wiser and the better
you will be. This little glass will give you a new set of teachers, and
you may learn fine lessons from them if you will,' said Mr Bhaer,
glad to see how interested the boys were in the matter.

'Could I see anybody's soul with this microscope if I looked
hard?' asked Demi, who was much impressed with the power of
the bit of glass.

'No, dear; it's not powerful enough for that, and never can be
made so. You must wait a long while before your eyes are clear
enough to see the most invisible of God's wonders. But looking at
the lovely things you can see will help you to understand the
lovelier things you can *not* see,' answered Uncle Fritz, with his
hand on the boy's head.

'Well, Daisy and I both think that if there are any angels, their
wings look like that butterfly's as we see it through the glass, only
more soft and gold.'

'Believe it if you like, and keep your own little wings as bright and beautiful, only don't fly away for a long time yet.'

'No, I won't,' and Demi kept his word.

'Goodbye, my boys; I must go now, but I leave you with our new Professor of Natural History;' and Mrs Jo went away well pleased with that composition day.

CHAPTER 18

Crops

The gardens did well that summer, and in September the little crops were gathered in with much rejoicing. Jack and Ned joined their farms and raised potatoes, those being a good saleable article. They got twelve bushels, counting little ones and all, and sold them to Mr Bhaer at a fair price, for potatoes went fast in that house. Emil and Franz devoted themselves to corn, and had a jolly little husking in the barn, after which they took their corn to the mill, and came proudly home with meal enough to supply the family with hasty-pudding and Johnny-cake for a long time. They would not take money for their crop; because, as Franz said, 'We never can pay Uncle for all he has done for us if we raised corn for the rest of our days.'

Nat had beans in such abundance that he despaired of ever shelling them, till Mrs Jo proposed a new way, which succeeded admirably. The dry pods were spread upon the barn floor, Nat fiddled, and the boys danced quadrilles on them, till they were thrashed out with much merriment and very little labour.

Tommy's six weeks' beans were a failure; for a dry spell early in the season hurt them, because he gave them no water; and after that he was so sure that they could take care of themselves, he let the poor things struggle with bugs and weeds till they were exhausted and died a lingering death. So Tommy had to dig his farm over again, and plant peas. But they were late; the birds ate many; the bushes, not being firmly planted, blew down, and when the poor peas came at last, no one cared for them, as their day was over, and spring lamb had grown into mutton. Tommy consoled himself with a charitable effort; for he transplanted all the thistles he could find, and tended them carefully for Toby, who was fond of the prickly delicacy, and had eaten all he could find on the place. The boys had great fun over Tom's thistle bed; but he insisted that it was better to care for poor Toby than for himself, and declared that he would devote his entire farm next year to thistles, worms, and snails, that Demi's turtles and Nat's pet owl might have the food they loved, as well as the donkey. So like shiftless, kind-hearted, happy-go-lucky Tommy!

Demi had supplied his grandmother with lettuce all summer, and in the autumn sent his grandfather a basket of turnips, each one scrubbed up till it looked like a great white egg. His Grandma was fond of salad, and one of his Grandpa's favourite quotations was:

> Lucullus, whom frugality could charm,
> Ate roasted turnips at the Sabine farm.

Therefore these vegetable offerings to the dear domestic god and goddess were affectionate, appropriate, and classical.

Daisy had nothing but flowers in her little plot, and it bloomed all summer long with a succession of gay or fragrant posies. She was very fond of her garden, and delved away in it at all hours, watching over her roses, and pansies, sweetpeas, and mignonette, as faithfully and tenderly as she did over her dolls or her friends. Little nosegays were sent into town on all occasions, and certain vases about the house were her especial care. She had all sorts of pretty fancies about her flowers, and loved to tell the children the story of the pansy, and show them how the stepmother-leaf sat up in her green chair in purple and gold; how the two own children in gay yellow had each its little seat, while the step-children, in dull colours, both sat on one small stool, and the poor little father in his red nightcap, was kept out of sight in the middle of the flower; that a monk's dark face looked out of the monk's-hood larkspur; that the flowers of the canary-vine were so like dainty birds fluttering their yellow wings, that one almost expected to see them fly away, and the snapdragons that went off like little pistol shots when you cracked them. Splendid dollies did she make out of scarlet and white poppies, with ruffled robes tied round the waist with grass-blade sashes, and astonishing hats of coreopsis on their green heads. Pea-pod boats, with rose-leaf sails, received these flower people, and floated them about a placid pool in the most charming style; for finding that there were no elves, Daisy made her own, and loved the fanciful little friends who played their parts in her summer life.

Nan went in for herbs, and had a fine display of useful plants, which she tended with steadily increasing interest and care. Very busy was she in September cutting, drying, and tying up her sweet harvest, and writing down in a little book how the different herbs are to be used. She had tried several experiments, and made several mistakes; so she wished to be particular lest she should give little Huz another fit by administering wormwood instead of catnip.

Dick, Dolly, and Rob each grubbed away on his small farm, and made more stir about it than all the rest put together. Parsnips and carrots were the crops of the two Ds; and they longed for it to be late enough to pull up the precious vegetables. Dick did privately examine his carrots, and plant them again, feeling that Silas was right in saying it was too soon for them yet.

Rob's crop was four small squashes and one immense pumpkin. It really was a 'bouncer', as everyone said; and I assure you that two small persons could sit on it side by side. It seemed to have absorbed all the goodness of the little garden, and all the sunshine that shone down on it, and lay there a great round, golden ball, full of rich suggestions of pumpkin pies for weeks to come. Robby was so proud of his mammoth vegetable that he took everyone to see it, and, when frosts began to nip, covered it up each night with an old bed quilt, tucking it round as if the pumpkin was a well-beloved baby. The day it was gathered he would let no one touch it but himself, and nearly broke his back tugging it to the barn in his little wheelbarrow, with Dick and Dolly harnessed in front to give a heave up the path. His mother promised him that the Thanksgiving pies should be made from it, and hinted vaguely that she had a plan in her head which would cover the prize pumpkin and its owner with glory.

Poor Billy had planted cucumbers, but unfortunately hoed them up and left the pig-weed. This mistake grieved him very much for ten minutes, then he forgot all about it, and sowed a handful of bright buttons which he had collected, evidently thinking in his feeble mind that they were money, and would come up and multiply, so that he might make many quarters, as Tommy did. No one disturbed him, and he did what he liked with his plot, which soon looked as if a series of small earthquakes had stirred it up. When the general harvest day came, he would have had nothing but stones and weeds to show, if kind old Asia had not hung half a dozen oranges on the dead tree he stuck up in the middle. Billy was delighted with his crop; and no one spoiled his pleasure in the little miracle which pity wrought for him, by making withered branches bear strange fruit.

Stuffy had various trials with his melons; for, being impatient to taste them, he had a solitary revel before they were ripe, and made himself so ill, that for a day or two it seemed doubtful if he would ever eat any more. But he pulled through it, and served up his first cantaloupe without tasting a mouthful himself. They were excellent melons, for he had a warm slope for them, and they ripened fast. The last and best were lingering on the vines, and Stuffy had announced that he should sell them to a neighbour. This disappointed the boys, who had hoped to eat the melons themselves, and they expressed their displeasure in a new and striking manner. Going one morning to gaze upon the three fine watermelons which he had kept for the market, Stuffy was horrified to find the word 'PIG' cut in white letters on the green rind, staring at him from every one. He was in a great rage, and flew to Mrs Jo for redress. She listened, condoled with him, and then said, 'If you want to turn the laugh, I'll tell you how, but you must give up the melons.'

'Well, I will; for I can't thrash all the boys, but I'd like to give them something to remember, the mean sneaks,' growled Stuffy, still in a fume.

Now Mrs Jo was pretty sure who had done the trick, for she had seen three heads suspiciously near to one another in the sofa-corner the evening before; and when these heads had nodded with chuckles and whispers, this experienced woman knew mischief was afoot. A moonlight night, a rustling in the old cherry tree near Emil's window, a cut on Tommy's finger, all helped to confirm her suspicions; and having cooled Stuffy's wrath a little, she bade him bring his maltreated melons to her room, and say not a word to anyone of what had happened. He did so, and the three wags were amazed to find their joke so quietly taken. It spoilt the fun, and the entire disappearance of the melons made them uneasy. So did Stuffy's good nature, for he looked more placid and plump than ever, and surveyed them with an air of calm pity that perplexed them very much.

At dinner-time they discovered why; for then Stuffy's vengeance fell upon them, and the laugh was turned against them. When the pudding was eaten, and the fruit was put on, Mary Ann reappeared in a high state of giggle, bearing a large watermelon; Silas followed with another; and Dan brought up the rear with a third. One was placed before each of the three guilty lads; and they read on the smooth green skins this addition to their own work, 'With the compliments of the PIG.' Everyone else read it also, and the whole table was in a roar, for the trick had been whispered about; so everyone understood the sequel. Emil, Ned, and Tommy did not know where to look, and had not a word to say for themselves; so they wisely joined in the laugh, cut up the melons, and handed them round, saying, what all the rest agreed to, that Stuffy had taken a wise and merry way to return good for evil.

Dan had no garden, for he was away or lame the greater part of the summer; so he had helped Silas wherever he could, chopped wood for Asia, and taken care of the lawn so well, that Mrs Jo always had smooth paths and nicely shaven turf before her door.

When the others got in their crops, he looked sorry that he had so little to show; but as autumn went on, he bethought himself of a woodland harvest which no one would dispute with him, and which was peculiarly his own. Every Saturday he was away alone to the forests, fields, and hills, and always came back loaded with spoils; for he seemed to know the meadows where the best flag-root grew, the thicket where the sassafras was spiciest, the haunts where the squirrels went for nuts, the white oak whose bark was most valuable, and the little gold-thread vine that Nursey liked to cure the canker with. All sorts of splendid red and yellow leaves did Dan bring home for Mrs Jo to dress her parlour with, graceful seeded grasses, clematis tassels, downy, soft, yellow wax-work berries, and mosses, red-brimmed, white, or emerald green.

'I need not sigh for the woods now, because Dan brings the woods to me,' Mrs Jo used to say, as she glorified the walls with yellow maple boughs and scarlet woodbine wreaths, or filled her vases with russet ferns, hemlock sprays full of delicate cones, and hardy autumn flowers; for Dan's crop suited her well.

The great garret was full of the children's little stores and for a time was one of the sights of the house. Daisy's flower seeds in neat little paper bags, all labelled, lay in a drawer of a three-legged table. Nan's herbs hung in bunches against the wall, filling the air with their aromatic breath. Tommy had a basket of thistledown with the tiny seeds attached, for he meant to plant them next year, if they did not all fly away before that time. Emil had bunches of popcorn hanging there to dry, and Demi laid up acorns and different sorts of grain for the pets. But Dan's crop made the best show, for fully one half of the floor was covered with the nuts he brought. All kinds were there, for he ranged the woods for miles round, climbed the tallest trees, and forced his way into the thickest hedges for his plunder. Walnuts, chestnuts, hazelnuts, and beechnuts lay in separate compartments, getting brown, and dry, and sweet, ready for winter revels.

There was one butternut tree on the place, and Rob and Teddy called it theirs. It bore well this year, and the great dingy nuts came dropping down to hide among the dead leaves, where the busy squirrels found them better than the lazy Bhaers. Their father had told them (the boys, not the squirrels) they should have the nuts if they would pick them up, but no one was to help. It was easy work, and Teddy liked it, only he soon got tired, and left his little basket half-full for another day. But the other day was slow to arrive, and, meantime, the sly squirrels were hard at work, scampering up and down the old elm trees stowing the nuts away till their holes were full, then all about in the crotches of the boughs, to be removed at their leisure. Their funny little ways amused the boys, till one day Silas said, 'Hev you sold them nuts to the squirrels?'

'No,' answered Rob, wondering what Silas meant.

'Wal, then, you'd better fly round, or them spry little fellers won't leave you none.'

'Oh, we can beat them when we begin. There are such lots of nuts we shall have a plenty.'

'There ain't many more to come down, and they have cleared the ground pretty well, see if they hain't.'

Robby ran to look, and was alarmed to find how few remained. He called Teddy, and they worked hard all one afternoon, while the squirrels sat on the fence and scolded.

'Now, Ted, we must keep watch, and pick up just as fast as they fall, or we shan't have more than a bushel, and everyone will laugh at us if we don't.'

'The naughty quillies tarn't have 'em. I'll pick fast and run and put 'em in the barn twick,' said Teddy, frowning at little Frisky, who chattered and whisked his tail indignantly.

That night a high wind blew down hundreds of nuts, and when Mrs Jo came to wake her little sons, she said, briskly, 'Come, my laddies, the squirrels are hard at it, and you will have to work well today, or they will have every nut on the ground.'

'No, they won't,' and Robby tumbled up in a great hurry, gobbled his breakfast, and rushed out to save his property.

Teddy went too, and worked like a little beaver, trotting to and fro with full and empty baskets. Another bushel was soon put away in the corn barn, and they were scrambling among the leaves for more nuts when the bell rang for school.

'Oh, Father! let me stay out and pick. Those horrid squirrels will have my nuts if you don't. I'll do my lessons by and by,' cried Rob, running into the school-room, flushed and tousled by the fresh cold wind and his eager work.

'If you had been up early and done a little every morning there would be no hurry now. I told you that, Rob, and you never minded. I cannot have the lessons neglected as the work has been. The squirrels will get more than their share this year, and they deserve it, for they have worked best. You may go an hour earlier, but that is all,' and Mr Bhaer led Rob to his place where the little man dashed at his books as if bent on making sure of the precious hour promised him.

It was almost maddening to sit still and see the wind shaking down the last nuts, and the lively thieves flying about, pausing now and then to eat one in his face, and flirt their tails, as if they said, saucily, 'We'll have them in spite of you, lazy Rob.' The only thing that sustained the poor child in this trying moment was the sight of Teddy working away all alone. It was really splendid the pluck and perseverance of the little lad. He picked and picked till his back ached; he trudged to and fro till his small legs were tired; and he defied wind, weariness, and wicked 'quillies', till his mother left her work and did the carrying for him, full of admiration for the kind little fellow who tried to help his brother. When Rob was dismissed, he found Teddy reposing in the bushel-basket quite used up, but unwilling to quit the field; for he flapped his hat at the thieves with one grubby little hand, while he refreshed himself with the big apple held in the other.

Rob fell to work and the ground was cleared before two o'clock, the nuts safely in the corn-barn loft, and the weary workers exulted in their success. But Frisky and his wife were not to be vanquished so easily; and when Rob went up to look at his nuts a few days later he was amazed to see how many had vanished. None of the boys could have stolen them, because the door had been locked; the doves could not have eaten them, and there were no rats about. There was great lamentation among the young Bhaers till Dick said, 'I saw Frisky on the roof of the corn barn, maybe he took them.'

'I know he did! I'll have a trap, and kill him dead,' cried Rob, disgusted with Frisky's grasping nature.

'Perhaps if you watch, you can find out where he puts them, and I may be able to get them back for you,' said Dan, who was much amused by the fight between the boys and squirrels.

So Rob watched and saw Mr and Mrs Frisky drop from the drooping elm boughs on to the roof of the corn barn, dodge in at one of the little doors, much to the disturbance of the doves, and come out with a nut in each mouth. So laden they could not get back the way they came, but ran down the low roof, along the wall, and leaping off at a corner they vanished a minute and re-appeared without their plunder. Rob ran to the place, and in a hollow under the leaves he found a heap of the stolen property hidden away to be carried off to the holes by and by.

'Oh, you little villains! I'll cheat you now, and not leave one,' said Rob. So he cleared the corner and the corn barn, and put the contested nuts in the garret, making sure that no broken window-pane could anywhere let in the unprincipled squirrels. They seemed to feel that the contest was over, and retired to their hole, but now and then could not resist throwing down nut-shells on Rob's head, and scolding violently as if they could not forgive him nor forget that he had the best of the battle.

Father and Mother Bhaer's crop was of a different sort, and not so easily described; but they were satisfied with it, felt that their summer work had prospered well, and by and by had a harvest that made them very happy.

CHAPTER 19

John Brooke

'Wake up, Demi, dear! I want you.'

'Why, I've just gone to bed; it can't be morning yet;' and Demi blinked like a little owl as he waked from his first sound sleep.

'It's only ten, but your father is ill, and we must go to him. Oh, my little John! my poor little John!' and Aunt Jo laid her head down on the pillow with a sob that scared sleep from Demi's eyes and filled his heart with fear and wonder; for he dimly felt why Aunt Jo called him 'John', and wept over him as if some loss had come that left him poor. He clung to her without a word, and in a minute she was quite steady again, and said, with a tender kiss as she saw his troubled face, 'We are going to say goodbye to him, my darling, and there is no time to lose; so dress quickly and come to me in my room. I must go to Daisy.'

'Yes, I will;' and when Aunt Jo was gone, little Demi got up quietly, dressed as if in a dream, and leaving Tommy fast asleep went away through the silent house, feeling that something new and sorrowful was going to happen – something that set him apart from the other boys for a time, and made the world seem as dark and still and strange as those familiar rooms did in the night. A carriage sent by Mr Laurie stood before the door. Daisy was soon ready, and the brother and sister held each other by the hand all the way into town, as they drove swiftly and silently with aunt and uncle through the shadowy roads to say goodbye to father.

None of the boys but Franz and Emil knew what had happened, and when they came down next morning, great was their wonderment and discomfort, for the house seemed forlorn without its master and mistress. Breakfast was a dismal meal with no cheery Mrs Jo behind the teapots; and when school-time came, Father Bhaer's place was empty. They wandered about in a disconsolate kind of way for an hour, waiting for news and hoping it would be all right with Demi's father, for good John Brooke was much beloved by the boys. Ten o'clock came, and no one arrived to relieve their anxiety. They did not feel like playing, yet the time dragged heavily, and they sat about listless and sober. All at once, Franz got up, and said, in his persuasive way, 'Look here, boys! let's go into school and do our lessons just as if Uncle was here. It will make the day go faster, and will please him, I know.'

'But who will hear us say them?' asked Jack.

'I will; I don't know much more than you do, but I'm the oldest here, and I'll try to fill Uncle's place till he comes, if you don't mind.'

Something in the modest, serious way Franz said this impressed the boys, for, though the poor lad's eyes were red with quiet crying for Uncle John in that long sad night, there was a new manliness about him, as if he had already begun to feel the cares and troubles of life, and tried to take them bravely.

'I will, for one,' and Emil went to his seat, remembering that obedience to his superior officer is a seaman's first duty.

The others followed; Franz took his uncle's seat, and for an hour order reigned. Lessons were learned and said, and Franz made a patient, pleasant teacher, wisely omitting such lessons as he was not equal to, and keeping order more by the unconscious dignity that sorrow gave him than by any words of his own. The little boys were reading when a step was heard in the hall, and everyone looked up to read the news in Mr Bhaer's face as he came in. The kind face told them instantly that Demi had no father now, for it was worn and pale, and full of tender grief, which left him no words with which to answer Rob, as he ran to him, saying, reproachfully, 'What made you go and leave me in the night, Papa?'

The memory of the other father who had left his children in the night, never to return, made Mr Bhaer hold his own boy close, and, for a minute, hide his face in Robby's curly hair. Emil laid his head down on his arms, Franz went to put his hand on his uncle's shoulder, his boyish face pale with sympathy and sorrow, and the others sat so still that the soft rustle of the falling leaves outside was distinctly heard.

Rob did not clearly understand what had happened, but he hated to see Papa unhappy, so he lifted up the bent head, and said, in his chirpy little voice, 'Don't cry, mein Vater! we were all so good, we did our lessons without you, and Franz was the master.'

Mr Bhaer looked up then, tried to smile, and said in a grateful tone that made the lads feel like saints, 'I thank you very much, my boys. It was a beautiful way to help and comfort me. I shall not forget it, I assure you.'

'Franz proposed it, and was a first-rate master, too,' said Nat; and the others gave a murmur of assent most gratifying to the young dominie.

Mr Bhaer put Rob down, and, standing up, put his arm round his tall nephew's shoulder, as he said, with a look of genuine pleasure, 'This makes my hard day easier, and gives me confidence in you all. I am needed there in town, and must leave you for some hours. I thought to give you a holiday, or send some of you home, but if you like to stay and go on as you have begun, I shall be glad and proud of my good boys.'

'We'll stay;' 'We'd rather;' 'Franz can see to us;' cried several, delighted with the confidence shown in them.

'Isn't Marmar coming home?' asked Rob, wistfully; for home without 'Marmar' was the world without the sun to him.

'We shall both come tonight; but dear Aunt Meg needs Mother more than you do now, and I know you like to lend her for a little while.'

'Well, I will; but Teddy's been crying for her, and he slapped Nursey, and was dreadful naughty,' answered Rob, as if the news might bring mother home.

'Where is my little man?' asked Mr Bhaer.

'Dan took him out, to keep him quiet. He's all right now,' said Franz, pointing to the window, through which they could see Dan drawing baby in his little wagon, with the dogs frolicking about him.

'I won't see him, it would only upset him again; but tell Dan I leave Teddy in his care. You older boys I trust to manage yourselves for a day. Franz will direct you, and Silas is here to oversee matters. So goodbye till tonight.'

'Just tell me a word about Uncle John,' said Emil, detaining Mr Bhaer, as he was about hurrying away again.

'He was only ill a few hours, and died as he has lived, so cheerfully, so peacefully, that it seems a sin to mar the beauty of it with any violent or selfish grief. We were in time to say goodbye: and Daisy and Demi were in his arms as he fell asleep on Aunt Meg's breast. No more now, I cannot bear it,' and Mr Bhaer went hastily away quite bowed with grief, for in John Brooke he had lost both friend and brother, and there was no one left to take his place.

All that day the house was very still; the small boys played quietly in the nursery; the others, feeling as if Sunday had come in the middle of the week, spent it in walking, sitting in the willow, or among their pets, all talking much of 'Uncle John', and feeling that something gentle, just, and strong, had gone out of their little world, leaving a sense of loss that deepened every hour. At dusk, Mr and Mrs Bhaer came home alone, for Demi and Daisy were their mother's best comfort now, and could not leave her. Poor Mrs Jo seemed quite spent, and evidently needed the same sort of comfort, for her first words, as she came up the stairs, were, 'Where is my baby?'

'Here I is,' answered a little voice, as Dan put Teddy into her arms, adding, as she hugged him close, 'My Danny tooked tare of me all day, and I was dood.'

Mrs Jo turned to thank the faithful nurse, but Dan was waving off the boys, who had gathered in the hall to meet her, and was saying, in a low voice, 'Keep back; she don't want to be bothered with us now.'

'No, don't keep back. I want you all. Come in and see me, my boys. I've neglected you all day,' and Mrs Jo held out her hands to them as they gathered round and escorted her into her own room, saying little, but expressing much by affectionate looks and clumsy little efforts to show their sorrow and sympathy.

'I am so tired, I will lie here and cuddle Teddy, and you shall bring me in some tea,' she said, trying to speak cheerfully for their sakes.

A general stampede into the dining-room followed, and the supper-table would have been ravaged if Mr Bhaer had not interfered. It was agreed that one squad should carry in the mother's tea, and another bring it out. The four nearest and dearest claimed the first honour, so Franz bore the teapot, Emil the bread, Rob the milk, and Teddy insisted on carrying the sugar basin, which was lighter by several lumps when it arrived than when it started. Some women might have found it annoying at such a time to have boys creaking in and out, upsetting cups and rattling spoons in violent efforts to be quiet and helpful; but it suited Mrs Jo, because just then her heart was very tender; and remembering that

many of her boys were fatherless or motherless, she yearned over
them, and found comfort in their blundering affection. It was the
sort of food that did her more good than the very thick bread and
butter that they gave her, and the rough Commodore's broken
whisper, 'Bear up, Aunty, it's a hard blow; but we'll weather it
somehow;' cheered her more than the sloppy cup he brought her,
full of tea as bitter as if some salt tear of his own had dropped
into it on the way. When supper was over, a second deputation
removed the tray; and Dan said, holding out his arms for sleepy
little Teddy, 'Let me put him to bed, you're so tired, Mother.'

'Will you go with him, lovey?' asked Mrs Jo of her small lord
and master, who lay on her arm among the sofa pillows.

'Torse I will;' and he was proudly carried off by his faithful bearer.

'I wish I could do something,' said Nat, with a sigh, as Franz
leaned over the sofa, and softly stroked Aunt Jo's hot forehead.

'You can, dear. Go and get your violin, and play me the sweet
little airs Uncle Teddy sent you last. Music will comfort me better
than anything else tonight.'

Nat flew for his fiddle, and, sitting just outside her door, played
as he had never done before, for now his heart was in it, and
seemed to magnetise his fingers. The other lads sat quietly upon
the steps, keeping watch that no newcomer should disturb the
house; Franz lingered at his post; and so, soothed, served, and
guarded by her boys, poor Mrs Jo slept at last, and forgot her
sorrow for an hour.

Two quiet days, and on the third Mr Bhaer came in just after
school, with a note in his hand, looking both moved and pleased.

'I want to read you something, boys,' he said; and as they stood
round him he read this:

'DEAR BROTHER FRITZ – I hear that you do not mean to bring
your flock today, thinking that I may not like it. Please do. The
sight of his friends will help Demi through the hard hour, and I
want the boys to hear what Father says of my John. It will do
them good, I know. If they would sing one of the sweet old
hymns you have taught them so well, I should like it better than
any other music, and feel that it was beautifully suited to the
occasion. Please ask them, with my love.

MEG.'

'Will you go?' and Mr Bhaer looked at the lads, who were greatly touched by Mrs Brooke's kind words and wishes.

'Yes,' they answered, like one boy; and an hour later they went away with Franz to bear their part in John Brooke's simple funeral.

The little house looked as quiet, sunny, and homelike as when Meg entered it as a bride, ten years ago, only then it was early summer, and roses blossomed everywhere; now it was early autumn, and dead leaves rustled softly down, leaving the branches bare. The bride was a widow now; but the same beautiful serenity shone in her face, and the sweet resignation of a truly pious soul made her presence a consolation to those who came to comfort her.

'O Meg! how can you bear it so?' whispered Jo, as she met them at the door with a smile of welcome, and no change in her gentle manner, except more gentleness.

'Dear Jo, the love that has blest me for ten happy years supports me still. It could not die, and John is more my own than ever,' whispered Meg; and in her eyes the tender trust was so beautiful and bright, that Jo believed her, and thanked God for the immortality of love like hers.

They were all there – Father and Mother, Uncle Teddy and Aunt Amy, old Mr Laurence, white-haired and feeble now, Mr and Mrs Bhaer, with their flock, and many friends, come to do honour to the dead. One would have said that modest John Brooke, in his busy, quiet, humble life, had had little time to make friends; but now they seemed to start up everywhere, old and young, rich and poor, high and low; for all unconsciously his influence had made itself widely felt, his virtues were remembered, and his hidden charities rose up to bless him. The group about his coffin was a far more eloquent eulogy than any Mr March could utter. There were the rich men whom he had served faithfully for years; the poor old women whom he cherished with his little store, in memory of his mother; the wife to whom he had given such happiness that death could not mar it utterly; the brothers and sisters in whose hearts he had made a place for ever; the little son and daughter, who already felt the loss of his strong arm and tender voice; the young children, sobbing for their kindest playmate, and the tall lads, watching with softened faces a scene which they never could forget. A very simple service, and very short; for the fatherly voice that had faltered in the marriage sacrament now failed entirely as Mr March

endeavoured to pay his tribute of reverence and love to the son
whom he most honoured. Nothing but the soft coo of Baby Josy's
voice upstairs broke the long hush that followed the last Amen, till,
at a sign from Mr Bhaer, the well-trained boyish voices broke out
in a hymn, so full of lofty cheer, that one by one all joined in it,
singing with full hearts, and finding their troubled spirits lifted
into peace on the wings of that brave, sweet psalm.

As Meg listened, she felt that she had done well; for not only
did the moment comfort her with the assurance that John's last
lullaby was sung by the young voices he loved so well, but in the
faces of the boys she saw that they had caught a glimpse of the
beauty of virtue in its most impressive form, and that the memory
of the good man lying dead before them would live long and
helpfully in their remembrance. Daisy's head lay in her lap, and
Demi held her hand, looking often at her, with eyes so like his
father's, and a little gesture that seemed to say, 'Don't be troubled,
mother; I am here;' and all about her were friends to lean upon and
love; so patient, pious Meg put by her heavy grief, feeling that her
best help would be to live for others, as her John had done.

That evening, as the Plumfield boys sat on the steps, as usual, in
the mild September moonlight, they naturally fell to talking of the
event of the day.

Emil began by breaking out, in his impetuous way, 'Uncle Fritz
is the wisest, and Uncle Laurie the jolliest, but Uncle John was the
best; and I'd rather be like him than any man I ever saw.'

'So would I. Did you hear what those gentlemen said to Grandpa
today? I would like to have that said of me when I was dead;' and
Franz felt with regret that he had not appreciated Uncle John
enough.

'What did they say?' asked Jack, who had been much impressed
by the scenes of the day.

'Why, one of the partners of Mr Laurence, where Uncle John
has been ever so long, was saying that he was conscientious
almost to a fault as a business man, and above reproach in all
things. Another gentleman said no money could repay the fidelity
and honesty with which Uncle John had served him, and then
Grandpa told them the best of all. Uncle John once had a place in
the office of a man who cheated, and when this man wanted
Uncle to help him do it, Uncle wouldn't, though he was offered a

big salary. The man was angry and said, "You will never get on in business with such strict principles;" and Uncle answered back, "I *never* will try to get on *without* them," and left the place for a much harder and poorer one.'

'Good!' cried several of the boys warmly, for they were in the mood to understand and value the little story as never before.

'He wasn't rich, was he?' asked Jack.

'No.'

'He never did anything to make a stir in the world, did he?'

'No.'

'He was only good?'

'That's all;' and Franz found himself wishing that Uncle John *had* done something to boast of, for it was evident that Jack was disappointed by his replies.

'Only good. That is *all* and everything,' said Mr Bhaer, who had overheard the last few words, and guessed what was going on the minds of the lads.

'Let me tell you a little about John Brooke, and you will see why men honour him, and why he was satisfied to be good rather than rich or famous. He simply did his duty in all things, and did it so cheerfully, so faithfully, that it kept him patient and brave, and happy through poverty and loneliness and years of hard work. He was a good son, and gave up his own plans to stay and live with his mother while she needed him. He was a good friend, and taught Laurie much beside his Greek and Latin, did it unconsciously, perhaps, by showing him an example of an upright man. He was a faithful servant, and made himself so valuable to those who employed him that they will find it hard to fill his place. He was a good husband and father, so tender, wise, and thoughtful, that Laurie and I learned much of him, and only knew how well he loved his family, when we discovered all he had done for them, unsuspected and unassisted.'

Mr Bhaer stopped a minute, and the boys sat like statues in the moonlight until he went on again, in a subdued, but earnest voice: 'As he lay dying, I said to him, "Have no care for Meg and the little ones; I will see that they never want." Then he smiled and pressed my hand, and answered, in his cheerful way, "No need of that; I have cared for them." And so he had, for when we looked among his papers, all was in order, not a debt remained; and safely put away was enough to keep Meg comfortable and independent. Then we knew why he had lived so plainly, denied himself so many pleasures, except that of charity, and worked so hard that I fear he shortened his good life. He never asked help for himself, though often for others, but bore his own burden and worked out his own task bravely and quietly. No one can say a word of complaint against him, so just and generous and kind was he; and now, when he is gone, all find so much to love and praise and honour, that I am proud to have been his friend, and would rather leave my children the legacy he leaves his than the largest fortune ever made. Yes! Simple, generous goodness is the best capital to found the business of this life upon. It lasts when fame and money fail, and is the only riches we can take out of this world with us. Remember that, my boys; and if you want to earn respect and confidence and love follow in the footsteps of John Brooke.'

When Demi returned to school, after some weeks at home, he seemed to have recovered from his loss with the blessed elasticity of childhood, and so he had in a measure; but he did not forget, for his was a nature into which things sank deeply, to be pondered over, and absorbed into the soil where the small virtues were growing fast. He played and studied, worked and sang, just as before, and few suspected any change; but there was one and Aunt Jo saw it for she watched over the boy with her whole heart, trying to fill John's place in her poor way. He seldom spoke of his loss, but Aunt Jo often heard a stifled sobbing in the little bed at night; and when she went to comfort him, all his cry was, 'I want my father! oh, I want my father!' for the tie between the two had been a very tender one, and the child's heart bled when it was broken. But time was kind to him, and slowly he came to feel that father was not lost, only invisible for a while, and sure to be found again, well and strong and fond as ever, even though his little son should see the purple asters blossom on his grave many, many times before they met. To this belief Demi held fast, and in it found both help and comfort, because it led him unconsciously through a tender longing for the father whom he had seen to a childlike trust in the Father whom he had not seen. Both were in heaven, and he prayed to both, trying to be good for love of them.

The outward change corresponded to the inward, for in those few weeks Demi seemed to have grown tall, and began to drop his childish plays, not as if ashamed of them, as some boys do, but as if he had outgrown them, and wanted something manlier. He took to the hated arithmetic, and held on so steadily that his uncle was charmed, though he could not understand the whim, until Demi said, 'I am going to be a bookkeeper when I grow up, like papa, and I must know about figures and things, else I can't have nice, neat ledgers like his.'

At another time he came to his aunt with a very serious face, and said, 'What can a small boy do to earn money?'

'Why do you ask, my deary?'

'My father told me to take care of mother and the little girls, and I want to, but I don't know how to begin.'

'He did not mean now, Demi, but by and by, when you are large.'

'But I wish to begin *now*, if I can, because I think I ought to make some money to buy things for the family. I am ten, and other boys no bigger than I earn pennies sometimes.'

'Well, then, suppose you rake up all the dead leaves and cover the strawberry bed. I'll pay you a dollar for the job,' said Aunt Jo.

'Isn't that a great deal? I could do it in one day. You must be fair, and no pay too much, because I want to truly earn it.'

'My little John, I will be fair, and not pay a penny too much. Don't work too hard; and when that is done I will have something else for you to do,' said Mrs Jo, much touched by his desire to help, and his sense of justice, so like his scrupulous father.

When the leaves were done, many barrowloads of chips were wheeled from the wood to the shed, and another dollar earned. Then Demi helped cover the schoolbooks, working in the evenings under Franz's direction, tugging patiently away at each book, letting no one help, and receiving his wages with such satisfaction that the dingy bills became quite glorified in his sight.

'Now, I have a dollar for each of them, and I should like to take my money to mother all myself, so she can see that I have minded my father.'

So Demi made a duteous pilgrimage to his mother, who received his little earnings as a treasure of great worth, and would have kept it untouched, if Demi had not begged her to buy some *useful* thing for herself and the women-children, whom he felt were left to his care.

This made him very happy, and, though he often forgot his responsibilities for a time, the desire to help was still there, strengthening with his years. He always uttered the words 'my father' with an air of gentle pride, and often said, as if he claimed a title full of honour, 'Don't call me Demi any more. I am John Brooke now.' So, strengthened by a purpose and a hope, the little lad of ten bravely began the world, and entered into his inheritance, the memory of a wise and tender father, the legacy of an honest name.

CHAPTER 20

Round the Fire

With the October frosts came the cheery fires in the great fire-places; and Demi's dry pine-chips helped Dan's oak-knots to blaze royally, and go roaring up the chimney with a jolly sound. All were glad to gather round the hearth, as the evenings grew longer, to play games, read, or lay plans for the winter. But the favourite amusement was story-telling, and Mr and Mrs Bhaer were expected to have a store of lively tales always on hand. Their supply occasionally gave out, and then the boys were thrown upon their own resources, which were not always successful. Ghost parties were the rage at one time; for the fun of the thing consisted in putting out the lights, letting the fire die down, and then sitting in the dark, and telling the most awful tales they could invent. As this resulted in scares of all sorts among the boys, Tommy's walking in his sleep on the shed roof, and a general state of nervousness in the little ones, it was forbidden, and they fell back on more harmless amusements.

One evening, when the small boys were snugly tucked in bed, and the older lads were lounging about the school-room fire, trying to decide what they should do, Demi suggested a new way of settling the question.

Seizing the hearth-brush, he marched up and down the room, saying, 'Row, row, row;' and when the boys, laughing and pushing, had got into line, he said, 'Now, I'll give you two minutes to think of a play.' Franz was writing, and Emil reading *The Life of Lord Nelson*, and neither joined the party, but the others thought hard, and when the time was up were ready to reply.

'Now, Tom!' and the poker softly rapped him on the head.

'Blind man's buff.'

'Jack!'

'Commerce; a good round game, and have cents for the pool.'

'Uncle forbids our playing for money. Dan, what do you want?'

'Let's have a battle between the Greeks and Romans.'

'Stuffy?'

'Roast apples, popcorn, and crack nuts.'

'Good! good!' cried several; and when the vote was taken, Stuffy's proposal carried the day.

Some went to the cellar for apples, some to the garret for nuts, and others looked up the popper and the corn.

'We had better ask the girls to come in, hadn't we?' said Demi, in a sudden fit of politeness.

'Daisy pricks chestnuts beautifully,' put in Nat, who wanted his little friend to share the fun.

'Nan pops corn tiptop, we must have her,' added Tommy.

'Bring in your sweethearts then, we don't mind,' said Jack, who laughed at the innocent regard the little people had for one another.

'You shan't call my sister a sweetheart; it is so silly!' cried Demi, in a way that made Jack laugh.

'She *is* Nat's darling, isn't she, old chirper?'

'Yes, if Demi don't mind. I can't help being fond of her, she is so good to me,' answered Nat, with bashful earnestness, for Jack's rough ways disturbed him.

'Nan is my sweetheart, and I shall marry her in about a year, so don't you get in the way, any of you,' said Tommy, stoutly; for he and Nan had settled their future, child fashion, and were to live in the willow, lower down a basket for food, and do other charmingly impossible things.

Demi was quenched by the decision of Bangs, who took him by the arm and walked him off to get the ladies. Nan and Daisy were sewing with Aunt Jo on certain small garments for Mrs Carney's newest baby.

'Please, ma'am, could you lend us the girls for a little while? We'll be very careful of them,' said Tommy, winking one eye to express apples, snapping his fingers to signify popcorn, and gnashing his teeth to convey the idea of nut cracking.

The girls understood this pantomime at once, and began to pull off their thimbles before Mrs Jo could decide whether Tommy was going into convulsions or was brewing some unusual piece of mischief. Demi explained with elaboration, permission was readily granted, and the boys departed with their prize.

'Don't you speak to Jack,' whispered Tommy, as he and Nan promenaded down the hall to get a fork to prick the apples.

'Why not?'

'He laughs at me, so I don't wish you to have anything to do with him.'

'Shall, if I like,' said Nan, promptly resenting this premature assumption of authority on the part of her lord.

'Then I won't have you for my sweetheart.'

'I don't care.'

'Why, Nan, I thought you were fond of me!' and Tommy's voice was full of tender reproach.

'If you mind Jack's laughing I don't care for you one bit.'

'Then you may take back your old ring; I won't wear it any longer;' and Tommy plucked off a horsehair pledge of affection which Nan had given him in return for one made of a lobster's feeler.

'I shall give it to Ned,' was her cruel reply; for Ned liked Mrs Giddygaddy, and had turned her clothes-pins, boxes, and spools enough to set up housekeeping with.

Tommy said, 'Thunder-turtles!' as the only vent equal to the pent-up anguish of the moment, and, dropping Nan's arm, retired in high dudgeon, leaving her to follow with the fork, a neglect which naughty Nan punished by proceeding to prick his heart with jealousy as if it were another sort of apple.

The hearth was swept, and the rosy Baldwins put down to roast. A shovel was heated, and the chestnuts danced merrily upon it, while the corn popped wildly in its wire prison. Dan cracked his best walnuts, and everyone chattered and laughed, while the rain beat on the windowpane and the wind howled round the house.

'Why is Billy like this nut?' asked Emil, who was frequently inspired with bad conundrums.

'Because he is cracked,' answered Ned.

'That's not fair; you mustn't make fun of Billy, because he can't hit back again. It's mean,' cried Dan, smashing a nut wrathfully.

'To what family of insects does Blake belong?' asked peace-maker Franz, seeing that Emil looked ashamed and Dan lowering.

'Gnats,' answered Jack.

'Why is Daisy like a bee?' cried Nat, who had been wrapped in thought for several minutes.

'Because she is queen of the hive,' said Dan.

'No.'

'Because she is sweet.'

'Bees are not sweet.'

'Give it up.'

'Because she makes sweet things, is always busy, and likes flowers,' said Nat, piling up his boyish compliments till Daisy blushed like a rosy clover.

'Why is Nan like a hornet?' demanded Tommy, glowering at her, and adding, without giving anyone time to answer, 'Because she *isn't* sweet, makes a great buzzing about nothing, and stings like fury.'

'Tommy's mad, and I'm glad,' cried Ned, as Nan tossed her head and answered quickly 'What thing in the china closet is Tom like?'

'A pepper pot,' answered Ned, giving Nan a nut meat with a tantalising laugh that made Tommy feel as if he would like to bounce up like a hot chestnut and hit somebody.

Seeing that ill-humour was getting the better of the small supply of wit in the company, Franz cast himself into the breach again.

'Let's make a law that the first person who comes into the room shall tell us a story. No matter who it is, he must do it, and it will be fun to see who comes first.'

The others agreed, and did not have to wait long, for a heavy step soon came clumping through the hall, and Silas appeared, bearing an armful of wood. He was greeted by a general shout, and stood staring about him with a bewildered grin on his big red face, till Franz explained the joke.

'Sho! I can't tell a story,' he said, putting down his load and preparing to leave the room. But the boys fell upon him, forced him into a seat, and held him there, laughing, and clamouring for their story, till the good-natured giant was overpowered.

'I don't know but jest one story, and that's about a horse,' he said, much flattered by the reception he received.

'Tell it! tell it!' cried the boys.

'Wal,' began Silas, tipping his chair back against the wall, and putting his thumbs in the armholes of his waistcoat, 'I jined a cavalry regiment durin' the war, and see a consid'able amount of fightin'. My horse, Major, was a fust-rate animal, and I was as fond on him as ef he'd ben a human critter. He warn't harnsome, but he was the best-tempered, stiddyest, lovenest brute I ever see. The fust battle we went into, he gave me a lesson that I didn't forgit in a hurry, and I'll tell you how it was. It ain't no use tryin' to picter the noise and hurry, and general horridness of a battle to you young fellers, for I ain't no words to do it in; but I'm free to confess that I got so sort of confused and upset at the fust on it, that I didn't know what I was about. We was ordered to charge, and went ahead like good ones, never stoppin' to pick up them that went down in the scrimmage. I got a shot in the arm, and was pitched out of the saddle – don't know how, but there I was left behind with two or three others, dead and wounded, for the rest went on, as I say. Wal, I picked myself up and looked round for Major, feeling as ef I'd had about enough for that spell. I didn't see him nowhere, and was kinder walking back to camp, when I heard a whinny that sounded nateral. I looked round, and there was Major stopping for me a long way off, and lookin' as ef he didn't understand why I was loiterin' behind. I whistled, and he trotted up to me as I'd trained him to do. I mounted as well as I could with my left arm bleedin' and was for going on to camp, for I declare I felt as sick and wimbly as a woman; folks often do in their fust battle. But, no sir! Major was the bravest of the two, and he wouldn't go, not a peg; he jest rared up, and danced, and snorted, and acted as ef the smell of powder and the noise had drove him half wild. I done my best, but he wouldn't give in, so I did; and what do you think that plucky brute done? He wheeled slap round, and galloped back like a hurricane, right into the thickest of the scrimmage!'

'Good for him!' cried Dan excitedly, while the other boys forgot apples and nuts in their interest.

'I wish I may die ef I warn't ashamed of myself,' continued Silas, warming up at the recollection of that day. 'I was as mad as a hornet, and I forgot my waound, and jest pitched in, rampagin' raound like fury till there come a shell into the midst of us, and in bustin' knocked a lot of us flat. I didn't know nothin' for a spell, and when I come-to, the fight was over just there, and I found myself layin' by a wall with poor Major long-side wuss wounded than I was. My leg was broke, and I had a ball in my shoulder, but he, poor old feller! was all tore in the side with a piece of that blasted shell.'

'Oh, Silas! what did you do?' cried Nan, pressing close to him with a face full of eager sympathy and interest.

'I dragged myself nigher, and tried to stop the bleedin' with sech rags as I could tear off of me with one hand. But it warn't no use, and he lay moanin' with horrid pain, and lookin' at me with them lovin' eyes of his, till I thought I couldn't bear it. I give him all the help I could, and when the sun got hotter and hotter, and he began to lap out his tongue, I tried to get to a brook that was a good piece away, but I couldn't do it, being stiff and faint, so I give it up and fanned him with my hat. Now you listen to this, and when you hear folks comin' down on the rebs, you jest remember what one on 'em did, and give him credit of it. A poor feller in grey laid not fur off, shot through the lungs and dyin' fast. I'd offered him my handkerchief to keep the sun off his face, and he'd thanked me kindly, for in sech times as that men don't stop to think on which side they belong, but jest buckle-to and help one another. When he see me mournin' over Major and tryin' to ease his pain, he looked up with his face all damp and white with sufferin', and sez he, "There's water in my canteen; take it, for it can't help me," and he flung it to me. I couldn't have took it ef I hadn't had a little brandy in a pocket flask, and I made him drink it. It done him good, and I felt as much set up as if I'd drunk it myself. It's surprisin' the good sech little things do folks sometime;' and Silas paused as if he felt again the comfort of that moment when he and his enemy forgot their feud, and helped one another like brothers.

'Tell about Major,' cried the boys, impatient for the catastrophe.

'I poured the water over his poor pantin' tongue, and ef ever a dumb critter looked grateful, he did then. But it warn't of much use, for the dreadful waound kep on tormentin' him, till I couldn't bear it any longer. It was hard, but I done it in mercy, and I know he forgive me.'

'What did you do?' asked Emil, as Silas stopped abruptly with a loud 'hem', and a look in his rough face that made Daisy go and stand by him with her little hand on his knee.

'I shot him.'

Quite a thrill went through the listeners as Silas said that, for Major seemed a hero in their eyes, and his tragic end roused all their sympathy.

'Yes, I shot him, and put him out of his misery. I patted him fust, and said, "Goodbye"; then I laid his head easy on the grass, give a last look into his lovin' eyes, and sent a bullet through his head. He hardly stirred, I aimed so true, and when I seen him quite still, with no more moanin' and pain, I was glad, and yet – wal, I don't know as I need be ashamed on't – I jest put my arms raound his neck and boo-hooed like a great baby. Sho! I didn't know I was sech a fool;' and Silas drew his sleeve across his eyes, as much touched by Daisy's sob, as by the memory of faithful Major.

No one spoke for a minute, because the boys were as quick to feel the pathos of the little story as tender-hearted Daisy, though they did not show it by crying.

'I'd like a horse like that,' said Dan, half-aloud.

'Did the rebel man die, too?' asked Nan, anxiously.

'Not then. We laid there all day, and at night some of our fellers came to look after the missing ones. They nat'rally wanted to take me fust, but I knew I could wait, and the rebel had but one chance, maybe, so I made them carry him off right away. He had jest strength enough to hold out his hand to me and say, "Thanky, comrade!" and them was the last words he spoke, for he died an hour after he got to the hospital-tent.'

'How glad you must have been that you were kind to him!' said Demi, who was deeply impressed by this story.

'Wal, I did take comfort thinkin' of it, as I laid there alone for a number of hours with my head on Major's neck, and see the moon come up. I'd like to have buried the poor beast decent, but it warn't possible; so I cut off a bit of his mane, and I've kep it ever sence. Want to see it, sissy?'

'Oh, yes, please,' answered Daisy, wiping away her tears to look.

Silas took out an old 'wallet', as he called his pocketbook, and produced from an inner fold a bit of brown paper, in which was a rough lock of white horsehair. The children looked at it silently, as it lay in the broad palm, and no one found anything to ridicule in the love Silas bore his good horse Major.

'That is a sweet story, and I like it, though it did make me cry. Thank you very much, Si,' and Daisy helped him fold and put away his little relic; while Nan stuffed a handful of popcorn into his pocket, and the boys loudly expressed their flattering opinions of his story, feeling that there had been two heroes in it.

He departed, quite overcome by his honours, and the little conspirators talked the tale over, while they waited for their next victim. It was Mrs Jo, who came in to measure Nan for some new pinafores she was making for her. They let her get well in, and then pounced upon her, telling her the law, and demanding the story. Mrs Jo was very much amused at the new trap, and consented at once, for the sound of happy voices had been coming across the hall so pleasantly that she quite longed to join them, and forget her own anxious thoughts of Sister Meg.

'Am I the first mouse you have caught, you sly pussies-in-boots?' she asked, as she was conducted to the big chair, supplied with refreshments, and surrounded by a flock of merry-faced listeners.

They told her about Silas and his contribution, and she slapped her forehead in despair, for she was quite at her wits' end, being called upon so unexpectedly for a brand new tale.

'What shall I tell about?' she said.

'Boys,' was the general answer.

'Have a party in it,' said Daisy.

'And something good to eat,' added Stuffy.

'That reminds me of a story, written years ago, by a dear old lady. I used to be very fond of it, and I fancy you will like it, for it has both boys, and "something good to eat" in it.'

'What is it called?' asked Demi.

'*The Suspected Boy*.'

Nat looked up from the nuts he was picking, and Mrs Jo smiled at him, guessing what was in his mind.

'Miss Crane kept a school for boys in a quiet little town, and a very good school it was, of the old-fashioned sort. Six boys lived in her house, and four or five more came in from the town. Among those who lived with her was one named Lewis White. Lewis was not a bad boy, but rather timid, and now and then he told a lie.

One day a neighbour sent Miss Crane a basket of gooseberries. There were not enough to go round, so kind Miss Crane, who liked to please her boys, went to work and made a dozen nice little gooseberry tarts.'

'I'd like to try gooseberry tarts. I wonder if she made them as I do my raspberry ones,' said Daisy, whose interest in cooking had lately revived.

'Hush,' said Nat, tucking a plump popcorn into her mouth to silence her, for he felt a particular interest in this tale, and thought it opened well.

'When the tarts were done, Miss Crane put them away in the best parlour closet, and said not a word about them, for she wanted to surprise the boys at tea-time. When the minute came and all were seated at table, she went to get her tarts, but came back looking much troubled, for what do you think had happened?'

'Somebody had hooked them!' cried Ned.

'No, there they were, but someone had stolen all the fruit out of them by lifting up the upper crust and then putting it down after the gooseberry had been scraped out.'

'What a mean trick!' and Nan looked at Tommy, as if to imply that he would do the same.

'When she told the boys her plan and showed them the poor little patties all robbed of their sweetness, the boys were much grieved and disappointed, and all declared that they knew nothing about the matter. "Perhaps the rats did it," said Lewis, who was among the loudest to deny any knowledge of the tarts. "No, rats would have nibbled crust and all, and never lifted it up and scooped out the fruit. Hands did that," said Miss Crane, who was more troubled about the lie that someone must have told than about her lost patties. Well, they had supper and went to bed, but in the night Miss Crane heard someone groaning, and going to see who it was she found Lewis in great pain. He had evidently eaten something that disagreed with him, and was so sick that Miss Crane was alarmed, and was going to send for the doctor, when Lewis moaned out, "It's the gooseberries; I ate them, and I must tell before I die," for the thought of a doctor frightened him. "If that is all, I'll give you an emetic and you will soon get over it," said Miss Crane. So Lewis had a good dose, and by morning was quite comfortable. "Oh, don't tell the boys; they will

laugh at me so," begged the invalid. Kind Miss Crane promised
not to, but Sally, the girl, told the story, and poor Lewis had no
peace for a long time. His mates called him Old Gooseberry, and
were never tired of asking him the price of tarts.'

'Served him right,' said Emil.

'Badness always gets found out,' added Demi, morally.

'No, it don't,' muttered Jack, who was tending the apples with
great devotion, so that he might keep his back to the rest and
account for his red face.

'Is that all?' asked Dan.

'No, that is only the first part; the second part is more interesting. Some time after this a peddler came by one day and stopped
to show his things to the boys, several of whom bought pocket-
combs, jew's-harps, and various trifles of that sort. Among the
knives was a little white-handled penknife that Lewis wanted very
much, but he had spent all his pocket money, and no one had any
to lend him. He held the knife in his hand, admiring and longing
for it, till the man packed up his goods to go, then he reluctantly
laid it down, and the man went on his way. The next day, however,
the peddler returned to say that he could not find that very knife,
and thought he must have left it at Miss Crane's. It was a very nice
one with a pearl handle, and he could not afford to lose it. Everyone looked, and everyone declared they knew nothing about it.
"This young gentleman had it last, and seemed to want it very
much. Are you quite sure you put it back?" said the man to Lewis,
who was much troubled at the loss, and vowed over and over again
that he did return it. His denials seemed to do no good, however,
for everyone was sure he had taken it, and after a stormy scene
Miss Crane paid for it, and the man went grumbling away.'

'Did Lewis have it?' cried Nat, much excited.

'You will see. Now poor Lewis had another trial to bear, for the
boys were constantly saying, "Lend me your pearl-handled knife,
Gooseberry," and things of that sort, till Lewis was so unhappy he
begged to be sent home. Miss Crane did her best to keep the boys
quiet, but it was hard work, for they would tease, and she could
not be with them all the time. That is one of the hardest things to
teach boys; they won't "hit a fellow when he is down", as they say,
but they will torment him in little ways till he would thank them
to fight it out all round.'

'I know that,' said Dan.

'So do I,' added Nat, softly.

Jack said nothing, but he quite agreed; for he knew that the elder boys despised him, and let him alone for that very reason.

'Do go on about poor Lewis, Aunt Jo. I don't believe he took the knife, but I want to be sure,' said Daisy, in great anxiety.

'Well, week after week went on and the matter was not cleared up. The boys avoided Lewis, and he, poor fellow, was almost sick with the trouble he had brought upon himself. He resolved never to tell another lie, and tried so hard that Miss Crane pitied and helped him, and really came at last to believe that he did not take the knife. Two months after the peddler's first visit, he came again, and the first thing he said was, "Well, ma'am, I found that knife after all. It had slipped behind the lining of my valise, and fell out the other day when I was putting in a new stock of goods. I thought I'd call and let you know, as you paid for it, and maybe would like it, so here it is."

'The boys had all gathered round, and at these words they felt much ashamed, and begged Lewis's pardon so heartily that he could not refuse to give it. Miss Crane presented the knife to him, and he kept it many years to remind him of the fault that had brought him so much trouble.'

'I wonder why it is that things you eat on the sly hurt you, and don't when you eat them at table,' observed Stuffy, thoughtfully.

'Perhaps your conscience affects your stomach,' said Mrs Jo, smiling at his speech.

'He is thinking of the cucumbers,' said Ned, and a gale of merriment followed the words, for Stuffy's last mishap had been a funny one.

He ate two large cucumbers in private, felt very ill, and confided his anguish to Ned, imploring him to do something. Ned good-naturedly recommended a mustard plaster and a hot flat iron to the feet; only in applying these remedies he reversed the order of things, and put the plaster on the feet, the flat iron on the stomach, and poor Stuffy was found in the barn with blistered soles and a scorched jacket.

'Suppose you tell another story, that was such an interesting one,' said Nat, as the laughter subsided.

Before Mrs Jo could refuse these insatiable Oliver Twists, Rob walked into the room trailing his little bed-cover after him, and wearing an expression of great sweetness as he said, steering straight to his mother as a sure haven of refuge, 'I heard a great noise, and I thought sumfin dreffle might have happened, so I came to see.'

'Did you think I would forget you, naughty boy?' asked his mother, trying to look stern.

'No; but I thought you'd feel better to see me right here,' responded the insinuating little party.

'I had much rather see you in bed, so march straight up again, Robin.'

'Everybody that comes in here has to tell a story, and you can't, so you'd better cut and run,' said Emil.

'Yes, I can! I tell Teddy lots of ones, all about bears and moons, and little flies that say things when they buzz,' protested Rob, bound to stay at any price.

'Tell one now, then, right away,' said Dan, preparing to shoulder and bear him off.

'Well, I will; let me fink a minute,' and Rob climbed into his mother's lap, where he was cuddled, with the remark, 'It is a family failing, this getting out of bed at wrong times. Demi used to do it; and as for me, I was hopping in and out all night long. Meg used to think the house was on fire, and send me down to see, and I used to stay and enjoy myself, as you mean to, my bad son.'

'I've finked now,' observed Rob, quite at his ease, and eager to win the entrée into this delightful circle.

Everyone looked and listened with faces full of suppressed merriment as Rob, perched on his mother's knee and wrapped in the gay coverlet, told the following brief but tragic tale with an earnestness that made it very funny: 'Once a lady had a million children, and one nice little boy. She went upstairs and said, "You mustn't go in the yard." But he wented, and fell into the pump, and was drowned dead.'

'Is that all?' asked Franz, as Rob paused out of breath with this startling beginning.

'No, there is another piece of it,' and Rob knit his downy eyebrows in the effort to evolve another inspiration.

'What did the lady do when he fell into the pump?' asked his mother, to help him on.

'Oh, she pumped him up, and wrapped him in a newspaper, and put him on a shelf to dry for seed.'

A general explosion of laughter greeted this surprising conclusion, and Mrs Jo patted the curly head, as she said, solemnly, 'My son, you inherit your mother's gift of story-telling. Go where glory waits thee.'

'Now I can stay, can't I? Wasn't it a good story?' cried Rob, in high feather at his superb success.

'You can stay till you have eaten these twelve popcorns,' said his mother, expecting to see them vanish at one mouthful.

But Rob was a shrewd little man, and got the better of her by eating them one by one very slowly, and enjoying every minute with all his might.

'Hadn't you better tell the other story, while you wait for him?' said Demi, anxious that no time should be lost.

'I really have nothing but a little tale about a wood-box,' said Mrs Jo, seeing that Rob had still seven corns to eat.

'Is there a boy in it?'

'It is all boy.'

'Is it true?' asked Demi.

'Every bit of it.'

'Goody! tell on, please.'

'James Snow and his mother lived in a little house, up in New Hampshire. They were poor, and James had to work to help his mother, but he loved books so well he hated work, and just wanted to sit and study all day long.'

'How could he! I hate books, and like work,' said Dan, objecting to James at the very outset.

'It takes all sorts of people to make a world; workers and students both are needed, and there is room for all. But I think the workers should study some, and the students should know how to work if necessary,' answered Mrs Jo, looking from Dan to Demi with a significant expression.

'I'm sure I do work,' and Demi showed three small hard spots in his little palm, with pride.

'And I'm sure I study,' added Dan, nodding with a groan toward the blackboard full of neat figures.

'See what James did. He did not mean to be selfish, but his mother was proud of him, and let him do as he liked, working by herself that he might have books and time to read them. One autumn James wanted to go to school, and went to the minister to see if he would help him, about decent clothes and books. Now the minister had heard the gossip about James's idleness, and was not inclined to do much for him, thinking that a boy who neglected his mother, and let her slave for him, was not likely to do very well even at school. But the good man felt more interested when he found how earnest James was, and being rather an odd man, he made this proposal to the boy, to try now sincere he was.

' "I will give you clothes and books on one condition, James."

' "What is that, sir?" and the boy brightened up at once.

' "You are to keep your mother's wood-box full all winter long, and do it yourself. If you fail, school stops." James laughed at the queer condition and readily agreed to it, thinking it a very easy one.

'He began school, and for a time got on capitally with the wood-box, for it was autumn, and chips and brushwood were plentiful. He ran out morning and evening and got a basket full, or chopped up the cat sticks for the little cooking stove, and as his mother was careful and saving, the task was not hard. But in November the frost came, the days were dull and cold, and wood went fast. His mother bought a load with her own earnings, but it seemed to melt away, and was nearly gone, before James remembered that *he* was to get the next. Mrs Snow was feeble and lame with rheumatism, and unable to work as she had done, so James had to put down the books, and see what he could do.

'It was hard, for he was going on well, and so interested in his lessons that he hated to stop except for food and sleep. But he knew the minister would keep his word, and much against his will James set about earning money in his spare hours, lest the wood-box should get empty. He did all sorts of things, ran errands, took care of a neighbour's cow, helped the old sexton dust and warm the church on Sundays, and in these ways got enough to buy fuel in small quantities. But it was hard work; the days were short, the winter was bitterly cold, and precious time went fast, and the dear books were so fascinating, that it was sad to leave them, for dull duties that never seemed done.

'The minister watched him quietly, and seeing that he was in earnest helped him without his knowledge. He met him often driving the wood sleds from the forest, where the men were chopping and as James plodded beside the slow oxen, he read or studied, anxious to use every minute. "The boy is worth helping, this lesson will do him good, and when he has learned it, I will give him an easier one," said the minister to himself, and on Christmas Eve a splendid load of wood was quietly dropped at the door of the little house, with a new saw and a bit of paper, saying only, "The Lord helps those who help themselves."

'Poor James expected nothing, but when he woke on that cold Christmas morning, he found a pair of warm mittens, knit by his mother, with her stiff painful fingers. This gift pleased him very much, but her kiss and tender look as she called him her "good son", was better still. In trying to keep her warm, he had warmed his own heart, you see, and in filling the wood-box he had also filled those months with duties faithfully done. He began to see this, to feel that there was something better than books, and to try to learn the lessons God set him, as well as those his schoolmaster gave.

'When he saw the great pile of oak and pine logs at his door, and read the little paper, he knew who sent it, and understood the minister's plan; thanked him for it, and fell to work with all his might. Other boys frolicked that day, but James sawed wood, and I think of all the lads in the town the happiest was the one in the new mittens, who whistled like a blackbird as he filled his mother's wood-box.'

'That's a first-rater!' cried Dan, who enjoyed a simple matter-of-fact story better than the finest fairy-tale; 'I like that fellow after all.'

'I could saw wood for you, Aunt Jo!' said Demi, feeling as if a new means of earning money for his mother was suggested by the story.

'Tell about a bad boy. I like them best,' said Nan.

'You'd better tell about a naughty crosspatch of a girl,' said Tommy, whose evening had been spoilt by Nan's unkindness. It made his apple taste bitter, his popcorn was insipid, his nuts were hard to crack, and the sight of Ned and Nan on one bench made him feel his life a burden.

But there were no more stories from Mrs Jo, for on looking down at Rob he was discovered to be fast asleep with his last corn firmly clasped in his chubby hand. Bundling him up in his coverlet, his mother carried him away and tucked him up with no fear of his popping out again.

'Now let's see who will come next,' said Emil, setting the door temptingly ajar.

Mary Ann passed first, and he called out to her, but Silas had warned her, and she only laughed and hurried on in spite of their enticements. Presently a door opened, and a strong voice was heard humming in the hall,

> 'Ich weiss nicht was soll es bedeuten
> Dass ich so traurig bin.'

'It's Uncle Fritz; all laugh loud and he will be sure to come in,' said Emil.

A wild burst of laughter followed, and in came Uncle Fritz, asking, 'What is the joke, my lads?'

'Caught! caught! you can't go out till you've told a story,' cried the boys, slamming the door.

'So! that is the joke then? Well, I have no wish to go, it is so pleasant here, and I pay my forfeit at once,' which he did by sitting down and beginning instantly.

'A long time ago your Grandfather, Demi, went to lecture in a great town, hoping to get some money for a home for little orphans that some good people were getting up. His lecture did well, and he put a considerable sum of money in his pocket, feeling very happy about it. As he was driving in a chaise to another town, he came to a lonely bit of road, late in the afternoon, and was just thinking what a good place it was for robbers when he saw a bad-looking man come out of the woods in front of him and go slowly along as if waiting till he came up. The thought of the money made Grandfather rather anxious, and at first he had a mind to turn round and drive away. But the horse was tired, and then he did not like to suspect the man, so he kept on, and when he got nearer and saw how poor and sick and ragged the stranger looked, his heart reproached him, and stopping, he said in a kind voice, "My friend, you look tired; let me give you a lift." The man seemed surprised, hesitated a minute, and then got in.

'He did not seem inclined to talk, but Grandfather kept on in his wise, cheerful way, speaking of what a hard year it had been, how much the poor had suffered, and how difficult it was to get on sometimes. The man slowly softened a little, and won by the kind chat, told his story. How he had been sick, could get no work, had a family of children, and was almost in despair. Grandfather was so full of pity that he forgot his fear, and, asking the man his name, said he would try to get him work in the next town, as he had friends there. Wishing to get at pencil and paper to write down the address, Grandfather took out his plump pocketbook, and the minute he did so, the man's eye was on it. Then Grandfather remembered what was in it and trembled for his money, but said quietly, "Yes, I have a little sum here for some poor orphans. I wish it was my own, I would so gladly give you some of it. I am not rich, but I know many of the trials of the poor; this five dollars is mine, and I want to give it to you for your children."

'The hard, hungry look in the man's eyes changed to a grateful one as he took the small sum, freely given, and left the orphans' money untouched. He rode on with Grandfather till they approached the town, then he asked to be set down. Grandpa shook hands with him, and was about to drive on, when the man said, as if something made him, "I was desperate when we met, and I meant to rob you, but you were so kind I couldn't do it. God bless you, sir, for keeping me from it!" '

'Did Grandpa ever see him again?' asked Daisy, eagerly.

'No; but I believe the man found work, and did not try robbery any more.'

'That was a curious way to treat him; I'd have knocked him down,' said Dan.

'Kindness is always better than force. Try it and see,' answered Mr Bhaer, rising.

'Tell another, please,' cried Daisy.

'You must, Aunt Jo did,' added Demi.

'Then I certainly won't, but keep my others for next time. Too many tales are as bad as too many bonbons. I have paid my forfeit and I go,' and Mr Bhaer ran for his life, with the whole flock in full pursuit. He had the start, however, and escaped safely into his study, leaving the boys to go rioting back again.

They were so stirred up by the race that they could not settle to their former quiet, and a lively game of blind man's buff followed, in which Tommy showed that he had taken the moral of the last story to heart, for, when he caught Nan, he whispered in her ear, 'I'm sorry I called you a crosspatch.'

Nan was not to be outdone in kindness, so, when they played 'Button, button, who's got the button?' and it was her turn to go round, she said, 'Hold fast all I give you,' with such a friendly smile at Tommy, that he was not surprised to find the horsehair ring in his hand instead of the button. He only smiled back at her then, but when they were going to bed, he offered Nan the best bite of his last apple; she saw the ring on his stumpy little finger, accepted the bite, and peace was declared. Both were ashamed of the temporary coldness, neither was ashamed to say, 'I was wrong, forgive me,' so the childish friendship remained unbroken, and the home in the willow lasted long, a pleasant little castle in the air.

CHAPTER 21

Thanksgiving

This yearly festival was always kept at Plumfield in the good old-fashioned way, and nothing was allowed to interfere with it. For days beforehand, the little girls helped Asia and Mrs Jo in store-room and kitchen, making pies and puddings, sorting fruit, dusting dishes, and being very busy and immensely important. The boys hovered on the outskirts of the forbidden ground, sniffing the savoury odours, peeping in at the mysterious performances, and occasionally being permitted to taste some delicacy in the process of preparation.

Something more than usual seemed to be on foot this year, for the girls were as busy upstairs as down, so were the boys in school-room and barn, and a general air of bustle pervaded the house. There was a great hunting up of old ribbons and finery, much cutting and pasting of gold paper, and the most remarkable quantity of straw, grey cotton, flannel, and big black beads, used by Franz and Mrs Jo. Ned hammered at strange machines in the workshop, Demi and Tommy went about murmuring to themselves as if learning something. A fearful racket was heard in

Emil's room at intervals, and peals of laughter from the nursery when Rob and Teddy were sent for and hidden from sight whole hours at a time. But the thing that puzzled Mr Bhaer the most was what became of Rob's big pumpkin. It had been borne in triumph to the kitchen, where a dozen golden-tinted pies soon after appeared. It would not have taken more than a quarter of the mammoth vegetable to make them, yet where was the rest? It disappeared, and Rob never seemed to care, only chuckled when it was mentioned, and told his father, 'To wait and see', for the fun of the whole thing was to surprise Father Bhaer at the end, and not let him know a bit about what was to happen.

He obediently shut eyes, ears, and mouth, and went about trying not to see what was in plain sight, not to hear the tell-tale sounds that filled the air, not to understand any of the perfectly transparent mysteries going on all about him. Being a German, he loved these simple domestic festivals, and encouraged them with all his heart, for they made home so pleasant that the boys did not care to go elsewhere for fun.

When at last the day came, the boys went off for a long walk, that they might have good appetites for dinner; as if they ever needed them! The girls remained at home to help set the table, and give last touches to various affairs which filled their busy little souls with anxiety. The school-room had been shut up since the night before, and Mr Bhaer was forbidden to enter it on pain of a beating from Teddy, who guarded the door like a small dragon, though he was dying to tell about it, and nothing but his father's heroic self-denial in not listening, kept him from betraying a grand secret.

'It's all done, and it's perfectly splendid,' cried Nan, coming out at last with an air of triumph.

'The – you know – goes beautifully, and Silas knows just what to do now,' added Daisy, skipping with delight at some unspeakable success.

'I'm blest if it ain't the 'cutest thing I ever see, them critters in particular,' and Silas, who had been let into the secret, went off laughing like a great boy.

'They are coming; I hear Emil roaring "Landlubbers lying down below", so we must run and dress,' cried Nan, and upstairs they scampered in a great hurry.

The boys came trooping home with appetites that would have made the big turkey tremble, if it had not been past all fear. They also retired to dress; and for half an hour there was a washing, brushing, and prinking that would have done any tidy woman's heart good to see. When the bell rang, a troop of fresh-faced lads with shiny hair, clean collars, and Sunday jackets on, filed into the dining-room, where Mrs Jo, in her one black silk, with a knot of her favourite white chrysanthemums in her bosom, sat at the head of the table, 'looking splendid', as the boys said, whenever she got herself up. Daisy and Nan were as gay as a posy bed in their new winter dresses, with bright sashes and hair ribbons. Teddy was gorgeous to behold in a crimson merino blouse, and his best button boots, which absorbed and distracted him as much as Mr Toot's wristbands did on one occasion.

As Mr and Mrs Bhaer glanced at each other down the long table, with those rows of happy faces on either side, they had a little thanksgiving all to themselves, and without a word, for one heart said to the other, 'Our work has prospered, let us be grateful and go on.'

The clatter of knives and forks prevented much conversation for a few minutes, and Mary Ann with an amazing pink bow in her hair 'flew round' briskly, handing plates and ladling out gravy. Nearly everyone had contributed to the feast, so the dinner was a peculiarly interesting ones to the eaters of it, who beguiled the pauses by remarks on their own productions.

'If these are not good potatoes I never saw any,' observed Jack, as he received his fourth big mealy one.

'Some of my herbs are in the stuffing of the turkey, that's why it's so nice,' said Nan, taking a mouthful with intense satisfaction.

'My ducks are prime anyway; Asia said she never cooked such fat ones,' added Tommy.

'Well, our carrots are beautiful, ain't they, and our parsnips will be ever so good when we dig them,' put in Dick, and Dolly murmured his assent from behind the bone he was picking.

'I helped make the pies with my pumpkin,' called out Robby, with a laugh which he stopped by retiring into his mug.

'I picked some of the apples that the cider is made of,' said Demi.

'I raked the cranberries for the sauce,' cried Nat.

'I got the nuts,' added Dan, and so it went on all round the table.

'Who made up Thanksgiving?' asked Rob, for being lately promoted to jacket and trousers he felt a new and manly interest in the institutions of his country.

'See who can answer that question,' and Mr Bhaer nodded to one or two of his best history boys.

'I know,' said Demi, 'the Pilgrims made it.'

'What for?' asked Rob, without waiting to learn who the Pilgrims were.

'I forget,' and Demi subsided.

'I believe it was because they were starved once, and so when they had a good harvest, they said, "We will thank God for it," and they had a day and called it Thanksgiving,' said Dan, who liked the story of the brave men who suffered so nobly for their faith.

'Good! I didn't think you would remember anything but natural history,' and Mr Bhaer tapped gently on the table as applause for his pupil.

Dan looked pleased; and Mrs Jo said to her son, 'Now do you understand about it, Robby?'

'No, I don't. I thought pil-grins were a sort of big bird that lived on rocks, and I saw pictures of them in Demi's book.'

'He means penguins. Oh, isn't he a little goosey!' and Demi leant back in his chair and laughed aloud.

'Don't laugh at him, but tell him all about it if you can,' said Mrs Bhaer, consoling Rob with more cranberry sauce for the general smile that went round the table at his mistake.

'Well, I will;' and, after a pause to collect his ideas, Demi delivered the following sketch of the Pilgrim Fathers, which would have made even those grave gentlemen smile if they could have heard it.

'You see, Rob, some of the people in England didn't like the king, or something, so they got into ships and sailed away to this country. It was all full of Indians, and bears, and wild creatures, and they lived in forts, and had a dreadful time.'

'The bears?' asked Robby, with interest.

'No; the Pilgrims, because the Indians troubled them. They hadn't enough to eat, and they went to church with guns, and ever so many died, and they got out of the ships on a rock, and it's called Plymouth Rock, and Aunt Jo saw it and touched it.

The Pilgrims killed all the Indians, and got rich; and hung the witches, and were very good; and some of the greatest great-grandpas came in the ships. One was the *Mayflower*; and they made Thanksgiving, and we have it always, and I like it. Some more turkey, please.'

'I think Demi will be an historian, there is such order and clearness in his account of events;' and Uncle Fritz's eyes laughed at Aunt Jo, as he helped the descendant of the Pilgrims to his third bit of turkey.

'I thought you must eat as much as ever you could on Thanksgiving. But Franz says you mustn't even then;' and Stuffy looked as if he had received bad news.

'Franz is right, so mind your knife and fork, and be moderate, or else you won't be able to help in the surprise by and by,' said Mrs Jo.

'I'll be careful; but everybody does eat lots, and I like it better than being moderate,' said Stuffy, who leaned to the popular belief that Thanksgiving must be kept by coming as near apoplexy as possible, and escaping with merely a fit of indigestion or a headache.

'Now, my "pilgrims" amuse yourselves quietly till tea-time, for you will have enough excitement this evening,' said Mrs Jo, as they rose from the table after a protracted sitting, finished by drinking everyone's health in cider.

'I think I will take the whole flock for a drive, it is so pleasant; then you can rest, my dear, or you will be worn out this evening,' added Mr Bhaer; and as soon as coats and hats could be put on, the great omnibus was packed full, and away they went for a long gay drive, leaving Mrs Jo to rest and finish sundry small affairs in peace.

An early and light tea was followed by more brushing of hair and washing of hands; then the flock waited impatiently for the company to come. Only the family was expected; for these small revels were strictly domestic, and such being the case, sorrow was not allowed to sadden the present festival. All came; Mr and Mrs March, with Aunt Meg, so sweet and lovely, in spite of her black dress and the little widow's cap that encircled her tranquil face. Uncle Teddy and Aunt Amy, with the Princess looking more fairylike than ever, in a sky-blue gown, and a great bouquet of hothouse flowers, which she divided among the boys, sticking one in each buttonhole, making them feel peculiarly elegant and festive. One strange face appeared, and Uncle Teddy led the unknown gentleman up to the Bhaers, saying, 'This is Mr Hyde; he has been enquiring about Dan, and I ventured to bring him tonight, that he might see how much the boy has improved.'

The Bhaers received him cordially, for Dan's sake, pleased that the lad had been remembered. But, after a few minutes' chat, they were glad to know Mr Hyde for his own sake, so genial, simple, and interesting was he. It was pleasant to see the boy's face light up when he caught sight of his friend; pleasanter still to see Mr Hyde's surprise and satisfaction in Dan's improved manners and appearance, and pleasantest of all to watch the two sit talking in a corner, forgetting the differences of age, culture, and position, in the one subject which interested both, as man and boy compared notes, and told the story of their summer life.

'The performance must begin soon, or the actors will go to sleep,' said Mrs Jo, when the first greetings were over.

So everyone went into the school-room, and took seats before a curtain made of two bed-covers. The children had already vanished; but stifled laughter, and funny little exclamations from behind the curtain, betrayed their whereabouts. The entertainment began with a spirited exhibition of gymnastics, led by Franz. The six elder lads, in blue trousers and red shirts, made a fine display of muscle with dumb-bells, clubs, and weights, keeping time to the music of the piano, played by Mrs Jo behind the scenes. Dan was so energetic in this exercise, that there was some danger of his knocking down his neighbours, like so many ninepins, or sending his beanbags whizzing among the audience; for he was excited by Mr Hyde's presence, and a burning desire to do honour to his teachers.

'A fine, strong lad. If I go on my trip to South America, in a year or two, I shall be tempted to ask you to lend him to me, Mr Bhaer,' said Mr Hyde, whose interest in Dan was much increased by the report he had just heard of him.

'You shall have him, and welcome, though we shall miss our young Hercules very much. It would do him a world of good, and I am sure he would serve his friend faithfully.'

Dan heard both question and answer, and his heart leaped with joy at the thought of travelling in a new country with Mr Hyde, and swelled with gratitude for the kindly commendation which rewarded his efforts to be all these friends desired to see him.

After the gymnastics, Demi and Tommy spoke the old school dialogue, 'Money makes the mare go'. Demi did very well, but Tommy was capital as the old farmer; for he imitated Silas in a way that convulsed the audience, and caused Silas himself to laugh so hard that Asia had to slap him on the back, as they stood in the hall enjoying the fun immensely.

Then Emil, who had got his breath by this time, gave them a sea-song in costume, with a great deal about 'stormy winds', 'lee shores', and a rousing chorus of 'Luff, boys, luff', which made the room ring; after which Ned performed a funny Chinese dance, and hopped about like a large frog in a pagoda hat. As this was the only public exhibition ever held at Plumfield, a few exercises in lightning-arithmetic, spelling, and reading were given. Jack quite amazed the public by his rapid calculations on the blackboard. Tommy won in the spelling match, and Demi read a little French fable so well that Uncle Teddy was charmed.

'Where are the other children?' asked everyone as the curtain fell, and none of the little ones appeared.

'Oh, that is the surprise. It's so lovely, I pity you because you don't know it,' said Demi, who had gone to get his mother's kiss, and stayed by her to explain the mystery when it should be revealed.

Goldilocks had been carried off by Aunt Jo, to the great amazement of her papa, who quite outdid Mr Bhaer in acting wonder, suspense, and wild impatience to know 'what was going to happen'.

At last, after much rustling, hammering, and very audible directions from the stage manager, the curtain rose to soft music, and Bess was discovered sitting on a stool beside a brown paper fireplace. A dearer little Cinderella was never seen; for the grey gown was very ragged, the tiny shoes all worn, the face so pretty under the bright hair, and the attitude so dejected, it brought tears, as well as smiles, to the fond eyes looking at the baby actress. She sat quite still, till a voice whispered, 'Now!' then she sighed a funny little sigh, and said, 'Oh I wish I tood go to the ball!' so naturally, that her father clapped frantically, and her mother called out, 'Little darling!' These highly improper expressions of feeling caused Cinderella to forget herself, and shake her head at them, saying, reprovingly, 'You mustn't 'peak to me.'

Silence instantly prevailed, and three taps were heard on the wall. Cinderella looked alarmed, but before she could remember to say, 'What is dat?' the back of the brown paper fireplace opened like a door, and, with some difficulty, the fairy godmother got herself and her pointed hat through. It was Nan, in a red cloak, a cap, and a wand, which she waved as she said decidedly, 'You *shall* go to the ball, my dear.'

'Now you must pull and show my pretty dess,' returned Cinderella, tugging at her brown gown.

'No, no; you must say, "How can I go in my rags?" ' said the godmother in her own voice.

'Oh yes, so I mus';' and the Princess said it, quite undisturbed by her forgetfulness.

'I change your rags into a splendid dress, because you are good,' said the godmother in her stage tones; and deliberately unbuttoning the brown pinafore, she displayed a gorgeous sight.

The little Princess really was pretty enough to turn the heads of any number of small princes, for her mamma had dressed her like a tiny court lady, in a rosy silk train with satin underskirt, and bits of bouquets here and there, quite lovely to behold. The godmother put a crown, with pink and white feathers drooping from it, on her head, and gave her a pair of silver paper slippers, which she put on, and then stood up, lifting her skirts to show them to the audience, saying, with pride, 'My dlass ones, ain't they pitty?'

She was so charmed with them, that she was with difficulty recalled to her part, and made to say, 'But I have no toach, Dodmother.'

'Behold it!' and Nan waved her wand with such a flourish, that she nearly knocked off the crown of the Princess.

Then appeared the grand triumph of the piece. First, a rope was seen to flap on the floor, to tighten with a twitch as Emil's voice was heard to say, 'Heave, ahoy!' and Silas's gruff one to reply, 'Stiddy, now, stiddy!' A shout of laughter followed, for four large grey rats appeared, rather shaky as to their legs, and queer as to their tails, but quite fine about the head, where black beads shone in the most lifelike manner. They drew, or were intended to appear as if they did, a magnificent coach made of half the mammoth pumpkin, mounted on the wheels of Teddy's wagon, painted yellow to match the gay carriage. Perched on a seat in front sat a jolly little coachman in a white cottonwool wig, cocked hat, scarlet breeches, and laced coat, who cracked a long whip and jerked the red reins so energetically, that the grey steeds reared finely. It was Teddy, and he beamed upon the company so affably that they gave him a round all to himself; and Uncle Laurie said, 'If I could find as sober a coachman as that one, I would engage him on the spot.' The coach stopped, the godmother lifted in the Princess, and she was trundled away in state, kissing her hand to the public, with her glass shoes sticking up in front, and her pink train sweeping the ground behind, for, elegant as the coach was, I regret to say that her Highness was rather a tight fit.

The next scene was the ball, and here Nan and Daisy appeared as gay as peacocks in all sorts of finery. Nan was especially good as the proud sister, and crushed many imaginary ladies as she swept about the palace hall. The Prince, in solitary state upon a somewhat unsteady throne, sat gazing about him from under an imposing crown, as he played with his sword and admired the rosettes in his shoes. When Cinderella came in he jumped up, and exclaimed, with more warmth than elegance, 'My gracious! who is that?' and immediately led the lady out to dance, while the sisters scowled and turned up their noses in the corner.

The stately jig executed by the little couple was very pretty, for the childish faces were so earnest, the costumes so gay, and the steps so peculiar, that they looked like the dainty quaint figures painted on a Watteau fan. The Princess's train was very much in her way, and the sword of Prince Rob nearly tripped him up several times. But they overcame these obstacles remarkably well, and finished the dance with much grace and spirit, considering that neither knew what the other was about.

'Drop your shoe,' whispered Mrs Jo's voice as the lady was about to sit down.

'Oh, I fordot!' and, taking off one of the silvery slippers, Cinderella planted it carefully in the middle of the stage, said to Rob, 'Now you must try and tatch me,' and ran away, while the Prince, picking up the shoe, obediently trotted after her.

The third scene, as everybody knows, is where the herald comes to try on the shoe. Teddy, still in coachman's dress, came in blowing a tin fish-horn melodiously, and the proud sisters each tried to put on the slipper. Nan insisted on playing cut off her toe with a carving knife, and performed that operation so well that the herald was alarmed, and begged her to be 'welly keerful'. Cinderella then was called, and came in with the pinafore half on, slipped her foot into the slipper, and announced, with satisfaction, 'I am the Pinsiss.'

Daisy wept, and begged pardon; but Nan, who liked tragedy, improved upon the story, and fell in a fainting-fit upon the floor, where she remained comfortably enjoying the rest of the play. It was not long, for the Prince ran in, dropped upon his knees, and kissed the hand of Goldilocks with great ardour, while the herald blew a blast that nearly deafened the audience. The curtain had no chance to fall, for the Princess ran off the stage to her father, crying, 'Didn't I do well?' while the Prince and herald had a fencing match with the tin horn and wooden sword.

'It was beautiful!' said everyone; and, when the raptures had a little subsided, Nat came out with his violin in his hand.

'Hush! hush!' cried all the children, and silence followed, for something in the boy's bashful manner and appealing eyes made everyone listen kindly.

The Bhaers thought he would play some of the old airs he knew so well, but, to their surprise, they heard a new and lovely melody, so softly, sweetly played, that they could hardly believe it could be Nat. It was one of those songs without words that touch the heart, and sing of all tender hymnlike hopes and joys, soothing and cheering those who listen to its simple music. Aunt Meg leaned her head on Demi's shoulder, Grandmother wiped her eyes, and Mrs Jo looked up at Mr Laurie, saying, in a choky whisper, 'You composed that.'

'I wanted your boy to do you honour, and thank you in his own way,' answered Laurie, leaning down to answer her.

When Nat made his bow and was about to go, he was called back by many hands, and had to play again. He did so with such a happy face, that it was good to see him, for he did his best, and gave them the gay old tunes that set the feet to dancing, and made quietude impossible.

'Clear the floor!' cried Emil; and in a minute the chairs were pushed back, the older people put safely in corners and the children gathered on the stage.

'Show your manners!' called Emil; and the boys pranced up to the ladies, old and young; with polite invitations to 'tread the mazy', as dear Dick Swiveller has it. The small lads nearly came to blows for the Princess, but she chose Dick, like a kind, little gentlewoman as she was, and let him lead her proudly to her place. Mrs Jo was not allowed to decline; and Aunt Amy filled Dan with unspeakable delight by refusing Franz and taking him. Of course Nan and Tommy, Nat and Daisy paired off, while Uncle Teddy went and got Asia, who was longing to 'jig it', and felt much elated by the honour done her. Silas and Mary Ann had a private dance in the hall; and for half an hour Plumfield was at its merriest.

The party wound up with a grand promenade of all the young folks, headed by the pumpkin-coach with the Princess and driver inside, and the rats in a wildly frisky state.

While the children enjoyed this final frolic, the elders sat in the parlour looking on as they talked together of the little people with the interest of parents and friends.

'What are you thinking of, all by yourself, with such a happy face, sister Jo?' asked Laurie, sitting down beside her on the sofa.

'My summer's work, Teddy, and amusing myself by imagining the future of my boys,' she answered, smiling as she made room for him.

'They are all to be poets, painters, and statesmen, famous soldiers, or at least merchant princes, I suppose.'

'No, I am not as aspiring as I once was, and I shall be satisfied if they are honest men. But I will confess that I do expect a little glory and a career for some of them. Demi is not a common child, and I think he will blossom into something good and great in the best sense of the word. The others will do well, I hope, especially my last two boys, for, after hearing Nat play tonight, I really think he has genius.'

'Too soon to say; talent he certainly has, and there is no doubt that the boy can soon earn his bread by the work he loves. Build him up for another year or so, and then I will take him off your hands, and launch him properly.'

'That is such a pleasant prospect for poor Nat, who came to me six months ago so friendless and forlorn. Dan's future is already plain to me. Mr Hyde will want him soon, and I mean to give him a brave and faithful little servant. Dan is one who can serve well if the wages are love and confidence, and he has the energy to carve out his own future in his own way. Yes, I am very happy over our success with these boys – one so weak, and one so wild; both so much better now, and so full of promise.'

'What magic did you use, Jo?'

'I only loved them, and let them see it. Fritz did the rest.'

'Dear soul! you look as if "only loving" had been rather hard work sometimes,' said Laurie, stroking her thin cheek with a look of more tender admiration than he had ever given her as a girl.

'I'm a faded old woman, but I'm a very happy one; so don't pity me, Teddy;' and she glanced about the room with eyes full of a sincere content.

'Yes, your plan seems to work better and better every year,' he said, with an emphatic nod of approval toward the cheery scene before him.

'How can it fail to work well when I have so much help from you all?' answered Mrs Jo, looking gratefully at her most generous patron.

'It is the best joke of the family, this school of yours and its success. So unlike the future we planned for you, and yet so suited to you after all. It was a regular inspiration, Jo,' said Laurie, dodging her thanks as usual.

'Ah! but you laughed at it in the beginning, and still make all manner of fun of me and my inspirations. Didn't you predict that having girls with the boys would be a dead failure? Now see how well it works;' and she pointed to the happy group of lads and lassies dancing, singing, and chattering together with every sign of kindly good fellowship.

'I give in, and when my Goldilocks is old enough I'll send her to you. Can I say more than that?'

'I shall be so proud to have your little treasure trusted to me. But really, Teddy, the effect of these girls has been excellent. I know you will laugh at me, but I don't mind, I'm used to it; so I'll tell you that one of my favourite fancies is to look at my family as a small world, to watch the progress of my little men, and, lately, to see how well the influence of my little women works upon them. Daisy is the domestic element, and they all feel the charm of her quiet, womanly ways. Nan is the restless, energetic, strong-minded one; they admire her courage, and give her a fair chance to work out her will, seeing that she has sympathy as well as strength, and the power to do much in their small world. Your Bess is the lady, full of natural refinement, grace, and beauty. She polishes them unconsciously, and fills her place as any lovely woman may, using her gentle influence to lift and hold them above the coarse, rough things of life, and keep them gentlemen in the best sense of the fine old word.'

'It is not always the ladies who do that best, Jo. It is sometimes the strong brave woman who stirs up the boy and makes a man of him;' and Laurie bowed to her with a significant laugh.

'No; I think the graceful woman, whom the boy you allude to married, has done more for him than the wild Nan of his youth; or, better still, the wise, motherly woman who watched over him, as Daisy watches over Demi, did more to make him what he is;' and Jo turned toward her mother, who sat a little apart with Meg, looking so full of the sweet dignity and beauty of old age, that Laurie gave her a glance of filial respect and love as he replied, in serious earnest, 'All three did much for him, and I can understand how well these little girls will help your lads.'

'Not more than the lads help them; it is mutual, I assure you. Nat does much for Daisy with his music; Dan can manage Nan better than any of us; and Demi teaches your Goldilocks so easily and well that Fritz calls them Roger Ascham and Lady Jane Grey. Dear me! if men and women would only trust, understand, and help one another as my children do, what a capital place the world would be!' and Mrs Jo's eyes grew absent, as if she was looking at a new and charming state of society in which people lived as happily and innocently as her flock at Plumfield.

'You are doing your best to help on the good time, my dear. Continue to believe in it, to work for it, and to prove its possibility by the success of your small experiment,' said Mr March, pausing as he passed to say an encouraging word, for the good man never lost his faith in humanity, and still hoped to see peace, goodwill, and happiness reign upon the earth.

'I am not so ambitious as that, Father. I only want to give these children a home in which they can be taught a few simple things which will help to make life less hard to them when they go out to fight their battles in the world. Honesty, courage, industry, faith in God, their fellow creatures, and themselves; that is all I try for.'

'That is everything. Give them these helps, then let them go to work out their life as men and women; and whatever their success or failure is, I think they will remember and bless your efforts, my good son and daughter.'

The Professor had joined them, and as Mr March spoke he gave a hand to each, and left them with a look that was a blessing. As Jo and her husband stood together for a moment talking quietly, and feeling that their summer work had been well done if Father approved, Mr Laurie slipped into the hall, said a word to the children, and all of a sudden the whole flock pranced into the room, joined hands and danced about Father and Mother Bhaer, singing blithely:

> 'Summer days are over,
> Summer work is done;
> Harvests have been gathered
> Gayly one by one.
> Now the feast is eaten,
> Finished is the play;
> But one rite remains for
> Our Thanksgiving-day.
>
> 'Best of all the harvest
> In the dear God's sight,
> Are the happy children
> In the home tonight;
> And we come to offer
> Thanks where thanks are due,
> With grateful hearts and voices,
> Father, Mother, unto you.'

With the last words the circle narrowed till the good Professor and his wife were taken prisoner by many arms, and half hidden by the bouquet of laughing young faces which surrounded them, proving that one plant had taken root and blossomed beautifully in all the little gardens. For love is a flower that grows in any soil, works its sweet miracles undaunted by autumn frost or winter snow, blooming fair and fragrant all the year, and blessing those who give and those who receive.

Jo's Boys
And How They Turned Out

CONTENTS

Preface

Having been written at long intervals during the past seven years, this story is more faulty than any of its very imperfect predecessors; but the desire to atone for an unavoidable disappointment, and to please my patient little friends, has urged me to let it go without further delay.

To account for the seeming neglect of AMY, let me add that, since the original of that character died, it has been impossible for me to write of her as when she was here to suggest, criticise and laugh over her namesake. The same excuse applies to MARMEE. But the folded leaves are not blank to those who knew and loved them and can find memorials of them in whatever is cheerful, true or helpful in these pages.

L. M. ALCOTT
Concord, 4 July 1886

CHAPTER I

Ten Years Later

'If anyone had told me what wonderful changes were to take place here in ten years, I wouldn't have believed it,' said Mrs Jo to Mrs Meg, as they sat on the piazza at Plumfield one summer day, looking about them with faces full of pride and pleasure.

'This is the sort of magic that money and kind hearts can work. I am sure Mr Laurence could have no nobler monument than the college he so generously endowed; and a home like this will keep Aunt March's memory green as long as it lasts,' answered Mrs Meg, always glad to praise the absent.

'We used to believe in fairies, you remember, and plan what we'd ask for if we could have three wishes. Doesn't it seem as if mine had been really granted at last? Money, fame, and plenty of the work I love,' said Mrs Jo, carelessly rumpling up her hair as she clasped her hands over her head just as she used to do when a girl.

'I have had mine, and Amy is enjoying hers to her heart's content. If dear Marmee, John, and Beth were here, it would be quite perfect,' added Meg, with a tender quiver in her voice; for Marmee's place was empty now.

Jo put her hand on her sister's, and both sat silent for a little while, surveying the pleasant scene before them with mingled sad and happy thoughts.

It certainly did look as if magic had been at work, for quiet Plumfield was transformed into a busy little world. The house seemed more hospitable than ever, refreshed now with new paint, added wings, well-kept lawn and garden, and a prosperous air it had not worn when riotous boys swarmed everywhere and it was rather difficult for the Bhaers to make both ends meet. On the hill, where kites used to be flown, stood the fine college which Mr Laurence's munificent legacy had built. Busy students were going to and fro along the paths once trodden by childish feet, and many young men and women were enjoying all the advantages that wealth, wisdom, and benevolence could give them.

Just inside the gates of Plumfield a pretty brown cottage, very like the Dovecote, nestled among the trees, and on the green slope westward Laurie's white-pillared mansion glittered in the sunshine; for when the rapid growth of the city shut in the old house, spoilt Meg's nest, and dared to put a soap factory under Mr Laurence's indignant nose, our friends emigrated to Plumfield, and the great changes began.

These were the pleasant ones; and the loss of the dear old people was sweetened by the blessings they left behind; so all prospered now in the little community, and Mr Bhaer as president, and Mr March as chaplain of the college, saw their long-cherished dream beautifully realised. The sisters divided the care of the young people among them, each taking the part that suited her best. Meg was the motherly friend of the young women, Jo the confidante and defender of all the youths, and Amy the lady Bountiful who delicately smoothed the way for needy students, and entertained them all so cordially that it was no wonder they named her lovely home Mount Parnassus, so full was it of music, beauty, and the culture hungry young hearts and fancies long for.

The original twelve boys had of course scattered far and wide during these years, but all that lived still remembered old Plumfield, and came wandering back from the four quarters of the earth to tell their various experiences, laugh over the pleasures of the past, and face the duties of the present with fresh courage; for such homecomings keep hearts tender and hands helpful with the memories of young and happy days. A few words will tell the history of each, and then we can go on with the new chapter of their lives.

Franz was with a merchant kinsman in Hamburg, a man of twenty-six now, and doing well. Emil was the jolliest tar that ever 'sailed the ocean blue'. His uncle sent him on a long voyage to disgust him with this adventurous life; but he came home so delighted with it that it was plain this was his profession, and the German kinsman gave him a good chance in his ships; so the lad was happy. Dan was a wanderer still; for after the geological researches in South America he tried sheep farming in Australia, and was now in California looking up mines. Nat was busy with music at the Conservatory, preparing for a year or two in Germany to finish him off. Tom was studying medicine and trying to like it. Jack was in business with his father, bent on getting rich. Dolly was in college with Stuffy and Ned reading law. Poor little Dick was dead, so was Billy; and no one could mourn for them, since life would never be happy, afflicted as they were in mind and body.

Rob and Teddy were called the 'Lion and the Lamb'; for the latter was as rampant as the king of beasts, and the former as gentle as any sheep that ever baaed. Mrs Jo called him 'my daughter', and found him the most dutiful of children, with plenty of manliness underlying the quiet manners and tender nature. But in Ted she seemed to see all the faults, whims, aspirations, and fun of her own youth in a new shape. With his tawny locks always in wild confusion, his long legs and arms, loud voice, and continual activity, Ted was a prominent figure at Plumfield. He had his moods of gloom, and fell into the Slough of Despond about once a week, to be hoisted out by patient Rob or his mother, who understood when to let him alone and when to shake him up. He was her pride and joy as well as torment, being a very bright lad for his age, and so full of all sorts of budding talent, that her maternal mind was much exercised as to what this remarkable boy would become.

Demi had gone through College with honour, and Mrs Meg had set her heart on his being a minister – picturing in her fond fancy the first sermon her dignified young parson would preach, as well as the long, useful, and honoured life he was to lead. But John, as she called him now, firmly declined the divinity school, saying he had had enough of books, and needed to know more of men and the world, and caused the dear woman much disappointment by deciding to try a journalist's career. It was a blow; but she knew that young minds cannot be driven, and that experience is the best teacher; so she let him follow his own inclinations, still hoping to see him in the pulpit. Aunt Jo raged when she found that there was to be a reporter in the family, and called him 'Jenkins' on the spot. She liked his literary tendencies, but had reason to detest official Paul Prys, as we shall see later. Demi knew his own mind, however, and tranquilly carried out his plans, unmoved by the tongues of the anxious mammas or the jokes of his mates. Uncle Teddy encouraged him, and painted a splendid career, mentioning

Dickens and other celebrities who began as reporters and ended as famous novelists or newspaper men.

The girls were all flourishing. Daisy, as sweet and domestic as ever, was her mother's comfort and companion. Josie at fourteen was a most original young person, full of pranks and peculiarities, the latest of which was a passion for the stage, which caused her quiet mother and sister much anxiety as well as amusement. Bess had grown into a tall, beautiful girl looking several years older than she was, with the same graceful ways and dainty tastes which the little Princess had, and a rich inheritance of both the father's and mother's gifts, fostered by every aid love and money could give. But the pride of the community was naughty Nan; for, like so many restless, wilful children, she was growing into a woman full of the energy and promise that suddenly blossoms when the ambitious seeker finds the work she is fitted to do well. Nan began to study medicine at sixteen, and at twenty was getting on bravely; for now, thanks to other intelligent women, colleges and hospitals were open to her. She had never wavered in her purpose from the childish days when she shocked Daisy in the old willow by saying: 'I don't want any family to fuss over. I shall have an office, with bottles and pestle things in it, and drive round and cure folks.' The future foretold by the little girl the young woman was rapidly bringing to pass, and finding so much happiness in it that nothing could win her from the chosen work. Several worthy young gentlemen had tried to make her change her mind and choose, as Daisy did, 'a nice little house and family to take care of'. But Nan only laughed, and routed the lovers by proposing to look at the tongue which spoke of adoration, or professionally felt the pulse in the manly hand offered for her acceptance. So all departed but one persistent youth, who was such a devoted Traddles it was impossible to quench him.

This was Tom, who was as faithful to his child sweetheart as she to her 'pestle things', and gave a proof of fidelity that touched her very much. He studied medicine for her sake alone, having no taste for it, and a decided fancy for a mercantile life. But Nan was firm, and Tom stoutly kept on, devoutly hoping he might not kill many of his fellow-beings when he came to practise. They were excellent friends, however, and caused much amusement to their comrades, by the vicissitudes of this merry love-chase.

Both were approaching Plumfield on the afternoon when Mrs Meg and Mrs Jo were talking on the piazza. Not together; for Nan was walking briskly along the pleasant road alone, thinking over a case that interested her, and Tom was pegging on behind to overtake her, as if by accident, when the suburbs of the city were past – a little way of his, which was part of the joke.

Nan was a handsome girl, with a fresh colour, clear eye, quick smile, and the self-poised look young women with a purpose always have. She was simply and sensibly dressed, walked easily, and seemed full of vigour, with her broad shoulders well back, arms swinging freely, and the elasticity of youth and health in every motion. The few people she met turned to look at her, as if it was a pleasant sight to see a hearty, happy girl walking countryward that lovely day; and the red-faced young man steaming along behind, hat off and every tight curl wagging with impatience, evidently agreed with them.

Presently a mild 'Hallo!' was borne upon the breeze, and pausing, with an effort to look surprised that was an utter failure, Nan said affably: 'Oh, is that you, Tom?'

'Looks like it. Thought you might be walking out today;' and Tom's jovial face beamed with pleasure.

'You knew it. How is your throat?' asked Nan in her professional tone, which was always a quencher to undue raptures.

'Throat? Oh, ah! yes, I remember. It is well. The effect of that prescription was wonderful. I'll never call homoeopathy a humbug again.'

'You were the humbug this time, and so were the unmedicated pellets I gave you. If sugar or milk can cure diphtheria in this remarkable manner, I'll make a note of it. O Tom, Tom, will you never be done playing tricks?'

'O Nan, Nan, will you never be done getting the better of me?' And the merry pair laughed at one another just as they did in the old times, which always came back freshly when they went to Plumfield.

'Well, I knew I shouldn't see you for a week if I didn't scare up some excuse for a call at the office. You are so desperately busy all the time I never get a word,' explained Tom.

'You ought to be busy too, and above such nonsense. Really, Tom, if you don't give your mind to your lectures, you'll never get on,' said Nan soberly.

'I have quite enough of them as it is,' answered Tom with an air of disgust. 'A fellow must lark a bit after dissecting corpuses all day. I can't stand it long at a time, though *some people* seem to enjoy it immensely.'

'Then why not leave it, and do what suits you better? I always thought it a foolish thing, you know,' said Nan, with a trace of anxiety in the keen eyes that searched for signs of illness in a face as ruddy as a Baldwin apple.

'You know why I chose it, and why I shall stick to it if it kills me. I may not *look* delicate, but I've a deep-seated heart complaint, and it will carry me off sooner or later; for only one doctor in the world can cure it, and she won't.'

There was an air of pensive resignation about Tom that was both comic and pathetic; for he was in earnest, and kept on giving hints of this sort, without the least encouragement.

Nan frowned; but she was used to it, and knew how to treat him.

'She is curing it in the best and only way; but a more refractory patient never lived. Did you go to that ball, as I directed?'

'I did.'

'And devote yourself to pretty Miss West?'

'Danced with her the whole evening.'

'No impression made on that susceptible organ of yours?'

'Not the slightest. I gaped in her face once, forgot to feed her, and gave a sigh of relief when I handed her over to her mamma.'

'Repeat the dose as often as possible, and note the symptoms. I predict that you'll "cry for it" by and by.'

'Never! I'm sure it doesn't suit my constitution.'

'We shall see. Obey orders!' sternly.

'Yes, Doctor,' meekly.

Silence reigned for a moment; then, as if the bone of contention was forgotten in the pleasant recollections called up by familiar objects, Nan said suddenly: 'What fun we used to have in that wood! Do you remember how you tumbled out of the big nut tree and nearly broke your collarbones?'

'Don't I! and how you steeped me in wormwood till I was a fine mahogany colour, and Aunt Jo wailed over my spoilt jacket,' laughed Tom, a boy again in a minute.

'And how you set the house afire?'

'And you ran off for your band-box?'

'Do you ever say "Thunder-turtles" now?'

'Do people ever call you "Giddygaddy"?'

'Daisy does. Dear thing, I haven't seen her for a week.'

'I saw Demi this morning, and he said she was keeping house for Mother Bhaer.'

'She always does when Aunt Jo gets into a vortex. Daisy is a model housekeeper; and you couldn't do better than make your bow to her, if you can't go to work and wait till you are grown up before you begin lovering.'

'Nat would break his fiddle over my head if I suggested such a thing. No, thank you. Another name is engraved upon my heart as indelibly as the blue anchor on my arm. "Hope" is my motto, and "No surrender", yours; see who will hold out longest.'

'You silly boys think we must pair off as we did when children; but we shall do nothing of the kind. How well Parnassus looks from here!' said Nan, abruptly changing the conversation again.

'It is a fine house; but I love old Plum best. Wouldn't Aunt March stare if she could see the changes here?' answered Tom, as they both paused at the great gate to look at the pleasant landscape before them.

A sudden whoop startled them, as a long boy with a wild yellow head came leaping over a hedge like a kangaroo, followed by a slender girl, who stuck in the hawthorn, and sat there laughing like a witch. A pretty little lass she was, with curly dark hair, bright eyes, and a very expressive face. Her hat was at her back, and her skirts a good deal the worse for the brooks she had crossed, the trees she had climbed, and the last leap, which added several fine rents.

'Take me down, Nan, please. Tom, hold Ted; he's got my book, and I *will* have it,' called Josie from her perch, not at all daunted by the appearance of her friends.

Tom promptly collared the thief, while Nan picked Josie from among the thorns and set her on her feet without a word of reproof; for having been a romp in her own girlhood, she was very indulgent to like tastes in others. 'What's the matter, dear?' she asked, pinning up the longest rip, while Josie examined the scratches on her hands. 'I was studying my part in the willow, and Ted came slyly up and poked the book out of my hands with his rod. It fell in the brook, and before I could scrabble down he was off. You wretch, give it back this moment or I'll box your ears,' cried Josie, laughing and scolding in the same breath.

Escaping from Tom, Ted struck a sentimental attitude, and with tender glances at the wet, torn young person before him, delivered Claude Melnotte's famous speech in a lackadaisical way that was irresistibly funny, ending with 'Dost like the picture, love?' as he made an object of himself by tying his long legs in a knot and distorting his face horribly.

The sound of applause from the piazza put a stop to these antics, and the young folks went up the avenue together very much in the old style when Tom drove four in hand and Nan was the best horse in the team. Rosy, breathless, and merry, they greeted the ladies and sat down on the steps to rest, Aunt Meg sewing up her daughter's rags while Mrs Jo smoothed the Lion's mane, and rescued the book. Daisy appeared in a moment to greet her friend, and all began to talk.

'Muffins for tea; better stay and eat 'em; Daisy's never fail,' said Ted hospitably.

'He's a judge; he ate nine last time. That's why he's so fat,' added Josie, with a withering glance at her cousin, who was as thin as a lath.

'I must go and see Lucy Dove. She has a whitlow, and it's time to lance it. I'll tea at college,' answered Nan, feeling in her pocket to be sure she had not forgotten her case of instruments.

'Thanks, I'm going there also. Tom Merryweather has granulated lids, and I promised to touch them up for him. Save a doctor's fee and be good practice for me. I'm clumsy with my thumbs,' said Tom, bound to be near his idol while he could.

'Hush! Daisy doesn't like to hear you sawbones talk of your work. Muffins suit us better;' and Ted grinned sweetly, with a view to future favours in the eating line.

'Any news of the Commodore?' asked Tom.

'He is on his way home, and Dan hopes to come soon. I long to see my boys together, and have begged the wanderers to come to Thanksgiving, if not before,' answered Mrs Jo, beaming at the thought.

'They'll come, every man of them, if they can. Even Jack will risk losing a dollar for the sake of one of our jolly old dinners,' laughed Tom.

'There's the turkey fattening for the feast. I never chase him now, but feed him well; and he's "swellin' wisibly", bless his drumsticks!' said Ted, pointing out the doomed fowl proudly parading in a neighbouring field.

'If Nat goes the last of the month we shall want a farewell frolic for him. I suppose the dear old Chirper will come home a second Ole Bull,' said Nan to her friend.

A pretty colour came into Daisy's cheek, and the folds of muslin on her breast rose and fell with a quick breath; but she answered placidly: 'Uncle Laurie says he has *real* talent, and after the training he will get abroad he can command a good living here, though he may never be famous.'

'Young people seldom turn out as one predicts, so it is of little use to expect anything,' said Mrs Meg with a sigh. 'If our children are good and useful men and women, we should be satisfied; yet it's very natural to wish them to be brilliant and successful.'

'They are like my chickens, mighty uncertain. Now, that finelooking cockerel of mine is the stupidest one of the lot, and the ugly, long-legged chap is the king of the yard, he's so smart; crows loud enough to wake the Seven Sleepers; but the handsome one croaks, and is no end of a coward. *I* get snubbed; but you wait till I grow up, and then see;' and Ted looked so like his own longlegged pet that everyone laughed at his modest prediction.

'I want to see Dan settled somewhere. "A rolling stone gathers no moss", and at twenty-five he is still roaming about the world without a tie to hold him, except this;' and Mrs Meg nodded towards her sister.

'Dan will find his place at last, and experience is his best teacher. He is rough still, but each time he comes home I see a change for the better, and never lose my faith in him. He may never do anything great, or get rich; but if the wild boy makes an honest man, I'm satisfied,' said Mrs Jo, who always defended the black sheep of her flock.

'That's right, Mother, stand by Dan! He's worth a dozen Jacks and Neds bragging about money and trying to be swells. You see if he doesn't do something to be proud of and take the wind out of their sails,' added Ted, whose love for his 'Danny' was now strengthened by a boy's admiration for the bold, adventurous man.

'Hope so, I'm sure. He's just the fellow to do rash things and come to glory – climbing the Matterhorn, taking a "header" into Niagara, or finding a big nugget. That's his way of sowing wild oats, and perhaps it's better than ours,' said Tom thoughtfully; for he had gained a good deal of experience in that sort of agriculture since he became a medical student.

'Much better!' said Mrs Jo emphatically. 'I'd rather send my boys off to see the world in that way than leave them alone in a city full of temptations, with nothing to do but waste time, money, and health, as so many are left. Dan has to work his way, and that teaches him courage, patience, and self-reliance. I don't worry about him as much as I do about George and Dolly at college, no more fit than two babies to take care of themselves.'

'How about John? He's knocking round town as a newspaper man, reporting all sorts of things, from sermons to prizefights,' asked Tom, who thought that sort of life would be much more to his own taste than medical lectures and hospital wards.

'Demi has three safeguards – good principles, refined tastes, and a wise mother. He won't come to harm, and these experiences will be useful to him when he begins to write, as I'm sure he will in time,' began Mrs Jo in her prophetic tone; for she was anxious to have some of her geese turn out swans.

'Speak of Jenkins, and you'll hear the rustling of his paper,' cried Tom, as a fresh-faced, brown-eyed young man came up the avenue, waving a newspaper over his head.

'Here's your *Evening Tattler*! Latest Edition! Awful murder! Bank clerk absconded! Powder-mill explosion, and great strike of the Latin School boys!' roared Ted, going to meet his cousin with the graceful gait of a young giraffe.

'The Commodore is in, and will cut his cable and run before the wind as soon as he can get off,' called Demi, with 'a nice derangement of nautical epitaphs', as he came up smiling over his good news.

Everyone talked together for a moment, and the paper passed from hand to hand that each eye might rest on the pleasant fact that the *Brenda*, from Hamburg, was safe in port.

'He'll come lurching out by tomorrow with his usual collection of marine monsters and lively yarns. I saw him, jolly and tarry and brown as a coffee-berry. Had a good run, and hopes to be second mate, as the other chap is laid up with a broken leg,' added Demi.

'Wish I had the setting of it,' said Nan to herself, with a professional twist of her hand.

'How's Franz?' asked Mrs Jo.

'He's going to be married! There's news for you. The first of the flock, Aunty, so say goodbye to him. Her name is Ludmilla Heldegard Blumenthal; good family, well-off, pretty, and of course an angel. The dear old boy wants Uncle's consent, and then he will settle down to be a happy and an honest burgher. Long life to him!'

'I'm glad to hear it. I do so like to settle my boys with a good wife and a nice little home. Now, if all is right, I shall feel as if Franz was off my mind,' said Mrs Jo, folding her hands contentedly; for she often felt like a distracted hen with a large brood of mixed chickens and ducks upon her hands.

'So do I,' sighed Tom, with a sly glance at Nan. 'That's what a fellow needs to keep him steady; and it's the duty of nice girls to marry as soon as possible, isn't it, Demi?'

'If there are enough nice fellows to go round. The female population exceeds the male, you know, especially in New England; which accounts for the high state of culture we are in, perhaps,' answered John, who was leaning over his mother's chair, telling his day's experiences in a whisper.

'It is a merciful provision, my dears; for it takes three or four women to get each man into, through, and out of the world. You are costly creatures, boys; and it is well that mothers, sisters, wives, and daughters love their duty and do it so well, or you would perish off the face of the earth,' said Mrs Jo solemnly, as she took up a basket filled with dilapidated hose; for the good Professor was still hard on his socks, and his sons resembled him in that respect.

'Such being the case, there is plenty for the "superfluous women" to do, in taking care of these helpless men and their families. I see that more clearly every day, and am very glad and grateful that my profession will make me a useful, happy, and independent spinster.'

Nan's emphasis on the last word caused Tom to groan, and the rest to laugh.

'I take great pride and solid satisfaction in you, Nan, and hope to see you very successful; for we do need just such helpful women in the world. I sometimes feel as if I've missed my vocation and ought to have remained single; but my duty seemed to point this way, and I don't regret it,' said Mrs Jo, folding a large and very ragged blue sock to her bosom.

'Neither do I. What should I ever have done without my dearest Mum?' added Ted, with a filial hug which caused both to disappear behind the newspaper in which he had been mercifully absorbed for a few minutes.

'My darling boy, if you would wash your hands semi-occasionally, fond caresses would be less disastrous to my collar. Never mind, my precious touslehead, better grass stains and dirt than no cuddlings at all;' and Mrs Jo emerged from that brief eclipse looking much refreshed, though her back hair was caught in Ted's buttons and her collar under one ear.

Here Josie, who had been studying her part at the other end of the piazza, suddenly burst forth with a smothered shriek, and gave Juliet's speech in the tomb so effectively that the boys applauded, Daisy shivered, and Nan murmured: 'Too much cerebral excitement for one of her age.'

'I'm afraid you'll have to make up your mind to it, Meg. That child is a born actress. We never did anything so well, not even the Witch's Curse,' said Mrs Jo, casting a bouquet of many-coloured socks at the feet of her flushed and panting niece, when she fell gracefully upon the doormat.

'It is a sort of judgement upon me for my passion for the stage when a girl. Now I know how dear Marmee felt when I begged to be an actress. I never can consent, and yet I may be obliged to give up my wishes, hopes, and plans again.'

There was an accent of reproach in his mother's voice, which made Demi pick up his sister with a gentle shake, and the stern command to 'drop that nonsense in public'.

'Drop me, Minion, or I'll give you the Maniac Bride, with my best *Ha-ha*!' cried Josie, glaring at him like an offended kitten. Being set on her feet, she made a splendid curtsy, and dramatically proclaiming, 'Mrs Woffington's carriage waits,' swept down the steps and round the corner, trailing Daisy's scarlet shawl majestically behind her.

'Isn't she great fun? I couldn't stop in this dull place if I hadn't that child to make it lively for me. If ever she turns prim, I'm off; so mind how you nip her in the bud,' said Teddy, frowning at Demi, who was now writing out shorthand notes on the steps.

Josie suddenly burst forth with a smothered shriek, and gave Juliet's speech in the tomb so effectively that the boys applauded

'You two are a team, and it takes a strong hand to drive you, but I rather like it. Josie ought to have been my child, and Rob yours, Meg. Then your house would have been all peace and mine all Bedlam. Now I must go and tell Laurie the news. Come with me, Meg, a little stroll will do us good;' and sticking Ted's straw hat on her head, Mrs Jo walked off with her sister, leaving Daisy to attend to the muffins, Ted to appease Josie, and Tom and Nan to give their respective patients a very bad quarter of an hour.

CHAPTER 2

Parnassus

It was well named; and the Muses seemed to be at home that day, for as the newcomers went up the slope appropriate sights and sounds greeted them. Passing an open window, they looked in upon a library presided over by Clio, Calliope, and Urania; Melpomene and Thalia were disporting themselves in the hall, where some young people were dancing and rehearsing a play; Erato was walking in the garden with her lover, and in the music-room Phoebus himself was drilling a tuneful choir.

A mature Apollo was our old friend Laurie, but comely and genial as ever; for time had ripened the freakish boy into a noble man. Care and sorrow, as well as ease and happiness, had done much for him; and the responsibility of carrying out his grandfather's wishes had been a duty most faithfully performed. Prosperity suits some people, and they blossom best in a glow of sunshine; others need the shade, and are the sweeter for a touch of frost. Laurie was one of the former sort, and Amy was another; so life had been a kind of poem to them since they married – not only harmonious and happy, but earnest, useful, and rich in the beautiful benevolence which can do so much when wealth and wisdom go hand in hand with charity. Their house was full of unostentatious beauty and comfort, and here the art-loving host and hostess attracted and entertained artists of all kinds. Laurie had music enough now, and was a generous patron to the class he most liked to help. Amy had her protégées among ambitious young painters and sculptors, and found her own art double dear as her daughter grew old enough to share its labours and delights with her; for she was one of those who prove that women can be faithful wives and mothers without sacrificing the special gift bestowed upon them for their own development and the good of others.

Her sisters knew where to find her, and Jo went at once to the studio, where mother and daughter worked together. Bess was busy with the bust of a little child, while her mother added the last touches to a fine head of her husband. Time seemed to have stood still with Amy, for happiness had kept her young and prosperity given her the culture she needed. A stately, graceful woman, who showed how elegant simplicity could be made by the taste with which she chose her dress and the grace with which she wore it. As someone said: 'I never know what Mrs Laurence has on, but I always receive the impression that she is the best-dressed lady in the room.'

It was evident that she adored her daughter, and well she might; for the beauty she had longed for seemed, to her fond eyes at least, to be impersonated in this younger self. Bess inherited her mother's Diana-like figure, blue eyes, fair skin, and golden hair, tied up in the same classic knot of curls. Also – ah! never-ending source of joy to Amy – she had her father's handsome nose and mouth, cast in a feminine mould. The severe simplicity of a long linen pinafore suited her; and she worked away with the entire absorption of the true artist, unconscious of the loving eyes upon her, till Aunt Jo came in exclaiming eagerly: 'My dear girls, stop your mud-pies and hear the news!'

Both artists dropped their tools and greeted the irrepressible woman cordially, though genius had been burning splendidly and her coming spoilt a precious hour. They were in the full tide of gossip when Laurie, who had been summoned by Meg, arrived, and sitting down between the sisters, with no barricade anywhere, listened with interest to the news of Franz and Emil.

'The epidemic has broke out, and now it will rage and ravage your flock. Be prepared for every sort of romance and rashness for the next ten years, Jo. Your boys are growing up and will plunge headlong into a sea of worse scrapes than any you have had yet,' said Laurie, enjoying her look of mingled delight and despair.

'I know it, and I hope I shall be able to pull them through and land them safely; but it's an awful responsibility, for they *will* come to me and insist that I can make their poor little loves run smoothly. I like it, though, and Meg is such a mush of sentiment she revels in the prospect,' answered Jo, feeling pretty easy about her own boys, whose youth made them safe for the present.

'I'm afraid she won't revel when our Nat begins to buzz too near her Daisy. Of course you see what all that means? As musical director I am also his confidante, and would like to know what advice to give,' said Laurie soberly. 'Hush! you forget that child,' began Jo, nodding towards Bess, who was at work again.

'Bless you! she's in Athens, and doesn't hear a word. She ought to leave off, though, and go out. My darling, put the baby to sleep, and go for a run. Aunt Meg is in the parlour; go and show her the new pictures till we come,' added Laurie, looking at his tall girl as Pygmalion might have looked at Galatea; for he considered her the finest statue in the house.

'Yes, Papa; but please tell me if it is good'; and Bess obediently put down her tools, with a lingering glance at the bust.

'My cherished daughter, truth compels me to confess that one cheek is plumper than the other; and the curls upon its infant brow are rather too much like horns for perfect grace; otherwise it rivals Raphael's Chanting Cherubs, and I'm proud of it.'

Laurie was laughing as he spoke; for these first attempts were so like Amy's early ones, it was impossible to regard them as soberly as the enthusiastic mamma did.

'You can't see beauty in anything but music,' answered Bess, shaking the golden head that made the one bright spot in the cool north lights of the great studio.

'Well, I see beauty in you, dear. And if you are not art, what is? I wish to put a little more nature into you, and get you away from this cold clay and marble into the sunshine, to dance and laugh as the others do. I want a flesh-and-blood girl, not a sweet statue in a grey pinafore, who forgets everything but her work.' As he spoke, two dusty hands came round his neck, and Bess said earnestly, punctuating her words with soft touches of her lips: 'I never forget *you*, Papa; but I do want to do something beautiful that you may be proud of me by and by. Mamma often tells me to stop; but when we get in here we forget there is any world outside, we are so busy and so happy. Now I'll go and run and sing, and be a girl to please you.' And throwing away the apron, Bess vanished from the room, seeming to take all the light with her.

'I'm glad you said that. The dear child is too much absorbed in her artistic dreams for one so young. It is my fault; but I sympathise so deeply in it all, I forget to be wise,' sighed Amy, carefully covering the baby with a wet towel.

'I think this power of living in our children is one of the sweetest things in the world; but I try to remember what Marmee once said to Meg – that fathers should have their share in the education of both girls and boys; so I leave Ted to his father all I can, and Fritz lends me Rob, whose quiet ways are as restful and good for me as Ted's tempests are for his father. Now I advise you, Amy, to let Bess drop the mud-pies for a time, and take up music with Laurie; then she won't be one-sided, and he won't be jealous.'

'Hear, hear! A Daniel – a very Daniel!' cried Laurie, well pleased. 'I thought you'd lend a hand, Jo, and say a word for me. I *am* a little jealous of Amy, and want more of a share in my girl. Come, my lady, let me have her this summer, and next year, when we go to Rome, I'll give her up to you and high art. Isn't that a fair bargain?'

'I agree; but in trying your hobby, nature, with music thrown in, don't forget that, though only fifteen, our Bess is older than most girls of that age, and cannot be treated like a child. She is so very precious to me, I feel as if I wanted to keep her always as pure and beautiful as the marble she loves so well.'

Amy spoke regretfully as she looked about the lovely room where she had spent so many happy hours with this dear child of hers.

' "Turn and turn about is fair play", as we used to say when we all wanted to ride on Ellen Tree or wear the russet boots,' said Jo briskly; 'so you must share your girl between you, and see who will do the most for her.'

'We will,' answered the fond parents, laughing at the recollections Jo's proverb brought up to them.

'How I did use to enjoy bouncing on the limbs of that old apple tree! No real horse ever gave me half the pleasure or the exercise,' said Amy, looking out of the high window as if she saw the dear old orchard again and the little girls at play there.

'And what fun I had with those blessed boots!' laughed Jo. 'I've got the relics now. The boys reduced them to rags; but I love them still, and would enjoy a good theatrical stalk in them if it were possible.'

'My fondest memories twine about the warming-pan and the sausage. What larks we had! And how long ago it seems!' said Laurie, staring at the two women before him as if he found it hard to realise that they ever had been little Amy and riotous Jo.

'Don't suggest that we are growing old, my lord. We have only bloomed; and a very nice bouquet we make with our buds about us,' answered Mrs Amy, shaking out the folds of her rosy muslin with much the air of dainty satisfaction the girl used to show in a new dress.

'Not to mention our thorns and dead leaves,' added Jo, with a sigh; for life had never been very easy to her, and even now she had her troubles both within and without.

'Come and have a dish of tea, old dear, and see what the young folks are about. You are tired, and want to be "stayed with flagons and comforted with apples",' said Laurie, offering an arm to each sister, and leading them away to afternoon tea, which flowed as freely on Parnassus as the nectar of old.

They found Meg in the summer parlour, an airy and delightful room, full now of afternoon sunshine and the rustle of trees; for the three long windows opened on the garden. The great music-room was at one end, and at the other, in a deep alcove hung with purple curtains, a little household shrine had been made. Three portraits hung there, two marble busts stood in the corners, and a couch, an oval table, with its urn of flowers, were the only articles of furniture the nook contained. The busts were John Brooke and Beth – Amy's work – both excellent likenesses, and both full of the placid beauty which always recalls the saying, that 'Clay represents life; plaster, death; marble, immortality'. On the right, as became the founder of the house, hung the portrait of Mr Laurence, with its expression of mingled pride and benevolence, as fresh and attractive as when he caught the girl Jo admiring it. Opposite was Aunt March – a legacy to Amy – in an imposing turban, immense sleeves, and long mittens decorously crossed on the front of her plum-coloured satin gown. Time had mellowed the severity of her aspect; and the fixed regard of the handsome old gentleman opposite seemed to account for the amiable simper on lips that had not uttered a sharp word for years.

In the place of honour, with the sunshine warm upon it, and a green garland always round it, was Marmee's beloved face, painted with grateful skill by a great artist whom she had befriended when poor and unknown. So beautifully lifelike was it that it seemed to smile down upon her daughters, saying cheerfully: 'Be happy; I am with you still.'

The three sisters stood a moment looking up at the beloved picture with eyes full of tender reverence and the longing that never left them; for this noble mother had been so much to them that no one could ever fill her place. Only two years since she had gone away to live and love anew, leaving such a sweet memory behind her that it was both an inspiration and a comforter to all the household. They felt this as they drew closer to one another, and Laurie put it into words as he said earnestly: 'I can ask nothing better for my child than that she may be a woman like our mother. Please God, she shall be, if I can do it; for I owe the best I have to this dear saint.'

Just then a fresh voice began to sing 'Ave Maria' in the music-room, and Bess unconsciously echoed her father's prayer for her as she dutifully obeyed his wishes. The soft sound of the air Marmee used to sing led the listeners back into the world again from that momentary reaching after the loved and lost, and they sat down together near the open windows enjoying the music, while Laurie brought them tea, making the little service pleasant by the tender care he gave to it.

Nat came in with Demi, soon followed by Ted and Josie, the Professor and his faithful Rob, all anxious to hear more about 'the boys'. The rattle of cups and tongues grew brisk, and the setting sun saw a cheerful company resting in the bright room after the varied labours of the day.

Professor Bhaer was grey now, but robust and genial as ever; for he had the work he loved, and did it so heartily that the whole college felt his beautiful influence. Rob was as much like him as it was possible for a boy to be, and was already called the 'young Professor', he so adored study and closely imitated his honoured father in all ways.

'Well, heart's dearest, we go to have our boys again, all two, and may rejoice greatly,' said Mr Bhaer, seating himself beside Jo with a beaming face and a handshake of congratulation.

'Oh, Fritz, I'm so delighted about Emil, and if you approve about Franz also. Did you know Ludmilla? Is it a wise match?' asked Mrs Jo, handing him her cup of tea and drawing closer, as if she welcomed her refuge in joy as well as sorrow.

'It all goes well. I saw the *Mädchen* when I went over to place Franz. A child then, but most sweet and charming. Blumenthal is satisfied, I think, and the boy will be happy. He is too German to be content away from Vaterland, so we shall have him as a link between the new and the old, and that pleases me much.'

'And Emil, he is to be second mate next voyage; isn't that fine? I'm so happy that both *your* boys have done well; you gave up so much for them and their mother. You make light of it, dear, but I never forget it,' said Jo, with her hand in his as sentimentally as if she was a girl again and her Fritz had come a-wooing.

He laughed his cheery laugh, and whispered behind her fan, 'If I had not come to America for the poor lads, I never should have found my Jo. The hard times are very sweet now, and I bless Gott for all I seemed to lose, because I gained the blessing of my life.'

'Spooning! spooning! Here's an awful flirtation on the sly,' cried Teddy, peering over the fan just at that interesting moment, much to his mother's confusion and his father's amusement; for the Professor never was ashamed of the fact that he still considered his wife the dearest woman in the world. Rob promptly ejected his brother from one window, to see him skip in at the other, while Mrs Jo shut her fan and held it ready to rap her unruly boy's knuckles if he came near her again.

Nat approached in answer to Mr Bhaer's beckoning teaspoon, and stood before them with a face full of the respectful affection he felt for the excellent man who had done so much for him.

'I have the letters ready for thee, my son. They are two old friends of mine in Leipzig, who will befriend thee in that new life. It is well to have them, for thou wilt be heartbroken with *Heimweh* at the first, Nat, and need comforting,' said the Professor, giving him several letters.

'Thanks, sir. Yes, I expect to be pretty lonely till I get started, then my music and the hope of getting on will cheer me up,' answered Nat, who both longed and dreaded to leave all these friends behind him and make new ones.

He was a man now; but the blue eyes were as honest as ever,

the mouth still a little weak, in spite of the carefully cherished moustache over it, and the broad forehead more plainly than ever betrayed the music-loving nature of the youth. Modest, affectionate, and dutiful, Nat was considered a pleasant though not a brilliant success by Mrs Jo. She loved and trusted him, and was sure he would do his best, but did not expect that he would be great in any way, unless the stimulus of foreign training and self-dependence made him a better artist and a stronger man than now seemed likely.

'I've marked all your things – or rather, Daisy did – and as soon as your books are collected, we can see about the packing,' said Mrs Jo, who was so used to fitting boys off for all quarters of the globe that a trip to the North Pole would not have been too much for her.

Nat grew red at mention of that name – or was it the last glow of sunset on his rather pale cheek? – and his heart beat happily at the thought of the dear girl working Ns and Bs on his humble socks and handkerchiefs; for Nat adored Daisy, and the cherished dream of his life was to earn a place for himself as a musician and win this angel for his wife. This hope did more for him than the Professor's counsels, Mrs Jo's care, or Mr Laurie's generous help. For her sake he worked, waited, and hoped, finding courage and patience in the dream of that happy future when Daisy should make a little home for him and he fiddle a fortune into her lap. Mrs Jo knew this; and though he was not exactly the man she would have chosen for her niece, she felt that Nat would always need just the wise and loving care Daisy could give him, and that without it there was danger of his being one of the amiable and aimless men who fail for want of the right pilot to steer them safely through the world. Mrs Meg decidedly frowned upon the poor boy's love, and would not hear of giving her dear girl to any but the best man to be found on the face of the earth. She was very kind, but as firm as such gentle souls can be; and Nat fled for comfort to Mrs Jo, who always espoused the interests of her boys heartily. A new set of anxieties was beginning now that the aforesaid boys were growing up, and she foresaw no end of worry as well as amusement in the love affairs already budding in her flock. Mrs Meg was usually her best ally and adviser, for she loved romances as well now as when a blooming girl herself. But in this case she hardened her heart, and would not hear a word of entreaty. 'Nat was not man enough, never would be, no one knew his family, a musician's life was a hard one; Daisy was too young, five or six years hence when time had proved both perhaps. Let us see what absence will do for him.' And that was the end of it, for when the maternal Pelican was roused she could be very firm, though for her precious children she would have plucked her last feather and given the last drop of her blood.

Mrs Jo was thinking of this as she looked at Nat while he talked with her husband about Leipzig, and she resolved to have a clear understanding with him before he went; for she was used to confidences, and talked freely with her boys about the trials and temptations that beset all lives in the beginning, and so often mar them, for want of the right word at the right moment.

This is the first duty of parents, and no false delicacy should keep them from the watchful care, the gentle warning, which makes self-knowledge and self-control the compass and pilot of the young as they leave the safe harbour of home.

'Plato and his disciples approach,' announced irreverent Teddy, as Mr March came in with several young men and women about him; for the wise old man was universally beloved, and ministered so beautifully to his flock that many of them thanked him all their lives for the help given to both hearts and souls.

Bess went to him at once; for since Marmee died, Grandpapa was her special care, and it was sweet to see the golden head bend over the silver one as she rolled out his easy chair and waited on him with tender alacrity.

'Aesthetic tea always on tap here, sir; will you have a flowing bowl or a bit of ambrosia?' asked Laurie, who was wandering about with a sugar basin in one hand and a plate of cake in the other; for sweetening cups and feeding the hungry was work he loved.

'Neither, thanks; this child has taken care of me;' and Mr March turned to Bess, who sat on one arm of his chair, holding a glass of fresh milk.

'Long may she live to do it, sir, and I be here to see this pretty contradiction of the song that "youth and age cannot live together"!' answered Laurie, smiling at the pair. ' "*Crabbed* age", Papa; that makes all the difference in the world,' said Bess quickly; for she loved poetry, and read the best.

' "Wouldst thou see fresh roses grow in a reverend bed of snow?" ' quoted Mr March, as Josie came and perched on the other arm, looking like a very thorny little rose; for she had been having a hot discussion with Ted, and had got the worst of it.

'Grandpa, must women always obey men and say they are the wisest, just because they are the strongest?' she cried, looking fiercely at her cousin, who came stalking up with a provoking smile on the boyish face that was always very comical atop of that tall figure.

'Well, my dear, that is the old-fashioned belief, and it will take some time to change it. But I think the woman's hour has struck; and it looks to me as if the boys must do their best, for the girls are abreast now, and may reach the goal first,' answered Mr March, surveying with paternal satisfaction the bright faces of the young women, who were among the best students in the college.

'The poor little Atalantas are sadly distracted and delayed by the obstacles thrown in their way – not golden apples, by any means – but I think they will stand a fair chance when they have learned to run better,' laughed Uncle Laurie, stroking Josie's breezy hair, which stood up like the fur of an angry kitten.

'Whole barrels of apples won't stop me when *I* start, and a dozen Teds won't trip me up, though they may try. I'll show him that a woman can act as well, if not better, than a man. It *has* been done, and will be again; and I'll never own that *my* brain isn't as good as his, though it may be smaller,' cried the excited young person.

'If you shake your head in that violent way you'll addle what brains you have got; and I'd take care of 'em, if I were you,' began teasing Ted.

'What started this civil war?' asked Grandpapa, with a gentle emphasis on the adjective, which caused the combatants to calm their ardour a little.

'Why, we were pegging away at the *Iliad* and came to where Zeus tells Juno not to enquire into his plans or he'll whip her, and Jo was disgusted because Juno meekly hushed up. I said it was all right, and agreed with the old fellow that women didn't know much and ought to obey men,' explained Ted, to the great amusement of his hearers.

'Goddesses may do as they like, but those Greek and Trojan

women were poor-spirited things if they minded men who couldn't fight their own battles and had to be hustled off by Pallas, and Venus, and Juno, when they were going to get beaten. The idea of two armies stopping and sitting down while a pair of heroes flung stones at one another! I don't think much of your old Homer. Give me Napoleon or Grant for my hero.'

Josie's scorn was as funny as if a hummingbird scolded at an ostrich, and everyone laughed as she sniffed at the immortal poet and criticised the gods.

'Napoleon's Juno had a nice time; didn't she? That's just the way girls argue – first one way and then the other,' jeered Ted.

'Like Johnson's young lady, who was "not categorical, but all wiggle-waggle",' added Uncle Laurie, enjoying the battle immensely.

'I was only speaking of them as soldiers. But if you come to the woman side of it, wasn't Grant a kind husband and Mrs Grant a happy woman? He didn't threaten to whip her if she asked a natural question; and if Napoleon did do wrong about Josephine, he could fight, and didn't want any Minerva to come fussing over him. They *were* a stupid set, from dandified Paris to Achilles sulking in his ships, and I won't change my opinion for all the Hectors and Agamemnons in Greece,' said Josie, still unconquered.

'You can fight like a Trojan, that's evident; and we will be the two obedient armies looking on while you and Ted have it out,' began Uncle Laurie, assuming the attitude of a warrior leaning on his spear.

'I fear we must give it up, for Pallas is about to descend and carry off our Hector,' said Mr March, smiling, as Jo came to remind her son that supper-time was near.

'We will fight it out later when there are no goddesses to interfere,' said Teddy, as he turned away with unusual alacrity, remembering the treat in store.

'Conquered by a muffin, by Jove!' called Josie after him, exulting in an opportunity to use the classical exclamation forbidden to her sex.

But Ted shot a Parthian arrow as he retired in good order by replying, with a highly virtuous expression: 'Obedience is a soldier's first duty.'

Bent on her woman's privilege of having the last word, Josie ran

after him, but never uttered the scathing speech upon her lips, for
a very brown young man in a blue suit came leaping up the steps
with a cheery 'Ahoy! ahoy! where is everybody?'

'Emil! Emil!' cried Josie, and in a moment Ted was upon him,
and the late enemies ended their fray in a joyful welcome to the
newcomer.

Muffins were forgotten, and towing their cousin like two fussy
little tugs with a fine merchantman, the children returned to the
parlour, where Emil kissed all the women and shook hands with
all the men except his uncle; him he embraced in the good old
German style, to the great delight of the observers.

'Didn't think I could get off today, but found I could, and
steered straight for old Plum. Not a soul there, so I luffed and
bore away for Parnassus, and here is every man Jack of you. Bless
your hearts, how glad I am to see you all!' exclaimed the sailor
boy, beaming at them, as he stood with his legs apart as if he still
felt the rocking deck under his feet.

'You ought to "shiver your timbers", not "bless our hearts",
Emil; it's not nautical at all. Oh, how nice and shippy and tarry
you do smell!' said Josie, sniffing at him with great enjoyment of
the fresh sea odours he brought with him. This was her favourite
cousin, and she was his pet; so she knew that the bulging pockets
of the blue jacket contained treasures for her at least.

'Avast, my hearty, and let me take soundings before you
dive,' laughed Emil, understanding her affectionate caresses, and
holding her off with one hand while with the other he rummaged
out sundry foreign little boxes and parcels marked with different
names, and handed them round with appropriate remarks, which
caused much laughter; for Emil was a wag.

'There's a hawser that will hold our little cock-boat still about
five minutes,' he said, throwing a necklace of pretty pink coral over
Josie's head; 'and here's something the mermaids sent to Undine,'
he added, handing Bess a string of pearly shells on a silver chain.

'I thought Daisy would like a fiddle, and Nat can find her a
beau,' continued the sailor, with a laugh, as he undid a dainty
filigree brooch in the shape of a violin.

'I know she will, and I'll take it to her,' answered Nat, as he
vanished, glad of an errand, and sure that *he* could find Daisy
though Emil had missed her.

Emil chuckled, and handed out a quaintly carved bear whose head opened, showing a capacious inkstand. This he presented, with a scrape, to Aunt Jo.

'Knowing your fondness for these fine animals, I brought this one to your pen.'

'Very good, Commodore! Try again,' said Mrs Jo, much pleased with her gift, which caused the Professor to prophesy 'works of Shakespeare' from its depths, so great would be the inspiration of the beloved bruin.

'As Aunt Meg *will* wear caps, in spite of her youth, I got Ludmilla to get me some bits of lace. Hope you'll like 'em;' and out of a soft paper came some filmy things, one of which soon lay like a net of snowflakes on Mrs Meg's pretty hair.

'I couldn't find anything swell enough for Aunt Amy, because she has everything she wants, so I brought a little picture that always makes me think of her when Bess was a baby;' and he handed her an oval ivory locket, on which was painted a golden-haired Madonna, with a rosy child folded in her blue mantle.

'How lovely!' cried everyone; and Aunt Amy at once hung it about her neck on the blue ribbon from Bess's hair, charmed with her gift; for it recalled the happiest year of her life.

'Now, I flatter myself I've got just the thing for Nan, neat but not gaudy, a sort of sign you see, and very appropriate for a doctor,' said Emil, proudly displaying a pair of lava earrings shaped like little skulls.

'Horrid!' And Bess, who hated ugly things, turned her eyes to her own pretty shells.

'She won't wear earrings,' said Josie.

'Well, she'll enjoy punching your ears then. She's never so happy as when she's overhauling her fellow creatures and going for 'em with a knife,' answered Emil, undisturbed. 'I've got a lot of plunder for you fellows in my chest, but I knew I should have no peace till my cargo for the girls was unloaded. Now tell me all the news.' And, seated on Amy's best marble-topped table, the sailor swung his legs and talked at the rate of ten knots an hour, till Aunt Jo carried them all off to a grand family tea in honour of the Commodore.

CHAPTER 3

Jo's Last Scrape

The March family had enjoyed a great many surprises in the course of their varied career, but the greatest of all was when the Ugly Duckling turned out to be, not a swan, but a golden goose, whose literary eggs found such an unexpected market that in ten years Jo's wildest and most cherished dream actually came true. How or why it happened she never clearly understood, but all of a sudden she found herself famous in a small way, and, better still, with a snug little fortune in her pocket to clear away the obstacles of the present and assure the future of her boys.

It began during a bad year when everything went wrong at Plumfield; times were hard, the school dwindled, Jo overworked herself and had a long illness; Laurie and Amy were abroad, and the Bhaers too proud to ask help even of those as near and dear as this generous pair. Confined to her room, Jo got desperate over the state of affairs, till she fell back upon the long-disused pen as the only thing she could do to help fill up the gaps in the income. A book for girls being wanted by a certain publisher, she hastily scribbled a little story describing a few scenes and adventures in the lives of herself and sisters, though boys were more in her line, and with very slight hopes of success sent it out to seek its fortune.

Things always went by contraries with Jo. Her first book, laboured over for years, and launched full of the high hopes and ambitious dreams of youth, foundered on its voyage, though the wreck continued to float long afterward, to the profit of the publisher at least. The hastily written story, sent away with no thought beyond the few dollars it might bring, sailed with a fair wind and a wise pilot at the helm into public favour, and came home heavily laden with an unexpected cargo of gold and glory.

A more astonished woman probably never existed than Josephine Bhaer when her little ship came into port with flags flying, cannon that had been silent before now booming gaily, and, better than all, many kind faces rejoicing with her, many friendly hands grasping hers with cordial congratulations. After that it was plain sailing, and she merely had to load her ships and send them off on prosperous trips, to bring home stores of comfort for all she loved and laboured for.

The fame she never did quite accept; for it takes very little fire to make a great deal of smoke nowadays, and notoriety is not real glory. The fortune she could not doubt, and gratefully received; though it was not half so large a one as a generous world reported it to be. The tide having turned continued to rise, and floated the family comfortably into a snug harbour where the older members could rest secure from storms, and whence the younger ones could launch their boats for the voyage of life.

All manner of happiness, peace, and plenty came in those years to bless the patient waiters, hopeful workers, and devout believers in the wisdom and justice of Him who sends disappointment, poverty, and sorrow to try the love of human hearts and make success the sweeter when it comes. The world saw the prosperity, and kind souls rejoiced over the improved fortunes of the family; but the success Jo valued most, the happiness that nothing could change or take away, few knew much about.

It was the power of making her mother's last years happy and serene; to see the burden of care laid down for ever, the weary hands at rest, the dear face untroubled by any anxiety, and the tender heart free to pour itself out in the wise charity which was its delight. As a girl, Jo's favourite plan had been a room where Marmee could sit in peace and enjoy herself after her hard, heroic life. Now the dream had become a happy fact, and Marmee sat in her pleasant chamber with every comfort and luxury about her, loving daughters to wait on her as infirmities increased, a faithful mate to lean upon, and grandchildren to brighten the twilight of life with their dutiful affection. A very precious time to all, for she rejoiced as only mothers can in the good fortunes of their children. She had lived to reap the harvest she sowed; had seen prayers answered, hopes blossom, good gifts bear fruit, peace and prosperity bless the home she had made; and then, like some brave, patient angel, whose work was done, turned her face heavenward, glad to rest.

This was the sweet and sacred side of the change; but it had its droll and thorny one, as all things have in this curious world of ours. After the first surprise, incredulity, and joy, which came to Jo, with the ingratitude of human nature, she soon tired of renown, and began to resent her loss of liberty. For suddenly the admiring public took possession of her and all her affairs, past, present, and to come. Strangers demanded to look at her, question, advise, warn, congratulate, and drive her out of her wits by well-meant but very wearisome attentions. If she declined to open her heart to them, they reproached her; if she refused to endow her pet charities, relieve private wants, or sympathise with every ill and trial known to humanity, she was called hard-hearted, selfish, and haughty; if she found it impossible to answer the piles of letters sent her, she was neglectful of her duty to the admiring public; and if she preferred the privacy of home to the pedestal upon which she was requested to pose, 'the airs of literary people' were freely criticised.

She did her best for the children, they being the public for whom she wrote, and laboured stoutly to supply the demand always in the mouths of voracious youth – 'More stories; more right away!' Her family objected to this devotion at their expense, and her health suffered; but for a time she gratefully offered herself up on the altar of juvenile literature, feeling that she owed a good deal to the little friends in whose sight she had found favour after twenty years of effort.

But a time came when her patience gave out; and wearying of being a lion, she became a bear in nature as in name, and returning to her den, growled awfully when ordered out. Her family enjoyed the fun, and had small sympathy with her trials, but Jo came to consider it the worse scrape of her life; for liberty had always been her dearest possession, and it seemed to be fast going from her. Living in a lantern soon loses its charm, and she was too old, too tired, and too busy to like it. She felt that she had done all that could reasonably be required of her when auto-graphs, photographs, and autobiographical sketches had been sown broadcast over the land; when artists had taken her home in all its aspects, and reporters had taken her in the grim one she always assumed on these trying occasions; when a series of en-thusiastic boarding-schools had ravaged her grounds for trophies, and a steady stream of amiable pilgrims had worn her doorsteps with their respectful feet; when servants left after a week's trial of the bell that rang all day; when her husband was forced to guard her at meals, and the boys to cover her retreat out of back windows on certain occasions when enterprising guests walked in unannounced at unfortunate moments.

A sketch of one day may perhaps explain the state of things, offer some excuse for the unhappy woman, and give a hint to the autograph-fiend now rampant in the land; for it is a true tale.

'There ought to be a law to protect unfortunate authors,' said Mrs Jo one morning soon after Emil's arrival, when the mail brought her an unusually large and varied assortment of letters. 'To me it is a more vital subject than international copyright; for time is money, peace is health, and I lose both with no return but less respect for my fellow creatures and a wild desire to fly into the wilderness, since I cannot shut my doors even in free America.'

'Lion hunters are awful when in search of their prey. If they could change places for a while it would do them good; and they'd see what bores they were when they "do themselves the honour of calling to express their admiration of our charming work",' quoted Ted, with a bow to his parent, now frowning over twelve requests for autographs.

'I have made up my mind on one point,' said Mrs Jo with great firmness. 'I will *not* answer this kind of letter. I've sent at least six to this boy, and he probably sells them. This girl writes from a seminary, and if I send her one all the other girls will at once write for more. All begin by saying they know they intrude, and that I am of course annoyed by these requests; but they venture to ask because I like boys, or they like the books, or it is only one. Emerson and Whittier put these things in the wastepaper-basket; and though only a literary nurserymaid who provides moral pap for the young, I will follow their illustrious example; for I shall have no time to eat or sleep if I try to satisfy these dear un-reasonable children;' and Mrs Jo swept away the entire batch with a sigh of relief.

'I'll open the others and let you eat your breakfast in peace, *liebe Mutter*,' said Rob, who often acted as her secretary. 'Here's one from the South;' and breaking an imposing seal, he read:

'MADAM– As it has pleased Heaven to bless your efforts with a large fortune, I feel no hesitation in asking you to supply funds to purchase a new communion-service for our church. To whatever denomination you belong, you will of course respond with liberality to such a request,

Respectfully yours,

MRS X. Y. ZAVIER.'

'Send a civil refusal, dear. All I have to give must go to feed and clothe the poor at my gates. That is my thank-offering for success. Go on,' answered his mother, with a grateful glance about her happy home.

'A literary youth of eighteen proposes that you put your name to a novel he has written; and after the first edition your name is to be taken off and his put on. There's a cool proposal for you. I guess you won't agree to that, in spite of your soft-heartedness towards most of the young scribblers.'

'Couldn't be done. Tell him so kindly, and don't let him send the manuscript. I have seven on hand now, and barely time to read my own,' said Mrs Jo, pensively fishing a small letter out of the slop-bowl and opening it with care, because the downhill address suggested that a child wrote it.

'I will answer this myself. A little sick girl wants a book, and she shall have it, but I can't write sequels to all the rest to please her. I should never come to an end if I tried to suit these voracious little Oliver Twists, clamouring for more. What next, Robin?'

'This is short and sweet.

DEAR MRS BHAER – I am now going to give you my opinion of your works. I have read them all many times, and call them first-rate. Please go ahead.

Your admirer,

BILLY BABCOCK.'

'Now that is what I like. Billy is a man of sense and a critic worth having, since he had read my works many times before expressing his opinion. He asks for no answer, so send my thanks and regards.'

'Here's a lady in England with seven girls, and she wishes to know your views upon education. Also what careers they shall follow the oldest being twelve. Don't wonder she's worried,' laughed Rob.

'I'll try to answer it. But as I have no girls, my opinion isn't worth much and will probably shock her, as I shall tell her to let them run and play and build up good, stout bodies before she talks about careers. They will soon show what they want, if they are let alone, and not all run in the same mould.'

'Here's a fellow who wants to know what sort of a girl he shall marry, and if you know of any like those in your stories.'

'Give him Nan's address, and see what he'll get,' proposed Ted, privately resolving to do it himself if possible.

'This is from a lady who wants you to adopt her child and lend her money to study art abroad for a few years. Better take it, and try your hand at a girl, mother.'

'No, thank you, I will keep to my own line of business. What is that blotted one? It looks rather awful, to judge by the ink,' asked Mrs Jo, who beguiled her daily task by trying to guess from the outside what was inside her many letters. This proved to be a poem from an insane admirer, to judge by its incoherent style.

'To J. M. B.

Oh, were I a heliotrope,
I would play poet,
And blow a breeze of fragrance
To you; and none should know it.

Your form like the stately elm
When Phoebus gilds the morning ray;
Your cheeks like the ocean bed
That blooms a rose in May.

Your words are wise and bright,
I bequeath them to you a legacy given;
And when your spirit takes its flight,
May it bloom an' flower in heaven.

My tongue in flattering language spoke,
And sweeter silence never broke
In busiest street or loneliest glen.
I take you with the flashes of my pen.

Consider the lilies, how they grow;
They toil not, yet are fair,
Gems and flowers and Solomon's seal.
The geranium of the world is J. M. Bhaer.

JAMES.'

While the boys shouted over this effusion – which is a true one – their mother read several liberal offers from budding magazines for her to edit them gratis; one long letter from a young girl inconsolable because her favourite hero died, and 'would dear Mrs Bhaer rewrite the tale, and make it end good?' Another from an irate boy denied an autograph, who darkly foretold financial ruin and loss of favour if she did not send him and all other fellows who asked autographs, photographs, and autobiographical sketches; a minister wished to know her religion; and an undecided maiden asked which of her two lovers she should marry. These samples will suffice to show a few of the claims made on a busy woman's time, and make my readers pardon Mrs Jo if she did not carefully reply to all.

'That job is done. Now I will dust a bit, and then go to my work. I'm all behind-hand, and serials can't wait; so deny me to everybody, Mary. I won't see Queen Victoria if she comes today.' And Mrs Bhaer threw down her napkin as if defying all creation.

'I hope the day will go well with thee, my dearest,' answered her husband, who had been busy with his own voluminous correspondence. 'I will dine at college with Professor Plock, who is to visit us today. The *Jünglings* can lunch on Parnassus; so thou shalt have a quiet time.' And smoothing the worried lines out of her forehead with his goodbye kiss, the excellent man marched away, both pockets full of books, an old umbrella in one hand, and a bag of stones for the geology class in the other.

'If all literary women had such thoughtful angels for husbands, they would live longer and write more. Perhaps that wouldn't be a blessing to the world though, as most of us write too much now,' said Mrs Jo, waving her feather duster to her spouse, who responded with flourishes of the umbrella as he went down the avenue.

Rob started for school at the same time, looking so much like him with his books and bag and square shoulders and steady air that his mother laughed as she turned away, saying heartily: 'Bless both my dear professors, for better creatures never lived!'

Emil was already gone to his ship in the city; but Ted lingered to steal the address he wanted, ravage the sugar bowl, and talk with 'Mum'; for the two had great larks together. Mrs Jo always arranged her own parlour, refilled her vases, and gave the little touches that left it cool and neat for the day. Going to draw down the curtain, she beheld an artist sketching on the lawn, and groaned as she hastily retired to the back window to shake her duster.

At that moment the bell rang and the sound of wheels was heard in the road.

'I'll go; Mary lets 'em in;' and Ted smoothed his hair as he made for the hall.

'Can't see anyone. Give me a chance to fly upstairs,' whispered Mrs Jo, preparing to escape. But before she could do so, a man appeared at the door with a card in his hand. Ted met him with a stern air, and his mother dodged behind the window curtains to bide her time for escape.

'I am doing a series of articles for the *Saturday Tattler*, and I called to see Mrs Bhaer the first of all,' began the newcomer in the insinuating tone of his tribe, while his quick eyes were taking in all they could, experience having taught him to make the most of his time, as his visits were usually short ones.

'Mrs Bhaer never sees reporters, sir.'

'But a few moments will be all I ask,' said the man, edging his way farther in.

'You can't see her, for she is out,' replied Teddy, as a backward glance showed him that his unhappy parent had vanished – through the window, he supposed, as she sometimes did when hard bestead.

'Very sorry. I'll call again. Is this her study? Charming room!' And the intruder fell back on the parlour, bound to see something and bag a fact if he died in the attempt. 'It is not,' said Teddy, gently but firmly backing him down the hall, devoutly hoping that his mother had escaped round the corner of the house.

'If you could tell me Mrs Bhaer's age and birthplace, date of marriage, and number of children, I should be much obliged,' continued the unabashed visitor as he tripped over the doormat.

'She is about sixty, born in Nova Zembla, married just forty years ago today, and has eleven daughters. Anything else, sir?' And Ted's sober face was such a funny contrast to his ridiculous reply that the reporter owned himself routed, and retired laughing just as a lady followed by three beaming girls came up the steps.

'We are all the way from Oshkosh, and couldn't go home without seein' dear Aunt Jo. My girls just admire her works, and are set on gettin' a sight of her. I know it's early; but we are goin' to see Holmes and Longfeller, and the rest of the celebrities, so we ran out here fust thing. Mrs Erastus Kingsbury Parmalee, of Oshkosh, tell her. We don't mind waitin'; we can look round a spell if she ain't ready to see folks yet.'

All this was uttered with such rapidity that Ted could only stand gazing at the buxom damsels, who fixed their six blue eyes upon him so beseechingly that his native gallantry made it impossible to deny them a civil reply at least.

'Mrs Bhaer is not visible today – out just now, I believe; but you can see the house and grounds if you like,' he murmured, falling back as the four pressed in gazing rapturously about them.

'Oh, thank you! Sweet, pretty place I'm sure! That's where she writes, ain't it? Do tell me if that's her picture! Looks just as I imagined her!'

With these remarks the ladies paused before a fine engraving of the Hon. Mrs Norton, with a pen in her hand and a rapt expression of countenance, likewise a diadem and pearl necklace.

Keeping his gravity with an effort, Teddy pointed to a very bad portrait of Mrs Jo, which hung behind the door, and afforded her much amusement, it was so dismal, in spite of a curious effect of light upon the end of the nose and cheeks as red as the chair she sat in.

'This was taken for my mother; but it is not very good,' he said, enjoying the struggles of the girls not to look dismayed at the sad difference between the real and the ideal. The youngest, aged twelve, could not conceal her disappointment, and turned away, feeling as so many of us have felt when we discover that our idols are very ordinary men and women.

'I thought she'd be about sixteen and have her hair braided in two tails down her back. I don't care about seeing her now,' said the honest child, walking off to the hall door, leaving her mother to apologise, and her sisters to declare that the bad portrait was 'perfectly lovely, so speaking and poetic, you know, 'specially about the brow'.

'Come, girls, we must be goin', if we want to get through today. You can leave your albums and have them sent when Mrs Bhaer has written a sentiment in 'em. We are a thousand times obliged. Give our best love to your ma, and tell her we are so sorry not to see her.' Just as Mrs Erastus Kingsbury Parmalee uttered the words her eye fell upon a middle-aged woman in a large checked apron, with a handkerchief tied over her head, busily dusting an end room which looked like a study.

'One peep at her sanctum since she is out,' cried the enthusiastic lady, and swept across the hall with her flock before Teddy could warn his mother, whose retreat had been cut off by the artist in front, the reporter at the back of the house – for he hadn't gone – and the ladies in the hall.

'They've got her!' thought Teddy, in comical dismay. 'No use for her to play housemaid since they've seen the portrait.'

Mrs Jo did her best, and being a good actress, would have escaped if the fatal picture had not betrayed her. Mrs Parmalee paused at the desk, and regardless of the meerschaum that lay there, the man's slippers close by, and a pile of letters directed to 'Prof. F. Bhaer', she clasped her hands, exclaiming impressively, 'Girls, this is the spot where she wrote those sweet, those moral tales which have thrilled us to the soul! Could I – ah, could I take one morsel of paper, an old pen, a postage stamp even, as a memento of this gifted woman?'

'Yes'm, help yourselves,' replied the maid, moving away with a glance at the boy, whose eyes were now full of merriment he could not suppress.

The oldest girl saw it, guessed the truth, and a quick look at the woman in the apron confirmed her suspicion. Touching her mother, she whispered: 'Ma, it's Mrs Bhaer herself. I know it is.'

'No? yes? it is! Well, I do declare, how nice that is!' And hastily pursuing the unhappy woman, who was making for the door, Mrs Parmalee cried eagerly: 'Don't mind us! I know you're busy, but just let me take your hand and then we'll go.'

Giving herself up for lost, Mrs Jo turned and presented her hand like a tea-tray, submitting to have it heartily shaken, as the matron said, with somewhat alarming hospitality, 'If ever you come to Oshkosh, your feet won't be allowed to touch the pavement; for you'll be borne in the arms of the populace, we shall be so dreadful glad to see you.'

Mentally resolving never to visit that effusive town, Jo responded as cordially as she could; and having written her name in the albums, provided each visitor with a memento, and kissed them all round, they at last departed, to call on 'Longfeller, Holmes, and the rest' – who were all out, it is devoutly to be hoped.

'You villain, why didn't you give me a chance to whip away? Oh, my dear, what fibs you told that man! I hope we shall be forgiven our sins in this line, but I don't know what *is* to become of us if we don't dodge. So many against one isn't fair play.' And Mrs Jo hung up her apron in the hall closet, with a groan at the trials of her lot.

'More people coming up the avenue! Better dodge while the coast is clear! I'll head them off!' cried Teddy, looking back from the steps, as he was departing to school.

Mrs Jo flew upstairs, and having locked her door, calmly viewed a young ladies' seminary camp on the lawn, and being denied the house, proceed to enjoy themselves by picking the flowers, doing up their hair, eating lunch, and freely expressing their opinion of the place and its possessors before they went.

A few hours of quiet followed, and she was just settling down to a long afternoon of hard work, when Rob came home to tell her that the Young Men's Christian Union would visit the college, and two or three of the fellows whom she knew wanted to pay their respects to her on the way.

'It is going to rain, so they won't come, I dare say; but father thought you'd like to be ready, in case they do call. You always see the boys, you know, though you harden your heart to the poor girls,' said Rob, who had heard from his brother about the morning visitations.

'Boys don't gush, so I can stand it. The last time I let in a party of girls one fell into my arms and said, "Darling, love me!" I wanted to shake her,' answered Mrs Jo, wiping her pen with energy.

'You may be sure the fellows won't do it, but they will want autographs, so you'd better be prepared with a few dozen,' said Rob, laying out a quire of notepaper, being a hospitable youth and sympathising with those who admired his mother.

'They can't outdo the girls. At X College I really believe I wrote three hundred during the day I was there, and I left a pile of cards and albums on my table when I came away. It is one of the most absurd and tiresome manias that ever afflicted the world.'

Nevertheless Mrs Jo wrote her name a dozen times, put on her black silk, and resigned herself to the impending call, praying for rain, however, as she returned to her work.

The shower came, and feeling quite secure, she rumpled up her hair, took off her cuffs, and hurried to finish her chapter; for thirty pages a day was her task, and she liked to have it well done before evening. Josie had brought some flowers for the vases, and was just putting the last touches when she saw several umbrellas bobbing down the hill.

'They are coming, Aunty! I see uncle hurrying across the field to receive them,' she called at the stair-foot.

'Keep an eye on them, and let me know when they enter the avenue. It will take but a minute to tidy up and run down,' answered Mrs Jo, scribbling away for dear life, because serials wait for no man, not even the whole Christian Union *en masse*.

'There are more than two or three. I see half a dozen at least,' called sister Ann from the hall door. 'No! a dozen, I do believe; Aunty, look out; they are all coming! What *shall* we do?' And Josie quailed at the idea of facing the black throng rapidly approaching.

'Mercy on us, there are hundreds! Run and put a tub in the back entry for their umbrellas to drip into. Tell them to go down the hall and leave them, and pile their hats on the table; the tree won't hold them all. No use to get mats; my poor carpets!' And down went Mrs Jo to prepare for the invasion, while Josie and the maids flew about dismayed at the prospect of so many muddy boots.

On they came, a long line of umbrellas, with splashed legs and flushed faces underneath; for the gentlemen had been having a good time all over the town, undisturbed by the rain. Professor Bhaer met them at the gate, and was making a little speech of welcome, when Mrs Jo, touched by their bedraggled state, appeared at the door, beckoning them in. Leaving their host to orate bare-headed in the wet, the young men hastened up the steps, merry, warm, and eager, clutching off their hats as they came, and struggling with their umbrellas, as the order was passed to march in and stack arms.

Tramp, tramp, tramp, down the hall went seventy-five pairs of boots; soon seventy-five umbrellas dripped sociably in the hos-pitable tub, while their owners swarmed all over the lower part of the house; and seventy-five hearty hands were shaken by the hostess without a murmur, though some were wet, some very warm, and nearly all bore trophies of the day's ramble. One impetuous party flourished a small turtle as he made his com-pliments; another had a load of sticks cut from noted spots; and all begged for some memento of Plumfield. A pile of cards mysteriously appeared on the table, with a written request for autographs; and despite her morning vow, Mrs Jo wrote every one, while her husband and boys did the honours of the house.

Josie fled to the back parlour, but was discovered by exploring youths, and mortally insulted by one of them, who innocently enquired if she was Mrs Bhaer. The reception did not last long, and the end was better than the beginning; for the rain ceased, and a rainbow shone beautifully over them as the good fellows stood upon the lawn singing sweetly for a farewell. A happy omen, that bow of promise arched over the young heads, as if Heaven smiled upon their union, and showed them that above the muddy earth and rainy skies the blessed sun still shone for all. Three cheers, and then away they went, leaving a pleasant recollection of their visit to amuse the family as they scraped the mud off the carpets with shovels and emptied the tub half-full of water.

'Nice, honest, hard-working fellows, and I don't begrudge my half-hour at all; but I must finish, so don't let anyone disturb me till tea-time,' said Mrs Jo, leaving Mary to shut up the house; for papa and the boys had gone off with the guests, and Josie had run home to tell her mother about the fun at Aunt Jo's.

Peace reigned for an hour, then the bell rang and Mary came giggling up to say: 'A queer kind of a lady wants to know if she can catch a grasshopper in the garden.'

'A what?' cried Mrs Jo, dropping her pen with a blot; for of all the odd requests ever made, this was the oddest.

'A grasshopper, ma'am. I said you was busy, and asked what she wanted, and says she: "I've got grasshoppers from the grounds of several famous folks, and I want one from Plumfield to add to my collection." Did you ever?' And Mary giggled again at the idea.

'Tell her to take all there are and welcome. I shall be glad to get rid of them; always bouncing in my face and getting in my dress,' laughed Mrs Jo.

Mary retired, to return in a moment nearly speechless with merriment.

'She's much obliged, ma'am, and she'd like an old gown or a pair of stockings of yours to put in a rug she's making. Got a vest of Emerson's, she says, and a pair of Mr Holmes's trousers, and a dress of Mrs Stowe's. She must be crazy!'

'Give her that old red shawl, then I shall make a gay show among the great ones in that astonishing rug. Yes, they are all lunatics, these lion hunters; but this seems to be a harmless maniac, for she doesn't take my time, and gives me a good laugh,' said Mrs Jo, returning to her work after a glance from the window, which showed her a tall, thin lady in rusty black, skipping wildly to and fro on the lawn in pursuit of the lively insect she wanted.

No more interruptions till the light began to fade, then Mary popped her head in to say a gentleman wished to see Mrs Bhaer, and wouldn't take no for an answer.

'He must. I shall *not* go down. This has been an awful day, and I won't be disturbed again,' replied the harassed authoress, pausing in the midst of the grand finale of her chapter.

'I told him so, ma'am; but he walked right in as bold as brass. I guess he's another crazy one, and I declare I'm 'most afraid of him, he's so big and black, and cool as cucumbers, though I will say he's good-looking,' added Mary, with a simper; for the stranger had evidently found favour in her sight despite his boldness.

'My day has been ruined, and I *will* have this last half-hour to finish. Tell him to go away; I *won't* go down,' cried Mrs Jo, fiercely.

Mary went; and listening, in spite of herself, her mistress heard first a murmur of voices, then a cry from Mary, and remembering the ways of reporters, also that her maid was both pretty and timid, Mrs Bhaer flung down her pen and went to the rescue. Descending with her most majestic air she demanded in an awe-inspiring voice, as she paused to survey the somewhat brigandish intruder, who seemed to be storming the staircase which Mary was gallantly defending: '*Who* is this person who insists on remaining when I have declined to see him?'

'I'm sure I don't know, ma'am. He won't give no name, and says you'll be sorry if you don't see him,' answered Mary, retiring flushed and indignant from her post.

'Won't you be sorry?' asked the stranger, looking up with a pair of black eyes full of laughter, the flash of white teeth through a long beard, and both hands out as he boldly approached the irate lady.

Mrs Jo gave one keen look, for the voice was familiar; then completed Mary's bewilderment by throwing both arms round the brigand's neck, exclaiming joyfully, 'My dearest boy, where did you come from?'

'California, on purpose to see you, Mother Bhaer. Now won't you be sorry if I go away?' answered Dan, with a hearty kiss.

'To think of my ordering you out of the house when I've been longing to see you for a year,' laughed Mrs Jo, and she went down to have a good talk with her returned wanderer, who enjoyed the joke immensely.

CHAPTER 4

Dan

Mrs Jo often thought that Dan had Indian blood in him, not only because of his love of a wild, wandering life, but his appearance; for as he grew up, this became more striking. At twenty-five he was very tall, with sinewy limbs, a keen, dark face, and the alert look of one whose senses were all alive; rough in manner, full of energy, quick with word and blow, eyes full of the old fire, always watchful as if used to keep guard, and a general air of vigour and freshness very charming to those who knew the dangers and delights of his adventurous life. He was looking his best as he sat talking with 'Mother Bhaer', one strong brown hand in hers, and a world of affection in his voice as he said: 'Forget old friends! How could I forget the only home I ever knew? Why, I was in such a hurry to come and tell my good luck that I didn't stop to fix up, you see; though I knew you'd think I looked more like a wild buffalo than ever,' with a shake of his shaggy black head, a tug at his beard, and a laugh that made the room ring.

'I like it; I always had a fancy for banditti – and you look just like one. Mary, being a newcomer, was frightened at your looks and manners. Josie won't know you, but Ted will recognise his Danny in spite of the big beard and flowing mane. They will all be here soon to welcome you; so before they come tell me more about yourself. Why, Dan, dear! it's nearly two years since you were here! Has it gone well with you?' asked Mrs Jo, who had been listening with maternal interest to his account of life in California, and the unexpected success of a small investment he had made.

'First-rate! I don't care for the money, you know. I only want a trifle to pay my way – rather earn as I go, and not be bothered with the care of a lot. It's the fun of the thing coming to me, and my being able to give away, that I like. No use to lay up; I shan't live to be old and need it – my sort never do,' said Dan, looking as if his little fortune rather oppressed him.

'But if you marry and settle somewhere, as I hope you will, you must have something to begin with, my son. So be prudent and invest your money; don't give it away, for rainy days come to all of us, and dependence would be very hard for you to bear,' answered Mrs Jo with a sage air, though she liked to see that the money-making fever had not seized her lucky boy yet.

Dan shook his head, and glanced about the room as if he already found it rather confined and longed for all out-of-doors again.

'Who would marry a jack-o'-lantern like me? Women like a steady-going man; I shall never be that.'

'My dear boy, when I was a girl I liked just such adventurous fellows as you are. Anything fresh and daring, free and romantic, is always attractive to us womenfolk. Don't be discouraged; you'll find an anchor someday, and be content to take shorter voyages and bring home a good cargo.'

'What should you say if I brought you an Indian squaw some-day?' asked Dan, with a glimmer of mischief in the eyes that rested on a marble bust of Galatea gleaming white and lovely in the corner.

'Welcome her heartily, if she was a good one. Is there a prospect of it?' and Mrs Jo peered at him with the interest which even literary ladies take in love affairs.

'Not at present, thank you. I'm too busy "to gallivant", as Ted calls it. How is the boy?' asked Dan, skilfully turning the conversation, as if he had had enough of sentiment.

Mrs Jo was off at once, and expatiated upon the talents and virtues of her sons till they came bursting in and fell upon Dan like two affectionate young bears, finding a vent for their joyful emotions in a sort of friendly wrestling-match; in which both got worsted, of course, for the hunter soon settled them. The Professor followed, and tongues went like mill-clappers while Mary lighted up and cook devoted herself to an unusually good supper, instinctively divining that this guest was a welcome one.

After tea Dan was walking up and down the long rooms as he talked, with occasional trips into the hall for a fresher breath of air, his lungs seeming to need more than those of civilised people. In one of these trips he saw a white figure framed in the dark doorway, and paused to look at it. Bess paused also, not recognising her old friend, and quite unconscious of the pretty picture she made standing, tall and slender, against the soft gloom of the summer night, with her golden hair like a halo round her head, and the ends of a white shawl blown out like wings by the cool wind sweeping through the hall. 'Is it Dan?' she asked, coming in with a gracious smile and outstretched hand.

'Looks like it; but I didn't know *you*, Princess. I thought it was a spirit,' answered Dan, looking down at her with a curious softness and wonder in his face.

'I've grown very much, but two years have changed you entirely;' and Bess looked up with girlish pleasure at the picturesque figure before her – for it was a decided contrast to the well-dressed people about her.

Before they could say more, Josie rushed in, and, forgetful of the newly acquired dignity of her teens, let Dan catch her up and kiss her like a child. Not till he set her down did he discover she also was changed, and exclaimed in comic dismay: 'Hallo! Why, you are growing up too! What am I going to do, with no young one to play with? Here's Ted going it like a beanstalk, and Bess a young lady, and even you, my mustard-seed, letting down your frocks and putting on airs.'

The girls laughed, and Josie blushed as she stared at the tall man, conscious that she had leaped before she looked. They made a pretty contrast, these two young cousins – one as fair as a lily, the other a little wild rose. And Dan gave a nod of satisfaction as he surveyed them; for he had seen many bonny girls in his travels, and was glad that these old friends were blooming so beautifully.

'Here! we can't allow any monopoly of Dan!' called Mrs Jo. 'Bring him back and keep an eye on him, or he will be slipping off for another little run of a year or two before we have half seen him.'

Led by these agreeable captors, Dan returned to the parlour to receive a scolding from Josie for getting ahead of all the other boys and looking like a man first.

'Emil is older; but he's only a boy, and dances jigs and sings sailor songs just as he used to. You look about thirty, and as big and black as a villain in a play. Oh, I've got a splendid idea! You are just the thing for Arbaces in *The Last Days of Pompeii*. We want to act it; have the lion and the gladiators and the eruption. Tom and Ted are going to shower bushels of ashes down and roll barrels of stones about. We wanted a dark man for the Egyptian; and you will be gorgeous in red and white shawls. Won't he, Aunt Jo?'

This deluge of words made Dan clap his hands over his ears; and before Mrs Bhaer could answer her impetuous niece the Laurences, with Meg and her family, arrived, soon followed by Tom and Nan, and all sat down to listen to Dan's adventures – told in brief yet effective manner, as the varying expressions of interest, wonder, merriment, and suspense painted on the circle of faces round him plainly showed. The boys all wanted to start at once for California and make fortunes; the girls could hardly wait for the curious and pretty things he had picked up for them in his travels; while the elders rejoiced heartily over the energy and good prospects of their wild boy.

'Of course you will want to go back for another stroke of luck; and I hope you will have it. But speculation is a dangerous game, and you may lose all you've won,' said Mr Laurie, who had enjoyed the stirring tale as much as any of the boys, and would have liked to rough it with Dan as well as they.

'I've had enough of it, for a while at least; too much like gambling. The excitement is all I care for, and it isn't good for me. I have a notion to try farming out West. It's grand on a large scale; and I feel as if steady work would be rather jolly after loafing round so long. I can make a beginning, and you can send me your black sheep to stock my place with. I tried sheep farming in Australia, and know something about black ones, anyway.'

A laugh chased away the sober look in Dan's face as he ended; and those who knew him best guessed that he had learned a lesson there in San Francisco, and dared not try again.

'That is a capital idea, Dan!' cried Mrs Jo, seeing great hope in this desire to fix himself somewhere and help others. 'We shall know where you are, and can go and see you, and not have half the world between us. I'll send my Ted for a visit. He's such a restless spirit, it would do him good. With you he would be safe while he worked off his surplus energies and learned a wholesome business.'

'I'll use the "shubble and de hoe" like a good one, if I get a chance out there; but the Speranza mines sound rather jollier,' said Ted, examining the samples of ore Dan had brought for the Professor.

'You go and start a new town, and when we are ready to swarm we will come out and settle there. You will want a newspaper very soon, and I like the idea of running one myself much better than grinding away as I do now,' observed Demi, panting to distinguish himself in the journalistic line.

'We could easily plant a new college there. These sturdy Westerners are hungry for learning, and very quick to see and choose the best,' added ever-young Mr March, beholding with his prophetic eye many duplicates of their own flourishing establishment springing up in the wide West.

'Go on, Dan. It is a fine plan, and we will back you up. I shouldn't mind investing in a few prairies and cowboys myself,' said Mr Laurie, always ready to help the lads to help themselves, both by his cheery words and ever-open purse.

'A little money sort of ballasts a fellow, and investing it in land anchors him – for a while, at least. I'd like to see what I can do, but I thought I'd consult you before I decided. Have my doubts about it suiting me for many years; but I can cut loose when I'm tired,' answered Dan, both touched and pleased at the eager interest of these friends in his plans.

'I know you *won't* like it. After having the whole world to roam over, one farm will seem dreadfully small and stupid,' said Josie, who much preferred the romance of the wandering life which brought her thrilling tales and pretty things at each return.

'Is there any art out there?' asked Bess, thinking what a good study in black and white Dan would make as he stood talking, half turned from the light.

'Plenty of nature, dear; and that is better. You will find splendid animals to model, and scenery such as you never saw in Europe to paint. Even prosaic pumpkins are grand out there. You can play Cinderella in one of them, Josie, when you open your theatre in Dansville,' said Mr Laurie, anxious that no cold water should be thrown on the new plan.

Stage-struck Josie was caught at once, and being promised all the tragic parts on the yet unbuilt stage, she felt a deep interest in the project and begged Dan to lose no time in beginning his experiment. Bess also confessed that studies from nature would be good for her, and wild scenery improve her taste, which might grow over-nice if only the delicate and beautiful were set before her.

'I speak for the practice of the new town,' said Nan, always eager for fresh enterprises. 'I shall be ready by the time you get well started – towns grow so fast out there.'

'Dan isn't going to allow any woman under forty in his place. He doesn't like them, 'specially young and pretty ones,' put in Tom, who was raging with jealousy, because he read admiration for Nan in Dan's eyes.

'That won't affect me, because doctors are exceptions to all rules. There won't be much sickness in Dansville, everyone will lead such active, wholesome lives, and only energetic young people will go there. But accidents will be frequent, owing to wild cattle, fast riding, Indian scrimmages, and the recklessness of Western life. That will just suit me. I long for broken bones, surgery is *so* interesting and I get so little here,' answered Nan, yearning to put out her shingle and begin.

'I'll have you, Doctor, and be glad of such a good sample of what we can do in the East. Peg away, and I'll send for you as soon as I have a roof to cover you. I'll scalp a few red fellows or smash up a dozen or so of cowboys for your special benefit,' laughed Dan, well pleased with the energy and fine physique which made Nan a conspicuous figure among other girls.

'Thanks. I'll come. Would you just let me feel your arm? Splendid biceps! Now, boys, see here: *this* is what I call muscle.' And Nan delivered a short lecture with Dan's sinewy arm to illustrate it. Tom retired to the alcove and glowered at the stars, while he swung his own right arm with a vigour suggestive of knocking someone down.

'Make Tom sexton; he'll enjoy burying the patients Nan kills. He's trying to get up the glum expression proper to the business. Don't forget him, Dan,' said Ted, directing attention to the blighted being in the corner.

But Tom never sulked long, and came out from his brief eclipse with the cheerful proposition, 'Look here, we'll get the city to ship out to Dansville all the cases of yellow fever, smallpox, and cholera that arrive; then Nan will be happy and her mistakes won't matter much with emigrants and convicts.'

'I should advise settling near Jacksonville, or some such city, that you might enjoy the society of cultivated persons. The Plato Club is there, and a most ardent thirst for philosophy. Everything from the East is welcomed hospitably, and new enterprises would flourish in such kindly soil,' observed Mr March, mildly offering a suggestion, as he sat among the elders enjoying the lively scene.

The idea of Dan studying Plato was very funny; but no one except naughty Ted smiled, and Dan made haste to unfold another plan seething in that active brain of his.

'I'm not sure the farming will succeed, and have a strong leaning towards my old friends the Montana Indians. They are a peaceful tribe, and need help awfully; hundreds have died of starvation because they don't get their share. The Sioux are fighters, thirty thousand strong, so Government fears 'em, and gives 'em all they want. I call that a damned shame!' Dan stopped short as the oath slipped out, but his eyes flashed, and he went on quickly: 'It *is* just that, and I won't beg pardon. If I'd had any money when I was there I'd have given every cent to those poor devils, cheated out of everything, and waiting patiently, after being driven from their own land to places where nothing will grow. Now, honest agents could do much, and I've a feeling that I ought to go and lend a hand. I know their lingo, and I like 'em. I've got a few thousands, and I ain't sure I have any right to spend it on myself and settle down to enjoy it. Hey?'

Dan looked very manly and earnest as he faced his friends, flushed and excited by the energy of his words; and all felt that little thrill of sympathy which links hearts together by the tie of pity for the wronged.

'Do it, do it!' cried Mrs Jo, fired at once; for misfortune was much more interesting to her than good luck.

'Do it, do it!' echoed Ted, applauding as if at a play, 'and take me along to help. I'm just raging to get among those fine fellows and hunt.'

'Let us hear more and see if it is wise,' said Mr Laurie, privately resolving to people his as yet unbought prairies with Montana Indians, and increase his donations to the society that sent missionaries to this much wronged people.

Dan plunged at once into the history of what he saw among

the Dakotas, and other tribes in the Northwest, telling of their wrongs, patience, and courage as if they were his brothers.

'They called me Dan Fire Cloud, because my rifle was the best they ever saw. And Black Hawk was as good a friend as a fellow would want; saved my life more than once, and taught me just what will be useful if I go back. They are down on their luck, now, and I'd like to pay my debts.'

By this time everyone was interested, and Dansville began to lose its charm. But prudent Mr Bhaer suggested that one honest agent among many could not do much, and noble as the effort would be, it was wiser to think over the matter carefully, get influence and authority from the right quarters, and meantime look at lands before deciding.

'Well, I will. I'm going to take a run to Kansas and see how that promises. Met a fellow in 'Frisco who'd been there, and he spoke well of it. The fact is, there's so much to be done *everywhere* that I don't know where to catch on, and half wish I hadn't any money,' answered Dan, knitting his brows in the perplexity all kind souls feel when anxious to help at the great task of the world's charity.

'I'll keep it for you till you decide. You are such an impetuous lad you'll give it to the first beggar that gets hold of you. I'll turn it over while you are prospecting, and hand it back when you are ready to invest, shall I?' asked Mr Laurie, who had learned wisdom since the days of his own extravagant youth.

'Thanky, sir, I'd be glad to get rid of it. You just hold on till I say the word; and if anything happens to me this time, keep it to help some other scamp as you helped me. This is my will, and you all witness it. Now I feel better.' And Dan squared his shoulders as if relieved of a burden, after handing over the belt in which he carried his little fortune.

No one dreamed how much was to happen before Dan came to take his money back, nor how nearly that act *was* his last will and testament; and while Mr Laurie was explaining how he would invest it, a cheery voice was heard singing:

> 'Oh, Peggy was a jolly lass,
>   Ye heave ho, boys, ye heave ho!
> She never grudged her Jack a glass,
>   Ye heave ho, boys, ye heave ho!

And when he sailed the raging main,
    She faithful was unto her swain,
        Ye heave ho, boys, ye heave ho!'

Emil always announced his arrival in that fashion, and in a moment he came hurrying in with Nat, who had been giving lessons in town all day. It was good to see the latter beam at his friend as he nearly shook his hand off; better still to see how Dan gratefully remembered all he owed Nat, and tried to pay the debt in his rough way; and best of all to hear the two travellers compare notes and reel off yarns to dazzle the landlubbers and home-keepers.

After this addition the house would not contain the gay youngsters, so they migrated to the piazza and settled on the steps, like a flock of night-loving birds. Mr March and the Professor retired to the study, Meg and Amy went to look after the little refection of fruit and cake which was to come, and Mrs Jo and Mr Laurie sat in the long window listening to the chat that went on outside.

'There they are, the flower of our flock!' she said, pointing to the group before them. 'The others are dead or scattered, but these seven boys and four girls are my especial comfort and pride. Counting Alice Heath, my dozen is made up, and my hands are full trying to guide these young lives as far as human skill can do it.'

'When we remember how different they are, from what some of them came, and the home influences about others, I think we may feel pretty well satisfied so far,' answered Mr Laurie soberly, as his eyes rested on one bright head among the black and brown ones, for the young moon shone alike on all.

'I don't worry about the girls; Meg sees to them, and is so wise and patient and tender they can't help doing well; but my boys are more care every year, and seem to drift farther away from me each time they go,' sighed Mrs Jo. 'They *will* grow up, and I can only hold them by one little thread, which may snap at any time, as it has with Jack and Ned. Dolly and George still like to come back, and I can say my word to them; and dear old Franz is too true ever to forget his own. But the three who are soon going out into the world again I can't help worrying about. Emil's good heart will keep him straight, I hope, and,"A sweet little cherub sits up aloft, To look out for the life of poor Jack."

'Nat is to make his first flight, and he's weak in spite of your strengthening influence; and Dan is still untamed. I fear it will take some hard lesson to do that.'

'He's a fine fellow, Jo, and I almost regret this farming project. A little polish would make a gentleman of him, and who knows what he might become here among us,' answered Mr Laurie, leaning over Mrs Bhaer's chair, just as he used to do years ago when they had mischievous secrets together.

'It wouldn't be safe, Teddy. Work and the free life he loves will make a good man of him, and that is better than any amount of polish, with the dangers an easy life in a city would bring him. We can't change his nature – only help it to develop in the right direction. The old impulses are there, and must be controlled, or he will go wrong. I see that; but his love for us is a safeguard, and we must keep a hold on him till he is older or has a stronger tie to help him.'

Mrs Jo spoke earnestly, for, knowing Dan better than anyone else, she saw that her colt was not thoroughly broken yet, and feared while she hoped, knowing that life would always be hard for one like him. She was sure that before he went away again, in some quiet moment he would give her a glimpse of his inner self, and then she could say the word of warning or encouragement that he needed. So she bided her time, studying him meanwhile, glad to see all that was promising, and quick to detect the harm the world was doing him. She was very anxious to make a success of her 'firebrand' because others predicted failure; but having learned that people cannot be moulded like clay, she contented herself with the hope that this neglected boy might become a good man, and asked no more. Even that was much to expect, so full was he of wayward impulses, strong passions, and the lawless nature born in him. Nothing held him but the one affection of his life – the memory of Plumfield, the fear of disappointing these faithful friends, the pride, stronger than principle, that made him want to keep the regard of the mates who always had admired and loved him in spite of all his faults.

'Don't fret, old dear; Emil is one of the happy-go-lucky sort who always fall on their legs. I'll see to Nat, and Dan is in a good way now. Let him take a look at Kansas, and if the farm plan loses its charm, he can fall back on poor Lo, and really do good out there. He's unusually fitted for that peculiar task and I hope he'll decide to do it. Fighting oppressors, and befriending the oppressed will keep those dangerous energies of his busy, and the life will suit him better than sheep-folds and wheat-fields.'

'I hope so. What is that?' and Mrs Jo leaned forward to listen, as exclamations from Ted and Josie caught her ear.

'A mustang! a real, live one; and we can ride it. Dan, you are a first-class trump!' cried the boy.

'A whole Indian dress for me! Now I can play Namioka, if the boys act *Metamora*,' added Josie, clapping her hands.

'A buffalo's head for Bess! Good gracious, Dan, why did you bring such a horrid thing as that to her?' asked Nan.

'Thought it would do her good to model something strong and natural. She'll never amount to anything if she keeps on making nambypamby gods and pet kittens,' answered irreverent Dan, remembering that when he was last here Bess was vibrating distractedly between a head of Apollo and her Persian cat as models.

'Thank you; I'll try it, and if I fail we can put the buffalo up in the hall to remind us of you,' said Bess, indignant at the insult offered the gods of her idolatry, but too well bred to show it except in her voice, which was as sweet and as cold as ice-cream.

'I suppose you won't come out to see our new settlement when the rest do? Too rough for you?' asked Dan, trying to assume the deferential air all the boys used when addressing their Princess.

'I am going to Rome to study for years. All the beauty and art of the world is there, and a lifetime isn't long enough to enjoy it,' answered Bess.

'Rome is a mouldy old tomb compared to the "Garden of the gods" and my magnificent Rockies. I don't care a hang for art; nature is as much as I can stand, and I guess I could show you things that would knock your old masters higher than kites. Better come, and while Josie rides the horses you can model 'em. If a drove of a hundred or so of wild ones can't show you beauty, I'll give up,' cried Dan, waxing enthusiastic over the wild grace and vigour which he could enjoy but had no power to describe.

'I'll come someday with Papa, and see if they are better than the horses of St Mark and those on Capitol Hill. Please don't abuse my gods, and I will try to like yours,' said Bess, beginning to think the West might be worth seeing, though no Raphael or Angelo had yet appeared there.

'That's a bargain! I do think people ought to see their own country before they go scooting off to foreign parts, as if the new world wasn't worth discovering,' began Dan, ready to bury the hatchet.

'It has some advantages, but not all. The women of England can vote, and we can't. I'm ashamed of America that she isn't ahead in *all* good things,' cried Nan, who held advanced views on all reforms, and was anxious about her rights, having had to fight for some of them.

'Oh, please don't begin on that. People always quarrel over that question, and call names, and never agree. Do let us be quiet and happy tonight,' pleaded Daisy, who hated discussion as much as Nan loved it.

'You shall vote as much as you like in our new town, Nan; be mayor and aldermen, and run the whole concern. It's going to be as free as air, or I can't live in it,' said Dan, adding, with a laugh, 'I see Mrs Giddygaddy and Mrs Shakespeare Smith don't agree any better than they used to.'

'If everyone agreed, we should never get on. Daisy is a dear, but inclined to be an old fogey; so I stir her up; and next fall she will go and vote with me. Demi will escort us to do the one thing we *are* allowed to do as yet.'

'Will you take 'em, Deacon?' asked Dan, using the old name as if he liked it. 'It works capitally in Wyoming.'

'I shall be proud to do it. Mother and the aunts go every year, and Daisy will come with me. She is my better half still; and I don't mean to leave her behind in anything,' said Demi, with an arm round his sister of whom he was fonder than ever.

Dan looked at them wistfully, thinking how sweet it must be to have such a tie; and his lonely youth seemed sadder than ever as he recalled its struggles. A gusty sigh from Tom made sentiment impossible, as he said pensively: 'I always wanted to be a twin. It's so sociable and so cosy to have someone glad to lean on a fellow and comfort him, if other girls are cruel.'

As Tom's unrequited passion was the standing joke of the family, this allusion produced a laugh, which Nan increased by whipping out a bottle of Nux, saying, with her professional air: 'I knew you ate too much lobster for tea. Take four pellets, and your dyspepsia will be all right. Tom always sighs and is silly when he's overeaten.'

'I'll take 'em. These are the only sweet things you ever give me.' And Tom gloomily crunched his dose.

' "Who can minister to a mind diseased, or pluck out a rooted sorrow?" ' quoted Josie tragically from her perch on the railing.

'Come with me, Tommy, and I'll make a man of you. Drop your pills and powders, and cavort round the world a spell, and you'll soon forget you've got a heart, or a stomach either,' said Dan, offering his one panacea for all ills.

'Ship with me, Tom. A good fit of seasickness will set you up, and a stiff north-easter blow your blue-devils away. Come along as surgeon – easy berth, and no end of larks.'

> 'And if your Nancy frowns, my lad,
> And scorns a jacket blue,
> Just hoist your sails for other ports,
> And find a maid more true.'

added Emil, who had a fragment of song to cheer every care and sorrow, and freely offered them to his friends.

'Perhaps I'll think of it when I've got my diploma. I'm not going to grind three mortal years and have nothing to show for it. Till then – '

'I'll never desert Mrs Micawber,' interrupted Teddy, with a gurgling sob. Tom immediately rolled him off the step into the wet grass below; and by the time this slight skirmish was over, the jingle of teaspoons suggested refreshments of a more agreeable sort. In former times the little girls waited on the boys, to save confusion; now the young men flew to serve the ladies, young and old; and that slight fact showed plainly how the tables were turned by time. And what a pleasant arrangement it was! Even Josie sat still, and let Emil bring her berries; enjoying her young ladyhood, till Ted stole her cake, when she forgot manners and chastised him with a rap on the knuckles. As guest of honour, Dan was only allowed to wait on Bess, who still held the highest place in this small world. Tom carefully selected the best of everything for Nan, to be crushed by the remark: 'I never eat at this hour; and you will have a nightmare if *you* do.'

So, dutifully curbing the pangs of hunger, he gave the plate to Daisy, and chewed rose-leaves for his supper.

When a surprising quantity of wholesome nourishment had been consumed, someone said, 'Let's sing!' and a tuneful hour followed. Nat fiddled, Demi piped, Dan strummed the old banjo, and Emil

warbled a doleful ballad about the wreck of the *Bounding Betsey*;
then everybody joined in the old songs till there was very decidedly
'music in the air'; and passersby said, as they listened smiling: 'Old
Plum is gay tonight!'

When all had gone Dan lingered on the piazza, enjoying the
balmy wind that blew up from the hayfields, and brought the breath
of flowers from Parnassus; and as he leaned there romantically in
the moonlight, Mrs Jo came to shut the door.

'Dreaming dreams, Dan?' she asked, thinking the tender moment
might have come. Imagine the shock when, instead of some
interesting confidence or affectionate word, Dan swung round,
saying bluntly: 'I was wishing I could smoke.'

Mrs Jo laughed at the downfall of her hopes, and answered
kindly, 'You may, in your room; but don't set the house afire.'

Perhaps Dan saw a little disappointment in her face, or the
memory of the sequel of that boyish frolic touched his heart; for he
stooped and kissed her, saying in a whisper: 'Good-night, mother.'
And Mrs Jo was half satisfied.

CHAPTER 5

Vacation

Everyone was glad of a holiday next morning, and all lingered
over the breakfast-table, till Mrs Jo suddenly exclaimed: 'Why,
there's a dog!' And on the threshold of the door appeared a great
deerhound, standing motionless, with his eyes fixed on Dan.

'Hallo, old boy! Couldn't you wait till I came for you? Have you
cut away on the sly? Own up now, and take your whipping like a
man,' said Dan, rising to meet the dog, who reared on his hind legs
to look his master in the face and bark as if uttering an indignant
denial of any disobedience.

'All right; Don never lies.' And Dan gave the tall beast a hug,
adding as he glanced out of the window, where a man and horse
were seen approaching, 'I left my plunder at the hotel overnight,
not knowing how I should find you. Come out and see Octoo,
my mustang; she's a beauty.' And Dan was off, with the family
streaming after him, to welcome the newcomer.

They found her preparing to go up the steps in her eagerness to reach her master, to the great dismay of the man, who was holding her back.

'Let her come,' called Dan; 'she climbs like a cat and jumps like a deer. Well, my girl, do you want a gallop?' he asked, as the pretty creature clattered up to him and whinnied with pleasure as he rubbed her nose and slapped her glossy flank.

'That's what I call a horse worth having,' said Ted, full of admiration and delight; for he was to have the care of her during Dan's absence.

'What intelligent eyes! She looks as if she would speak,' said Mrs Jo.

'She talks like a human in her way. Very little that she *don't* know. Hey, old lass?' and Dan laid his cheek to hers as if the little black mare was very dear to him.

'What does "Octoo" mean?' asked Rob.

'Lightning; she deserves it, as you'll see. Black Hawk gave her to me for my rifle, and we've had high times together out yonder. She's saved my life more than once. Do you see that scar?'

Dan pointed to a small one, half hidden by the long mane; and standing with his arm about Octoo's neck, he told the story of it.

'Black Hawk and I were after buffalo one time, but didn't find 'em as soon as we expected; so our food gave out, and there we were a hundred miles from Red Deer River, where our camp was. I thought we were done for, but my brave pal says, "Now I'll show you how we can live till we find the herds." We were unsaddling for the night by a little pond; there wasn't a living creature in sight anywhere, not even a bird, and we could see for miles over the prairies. What do you think we did?' And Dan looked into the faces round him.

'Ate worms like the Australian fellows,' said Rob. 'Boiled grass or leaves,' added Mrs Jo.

'Perhaps filled the stomach with clay, as we read of savages doing?' suggested Mr Bhaer.

'Killed one of the horses,' cried Ted, eager for bloodshed of some sort.

'No; but we bled one of them. See, just here; filled a tin cup, put some wild sage leaves in it, with water, and heated it over a fire of sticks. It was good, and we slept well.'

'I guess Octoo didn't.' And Josie patted the animal, with a face full of sympathy.

'Never minded it a bit. Black Hawk said we could live on the horses several days and still travel before they felt it. But by another morning we found the buffalo, and I shot the one whose head is in my box, ready to hang up and scare brats into fits. He's a fierce old fellow, you bet.'

'What is this strap for?' asked Ted, who was busily examining the Indian saddle, the single rein and snaffle, with lariat, and round the neck the leather band he spoke of.

'We hold on to that when we lie along the horse's flank farthest from the enemy, and fire under the neck as we gallop round and round. I'll show you.' And springing into the saddle, Dan was off down the steps, tearing over the lawn at a great pace, sometimes on Octoo's back, sometimes half hidden as he hung by stirrup and strap, and sometimes off altogether, running beside her as she loped along, enjoying the fun immensely; while Don raced after, in a canine rapture at being free again and with his mates.

It was a fine sight – the three wild things at play, so full of vigour, grace, and freedom, that for the moment the smooth lawn seemed a prairie; and the spectators felt as if this glimpse of another life made their own seem rather tame and colourless.

'This is better than a circus!' cried Mrs Jo, wishing she were a girl again, that she might take a gallop on this chained lightning of a horse. 'I foresee that Nan will have her hands full setting bones, for Ted will break every one of his trying to rival Dan.'

'A few falls will not harm, and this new care and pleasure will be good for him in all ways. But I fear Dan will never follow a plough after riding a Pegasus like that,' answered Mr Bhaer, as the black mare leaped the gate and came flying up the avenue, to stop at a word and stand quivering with excitement, while Dan swung himself off and looked up for applause.

He received plenty of it, and seemed more pleased for his pet's sake than for his own. Ted clamoured for a lesson at once, and was soon at ease in the queer saddle, finding Octoo gentle as a lamb, as he trotted away to show off at college. Bess came hastening down the hill, having seen the race from afar; and all collected on the piazza while Dan 'yanked' the cover off the big box the express had 'dumped' before the door – to borrow his own words.

Dan usually travelled in light marching order, and hated to have more luggage than he could carry in his well-worn valise. But now that he had a little money of his own, he had cumbered himself with a collection of trophies won by his bow and spear, and brought them home to bestow upon his friends.

'We shall be devoured with moths,' thought Mrs Jo, as the shaggy head appeared, followed by a wolfskin rug for her feet, a bearskin ditto for the Professor's study, and Indian garments bedecked with foxes' tails for the boys.

All nice and warm for a July day, but received with delight nevertheless. Ted and Josie immediately 'dressed up', learned the war-whoop, and proceeded to astonish their friends by a series of skirmishes about the house and grounds, with tomahawks and bows and arrows, till weariness produced a lull.

Gay birds' wings, plumy pampas grass, strings of wampum, and pretty work in beads, bark, and feathers, pleased the girls. Minerals, arrowheads, and crude sketches interested the Professor; and when the box was empty, Dan gave Mr Laurie, as his gift, several plaintive Indian songs written on birch-bark.

'We only want a tent over us to be quite perfect. I feel as if I ought to give you parched corn and dried meat for dinner, my braves. Nobody will want lamb and green peas after this splendid powwow,' said Mrs Jo, surveying the picturesque confusion of the long hall, where people lay about on the rugs, all more or less bedecked with feathers, moccasins, or beads.

'Moose noses, buffalo tongues, bear steaks, and roasted marrow-bones would be the thing, but I don't mind a change; so bring on your baa-baa and green meat,' answered Dan from the box, where he sat in state like a chief among his tribe, with the great hound at his feet.

The girls began to clear up, but made little headway; for everything they touched had a story, and all were thrilling, comical, or wild; so they found it hard to settle to their work, till Dan was carried off by Mr Laurie.

This was the beginning of the summer holiday, and it was curious to see what a pleasant little stir Dan's and Emil's coming made in the quiet life of the studious community; for they seemed to bring a fresh breeze with them that enlivened everyone. Many of the collegians remained during vacation; and Plumfield and

Parnassus did their best to make these days pleasant for them, since most came from distant States, were poor, and had few opportunities but this for culture or amusement. Emil was hail-fellow-well-met with men and maids, and went rollicking about in true sailor fashion; but Dan stood rather in awe of the 'fair girl graduates', and was silent when among them, eyeing them as an eagle might a flock of doves. He got on better with the young men, and was their hero at once. Their admiration for his manly accomplishments did him good; because he felt his educational defects keenly, and often wondered if he could find anything in books to satisfy him as thoroughly as did the lessons he was learning from Nature's splendidly illustrated volume. In spite of his silence, the girls found out his good qualities, and regarded 'the Spaniard', as they named him, with great favour; for his black eyes were more eloquent than his tongue, and the kind creatures tried to show their friendly interests in many charming ways.

He saw this, and endeavoured to be worthy of it – curbing his free speech, toning down his rough manners, and watching the effect of all he said and did, anxious to make a good impression. The social atmosphere warmed his lonely heart, the culture excited him to do his best, and the changes which had taken place during his absence, both in himself and others, made the old home seem like a new world. After the life in California, it was sweet and restful to be here, with these familiar faces round him, helping him to forget much that he regretted, and to resolve to deserve more entirely the confidence of these good fellows, the respect of these innocent girls.

So there was riding, rowing, and picnicking by day, music, dancing, and plays by night; and everyone said there had not been so gay a vacation for years. Bess kept her promise, and let the dust gather on her beloved clay while she went pleasuring with her mates or studied music with her father, who rejoiced over the fresh roses in her cheeks and the laughter which chased away the dreamy look she used to wear. Josie quarrelled less with Ted; for Dan had a way of looking at her which quelled her instantly, and had almost as good an effect upon her rebellious cousin. But Octoo did even more for the lively youth, who found that her charms entirely eclipsed those of the bicycle which had been his heart's delight before. Early and late he rode this untiring beast, and began to gain flesh – to the great joy of his mother, who feared that her beanstalk was growing too fast for health.

Demi, finding business dull, solaced his leisure by photographing everybody he could induce to sit or stand to him, producing some excellent pictures among many failures; for he had a pretty taste in grouping, and endless patience. He might be said to view the world through the lens of his camera, and seemed to enjoy himself very much squinting at his fellow beings from under a bit of black cambric. Dan was a treasure to him; for he took well, and willingly posed in his Mexican costume, with horse and hound, and all wanted copies of these effective photographs. Bess, also, was a favourite sitter; and Demi received a prize at the Amateur Photographic Exhibition for one of his cousin with all her hair about her face, which rose from the cloud of white lace draping the shoulders. These were freely handed round by the proud artist; and one copy had a tender little history yet to be told.

Nat was snatching every minute he could get with Daisy before the long parting; and Mrs Meg relented somewhat, feeling sure that absence would quite cure this unfortunate fancy. Daisy said little; but her gentle face was sad when she was alone, and a few quiet tears dropped on the handkerchiefs she marked so daintily with her own hair. She was sure Nat would *not* forget her; and life looked rather forlorn without the dear fellow who had been her friend since the days of patty pans and confidences in the willow tree. She was an old-fashioned daughter, dutiful and docile, with such love and reverence for her mother that her will was law; and if love was forbidden, friendship must suffice. So she kept her little sorrow to herself, smiled cheerfully at Nat, and made his last days of home-life very happy with every comfort and pleasure she could give, from sensible advice and sweet words to a well-filled workbag for his bachelor establishment and a box of goodies for the voyage.

Tom and Nan took all the time they could spare from their studies to enjoy high jinks at Plumfield with their old friends; for Emil's next voyage was to be a long one, Nat's absence was uncertain, and no one ever knew when Dan would turn up again. They all seemed to feel that life was beginning to grow serious; and even while they enjoyed those lovely summer days together they were conscious that they were children no longer, and often in the pauses of their fun talked soberly of their plans and hopes, as if anxious to know and help one another before they drifted farther apart on their different ways.

A few weeks were all they had; then the *Brenda* was ready, Nat was to sail from New York, and Dan went along to see him off; for his own plans fermented in his head, and he was eager to be up and doing. A farewell dance was given on Parnassus in honour of the travellers, and all turned out in their best array and gayest spirits. George and Dolly came with the latest Harvard airs and graces, radiant to behold, in dress-suits and 'crushed hats', as Josie called the especial pride and joy of their boyish souls. Jack and Ned sent regrets and best wishes, and no one mourned their absence; for they were among what Mrs Jo called her failures. Poor Tom got into trouble, as usual, by deluging his head with some highly scented preparation in the vain hope of making his tight curls lie flat and smooth, as was the style. Unhappily, his rebellious crop only kinked the closer, and the odour of many barbers' shops clung to him in spite of his frantic efforts to banish it. Nan wouldn't allow him near her, and flapped her fan vigorously whenever he was in sight; which cut him to the heart, and made him feel like the Peri shut out from Paradise. Of course his mates jeered at him, and nothing but the unquenchable jollity of his nature kept him from despair.

Emil was resplendent in his new uniform, and danced with an abandon which only sailors know. His pumps seemed to be everywhere, and his partners soon lost breath trying to keep up with him; but the girls all declared he steered like an angel, and in spite of his pace no collisions took place; so he was happy, and found no lack of damsels to ship with him.

Having no dress-suit, Dan had been coaxed to wear his Mexican costume, and feeling at ease in the many-buttoned trousers, loose jacket, and gay sash, flung his serape over his shoulder with a flourish and looked his best, doing great execution with his long spurs, as he taught Josie strange steps or rolled his black eyes admiringly after certain blonde damsels whom he dared not address.

The mammas sat in the alcove, supplying pins, smiles, and kindly words to all, especially the awkward youths new to such scenes, and the bashful girls conscious of faded muslins and cleaned gloves. It was pleasant to see stately Mrs Amy promenade on the arm of a tall country boy, with thick boots and a big fore-head, or Mrs Jo dance like a girl with a shy fellow whose arms went like pump-handles, and whose face was scarlet with confusion and pride at the honour of treading on the toes of the president's wife. Mrs Meg always had room on her sofa for two or three girls, and Mr Laurie devoted himself to these plain, poorly dressed damsels with a kindly grace that won their hearts and made them happy. The good Professor circulated like refreshments, and his cheerful face shone on all alike, while Mr March discussed Greek comedy in the study with such serious gentlemen as never unbent their mighty minds to frivolous joys.

The long music-room, parlour, hall, and piazza were full of white-gowned maidens with attendant shadows; the air was full of lively voices, and hearts and feet went lightly together as the home band played vigorously, and the friendly moon did her best to add enchantment to the scene.

'Pin me up, Meg; that dear Dunbar boy has nearly rent me "in sunder", as Mr Peggotty would say. But didn't he enjoy himself, bumping against his fellow men and swinging me round like a mop. On these occasions I find that I'm not as young as I was, nor as light of foot. In ten years more we shall be meal-bags, sister; so be resigned.' And Mrs Jo subsided into a corner, much dishevelled by her benevolent exertions.

'I know I shall be stout; but you won't keep still long enough to get much flesh on your bones, dear; and Amy will always keep her lovely figure. She looks about eighteen tonight, in her white gown and roses,' answered Meg, busily pinning up one sister's torn frills, while her eyes fondly followed the other's graceful movements; for Meg still adored Amy in the old fashion.

It was one of the family jokes that Jo was getting fat, and she kept it up, though as yet she had only acquired a matronly outline, which was very becoming. They were laughing over the impending double chins, when Mr Laurie came off duty for a moment.

'Repairing damages as usual, Jo? You never could take a little gentle exercise without returning in rags. Come and have a quiet stroll with me and cool off before supper. I've a series of pretty tableaux to show you while Meg listens to the raptures of lisping Miss Carr, whom I made happy by giving her Demi for a partner.'

As he spoke, Laurie led Jo to the music-room, nearly empty now after a dance which sent the young people into garden and hall. Pausing before the first of the four long windows that opened on a very wide piazza, he pointed to a group outside, saying: 'The name of this is "Jack Ashore".'

A pair of long, blue legs, ending in very neat pumps, hung from the veranda roof among the vines; and roses, gathered by unseen hands, evidently appertaining to aforesaid legs, were being dropped into the laps of several girls perched like a flock of white birds on the railing below; while a manly voice 'fell like a falling star', as it sung this pensive ditty to a most appreciative audience:

Mary's Dream

'The moon had climbed the eastern hill
    Which rises o'er the sands of Dee,
And from its highest summit shed
    A silver light on tower and tree,
When Mary laid her down to sleep
    (Her thoughts on Sandy far at sea);
When soft and low a voice was heard,
    Saying, "Mary, weep no more for me."

'She from her pillow gently raised
    Her head, to see who there might be,
And saw young Sandy, shivering, stand
    With visage pale and hollow e'e.
"Oh Mary dear, cold is my clay;
    It lies beneath the stormy sea;
Far, far from thee, I sleep in death.
    Dear Mary, weep no more for me.

' "Three stormy nights and stormy days
    We tossed upon the raging main.
And long we strove our bark to save;
    But all our striving was in vain.
E'en then, when terror chilled my blood,
    My heart was filled with love of thee.
The storm is past, and I'm at rest;
    So, Mary, weep no more for me.

' "Oh maiden dear, yourself prepare;
   We soon shall meet upon that shore
Where love is free from doubt and care,
   And you and I shall part no more."
Loud crew the cock, the shadow fled;
   No more her Sandy did she see;
But soft the passing spirit said,
   "Sweet Mary, weep no more for me." '

'The constant jollity of that boy is worth a fortune to him. He'll never sink with such a buoyant spirit to keep him afloat through life,' said Mrs Jo, as the roses were tossed back with much applause when the song ended.

'Not he; and it's a blessing to be grateful for, isn't it? We moody people know its worth. Glad you like my first tableau. Come and see number two. Hope it isn't spoilt; it was very pretty just now. This is "Othello telling his adventures to Desdemona".'

The second window framed a very picturesque group of three. Mr March in an armchair, with Bess on a cushion at his feet, was listening to Dan, who, leaning against a pillar, was talking with unusual animation. The old man was in shadow, but little Desdemona was looking up with the moonlight full upon her into young Othello's face, quite absorbed in the story he was telling so well. The gay drapery over Dan's shoulder, his dark colouring, and the gesture of his arm made the picture very striking, and both spectators enjoyed it with silent pleasure, till Mrs Jo said in a quick whisper, 'I'm glad he's going away. He's too picturesque to have here among so many romantic girls. Afraid his "grand, gloomy, and peculiar" style will be too much for our simple maids.'

'No danger; Dan is in the rough as yet, and always will be, I fancy; though he is improving in many ways. How well Queenie looks in that soft light!'

'Dear little Goldilocks looks well everywhere.' And with a backward glance full of pride and fondness, Mrs Jo went on. But that scene returned to her long afterward and her own prophetic words also.

Number three was a tragical tableau at first sight; and Mr Laurie stifled a laugh as he whispered 'The Wounded Knight', pointing to Tom with his head enveloped in a large handkerchief, as he knelt before Nan, who was extracting a thorn or splinter from the palm of his hand with great skill, to judge from the patient's blissful expression of countenance.

'Do I hurt you?' she asked, turning the hand to the moonlight for a better view.

'Not a bit; dig away; I like it,' answered Tom, regardless of his aching knees and the damage done to his best trousers.

'I won't keep you long.'

'Hours, if you please. Never so happy as here.'

Quite unmoved by this tender remark, Nan put on a pair of large, round-eyed glasses, saying in a matter-of-fact tone: 'Now I see it. Only a splinter, and there it is.'

'My hand is bleeding; won't you bind it up?' asked Tom, wishing to prolong the situation.

'Nonsense; suck it. Only take care of it tomorrow if you dissect. Don't want any more blood-poisoning.'

'That was the only time you were kind to me. Wish I'd lost my arm.'

'I wish you'd lost your head; it smells more like turpentine and kerosene than ever. Do take a run in the garden and air it.'

Fearing to betray themselves by laughter, the watchers went on, leaving the Knight to rush away in despair, and the Lady to bury her nose in the cup of a tall lily for refreshment.

'Poor Tom, his fate is a hard one, and he's wasting his time! Do advise him to quit philandering and go to work, Jo.'

'I have, Teddy, often; but it will take some great shock to make that boy wise. I wait with interest to see what it will be. Bless me! what is all this?'

She might well ask; for on a rustic stool stood Ted trying to pose on one foot, with the other extended, and both hands waving in the air. Josie, with several young mates, was watching his contortions with deep interest as they talked about 'little wings', 'gilded wire twisted', and a 'cunning skullcap'.

'This might be called "Mercury Trying to Fly",' said Mr Laurie, as they peeped through the lace curtains.

'Bless the long legs of that boy! how does he expect to manage them? They are planning for the Owlsdark Marbles, and a nice muddle they will make of my gods and goddesses with no one to

show them how,' answered Mrs Jo, enjoying this scene immensely.
'Now, he's got it!' 'That's perfectly splendid!' 'See how long you
can keep so!' cried the girls, as Ted managed to maintain his
equilibrium a moment by resting one toe on the trellis. Unfortunately this brought all his weight on the other foot; the
straw seat of the stool gave way, and the flying Mercury came
down with a crash, amid shrieks of laughter from the girls. Being
accustomed to ground and lofty tumbling, he quickly recovered
himself, and hopped gaily about, with one leg through the stool
as he improvised a classic jig.

'Thanks for four nice little pictures. You have given me an idea,
and I think sometime we will get up regular tableaux of this sort
and march our company round a set of dissolving views. New and
striking; I'll propose it to our manager and give you all the glory,'
said Mrs Jo, as they strolled towards the room whence came the
clash of glass and china, and glimpses of agitated black coats.

Let us follow the example of our old friends and stroll about
among the young people, eavesdropping, so gathering up various
little threads to help in the weaving of the story. George and Dolly
were at supper, and having served the ladies in their care stood in a
corner absorbing nourishment of all kinds with a vain attempt to
conceal hearty appetites under an air of elegant indifference.

'Good spread, this; Laurence does things in style. First-rate
coffee, but no wine, and that's a mistake,' said Stuffy, who still
deserved his name, and was a stout youth with a heavy eye and
bilious complexion.

'Bad for boys, he says. Jove! wish he could see us at some of
our wines. Don't we just "splice the main brace" as Emil says,'
answered Dolly, the dandy, carefully spreading a napkin over the
glossy expanse of shirtfront whereon a diamond stud shone like a
lone star. His stutter was nearly outgrown; but he, as well as
George, spoke in the tone of condescension, which, with the blasé
airs they assumed, made a very funny contrast to their youthful
faces and foolish remarks. Good-hearted little fellows both, but
top-heavy with the pride of being Sophs and the freedom that
college life gave them.

'Little Jo is getting to be a deuced pretty girl, isn't she?' said
George, with a long sigh of satisfaction as his first mouthful of ice
went slowly down his throat.

'H'm – well, fairish. The Princess is rather more to my taste. I like 'em blonde and queenly and elegant, don't you know.'

'Yes, Jo *is* too lively; might as well dance with a grasshopper. I've tried her, and she's one too many for me. Miss Perry is a nice, easy-going girl. Got her for the German.'

'You'll never be a dancing man. Too lazy. Now I'll undertake to steer any girl and dance down any fellow you please. Dancing's my forte.' And Dolly glanced from his trim feet to his flashing gem with the defiant air of a young turkeycock on parade.

'Miss Grey is looking for you. Wants more grub. Just see if Miss Nelson's plate is empty, there's a good fellow. Can't eat ice in a hurry.' And George remained in his safe corner, while Dolly struggled through the crowd to do his duty, coming back in a fume, with a splash of salad dressing on his coat-cuff.

'Confound these country chaps! they go blundering round like so many dor-bugs, and make a deuce of a mess. Better stick to books and not try to be society men. Can't do it. Beastly stain. Give it a rub, and let me bolt a mouthful, I'm starved. Never saw girls eat such a lot. It proves that they ought not to study so much. Never liked co-ed,' growled Dolly, much ruffled in spirit.

'So they do. 'Tisn't ladylike. Ought to be satisfied with an ice and a bit of cake, and eat it prettily. Don't like to see a girl feed. We hard-working men need it, and, by Jove, I mean to get some more of that meringue if it's not all gone. Here, waiter! bring along that dish over there, and be lively,' commanded Stuffy, poking a young man in a rather shabby dress-suit, who was passing with a tray of glasses.

His order was obeyed promptly; but George's appetite was taken away the next moment by Dolly's exclaiming, as he looked up from his damaged coat, with a scandalised face: 'You've put your foot in it now, old boy! that's Morton, Mr Bhaer's crack man. Knows everything, no end of a "dig", and bound to carry off all the honours. You won't hear the last of it in a hurry.' And Dolly laughed so heartily that a spoonful of ice flew upon the head of a lady sitting below him, and got him into a scrape also.

Leaving them to their despair, let us listen to the whispered chat of two girls comfortably seated in a recess waiting till their escorts were fed.

'I do think the Laurences give lovely parties. Don't you enjoy

*Dolly laughed so heartily that a spoonful of ice flew upon
the head of a lady sitting below him*

them?' asked the younger, looking about her with the eager air of one unused to this sort of pleasure.

'Very much, only I never feel as if I was dressed right. My things seemed elegant at home, and I thought I'd be *over* over-dressed if anything; but I look countrified and dowdy here. No time or money to change now, even if I knew how to do it,' answered the other, glancing anxiously at her bright pink silk grown, trimmed with cheap lace.

'You must get Mrs Brooke to tell you how to fix your things. She was very kind to me. I had a green silk, and it looked so cheap and horrid by the side of the nice dresses here I felt regularly unhappy about it, and asked her how much a dress like one Mrs Laurence had would cost. That looked so simple and elegant I thought it wouldn't be costly; but it was India mull and Valenciennes lace, so, of course, I couldn't have it. Then Mrs Brooke said: "Get some muslin to cover the green silk, and wear hops or some white flowers, instead of pink, in your hair, and you will have a pretty suit." Isn't it lovely and becoming?' And Miss Burton surveyed herself with girlish satisfaction; for a little taste had softened the harsh green, and hop-bells became her red hair better than roses.

'It's sweet: I've been admiring it. I'll do mine so and ask about my purple one. Mrs Brooke has helped me to get rid of my head-aches, and Mary Clay's dyspepsia is all gone since she gave up coffee and hot bread.'

'Mrs Laurence advised me to walk and run and use the gymnasium to cure my round shoulders and open my chest, and I'm a much better figure than I was.'

'Did you know that Mr Laurence pays all Amelia Merrill's bills? Her father failed, and she was heartbroken at having to leave college; but that splendid man just stepped in and made it all right.' 'Yes, and Professor Bhaer has several of the boys down at his house evenings to help them along so they can keep up with the rest; and Mrs Bhaer took care of Charles Mackey herself when he had a fever last year. I do think they are the best and kindest people in the world.'

'So do I, and my time here will be the happiest and most useful years of my life.'

And both girls forgot their gowns and their suppers for a moment to look with grateful, affectionate eyes at the friends who tried to care for bodies and for souls as well as minds.

Now come to a lively party supping on the stairs, girls like foam at the top, and a substratum of youths below, where the heaviest particles always settle. Emil, who never sat if he could climb or perch, adorned the newel-post; Tom, Nat, Demi, and Dan were camped on the steps, eating busily, as their ladies were well served and they had earned a moment's rest, which they enjoyed with their eyes fixed on the pleasing prospect above them.

'I'm so sorry the boys are going. It will be dreadfully dull without them. Now they have stopped teasing and are polite, I really enjoy them,' said Nan, who felt unusually gracious tonight as Tom's mishap kept him from annoying her.

'So do I; and Bess was mourning about it today, though as a general thing she doesn't like boys unless they are models of elegance. She has been doing Dan's head, and it is not quite finished. I never saw her so interested in any work, and it's very well done. He is so striking and big he always makes me think of the Dying Gladiator or some of those antique creatures. There's Bess now. Dear child, how sweet she looks tonight!' answered Daisy, waving her hand as the Princess went by with Grandpa on her arm.

'I never thought he would turn out so well. Don't you remember how we used to call him "the bad boy" and be sure he would become a pirate or something awful because he glared at us and swore sometimes? Now he is the handsomest of all the boys, and very entertaining with his stories and plans. I like him very much; he's so big and strong and independent. I'm tired of mollycoddles and bookworms,' said Nan in her decided way.

'Not handsomer that Nat!' cried loyal Daisy, contrasting two faces below, one unusually gay, the other sentimentally sober even in the act of munching cake. 'I like Dan, and am glad he is doing well; but he tires me, and I'm still a little afraid of him. Quiet people suit me best.'

'Life is a fight, and I like a good soldier. Boys take things too easily, don't see how serious it all is and go to work in earnest. Look at that absurd Tom, wasting his time and making an object of himself just because he can't have what he wants, like a baby crying for the moon. I've no patience with such nonsense,' scolded

Nan, looking down at the jovial Thomas, who was playfully putting macaroons in Emil's shoes, and trying to beguile his exile as best he could.

'Most girls would be touched by such fidelity. I think it's beautiful,' said Daisy behind her fan; for other girls sat just below.

'You are a sentimental goose and not a judge. Nat will be twice the man when he comes back after his trip. I wish Tom was going with him. My idea is that if we girls have any influence we should use it for the good of these boys, and not pamper them up, making slaves of ourselves and tyrants of them. Let them prove what they can do and be before they ask anything of us, and give us a chance to do the same. Then we know where we are, and shall not make mistakes to mourn over all our lives.'

'Hear, hear!' cried Alice Heath, who was a girl after Nan's own heart, and had chosen a career, like a brave and sensible young woman. 'Only give us a chance, and have patience till we can do our best. Now we are expected to be as wise as men who have had generations of all the help there is, and we scarcely anything. Let us have equal opportunities, and in a few generations we will see what the judgement is. I like justice, and we get very little of it.'

'Still shouting the battle-cry of freedom?' asked Demi, peering through the banisters at this moment. 'Up with your flag! I'll stand by and lend a hand if you want it. With you and Nan to lead the van, I think you won't need much help.'

'You are a great comfort, Demi, and I'll call on you in all emergencies; for you are an honest boy, and don't forget that you owe much to your mother and your sisters and your aunts,' continued Nan. 'I do like men who come out frankly and own that they are *not* gods. How can *we* think them so when such awful mistakes are being made all the time by these great creatures? See them sick, as I do, then you know them.'

'Don't hit us when we are down; be merciful, and set us up to bless and believe in you evermore,' pleaded Demi from behind the bars.

'We'll be kind to you if you will be just to us. I don't say generous, only just. I went to a suffrage debate in the Legislature last winter; and of all the feeble, vulgar twaddle I ever heard, that was the worst; and those men were *our* representatives. I blushed for them, and their wives and mothers. I want an intelligent man to represent *me*, if I can't do it myself, not a fool.'

'Nan is on the stump. Now we shall catch it,' cried Tom, putting up an umbrella to shield his unhappy head; for Nan's earnest voice was audible, and her indignant eye happened to rest on him as she spoke.

'Go on, go on! I'll take notes, and put in "great applause" liberally,' added Demi, producing his ball-book and pencil, with his Jenkins air.

Daisy pinched his nose through the bars, and the meeting was rather tumultuous for a moment, for Emil called: 'Avast, avast, here's a squall to wind'ard'; Tom applauded wildly; Dan looked up as if the prospect of a fight, even with words, pleased him, and Nat went to support Demi, as his position seemed to be a good one. At this crisis, when everyone laughed and talked at once, Bess came floating through the upper hall and looked down like an angel of peace upon the noisy group below, as she asked, with wondering eyes and smiling lips: 'What is it?'

'An indignation meeting. Nan and Alice are on the rampage, and we are at the bar to be tried for our lives. Will Your Highness preside and judge between us?' answered Demi, as a lull at once took place; for no one rioted in the presence of the Princess.

'I'm not wise enough. I'll sit here and listen. Please go on.' And Bess took her place above them all as cool and calm as a little statue of Justice, with fan and nosegay in place of sword and scales.

'Now, ladies, free your minds, only spare us till morning; for we've got a German to dance as soon as everyone is fed, and Parnassus expects every man to do his duty. Mrs President Giddygaddy has the floor,' said Demi, who liked this sort of fun better than the very mild sort of flirtation which was allowed at Plumfield, for the simple reason that it could not be entirely banished, and is a part of all education, co- or otherwise.

'I have only one thing to say, and it is this,' began Nan soberly, though her eyes sparkled with a mixture of fun and earnestness. 'I want to ask every boy of you what you really think on this subject. Dan and Emil have seen the world and ought to know their own minds. Tom and Nat have had fine examples before them for years. Demi is ours and we are proud of him. So is Rob. Ted is a weathercock, and Dolly and George, of course, are fogies in spite of the Annex, and girls at Girton going ahead of the men. Commodore, are you ready for the question?'

'Ay, ay, skipper.'

'Do you believe in Woman's Suffrage?'

'Bless your pretty figgerhead! I do, and I'll ship a crew of girls any time you say so. Aren't they worse than a press gang to carry a fellow out of his moorings? Don't we all need one as pilot to steer us safe to port? and why shouldn't they share our mess afloat and ashore since we are sure to be wrecked without 'em?'

'Good for you, Emil! Nan will take you for first mate after that handsome speech,' said Demi, as the girls applauded, and Tom glowered. 'Now, Dan, you love liberty so well yourself, are you willing we should have it?'

'All you can get, and I'll fight any man who's mean enough to say you don't deserve it.'

This brief and forcible reply delighted the energetic President, and she beamed upon the member from California, as she said briskly, 'Nat wouldn't dare to say he was on the other side even if he were, but I hope he has made up his mind to pipe for us, at least when we take the field, and not be one of those who wait till the battle is won, and then beat the drums and share the glory.'

Mrs Giddygaddy's doubts were most effectually removed, and her sharp speech regretted, as Nat looked up blushing, but with a new sort of manliness in face and manner, saying, in a tone that touched them all, 'I should be the most ungrateful fellow alive if I did not love, honour, and serve women with all my heart and might, for to them I owe everything I am or ever shall be.'

Daisy clapped her hands, and Bess threw her bouquet into Nat's lap, while the other girls waved their fans, well pleased; for real feeling made his little speech eloquent.

'Thomas B. Bangs, come into court, and tell the truth, the whole truth, and nothing but the truth, if you can,' commanded Nan, with a rap to call the meeting to order.

Tom shut the umbrella, and standing up raised his hand, saying solemnly, 'I believe in suffrage of *all* kinds. I adore *all* women, and will die for them at any moment if it will help the cause.'

'Living and working for it is harder, and therefore more honourable. Men are always ready to die for us, but not to make our lives worth having. Cheap sentiment and bad logic. You will pass, Tom, only don't twaddle. Now, having taken the sense of the meeting we will adjourn, as the hour for festive gymnastics has arrived. I am glad to see that old Plum has given six true men to the world, and hope they will continue to be staunch to her and the principles she has taught them, wherever they may go. Now, girls, don't sit in draughts, and, boys, beware of ice-water when you are warm.'

With this characteristic close Nan retired from office, and the girls went to enjoy one of the few rights allowed them.

CHAPTER 6

Last Words

The next day was Sunday, and a goodly troop of young and old set forth to church – some driving, some walking, all enjoying the lovely weather and the happy quietude which comes to refresh us when the work and worry of the week are over. Daisy had a headache; and Aunt Jo remained at home to keep her company, knowing very well that the worst ache was in the tender heart struggling dutifully against the love that grew stronger as the parting drew nearer.

'Daisy knows my wishes, and I trust her. You must keep an eye on Nat, and let him clearly understand that there is to be no "lovering", or I shall forbid the letter-writing. I hate to seem cruel, but it is too soon for my dear girl to bind herself in any way,' said Mrs Meg, as she rustled about in her best grey silk, while waiting for Demi, who always escorted his pious mother to church as a peace offering for crossing her wishes in other things.

'I will, dear; I'm lying in wait for all three boys today, like an old spider; and I will have a good talk with each. They know I understand them, and they always open their hearts sooner or later. You look like a nice, plump little Quakeress, Meg; and no one will believe that big boy is your son,' added Mrs Jo, as Demi came in shining with Sunday neatness, from his well-blacked boots to his smooth brown head.

'You flatter me, to soften my heart toward *your* boy. I know your ways, Jo, and I don't give in. Be firm, and spare me a scene by and by. As for John, as long as he is satisfied with his old mother, I don't care what people think,' answered Mrs Meg, accepting with a smile the little posy of sweetpeas and mignonette Demi brought her.

Then, having buttoned her dove-coloured gloves with care, she took her son's arm and went proudly away to the carriage, where Amy and Bess waited, while Jo called after them, just as Marmee used to do, 'Girls, *have* you got nice pocket-handkerchiefs?' They all smiled at the familiar words, and three white banners waved as they drove away, leaving the spider to watch for her first fly. She did not wait long. Daisy was lying down with a wet cheek on the little hymnbook out of which she and Nat used to sing together; so Mrs Jo strolled about the lawn, looking very like a wandering mushroom with her large buff umbrella.

Dan had gone for a ten-mile stroll; and Nat was supposed to have accompanied him, but presently came sneaking back, unable to tear himself away from the Dovecote or lose a moment of nearness to his idol that last day. Mrs Jo saw him at once, and beckoned him to a rustic seat under the old elm, where they could have their confidences undisturbed, and both keep an eye on a certain white-curtained window, half hidden in vines.

'Nice and cool here. I'm not up to one of Dan's tramps today – it's so warm, and he goes so like a steam engine. He headed for the swamp where his pet snakes used to live, and I begged to be excused,' said Nat, fanning himself with his straw hat, though the day was not oppressive.

'I'm glad you did. Sit and rest with me, and have one of our good old talks. We've both been so busy lately, I feel as if I didn't half know your plans; and I want to,' answered Mrs Jo, feeling sure that though they might start with Leipzig they would bring up at Plumfield.

'You are very kind, and there's nothing I'd like better. I don't realise I'm going so far – suppose I shan't till I get afloat. It's a splendid start, and I don't know how I can ever thank Mr Laurie for all he's done, or you either,' added Nat, with a break in his voice; for he was a tender-hearted fellow, and never forgot a kindness.

'You can thank us beautifully by being and doing all we hope

and expect of you, my dear. In the new life you are going to there
will be a thousand trials and temptations, and only your own wit
and wisdom to rely on. That will be the time to test the principles
we have tried to give you, and see how firm they are. Of course,
you will make mistakes – we all do; but don't let go of your conscience and drift along blindly. Watch and pray, dear Nat; and
while your hand gains skill, let your head grow wiser, and keep
your heart as innocent and warm as it is now.'

'I'll try, Mother Bhaer, my very best to be a credit to you. I
know I shall improve in my music – can't help it there; but I never
shall be very wise, I'm afraid. As for my heart, you know, I leave it
behind me in good keeping.'

As he spoke, Nat's eyes were fixed on the window with a look of
love and longing that made his quiet face both manly and sad –
plainly showing how strong a hold this boyish affection had upon
him.

'I want to speak of that; and I know you will forgive what seems
hard, because I do most heartily sympathise with you,' said Mrs
Jo, glad to have her say.

'Yes, do talk about Daisy! I think of nothing but leaving and
losing her. I have no hope – I suppose it is too much to ask; only I
can't help loving her, wherever I am!' cried Nat, with a mixture of
defiance and despair in his face that rather startled Mrs Jo.

'Listen to me and I'll try to give you both comfort and good
advice. We all know that Daisy is fond of you, but her mother
objects, and being a good girl she tries to obey. Young people
think they never can change, but they do in the most wonderful
manner, and very few die of broken hearts.' Mrs Jo smiled as she
remembered another boy whom she had once tried to comfort,
and then went soberly on while Nat listened as if his fate hung
upon her lips.

'One of two things will happen. You will find someone else to
love, or, better still, be so busy and happy in your music that you
will be willing to wait for time to settle the matter for you both.
Daisy will perhaps forget when you are gone, and be glad you are
only friends. At any rate it is much wiser to have no promises
made; then both are free, and in a year or two may meet to laugh
over the little romance nipped in the bud.'

'Do you honestly think that?' asked Nat, looking at her so keenly that the truth had to come; for all his heart was in those frank blue eyes of his.

'No, I don't!' answered Mrs Jo.

'Then if you were in my place, what would you do?' he added, with a tone of command never heard in his gentle voice before.

'Bless me! the boy is in dead earnest, and I shall forget prudence in sympathy I'm afraid,' thought Mrs Jo, surprised and pleased by the unexpected manliness Nat showed.

'I'll tell you what I should do. I'd say to myself: "I'll prove that my love is strong and faithful, and make Daisy's mother proud to give her to me by being not only a good musician but an excellent man, and so command respect and confidence. This I will try for; and if I fail, I shall be the better for the effort, and find comfort in the thought that I did my best for her sake."'

'That is what I meant to do. But I wanted a word of hope to give me courage,' cried Nat, firing up as if the smouldering spark was set ablaze by a breath of encouragement. 'Other fellows, poorer and stupider than I, have done great things and come to honour. Why may not I, though I'm nothing now? I know Mrs Brooke remembers what I came from, but my father was *honest* though everything went wrong; and I have nothing to be ashamed of though I *was* a charity boy. I never will be ashamed of my people or myself, and I'll make other folks respect me if I can.'

'Good! that's the right spirit, Nat. Hold to it and make yourself a man. No one will be quicker to see and admire the brave work than my sister Meg. She does not despise your poverty or your past; but mothers are very tender over their daughters, and we Marches, though we have been poor, *are*, I confess, a little proud of our good family. We don't care for money; but a long line of virtuous ancestors *is* something to desire and to be proud of.'

'Well, the Blakes are a good lot. I looked 'em up, and not one was ever in prison, hanged, or disgraced in any way. We used to be rich and honoured years ago, but we've died out and got poor, and father was a street musician rather than beg; and I'll be one again before I'll do the mean things some men do and pass muster.'

Nat was so excited that Mrs Jo indulged in a laugh to calm him, and both went on more quietly.

'I told my sister all that and it pleased her. I am sure if you do well these next few years that she will relent and all be happily settled, unless that wonderful change, which you don't believe possible, should occur. Now, cheer up; don't be lackadaisical and blue. Say goodbye cheerfully and bravely, show a manly front, and leave a pleasant memory behind you. We all wish you well and hope much for you. Write to me every week and I'll send a good, gossipy answer. Be careful what you write to Daisy; don't gush or wail, for sister Meg will see the letters; and you can help your cause very much by sending sensible, cheery accounts of your life to us all.'

'I will; I will; it looks brighter and better already, and I won't lose my one comfort by any fault of my own. Thank you so much, Mother Bhaer, for taking my side. I felt so ungrateful and mean and crushed when I thought you all considered me a sneak who had no business to love such a precious girl as Daisy. No one said anything, but I knew how you felt, and that Mr Laurie sent me off partly to get me out of the way. Oh dear, life is pretty tough sometimes, isn't it?' And Nat took his head in both hands as if it ached with the confusion of hopes and fears, passions and plans that proved boyhood was past and manhood had begun.

'Very tough, but it is that very struggle with obstacles which does us good. Things have been made easy for you in many ways, but no one can do everything. You must paddle your own canoe now, and learn to avoid the rapids and steer straight to the port you want to reach. I don't know just what your temptations will be for you have no bad habits and seem to love music so well, nothing can lure you from it. I only hope you won't work too hard.'

'I feel as if I *could* work like a horse, I'm so eager to get on; but I'll take care. Can't waste time being sick, and you've given me doses enough to keep me all right, I guess.' Nat laughed as he remembered the book of directions Mrs Jo had written for him to consult on all occasions.

She immediately added some verbal ones on the subject of foreign messes, and having mounted one of her pet hobbies, was in full gallop when Emil was seen strolling about on the roof of the old house, that being his favourite promenade; for there he could fancy himself walking the deck, with only blue sky and fresh air about him.

'I want a word with the Commodore, and up there we shall be nice and quiet. Go and play to Daisy: it will put her to sleep and do you both good. Sit in the porch, so I can keep an eye on you as I promised;' and with a motherly pat on the shoulder Mrs Jo left Nat to his delightful task and briskly ascended to the housetop, not up the trellis as of old but by means of the stairs inside.

Emerging on the platform she found Emil cutting his initials afresh in the woodwork and singing 'Pull for the Shore', like the tuneful mariner he was.

'Come aboard and make yourself at home, Aunty,' he said, with a playful salute. 'I'm just leaving a P.P.C. in the old place, so when you fly up here for refuge you'll remember me.'

'Ah, my dear, I'm not likely to forget you. It doesn't need E. B. H. cut on all the trees and railings to remind me of my sailor boy;' and Mrs Jo took the seat nearest the blue figure astride the balustrade, not quite sure how to begin the little sermon she wanted to preach.

'Well, you don't pipe your eye and look squally when I sheer off as you used to, and that's a comfort. I like to leave port in fair weather and have a jolly send-off all round. Specially this time, for it will be a year or more before we drop anchor here again,' answered Emil, pushing his cap back, and glancing about him as if he loved old Plum and would be sorry never to see it any more.

'You have salt water enough without my adding to it. I'm going to be quite a Spartan mother, and send my sons to battle with no wailing, only the command, "With your shield or on it",' said Mrs Jo cheerfully, adding after a pause, 'I often wish I could go too, and someday I will, when you are captain and have a ship of your own – as I've no doubt you will before long, with Uncle Herman to push you on.'

'When I do I'll christen her the *Jolly Jo* and take you as first mate. It would be regular larks to have you aboard, and I'd be a proud man to carry you round the world you've wanted to see so long and never could,' answered Emil, caught at once by this splendid vision.

'I'll make my first voyage with you and enjoy myself immensely in spite of seasickness and all the stormy winds that blow. I've always thought I'd like to see a wreck, a nice safe one with all saved after great danger and heroic deeds, while we clung like Mr Pillicoddy to main-top jibs and lee scuppers.'

'No wrecks yet, ma'am, but we'll try to accommodate customers.

Captain says I'm a lucky dog and bring fair weather, so we'll save the dirty weather for you if you want it,' laughed Emil, digging at the ship in full sail which he was adding to his design.

'Thanks, I hope you will. This long voyage will give you new experiences, and being an officer, you will have new duties and responsibilities. Are you ready for them? You take everything so gaily, I've been wondering if you realised that now you will have not only to obey but to command also, and power is a dangerous thing. Be careful that you don't abuse it or let it make a tyrant of you.'

'Right you are, ma'am. I've seen plenty of that, and have got my bearings pretty well, I guess. I shan't have very wide swing with Peters over me, but I'll see that the boys don't get abused when he's bowsed up his jib. No right to speak before, but now I won't stand it.'

'That sounds mysteriously awful; could I ask what nautical torture "bowsing jibs" is?' asked Mrs Jo, in a tone of deep interest.

'Getting drunk. Peters can hold more grog than any man I ever saw; he keeps right side up, but is as savage as a norther, and makes things lively all round. I've seen him knock a fellow down with a belaying pin, and couldn't lend a hand. Better luck now, I hope.' And Emil frowned as if he already trod the quarterdeck, lord of all he surveyed.

'Don't get into trouble, for even Uncle Herman's favour won't cover insubordination, you know. You have proved yourself a good sailor; now be a good officer, which is a harder thing, I fancy. It takes a fine character to rule justly and kindly; you will have to put by your boyish ways and remember your dignity. That will be excellent training for you, Emil, and sober you down a bit. No more skylarking except here, so mind your ways, and do honour to your buttons,' said Mrs Jo, tapping one of the very bright brass ones that ornamented the new suit Emil was so proud of.

'I'll do my best. I know my time for skrimshander [chaff] is over, and I must steer a straighter course; but don't you fear, Jack ashore is a very different craft from what he is with blue water under his keel. I had a long talk with Uncle last night and got my orders; I won't forget 'em nor all I owe him. As for you, I'll name my first ship as I say, and have your bust for the figurehead, see if I don't,' and Emil gave his aunt a hearty kiss to seal the vow, which proceeding much amused Nat, playing softly in the porch of the Dovecote.

'You do me proud, Captain. But, dear, I want to say one thing and then I'm done; for you don't need much advice of mine after my good man has spoken. I read somewhere that every inch of rope used in the British Navy has a strand of red in it, so that wherever a bit of it is found it is known. That is the text of my little sermon to you. Virtue, which means honour, honesty, courage, and all that makes character, is the red thread that marks a good man wherever he is. Keep that always and everywhere, so that even if wrecked by misfortune, that sign shall still be found and recognised. Yours is a rough life, and your mates not all we could wish, but you can be a gentleman in the true sense of the word; and no matter what happens to your body, keep your soul clean, your heart true to those who love you, and do your duty to the end.'

As she spoke Emil had risen and stood listening with his cap off and a grave, bright look as if taking orders from a superior officer; when she ended, he answered briefly, but heartily, 'Please God, I will!'

'That's all; I have little fear for you, but one never knows when or how the weak moment may come, and sometimes a chance word helps us, as so many my dear mother spoke come back to me now for my own comfort and the guidance of my boys,' said Mrs Jo, rising; for the words had been said and no more were needed.

'I've stored 'em up and know where to find 'em when wanted. Often and often in my watch I've seen old Plum, and heard you and Uncle talking so plainly, I'd have sworn I was here. It is a rough life, Aunty, but a wholesome one if a fellow loves it as I do, and has an anchor to windward as I have. Don't worry about me, and I'll come home next year with a chest of tea that will cheer your heart and give you ideas enough for a dozen novels. Going below? All right, steady in the gangway! I'll be along by the time you've got out the cake-box. Last chance for a good old lunch ashore.'

Mrs Jo descended laughing, and Emil finished his ship whistling cheerfully, neither dreaming when and where this little chat on the housetop would return to the memory of one of them.

Dan was harder to catch, and not until evening did a quiet moment come in that busy family; when, while the rest were roaming about, Mrs Jo sat down to read in the study, and presently Dan looked in at the window.

'Come and rest after your long tramp; you must be tired,' she called, with an inviting nod towards the big sofa where so many boys had reposed – as much as that active animal ever does.

'Afraid I shall disturb you;' but Dan looked as if he wanted to stay his restless feet somewhere.

'Not a bit; I'm always ready to talk, shouldn't be a woman if I were not,' laughed Mrs Jo, as Dan swung himself in and sat down with an air of contentment very pleasant to see.

'Last day is over, yet somehow I don't seem to hanker to be off. Generally, I'm rather anxious to cut loose after a short stop. Odd, ain't it?' asked Dan, gravely picking grass and leaves out of his hair and beard; for he had been lying on the grass, thinking many thoughts in the quiet summer night.

'Not at all; you are beginning to get civilised. It's a good sign, and I'm glad to see it,' answered Mrs Jo promptly. 'You've had your swing, and want a change. Hope the farming will give it to you, though helping the Indians pleases me more, it is so much better to work for others than for oneself alone.'

'So 'tis,' assented Dan heartily. 'I seem to want to root somewhere and have folks of my own to take care of. Tired of my own company, I suppose, now I've seen so much better. I'm a rough, ignorant lot, and I've been thinking maybe I've missed it loafing round creation, instead of going in for education as the other chaps did. Hey?'

He looked anxiously at Mrs Jo; and she tried to hide the surprise this new outburst caused her; for till now Dan had scorned books and gloried in his freedom.

'No; I don't think so in your case. So far I'm sure the free life was best. Now that you are a man you can control that lawless nature better; but as a boy only great activity and much adventure could keep you out of mischief. Time is taming my colt, you see, and I shall yet be proud of him, whether he makes a packhorse of himself to carry help to the starving or goes to ploughing as Pegasus did.'

Dan liked the comparison, and smiled as he lounged in the sofa-corner, with the new thoughtfulness in his eyes.

'Glad you think so. The fact is it's going to take a heap of taming to make me go well in harness anywhere. I want to, and I try now and then, but always kick over the traces and run away. No lives lost yet; but I shouldn't wonder if there was sometime, and a general smash-up.'

'Why, Dan, did you have any dangerous adventures during this last absence? I fancied so, but didn't ask before, knowing you'd tell me if I could help in any way. Can I?' And Mrs Jo looked anxiously at him; for a sudden lowering expression had come into his face, and he leaned forward as if to hide it.

'Nothing very bad; but 'Frisco isn't just a heaven on earth, you know, and it's harder to be a saint there than here,' he answered slowly; then, as if he had made up his mind to ' 'fess', as the children used to say, he sat up, and added rapidly, in a half-defiant, half-shamefaced way, 'I tried gambling, and it wasn't good for me.'

'Was that how you made your money?'

'Not a penny of it! That's all honest, if speculation isn't a bigger sort of gambling. I won a lot; but I lost or gave it away, and cut the whole concern before it got the better of me.'

'Thank heaven for that! Don't try it again; it may have the terrible fascination for you it has for so many. Keep to your mountains and prairies, and shun cities, if these things tempt you, Dan. Better lose your life than your soul, and one such passion leads to worse sins, as you know better than I.'

Dan nodded, and seeing how troubled she was, said, in a lighter tone, though still the shadow of that past experience remained, 'Don't be scared; I'm all right now; and a burnt dog dreads the fire. I don't drink, or do the things you dread; don't care for 'em; but I get excited, and then this devilish temper of mine is more than I can manage. Fighting a moose or a buffalo is all right; but when you pitch into a man, no matter how great a scamp he is, you've got to look out. I shall kill someone someday; that's all I'm afraid of. I do hate a sneak!' And Dan brought his fist down on the table with a blow that made the lamp totter and the books skip.

'That always was your trial, Dan, and I can sympathise with you; for I've been trying to govern my own temper all my life, and haven't learnt yet,' said Mrs Jo, with a sigh. 'For heaven's sake, guard your demon well, and don't let a moment's fury ruin all your life. As I said to Nat, watch and pray, my dear boy. There is no other help or hope for human weakness but God's love and patience.'

Tears were in Mrs Jo's eyes as she spoke; for she felt this deeply, and knew how hard a task it is to rule these bosom sins of ours. Dan looked touched, also uncomfortable, as he always did when religion of any sort was mentioned, though he had a simple creed of his own, and tried to live up to it in his blind way.

'I don't do much praying; don't seem to come handy to me; but I can watch like a redskin, only it's easier to mount guard over a lurking grizzly than my own cursed temper. It's that I'm afraid of, if I settle down. I can get on with wild beasts first-rate; but men rile me awfully, and I can't take it out in a free fight, as I can with a bear or a wolf. Guess I'd better head for the Rockies, and stay there a spell longer – till I'm tame enough for decent folks, if I ever am.' And Dan leaned his rough head on his hands in a despondent attitude.

'Try my sort of help, and don't give up. Read more, study a little, and try to meet a better class of people, who won't "rile", but soothe and strengthen you. We don't make you savage, I'm sure; for you have been as meek as a lamb, and made us very happy.'

'Glad of it; but I've felt like a hawk in a henhouse all the same, and wanted to pounce and tear more than once. Not so much as I used, though,' added Dan, after a short laugh at Mrs Jo's surprised face. 'I'll try your plan, and keep good company this bout if I can; but a man can't pick and choose, knocking about as I do.'

'Yes, you can this time; for you are going on a peaceful errand and can keep clear of temptation if you try. Take some books and read; that's an immense help; and books are always good company if you have the right sort. Let me pick out some for you.' And Mrs Jo made a beeline to the well-laden shelves, which were the joy of her heart and the comfort of her life.

'Give me travels and stories, please; don't want any pious works, can't seem to relish 'em, and won't pretend I do,' said Dan, following to look over her head with small favour at the long lines of well-worn volumes.

Mrs Jo turned short round, and putting a hand on either broad shoulder, looked him in the eye, saying soberly: 'Now, Dan, see here; never sneer at good things or pretend to be worse than you are. Don't let false shame make you neglect the religion without which no man can live. You needn't talk about it if you don't like, but don't shut your heart to it in whatever shape it comes. Nature is your God now; she has done much for you; let her do more, and lead you to know and love a wiser and more tender teacher, friend, and comforter than she can ever be. That is your only hope; don't throw it away, and waste time; for sooner or later you will feel the need of Him, and He will come to you and hold you up when all other help fails.'

Dan stood motionless, and let her read in his softened eyes the dumb desire that lived in his heart, though he had no words to tell it, and only permitted her to catch a glimpse of the divine spark which smoulders or burns clearly in every human soul. He did not speak; and glad to be spared some answer which should belie his real feelings, Mrs Jo hastened to say, with her most motherly smile: 'I saw in your room the little Bible I gave you long ago; it was well worn *outside*, but fresh within, as if not much read. Will you promise me to read a little once a week, dear, for my sake? Sunday is a quiet day everywhere, and this book is never old nor out of place. Begin with the stories you used to love when I told them to you boys. David was your favourite, you remember? Read him again; he'll suit you even better now, and you'll find his sins and repentance useful reading till you come to the life and work of a diviner example than he. You will do it, for love of mother Bhaer, who always loved her "firebrand" and hoped to save him?'

'I will,' answered Dan, with a sudden brightening of face that was like a sunburst through a cloud, full of promise though so short-lived and rare.

Mrs Jo turned at once to the books and began to talk of them, knowing well that Dan would not hear any more just then. He seemed relieved; for it was always hard for him to show his inner self, and he took pride in hiding it as an Indian does in concealing pain or fear.

'Hallo, here's old Sintram! I remember him; used to like him and his tantrums, and read about 'em to Ted. There he is riding ahead with Death and the Devil alongside.'

As Dan looked at the little picture of the young man with horse and hound going bravely up the rocky defile, accompanied by the companions who ride beside most men through this world, a curious impulse made Mrs Jo say quickly: 'That's you, Dan, just you at this time! Danger and sin are near you in the life you lead;

moods and passions torment you; the bad father left you to fight alone, and the wild spirit drives you to wander up and down the world looking for peace and self-control. Even the horse and hound are there, your Octoo and Don, faithful friends, unscared by the strange mates that go with you. You have not got the armour yet, but I'm trying to show you where to find it. Remember the mother Sintram loved and longed to find, and did find when his battle was bravely fought, his reward well earned? You can recollect your mother; and I have always felt that all the good qualities you possess come from her. Act out the beautiful old story in this as in the other parts, and try to give her back a son to be proud of.'

Quite carried away by the likeness of the quaint tale to Dan's life and needs, Mrs Jo went on pointing to the various pictures which illustrated it, and when she looked up was surprised to see how struck and interested he seemed to be. Like all people of his temperament he was very impressionable, and his life among hunters and Indians had made him superstitious; he believed in dreams, liked weird tales, and whatever appealed to the eye or mind, vividly impressed him more than the wisest words. The story of poor, tormented Sintram came back clearly as he looked and listened, symbolising his secret trials even more truly than Mrs Jo knew; and just at that moment this had an effect upon him that never was forgotten. But all he said was: 'Small chance of that. I don't take much stock in the idea of meeting folks in heaven. Guess mother won't remember the poor little brat she left so long ago; why should she?'

'Because true mothers never forget their children; and I know she was one, from the fact that she ran away from the cruel husband, to save her little son from bad influences. Had she lived, life would have been happier for you, with this tender friend to help and comfort you. Never forget that she risked everything for your sake, and don't let it be in vain.'

Mrs Jo spoke very earnestly, knowing that this was the one sweet memory of Dan's early life, and glad to have recalled it at this moment; for suddenly a great tear splashed down on the page where Sintram kneels at his mother's feet, wounded, but victorious over sin and death. She looked up, well pleased to have touched Dan to the heart's core, as that drop proved; but a sweep of the arm brushed away the tell-tale, and his beard hid the mate to it, as he shut the book, saying with a suppressed quiver in his strong voice: 'I'll keep this, if nobody wants it. I'll read it over, and maybe it will do me good. I'd like to meet her anywhere, but don't believe I ever shall.'

'Keep it and welcome. My mother gave it to me; and when you read it try to believe that neither of your mothers will ever forget you.'

Mrs Jo gave the book with a caress; and simply saying: 'Thanks; good-night,' Dan thrust it into his pocket, and walked straight away to the river to recover from this unwonted mood of tenderness and confidence.

Next day the travellers were off. All were in good spirits, and a cloud of handkerchiefs whitened the air as they drove away in the old bus, waving their hats to everyone and kissing their hands, especially to Mother Bhaer, who said in her prophetic tone as she wiped her eyes, when the familiar rumble died away, 'I have a feeling that something is going to happen to some of them, and they will never come back to me, or come back changed. Well, I can only say, "God be with my boys"!'

And He was.

CHAPTER 7

The Lion and the Lamb

When the boys were gone a lull fell upon Plumfield, and the family scattered to various places for brief outings, as August had come and all felt the need of change. The Professor took Mrs Jo to the mountains. The Laurences were at the seashore, and there Meg's family and the Bhaer boys took turns to visit, as someone must always be at home to keep things in order.

Mrs Meg, with Daisy, was in office when the events occurred which we are about to relate. Rob and Ted were just up from Rocky Nook, and Nan was passing a week with her friend as the only relaxation she allowed herself. Demi was off on a run with Tom, so Rob was man of the house, with old Silas as general overseer. The sea air seemed to have gone to Ted's head, for he was unusually freakish, and led his gentle aunt and poor Rob a life of it with his pranks. Octoo was worn out with the wild rides he took, and Don openly rebelled when ordered to leap and show off his accomplishments; while the girls at college were both amused and worried by the ghosts who haunted the grounds at night, the unearthly melodies that disturbed their studious hours, and the hairbreadth escapes of this restless boy by flood and field and fire. Something happened at length which effectually sobered Ted and made a lasting impression on both the boys; for sudden danger and a haunting fear turned the Lion into a lamb and the Lamb into a lion, as far as courage went.

On the first of September – the boys never forgot the date – after a pleasant tramp and good luck with their fishing, the brothers were lounging in the barn; for Daisy had company, and the lads kept out of the way.

'I tell you what it is, Bobby, that dog is sick. He won't play, nor eat, nor drink, and acts queerly. Dan will kill us if anything happens to him,' said Ted, looking at Don, who lay near his kennel resting a moment after one of the restless wanderings which kept him vibrating between the door of Dan's room and the shady corner of the yard, where his master had settled him with an old cap to guard till he came back.

'It's the hot weather, perhaps. But I sometimes think he's pining for Dan. Dogs do, you know, and the poor fellow has been low in his mind ever since the boys went. Maybe something has happened to Dan. Don howled last night and can't rest. I've heard of such things,' answered Rob thoughtfully.

'Pooh! he can't know. He's cross. I'll stir him up and take him for a run. Always makes me feel better. Hi, boy! wake up and be jolly;' and Ted snapped his fingers at the dog, who only looked at him with grim indifference.

'Better let him alone. If he isn't right tomorrow, we'll take him to Dr Watkins and see what he says.' And Rob went on watching the swallows as he lay in the hay polishing up some Latin verses he had made.

The spirit of perversity entered into Ted, and merely because he was told not to tease Don he went on doing it, pretending that it was for the dog's good. Don took no heed of his pats, commands, reproaches, or insults, till Ted's patience gave out; and seeing a convenient switch near by he could not resist the temptation to conquer the great hound by force, since gentleness failed to win obedience. He had the wisdom to chain Don up first; for a blow from any hand but his master's made him savage, and Ted had more than once tried the experiment, as the dog remembered. This indignity roused Don and he sat up with a growl. Rob heard it, and seeing Ted raise the switch, ran to interfere, exclaiming, 'Don't touch him! Dan forbade it! Leave the poor thing in peace; I won't allow it.'

Rob seldom commanded, but when he did Master Ted had to give in. His temper was up, and Rob's masterful tone made it impossible to resist one cut at the rebellious dog before he submitted. Only a single blow, but it was a costly one; for as it fell, the dog sprang at Ted with a snarl, and Rob, rushing between the two, felt the sharp teeth pierce his leg. A word made Don let go and drop remorsefully at Rob's feet, for he loved him and was evidently sorry to have hurt his friend by mistake. With a forgiving pat Rob left him, to limp to the barn followed by Ted, whose wrath was changed to shame and sorrow when he saw the red drops on Rob's sock and the little wounds in his leg.

'I'm awfully sorry. Why *did* you get in the way? Here, wash it up, and I'll get a rag to tie on it,' he said quickly filling a sponge with water and pulling out a very demoralised handkerchief. Rob usually made light of his own mishaps and was over ready to forgive if others were to blame; but now he sat quite still, looking at the purple marks with such a strange expression on his white face that Ted was troubled, though he added with a laugh, 'Why, you're not afraid of a little dig like that, are you, Bobby?'

'I am afraid of hydrophobia. But if Don *is* mad I'd rather be the one to have it,' answered Rob, with a smile and a shiver.

At that dreadful word Ted turned whiter than his brother, and, dropping sponge and handkerchief, stared at him with a frightened face, whispering in a tone of despair: 'Oh, Rob, don't say it! What shall we do, what *shall* we do?'

'Call Nan; she will know. Don't scare Aunty, or tell a soul but Nan; she's on the back piazza; get her out here as quick as you can. I'll wash it till she comes. Maybe it's nothing; don't look so staggered, Ted. I only thought it might be, as Don is queer.'

Rob tried to speak bravely; but Ted's long legs felt strangely weak as he hurried away, and it was lucky he met no one, for his face would have betrayed him. Nan was swinging luxuriously in a hammock, amusing herself with a lively treatise on croup, when an agitated boy suddenly clutched her, whispering, as he nearly pulled her overboard: 'Come to Rob in the barn! Don's mad and he's bitten him, and we don't know what to do; it's all my fault; no one must know. Oh, do be quick!'

Nan was on her feet at once, startled, but with her wits about her, and both were off without more words as they dodged round the house where unconscious Daisy chatted with her friends in the parlour and Aunt Meg peacefully took her afternoon nap upstairs.

Rob was braced up, and was as calm and steady as ever when they found him in the harness-room, whither he had wisely retired, to escape observation. The story was soon told, and after a look at Don, now in his kennel, sad and surly, Nan said slowly, with her eye on the full water-pan: 'Rob, there is one thing to do for the sake of safety, and it must be done at once. We can't wait to see if Don is – sick – or to go for a doctor. I *can* do it, and I *will*; but it is very painful, and I hate to hurt you, dear.'

A most unprofessional quiver got into Nan's voice as she spoke, and her keen eyes dimmed as she looked at the two anxious young faces turned so confidingly to her for help.

'I know, burn it; well, do it, please; I can bear it. But Ted better go away,' said Rob, with a firm setting of his lips, and a nod at his afflicted brother.

'I won't stir; I can stand it if he can, only it ought to be me!' cried Ted, with a desperate effort not to cry, so full of grief and fear and shame was he that it seemed as if he couldn't bear it like a man.

'He'd better stay and help; do him good,' answered Nan sternly, because, her heart was faint within her, knowing as she did all that might be in store for both poor boys. 'Keep quiet; I'll be back in a minute,' she added, going towards the house, while her quick mind hastily planned what was best to be done.

It was ironing day, and a hot fire still burned in the empty kitchen, for the maids were upstairs resting. Nan put a slender poker to heat, and as she sat waiting for it, covered her face with her hands, asking help in this sudden need for strength, courage, and wisdom; for there was no one else to call upon, and young as she was, she knew what was to be done if she only had the nerve to do it. Any other patient would have been calmly interesting, but dear, good Robin, his father's pride, his mother's comfort, everyone's favourite and friend, that he should be in danger was very terrible; and a few hot tears dropped on the well-scoured table as Nan tried to calm her trouble by remembering how very likely it was to be all a mistake, a natural but vain alarm.

'I must make light of it, or the boys will break down, and then there will be a panic. Why afflict and frighten everyone when all is in doubt? I won't. I'll take Rob to Dr Morrison at once, and have the dog man see Don. Then, having done all we can, we will either laugh at our scare – if it is one – or be ready for whatever comes. Now for my poor boy.'

Armed with the red-hot poker, a pitcher of ice-water, and several handkerchiefs from the clothes horse, Nan went back to the barn ready to do her best in this her most serious 'emergency case'. The boys sat like statues, one of despair, the other of resignation; and it took all Nan's boasted nerve to do her work quickly and well.

'Now, Rob, only a minute, then we are safe. Stand by, Ted; he may be a bit faintish.'

Rob shut his eyes, clinched his hands, and sat like a hero. Ted knelt beside him, white as a sheet, and as weak as a girl; for the pangs of remorse were rending him, and his heart failed at the thought of all this pain because of his wilfulness. It was all over in a moment, with only one little groan; but when Nan looked to her assistant to hand the water, poor Ted needed it the most, for he had fainted away, and lay on the floor in a pathetic heap of arms and legs.

Rob laughed, and, cheered by that unexpected sound, Nan bound up the wound with hands that never trembled, though great drops stood on her forehead; and she shared the water with patient number one before she turned to patient number two. Ted was much ashamed, and quite broken in spirit, when he found how he had failed at the critical moment, and begged them not to tell, as he really could not help it; then by way of finishing his utter humiliation, a burst of hysterical tears disgraced his manly soul, and did him a world of good.

'Never mind, never mind, we are all right now, and no one need be the wiser,' said Nan briskly, as poor Ted hiccoughed on Rob's shoulder, laughing and crying in the most tempestuous manner, while his brother soothed him, and the young doctor fanned both with Silas's old straw hat.

'Now, boys, listen to me and remember what I say. We won't alarm anyone *yet*, for I've made up my mind our scare is all nonsense. Don was out lapping the water as I came by, and I don't believe he's mad any more than I am. Still, to ease our minds and compose our spirits, and get our guilty faces out of sight for a while, I think we had better drive into town to my old friend Dr Morrison, and let him just take a look at my work, and give us some quieting little dose; for we are all rather shaken by this flurry. Sit still, Rob; and Ted, you harness up while I run and get my hat and tell Aunty to excuse me to Daisy. I don't know those Penniman girls, and she will be glad of our room at tea, and we'll have a cosy bite at my house, and come home as gay as larks.'

Nan talked on as a vent for the hidden emotions which professional pride would not allow her to show, and the boys approved her plan at once; for action is always easier than quiet waiting. Ted went staggering away to wash his face at the pump, and rub some colour into his cheeks before he harnessed the horse. Rob lay tranquilly on the hay, looking up at the swallows again as he lived through some very memorable moments. Boy as he was, the thought of death coming suddenly to him, and in this way, might well make him sober; for it is a very solemn thing to be arrested in the midst of busy life by the possibility of the great change. There were no sins to be repented of, few faults, and many happy, dutiful years to remember with infinite comfort. So Rob had no fears to daunt him, no regrets to sadden, and best of all, a very strong and simple piety to sustain and cheer him.

'Mein Vater,' was his first thought; for Rob was very near the Professor's heart, and the loss of his eldest would have been a bitter blow. These words, whispered with a tremble of the lips that had been so firm when the hot iron burned, recalled that other Father who is always near, always tender and helpful; and, folding his hands, Rob said the heartiest little prayer he ever prayed, there on the hay, to the soft twitter of the brooding birds. It did him good; and wisely laying all his fear and doubt and trouble in God's hand, the boy felt ready for whatever was to come, and from that hour kept steadily before him the one duty that was plain – to be brave and cheerful, keep silent, and hope for the best.

Nan stole her hat, and left a note on Daisy's pincushion, saying she had taken the boys to drive, and all would be out of the way till after tea. Then she hurried back and found her patients much better, the one for work, the other for rest. In they got, and, putting Rob on the back seat with his leg up drove away, looking as gay and carefree as if nothing had happened.

Dr Morrison made light of the affair, but told Nan she had done right; and as the much-relieved lads went downstairs, he added in a whisper, 'Send the dog off for a while, and keep your eye on the boy. Don't let him know it, and report to me if anything seems wrong. One never knows in these cases. No harm to be careful.'

Nan nodded, and feeling much relieved now that the responsibility was off her shoulders, took the lads to Dr Watkins, who promised to come out later and examine Don. A merry tea at Nan's house, which was kept open for her all summer, did them good, and by the time they got home in the cool of the evening no sign of the panic remained but Ted's heavy eyes, and a slight limp when Rob walked. As the guests were still chattering on the front piazza they retired to the back, and Ted soothed his remorseful soul by swinging Rob in the hammock, while Nan told stories till the dog man arrived.

He said Don was a little under the weather, but no more mad than the grey kitten that purred round his legs while the examination went on.

'He wants his master, and feels the heat. Fed too well, perhaps. I'll keep him a few weeks and send him home all right,' said Dr Watkins, as Don laid his great head in his hand, and kept his intelligent eyes on his face, evidently feeling that this man understood his trials, and knew what to do for him.

So Don departed without a murmur, and our three conspirators took counsel together how to spare the family all anxiety, and give Rob the rest his leg demanded. Fortunately, he always spent many hours in his little study, so he could lie on the sofa with a book in his hand as long as he liked, without exciting any remark. Being of a quiet temperament, he did not worry himself or Nan with useless fears, but believed what was told him, and dismissing all dark possibilities, went cheerfully on his way, soon recovering from the shock of what he called 'our scare'.

But excitable Ted was harder to manage, and it took all Nan's wit and wisdom to keep him from betraying the secret; for it was best to say nothing and spare all discussion of the subject for Rob's sake. Ted's remorse preyed upon him, and having no 'Mum' to confide in, he was very miserable. By day he devoted himself to Rob, waiting on him, talking to him, gazing anxiously at him, and worrying the good fellow very much; though he wouldn't own it, since Ted found comfort in it. But at night, when all was quiet, Ted's lively imagination and heavy heart got the better of him, and kept him awake, or set him walking in his sleep. Nan had her eye on him, and more than once administered a little dose to give him a rest, read to him, scolded him, and when she caught him haunting the house in the watches of the night, threatened to lock him up if he did not stay in his bed. This wore off after a while; but a change came over the freakish boy, and everyone observed it, even before his mother returned to ask what they had done to quench the Lion's spirits. He was gay, but not so heedless; and often when the old wilfulness beset him, he would check it sharply, look at Rob, and give up, or stalk away to have his sulk out alone. He no longer made fun of his brother's old-fashioned ways and bookish tastes, but treated him with a new and very marked respect, which touched and pleased modest Rob, and much amazed all observers. It seemed as if he felt that he owed him reparation for the foolish act that might have cost him his life; and love being stronger than will, Ted forgot his pride, and paid his debt like an honest boy.

'I don't understand it,' said Mrs Jo, after a week of home life, much impressed by the good behaviour of her younger son. 'Ted is such a saint, I'm afraid we are going to lose him. Is it Meg's sweet influence, or Daisy's fine cooking, or the pellets I catch Nan giving him on the sly? Some witchcraft has been at work during my absence, and this will-o'-the-wisp is so amiable, quiet, and obedient, I don't know him.'

'He is growing up, heart's dearest, and being a precocious plant, he begins to bloom early. I also see a change in my Robchen. He is more manly and serious than ever, and is seldom far from me, as if his love for the old papa was growing with his growth. Our boys will often surprise us in this way, Jo, and we can only rejoice over them and leave them to become what Gott pleases.'

As the Professor spoke, his eyes rested proudly on the brothers, who came walking up the steps together, Ted's arm over Rob's shoulder as he listened attentively to some geological remarks Rob was making on a stone he held. Usually, Ted made fun of such tastes, and loved to lay boulders in the student's path, put brickbats under his pillow, gravel in his shoes, or send parcels of dirt by express to 'Prof. R. M. Bhaer'. Lately, he had treated Rob's hobbies respectfully, and had begun to appreciate the good qualities of this quiet brother whom he had always loved but rather undervalued, till his courage under fire won Ted's admiration, and made it impossible to forget a fault, the consequences of which might have been so terrible. The leg was still lame, though doing well, and Ted was always offering an arm as support, gazing anxiously at his brother, and trying to guess his wants; for regret was still keen in Ted's soul, and Rob's forgiveness only made it deeper. A fortunate slip on the stairs gave Rob an excuse for limping, and no one but Nan and Ted saw the wound; so the secret was safe up to this time.

'We are talking about you, my lads. Come in and tell us what good fairy has been at work while we were gone. Or is it because absence sharpens our eyes, that we find such pleasant changes when we come back?' said Mrs Jo, patting the sofa on either side, while the Professor forgot his piles of letters to admire the pleasing prospect of his wife in a bower of arms, as the boys sat down beside her, smiling affectionately, but feeling a little guilty; for till now 'Mum' and 'Vater' knew every event in their boyish lives.

'Oh, it's only because Bobby and I have been alone so much; we are sort of twins. I stir him up a bit, and he steadies me a great deal. You and father do the same, you know. Nice plan. I like it;' and Ted felt that he had settled the matter capitally.

'Mother won't thank you for comparing yourself to her, Ted. I'm flattered at being like father in any way. I try to be,' answered Rob, as they laughed at Ted's compliment.

'I do thank him, for it's true; and if you, Robin, do half as much for your brother as Papa has for me, your life won't be a failure,' said Mrs Jo heartily. 'I'm very glad to see you helping one another. It's the right way, and we can't begin too soon to try to understand the needs, virtues, and failings of those nearest us. Love should not make us blind to faults, nor familiarity make us too ready to blame the shortcomings we see. So work away, my sonnies, and give us more surprises of this sort as often as you like.'

'The liebe Mutter has said all. I too am well pleased at the friendly brother-warmth I find. It is good for everyone; long may it last!' and Professor Bhaer nodded at the boys, who looked gratified, but rather at a loss how to respond to these flattering remarks.

Rob wisely kept silent, fearing to say too much; but Ted burst out, finding it impossible to help telling something: 'The fact is I've been finding out what a brave good chap Bobby is, and I'm trying to make up for all the bother I've been to him. I knew he was awfully wise, but I thought him rather soft, because he liked books better than larks, and was always fussing about his conscience. But I begin to see that it isn't the fellows who talk the loudest and show off best that are the manliest. No, sir! quiet old Bob is a hero and a trump, and I'm proud of him; so would you be if you knew all about it.'

Here a look from Rob brought Ted up with a round turn; he stopped short, grew red, and clapped his hand on his mouth in dismay.

'Well, are we not to "know all about it"?' asked Mrs Jo quickly; for her sharp eye saw signs of danger and her maternal heart felt that something had come between her and her sons. 'Boys,' she went on solemnly, 'I suspect that the change we talk about is not altogether the effect of growing up, as we say. It strikes me that Ted has been in mischief and Rob has got him out of some scrape; hence the lovely mood of my bad boy and the sober one of my conscientious son, who never hides anything from his mother.'

Rob was as red as Ted now, but after a moment's hesitation he looked up and answered with an air of relief, 'Yes, mother, that's it; but it's all over and no harm done, and I think we'd better let it be, for a while at least. I did feel guilty to keep anything from you, but now you know so much I shall not worry and you needn't either. Ted's sorry, I don't mind, and it has done us both good.'

Mrs Jo looked at Ted, who winked hard but bore the look like a man; then she turned to Rob, who smiled at her so cheerfully that she felt reassured; but something in his face struck her, and she saw what it was that made him seem older, graver, yet more lovable than ever. It was the look pain of mind, as well as body, brings, and the patience of a sweet submission to some inevitable trial. Like a flash she guessed that some danger had been near her boy, and the glances she had caught between the two lads and Nan confirmed her fears.

'Rob, dear, you have been ill, hurt, or seriously troubled by Ted? Tell me at once; I will not have any secrets now. Boys sometimes suffer all their lives from neglected accidents or carelessness. Fritz, make them speak out!'

Mr Bhaer put down his papers and came to stand before them, saying in a tone that quieted Mrs Jo, and gave the boys courage, 'My sons, give us the truth. We can bear it; do not hold it back to spare us. Ted knows we forgive much because we love him, so be frank, all two.'

Ted instantly dived among the sofa pillows and kept there, with only a pair of scarlet ears visible, while Rob in a few words told the little story, truthfully, but as gently as he could, hastening to add the comfortable assurance that Don was *not* mad, the wound nearly well, and no danger would ever come of it.

But Mrs Jo grew so pale he had to put his arms about her, and his father turned and walked away, exclaiming: 'Ach Himmel!' in a tone of such mingled pain, relief, and gratitude, that Ted pulled an extra pillow over his head to smother the sound. They were all right in a minute; but such news is always a shock, even if the peril is past, and Mrs Jo hugged her boy close till his father came and took him away, saying with a strong shake of both hands and a quiver in his voice, 'To be in danger of one's life tries a man's mettle, and you bear it well; but I cannot spare my good boy yet; thank Gott, we keep him safe!'

A smothered sound, between a choke and a groan, came from under the pillows, and the writhing of Ted's long legs so plainly expressed despair that his mother relented towards him, and burrowing till she found a tousled yellow head, pulled it out and smoothed it, exclaiming with an irrepressible laugh, though her cheeks were wet with tears, 'Come and be forgiven, poor sinner! I know you have suffered enough, and I won't say a word; only if harm *had* come to Rob you would have made me more miserable than yourself. Oh, Teddy, Teddy, do try to cure that wilful spirit of yours before it is too late!'

'Oh, Mum, I do try! I never can forget this – I hope it's cured me; if it hasn't, I am afraid I ain't worth saving,' answered Ted, pulling his own hair as the only way of expressing his deep remorse.

'Yes, you are, my dear; I felt just so at fifteen when Amy was nearly drowned, and Marmee helped me as I'll help you. Come to me, Teddy, when the evil one gets hold of you, and together we'll rout him. Ah, me! I've had many a tussle with that old Apollyon, and often got worsted, but not always. Come under my shield, and we'll fight till we win.'

No one spoke for a minute as Ted and his mother laughed and cried in one handkerchief, and Rob stood with his father's arm round him so happy that all was told and forgiven, though never to be forgotten; for such experiences do one good, and knit hearts that love more closely together.

Presently Ted rose straight up and going to his father, said bravely and humbly, 'I ought to be punished. Please do it; but first say you forgive me, as Rob does.'

'Always that, mein Sohn, seventy time seven, if needs be, else I am not worthy the name you give me. The punishment has come; I can give no greater. Let it not be in vain. It will not with the help of the mother and the All Father. Room here for both, always!'

The good Professor opened his arms and embraced his boys like a true German, not ashamed to express by gesture or by word the fatherly emotions an American would have compressed into a slap on the shoulder and a brief 'All right'.

Mrs Jo sat and enjoyed the prospect like a romantic soul as she was, and then they had a quiet talk together, saying freely all that was in their hearts, and finding much comfort in the confidence which comes when love casts out fear. It was agreed that nothing be said except to Nan, who was to be thanked and rewarded for her courage, discretion, and fidelity.

'I always knew that girl had the making of a fine woman in her, and this proves it. No panics and shrieks and faintings and fuss, but calm sense and energetic skill. Dear child, what can I give or do to show my gratitude?' said Mrs Jo enthusiastically.

'Make Tom clear out and leave her in peace,' suggested Ted, almost himself again, though a pensive haze still partially obscured his native gaiety.

'Yes, do! he frets her like a mosquito. She forbade him to come out here while she stayed, and packed him off with Demi. I like old Tom, but he is a regular noodle about Nan,' added Rob, as he went away to help his father with the accumulated letters.

'I'll do it!' said Mrs Jo decidedly. 'That girl's career shall *not* be hampered by a foolish boy's fancy. In a moment of weariness she may give in, and then it's all over. Wiser women have done so and regretted it all their lives. Nan shall earn her place first, and prove that she can fill it; then she may marry if she likes, and can find a man worthy of her.'

But Mrs Jo's help was not needed; for love and gratitude can work miracles, and when youth, beauty, accident, and photography are added, success is sure; as was proved in the case of the unsuspecting but too susceptible Thomas.

CHAPTER 8

Josie Plays Mermaid

While the young Bhaers were having serious experiences at home, Josie was enjoying herself immensely at Rocky Nook; for the Laurences knew how to make summer idleness both charming and wholesome. Bess was very fond of her little cousin; Mrs Amy felt that whether her niece was an actress or not she *must* be a gentlewoman, and gave her the social training which marks the well-bred woman everywhere; while Uncle Laurie was never happier than when rowing, riding, playing, or lounging with two gay girls beside him. Josie bloomed like a wild flower in this free life, Bess grew rosy, brisk, and merry, and both were great favourites with the neighbours, whose villas were by the shore or perched on the cliffs along the pretty bay.

One crumpled rose-leaf disturbed Josie's peace, one baffled wish filled her with a longing which became a mania, and kept her as restless and watchful as a detective with a case to 'work up'. Miss Cameron, the great actress, had hired one of the villas and retired thither to rest and 'create' a new part for next season. She saw no one but a friend or two, had a private beach, and was invisible except during her daily drive, or when the opera-glasses of curious gazers were fixed on a blue figure disporting itself in the sea. The Laurences knew her, but respected her privacy, and after a call left her in peace till she expressed a wish for society – a courtesy which she remembered and repaid later, as we shall see.

But Josie was like a thirsty fly buzzing about a sealed honeypot, for this nearness to her idol was both delightful and maddening. She pined to see, hear, talk with, and study this great and happy woman who could thrill thousands by her art, and win friends by her virtue, benevolence, and beauty. This was the sort of actress the girl meant to be, and few could object if the gift was really hers; for the stage needs just such women to purify and elevate the profession which should teach as well as amuse. If kindly Miss Cameron had known what passionate love and longing burned in the bosom of the little girl whom she idly observed skipping over the rocks, splashing about the beach, or galloping past her gate on a Shetland pony, she would have made her happy by a look or a word. But being tired with her winter's work and busy with her new part, the lady took no more notice of this young neighbour than of the seagulls in the bay or the daisies dancing in the fields. Nosegays left on her doorstep, serenades under her garden wall, and the fixed stare of admiring eyes were such familiar things that she scarcely minded them; and Josie grew desperate when all her little attempts failed.

'I might climb that pine tree and tumble off on her piazza roof, or get Sheltie to throw me just at her gate and be taken in fainting. It's no use to try to drown myself when she is bathing. I can't sink, and she'd only send a man to pull me out. What can I do? I *will* see her and tell her my hopes and make her say I can act someday. Mamma would believe *her*; and if – oh, if she only *would* let me study with her, what perfect joy that would be!'

Josie made these remarks one afternoon as she and Bess prepared for a swim, a fishing party having prevented their morning bathe.

'You must bide your time, dear, and not be so impatient. Papa promised to give you a chance before the season is over, and he always manages things nicely. That will be better than any queer prank of yours,' answered Bess, tying her pretty hair in a white net to match her suit, while Josie made a little lobster of herself in scarlet.

'I hate to wait; but I suppose I must. Hope she will bathe this afternoon, though it is low tide. She told Uncle she should have to go in then because in the morning people stared so and went on her beach. Come and have a good dive from the big rock. No one round but nurses and babies, so we can romp and splash as much as we like.'

Away they went to have a fine time; for the little bay was free from other bathers, and the babies greatly admired their aquatic gymnastics, both being expert swimmers.

As they sat dripping on the big rock Josie suddenly gave a clutch that nearly sent Bess overboard, as she cried excitedly: 'There she is! Look! coming to bathe. How splendid! Oh, if she only would drown a little and let me save her! or even get her toe nipped by a crab; anything so I could go and speak!'

'Don't seem to look; she comes to be quiet and enjoy herself. Pretend we don't see her, that's only civil,' answered Bess, affecting to be absorbed in a white-winged yacht going by.

'Let's carelessly float that way as if going for seaweed on the rocks. She can't mind if we are flat on our backs, with only our noses out. Then when we can't help seeing her, we'll swim back as if anxious to retire. That will impress her, and she may call to thank the very polite young ladies who respect her wishes,' proposed Josie, whose lively fancy was always planning dramatic situations.

Just as they were going to slip from their rock, as if Fate relented at last, Miss Cameron was seen to beckon wildly as she stood waist-deep in the water, looking down. She called to her maid, who seemed searching along the beach for something, and not finding what she sought, waved a towel towards the girls as if summoning them to help her.

'Run, fly! she wants us, she wants us!' cried Josie, tumbling into the water like a very energetic turtle, and swimming away in her best style towards this long desired haven of joy. Bess followed more slowly, and both came panting and smiling up to Miss Cameron, who never lifted her eyes, but said in that wonderful voice of hers: 'I've dropped a bracelet. I see it, but can't get it. Will the little boy find me a long stick? I'll keep my eye on it, so the water shall not wash it away.'

'I'll dive for it with pleasure; but I'm not a boy,' answered Josie, laughing as she shook the curly head which at a distance had deceived the lady.

'I beg your pardon. Dive away, child; the sand is covering it fast. I value it very much. Never forgot to take it off before.'

'I'll get it!' and down went Josie, to come up with a handful of pebbles, but no bracelet.

'It's gone; never mind – my fault,' said Miss Cameron, disappointed, but amused at the girl's dismay as she shook the water out of her eyes and gasped bravely, 'No, it isn't. I'll have it, if I stay down all night!' and with one long breath Josie dived again, leaving nothing but a pair of agitated feet to be seen.

'I'm afraid she will hurt herself,' said Miss Cameron, looking at Bess, whom she recognised by her likeness to her mother.

'Oh, no; Josie is a little fish. She likes it;' and Bess smiled happily at this wonderful granting of her cousin's desire.

'You are Mr Laurence's daughter, I think? How d'ye do, dear? Tell papa I'm coming to see him soon. Too tired before. Quite savage. Better now. Ah! here's our pearl of divers. What luck?' she asked, as the heels went down and a dripping head came up.

Josie could only choke and splutter at first, being half strangled; but though her hands had failed again, her courage had not; and with a resolute shake of her wet hair, a bright look at the tall lady, and a series of puffs to fill her lungs, she said calmly, ' "Never give up" is my motto. I'm going to get it, if I go to Liverpool for it! Now, then!' and down went the mermaid quite out of sight this time, groping like a real lobster at the bottom of the sea.

'Plucky little girl! I like that. Who is she?' asked the lady, sitting down on a half-covered stone to watch her diver, since the bracelet was lost sight of.

Bess told her, adding, with the persuasive smile of her father, 'Josie longs to be an actress, and has waited for a month to see you. This is a great happiness for her.'

'Bless the child! why didn't she come and call? I'd have let her in; though usually I avoid stage-struck girls as I do reporters,' laughed Miss Cameron.

There was no time for more; a brown hand, grasping the bracelet, rose from the sea, followed by a purple face as Josie came up so blind and dizzy she had to cling to Bess, half drowned but triumphant.

Miss Cameron drew her to the rock where she sat, and pushing the hair out of her eyes, revived her with a hearty 'Bravo! bravo!' which assured the girl that her first act was a hit. Josie had often imagined her meeting with the great actress – the dignity and grace with which she would enter and tell her ambitious hopes, the effective dress she would wear, the witty things she would say, the deep impression her budding genius would make. But never in her wildest moments had she imagined an interview like this; scarlet, sandy, streaming, and speechless she leaned against the illustrious shoulder, looking like a beautiful seal as she blinked and wheezed till she could smile joyfully and exclaim proudly, 'I did get it! I'm so glad!'

'Now get your breath, my dear; then I shall be glad also. It was very nice of you to take all that trouble for me. How shall I thank you?' asked the lady, looking at her with the beautiful eyes that could say so many things without words.

Josie clasped her hands with a wet spat which rather destroyed the effect of the gesture, and answered in a beseeching tone that would have softened a far harder heart than Miss Cameron's, 'Let me come and see you once – only once! I want you to tell me if I can act; you will know. I'll abide by what you say; and if you think I can – by and by, when I've studied very hard – I shall be the happiest girl in the world. May I?'

'Yes; come tomorrow at eleven. We'll have a good talk; you shall show me what you can do, and I'll give you my opinion. But you won't like it.'

'I will, no matter if you tell me I'm a fool. I want it settled; so does Mamma. I'll take it bravely if you say no; and if you say yes, I'll never give up till I've done my best – as you did.'

'Ah, my child, it's a weary road, and there are plenty of thorns among the roses when you've won them. I think you have the courage, and this proves that you have perseverance. Perhaps you'll do. Come, and we'll see.'

Miss Cameron touched the bracelet as she spoke, and smiled so kindly that impetuous Josie wanted to kiss her; but wisely refrained, though her eyes were wet with softer water than any in the sea as she thanked her.

'We are keeping Miss Cameron from her bathe, and the tide is going out. Come, Josie,' said thoughtful Bess, fearing to outstay their welcome.

'Run over the beach and get warm. Thank you very much, little mermaid. Tell papa to bring his daughter to see me any time. Goodbye;' and with a wave of her hand the tragedy queen dismissed her court, but remained on her weedy throne watching the two lithe figures race over the sand with twinkling feet till they were out of sight. Then, as she calmly bobbed up and down in the water, she said to herself, 'The child has a good stage face, vivid, mobile; fine eyes, abandon, pluck, will. Perhaps she'll do. Good stock – talent in the family. We shall see.'

Of course Josie never slept a wink, and was in a fever of joyful excitement next day. Uncle Laurie enjoyed the episode very much, and Aunt Amy looked out her most becoming white dress for the grand occasion; Bess lent her most artistic hat, and Josie ranged the wood and marsh for a bouquet of wild roses, sweet white azalea, ferns, and graceful grasses, as the offering of a very grateful heart.

At ten she solemnly arrayed herself, and then sat looking at her neat gloves and buckled shoes till it was time to go, growing pale and sober with the thought that her fate was soon to be decided; for, like all young people she was sure that her whole life could be settled by one human creature, quite forgetting how wonderfully Providence trains us by disappointment, surprises us with unexpected success, and turns our seeming trials into blessings.

'I will go alone: we shall be freer so. Oh, Bess, pray that she may tell me rightly! So much depends on that! Don't laugh, Uncle! It *is* a very serious moment for me. Miss Cameron knows that, and will tell you so. Kiss me, Aunt Amy, since Mamma isn't here. If you say I look nice, I'm quite satisfied. Goodbye.' And with a wave of the hand as much like her model's as she could make it, Josie departed, looking very pretty and feeling very tragical.

Sure now of admittance, she boldly rang at the door which excluded so many, and being ushered into a shady parlour, feasted her eyes upon several fine portraits of great actors while she waited. She had read about most of them, and knew their trials and triumphs so well that she soon forgot herself, and tried to imitate Mrs Siddons as Lady Macbeth, looking up at the engraving as she held her nosegay like the candle in the sleep-walking scene, and knit her youthful brows distressfully while murmuring the speech of the haunted queen. So busy was she that Miss Cameron watched her for several minutes unseen, then startled her by suddenly sweeping in with the words upon her lips, the look upon her face, which made that one of her greatest scenes.

'I never can do it like that; but I'll keep trying, if you say I may,' cried Josie, forgetting her manners in the intense interest of the moment.

'Show me what you *can* do,' answered the actress, wisely plunging into the middle of things at once, well knowing that no common chat would satisfy this very earnest little person.

'First let me give you these. I thought you'd like wild things better than hot-house flowers; and I loved to bring them, as I'd no other way to thank you for your great kindness to me,' said Josie, offering her nosegay with a simple warmth that was very sweet.

'I do love them best, and keep my room full of the posies some good fairy hangs on my gate. Upon my word, I think I've found the fairy out – these are so like,' she added quickly, as her eye went from the flowers in her hand to others that stood near by, arranged with the same taste.

Josie's blush and smile betrayed her before she said, with a look full of girlish adoration and humility, 'I couldn't help it; I admire you so much. I know it was a liberty; but as I couldn't get in myself, I loved to think my posies pleased you.'

Something about the child and her little offering touched the woman, and, drawing Josie to her, she said, with no trace of actress in face or voice, 'They did please me, dear, and so do you. I'm tired of praise; and love is very sweet, when it is simple and sincere like this.'

Josie remembered to have heard, among many other stories, that Miss Cameron lost her lover years ago, and since had lived only for art. Now she felt that this might have been true; and pity for the splendid, lonely life made her face very eloquent, as well as grateful. Then, as if anxious to forget the past, her new friend said, in the commanding way that seemed natural to her, 'Let me see what you can do. Juliet, of course. All begin with that. Poor soul, how she is murdered!'

Now, Josie *had* intended to begin with Romeo's much-enduring sweetheart, and follow her up with Bianca, Pauline, and several of the favourite idols of stage-struck girls; but being a shrewd little person, she suddenly saw the wisdom of Uncle Laurie's advice, and resolved to follow it. So instead of the rant Miss Cameron expected, Josie gave poor Ophelia's mad scene, and gave it very well, having been trained by the college professor of elocution and done it many times. She was too young, of course, but the white gown, the loose hair, the real flowers she scattered over the imaginary grave, added to the illusion; and she sung the songs sweetly, dropped her pathetic curtsies, and vanished behind the curtain that divided the rooms with a backward look that surprised her critical auditor into a quick gesture of applause. Cheered by that welcome sound, Josie ran back as a little hoyden in one of the farces she had often acted, telling a story full of fun and naughtiness at first, but ending with a sob of repentance and an earnest prayer for pardon.

'Very good! Try again. Better than I expected,' called the voice of the oracle.

Josie tried Portia's speech, and recited very well, giving due emphasis to each fine sentence. Then, unable to refrain from what she considered her greatest effort, she burst into Juliet's balcony scene, ending with the poison and the tomb. She felt sure that she surpassed herself, and waited for applause. A ringing laugh made her tingle with indignation and disappointment, as she went to stand before Miss Cameron, saying in a tone of polite surprise, 'I have been told that I did it *very well*. I'm sorry you don't think so.'

'My dear, it's very bad. How can it help being so? What can a child like you know of love and fear and death? Don't try it yet. Leave tragedy alone till you are ready for it.'

'But you clapped Ophelia.'

'Yes, that was very pretty. Any clever girl can do it effectively. But the real meaning of Shakespeare is far above you yet, child. The comedy bit was best. There you showed real talent. It was both comic and pathetic. That's art. Don't lose it. The Portia was good declamation. Go on with that sort of thing; it trains the voice – teaches shades of expression. You've a good voice and natural grace – great helps both, hard to acquire.'

'Well, I'm glad I've got something,' sighed Josie, sitting meekly on a stool, much crestfallen, but not daunted yet, and bound to have her say out.

'My dear little girl, I told you that you would not like what I should say to you; yet I must be honest if I would really help you.

I've had to do it for many like you; and most of them have never forgiven me, though my words have proved true, and they are what I advised them to be – good wives and happy mothers in quiet homes. A few have kept on, and done fairly well. One you will hear of soon, I think; for she has talent, indomitable patience, and mind as well as beauty. You are too young to show to which class you belong. Geniuses are very rare, and even at fifteen seldom give much promise of future power.'

'Oh, I don't think I'm a genius!' cried Josie, growing calm and sober as she listened to the melodious voice and looked into the expressive face that filled her with confidence, so strong, sincere, and kindly was it. 'I only want to find out if I have talent enough to go on, and after years of study to be able to act well in any of the good plays people never tire of seeing. I don't expect to be a Mrs Siddons or a Miss Cameron, much as I long to be; but it *does* seem as if I had something in me which can't come out in any way but this. When I act I'm perfectly happy. I seem to live, to be in my own world, and each new part is a new friend. I love Shakespeare, and am never tired of his splendid people. Of course, I don't understand it all; but it's like being alone at night with the mountains and the stars, solemn and grand, and I try to imagine how it will look when the sun comes up, and all is glorious and clear to me. I can't see, but I feel the beauty, and long to express it.'

As she spoke with the most perfect self-forgetfulness Josie was pale with excitement, her eyes shone, her lips trembled, and all her little soul seemed trying to put into words the emotions that filled it to overflowing. Miss Cameron understood, felt that this was something more than a girlish whim; and when she answered there was a new tone of sympathy in her voice, a new interest in her face, though she wisely refrained from saying all she thought, well knowing what splendid dreams young people build upon a word, and how bitter is the pain when the bright bubbles burst.

'If you feel this, I can give you no better advice than to go on loving and studying our great master,' she said slowly; but Josie caught the changed tone, and felt, with a thrill of joy, that her new friend was speaking to her now as to a comrade. 'It is an education in itself, and a lifetime is not long enough to teach you all his secret. But there is much to do before you can hope to echo his words. Have you the patience, courage, strength, to begin at the beginning, and slowly, painfully, lay the foundation for future work? Fame is a pearl many dive for and only a few bring up. Even when they do, it is not perfect, and they sigh for more, and lose better things in struggling for them.'

The last words seemed spoken more to herself than to her hearer, but Josie answered quickly, with a smile and an expressive gesture, 'I got the bracelet in spite of all the bitter water in my eyes.'

'You did! I don't forget it. A good omen. We will accept it.'

Miss Cameron answered the smile with one that was like sunshine to the girl, and stretched her white hands as if taking some invisible gift. Then added in a different tone, watching the effect of her words on the expressive face before her, 'Now you will be disappointed, for instead of telling you to come and study with me, or go and act in some second-rate theatre at once, I advise you to go back to school and finish your education. That is the first step, for all accomplishments are needed, and a single talent makes a very imperfect character. Cultivate mind and body, heart and soul, and make yourself an intelligent, graceful, beautiful, and healthy girl. Then, at eighteen or twenty, go into training and try your powers. Better start for the battle with your arms in order, and save the hard lesson which comes when we rush on too soon. Now and then genius carries all before it, but not often. We have to climb slowly, with many slips and falls. Can you wait as well as work?'

'I will!'

'We shall see. It would be pleasant to me to know that when I quit the stage I leave behind me a well-trained, faithful, gifted comrade to more than fill my place, and carry on what I have much at heart – the purification of the stage. Perhaps you are she; but remember, mere beauty and rich costumes do not make an actress, nor are the efforts of a clever little girl to play great characters real art. It is all dazzle and sham, and a disgrace and disappointment now. Why will the public be satisfied with opera bouffe, or the trash called society plays when a world of truth and beauty, poetry and pathos lies waiting to be interpreted and enjoyed?'

Miss Cameron had forgotten to whom she spoke, and walked to and fro, full of the noble regret all cultivated people feel at the low state of the stage nowadays.

'That's what Uncle Laurie says; and he and Aunt Jo try to plan plays about true and lovely things – simple domestic scenes that touch people's hearts, and make them laugh and cry and feel better. Uncle says that sort is my style, and I must not think of tragedy. But it's so much nicer to sweep about in crowns and velvet trains than to wear everyday clothes, and just be myself, though it is so easy.'

'Yet that is high art, child, and what we need for a time till we are ready for the masters. Cultivate that talent of yours. It is a special gift, this power to bring tears and smiles, and a sweeter task to touch the heart than to freeze the blood or fire the imagination. Tell your uncle he is right, and ask your aunt to try a play for you. I'll come and see it when you are ready.'

'Will you? Oh! will you? We are going to have some at Christmas, with a nice part for me. A simple little thing, but I can do it, and should be so proud, so happy to have you there.'

Josie rose as she spoke, for a glance at the clock showed her that her call was a long one; and hard as it was to end this momentous interview, she felt that she must go. Catching up her hat she went to Miss Cameron, who stood looking at her so keenly that she felt as transparent as a pane of glass, and coloured prettily as she looked up, saying, with a grateful little tremor in her voice, 'I can never thank you for this hour and all you have told me. I shall do just what you advise, and Mamma will be very glad to see me settled at my books again. I can study now with all my heart, because it is to help me on; and I won't hope too much, but work and wait, and try to please you, as the only way to pay my debt.'

'That reminds me that I have not paid mine. Little friend, wear this for my sake. It is fit for a mermaid, and will remind you of your first dive. May the next bring up a better jewel, and leave no bitter water on your lips!'

As she spoke, Miss Cameron took from the lace at her throat a pretty pin of aquamarine, and fastened it like an order on Josie's proud bosom; then lifting the happy little face, she kissed it very tenderly, and watched it go smiling away with eyes that seemed to see into a future full of the trials and the triumphs which she knew so well.

Bess expected to see Josie come flying in, all raptures and excitement, or drowned in tears of disappointment, but was surprised at the expression of calm content and resolution which she wore. Pride and satisfaction, and a new feeling of responsibility both sobered and sustained her, and she felt that any amount of dry study and long waiting would be bearable, if in the glorious future she could be an honour to her profession and a comrade to the new friend whom she already adored with girlish ardour.

She told her little story to a deeply interested audience, and all felt that Miss Cameron's advice was good. Mrs Amy was relieved at the prospect of delay; for she did not want her niece to be an actress and hoped the fancy would die out.

Uncle Laurie was full of charming plans and prophecies and wrote one of his most delightful notes to thank their neighbour for her kindness; while Bess, who loved art of all kinds, fully sympathised with her cousin's ambitious hopes, only wondering why she preferred to act out her visions rather than embody them in marble.

That first interview was not the last; for Miss Cameron was really interested, and had several memorable conversations with the Laurences, while the girls sat by, drinking in every word with the delight all artists feel in their own beautiful world, and learning to see how sacred good gifts are, how powerful, and how faithfully they should be used for high ends, each in its own place helping to educate, refine, and refresh.

Josie wrote reams to her mother; and when the visit ended rejoiced her heart by bringing her a somewhat changed little daughter, who fell to work at the once-detested books with a patient energy which surprised and pleased everyone. The right string had been touched, and even French exercises and piano practice became endurable, since accomplishments would be useful by and by; dress, manners, and habits were all interesting now, because 'mind and body, heart and soul, must be cultivated', and while training to become an 'intelligent, graceful, healthy girl', little Josie was unconsciously fitting herself to play her part well on whatever stage the great Manager might prepare for her.

CHAPTER 9

The Worm Turns

Two very superior bicycles went twinkling up the road to Plumfield one September afternoon, bearing two brown and dusty riders evidently returning from a successful run, for though their legs might be a trifle weary, their faces beamed as they surveyed the world from their lofty perches with the air of calm content all wheelmen wear *after* they have learned to ride; before that happy period anguish of mind and body is the chief expression of the manly countenance.

'Go ahead and report, Tom; I'm due here. See you later,' said Demi, swinging himself down at the door of the Dovecote.

'Don't peach, there's a good fellow. Let me have it out with Mother Bhaer first,' returned Tom, wheeling in at the gate with a heavy sigh.

Demi laughed, and his comrade went slowly up the avenue, devoutly hoping that the coast was clear; for he was the bearer of tidings which would, he thought, convulse the entire family with astonishment and dismay.

To his great joy Mrs Jo was discovered alone in a grove of proof-sheets, which she dropped to greet the returning wanderer cordially. But after the first glance she saw that something was the matter, recent events having made her unusually sharp-eyed and suspicious.

'What is it now, Tom?' she asked, as he subsided into an easy chair with a curious expression of mingled fear, shame, amusement, and distress in his brick-red countenance.

'I'm in an awful scrape, ma'am.'

'Of course; I'm always prepared for scrapes when you appear. What is it? Run over some old lady who is going to law about it?' asked Mrs Jo cheerfully.

'Worse than that,' groaned Tom.

'Not poisoned some trusting soul who asked you to prescribe, I hope?'

'Worse than that.'

'You haven't let Demi catch any horrid thing and left him behind, have you?'

'Worse even than that.'

'I give it up. Tell me quick; I hate to wait for bad news.'

Having got his listener sufficiently excited, Tom launched his thunderbolt in one brief sentence, and fell back to watch the effect.

'I'm engaged!'

Mrs Jo's proof-sheets flew wildly about as she clasped her hands, exclaiming in dismay, 'If Nan has yielded, I'll never forgive her!'

'She hasn't; it's another girl.'

Tom's face was so funny as he said the words, that it was impossible to help laughing; for he looked both sheepish and pleased, besides very much perplexed and worried.

'I'm glad, very glad indeed! Don't care who it is; and I hope you'll be married soon. Now tell me all about it,' commanded Mrs Jo, so much relieved that she felt ready for anything.

'What will Nan say?' demanded Tom, rather taken aback at this view of his predicament.

'She will be rejoiced to get rid of the mosquito who has plagued her so long. Don't worry about Nan. Who is this "other girl"?'

'Demi hasn't written about her?'

'Only something about your upsetting a Miss West down at Quitno; I thought that was scrape enough.'

'That was only the beginning of a series of scrapes. Just my luck! Of course after sousing the poor girl I had to be attentive to her, hadn't I? Everyone seemed to think so, and I couldn't get away, and so I was lost before I knew it. It's all Demi's fault, he would stay there and fuss with his old photos, because the views were good and all the girls wanted to be taken. Look at these, will you, ma'am? That's the way we spent our time when we weren't playing tennis;' and Tom pulled a handful of pictures from his pocket, displaying several in which he was conspicuous, either holding a sun-umbrella over a very pretty young lady on the rocks, reposing at her feet in the grass, or perched on a piazza railing with other couples in seaside costumes and effective attitudes.

'This is *she* of course?' asked Mrs Jo, pointing to the much-ruffled damsel with the jaunty hat, coquettish shoes, and racquet in her hand.

'That's Dora. Isn't she lovely?' cried Tom, forgetting his tribulations for a moment and speaking with lover-like ardour.

'Very nice little person to look at. Hope she is not a Dickens Dora? That curly crop looks like it.'

'Not a bit; she's very smart; can keep house, and sew, and do lots of things, I assure you, ma'am. All the girls like her, and she's sweet-tempered and jolly, and sings like a bird, and dances beautifully, and loves books. Thinks yours are splendid, and made me talk about you no end.'

'That last sentence is to flatter me and win my help to get you out of the scrape. Tell me first how you got in;' and Mrs Jo settled herself to listen with interest, never tired of boys' affairs.

Tom gave his head a rousing rub all over to clear his wits, and plunged into his story with a will.

'Well, we've met her before, but I didn't know she was there. Demi wanted to see a fellow, so we went, and finding it nice and cool rested over Sunday. Found some pleasant people and went out rowing; I had Dora, and came to grief on a confounded rock. She could swim, no harm done, only the scare and the spoilt gown. She took it well, and we got friendly at once – couldn't help it, scrambling into that beast of a boat while the rest laughed at us. Of course we had to stay another day to see that Dora was all right. Demi wanted to. Alice Heath is down there and two other girls from our college, so we sort of lingered along, and Demi kept taking pictures, and we danced, and got into a tennis tournament; and that was as good exercise as wheeling, we thought. Fact is, tennis is a dangerous game, ma'am. A great deal of courting goes on in those courts, and we fellows find that sort of "serving" mighty agreeable, don't you know?'

'Not much tennis in my day, but I understand perfectly,' said Mrs Jo, enjoying it all as much as Tom did.

'Upon my word, I hadn't the least idea of being serious,' he continued slowly, as if this part of his tale was hard to tell; 'but everyone else spooned, so I did. Dora seemed to like it and expect it, and of course I was glad to be agreeable. *She* thought I amounted to something, though Nan does not, and it was pleasant to be appreciated after years of snubbing. Yes, it was right down jolly to have a sweet girl smile at you all day, and blush prettily when you said a neat thing to her, and look glad when you came, sorry when you left, and admire all you did, and make you feel like a man and act your best. That's the sort of treatment a fellow enjoys and ought to get if he behaves himself; not frowns and cold shoulders year in and year out, and made to look like a fool when he means well, and is faithful, and has loved a girl ever since he was a boy. No, by Jove, it's not fair, and I won't stand it!'

Tom waxed warm and eloquent as he thought over his wrongs, and bounced up to march about the room, wagging his head and trying to feel aggrieved as usual, but surprised to find that his heart did not ache a bit.

'I wouldn't. Drop the old fancy, for it was nothing more, and take up the new one, if it is genuine. But how came you to propose, Tom, as you must have done to be engaged?' asked Mrs Jo, impatient for the crisis of the tale.

'Oh, that was an accident. I didn't mean it at all; the donkey did it, and I couldn't get out of the scrape without hurting Dora's feelings, you see,' began Tom, seeing that the fatal moment had come.

'So there were two donkeys in it, were there?' said Mrs Jo, foreseeing fun of some sort.

'Don't laugh! It sounds funny, I know; but it might have been awful,' answered Tom darkly, though a twinkle of the eye showed that his love trials did not quite blind him to the comic side of the adventure.

'The girls admired our new wheels, and of course we liked to show off. Took 'em to ride, and had larks generally. Well, one day, Dora was on behind, and we were going nicely along a good bit of road, when a ridiculous old donkey got right across the way. I thought he'd move, but he didn't, so I gave him a kick; he kicked back, and over we went in a heap, donkey and all. Such a mess! I thought only of Dora, and she had hysterics; at least, she laughed till she cried, and that beast brayed, and I lost my head. Any fellow would, with a poor girl gasping in the road, and he wiping her tears and begging pardon, not knowing whether her bones were broken or not. I called her my darling, and went on like a fool in my flurry, till she grew calmer, and said, with such a look, "I forgive you, Tom. Pick me up, and let us go on again."

'Wasn't that sweet now, after I'd upset her for the second time? It touched me to the heart; and I said I'd like to go on for ever with such an angel to steer for, and – well I don't know *what* I did say; but you might have knocked me down with a feather when she put her arm round my neck and whispered, "Tom, dear, with you I'm not afraid of any lions in the path." She might have said *donkeys*; but she was in earnest, and she spared my feelings. Very nice of the dear girl; but there I am with two sweethearts on my hands, and in a deuce of a scrape.'

Finding it impossible to contain herself another moment, Mrs Jo laughed till the tears ran down her cheeks at this characteristic episode; and after one reproachful look, which only added to her merriment, Tom burst into a jolly roar that made the room ring.

'Tommy Bangs! Tommy Bangs! who but you could ever get into such a catastrophe?' said Mrs Jo, when she recovered her breath.

'Isn't it a muddle all round, and won't everyone chaff me to death about it? I shall have to quit old Plum for a while,' answered Tom, as he mopped his face, trying to realise the full danger of his position.

'No, indeed; I'll stand by you, for I think it the best joke of the season. But tell me how things ended. Is it really serious, or only a summer flirtation? I don't approve of them, but boys and girls will play with edged tools and cut their fingers.'

'Well, Dora considers herself engaged, and wrote to her people at once. I couldn't say a word when she took it all in solemn earnest and seemed so happy. She's only seventeen, never liked anyone before, and is sure all will be all right; as her father knows mine, and we are both well off. I was so staggered that I said, ' "Why, you can't love me really when we know so little of one another?" But she answered right out of her tender little heart, "Yes, I do, dearly, Tom; you are so gay and kind and honest, I couldn't help it." Now, after that what could I do but go ahead and make her happy while I stayed, and trust to luck to straighten the snarl out afterwards?'

'A truly Tomian way of taking things easy. I hope you told your father at once.'

'Oh yes, I wrote off and broke it to him in three lines. I said, "Dear Father, I'm engaged to Dora West, and I hope she will suit the family. She suits me tiptop. Yours ever, Tom." He was all right, never liked Nan, you know; but Dora will suit him down to the ground.' And Tom looked entirely satisfied with his own tact and taste.

'What did Demi say to this rapid and funny lovemaking? Wasn't he scandalised?' asked Mrs Jo, trying not to laugh again as she thought of the unromantic spectacle of donkey, bicycle, boy, and girl all in the dust together.

'Not a bit. He was immensely interested and very kind; talked to me like a father; said it was a good thing to steady a fellow, only I must be honest with her and myself and not trifle a moment. Demi is a regular Solomon, especially when he is in the same boat,' answered Tom, looking wise.

'You don't mean – ?' gasped Mrs Jo, in sudden alarm at the bare idea of more love-affairs just yet.

'Yes, I do, please, ma'am; it's a regular sell all the way through, and I owe Demi one for taking me into temptation blindfold. He *said* he went to Quitno to see Fred Wallace, but he never saw the fellow. How could he, when Wallace was off in his yacht all the time we were there? Alice was the real attraction, and I was left to my fate, while they were maundering round with that old camera. There were three donkeys in this affair, and I'm not the worst one, though I shall have to bear the laugh. Demi will look innocent and sober, and no one will say a word to him.'

'The midsummer madness has broken out, and no one knows who will be stricken next. Well, leave Demi to his mother, and let us see what you are going to do, Tom.'

'I don't know exactly; it's awkward to be in love with two girls at once. What do you advise?'

'A common-sense view of the case, by all means. Dora loves you and thinks you love her. Nan does not care for you, and you only care for her as a friend, though you have tried to do more. It is my opinion, Tom, that you love Dora, or are on the way to it; for in all these years I've never seen you look or speak about Nan as you do about Dora. Opposition has made you obstinately cling to her till accident has shown you a more attractive girl. Now, I think you had better take the old love for a friend, the new one for a sweetheart, and in due time, if the sentiment is genuine, marry her.'

If Mrs Jo had any doubts about the matter, Tom's face would have proved the truth of her opinion; for his eyes shone, his lips smiled, and in spite of dust and sunburn a new expression of happiness quite glorified him as he stood silent for a moment, trying to understand the beautiful miracle which real love works when it comes to a young man's heart.

'The fact is I meant to make Nan jealous, for she knows Dora, and I was sure would hear of our doings. I was tired of being walked on, and I thought I'd try to break away and not be a bore and a laughing-stock any more,' he said slowly, as if it relieved him to pour out his doubts and woes and hopes and joys to his old friend. 'I was regularly astonished to find it so easy and so pleasant. I didn't mean to do any harm, but drifted along beautifully, and told Demi to mention things in his letters to Daisy, so Nan might know. Then I forgot Nan altogether, and saw, heard, felt, cared for no one but Dora, till the donkey – bless his old heart! – pitched her into my arms and I found she loved me. Upon my soul, I don't see why she should! I'm not half good enough.'

'Every honest man feels that when an innocent girl puts her hand in his. Make yourself worthy of her, for she isn't an angel, but a woman with faults of her own for you to bear, and forgive, and you must help one another,' said Mrs Jo, trying to realise that this sober youth was her scapegrace Tommy.

'What troubles me is that I didn't mean it when I began, and was going to use the dear girl as an instrument of torture for Nan. It wasn't right, and I don't deserve to be so happy. If all my scrapes ended as well as this, what a state of bliss I should be in!' and Tom beamed again at the rapturous prospect.

'My dear boy, it is not a scrape, but a very sweet experience suddenly dawning upon you,' answered Mrs Jo, speaking very soberly; for she saw he was in earnest. 'Enjoy it wisely and be worthy of it, for it is a serious thing to accept a girl's love and trust, and let her look up to you for tenderness and truth in return. Don't let little Dora look in vain, but be a man in all things for her sake, and make this affection a blessing to you both.'

'I'll try. Yes, I do love her, only I can't believe it just yet. Wish you knew her. Dear little soul, I long to see her already! She cried when we parted last night and I hated to go.' Tom's hand went to his cheek as if he still felt the rosy little seal Dora had set upon his promise not to forget her, and for the first time in his happy-go-lucky life Tommy Bangs understood the difference between sentiment and sentimentality. The feeling recalled Nan, for he had never known that tender thrill when thinking of her, and the old friendship seemed rather a prosaic affair beside this delightful mingling of romance, surprise, love, and fun. 'I declare, I feel as if a weight was off me, but what the dickens *will* Nan say when she knows it!' he exclaimed with a chuckle.

'Knows what?' asked a clear voice that made both start and turn, for there was Nan calmly surveying them from the doorway.

Anxious to put Tom out of suspense and see how Nan would take the news, Mrs Jo answered quickly, 'Tom's engagement to Dora West.'

'Really?' and Nan looked so surprised that Mrs Jo was afraid she might be fonder of her old playmate than she knew; but her next words set the fear at rest, and made everything comfortable and merry at once.

'I knew my prescription would work wonders if he only took it long enough. Dear old Tom, I'm so glad. Bless you! bless you!' And she shook both his hands with hearty affection.

'It was an accident, Nan. I didn't mean to, but I'm always getting into messes, and I couldn't seem to get out of this any other way. Mother Bhaer will tell you all about it. I must go and make myself tidy. Going to tea with Demi. See you later.'

Stammering, blushing, and looking both sheepish and gratified, Tom suddenly bolted, leaving the elder lady to enlighten the younger at length, and have another laugh over this new sort of courtship, which might well be called accidental. Nan was deeply interested, for she knew Dora, thought her a nice little thing, and predicted that in time she would make Tom an excellent wife, since she admired and 'appreciated' him so much.

'I shall miss him of course, but it will be a relief to me and better for him; dangling is so bad for a boy. Now he will go into business with his father and do well, and everyone be happy. I shall give Dora an elegant family medicine-chest for a wedding-present, and teach her how to use it. Tom can't be trusted, and is no more fit for the profession than Silas.'

The latter part of this speech relieved Mrs Jo's mind, for Nan had looked about her as if she had lost something valuable when she began; but the medicine-chest seemed to cheer her, and the thought of Tom in a *safe* profession was evidently a great comfort.

'The worm has turned at last, Nan, and your bond-man is free. Let him go, and give your whole mind to your work; for *you* are fitted for the profession, and will be an honour to it by and by,' she said approvingly.

'I hope so. That reminds me – measles are in the village, and you had better tell the girls not to call where there are children. It would be bad to have a run of them just as term begins. Now I'm off to Daisy. Wonder what she will say to Tom. Isn't he great fun?' And Nan departed, laughing over the joke with such genuine satisfaction that it was evident no sentimental regrets disturbed her 'maiden meditation, fancy-free'.

'I shall have my eye on Demi, but won't say a word. Meg likes to manage her children in her own way, and a very good way it is. But the dear Pelican will be somewhat ruffled if her boy has caught the epidemic which seems to have broken out among us this summer.'

Mrs Jo did not mean the measles, but that more serious malady called love, which is apt to ravage communities, spring and autumn, when winter gaiety and summer idleness produce whole bouquets of engagements, and set young people to pairing off like the birds. Franz began it, Nat was a chronic and Tom a sudden case; Demi seemed to have the symptoms; and worst of all, her own Ted had only the day before calmly said to her, 'Mum, I think I should be happier if I had a sweetheart, like the other boys.' If her cherished son had asked her for dynamite to play with, she would hardly have been more startled, or have more decidedly refused the absurd request.

'Well, Barry Morgan said I ought to have one and offered to pick me out a nice one among our set. I asked Josie first, and she hooted at the idea, so I thought I'd let Barry look round. You say it steadies a fellow, and I want to be steady,' explained Ted in a serious tone, which would have convulsed his parent at any other time.

'Good lack! What are we coming to in this fast age when babes and boys make such demands and want to play with one of the most sacred things in life?' exclaimed Mrs Jo, and having in a few words set the matter in its true light, sent her son away to wholesome baseball and Octoo for a safe sweetheart.

Now, here was Tom's bombshell to explode in their midst, carrying widespread destruction, perhaps; for though one swallow does not make a summer, one engagement is apt to make several, and her boys were, most of them, at the inflammable age when a spark ignites the flame, which soon flickers and dies out, or burns warm and clear for life. Nothing could be done about it but to help them make wise choices, and be worthy of good mates. But of all the lessons Mrs Jo had tried to teach her boys, this great one was the hardest; for love is apt to make lunatics of even saints and sages, so young people cannot be expected to escape the delusions, disappointments, and mistakes, as well as the delights, of this sweet madness.

'I suppose it is inevitable, since we live in America, so I won't borrow trouble, but hope that some of the new ideas of education will produce a few hearty, happy, capable, and intelligent girls for my lads. Lucky for me that I haven't the whole twelve on my hands, I should lose my wits if I had, for I foresee complications and troubles ahead worse than Tom's boats, bicycles, donkeys, and Doras,' meditated Mrs Jo, as she went back to her neglected proof-sheets.

Tom was quite satisfied with the tremendous effect his engagement produced in the little community at Plumfield.

'It was paralysing,' as Demi said; and astonishment left most of Tom's mates little breath for chaff. That he, the faithful one, should turn from the idol to strange goddesses, was a shock to the romantic and a warning to the susceptible. It was comical to see the airs our Thomas put on; for the most ludicrous parts of the affair were kindly buried in oblivion by the few who knew them, and Tom burst forth as a full-blown hero who had rescued the maiden from a watery grave, and won her gratitude and love by his daring deed. Dora kept the secret, and enjoyed the fun when she came to see Mother Bhaer and pay her respects to the family generally. Everyone liked her at once, for she was a gay and winning little soul; fresh, frank, and so happy, it was beautiful to see her innocent pride in Tom, who was a new boy, or man rather; for with this change in his life a great change took place in him. Jolly he would always be, and impulsive, but he tried to become all that Dora believed him, and his best side came uppermost for everyday wear. It was surprising to see how many good traits Tom had; and his efforts to preserve the manly dignity belonging to his proud position as an engaged man was very comical. So was the entire change from his former abasement and devotion to Nan to a somewhat lordly air with his little betrothed; for Dora made an idol of him, and resented the idea of a fault or a flaw in her Tom. This new state of things suited both, and the once blighted being bloomed finely in the warm atmosphere of appreciation, love, and confidence. He was very fond of the dear girl, but meant to be a slave no longer, and enjoyed his freedom immensely, quite unconscious that the great tyrant of the world had got hold of him for life.

To his father's satisfaction he gave up his medical studies, and prepared to go into business with the old gentleman, who was a flourishing merchant, ready now to make the way smooth and smile upon his marriage with Mr West's well-endowed daughter. The only thorn in Tom's bed of roses was Nan's placid interest in his affairs, and evident relief at his disloyalty. He did not want her to suffer, but a decent amount of regret at the loss of such a lover would have gratified him; a slight melancholy, a word of reproach, a glance of envy as he passed with adoring Dora on his arm, seemed but the fitting tribute to such years of faithful service and sincere affection. But Nan regarded him with a maternal sort of air that nettled him very much, and patted Dora's curly head with a worldly wise air worthy of the withered spinster, Julia Mills, in *David Copperfield*.

It took some time to get the old and the new emotions comfortably adjusted, but Mrs Jo helped him, and Mr Laurie gave him some wise advice upon the astonishing gymnastic feats the human heart can perform, and be all the better for it if it only held fast to the balancing-pole of truth and common sense. At last our Tommy got his bearings, and as autumn came on Plumfield saw but little of him; for his new lode star was in the city, and business kept him hard at work. He was evidently in his right place now, and soon throve finely, to his father's great contentment; for his jovial presence pervaded the once quiet office like a gale of fresh wind, and his lively wits found managing men and affairs much more congenial employment than studying disease, or playing unseemly pranks with skeletons.

Here we will leave him for a time and turn to the more serious adventures of his mates, though this engagement, so merrily made, was the anchor which kept our mercurial Tom happy, and made a man of him.

CHAPTER 10

Demi Settles

'Mother, can I have a little serious conversation with you?' asked Demi one evening, as they sat together enjoying the first fire of the season, while Daisy wrote letters upstairs and Josie was studying in the little library close by.

'Certainly, dear. No bad news, I hope?' and Mrs Meg looked up from her sewing with a mixture of pleasure and anxiety on her motherly face; for she dearly loved a good talk with her son, and knew that he always had something worth telling.

'It will be good news for you, I think,' answered Demi, smiling as he threw away his paper and went to sit beside her on the little sofa which just held two.

'Let me hear it, then, at once.'

'I know you don't like the reporting, and will be glad to hear that I have given it up.'

'I am very glad! It is too uncertain a business, and there is no prospect of getting on for a long time. I want you settled in some good place where you can stay, and in time make money. I wish you liked a profession; but as you don't, any clean, well-established business will do.'

'What do you say to a railroad office?'

'I don't like it. A noisy, hurried kind of place, I know, with all sorts of rough men about. I hope it isn't that, dear?'

'I could have it; but does bookkeeping in a wholesale leather business please you better?'

'No; you'll get round-shouldered writing at a tall desk; and they say, once a bookkeeper always a bookkeeper.'

'How does a travelling agent suit your views?'

'Not at all; with all those dreadful accidents, and the exposure and bad food as you go from place to place, you are sure to get killed or lose your health.'

'I could be private secretary to a literary man; but the salary is small, and may end any time.'

'That would be better, and more what I want. It isn't that I object to honest work of any kind; but I don't want my son to spend his best years grubbing for a little money in a dark office, or be knocked about in a rough-and-tumble scramble to get on. I want to see you in some business where your tastes and talents can be developed and made useful; where you can go on rising, and in time put in your little fortune and be a partner; so that your years of apprenticeship will not be wasted, but fit you to take your place among the honourable men who make their lives and work useful and respected. I talked it all over with your dear father when you were a child; and if he had lived he would have shown you what I mean, and helped you to be what he was.'

Mrs Meg wiped away a quiet tear as she spoke; for the memory of her husband was a very tender one, and the education of his children had been a sacred task to which she gave all her heart and life, and so far she had done wonderfully well – as her good son and loving daughters tried to prove. Demi's arm was round her now, as he said, in a voice so like his father's that it was the sweetest music to her ear, 'Mother dear, I think I have got just what you want for me; and it shall not be my fault if I don't become the man you hope to see me. Let me tell you all about it. I didn't say anything till it was sure because it would only worry you; but Aunt Jo and I have been on the look-out for it some time, and now it has come. You know her publisher, Mr Tiber, is one of the most successful men in the business; also generous, kind, and the soul of honour – as his treatment of Aunty proves. Well, I've rather hankered for that place; for I love books, and as I can't make them I'd like to publish them. That needs some literary taste and judgement, it brings you in contact with fine people, and is an education in itself. Whenever I go into that large, handsome room to see Mr Tiber for Aunt Jo, I always want to stay; for it's lined with books and pictures, famous men and women come and go, and Mr Tiber sits at his desk like a sort of king, receiving his subjects; for the greatest authors are humble to him, and wait his Yes or No with anxiety. Of course I've nothing to do with all that, and may never have; but I like to see it, and the atmosphere is so different from the dark offices and hurly-burly of many other trades, where nothing but money is talked about, that it seems another world, and I feel at home in it. Yes, I'd rather beat the doormats and make fires there than be head clerk in the great hide and leather store at a big salary.' Here Demi paused for breath; and Mrs Meg, whose face had been growing brighter and brighter, exclaimed eagerly, 'Just what I should like! Have you got it? Oh, my dear boy! your fortune is made if you go to that well-established and flourishing place, with those good men to help you along!'

'I think I have, but we mustn't be too sure of anything yet. I may not suit; I'm only on trial, and must begin at the beginning and work my way up faithfully. Mr Tiber was very kind, and will push me on as fast as is fair to the other fellows, and as I prove myself fit to go up. I'm to begin the first of next month in the book-room, filling orders; and I go round and get orders, and do various other things of the sort. I like it. I am ready to do anything about books, if it's only to dust them,' laughed Demi, well pleased with his prospects, for, after trying various things, he seemed at last to have found the sort of work he liked, and a prospect that was very inviting to him.

'You inherit that love of books from grandpa; he can't live without them. I'm glad of it. Tastes of that kind show a refined nature, and are both a comfort and a help all one's life. I am truly glad and grateful, John, that at last you want to settle, and have got such an entirely satisfactory place. Most boys begin much earlier; but I don't believe in sending them out to face the world so young, just when body and soul need home care and watchfulness. Now you are a man, and must begin your life for yourself. Do your best, and be as honest, useful, and happy as your father, and I won't care about making a fortune.'

'I'll try, Mother. Couldn't have a better chance; for Tiber & Co. treat their people like gentlemen, and pay generously for faithful work. Things are done in a businesslike way there, and that suits me. I hate promises that are not kept, and shiftless or tyrannical ways anywhere. Mr Tiber said, "This is only to teach you the ropes, Brooke; I shall have other work for you by and by." Aunty told him I had done book notices, and had rather a fancy for literature; so though I can't produce any "works of Shakespeare", as she says, I may get up some little things later. If I don't, I think it a very honourable and noble profession to select and give good books to the world; and I'm satisfied to be a humble helper in the work.'

'I'm glad you feel so. It adds so much to one's happiness to love the task one does. I used to hate teaching; but housekeeping for my own family was always sweet, though much harder in many ways. Isn't Aunt Jo pleased about all this?' asked Mrs Meg, already seeing in her mind's eye a splendid sign with 'Tiber, Brooke & Co.' over the door of a famous publishing house.

'So pleased that I could hardly keep her from letting the cat out of the bag too soon. I've had so many plans, and disappointed you so often, I wanted to be very sure this time. I had to bribe Rob and Ted to keep her at home tonight till I'd told my news, she was eager to rush down and tell you herself. The castles that dear woman has built for me would fill all Spain, and have kept us jolly while we waited to know our fate. Mr Tiber doesn't do things in a hurry; but when he makes up his mind, you are all right; and I feel that I am fairly launched.'

'Bless you, dear, I hope so! It is a happy day for me, because I've been so anxious lest, with all my care, I have been too easy and indulgent, and my boy, with his many good gifts, might fritter his time away in harmless but unsatisfactory things. Now I am at ease about you. If only Daisy can be happy, and Josie give up her dream, I shall be quite contented.'

Demi let his mother enjoy herself for a few minutes, while he smiled over a certain little dream of his own, not ready yet for the telling; then he said, in the paternal tone which he unconsciously used when speaking of his sisters, 'I'll see to the girls; but I begin to think grandpa is right in saying we must each be what God and nature makes us. We can't change it much – only help to develop the good and control the bad elements in us. I have fumbled my way into my right place at last, I hope. Let Daisy be happy in her way, since it is a good and womanly one. If Nat comes home all right, I'd say, "Bless you, my children," and give them a nest of their own. Then you and I will help little Jo to find out if it is to be "All the world's a stage" or "Home, sweet home", for her.'

'I suppose we must, John; but I can't help making plans, and hoping they will come to pass. I see that Daisy is bound up in Nat; and if he is worthy of her I shall let them be happy in their own way, as my parents let me. But Josie will be a trial, I foresee; and much as I love the stage, and always did, I don't see how I can ever let my little girl be an actress, though she certainly has great talent for it.'

'Whose fault is that?' asked Demi, smiling, as he remembered his mother's early triumphs and unquenchable interest in the dramatic efforts of the young people round her.

'Mine, I know. How could it be otherwise when I acted "Babes in the Wood" with you and Daisy before you could speak, and taught Josie to declaim "Mother Goose" in her cradle. Ah, me! the tastes of the mother come out in her children, and she must atone for them by letting them have their own way, I suppose.' And Mrs Meg laughed, even while she shook her head over the undeniable fact that the Marches were a theatrical family.

'Why not have a great actress of our name, as well as an authoress, a minister, and an eminent publisher? We don't choose our talents, but we needn't hide them in a napkin because they are not just what we want. I say, let Jo have her way, and do what she can. Here am I to take care of her; and you can't deny you'd enjoy fixing her furbelows, and seeing her shine before the footlights, where you used to long to be. Come, mother, better face the music and march gaily, since your wilful children will "gang their ain gait".'

'I don't see but I must, and "leave the consequences to the Lord", as Marmee used to say when she had to decide, and only saw a step of the road. I *should* enjoy it immensely, if I could only feel that the life would not hurt my girl, and leave her unsatisfied when it was too late to change; for nothing is harder to give up than the excitements of that profession. I know something of it; and if your blessed father had not come along, I'm afraid I should have been an actress in spite of Aunt March and all our honoured ancestors.'

'Let Josie add new honour to the name, and work out the family talent in its proper place. I'll play dragon to her, and you play nurse, and no harm can come to our little Juliet, no matter how many Romeos spoon under her balcony. Really, ma'am, opposition comes badly from an old lady who is going to wring the hearts of our audience in the heroine's part in Aunty's play next Christmas.

It's the most pathetic thing I ever saw, mother; and I'm sorry you didn't become an actress, though we should be nowhere if you had.'

Demi was on his legs now, with his back to the fire, in the lordly attitude men like to assume when things go well with them, or they want to lay down the law on any subject.

Mrs Meg actually blushed at her son's hearty praise, and could not deny that the sound of applause was as sweet now as when she played the 'Witch's Curse' and 'The Moorish Maiden's Vow' long years ago.

'It's perfectly absurd for me to do it, but I couldn't resist when Jo and Laurie made the part for me, and you children were to act in it. The minute I get on the old mother's dress I forget myself and feel the same thrill at the sound of the bell that I used to feel when we got up plays in the garret. If Daisy would only take the daughter's part it would be so complete; for with you and Josie I am hardly acting, it is all so real.'

'Especially the hospital scene, where you find the wounded son. Why, mother, do you know when we did that at last rehearsal my face was wet with real tears as you cried over me. It will bring down the house; but don't forget to wipe 'em off, or I shall sneeze,' said Demi, laughing at the recollection of his mother's hit.

'I won't; but it almost broke my heart to see you so pale and dreadful. I hope there will never be another war in my time, for I should have to let you go; and I never want to live through the same experience we had with Father.'

'Don't you think Alice does the part better than Daisy would? Daisy hasn't a bit of the actress in her, and Alice puts life into the dullest words she speaks. I think the Marquise is just perfect in our piece,' said Demi, strolling about the room as if the warmth of the fire sent a sudden colour to his face.

'So do I. She is a dear girl, and I'm proud and fond of her. Where is she tonight?'

'Pegging away at her Greek, I suppose. She usually is in the evening. More's the pity,' added Demi, in a low tone, as he stared intently at the bookcase, though he couldn't read a title.

'Now, there is a girl after my own heart. Pretty, well-bred, well-educated, and yet domestic, a real companion as well as help-meet for some good and intelligent man. I hope she will find one.'

'So do I,' muttered Demi.

Mrs Meg had taken up her work again, and was surveying a half-finished buttonhole with so much interest that her son's face escaped her eye. He shed a beaming smile upon the rows of poets, as if even in their glass prison they could sympathise and rejoice with him at the first rosy dawn of the great passion which they knew so well. But Demi was a wise youth, and never leaped before looking carefully. He hardly knew his own heart yet, and was contented to wait till the sentiment, the fluttering of those folded wings he began to feel, should escape from the chrysalis and be ready to soar away in the sunshine to seek and claim its lovely mate. He had said nothing; but the brown eyes were eloquent, and there was an unconscious underplot to all the little plays he and Alice Heath acted so well together. She was busy with her books, bound to graduate with high honours, and he was trying to do the same in that larger college open to all, and where each man has his own prize to win or lose. Demi had nothing but himself to offer and, being a modest youth, considered that a poor gift till he had proved his power to earn his living, and the right to take a woman's happiness into his keeping.

No one guessed that he had caught the fever except sharp-eyed Josie, and she, having a wholesome fear of her brother – who could be rather awful when she went too far – wisely contented herself with watching him like a little cat, ready to pounce on the first visible sign of weakness. Demi had taken to playing pensively upon his flute after he was in his room for the night, making this melodious friend his confidante, and breathing into it all the tender hopes and fears that filled his heart. Mrs Meg, absorbed in domestic affairs, and Daisy, who cared for no music but Nat's violin, paid no heed to these chamber concerts, but Josie always murmured to herself, with a naughty chuckle, 'Dick Swiveller is thinking of his Sophy Wackles,' and bided her time to revenge certain wrongs inflicted upon her by Demi, who always took Daisy's side when she tried to curb the spirits of her unruly little sister.

This evening she got her chance, and made the most of it. Mrs Meg was just rounding off her buttonhole, and Demi still strolling restlessly about the room, when a book was heard to slam in the study, followed by an audible yawn and the appearance of the student looking as if sleep and a desire for mischief were struggling which should be master.

'I heard my name; have you been saying anything bad about me?' she demanded, perching on the arm of an easy chair.

Her mother told the good news, over which Josie duly rejoiced, and Demi received her congratulations with a benignant air which made her feel that too much satisfaction was not good for him, and incited her to put a thorn into his bed of roses at once.

'I caught something about the play just now, and I want to tell you that I'm going to introduce a song into my part to liven it up a bit. How would this do?' and seating herself at the piano she began to sing to these words the air of 'Kathleen Mavourneen':

> 'Sweetest of maidens, oh, how can I tell
>   The love that transfigures the whole earth to me?
> The longing that causes my bosom to swell,
>   When I dream of a life all devoted to thee?'

She got no further, for Demi, red with wrath, made a rush at her, and the next moment a very agile young person was seen dodging round tables and chairs with the future partner of Tiber & Co. in hot pursuit. 'You monkey, how dare you meddle with my papers?' cried the irate poet, making futile grabs at the saucy girl, who skipped to and fro, waving a bit of paper tantalisingly before him.

'Didn't; found it in the big "Dic". Serves you right if you leave your rubbish about. Don't you like my song? It's very pretty.'

'I'll teach you one that you won't like if you don't give me my property.'

'Come and get it if you can;' and Josie vanished into the study to have out her squabble in peace, for Mrs Meg was already saying, 'Children, children! don't quarrel.'

The paper was in the fire by the time Demi arrived and he at once calmed down, seeing that the bone of contention was out of the way.

'I'm glad it's burnt; I don't care for it, only some verse I was trying to set to music for one of the girls. But I'll trouble you to let my papers alone, or I shall take back the advice I gave mother tonight about allowing you to act as much as you like.'

Josie was sobered at once by this dire threat, and in her most wheedling tone begged to know what he had said. By way of heaping coals of fire on her head he told her, and this diplomatic performance secured him an ally on the spot.

'You dear old boy! I'll never tease you again though you moon and spoon both day and night. If you stand by me, I'll stand by you and never say a word. See here! I've got a note for you from Alice. Won't that be a peace offering and soothe your little feelings?'

Demi's eyes sparkled as Josie held up a paper cocked hat, but as he knew what was probably in it, he took the wind out of Josie's sails, and filled her with blank astonishment by saying carelessly, 'That's nothing; it's only to say whether she will go to the concert with us tomorrow night. You can read it if you like.'

With the natural perversity of her sex Josie ceased to be curious the moment she was told to read it, and meekly handed it over; but she watched Demi as he calmly read the two lines it contained and then threw it into the fire. 'Why, Jack, I thought you'd treasure every scrap the "sweetest maid" touched. Don't you care for her?'

'Very much; we all do; but "mooning and spooning", as you elegantly express it, is not in my line. My dear little girl, your plays make you romantic, and because Alice and I act lovers sometimes you take it into your silly head that we are really so. Don't waste time hunting mare's nests, but attend to your own affairs and leave me to mine. I forgive you, but don't do it again; it's bad taste, and tragedy queens don't romp.'

The last cut finished Josie; she humbly begged pardon and went off to bed, while Demi soon followed, feeling that he had not only settled himself but his too inquisitive little sister also. But if he had seen her face as she listened to the soft wailing of his flute he would not have been so sure, for she looked as cunning as a magpie as she said, with a scornful sniff, 'Pooh, you can't deceive me; I *know* Dick is serenading Sophy Wackles.'

CHAPTER II

Emil's Thanksgiving

The *Brenda* was scudding along with all sail set to catch the rising wind, and everyone on board was rejoicing, for the long voyage was drawing towards an end.

'Four weeks more, Mrs Hardy, and we'll give you a cup of tea such as you never had before,' said second mate Hoffmann, as he paused beside two ladies sitting in a sheltered corner of the deck.

'I shall be glad to get it, and still gladder to put my feet on solid ground,' answered the elder lady, smiling; for our friend Emil was a favourite, as well he might be, since he devoted himself to the captain's wife and daughter, who were the only passengers on board.

'So shall I, even if I have to wear a pair of shoes like Chinese junks. I've tramped up and down the deck so much, I shall be barefooted if we don't arrive soon,' laughed Mary, the daughter, showing two shabby little boots as she glanced up at the companion of these tramps, remembering gratefully how pleasant he had made them.

'Don't think there are any small enough in China,' answered Emil, with a sailor's ready gallantry, privately resolving to hunt up the handsomest shoes he could find the moment he landed.

'I don't know what you would have done for exercise, dear, if Mr Hoffmann had not made you walk every day. This lazy life is bad for young people, though it suits an old body like me well enough in calm weather. Is this likely to be a gale, think ye?' added Mrs Hardy, with an anxious glance at the west, where the sun was setting redly.

'Only a capful of wind, ma'am, just enough to send us along lively,' answered Emil, with a comprehensive glance aloft and alow.

'Please sing, Mr Hoffmann, it's so pleasant to have music at this time. We shall miss it very much when we get ashore,' said Mary, in a persuasive tone which would have won melody from a shark, if such a thing were possible.

Emil had often blessed his one accomplishment during these months, for it cheered the long days, and made the twilight hour his happiest time, wind and weather permitting. So now he gladly tuned his pipe, and leaning on the taffrail near the girl, watched the brown locks blowing in the wind as he sang her favourite song:

> 'Give me freshening breeze, my boys,
>   A white and swelling sail,
> A ship that cuts the dashing waves,
>   And weathers every gale.
> What life is like a sailor's life,
>   So free, so bold, so brave?
> His home the ocean's wide expanse,
>   A coral bed his grave.'

Just as the last notes of the clear, strong voice died away, Mrs Hardy suddenly exclaimed: 'What's that?' Emil's quick eye saw at once the little puff of smoke coming up a hatchway where no smoke should be, and his heart seemed to stand still for an instant as the dread word 'Fire!' flashed through his mind. Then he was quite steady, and strolled away saying quietly, 'Smoking not allowed there, I'll go and stop it.' But the instant he was out of sight his face changed, and he leaped down the hatchway, thinking, with a queer smile on his lips: 'If we *are* afire, shouldn't wonder if I did make a coral bed my grave!'

He was gone a few minutes, and when he came up, half stifled with smoke, he was as white as a very brown man could be, but calm and cool as he went to report to the captain.

'Fire in the hold, sir.'

'Don't frighten the women,' was Captain Hardy's first order; then both bestirred themselves to discover how strong the treacherous enemy was, and to rout it if possible.

The *Brenda*'s cargo was a very combustible one, and in spite of the streams of water poured into the hold it was soon evident that the ship was doomed. Smoke began to ooze up between the planks everywhere, and the rising gale soon fanned the smouldering fire to flames that began to break out here and there, telling the dreadful truth too plainly for anyone to hide. Mrs Hardy and Mary bore the shock bravely when told to be ready to quit the ship at a minute's notice; the boats were hastily prepared, and the men worked with a will to batten down every loophole whence the fire might escape. Soon the poor *Brenda* was a floating furnace, and the order to 'Take to the boats!' came for all. The women first, of course, and it was fortunate that, being a merchantman, there were no more passengers on board, so there was no panic, and one after the other the boats pushed off. That in which the women were lingered near, for the brave captain would be the last to leave his ship.

Emil stayed by him till ordered away, and reluctantly obeyed; but it was well for him he went, for just as he had regained the boat, rocking far below, half hidden by a cloud of smoke, a mast, undermined by the fire now raging in the bowels of the ship, fell with a crash, knocking Captain Hardy overboard. The boat soon reached him as he floated out from the wreck, and Emil sprung into the sea to rescue him, for he was wounded and senseless. This accident made it necessary for the young man to take command, and he at once ordered the men to pull for their lives, as an explosion might occur at any moment.

The other boats were out of danger and all lingered to watch the splendid yet awesome spectacle of the burning ship alone on the wide sea, reddening the night and casting a lurid glare upon the water, where floated the frail boats filled with pale faces, all turned for a last look at the fated *Brenda*, slowly settling to her watery grave. No one saw the end, however, for the gale soon swept the watchers far away and separated them, some never to meet again till the sea gives up its dead.

The boat whose fortunes we must follow was alone when dawn came up, showing these survivors all the dangers of their situation. Food and water had been put in, and such provision for comfort and safety as time allowed; but it was evident that with a badly wounded man, two women, and seven sailors, their supply would not last long, and help was sorely needed. Their only hope was in meeting a ship, although the gale, which had raged all night, had blown them out of their course. To this hope all clung, and whiled away the weary hours, watching the horizon and cheering one another with prophecies of speedy rescue.

Second mate Hoffmann was very brave and helpful, though his unexpected responsibility weighed heavily on his shoulders; for the captain's state seemed desperate, the poor wife's grief wrung his heart, and the blind confidence of the young girl in his power to save them made him feel that no sign of doubt or fear must lessen it. The men did their part readily now, but Emil knew that if starvation and despair made brutes of them, his task might be a terrible one. So he clutched his courage with both hands, kept up a manly front, and spoke so cheerily of their good chances, that all instinctively turned to him for guidance and support.

The first day and night passed in comparative comfort, but when the third came, things looked dark and hope began to fail. The wounded man was delirious, the wife worn out with anxiety and suspense, the girl weak for want of food, having put away half her biscuit for her mother, and given her share of water to wet her father's feverish lips. The sailors ceased rowing and sat grimly waiting, openly reproaching their leader for not following their advice, others demanding more food, all waxing dangerous as privation and pain brought out the animal instincts lurking in them. Emil did his best, but mortal man was helpless there, and he could only turn his haggard face from the pitiless sky, that dropped no rain for their thirst, to the boundless sea where no sail appeared to gladden their longing eyes. All day he tried to cheer and comfort them, while hunger gnawed, thirst parched, and growing fear lay heavy at his heart. He told stories to the men, implored them to bear up for the helpless women's sake, and promised rewards if they would pull while they had strength to regain the lost route, as nearly as he could make it out, and increase their chance of rescue. He rigged an awning of sailcloth over the suffering man and tended him like a son, comforted the wife, and tried to make the pale girl forget herself, by singing every song he knew or recounting his adventures by land and sea, till she smiled and took heart; for all ended well.

The fourth day came and the supply of food and water was nearly gone. Emil proposed to keep it for the sick man and the women, but two of the men rebelled, demanding their share. Emil gave up his as an example, and several of the good fellows followed it, with the quiet heroism which so often crops up in rough but manly natures. This shamed the others, and for another day an ominous peace reigned in that little world of suffering and suspense. But during the night, while Emil, worn out with fatigue, left the watch to the most trustworthy sailor, that he might snatch an hour's rest, these two men got at the stores and stole the last of the bread and water, and the one bottle of brandy, which was carefully hoarded to keep up their strength and make the brackish water drinkable. Half mad with thirst, they drank greedily and by morning one was in a stupor, from which he never woke; the other so crazed by the strong stimulant, that when Emil tried to control him, he leaped overboard and was lost. Horror-stricken by this terrible scene, the other men were submissive henceforth, and the boat floated on and on with its sad freight of suffering souls and bodies.

Another trial came to them that left all more despairing than before. A sail appeared, and for a time a frenzy of joy prevailed, to be turned to bitterest disappointment when it passed by, too far away to see the signals waved to them or hear the frantic cries for help that rang across the sea. Emil's heart sank then, for the captain seemed dying, and the women could not hold out much longer. He kept up till night came; then in the darkness, broken only by the feeble murmuring of the sick man, the whispered prayers of the poor wife, the ceaseless swash of waves, Emil hid his face, and had an hour of silent agony that aged him more than years of happy life could have done. It was not the physical hardship that daunted him, though want and weakness tortured him; it was his dreadful power- lessness to conquer the cruel fate that seemed hanging over them. The men he cared little for, since these perils were but a part of the life they chose; but the master he loved, the good woman who had been so kind to him, the sweet girl whose winsome presence had made the long voyage so pleasant for them all – if he could only save these dear and innocent creatures from a cruel death, he felt that he could willingly give his life for them.

As he sat there with his head in his hands, bowed down by the first great trial of his young life, the starless sky overhead, the restless sea beneath, and all around him suffering, for which he had no help, a soft sound broke the silence, and he listened like one in a dream. It was Mary singing to her mother, who lay sobbing in her arms, spent with this long anguish. A very faint and broken voice it was, for the poor girl's lips were parched with thirst; but the loving heart turned instinctively to the great Helper in this hour of de- spair, and He heard her feeble cry. It was a sweet old hymn often sung at Plumfield; and as he listened, all the happy past came back so clearly that Emil forgot the bitter present, and was at home again. His talk on the housetop with Aunt Jo seemed but yesterday, and, with a pang of self-reproach, he thought, 'The scarlet strand! I must remember it, and do my duty to the end. Steer straight, old boy; and if you can't come into port, go down with all sail set.'

Then, as the soft voice crooned on to lull the weary woman to a fitful sleep, Emil for a little while forgot his burden in a dream of Plumfield. He saw them all, heard the familiar voices, felt the grip of welcoming hands, and seemed to say to himself, 'Well, they shall not be ashamed of me if I never see them any more.'

A sudden shout startled him from that brief rest, and a drop on his forehead told him that the blessed rain had come at last, bringing salvation with it; for thirst is harder to bear than hunger, heat, or cold. Welcomed by cries of joy, all lifted up their parched lips, held out their hands, and spread their garments to catch the great drops that soon came pouring down to cool the sick man's fever, quench the agony of thirst, and bring refreshment to every weary body in the boat. All night it fell, all night the castaways revelled in the saving shower, and took heart again, like dying plants revived by heaven's dew. The clouds broke away at dawn, and Emil sprung up, wonderfully braced and cheered by those hours of silent gratitude for this answer to their cry for help. But this was not all; as his eye swept the horizon, clear against the rosy sky shone the white sails of a ship, so near that they could see the pennon at her masthead and black figures moving on the deck.

One cry broke from all those eager throats, and rang across the sea, as every man waved hat or handkerchief and the women stretched imploring hands towards this great white angel of deliverance coming down upon them as if the fresh wind filled every sail to help her on.

No disappointment now; answering signals assured them of help; and in the rapture of that moment the happy women fell on Emil's neck, giving him his reward in tears and blessings as their grateful hearts overflowed. He always said that was the proudest moment of his life, as he stood there holding Mary in his arms; for the brave girl, who had kept up so long, broke down then, and clung to him half fainting; while her mother busied herself about the invalid, who seemed to feel the joyful stir, and gave an order, as if again on the deck of his lost ship.

It was soon over; and then all were safely aboard the good *Urania*, homeward bound. Emil saw his friends in tender hands, his men among their mates, and told the story of the wreck before he thought of himself. The savoury odour of the soup, carried by to the cabin for the ladies, reminded him that he was starving, and a sudden stagger betrayed his weakness. He was instantly borne away, to be half killed by kindness, and being fed, clothed, and comforted, was left to rest. Just as the surgeon left the stateroom, he asked in his broken voice, 'What day is this? My head is so confused, I've lost my reckoning.'

'Thanksgiving Day, man! And we'll give you a regular New England dinner, if you'll eat it,' answered the surgeon heartily.

But Emil was too spent to do anything, except lie still and give thanks, more fervently and gratefully than ever before, for the blessed gift of life, which was the sweeter for a sense of duty faithfully performed.

CHAPTER 12

Dan's Christmas

Where was Dan? In prison. Alas for Mrs Jo! how her heart would have ached if she had known that while old Plum shone with Christmas cheer her boy sat alone in his cell, trying to read the little book she gave him, with eyes dimmed now and then by the hot tears no physical suffering had ever wrung from him, and longing with a homesick heart for all that he had lost.

Yes, Dan was in prison; but no cry for help from him as he faced the terrible strait he was in with the dumb despair of an Indian at the stake; for his own bosom sin had brought him there, and this was to be the bitter lesson that tamed the lawless spirit and taught him self-control.

The story of his downfall is soon told; for it came, as so often happens, just when he felt unusually full of high hopes, good resolutions, and dreams of a better life. On his journey he met a pleasant young fellow, and naturally felt an interest in him, as

Blair was on his way to join his elder brothers on a ranch in Kansas. Card-playing was going on in the smoking-car, and the lad – for he was barely twenty – tired with the long journey, beguiled the way with such partners as appeared, being full of spirits, and a little intoxicated with the freedom of the West. Dan, true to his promise, would not join, but watched with intense interest the games that went on, and soon made up his mind that two of the men were sharpers anxious to fleece the boy, who had imprudently displayed a well-filled pocketbook. Dan always had a soft spot in his heart for any younger, weaker creature whom he met, and something about the lad reminded him of Teddy; so he kept an eye on Blair, and warned him against his new friends.

Vainly, of course; for when all stopped overnight in one of the great cities, Dan missed the boy from the hotel whither he had taken him for safekeeping; and learning who had come for him, went to find him, calling himself a fool for his pains, yet unable to leave the confiding boy to the dangers that surrounded him.

He found him gambling in a low place with the men, who were bound to have his money; and by the look of relief on Blair's anxious face when he saw him Dan knew without words that things were going badly with him, and he saw the peril too late.

'I can't come yet – I've lost; it's not my money; I must get it back, or I dare not face my brothers,' whispered the poor lad, when Dan begged him to get away without further loss. Shame and fear made him desperate; and he played on, sure that he could recover the money confided to his care. Seeing Dan's resolute face, keen eye, and travelled air, the sharpers were wary, played fair, and let the boy win a little; but they had no mind to give up their prey, and finding that Dan stood sentinel at the boy's back, an ominous glance was exchanged between them, which meant, 'We must get this fellow out of the way.'

Dan saw it, and was on his guard; for he and Blair were strangers, evil deeds are easily done in such places, and no tales told. But he would not desert the boy, and still kept watch of every card till he plainly detected false play, and boldly said so. High words passed, Dan's indignation overcame his prudence; and when the cheat refused to restore his plunder with insulting words and drawn pistol, Dan's hot temper flashed out, and he knocked the man down with a blow that sent him crashing head first against a stove, to roll senseless and bleeding to the floor. A wild scene followed, but in the midst of it Dan whispered to the boy, 'Get away, and hold your tongue. Don't mind me.'

Frightened and bewildered, Blair quitted the city at once, leaving Dan to pass the night in the lock-up, and a few days later to stand in court charged with manslaughter; for the man was dead. Dan had no friends, and having once briefly told the story, held his peace, anxious to keep all knowledge of this sad affair from those at home. He even concealed his name – giving that of David Kent, as he had done several times before in emergencies. It was all over very soon; but as there were extenuating circumstances his sentence was a year in prison, with hard labour.

Dazed by the rapidity with which this horrible change in his life came upon him, Dan did not fully realise it till the iron door clanged behind him and he sat alone in a cell as narrow, cold, and silent as a tomb. He knew that a word would bring Mr Laurie to help and comfort him; but he could not bear to tell of this disgrace, or see the sorrow and the shame it would cause the friends who hoped so much for him.

'No,' he said, clenching his fist, 'I'll let them think me dead first. I shall be if I am kept here long;' and he sprang up to pace the stone floor like a caged lion, with a turmoil of wrath and grief, rebellion and remorse, seething in heart and brain, till he felt as if he should go mad and beat upon the walls that shut him away from the liberty which was his life. For days he suffered terribly, then worn out, sank into a black melancholy sadder to see than his excitement.

The warden of this prison was a rough man who had won the ill-will of all by unnecessary harshness, but the chaplain was full of sympathy, and did his hard duty faithfully and tenderly. He laboured with poor Dan, but seemed to make no impression, and was forced to wait till work had soothed the excited nerves and captivity tamed the proud spirit that would suffer but not complain.

Dan was put in the brush-shop, and feeling that activity was his only salvation, worked with a feverish energy that soon won the approval of the master and the envy of less skilful mates. Day after day he sat in his place, watched by an armed overseer, forbidden any but necessary words, no intercourse with the men beside him, no change but from cell to shop, no exercise but the dreary marches to and fro, each man's hand on the other's shoulder keeping step with the dreary tramp so different from the ringing tread of soldiers. Silent, gaunt, and grim, Dan did his daily task, ate his bitter bread, and obeyed commands with a rebellious flash of the eye, that made the warden say, 'That's a dangerous man. Watch him. He'll break out someday.'

There were others more dangerous than he, because older in crime and ready for any desperate outbreak to change the monotony of long sentences. These men soon divined Dan's mood, and in the mysterious way convicts invent, managed to convey to him before a month was over that plans were being made for a mutiny at the first opportunity. Thanksgiving Day was one of the few chances for them to speak together as they enjoyed an hour of freedom in the prison yard. Then all would be settled and the rash attempt made if possible, probably to end in bloodshed and defeat for most, but liberty for a few. Dan had already planned his own escape and bided his time, growing more and more moody, fierce, and rebellious, as loss of liberty wore upon soul and body; for this sudden change from his free, healthy life to such a narrow, gloomy, and miserable one, could not but have a terrible effect upon one of Dan's temperament and age.

He brooded over his ruined life, gave up all his happy hopes and plans, felt that he could never face dear old Plumfield again, or touch those friendly hands, with the stain of blood upon his own. He did not care for the wretched man whom he had killed, for such a life was better ended, he thought; but the disgrace of prison would never be wiped out of his memory, though the cropped hair would grow again, the grey suit easily be replaced, and the bolts and bars left far behind.

'It's all over with me; I've spoilt my life, now let it go. I'll give up the fight and get what pleasure I can anywhere, anyhow. They shall think me dead and so still care for me, but never know what I am. Poor Mother Bhaer! she tried to help me, but it's no use; the firebrand can't be saved.'

And dropping his head in his hands as he sat on his low bed, Dan would mourn over all he had lost in tearless misery, till merciful sleep would comfort him with dreams of the happy days when the boys played together, or those still later and happier ones when all smiled on him, and Plumfield seemed to have gained a new and curious charm.

There was one poor fellow in Dan's shop whose fate was harder than his, for his sentence expired in the spring, but there was little hope of his living till that time; and the coldest-hearted man pitied poor Mason as he sat coughing his life away in that close place and counting the weary days yet to pass before he could see his wife and little child again. There was some hope that he might be pardoned out, but he had no friends to bestir themselves in the matter, and it was evident that the great Judge's pardon would soon end his patient pain for ever.

Dan pitied him more than he dared to show, and this one tender emotion in that dark time was like the little flower that sprung up between the stones of the prison yard and saved the captive from despair, in the beautiful old story. Dan helped Mason with his work when he was too feeble to finish his task, and the grateful look that thanked him was a ray of sunshine to cheer his cell when he was alone. Mason envied the splendid health of his neighbour, and mourned to see it wasting there. He was a peaceful soul and tried, as far as a whispered word or warning glance could do it, to deter Dan from joining the 'bad lot', as the rebels were called. But having turned his face from the light, Dan found the downward way easy, and took a grim satisfaction in the prospect of a general outbreak during which he might revenge himself upon the tyrannical warden, and strike a blow for his own liberty, feeling that an hour of insurrection would be a welcome vent for the pent-up passions that tormented him. He had tamed many a wild animal, but his own lawless spirit was too much for him, till he found the curb that made him master of himself.

The Sunday before Thanksgiving, as he sat in chapel, Dan observed several guests in the seats reserved for them, and looked anxiously to see if any familiar face was there; for he had a mortal fear that someone from home would suddenly confront him. No, all were strangers, and he soon forgot them in listening to the chaplain's cheerful words, and the sad singing of many heavy hearts. People often spoke to the convicts, so it caused no surprise when, on being invited to address them, one of the ladies rose and said she would tell them a little story; which announcement caused the younger listeners to prick up their ears, and even the older ones to look interested; for any change in their monotonous life was welcome.

The speaker was a middle-aged woman in black, with a sympathetic face, eyes full of compassion, and a voice that seemed to warm the heart, because of certain motherly tones in it. She reminded Dan of Mrs Jo, and he listened intently to every word, feeling that each was meant for him, because by chance, they came at the moment when he needed a softening memory to break up the ice of despair which was blighting all the good impulses of his nature.

It was a very simple little story, but it caught the men's attention at once, being about two soldiers in a hospital during the late war, both badly wounded in the right arm, and both anxious to save these breadwinners and go home unmaimed. One was patient, docile, and cheerfully obeyed orders, even when told that the arm must go. He submitted and after much suffering recovered, grateful for life, though he could fight no more. The other rebelled, would listen to no advice, and having delayed too long, died a lingering death, bitterly regretting his folly when it was too late. 'Now, as all stories should have a little moral, let me tell you mine,' added the lady, with a smile, as she looked at the row of young men before her, sadly wondering what brought them there.

'This is a hospital for soldiers wounded in life's battle; here are sick souls, weak wills, insane passions, blind consciences, all the ills that come from broken laws, bringing their inevitable pain and punishment with them. There is hope and help for everyone, for God's mercy is infinite and man's charity is great; but penitence and submission must come before the cure is possible. Pay the forfeit manfully, for it is just; but from the suffering and shame wring new strength for a nobler life. The scar will remain, but it is better for a man to lose both arms than his soul; and these hard years, instead of being lost, may be made the most precious of your lives, if they teach you to rule yourselves. O friends, try to outlive the bitter past, to wash the sin away, and begin anew. If not for your own sakes, for that of the dear mothers, wives, and children, who wait and hope so patiently for you. Remember them, and do not let them love and long in vain. And if there be any here so forlorn that they have no friend to care for them, never forget the Father whose arms are always open to receive, forgive, and comfort His prodigal sons, even at the eleventh hour.'

There the little sermon ended; but the preacher of it felt that her few hearty words had not been uttered in vain, for one boy's head was down, and several faces wore the softened look which told that a tender memory was touched. Dan was forced to set his lips to keep them steady, and drop his eyes to hide the sudden dew that dimmed them when waiting, hoping friends were spoken of. He was glad to be alone in his cell again, and sat thinking deeply, instead of trying to forget himself in sleep. It seemed as if those words were just what he needed to show him where he stood and how fateful the next few days might be to him. Should he join the 'bad lot', and perhaps add another crime to the one already committed, lengthen the sentence already so terrible to bear, deliberately turn his back on all that was good, and mar the future that might yet be redeemed? Or should he, like the wiser man in the story, submit, bear the just punishment, try to be better for it; and though the scar would remain, it might serve as a reminder of a battle not wholly lost, since he had saved his soul though innocence was gone? Then he would dare go home, perhaps, confess, and find fresh strength in the pity and consolation of those who never gave him up.

Good and evil fought for Dan that night as did the angel and the devil for Sintram, and it was hard to tell whether lawless nature or loving heart would conquer. Remorse and resentment, shame and sorrow, pride and passion, made a battlefield of that narrow cell, and the poor fellow felt as if he had fiercer enemies to fight now than any he had met in all his wanderings. A little thing turned the scale, as it so often does in these mysterious hearts of ours, and a touch of sympathy helped Dan decide the course which would bless or ban his life.

In the dark hour before the dawn, as he lay wakeful on his bed, a ray of light shone through the bars, the bolts turned softly, and a man came in. It was the good chaplain, led by the same instinct that brings a mother to her sick child's pillow; for long experience as nurse of souls had taught him to see the signs of hope in the hard faces about him, and to know when the moment came for a helpful word and the cordial of sincere prayer that brings such comfort and healing to tried and troubled hearts. He had been to Dan before at unexpected hours, but always found him sullen, indifferent, or rebellious, and had gone away to patiently bide his time. Now it had come; a look of relief was in the prisoner's face as the light shone on it, and the sound of a human voice was strangely comfortable after listening to the whispers of the passions, doubts, and fears which had haunted the cell for hours, dismaying Dan by their power, and showing him how much he needed help to fight the good fight, since he had no armour of his own.

'Kent, poor Mason has gone. He left a message for you, and I felt impelled to come and give it now, because I think you were touched by what we heard today, and in need of the help Mason tried to give you,' said the chaplain, taking the one seat and fixing his kind eyes on the grim figure in the bed.

'Thank you, sir, I'd like to hear it,' was all Dan's answer; but he forgot himself in pity for the poor fellow dead in prison, with no last look at wife or child.

'He went suddenly, but remembered you, and begged me to say these words, "Tell him not to do it, but to hold on, do his best, and when his time is out go right to Mary, and she'll make him welcome for my sake. He's got no friends in these parts and will feel lonesome, but a woman's always safe and comfortable when a fellow's down on his luck. Give him my love and goodbye for he was kind to me, and God will bless him for it." Then he died quietly, and tomorrow will go home with God's pardon, since man's came too late.'

Dan said nothing, but laid his arm across his face and lay quite still. Seeing that the pathetic little message had done its work even better than he hoped, the chaplain went on, unconscious how soothing his paternal voice was to the poor prisoner who longed to 'go home', but felt he had forfeited the right.

'I hope you won't disappoint this humble friend whose last thought was for you. I know that there is trouble brewing, and fear that you may be tempted to lend a hand on the wrong side. Don't do it, for the plot will not succeed – it never does – and it would be a pity to spoil your record which is fair so far. Keep up your courage, my son, and go out at the year's end better, not worse, for this hard experience. Remember a grateful woman waits to welcome and thank you if you have no friends of your own; if you have, do your best for their sake, and let us ask God to help you as He only can.'

Then waiting for no answer the good man prayed heartily, and Dan listened as he never had before; for the lonely hour, the dying message, the sudden uprising of his better self, made it seem as if some kind angel had come to save and comfort him. After that night there was a change in Dan, though no one knew it but the chaplain; for to all the rest he was the same silent, stern, unsocial fellow as before, and turning his back on the bad and the good alike, found his only pleasure in the books his friend brought him. Slowly, as the steadfast drop wears away the rock, the patient kindness of this man won Dan's confidence, and led by him he began to climb out of the Valley of Humiliation towards the mountains, whence, through the clouds, one can catch glimpses of the Celestial City whither all true pilgrims sooner or later turn their wistful eyes and stumbling feet. There were many back-slidings, many struggles with Giant Despair and fiery Apollyon, many heavy hours when life did not seem worth living and Mason's escape the only hope. But through all, the grasp of a friendly hand, the sound of a brother's voice, the unquenchable desire to atone for the past by a better future, and win the right to see home again, kept poor Dan to his great task as the old year drew to its end, and the new waited to turn another leaf in the book whose hardest lesson he was learning now.

At Christmas he yearned so for Plumfield that he devised a way to send a word of greeting to cheer their anxious hearts, and comfort his own. He wrote to Mary Mason, who lived in another State, asking her to mail the letter he enclosed. In it he merely said he was well and busy, had given up the farm, and had other plans which he would tell later; would not be home before autumn probably, nor write often, but was all right, and sent love and merry Christmas to everyone.

Then he took up his solitary life again, and tried to pay his forfeit manfully.

CHAPTER 13

Nat's New Year

'I don't expect to hear from Emil yet, and Nat writes regularly, but where is Dan? Only two or three postals since he went. Such an energetic fellow as he is could buy up all the farms in Kansas by this time,' said Mrs Jo one morning when the mail came in and no card or envelope bore Dan's dashing hand.

'He never writes often, you know, but does his work and then comes home. Months and years seem to mean little to him, and he is probably prospecting in the wilderness, forgetful of time,' answered Mr Bhaer, deep in one of Nat's long letters from Leipzig.

'But he promised he would let me know how he got on, and Dan keeps his word if he can. I'm afraid something has happened to him;' and Mrs Jo comforted herself by patting Don's head, as he came at the sound of his master's name to look at her with eyes almost human in their wistful intelligence.

'Don't worry, Mum dear, nothing ever happens to the old fellow. He'll turn up all right, and come stalking in someday with a gold-mine in one pocket and a prairie in the other, as jolly as a grig,' said Ted, who was in no haste to deliver Octoo to her rightful owner.

'Perhaps he has gone to Montana and given up the farm plan. He seemed to like Indians best, I thought;' and Rob went to help his mother with her pile of letters and his cheerful suggestions.

'I hope so, it would suit him best. But I am sure he would have told us his change of plan and sent for some money to work with. No, I feel in my prophetic bones that something is wrong,' said Mrs Jo, looking as solemn as Fate in a breakfast-cap.

'Then we shall hear; ill news always travels fast. Don't borrow trouble, Jo, but hear how well Nat is getting on. I'd no idea the boy would care for anything but music. My good friend Baumgarten has launched him well, and it will do him good if he lose not his head. A good lad, but new to the world, and Leipzig is full of snares for the unwary. Gott be with him!'

The Professor read Nat's enthusiastic account of certain literary and musical parties he had been to, the splendours of the opera, the kindness of his new friends, the delight of studying under such a master as Bergmann, his hopes of rapid gain, and his great gratitude to those who had opened this enchanted world to him.

'That, now, is satisfactory and comfortable. I felt that Nat had unsuspected power in him before he went away; he was so manly and full of excellent plans,' said Mrs Jo, in a satisfied tone.

'We shall see. He will doubtless get his lesson and be the better for it. That comes to us all in our young days. I hope it will not be too hard for our good *Jüngling*,' answered the Professor, with a wise smile, remembering his own student life in Germany.

He was right; and Nat was already getting his lesson in life with a rapidity which would have astonished his friends at home. The manliness over which Mrs Jo rejoiced was developing in unexpected ways, and quiet Nat had plunged into the more harmless dissipations of the gay city with all the ardour of an inexperienced youth taking his first sip of pleasure. The entire freedom and sense of independence was delicious, for many benefits began to burden him, and he longed to stand on his own legs and make his own way. No one knew his past here; and with a well-stocked wardrobe, a handsome sum at his banker's, and the best teacher in Leipzig, he made his debut as a musical young gentleman, presented by the much-respected Professor Bhaer and the wealthy Mr Laurence, who had many friends glad to throw open their houses to his protégé. Thanks to these introductions, his fluent German, modest manners, and undeniable talent, the stranger was cordially welcomed, and launched at once into a circle which many an ambitious young man strove in vain to enter.

All this rather turned Nat's head; and as he sat in the brilliant opera house, chatted among the ladies at some select coffee party, or whisked an eminent professor's amiable daughter down the room, trying to imagine she was Daisy, he often asked himself if this gay fellow could be the poor homeless little street musician who once stood waiting in the rain at the gates of Plumfield. His heart was true, his impulses good, and his ambitions high; but the weak side of his nature came uppermost here; vanity led him astray, pleasure intoxicated him, and for a time he forgot everything but the delights of this new and charming life. Without meaning to deceive, he allowed people to imagine him a youth of good family and prospects; he boasted a little of Mr Laurie's wealth and influence, of Professor Bhaer's eminence, and the flourishing college at which he himself had been educated. Mrs Jo was introduced to the sentimental Fräuleins who read her books, and the charms and virtues of his own dear *Mädchen* confided to sympathetic mammas. All these boyish boastings and innocent vanities were duly circulated among the gossips, and his importance much increased thereby, to his surprise and gratification, as well as some shame.

But they bore fruit that was bitter in the end; for, finding that he was considered one of the upper class, it very soon became impossible for him to live in the humble quarters he had chosen, or to lead the studious, quiet life planned for him. He met other students, young officers, and gay fellows of all sorts, and was flattered at being welcomed among them; though it was a costly pleasure, and often left a thorn of regret to vex his honest conscience. He was tempted to take better rooms in a more fashionable street, leaving good Frau Tetzel to lament his loss, and his artist neighbour, Fräulein Vogelstein, to shake her grey ringlets and predict his return, a sadder and a wiser man.

The sum placed at his disposal for expenses and such simple pleasures as his busy life could command seemed a fortune to Nat, though it was smaller than generous Mr Laurie first proposed. Professor Bhaer wisely counselled prudence, as Nat was unused to the care of money, and the good man knew the temptations that a well-filled purse makes possible at this pleasure-loving age. So Nat enjoyed his handsome little apartment immensely, and insensibly let many unaccustomed luxuries creep in. He loved his music and never missed a lesson; but the hours he should have spent in patient practice were too often wasted at theatre, ball, beer garden, or club – doing no harm beyond that waste of precious time, and money not his own; for he had no vices, and took his recreation like a gentleman, so far. But slowly a change for the worse was beginning to show itself, and he felt it. These first steps along the flowery road were downward, not upward; and the constant sense of disloyalty which soon began to haunt him made Nat feel, in the few quiet hours he gave himself, that all was not well with him, in spite of the happy whirl in which he lived.

'Another month, and then I will be steady,' he said more than once, trying to excuse the delay by the fact that all was new to him, that his friends at home wished him to be happy, and that society was giving him the polish he needed. But as each month slipped away it grew harder to escape; he was inevitably drawn on, and it was so easy to drift with the tide that he deferred the evil day as long as possible. Winter festivities followed the more wholesome summer pleasures, and Nat found them more costly; for the hospitable ladies expected some return from the stranger; and carriages, bouquets, theatre tickets, and all the little expenses a young man cannot escape at such times, told heavily on the purse which seemed bottomless at first. Taking Mr Laurie for his model, Nat became quite a gallant, and was universally liked; for through all the newly acquired airs and graces the genuine honesty and simplicity of his character plainly shone, winning confidence and affection from all who knew him.

Among these was a certain amiable old lady with a musical daughter – well-born but poor, and very anxious to marry the aforesaid daughter to some wealthy man. Nat's little fictions concerning his prospects and friends charmed the *gnädige* Frau as much as his music and devoted manners did the sentimental Minna. Their quiet parlour seemed homelike and restful to Nat, when tired of gayer scenes; and the motherly interest of the elder lady was sweet and comfortable to him; while the tender blue eyes of the pretty girl were always so full of welcome when he came, of regret when he left, and of admiration when he played to her, that he found it impossible to keep away from this attractive spot. He meant no harm, and feared no danger, having confided to the Frau Mamma that he was betrothed; so he continued to call, little dreaming what ambitious hopes the old lady cherished, nor the peril there was in receiving the adoration of a romantic German girl, till it was too late to spare her pain and himself great regret.

Of course some inkling of these new and agreeable experiences got into the voluminous letters he never was too gay, too busy, or too tired to write each week; and while Daisy rejoiced over his happiness and success, and the boys laughed at the idea of 'old

Chirper coming out as a society man', the elders looked sober, and said among themselves, 'He is going too fast; he must have a word of warning, or trouble may come.'

But Mr Laurie said: 'Oh, let him have his fling; he's been dependent and repressed long enough. He can't go far with the money he has, and I've no fear of his getting into debt. He's too timid and too honest to be reckless. It is his first taste of freedom; let him enjoy it, and he'll work the better by and by; I know – and I'm sure I'm right.'

So the warnings were very gentle, and the good people waited anxiously to hear more of hard study, and less of 'splendid times'. Daisy sometimes wondered, with a pang of her faithful heart, if one of the charming Minnas, Hildegardes, and Lottchens mentioned were not stealing her Nat away from her; but she never asked, always wrote calmly and cheerfully, and looked in vain for any hint of change in the letters that were worn out with much reading.

Month after month slipped away, till the holidays came with gifts, good wishes, and brilliant festivities. Nat expected to enjoy himself very much, and did at first; for a German Christmas is a spectacle worth seeing. But he paid dearly for the abandon with which he threw himself into the gaieties of that memorable week; and on New Year's Day the reckoning came. It seemed as if some malicious fairy had prepared the surprises that arrived, so unwelcome were they, so magical the change they wrought, turning his happy world into a scene of desolation and despair as suddenly as a transformation at the pantomime.

The first came in the morning when, duly armed with costly bouquets and bonbons, he went to thank Minna and her mother for the braces embroidered with forget-me-nots and the silk socks knit by the old lady's nimble fingers, which he had found upon his table that day. The Frau Mamma received him graciously; but when he asked for the daughter the good lady frankly demanded what his intentions were, adding that certain gossip which had reached her ear made it necessary for him to declare himself or come no more, as Minna's peace must not be compromised.

A more panic-stricken youth was seldom seen than Nat as he received this unexpected demand. He saw too late that his American style of gallantry had deceived the artless girl, and might be used with terrible effect by the artful mother, if she

chose to do it. Nothing but the truth could save him, and he had
the honour and honesty to tell it faithfully. A sad scene followed;
for Nat was obliged to strip off his fictitious splendour, confess
himself only a poor student, and humbly ask pardon for the
thoughtless freedom with which he had enjoyed their too confiding hospitality. If he had any doubts of Frau Schomburg's
motives and desires, they were speedily set at rest by the frankness
with which she showed her disappointment, the vigour with which
she scolded him, and the scorn with which she cast him off when
her splendid castles in the air collapsed.

The sincerity of Nat's penitence softened her a little and she
consented to a farewell word with Minna, who had listened at the
keyhole, and was produced drenched in tears, to fall on Nat's
bosom, crying, 'Ah, thou dear one, never can I forget thee, though
my heart is broken!'

This was worse than the scolding; for the stout lady also wept,
and it was only after much German gush and twaddle that he
escaped, feeling like another Werther; while the deserted Lotte
consoled herself with the bonbons, her mother with the more
valuable gifts.

The second surprise arrived as he dined with Professor Baumgarten. His appetite had been effectually taken away by the scene
of the morning, and his spirits received another damper when a
fellow student cheerfully informed him that he was about to go to
America, and should make it his agreeable duty to call on the
'lieber Herr Professor Bhaer', to tell him how gaily his protégé
was disporting himself at Leipzig. Nat's heart died within him
as he imagined the effect these glowing tales would have at
Plumfield – not that he had wilfully deceived them, but in his
letters many things were left untold; and when Carlsen added,
with a friendly wink, that he would merely hint at the coming
betrothal of the fair Minna and his 'heart's friend', Nat found
himself devoutly hoping that this other inconvenient heart's friend
might go to the bottom of the sea before he reached Plumfield to
blast all his hopes by these tales of a mis-spent winter. Collecting
his wits, he cautioned Carlsen with what he flattered himself was
Mephistophelian art, and gave him such confused directions that
it would be a miracle if he ever found Professor Bhaer. But the
dinner was spoilt for Nat, and he got away as soon as possible, to

wander disconsolately about the streets, with no heart for the theatre or the supper he was to share with some gay comrades afterwards. He comforted himself a little by giving alms to sundry beggars, making two children happy with gilded gingerbread, and drinking a lonely glass of beer, in which he toasted his Daisy and wished himself a better year than the last had been.

Going home at length, he found a third surprise awaiting him in the shower of bills which had descended upon him like a snow-storm, burying him in an avalanche of remorse, despair, and self-disgust. These bills were so many and so large that he was startled and dismayed; for, as Mr Bhaer wisely predicted, he knew little about the value of money. It would take every dollar at the bankers to pay them all at once, and leave him penniless for the next six months, unless he wrote home for more. He would rather starve than do that; and his first impulse was to seek help at the gaming-table, whither his new friends had often tempted him. But he had promised Mr Bhaer to resist what then had seemed an impossible temptation; and now he would not add another fault to the list already so long. Borrow he would not, nor beg. What could he do? For these appalling bills must be paid, and the lessons go on; or his journey was an ignominious failure. But he must live meantime. And how? Bowed down with remorse for the folly of these months, he saw too late whither he was drifting, and for hours paced up and down his pretty rooms, floundering in a Slough of Despond, with no helping hand to pull him out – at least he thought so till letters were brought in, and among fresh bills lay one well-worn envelope with an American stamp in the corner.

Ah, how welcome it was! how eagerly he read the long pages full of affectionate wishes from all at home! For everyone had sent a line, and as each familiar name appeared, his eyes grew dimmer and dimmer till, as he read the last – 'God bless my boy! Mother Bhaer' – he broke down; and laying his head on his arms, blistered the paper with a rain of tears that eased his heart and washed away the boyish sins that now lay so heavy on his conscience.

'Dear people, how they love and trust me! And how bitterly they would be disappointed if they knew what a fool I've been! I'll fiddle in the streets again before I'll ask for help from them!' cried Nat, brushing away the tears of which he was ashamed, although he felt the good they had done.

Now he seemed to see more clearly what to do; for the helping hand had been stretched across the sea, and Love, the dear Evangelist, had lifted him out of the slough and shown him the narrow gate, beyond which deliverance lay. When the letter had been reread, and one corner where a daisy was painted, passionately kissed, Nat felt strong enough to face the worst and conquer it. Every bill should be paid, every saleable thing of his own sold, these costly rooms given up; and once back with thrifty Frau Tetzel, he would find work of some sort by which to support himself, as many another student did. He must give up the new friends, turn his back on the gay life, cease to be a butterfly, and take his place among the grubs. It was the only honest thing to do, but very hard for the poor fellow to crush his little vanities, renounce the delights so dear to the young, own his folly, and step down from his pedestal to be pitied, laughed at, and forgotten.

It took all Nat's pride and courage to do this, for his was a sensitive nature; esteem was very precious to him, failure very bitter, and nothing but the inborn contempt for meanness and deceit kept him from asking help or trying to hide his need by some dishonest device. As he sat alone that night, Mr Bhaer's words came back to him with curious clearness, and he saw himself a boy again at Plumfield, punishing his teacher as a lesson to himself, when timidity had made him lie.

'He shall not suffer for me again, and I won't be a sneak if I am a fool. I'll go and tell Professor Baumgarten all about it and ask his advice. I'd rather face a loaded cannon; but it must be done. Then I'll sell out, pay my debts, and go back where I belong. Better be an honest pauper than a jackdaw among peacocks;' and Nat smiled in the midst of his trouble, as he looked about him at the little elegancies of his room, remembering what he came from.

He kept his word manfully, and was much comforted to find that his experience was an old story to the professor, who approved his plan, thinking wisely that the discipline would be good for him, and was very kind in offering help and promising to keep the secret of his folly from his friend Bhaer till Nat had redeemed himself.

The first week of the new year was spent by our prodigal in carrying out his plan with penitent dispatch, and his birthday found him alone in the little room high up at Frau Tetzel's, with nothing of his former splendour, but sundry unsaleable keepsakes from the buxom maidens, who mourned his absence deeply. His male friends had ridiculed, pitied, and soon left him alone, with one or two exceptions, who offered their purses generously and promised to stand by him. He was lonely and heavy-hearted, and sat brooding over his small fire as he remembered the last New Year's Day at Plumfield, when at this hour he was dancing with his Daisy.

A tap at the door roused him, and with a careless 'Herein', he waited to see who had climbed so far for his sake. It was the good Frau proudly bearing a tray, on which stood a bottle of wine and an astonishing cake bedecked with sugarplums of every hue, and crowned with candles. Fräulein Vogelstein followed, embracing a blooming rose tree, above which her grey curls waved and her friendly face beamed joyfully as she cried, 'Dear Herr Blak, we bring you greetings and a little gift or two in honour of this ever-to-be-remembered day. Best wishes! and may the new year bloom for you as beautifully as we your heart-warm friends desire.'

'Yes, yes, in truth we do, dear Herr,' added Frau Tetzel. 'Eat of this with-joy-made Kuchen, and drink to the health of the faraway beloved ones in the good wine.'

Amused, yet touched by the kindness of the good souls, Nat thanked them both, and made them stay to enjoy the humble feast with him. This they gladly did, being motherly women full of pity for the dear youth, whose straits they knew, and having substantial help to offer, as well as kind words and creature comforts.

Frau Tetzel, with some hesitation, mentioned a friend of hers who, forced by illness to leave his place in the orchestra of a second-rate theatre, would gladly offer it to Nat, if he could accept so humble a position. Blushing and toying with the roses like a shy girl, good old Vogelstein asked if in his leisure moments he could give English lessons in the young ladies' school where she taught painting, adding that a small but certain salary would be paid him.

Gratefully Nat accepted both offers, finding it less humiliating to be helped by women than by friends of his own sex. This work would support him in a frugal way, and certain musical drudgery promised by his master assured his own teaching. Delighted with the success of their little plot, these friendly neighbours left him with cheery words, warm hand-grasps, and faces beaming with feminine satisfaction at the hearty kiss Nat put on each faded cheek, as the only return he could make for all their helpful kindness.

It was strange how much brighter the world looked after that; for hope was a better cordial than the wine, and good resolutions bloomed as freshly as the little rose tree that filled the room with fragrance, as Nat woke the echoes with the dear old airs, finding now as always his best comforter in music, to whom henceforth he swore to be a more loyal subject.

CHAPTER 14

Plays at Plumfield

As it is as impossible for the humble historian of the March family to write a story without theatricals in it as for our dear Miss Yonge to get on with less than twelve or fourteen children in her interesting tales, we will accept the fact, and at once cheer ourselves after the last afflicting events, by proceeding to the Christmas plays at Plumfield; for they influence the fate of several of our characters, and cannot well be skipped.

When the college was built Mr Laurie added a charming little theatre which not only served for plays, but declamations, lectures, and concerts. The drop-curtain displayed Apollo with the Muses grouped about him; and as a compliment to the donor of the hall the artist had given the god a decided resemblance to our friend, which was considered a superb joke by everyone else. Home talent furnished stars, stock company, orchestra, and scene painter; and astonishing performances were given on this pretty little stage.

Mrs Jo had been trying for some time to produce a play which should be an improvement upon the adaptations from the French then in vogue, curious mixtures of fine toilettes, false sentiment, and feeble wit, with no touch of nature to redeem them. It was easy to plan plays full of noble speeches and thrilling situations, but very hard to write them; so she contented herself with a few scenes of humble life in which the comic and pathetic were mingled; and as she fitted her characters to her actors, she hoped the little venture would prove that truth and simplicity had not entirely lost their power to charm. Mr Laurie helped her, and they called themselves Beaumont and Fletcher, enjoying their joint labour very much; for Beaumont's knowledge of dramatic art was of great use in curbing Fletcher's too-aspiring pen, and they flattered themselves that they had produced a neat and effective bit of work as an experiment.

All was ready now; and Christmas Day was much enlivened by last rehearsals, the panics of timid actors, the scramble for forgotten properties, and the decoration of the theatre. Evergreen and holly from the woods, blooming plants from the hothouse on Parnassus, and flags of all nations made it very gay that night in honour of the guests who were coming, chief among them, Miss Cameron, who kept her promise faithfully. The orchestra tuned their instruments with unusual care, the scene-shifters set their stage with lavish elegance, the prompter heroically took his seat in the stifling nook provided for him, and the actors dressed with trembling hands that dropped the pins, and perspiring brows whereon the powder wouldn't stick. Beaumont and Fletcher were everywhere, feeling that their literary reputation was at stake; for sundry friendly critics were invited, and reporters, like mosquitoes, cannot be excluded from any earthly scene, be it a great man's deathbed or a dime museum.

'Has she come?' was the question asked by every tongue behind the curtain; and when Tom, who played an old man, endangered his respectable legs among the footlights to peep, announced that he saw Miss Cameron's handsome head in the place of honour, a thrill pervaded the entire company, and Josie declared with an excited gasp that she was going to have stage fright for the first time in her life.

'I'll shake you if you do,' said Mrs Jo, who was in such a wild state of dishevelment with her varied labours that she might have gone on as Madge Wildlife, without an additional rag or crazy elf-lock.

'You'll have time to get your wits together while we do our piece. We are old stagers and calm as clocks,' answered Demi, with a nod towards Alice, ready in her pretty dress and all her properties at hand.

But both clocks were going rather faster than usual, as heightened colour, brilliant eyes, and a certain flutter under the laces and

velvet coat betrayed. They were to open the entertainment with a
gay little piece which they had played before and did remarkably
well. Alice was a tall girl, with dark hair and eyes, and a face which
intelligence, health, and a happy heart made beautiful. She was
looking her best now, for the brocades, plumes, and powder of the
Marquise became her stately figure; and Demi in his court suit,
with sword, three-cornered hat, and white wig, made as gallant a
Baron as one would wish to see. Josie was the maid, and looked
her part to the life, being as pretty, pert, and inquisitive as any
French soubrette. These three were all the characters; and the
success of the piece depended on the spirit and skill with which
the quickly changing moods of the quarrelsome lovers were given,
their witty speeches made to tell, and byplay suited to the courtly
period in which the scene was laid.

Few would have recognised sober John and studious Alice in the
dashing gentleman and coquettish lady, who kept the audience
laughing at their caprices; while they enjoyed the brilliant
costumes, and admired the ease and grace of the young actors.
Josie was a prominent figure in the plot, as she listened at key-
holes, peeped into notes, and popped in and out at all the most
inopportune moments, with her nose in the air, her hands in her
apron pockets, and curiosity pervading her little figure from the
topmost bow of her jaunty cap to the red heels of her slippers. All
went smoothly; and the capricious Marquise, after tormenting the
devoted Baron to her heart's content, owned herself conquered in
the war of wits, and was just offering the hand he had fairly won,
when a crash startled them, and a heavily decorated side-scene
swayed forward, ready to fall upon Alice. Demi saw it and sprung
before her to catch and hold it up, standing like a modern Samson
with the wall of a house on his back. The danger was over in a
moment, and he was about to utter his last speech, when the
excited young scene-shifter, who had flown up a ladder to repair
the damage, leaned over to whisper 'All right', and release Demi
from his spreadeagle attitude: as he did so, a hammer slipped out
of his pocket, to fall upon the upturned face below, inflicting a
smart blow and literally knocking the Baron's part out of his head.

'A quick curtain' robbed the audience of a pretty little scene
not down on the bill; for the Marquise flew to staunch the blood
with a cry of alarm, 'Oh! John, you are hurt! Lean on me' –

which John gladly did for a moment, being a trifle dazed yet quite able to enjoy the tender touch of the hands busied about him and the anxiety of the face so near his own; for both told him something which he would have considered cheaply won by a rain of hammers and the fall of the whole college on his head.

Nan was on the spot in a moment with the case that never left her pocket; and the wound was neatly plastered up by the time Mrs Jo arrived, demanding tragically, 'Is he too much hurt to go on again? If he is, my play is lost!'

'I'm all the fitter for it, Aunty; for here's a real instead of a painted wound. I'll be ready; don't worry about me.' And catching up his wig, Demi was off, with only a very eloquent look of thanks to the Marquise, who had spoilt her gloves for his sake, but did not seem to mind it at all, though they reached above her elbows, and were most expensive.

'How are your nerves, Fletcher?' asked Mr Laurie as they stood together during the breathless minute before the last bell rings.

'About as calm as yours, Beaumont,' answered Mrs Jo, gesticulating wildly to Mrs Meg to set her cap straight.

'Bear up, partner! I'll stand by you whatever comes!'

'I feel that it ought to go; for, though it's a mere trifle, a good deal of honest work and truth have gone into it. Doesn't Meg look the picture of a dear old country woman?'

She certainly did, as she sat in the farmhouse kitchen by a cheery fire, rocking a cradle and darning stockings, as if she had done nothing else all her life. Grey hair, skilfully drawn lines on the forehead, and a plain gown, with cap, little shawl, and check apron, changed her into a comfortable, motherly creature who found favour the moment the curtain went up and discovered her rocking, darning, and crooning an old song. In a short soliloquy about Sam, her boy, who wanted to enlist; Dolly, her discontented little daughter, who longed for city ease and pleasures; and poor 'Elizy', who had married badly, and came home to die, bequeathing her baby to her mother, lest its bad father should claim it, the little story was very simply opened, and made effective by the real boiling of the kettle on the crane, the ticking of a tall clock, and the appearance of a pair of blue worsted shoes which waved fitfully in the air to the soft babble of a baby's voice. Those shapeless little shoes won the first applause; and Mr Laurie, forgetting elegance in satisfaction, whispered to his coadjutor, 'I thought the baby would fetch them!'

'If the dear thing won't squall in the wrong place, we are saved. But it is risky. Be ready to catch it if all Meg's cuddlings prove in vain,' answered Mrs Jo, adding, with a clutch at Mr Laurie's arm as a haggard face appeared at the window: 'Here's Demi! I hope no one will recognise him when he comes on as the son. I'll never forgive you for not doing the villain yourself.'

'Can't run the thing and act too. He's capitally made up, and likes a bit of melodrama.'

'This scene ought to have come later; but I wanted to show that the mother was the heroine as soon as possible. I'm tired of love-sick girls and runaway wives. We'll prove that there's romance in old women also. Now he's coming!'

And in slouched a degraded-looking man, shabby, unshaven, and evil-eyed, trying to assume a masterful air as he dismayed the tranquil old woman by demanding his child. A powerful scene followed; and Mrs Meg surprised even those who knew her best by the homely dignity with which she at first met the man she dreaded; then, as he brutally pressed his claim, she pleaded with trembling voice and hands to keep the little creature she had promised the dying mother to protect; and when he turned to take it by force, quite a thrill went through the house as the old woman sprung to snatch it from the cradle, and holding it close, defied him in God's name to tear it from that sacred refuge. It was really well done; and the round of applause that greeted the fine tableau of the indignant old woman, the rosy, blinking baby clinging to her neck, and the daunted man who dared not execute his evil purpose with such a defender for helpless innocence, told the excited authors that their first scene was a hit.

The second was quieter, and introduced Josie as a bonny country lass setting the supper-table in a bad humour. The pettish way in which she slapped down the plates, hustled the cups, and cut the big brown loaf, as she related her girlish trials and ambitions, was capital. Mrs Jo kept her eye on Miss Cameron, and saw her nod approval several times at some natural tone or gesture, some good bit of byplay or a quick change of expression in the young face, which was as variable as an April day. Her struggle with the toasting-fork made much merriment; so did her contempt for the brown sugar, and the relish with which she sweetened her irksome duties by eating it; and when she sat, like Cinderella, on the hearth, tearfully watching the flames dance on the homely room, a girlish voice was heard to exclaim impulsively, 'Poor little thing! she ought to have *some* fun!'

The old woman enters; and mother and daughter have a pretty scene, in which the latter coaxes and threatens, kisses and cries, till she wins the reluctant consent of the former to visit a rich relation in the city; and from being a little thundercloud Dolly becomes bewitchingly gay and good, as soon as her wilful wish is granted. The poor old soul has hardly recovered from this trial when the son enters, in army blue, tells he has enlisted and must go. That is a hard blow; but the patriotic mother bears it well, and not till the thoughtless young folks have hastened away to tell their good news elsewhere does she break down. Then the country kitchen becomes pathetic as the old mother sits alone mourning over her children, till the grey head is hidden in the hands as she kneels down by the cradle to weep and pray, with only Baby to comfort her fond and faithful heart.

Sniffs were audible all through the latter part of this scene; and when the curtain fell, people were so busy wiping their eyes that for a moment they forgot to applaud. That silent moment was more flattering than noise; and as Mrs Jo wiped the real tears off her sister's face, she said as solemnly as an unconscious dab of rouge on her nose permitted, 'Meg, you have saved my play! Oh, why aren't you a real actress, and I a real playwright?'

'Don't gush now, dear, but help me dress Josie; she's in such a quiver of excitement, I can't manage her, and this is her best scene, you know.'

So it was; for her aunt had written it especially for her, and little Jo was happy in a gorgeous dress, with a train long enough to satisfy her wildest dreams. The rich relation's parlour was in festival array, and the country cousin sails in, looking back at her sweeping flounces with such artless rapture that no one had the heart to laugh at the pretty jay in borrowed plumes. She has confidences with herself in the mirror, from which it is made evident that she had discovered all is not gold that glitters, and has found greater temptations than those a girlish love of pleasure, luxury, and flattery bring her. She is sought by a rich lover; but her honest heart resists the allurements he offers, and in its innocent perplexity wishes 'mother' was there to comfort and counsel.

A gay little dance, in which Dora, Nan, Bess, and several of the boys took part, made a good background for the humble figure of the old woman in her widow's bonnet, rusty shawl, big umbrella, and basket. Her naïve astonishment, as she surveys the spectacle, feels the curtains, and smooths her old gloves during the moment she remains unseen, was very good; but Josie's unaffected start when she sees her, and the cry, 'Why, there's mother!' was such a hearty little bit of nature, it hardly needed the impatient tripping over her train as she ran into the arms that seemed now to be her nearest refuge.

The lover plays his part; and ripples of merriment greeted the old woman's searching questions and blunt answers during the interview which shows the girl how shallow his love is, and how near she had been to ruining her life as bitterly as poor 'Elizy' did. She gives her answer frankly, and when they are alone, looks from her own bedizened self to the shabby dress, work-worn hands, and tender face, crying with a repentant sob and kiss, 'Take me home, mother, and keep me safe. I've had enough of this!'

'That will do you good, Maria; don't forget it,' said one lady to her daughter as the curtain went down; and the girl answered, 'Well, I'm sure I don't see why it's touching; but it is,' as she spread her lace handkerchief to dry.

Tom and Nan came out strong in the next scene; for it was a ward in an army hospital, and surgeon and nurse went from bed to bed, feeling pulses, administering doses, and hearing complaints with an energy and gravity which convulsed the audience. The tragic element, never far from the comic at such times and places, came in when, while they bandaged an arm, the doctor told the nurse about an old woman who was searching through the hospital for her son, after days and nights on battlefields, through ambulances, and among scenes which would have killed most women.

'She will be here directly, and I dread her coming, for I'm afraid the poor lad who has just gone is her boy. I'd rather face a cannon than these brave women, with their hope and courage and great sorrow,' says the surgeon.

'Ah, these poor mothers break my heart!' adds the nurse, wiping her eyes on her big apron; and with the words Mrs Meg came in.

There was the same dress, the basket and umbrella, the rustic speech, the simple manners; but all were made pathetic by the terrible experience which had changed the tranquil old woman to that haggard figure with wild eyes, dusty feet, trembling hands, and an expression of mingled anguish, resolution, and despair which gave the homely figure a tragic dignity and power that touched all hearts. A few broken words told the story of her vain search, and then the sad quest began again. People held their breath as, led by the nurse, she went from bed to bed, showing in her face the alternations of hope, dread, and bitter disappointment as each was passed. On a narrow cot was a long figure covered with a sheet, and here she paused to lay one hand on her heart and one on her eyes, as if to gather courage to look at the nameless dead. Then she drew down the sheet, gave a long shivering sigh of relief, saying softly, 'Not my son, thank God! but some mother's boy.' And stooping down, she kissed the cold forehead tenderly.

Somebody sobbed there, and Miss Cameron shook two tears out of her eyes, anxious to lose no look or gesture as the poor soul, nearly spent with the long strain, struggled on down the long line. But her search was happily ended for, as if her voice had roused him from his feverish sleep, a gaunt, wild-eyed man sat up in his bed, and stretching his arms to her, cried in a voice that echoed through the room, 'Mother, mother! I knew you'd come to me!'

She did go to him, with a cry of love and joy that thrilled every listener, as she gathered him in her arms with the tears and prayers and blessing such as only a fond and faithful old mother could give.

The last scene was a cheerful contrast to this; for the country kitchen was bright with Christmas cheer, the wounded hero, with black patch and crutches well displayed, sat by the fire in the old chair whose familiar creak was soothing to his ear; pretty Dolly was stirring about, gaily trimming dresser, settle, high chimney piece, and old-fashioned cradle with mistletoe and holly; while the mother rested beside her son, with that blessed baby on her knee. Refreshed by a nap and nourishment, this young actor now covered himself with glory by his ecstatic prancings, incoherent remarks to the audience, and vain attempts to get to the footlights, as he blinked approvingly at these brilliant toys. It was good to see

Mrs Meg pat him on the back, cuddle the fat legs out of sight, and appease his vain longings with a lump of sugar, till Baby embraced her with a grateful ardour that brought him a round of applause all for his little self.

A sound of singing outside disturbs the happy family, and, after a carol in the snowy moonlight, a flock of neighbours troop in with Christmas gifts and greetings. Much byplay made this a lively picture; for Sam's sweetheart hovered round him with a tenderness the Marquise did not show the Baron; and Dolly had a pretty bit under the mistletoe with her rustic adorer, who looked so like Ham Peggotty in his cowhide boots, rough jacket, and dark beard and wig, that no one would have recognised Ted but for the long legs, which no extent of leather could disguise. It ended with a homely feast, brought by the guests; and as they sat round the table covered with doughnuts and cheese, pumpkin-pie, and other delicacies, Sam rises on his crutches to propose the first toast, and holding up his mug of cider, says, with a salute, and a choke in his voice, 'Mother, God bless her!' All drink it standing, Dolly with her arm round the old woman's neck, as she hides her happy tears on her daughter's breast; while the irrepressible baby beat rapturously on the table with a spoon, and crowed audibly as the curtain went down.

They had it up again in a jiffy to get a last look at the group about that central figure, which was showered with bouquets, to the great delight of the infant Roscius; till a fat rosebud hit him on the nose, and produced the much-dreaded squall, which, fortunately, only added to the fun at that moment.

'Well, that will do for a beginning,' said Beaumont, with a sigh of relief, as the curtain descended for the last time, and the actors scattered to dress for the closing piece.

'As an experiment, it is a success. Now we can venture to begin our great American drama,' answered Mrs Jo, full of satisfaction and grand ideas for the famous play – which, we may add, she did not write that year, owing to various dramatic events in her own family.

'The Owlsdark Marbles' closed the entertainment, and, being something new, proved amusing to this very indulgent audience. The gods and goddesses on Parnassus were displayed in full conclave; and, thanks to Mrs Amy's skill in draping and posing, the white wigs and cotton-flannel robes were classically correct and graceful, though sundry modern additions somewhat marred the effect, while adding point to the showman's learned remarks. Mr Laurie was Professor Owlsdark, in cap and gown; and, after a high-flown introduction, he proceeded to exhibit and explain his marbles. The first figure was a stately Minerva; but a second glance produced a laugh, for the words 'Women's Rights' adorned her shield, a scroll bearing the motto 'Vote early and often' hung from the beak of the owl perched on her lance, and a tiny pestle and mortar ornamented her helmet. Attention was drawn to the firm mouth, the piercing eye, the awe-inspiring brow, of the strong-minded woman of antiquity, and some scathing remarks made upon the degeneracy of her modern sisters who failed to do their duty. Mercury came next, and was very fine in his airy attitude, though the winged legs quivered as if it was difficult to keep the lively god in his place. His restless nature was dilated upon, his mischievous freaks alluded to, and a very bad character given to the immortal messenger-boy; which delighted his friends and caused the marble nose of the victim to curl visibly with scorn when derisive applause greeted a particularly hard hit. A charming little Hebe stood next, pouring nectar from a silver teapot into a blue china teacup. She also pointed a moral; for the Professor explained that the nectar of old was the beverage which cheers but does not inebriate, and regretted that the excessive devotion of American women to this classic brew proved so harmful, owing to the great development of brain their culture produced. A touch at modern servants, in contrast to this accomplished table-girl, made the statue's cheeks glow under the chalk, and brought her a hearty round as the audience recognised Dolly and the smart soubrette.

Jove in all his majesty followed, as he and his wife occupied the central pedestals in the half-circle of immortals. A splendid Jupiter, with hair well set up off the fine brow, ambrosial beard, silver thunderbolts in one hand, and a well-worn ferrule in the other. A large stuffed eagle from the museum stood at his feet; and the benign expression of his august countenance showed that he was in a good humour – as well he might be, for he was paid some handsome compliments upon his wise rule, the peaceful state of his kingdom, and the brood of all-accomplished Pallases that yearly issued from his mighty brain. Cheers greeted this and other pleasant words, and caused the thunderer to bow his thanks; for 'Jove nods', as everyone knows, and flattery wins the heart of gods and men.

Mrs Juno, with her peacocks, darning-needle, pen, and cooking-spoon, did not get off so easily; for the Professor was down on her with all manner of mirth-provoking accusations, criticisms, and insults even. He alluded to her domestic infelicity, her meddle-some disposition, sharp tongue, bad temper, and jealousy, closing, however, with a tribute to her skill in caring for the wounds and settling the quarrels of belligerent heroes, as well as her love for youths in Olympus and on earth. Gales of laughter greeted these hits, varied by hisses from some indignant boys, who would not bear, even in joke, any disrespect to dear Mother Bhaer, who, however, enjoyed it all immensely, as the twinkle in her eye and the irrepressible pucker of her lips betrayed.

A jolly Bacchus astride of his cask took Vulcan's place, and appeared to be very comfortable with a beer mug in one hand, a champagne bottle in the other, and a garland of grapes on his curly head. He was the text of a short temperance lecture, aimed directly at a row of smart young gentlemen who lined the walls of the auditorium. George Cole was seen to dodge behind a pillar at one point, Dolly nudged his neighbour at another, and there was laughter all along the line as the Professor glared at them through his big glasses, and dragged their bacchanalian orgies to the light and held them up to scorn.

Seeing the execution he had done, the learned man turned to the lovely Diana, who stood as white and still as the plaster stag beside her, with sandals, bow, and crescent; quite perfect, and altogether the best piece of statuary in the show. She was very tenderly treated by the paternal critic who, merely alluding to her confirmed spinsterhood, fondness for athletic sports, and oracular powers, gave a graceful little exposition of true art and passed on to the last figure.

This was Apollo in full fig, his curls skilfully arranged to hide a well-whitened patch over the eye, his handsome legs correctly poised, and his gifted fingers about to draw divine music from the silvered gridiron which was his lyre. His divine attributes were described, as well as his little follies and failings, among which were his weakness for photography and flute-playing, his attempts to run a newspaper, and his fondness for the society of the Muses; which latter slap produced giggles and blushes among the girl-graduates, and much mirth among the stricken youths; for misery loves company, and after this they began to rally.

Then, with a ridiculous conclusion, the Professor bowed his thanks; and after several recalls the curtain fell, but not quickly enough to conceal Mercury, wildly waving his liberated legs, Hebe dropping her teapot, Bacchus taking a lovely roll on his barrel, and Mrs Juno rapping the impertinent Owlsdark on the head with Jove's ruler.

While the audience filed out to supper in the hall, the stage was a scene of dire confusion as gods and goddesses, farmers and barons, maids and carpenters, congratulated one another on the success of their labours. Assuming various costumes, actors and actresses soon joined their guests, to sip bounteous draughts of praise with their coffee, and cool their modest blushes with ice cream. Mrs Meg was a proud and happy woman when Miss Cameron came to her as she sat by Josie, with Demi serving both, and said, so cordially that it was impossible to doubt the sincerity of her welcome words, 'Mrs Brooke, I no longer wonder where your children get their talent. I make my compliments to the Baron and next summer you must let me have little "Dolly" as a pupil when we are at the beach.'

One can easily imagine how this offer was received, as well as the friendly commendation bestowed by the same kind critic on the work of Beaumont and Fletcher, who hastened to explain that this trifle was only an attempt to make nature and art go hand in hand, with little help from fine writing or imposing scenery. Everybody was in the happiest mood, especially 'little Dolly', who danced like a will-o'-the-wisp with light-footed Mercury and Apollo as he promenaded with the Marquise on his arm, who seemed to have left her coquetry in the green room with her rouge.

When all was over, Mrs Juno said to Jove, to whose arm she clung as they trudged home along the snowy paths, 'Fritz dear, Christmas is a good time for new resolutions, and I've made one never to be impatient or fretful with my beloved husband again. I know I am, though you won't own it; but Laurie's fun had some truth in it, and I felt hit in a tender spot. Henceforth I am a model wife, else I don't deserve the dearest, best man ever born;' and being in a dramatic mood, Mrs Juno tenderly embraced her excellent Jove in the moonlight, to the great amusement of sundry lingerers behind them.

So all three plays might be considered successes, and that merry Christmas night a memorable one in the March family; for Demi got an unspoken question answered, Josie's fondest wish was granted, and, thanks to Professor Owlsdark's jest, Mrs Jo made Professor Bhaer's busy life quite a bed of roses by the keeping of her resolution. A few days later she had her reward for this burst of virtue in Dan's letter, which set her fears at rest and made her very happy, though she was unable to tell him so, because he sent her no address.

CHAPTER 15

Waiting

'My wife, I have bad news for thee,' said Professor Bhaer, coming in one day early in January.

'Please tell it at once. I can't bear to wait, Fritz,' cried Mrs Jo, dropping her work and standing up as if to take the shot bravely.

'But we must wait and hope, heart's dearest. Come and let us bear it together. Emil's ship is lost, and as yet no news of him.'

It was well Mr Bhaer had taken his wife into his strong arms, for she looked ready to drop, but bore up after a moment, and sitting by her good man, heard all that there was to tell. Tidings had been sent to the shipowners at Hamburg by some of the survivors, and telegraphed at once by Franz to his uncle. As one boatload was safe, there was hope that others might also escape, though the gale had sent two to the bottom. A swift-sailing steamer had brought these scanty news, and happier ones might come at any hour; but kind Franz had not added that the sailors reported the captain's boat as undoubtedly wrecked by the falling mast, since the smoke hid its escape, and the gale soon drove all far asunder. But this sad rumour reached Plumfield in time; and deep was the mourning for the happy-hearted Commodore, never to come singing home again. Mrs Jo refused to believe it, stoutly insisting that Emil would outlive any storm and yet turn up safe and gay. It was well she clung to this hopeful view, for poor Mr Bhaer was much afflicted by the loss of his boy, because his sister's sons had been his so long he scarcely knew a different love for his very own. Now was a chance for Mrs Juno to keep her word; and she did, speaking cheerily of Emil, even when hope waxed faint and her heart was heavy. If anything could comfort the Bhaers for the loss of one boy, it would have been the affection and sorrow shown by all the rest. Franz kept the cable busy with his varying messages, Nat sent loving letters from Leipzig, and Tom harassed the shipping agents for news. Even busy Jack wrote them with unusual warmth; Dolly and George came often, bearing the loveliest flowers and the daintiest bonbons to cheer Mrs Bhaer and sweeten Josie's grief; while good-hearted Ned travelled all the way from Chicago to press their hands and say, with a tear in his eye, 'I was so anxious to hear all about the dear old boy, I couldn't keep away.'

'That's right comfortable, and shows me that if I didn't teach my boys anything else, I did give them the brotherly love that will make them stand by one another all their lives,' said Mrs Jo, when he had gone.

Rob answered reams of sympathising letters, which showed how many friends they had; and the kindly praises of the lost man would have made Emil a hero and a saint, had they all been true. The elders bore it quietly, having learned submission in life's hard school; but the younger people rebelled; some hoped against hope and kept up, others despaired at once, and little Josie, Emil's pet cousin and playmate, was so broken-hearted nothing could comfort her. Nan dosed in vain, Daisy's cheerful words went by like the wind, and Bess's devices to amuse her all failed utterly. To cry in mother's arms and talk about the wreck, which haunted her even in her sleep, was all she cared to do; and Mrs Meg was getting anxious when Miss Cameron sent Josie a kind note bidding her learn bravely her first lesson in real tragedy, and be like the self-sacrificing heroines she loved to act. That did the little girl good, and she made an effort in which Teddy and Octoo helped her much; for the boy was deeply impressed by this sudden eclipse of the firefly whose light and life all missed when they were gone, and lured her out every day for long drives behind the black mare, who shook her silvery bells till they made such merry music Josie could not help listening to it, and whisked her over the snowy roads at a pace which set the blood dancing in her veins and sent her home strengthened and comforted by sunshine, fresh air, and congenial society – three aids young sufferers seldom can resist.

As Emil was helping nurse Captain Hardy, safe and well, aboard the ship, all this sorrow would seem wasted; but it was not, for it drew many hearts more closely together by a common grief, taught some patience, some sympathy, some regret for faults that lie heavy on the conscience when the one sinned against is gone, and all of them the solemn lesson to be ready when the summons comes. A hush lay over Plumfield for weeks, and the studious faces on the hill reflected the sadness of those in the valley. Sacred music sounded from Parnassus to comfort all who heard; the brown cottage was beseiged with gifts for the little mourner, and Emil's flag hung at half-mast on the roof where he last sat with Mrs Jo.

So the weeks went heavily by till suddenly, like a thunderbolt out of a clear sky, came the news, 'All safe, letters on the way.' Then up went the flag, out rang the college bells, bang went Teddy's long-unused cannon, and a chorus of happy voices cried, 'Thank God', as people went about, laughing, crying, and embracing one another in a rapture of delight. By and by the longed-for letters came, and all the story of the wreck was told; briefly by Emil, eloquently by Mrs Hardy, gratefully by the captain, while Mary added a few tender words that went straight to their hearts and seemed the sweetest of all. Never were letters so read, passed round, admired, and cried over as these; for Mrs Jo carried them in *her* pocket when Mr Bhaer did not have them in his, and both took a look at them when they said their prayers at night. Now the Professor was heard humming like a big bee again as he went to his classes, and the lines smoothed out of Mother Bhaer's forehead, while she wrote this real story to anxious friends and let her romances wait. Now messages of congratulation flowed in, and beaming faces showed everywhere. Rob amazed his parents by producing a poem which was remarkably good for one of his years, and Demi set it to music that it might be sung when the sailor boy returned. Teddy stood on his head literally, and tore about the neighbourhood on Octoo, like a second Paul Revere – only *his* tidings were good. But best of all, little Josie lifted up her head as the snowdrops did, and began to bloom again, growing tall and quiet, with the shadow of past sorrow to tone down her former vivacity and show that she *had* learned a lesson in trying to act well her part on the real stage, where all have to take their share in the great drama of life.

Now another sort of waiting began; for the travellers were on their way to Hamburg, and would stay there awhile before coming home, as Uncle Hermann owned the *Brenda*, and the captain must report to him. Emil must remain to Franz's wedding, deferred till now because of the season of mourning, so happily ended. These plans were doubly welcome and pleasant after the troublous times which went before, and no spring ever seemed so beautiful as this one; for, as Teddy put it: 'Now is the winter of our discontent made glorious summer by these sons of Bhaer!' – Franz and Emil being regarded in the light of elder brothers by the real 'sons of Bhaer'.

There was great scrubbing and dusting among the matrons as they set their houses in order not only for Class Day, but to receive the bride and groom, who were to come to them for the honeymoon trip. Great plans were made, gifts prepared, and much joy felt at the prospect of seeing Franz again; though Emil, who was to accompany them, would be the greater hero. Little did the dear souls dream what a surprise was in store for them, as they innocently laid their plans and wished all the boys could be there to welcome home their eldest and their Casabianca.

While they wait and work so happily, let us see how our other absent boys are faring as they too wait and work and hope for better days. Nat was toiling steadily along the path he had wisely chosen, though it was by no means strewn with flowers – quite thorny was it, in fact, and hard to travel, after the taste of ease and pleasure he had got when nibbling at forbidden fruit. But his crop of wild oats was a light one, and he resolutely reaped what he had sowed, finding some good wheat among the tares. He taught by day; he fiddled night after night in the dingy little theatre, and he studied so diligently that his master was well pleased, and kept him in mind as one to whom preferment was due, if any chance occurred. Gay friends forgot him; but the old ones stood fast, and cheered him up when *Heimweh* and weariness made him sad. As spring came on things mended – expenses grew less, work pleasanter, and life more bearable than when wintry storms beat on his thinly clad back, and frost pinched the toes that patiently trudged in old boots. No debts burdened him; the year of absence was nearly over; and if he chose to stay, Herr Bergmann had hopes for him that would bring independence for a time at least. So he walked under the lindens with a lighter heart, and in the May evenings went about the city with a band of strolling students, making music before houses where he used to sit as guest. No one recognised him in the darkness, though old friends often listened to the band; and once Minna threw him money, which he humbly received as part of his penance, being morbid on the subject of his sins.

His reward came sooner than he expected, and was greater than he deserved, he thought, though his heart leaped with joy when his master one day informed him that he was chosen, with several other of his most promising pupils, to join the musical society which was to take part in the great festival in London the next July. Here was not only honour for the violinist but happiness for the man, as it brought him nearer home, and would open a chance of further promotion and profit in his chosen profession.

'Make thyself useful to Bachmeister there in London with thy English, and if all goes well with him, he will be glad to take thee to America, whither he goes in the early autumn for winter concerts. Thou hast done well these last months, and I have hopes of thee.'

As the great Bergmann seldom praised his pupils, these words filled Nat's soul with pride and joy, and he worked yet more diligently than before to fulfil his master's prophecy. He thought the trip to England happiness enough, but found room for more when, early in June, Franz and Emil paid him a flying visit, bringing all sorts of good news, kind wishes, and comfortable gifts for the lonely fellow, who could have fallen on their necks and cried like a girl at seeing his old mates again. How glad he was to be found in his little room busy at his proper work, not living like an idle gentleman on borrowed money! How proud he was to tell his plans, assure them that he had no debts, and receive their praises for his improvement in music, their respect for his economy and steadfastness in well-doing! How relieved when, having honestly confessed his shortcomings, they only laughed, and owned that they also had known like experiences, and were the wiser for them. He was to go to the wedding late in June, and join his comrades in London. As best man, he could not refuse the new suit Franz insisted on ordering for him; and a cheque from home about that time made him feel like a millionaire – and a happy one; for this was accompanied by such kind letters full of delight in his success, he felt that he had earned it, and waited for his joyful holiday with the impatience of a boy.

Dan meantime was also counting the weeks till August, when he would be free. But neither marriage-bells nor festival music awaited him; no friends would greet him as he left the prison; no hopeful prospect lay before him; no happy home-going was to be his. Yet his success was far greater than Nat's, though only God and one good man saw it. It was a hard-won battle; but he would never have to fight so terrible a one again; for though enemies would still assail from within and from without, he had found the little guidebook that Christian carried in his bosom, and Love, Penitence, and Prayer, the three sweet sisters, had given him the armour which would keep him safe. He had not learned to wear it yet, and chafed against it, though he felt its value, thanks to the faithful friend who had stood by him all that bitter year.

Soon he was to be free again, worn and scarred in the fray, but out among men in the blessed sun and air. When he thought of it Dan felt as if he could not wait, but must burst that narrow cell and fly away, as the caddis worms he used to watch by the brook-side shed their stony coffins, to climb the ferns and soar into the sky. Night after night he lulled himself to sleep with planning how, when he had seen Mary Mason according to his promise, he would steer straight for his old friends, the Indians, and in the wilderness hide his disgrace and heal his wounds. Working to save the many would atone for the sin of killing one, he thought; and the old free life would keep him safe from the temptations that beset him in cities.

'By and by, when I'm all right again, and have something to tell that I'm not ashamed of, I'll go home,' he said, with a quicker beat of the impetuous heart that longed to be there so intensely, he found it as hard to curb as one of his unbroken horses on the plains. 'Not yet. I must get over this first. They'd see and smell and feel the prison taint on me, if I went now, and I couldn't look them in the face and hide the truth. I *can't* lose Ted's love, Mother Bhaer's confidence, and the respect of – of – the girls, for they did respect my strength, anyway; but now they wouldn't touch me.' And poor Dan looked with a shudder at the brown fist he clenched involuntarily as he remembered what it had done since a certain little white hand had laid in it confidingly. 'I'll make 'em proud of me yet; and no one shall ever know of this awful year. I *can* wipe it out, and I will, so help me God!' And the clenched hand was held up as if to take a solemn oath that this lost year should yet be made good, if resolution and repentance could work the miracle.

CHAPTER 16

In the Tennis Court

Athletic sports were in high favour at Plumfield; and the river where the old punt used to wabble about with a cargo of small boys, or echo to the shrill screams of little girls trying to get lilies, now was alive with boats of all kinds, from the slender wherry to the trim pleasure-craft, gay with cushions, awnings, and fluttering pennons. Everyone rowed, and the girls as well as the youths had their races, and developed their muscles in the most scientific manner. The large, level meadow near the old willow was now the college playground, and here baseball battles raged with fury, varied by football, leaping, and kindred sports fitted to split the fingers, break the ribs, and strain the backs of the too ambitious participants. The gentler pastimes of the damsels were at a safe distance from this Champ de Mars; croquet mallets clicked under the elms that fringed the field, rackets rose and fell energetically in several tennis courts, and gates of different heights were handy to practise the graceful bound by which every girl expected to save her life someday when the mad bull, which was always coming but never seemed to arrive, should be bellowing at her heels.

One of these tennis grounds was called 'Jo's Court', and here the little lady ruled like a queen; for she was fond of the game, and being bent on developing her small self to the highest degree of perfection, she was to be found at every leisure moment with

Croquet mallets clicked under the elms that fringed the field

some victim hard at it. On a certain pleasant Saturday afternoon she had been playing with Bess and beating her; for, though more graceful, the Princess was less active than her cousin, and cultivated her roses by quieter methods.

'Oh dear! you are tired, and every blessed boy is at that stupid baseball match. What shall I do?' sighed Josie, pushing back the great red hat she wore, and gazing sadly round her for more worlds to conquer.

'I'll play presently, when I'm a little cooler. But it is dull work for me, as I never win,' answered Bess, fanning herself with a large leaf.

Josie was about to sit down beside her on the rustic seat and wait, when her quick eye saw afar off two manly forms arrayed in white flannel; their blue legs seemed bearing them towards the battle going on in the distance; but they never reached the fray; for with a cry of joy, Jo raced away to meet them, bent on securing this heaven-sent reinforcement. Both paused as she came flying up, and both raised their hats; but oh, the difference there was in the salutes! The stout youth pulled his off lazily and put it on again at once, as if glad to get the duty over; the slender being, with the crimson tie, lifted his with a graceful bend, and held it aloft while he accosted the rosy, breathless maid, thus permitting her to see his raven locks smoothly parted, with one little curl upon the brow. Dolly prided himself upon that bow, and practised it before his glass, but did not bestow it upon all alike, regarding it as a work of art, fit only for the fairest and most favoured of his female admirers; for he was a pretty youth, and fancied himself an Adonis.

Eager Josie evidently did not appreciate the honour he did her, for with a nod she begged them both to 'come along and play tennis, not go and get all hot and dirty with the boys'. These two adjectives won the day; for Stuffy was already warmer than he liked to be, and Dolly had on a new suit which he desired to keep immaculate as long as possible, conscious that it was very becoming.

'Charmed to oblige,' answered the polite one, with another bend.

'You play, I'll rest,' added the fat boy, yearning for repose and gentle converse with the Princess in the cooling shade.

'Well, you can comfort Bess, for I've beaten her all to bits and she needs amusing. I know you've got something nice in your pocket,

George; give her some, and 'Dolphus can have her racket. Now then, fly round;' and driving her prey before her, Josie returned in triumph to the court.

Casting himself ponderously upon the bench, which creaked under his weight, Stuffy – as we will continue to call him, though no one else dared to use the old name now – promptly produced the box of confectionery, without which he never travelled far, and regaled Bess with candied violets and other dainties, while Dolly worked hard to hold his own against a most accomplished antagonist. He would have beaten her if an unlucky stumble, which produced an unsightly stain upon the knee of those new shorts, had not distracted his mind and made him careless. Much elated at her victory, Josie permitted him to rest, and offered ironical consolation for the mishap which evidently weighed upon his mind.

'Don't be an old Betty; it can be cleaned. You must have been a cat in some former state, you are so troubled about dirt; or a tailor, and lived for clothes.'

'Come now, don't hit a fellow when he is down,' responded Dolly from the grass where he and Stuffy now lay to make room for both girls on the seat. One handkerchief was spread under him, and his elbow leaned upon another, while his eyes were sadly fixed upon the green and brown spot which afflicted him. 'I like to be neat; don't think it civil to cut about in old shoes and grey flannel shirts before ladies. *Our* fellows are gentlemen, and dress as such,' he added, rather nettled at the word 'tailor'; for he owed one of those too attractive persons an uncomfortably big bill.

'So are ours; but good clothes alone don't make a gentleman *here*. We require a good deal more,' flashed Josie, in arms at once to defend her college. 'You will hear of some of the men in "old boots and grey flannel" when you and your fine gentlemen are twiddling your ties and scenting your hair in obscurity. I *like* old boots and wear them, and I hate dandies; don't you, Bess?'

'Not when they are kind to me, and belong to our old set,' answered Bess, with a nod of thanks to Dolly, who was carefully removing an inquisitive caterpillar from one of her little russet shoes.

'*I* like a lady who is always polite, and doesn't snap a man's head off if he has a mind of his own; don't you, George?' asked Dolly, with his best smile for Bess and a Harvard stare of disapprobation for Josie.

A tranquil snore was Stuffy's sole reply, and a general laugh restored peace for the moment. But Josie loved to harass the lords of creation who asserted themselves too much, and bided her time for another attack till she had secured more tennis. She got another game; for Dolly was a sworn knight of dames, so he obeyed her call, leaving Bess to sketch George as he lay upon his back, his stout legs crossed, and his round red face partially eclipsed by his hat. Josie got beaten this time and came back rather cross, so she woke the peaceful sleeper by tickling his nose with a straw till he sneezed himself into a sitting posture, and looked wrathfully about for 'that confounded fly'.

'Come, sit up and let us have a little elegant conversation; you "howling swells" ought to improve our minds and manners, for we are only poor "country girls in dowdy gowns and hats",' began the gadfly, opening the battle with a sly quotation from one of Dolly's unfortunate speeches about certain studious damsels who cared more for books than finery.

'I didn't mean you! Your gowns are all right, and those hats the latest thing out,' began poor 'Dolphus, convicting himself by the incautious exclamation.

'Caught you that time; I thought you fellows were all *gentlemen*, civil as well as nice. But you are always sneering at girls who don't dress well and that is a very unmanly thing to do; my mother said so;' and Josie felt that she had dealt a shrewd blow at the elegant youth who bowed at many shrines if they were well-decorated ones.

'Got you there, old boy, and she's right. You never hear *me* talk about clothes and such twaddle,' said Stuffy, suppressing a yawn, and feeling for another bonbon wherewith to refresh himself.

'You talk about eating, and that is even worse for a man. You will marry a cook and keep a restaurant someday,' laughed Josie, down on him at once.

This fearful prediction kept him silent for several moments; but Dolly rallied, and wisely changing the subject, carried war into the enemy's camp.

'As you wanted us to improve your manners, allow me to say that young ladies in good society don't make personal remarks or deliver lectures. Little girls who are not out do it, and think it witty; but I assure you it's not good form.'

Josie paused a moment to recover from the shock of being called 'a little girl', when all the honours of her fourteenth birthday were fresh upon her; and Bess said, in the lofty tone which was infinitely more crushing than Jo's impertinence, 'That is true; but we have lived all our lives with superior people, so we have no society talk like your young ladies. We are so accustomed to sensible conversation, and helping one another by telling our faults, that we have no gossip to offer you.'

When the Princess reproved, the boys seldom resented it; so Dolly held his peace, and Josie burst out, following her cousin's lead, which she thought a happy one, '*Our* boys like to have us talk with them, and take kindly any hints we give. *They* don't think they know everything and are quite perfect at eighteen, as I've observed the Harvard men do, especially the *very young* ones.'

Josie took immense satisfaction in that return shot; and Dolly showed that he was hit, by the nettled tone in which he answered, with a supercilious glance at the hot, dusty, and noisy crowd on the baseball ground, 'The class of fellows you have here need all the polish and culture you can give them; and I'm glad they get it. Our men are largely from the best families all over the country, so we don't need girls to teach us anything.'

'It's a pity you don't have more of such "fellows" as ours. They value and use well what college gives them, and aren't satisfied to slip through, getting all the fun they can and shirking the work. Oh, I've heard you "men" talk, and heard your fathers say they wish they hadn't wasted time and money just that you might say you'd been through college. As for the girls, you'll be much better off in all ways when they do get in, and keep you lazy things up to the mark, as we do here.'

'If you have such a poor opinion of us, why do you wear our colour?' asked Dolly, painfully conscious that he was not improving the advantages his Alma Mater offered him, but bound to defend her.

'I don't; my hat is scarlet, not crimson. Much you know about a colour,' scoffed Josie.

'I know that a cross cow would soon set you scampering, if you flaunted that red tile under her nose,' retorted Dolly.

'I'm ready for her. Can your fine young ladies do this? or you either?' and burning to display her latest accomplishment, Josie ran to the nearest gate, put one hand on the top rail, and vaulted over as lightly as a bird.

Bess shook her head, and Stuffy languidly applauded; but Dolly scorning to be braved by a girl, took a flying leap and landed on his feet beside Josie, saying calmly, 'Can you do that?'

'Not yet; but I will by and by.'

As his foe looked a little crestfallen, Dolly relented, and affably added sundry feats of a like nature, quite unconscious that he had fallen into a dreadful snare; for the dull red paint on the gate, not being used to such vigorous handling, came off in streaks upon his shoulders when he turned a backward swing and came up smiling, to be rewarded with the aggravating remark, 'If you want to know what crimson is, look at your back; it's nicely stamped on and won't wash out, I think.'

'The deuce it won't!' cried Dolly, trying to get an impossible view, and giving it up in great disgust.

'I guess we'd better be going, 'Dolf,' said peaceable Stuffy, feeling that it would be wise to retreat before another skirmish took place, as his side seemed to be getting the worst of it.

'Don't hurry, I beg; stay and rest; you must need it after the tremendous amount of brain work you've done this week. It is time for our Greek. Come, Bess. Good-afternoon, *gentlemen*.' And, with a sweeping courtesy, Josie led the way, with her hat belligerently cocked up, and her racket borne like a triumphal banner over one shoulder; for having had the last word, she felt that she could retire with the honours of war.

Dolly gave Bess his best bow, with the chill on; and Stuffy subsided luxuriously, with his legs in the air, murmuring in a dreamy tone, 'Little Jo is as cross as two sticks today. I'm going in for another nap: too hot to play anything.'

'So it is. Wonder if Spitfire was right about these beastly spots?' And Dolly sat down to try dry cleansing with one of his hand-kerchiefs. 'Asleep?' he asked, after a few moments of this cheerful occupation, fearing that his chum might be too comfortable when he was in a fume himself.

'No. I was thinking that Jo wasn't far wrong about shirking. 'Tis a shame to get so little done, when we ought to be grinding like

Morton and Torry and that lot. I never wanted to go to college; but my governor made me. Much good it will do either of us!' answered Stuffy, with a groan; for he hated work, and saw two more long years of it before him.

'Gives a man prestige, you know. No need to dig. I mean to have a gay old time, and be a "howling swell", if I choose. Between you and me though, it *would* be no end jolly to have the girls along. Study be hanged! But if we've got to turn the grindstone, it would be mighty nice to have some of the little dears to lend a hand. Wouldn't it now?'

'I'd like three this minute – one to fan me, one to kiss me, and one to give me some iced lemonade!' sighed Stuffy, with a yearning glance towards the house, whence no succour appeared.

'How would root beer do?' asked a voice behind them, which made Dolly spring to his feet and Stuffy roll over like a startled porpoise.

Sitting on the stile that crossed the wall near by was Mrs Jo, with two jugs slung over her shoulder by a strap, several tin mugs in her hand, and an old-fashioned sun-bonnet on her head.

'I knew the boys would be killing themselves with ice-water; so I strolled down with some of my good, wholesome beer. They drank like fishes. But Silas was with me; so my cruse still holds out. Have some?'

'Yes, thanks, very much. Let us pour it.' And Dolly held the cup while Stuffy joyfully filled it; both very grateful, but rather afraid she had heard what went before the wish she fulfilled.

She proved that she had by saying, as they stood drinking her health, while she sat between them, looking like a middle-aged *vivandière*, with her jugs and mugs, 'I was glad to hear you say you would like to have girls at your college; but I hope you will learn to speak more respectfully of them before they come; for that will be the first lesson they will teach you.'

'Really, ma'am, I was only joking,' began Stuffy, gulping down his beer in a hurry.

'So was I. I'm sure I – I'm devoted to 'em,' stuttered Dolly, panic-stricken; for he saw that he was in for a lecture of some sort.

'Not in the right way. Frivolous girls may like to be called "little dears" and things of that sort; but the girls who love study wish to be treated like reasonable beings, not dolls to flirt with. Yes, I'm going to preach; that's my business; so stand up and take it like men.'

Mrs Jo laughed; but she was in earnest; for by various hints and signs during the past winter she knew that the boys were beginning to 'see life' in the way she especially disapproved. Both were far from home, had money enough to waste, and were as inexperienced, curious, and credulous as most lads of their age. Not fond of books, therefore without the safeguard which keeps many studious fellows out of harm; one self-indulgent, indolent, and so used to luxury that pampering of the senses was an easy thing; the other vain, as all comely boys are, full of conceit, and so eager to find favour in the eyes of his comrades that he was ready for anything which would secure it. These traits and foibles made both peculiarly liable to the temptations which assail pleasure-loving and weak-willed boys. Mrs Jo knew them well, and had dropped many a warning word since they went to college; but till lately they seemed not to understand some of her friendly hints; now she was sure they would, and meant to speak out: for long experience with boys made her both bold and skilful in handling some of the dangers usually left to silence, till it is too late for anything but pity and reproach.

'I'm going to talk to you like a mother, because yours are far away; and there are things that mothers can manage best, if they do their duty,' she solemnly began from the depths of the sun-bonnet.

'Great Scott! We're in for it now!' thought Dolly, in secret dismay; while Stuffy got the first blow by trying to sustain himself with another mug of beer.

'That won't hurt you; but I must warn you about drinking other things, George. Overeating is an old story; and a few more fits of illness will teach you to be wise. But drinking is a more serious thing, and leads to worse harm than any that can afflict your body alone. I hear you talk about wines as if you knew them and cared more for them than a boy should; and several times I've heard jokes that meant mischief. For heaven's sake, don't begin to play with this dangerous taste "for fun", as you say, or because it's the fashion, and the other fellows do. Stop at once, and learn that temperance in all things is the only safe rule.'

'Upon my honour, I only take wine and iron. I need a tonic,

mother says, to repair the waste of brain tissue while I'm studying,'
protested Stuffy, putting down the mug as if it burnt his fingers.

'Good beef and oatmeal will repair your tissues much better
than any tonic of that sort. Work and plain fare are what you
want; and I wish I had you here for a few months out of harm's
way. I'd Banting you, and fit you to run without puffing, and get
on without four or five meals a day. What an absurd hand that is
for a man! You ought to be ashamed of it!' And Mrs Jo caught up
the plump fist, with deep dimples at each knuckle, which was
fumbling distressfully at the buckle of the belt girt about a waist
far too large for a youth of his age.

'I can't help it – we all grow fat; it's in the family,' said Stuffy in
self-defence.

'All the more reason you should live carefully. Do you want to
die early, or be an invalid all your life?'

'No, ma'am!'

Stuffy looked so scared that Mrs Jo could not be hard upon his
budding sins, for they lay at his over-indulgent mother's door in a
great measure; so she softened the tone of her voice, and added,
with a little slap on the fat hand, as she used to do when it was
small enough to pilfer lumps of sugar from her bowl, 'Then be
careful; for a man writes his character in his face; and you don't
want gluttony and intemperance in yours, I know.'

'I'm sure I don't! Please make out a wholesome bill of fare, and
I'll stick to it, if I can. I *am* getting stout, and I don't like it; and my
liver's torpid, and I have palpitations and headache. Overwork,
mother says; but it may be overeating.' And Stuffy gave a sigh of
mingled regret for the good things he renounced, and relief as he
finished loosening his belt as soon as his hand was free.

'I will; follow it, and in a year you'll be a man and not a meal-
bag. Now, Dolly;' and Mrs Jo turned to the other culprit, who
shook in his shoes and wished he hadn't come.

'Are you studying French as industriously as you were last
winter?'

'No ma'am; I don't care for it – that is, I, I'm busy with G–
Greek just now,' answered Dolly, beginning bravely, quite in the
dark as to what that odd question meant till a sudden memory
made him stutter and look at his shoes with deep interest.

'Oh, he doesn't study it; only reads French novels and goes to the theatre when the Opera Bouffe is here,' said Stuffy, innocently confirming Mrs Jo's suspicions.

'So I understood; and that is what I want to speak about. Ted had a sudden desire to learn French in that way, from something you said, Dolly; so I went myself, and was quite satisfied that it was no place for a decent boy. Your men were out in full force; and I was glad to see that some of the younger ones looked as ashamed as I felt. The older fellows enjoyed it, and when we came out were waiting to take those painted girls to supper. Did you ever go with them?'

'Once.'

'Did you like it?'

'No, 'm; I – I came away early,' stammered Dolly, with a face as red as his splendid tie.

'I'm glad you have not lost the grace of blushing yet; but you will soon, if you keep up this sort of study and forget to be ashamed. The society of such women will unfit you for that of good ones, and lead you into trouble and sin and shame. Oh, why don't the city fathers stop that evil thing, when they know the harm it does? It made my heart ache to see those boys, who ought to be at home and in their beds, going off for a night of riot which would help to ruin some of them for ever.'

The youths looked scared at Mrs Jo's energetic protest against one of the fashionable pleasures of the day, and waited in conscience-stricken silence – Stuffy glad that he never went to those gay suppers, and Dolly deeply grateful that he 'came away early'. With a hand on either shoulder, and all the terrors smoothed from her brow, Mrs Jo went on in her most motherly tone, anxious to do for them what no other woman would, and do it kindly, 'My dear boys, if I didn't love you, I would not say these things. I know they are not pleasant; but my conscience won't let me hold my peace when a word may keep you from two of the great sins that curse the world and send so many young men to destruction. You are just beginning to feel the allurement of them, and soon it will be hard to turn away. Stop now, I beg of you, and not only save yourselves but help others by a brave example. Come to me if things worry you; don't be afraid or ashamed; I have heard many sadder confessions than any you are ever likely to bring me, and been able to comfort many poor fellows, gone wrong for want of a word in time. Do this, and you will be able to kiss your mothers with clean lips, and by and by have the right to ask innocent girls to love you.'

'Yes, 'm, thank you. I suppose you're right; but it's pretty hard work to toe the mark when ladies give you wine and gentlemen take their daughters to see Aimée,' said Dolly, foreseeing tribulations ahead though he knew it was time to 'pull up'.

'So it is; but all the more honour to those who are brave and wise enough to resist public opinion, and the easy-going morals of bad or careless men and women. Think of the persons whom you respect most, and in imitating them you will secure the respect of those who look up to you. I'd rather my boys should be laughed at and cold-shouldered by a hundred foolish fellows than lose what, once gone, no power can give them back – innocence and self-respect. I don't wonder you find it "hard to toe the mark", when books, pictures, ballrooms, theatres, and streets offer temptations; yet you *can* resist, if you try. Last winter Mrs Brooke used to worry about John's being out so late reporting; but when she spoke to him about the things he must see and hear on his way to and fro from the office at midnight, he said in his sober way, "I know what you mean, mother; but no fellow need to go wrong unless he *wants* to." '

'That's like the Deacon!' exclaimed Stuffy, with an approving smile on his fat face.

'I'm glad you told me that. He's right; and it's because he doesn't want to go wrong we all respect him so,' added Dolly, looking up now with an expression which assured his Mentor that the right string had been touched, and a spirit of emulation roused, more helpful, perhaps, than any words of hers. Seeing this, she was satisfied, and said, as she prepared to leave the bar before which her culprits had been tried and found guilty, but recommended to mercy, 'Then be to others what John is to you – a good example. Forgive me for troubling you, my dear lads, and remember my little preachment. I think it will do you good, though I may never know it. Chance words spoken in kindness often help amazingly; and that's what old people are here for – else their experience is of little use. Now, come and find the young folk. I hope I shall never have to shut the gates of Plumfield upon *you*, as I have on some of your "gentlemen". I mean to keep my boys and girls safe if I can, and this a wholesome place where the good old-fashioned virtues are lived and taught.'

Much impressed by that dire threat, Dolly helped her from her perch with deep respect; and Stuffy relieved her of her empty jugs, solemnly vowing to abstain from all fermented beverages except root beer, as long as feeble flesh could hold out. Of course they made light of 'Mother Bhaer's lecture' when they were alone – that was to be expected of 'men of our class' but in their secret souls they thanked her for giving their boyish consciences a jog, and more than once afterward had cause to remember gratefully that half-hour in the tennis court.

CHAPTER 17

Among the Maids

Although this story is about Jo's boys, her girls cannot be neglected, because they held a high place in this little republic, and especial care was taken to fit them to play their parts worthily in the great republic which offered them wider opportunities and more serious duties. To many the social influence was the better part of the training they received; for education is not confined to books, and the finest characters often graduate from no college, but make experience their master, and life their book. Others cared only for the mental culture, and were in danger of over-studying, under the delusion which pervades New England that learning must be had at all costs, forgetting that health and real wisdom are better. A third class of ambitious girls hardly knew what they wanted, but were hungry for whatever could fit them to face the world and earn a living, being driven by necessity, the urgency of some half-conscious talent, or the restlessness of strong young natures to break away from the narrow life which no longer satisfied.

At Plumfield all found something to help them; for the growing institution had not yet made its rules as fixed as the laws of the Medes and Persians, and believed so heartily in the right of all sexes, colours, creeds, and ranks to education, that there was room for everyone who knocked, and a welcome to the shabby youths from up country, the eager girls from the West, the awkward freedman or woman from the South, or the well-born student whose poverty made this college a possibility when other doors were barred. There still was prejudice, ridicule, neglect in high places, and prophecies of failure to contend against; but the Faculty was composed of cheerful, hopeful men and women who had seen greater reforms spring from smaller roots, and after stormy seasons blossom beautifully, to add prosperity and honour to the nation. So they worked on steadily and bided their time, full of increasing faith in their attempt as year after year their numbers grew, their plans succeeded, and the sense of usefulness in this most vital of all professions blessed them with its sweet rewards.

Among the various customs which had very naturally sprung up was one especially useful and interesting to 'the girls', as the young women liked to be called. It all grew out of the old sewing hour still kept up by the three sisters long after the little work-boxes had expanded into big baskets full of household mending. They were busy women, yet on Saturdays they tried to meet in one of the three sewing-rooms; for even classic Parnassus had its nook where Mrs Amy often sat among her servants, teaching them to make and mend, thereby giving them a respect for economy, since the rich lady did not scorn to darn her hose, and sew on buttons. In these household retreats, with books and work, and their daughters by them, they read and sewed and talked in the sweet privacy that domestic women love, and can make so helpful by a wise mixture of cooks and chemistry, table linen and theology, prosaic duties and good poetry.

Mrs Meg was the first to propose enlarging this little circle; for as she went her motherly rounds among the young women she found a sad lack of order, skill, and industry in this branch of education. Latin, Greek, the higher mathematics, and science of all sorts prospered finely; but the dust gathered on the work-baskets, frayed elbows went unheeded, and some of the blue stockings sadly needed mending. Anxious lest the usual sneer at learned women should apply to 'our girls', she gently lured two or three of the most untidy to her house, and made the hour so pleasant, the lesson so kindly, that they took the hint, were grateful for the favour, and asked to come again. Others soon begged to make the detested weekly duty lighter by joining the party, and soon it was a privilege so much desired that the old museum was refitted with sewing-machines, tables, rocking-chair, and a cheerful fireplace, so that, rain or shine, the needles might go on undisturbed.

Here Mrs Meg was in her glory, and stood wielding her big shears like a queen as she cut out white work, fitted dresses, and directed Daisy, her special aide, about the trimming of hats, and completing the lace and ribbon trifles which add grace to the simplest costume and save poor or busy girls so much money and time. Mrs Amy contributed taste, and decided the great question of colours and complexions; for few women, even the most learned, are without that desire to look well which makes many a plain face comely, as well as many a pretty one ugly for want of skill and knowledge of the fitness of things. She also took her turn to provide books for the readings, and as art was her forte she gave them selections from Ruskin, Hamerton, and Mrs Jameson, who is never old. Bess read these aloud as her contribution, and Josie took her turn at the romances, poetry, and plays her uncles recommended. Mrs Jo gave little lectures on health, religion, politics, and the various questions in which all should be interested, with copious extracts from Miss Cobbe's *Duties of Women*, Miss Brackett's *Education of American Girls*, Mrs Duffy's *No Sex in Education*, Mrs Woolson's *Dress Reform*, and many of the other excellent books wise women write for their sisters, now that they are waking up and asking, 'What shall we do?'

It was curious to see the prejudices melt away as ignorance was enlightened, indifference change to interest, and intelligent minds set thinking, while quick wits and lively tongues added spice to the discussions which inevitably followed. So the feet that wore the neatly mended hose carried wiser heads than before, the pretty gowns covered hearts warmed with higher purposes, and the hands that dropped the thimbles for pens, lexicons, and celestial globes, were better fitted for life's work, whether to rock cradles, tend the sick, or help on the great work of the world.

One day a brisk discussion arose concerning careers for women. Mrs Jo had read something on the subject and asked each of the dozen girls sitting about the room, what she intended to do on leaving college. The answers were as usual: 'I shall teach, help mother, study medicine, art,' etc.; but nearly all ended with, 'Till I marry.'

'But if you don't marry, what then?' asked Mrs Jo, feeling like a girl again as she listened to the answers, and watched the thoughtful, gay, or eager faces.

'Be old maids, I suppose. Horrid, but inevitable, since there are so many superfluous women,' answered a lively lass, too pretty to fear single blessedness unless she chose it.

'It is well to consider that fact, and fit yourselves to be useful, not superfluous women. That class, by the way, is largely made up of widows, I find; so don't consider it a slur on maidenhood.'

'That's a comfort! Old maids aren't sneered at half as much as they used to be, since some of them have grown famous and proved that woman isn't a half but a whole human being, and can stand alone.'

'Don't like it all the same. We can't all be like Miss Cobbe, Miss Nightingale, Miss Phelps, and the rest. So what can we do but sit in a corner and look on?' asked a plain girl with a dissatisfied expression.

'Cultivate cheerfulness and content, if nothing else. But there are so many little odd jobs waiting to be done that nobody need "sit idle and look on", unless she chooses,' said Mrs Meg, with a smile, laying on the girl's head the new hat she had just trimmed.

'Thank you very much. Yes, Mrs Brooke, I see; it's a little job, but it makes me neat and happy – and grateful,' she added, looking up with brighter eyes as she accepted the labour of love and the lesson as sweetly as they were given.

'One of the best and most beloved women I know has been doing odd jobs for the Lord for years, and will keep at it till her dear hands are folded in her coffin. All sorts of things she does – picks up neglected children and puts them in safe homes, saves lost girls, nurses poor women in trouble, sews, knits, trots, begs, works for the poor day after day with no reward but the thanks of the needy, the love and honour of the rich who make Saint Matilda their almoner. That's a life worth living; and I think that quiet little woman will get a higher seat in Heaven than many of those of whom the world has heard.'

'I know it's lovely, Mrs Bhaer; but it's dull for young folks. We do want a little fun before we buckle to,' said a Western girl with a wide-awake face.

'Have your fun, my dear; but if you must earn your bread, try to make it sweet with cheerfulness, not bitter with the daily regret that it isn't cake. I used to think mine was a very hard fate because I had to amuse a somewhat fretful old lady; but the books I read in that lonely library have been of immense use to me since, and the dear old soul bequeathed me Plumfield for my "cheerful service and affectionate care". I didn't deserve it, but I did use to try to be jolly and kind, and get as much honey out of duty as I could, thanks to my dear mother's help and advice.'

'Gracious! if I could earn a place like this, I'd sing all day and be an angel; but you have to take your chance, and get nothing for your pains, perhaps. I never do,' said the Westerner, who had a hard time with small means and large aspirations.

'Don't do it for the reward; but be sure it will come, though not in the shape you expect. I worked hard for fame and money one winter; but I got neither, and was much disappointed. A year afterwards I found I had earned two prizes: skill with my pen, and – Professor Bhaer.'

Mrs Jo's laugh was echoed blithely by the girls, who liked to have these conversations enlivened by illustrations from life.

'You are a very lucky woman,' began the discontented damsel, whose soul soared above new hats, welcome as they were, but did not quite know where to steer.

'Yet her name used to be "Luckless Jo", and she never had what she wanted till she had given up hoping for it,' said Mrs Meg.

'I'll give up hoping, then, right away, and see if my wishes will come. I only want to help my folks, and get a good school.'

'Take this proverb for your guide: "Get the distaff ready, and the Lord will send the flax",' answered Mrs Jo.

'We'd better all do that, if we are to be spinsters,' said the pretty one, adding gaily, 'I think I should like it, on the whole – they are so independent. My Aunt Jenny can do just what she likes, and ask no one's leave; but Ma has to consult Pa about everything. Yes, I'll give you my chance, Sally, and be a "superfluum", as Mr Plock says.'

'You'll be one of the first to go into bondage, see if you aren't. Much obliged, all the same.'

'Well, I'll get my distaff ready, and take whatever flax the Fates send – single, or double-twisted, as the powers please.'

'That is the right spirit, Nelly. Keep it up, and see how happy life will be with a brave heart, a willing hand, and plenty to do.'

'No one objects to plenty of domestic work or fashionable pleasure, I find; but the minute we begin to study, people tell us we can't bear it, and warn us to be very careful. I've tried the other things, and got so tired I came to college; though my people predict nervous exhaustion and an early death. Do you think there is any danger?' asked a stately girl, with an anxious glance at the blooming face reflected in the mirror opposite.

'Are you stronger or weaker than when you came two years ago, Miss Winthrop?'

'Stronger in body, and much happier in mind. I think I was dying of ennui; but the doctors called it inherited delicacy of constitution. That is why mamma is so anxious, and I wish not to go too fast.'

'Don't worry, my dear; that active brain of yours was starving for good food; it has plenty now, and plain living suits you better than luxury and dissipation. It is all nonsense about girls not being able to study as well as boys. Neither can bear cramming; but with proper care both are better for it; so enjoy the life your instinct led you to, and we will prove that wise headwork is a better cure for that sort of delicacy than tonics, and novels on the sofa, where far too many of our girls go to wreck nowadays. They burn the candle at both ends; and when they break down they blame the books, not the balls.'

'Dr Nan was telling me about a patient of hers who thought she had heart-complaint, till Nan made her take off her corsets, stopped her coffee and dancing all night, and made her eat, sleep, walk, and live regularly for a time; and now she's a brilliant cure. Common sense versus custom, Nan said.'

'I've had no headaches since I came here, and can do twice as much studying as I did at home. It's the air, I think, and the fun of going ahead of the boys,' said another girl, tapping her big forehead with her thimble, as if the lively brain inside was in good working order and enjoyed the daily gymnastics she gave it.

'Quality, not quantity, wins the day, you know. Our brains may be smaller, but I don't see that they fall short of what is required of them; and if I'm not mistaken, the largest-headed man in our class is the dullest,' said Nelly, with a solemn air which produced a gale of merriment; for all knew that the young Goliath she mentioned had been metaphorically slain by this quick-witted David on many a battlefield, to the great disgust of himself and his mates.

'Mrs Brooke, do I gauge on the right or the wrong side?' asked the best Greek scholar of her class, eyeing a black silk apron with a lost expression.

'The right, Miss Pierson; and leave a space between the tucks; it looks prettier so.'

'I'll never make another; but it will save my dresses from ink-stains, so I'm glad I've got it;' and the erudite Miss Pierson laboured on, finding it a harder task than any Greek root she ever dug up.

'We paper-stainers must learn how to make shields, or we are lost. I'll give you a pattern of the pinafore I used to wear in my "blood-and-thunder days", as we call them,' said Mrs Jo, trying to remember what became of the old tin-kitchen which used to hold her works.

'Speaking of writers reminds me that my ambition is to be a George Eliot, and thrill the world! It must be so splendid to know that one has such power, and to hear people own that one possesses a "masculine intellect"! I don't care for most women's novels, but hers are immense; don't you think so, Mrs Bhaer?' asked the girl with the big forehead, and torn braid on her skirt.

'Yes; but they don't thrill me as little Charlotte Brontë's books do. The brain is there, but the heart seems left out. I admire, but I don't love, George Eliot; and her life is far sadder to me than Miss Brontë's, because, in spite of the genius, love, and fame, she missed the light without which no soul is truly great, good, or happy.'

'Yes, 'm, I know; but still it's so romantic and sort of new and mysterious, and she *was* great in one sense. Her nerves and dyspepsia do rather destroy the illusion; but I adore famous people and mean to go and see all I can scare up in London someday.'

'You will find some of the best of them busy about just the work I recommend to you; and if you want to see a great lady, I'll tell you that Mrs Laurence means to bring one here today. Lady Abercrombie is lunching with her, and after seeing the college is to call on us. She especially wanted to see our sewing-school, as she is interested in things of this sort, and gets them up at home.'

'Bless me! I always imagined lords and ladies did nothing but ride round in a coach and six, go to balls, and be presented to the Queen in cocked hats, and trains and feathers,' exclaimed an artless young person from the wilds of Maine, whither an illustrated paper occasionally wandered.

'Not at all; Lord Abercrombie is over here studying up our American prison system, and my lady is busy with the schools – both very high-born, but the simplest and most sensible people I've met this long time. They are neither of them young nor handsome, and dress plainly; so don't expect anything splendid. Mr Laurence was telling me last night about a friend of his who met my lord in the hall, and owing to a rough greatcoat and a red face, mistook him for a coachman, and said, "Now, my man, what do you want here?" Lord Abercrombie mildly mentioned who he was, and that he had come to dinner. And the poor host was much afflicted, saying afterward, "Why didn't he wear his stars and garters? then a fellow would know he was a lord." '

The girls laughed again, and a general rustle betrayed that each was prinking a bit before the titled guest arrived. Even Mrs Jo settled her collar, and Mrs Meg felt if her cap was right, while Bess shook out her curls and Josie boldly consulted the glass; for they were women, in spite of philosophy and philanthropy.

'Shall we all rise?' asked one girl, deeply impressed by the impending honour.

'It would be courteous.'

'Shall we shake hands?'

'No, I'll present you *en masse*, and your pleasant faces will be introduction enough.'

'I wish I'd worn my best dress. Ought to have told us,' whispered Sally.

'Won't my folks be surprised when I tell them we have had a real lady to call on us?' said another.

'Don't look as if you'd never seen a gentlewoman before, Milly. We are not all fresh from the wilderness,' added the stately damsel who, having Mayflower ancestors, felt that she was the equal of all the crowned heads of Europe.

'Hush, she's coming! Oh, my heart, what a bonnet!' cried the gay girl in a stage whisper; and every eye was demurely fixed upon the busy hands as the door opened to admit Mrs Laurence and her guest.

It *was* rather a shock to find, after the general introduction was over, that this daughter of a hundred earls was a stout lady in a plain gown, and a rather weather-beaten bonnet, with a bag of papers in one hand and a notebook in the other. But the face was full of benevolence, the sonorous voice very kind, the genial manners very winning, and about the whole person an indescribable air of high breeding which made beauty of no consequence, costume soon forgotten, and the moment memorable to the keen-eyed girls whom nothing escaped.

A little chat about the rise, growth, and success of this particular class, and then Mrs Jo led the conversation to the English lady's work, anxious to show her pupils how rank dignifies labour, and charity blesses wealth.

It was good for these girls to hear of the evening-schools supported and taught by women whom they knew and honoured; of Miss Cobbe's eloquent protest winning the protection of the law for abused wives; Mrs Butler saving the lost; Mrs Taylor, who devoted one room in her historic house to a library for the servants; Lord Shaftesbury, busy with his new tenement houses in the slums of London; of prison reforms; and all the brave work being done in God's name by the rich and great for the humble and the poor. It impressed them more than many quiet home lectures would have done, and roused an ambition to help when their time should come, well knowing that even in glorious America there is still plenty to be done before she is what she should be – truly just, and free, and great. They were also quick to see that Lady Abercrombie treated all there as her equals, from stately Mrs Laurence, to little Josie, taking notes of everything and privately resolving to have some thick-soled English boots as soon as possible. No one would have guessed that she had a big house in London, a castle in Wales, and a grand country seat in Scotland, as she spoke of Parnassus with admiration, Plumfield as a 'dear old home', and the college as an honour to all concerned in it. At that, of course, every head went up a little, and when my lady left, every hand was ready for the hearty shake the noble Englishwoman gave them, with words they long remembered, 'I am very pleased to see this much-neglected branch of a woman's education so well conducted here, and I have to thank my friend Mrs Laurence for one of the most charming pictures I've seen in America – Penelope among her maids.'

A group of smiling faces watched the stout boots trudge away, respectful glances followed the shabby bonnet till it was out of sight, and the girls felt a truer respect for their titled guest than if she had come in the coach and six, with all her diamonds on.

'I feel better about the "odd jobs" now. I only wish I could do them as well as Lady Abercrombie does,' said one.

'I thanked my stars my buttonholes were nice, for she looked at them and said, "Quite workmanlike, upon me word",' added another, feeling that her gingham gown had come to honour.

'Her manners were as sweet and kind as Mrs Brooke's. Not a bit stiff or condescending, as I expected. I see now what you meant, Mrs Bhaer, when you said once that well-bred people were the same all the world over.'

Mrs Meg bowed her thanks for the compliment, and Mrs Bhaer said, 'I know them when I see them, but never shall be a model of deportment myself. I'm glad you enjoyed the little visit. Now, if you young people don't want England to get ahead of us in many ways, you must bestir yourselves and keep abreast; for our sisters are in earnest, you see, and don't waste time worrying about their sphere, but make it wherever duty calls them.'

'We will do our best, ma'am,' answered the girls heartily, and trooped away with their work-baskets, feeling that though they might never be Harriet Martineaus, Elizabeth Brownings, or George Eliots, they might become noble, useful, and independent women, and earn for themselves some sweet title from the grateful lips of the poor, better than any a queen could bestow.

CHAPTER 18

Class Day

The clerk of the weather evidently has a regard for young people, and sends sunshine for class days as often as he can. An especially lovely one shone over Plumfield as this interesting anniversary came round, bringing the usual accompaniments of roses, strawberries, white-gowned girls, beaming youths, proud friends, and stately dignitaries full of well-earned satisfaction with the yearly harvest. As Laurence College was a mixed one, the presence of young women as students gave to the occasion a grace and animation entirely wanting where the picturesque half of creation appear merely as spectators. The hands that turned the pages of wise books also possessed the skill to decorate the hall with flowers; eyes tired with study shone with hospitable warmth on the assembling guests; and under the white muslins beat hearts as full of ambition, hope, and courage as those agitating the broadcloth of the ruling sex.

College Hill, Parnassus, and old Plum swarmed with cheery faces, as guests, students, and professors hurried to and fro in the pleasant excitement of arriving and receiving. Everyone was welcomed cordially, whether he rolled up in a fine carriage, or trudged afoot to see the good son or daughter come to honour on the happy day that rewarded many a mutual sacrifice. Mr Laurie and his wife were on the reception committee, and their lovely house was overflowing. Mrs Meg, with Daisy and Jo as aides, was in demand among the girls, helping on belated toilettes, giving an eye to spreads, and directing the decorations. Mrs Jo had her hands full as President's lady, and the mother of Ted; for it took all the power and skill of that energetic woman to get her son into his Sunday best.

Not that he objected to be well arrayed; far from it; he adored good clothes, and owing to his great height already revelled in a dress-suit, bequeathed him by a dandy friend. The effect was very funny; but he would wear it in spite of the jeers of his mates, and sighed vainly for a beaver, because his stern parent drew the line there. He pleaded that English lads of ten wore them and were 'no end nobby'; but his mother only answered, with a consoling pat of the yellow mane, 'My child, you are absurd enough now; if I let you add a tall hat, Plumfield wouldn't hold either of us, such would be the scorn and derision of all beholders. Content yourself with looking like the ghost of a waiter, and don't ask for the most ridiculous headgear in the known world.'

Denied this noble badge of manhood, Ted soothed his wounded soul by appearing in collars of an amazing height and stiffness, and ties which were the wonder of all female eyes. This freak was a sort of vengeance on his hard-hearted mother; for the collars drove the laundress to despair, never being just right, and the ties required such art in the tying that three women sometimes laboured long before – like Beau Brummel – he turned from a heap of 'failures' with the welcome words, 'That will do.' Rob was devoted on these trying occasions, his own toilet being distinguished only by its speed, simplicity, and neatness. Ted was usually in a frenzy before he was suited, and roars, whistles, commands, and groans were heard from the den wherein the Lion raged and the Lamb patiently toiled. Mrs Jo bore it till boots were hurled and a rain of hairbrushes set in, then, fearing for the safety of her eldest, she would go to the rescue, and by a wise mixture of fun and authority finally succeed in persuading Ted that he was 'a thing of beauty', if not 'a joy for ever'. At last he would stalk majestically forth, imprisoned in collars compared to which those worn by Dickens's afflicted Biler were trifles not worth mentioning. The dress-coat was a little loose in the shoulders, but allowed a noble expanse of glossy bosom to be seen, and with a delicate handkerchief negligently drooping at the proper angle, had a truly fine effect. Boots that shone, and likewise pinched, appeared at one end of the 'long, black clothes-pin' – as Josie called him – and a youthful but solemn face at the other, carried at an angle which, if long continued, would have resulted in spinal curvature. Light gloves, a cane, and – oh, bitter drop in the cup of joy! – an ignominious straw hat, not to mention a choice floweret in the buttonhole, and a festoon of watch-guard below, finished off this impressive boy.

'How's that for style?' he asked, appearing to his mother and cousins whom he was to escort to the hall on this particular occasion.

A shout of laughter greeted him, followed by exclamations of horror; for he had artfully added the little blond moustache he often wore when acting. It was very becoming, and seemed the only balm to heal the wound made by the loss of the beloved hat.

'Take it off this moment, you audacious boy! What *would* your father say to such a prank on this day when we must all behave our best?' said Mrs Jo, trying to frown, but privately thinking that among the many youths about her none were so beautiful and original as her long son.

'Let him wear it, Aunty; it's so becoming. No one will ever guess he isn't eighteen at least,' cried Josie, to whom disguise of any sort was always charming.

'Father won't observe it; he'll be absorbed in his bigwigs and the girls. No matter if he does, he'll enjoy the joke and introduce me as his oldest son. Rob is nowhere when I'm in full fig;' and Ted took the stage with a tragic stalk, like Hamlet in a tailcoat and choker.

'My son, obey me!' and when Mrs Jo spoke in that tone her word was law. Later, however, the moustache appeared, and many strangers firmly believed that there were three young Bhaers. So Ted found one ray of joy to light his gloom.

Mr Bhaer was a proud and happy man when, at the appointed hour, he looked down upon the parterre of youthful faces before him, thinking of the 'little gardens' in which he had hopefully and faithfully sowed good seed years ago, and from which this beautiful harvest seemed to have sprung. Mr March's fine old face shone with the serenest satisfaction, for this was the dream of his life fulfilled after patient waiting; and the love and reverence in the countenances of the eager young men and women looking up at him plainly showed that the reward he coveted was his in fullest measure. Laurie always effaced himself on these occasions as much as courtesy would permit; for everyone spoke gratefully in ode, poem, and oration of the founder of the college and noble dispenser of his beneficence. The three sisters beamed with pride as they sat among the ladies, enjoying, as only women can, the honour done the men they loved; while 'the original Plums', as the younger ones called themselves, regarded the whole affair as their work, receiving the curious, admiring, or envious glances of strangers with a mixture of dignity and delight rather comical to behold.

The music was excellent, and well it might be when Apollo waved the baton. The poems were – as usual on such occasions – of varied excellence, as the youthful speakers tried to put old truths into new words, and made them forceful by the enthusiasm of their earnest faces and fresh voices. It was beautiful to see the eager interest with which the girls listened to some brilliant brother student, and applauded him with a rustle as of wind over a bed of flowers. It was still more significant and pleasant to watch the young men's faces when a slender white figure stood out against the background of black-coated dignitaries, and with cheeks that flushed and paled, and lips that trembled till earnest purpose conquered maiden fear, spoke to them straight out of a woman's heart and brain concerning the hopes and doubts, the aspirations and rewards all must know, desire, and labour for. This clear, sweet voice seemed to reach and rouse all that was noblest in the souls of these youths, and to set a seal upon the years of comradeship which made them sacred and memorable for ever.

Alice Heath's oration was unanimously pronounced the success of the day; for without being flowery or sentimental, as is too apt to be the case with these first efforts of youthful orators, it was earnest, sensible, and so inspiring that she left the stage in a storm of applause, the good fellows being as much fired by her stirring appeal to 'march shoulder to shoulder', as if she had chanted the 'Marseillaise' then and there. One young man was so excited that he nearly rushed out of his seat to receive her as she hastened to hide herself among her mates, who welcomed her with faces full of tender pride and tearful eye. A prudent sister detained him, however, and in a moment he was able to listen with composure to the President's remarks.

They were worth listening to, for Mr Bhaer spoke like a father to the children whom he was dismissing to the battle of life; and his tender, wise, and helpful words lingered in their hearts long after the praise was forgotten. Then came other exercises peculiar to Plumfield, and the end. Why the roof did not fly off when the sturdy lungs of the excited young men pealed out the closing hymn will for ever be a mystery; but it remained firm, and only the fading garlands vibrated as the waves of music rolled up and died away, leaving sweet echoes to haunt the place for another year.

Dinners and spreads consumed the afternoon, and at sunset came a slight lull as everyone sought some brief repose before the festivities of the evening began. The President's reception was one of the enjoyable things in store, also dancing on Parnassus, and as much strolling, singing, and flirting, as could be compressed into a few hours by youths and maidens just out of school.

Carriages were rolling about, and gay groups on piazzas, lawns, and window-seats idly speculated as to who the distinguished guests might be. The appearance of a very dusty vehicle loaded with trunks at Mr Bhaer's hospitably open door caused much curious comment among the loungers, especially as two rather foreign-looking gentlemen sprang out, followed by two young ladies, all four being greeted with cries of joy and much embracing by the Bhaers. Then they all disappeared into the house, the luggage followed, and the watchers were left to wonder who the mysterious strangers were, till a fair collegian declared that they must be the Professor's nephews, one of whom was expected on his wedding journey.

She was right; Franz proudly presented his blonde and buxom bride, and she was hardly kissed and blessed when Emil led up his bonny English Mary, with the rapturous announcement, 'Uncle, Aunt Jo, here's another daughter! Have you room for *my* wife, too?'

There could be no doubt of that; and Mary was with difficulty rescued from the glad embraces of her new relatives, who, remembering all the young pair had suffered together, felt that this was the natural and happy ending of the long voyage so perilously begun.

'But why not tell us, and let us be ready for two brides instead of one?' asked Mrs Jo, looking as usual rather demoralised in a wrapper and crimping-pins, having rushed down from her chamber, where she was preparing for the labours of the evening.

'Well, I remembered what a good joke you all considered Uncle Laurie's marriage, and I thought I'd give you another nice little surprise,' laughed Emil. 'I'm off duty, and it seemed best to take advantage of wind and tide, and come along as convoy to the old boy here. We hoped to get in last night, but couldn't fetch it, so here we are in time for the end of the jollification, anyway.'

'Ah, my sons, it is too feeling-full to see you both so happy and again in the old home. I haf no words to outpour my gratitude, and can only ask of the dear Gott in Himmel to bless and keep you all,' cried Professor Bhaer, trying to gather all four into his arms at once, while tears rolled down his cheeks, and his English failed him.

An April shower cleared the air and relieved the full hearts of the happy family; then of course everyone began to talk – Franz and Ludmilla in German with the uncle, Emil and Mary with the aunts; and round this group gathered the young folk, clamouring to hear all about the wreck, and the rescue, and the homeward voyage. It was a very different story from the written one; and as they listened to Emil's graphic words, with Mary's soft voice breaking in now and then to add some fact that brought out the courage, patience, and self-sacrifice he so lightly touched upon, it became a solemn and pathetic thing to see and hear these happy creatures tell of that great danger and deliverance.

'I never hear the patter of rain now that I don't want to say my prayers; and as for women, I'd like to take my hat off to every one of 'em, for they are braver than any man I ever saw,' said Emil, with the new gravity that was as becoming to him as the new gentleness with which he treated everyone.

'If women are brave, some men are as tender and self-sacrificing as women. I know one who in the night slipped his share of food into a girl's pocket, though starving himself, and sat for hours rocking a sick man in his arms that he might get a little sleep. No, love, I will tell, and you must let me!' cried Mary, holding in both her own the hand he laid on her lips to silence her.

'Only did my duty. If that torment had lasted much longer I might have been as bad as poor Barry and the boatswain. Wasn't that an awful night?' And Emil shuddered as he recalled it.

'Don't think of it, dear. Tell about the happy days on the *Urania*, when Papa grew better and we were all safe and homeward bound,' said Mary, with the trusting look and comforting touch which seemed to banish the dark and recall the bright side of that terrible experience.

Emil cheered up at once, and sitting with his arm about his 'dear lass', in true sailor fashion told the happy ending of the tale.

'Such a jolly old time as we had at Hamburg! Uncle Hermann couldn't do enough for the captain, and while Mamma took care of him, Mary looked after me. I had to go into dock for repairs; fire hurt my eyes, and watching for a sail and want of sleep made 'em as hazy as a London fog. She was pilot and brought me in all right, you see, only I couldn't part company, so she came aboard as first mate, and I'm bound straight for glory now.'

'Hush! that's silly, dear,' whispered Mary, trying in her turn to stop him, with English shyness about tender topics. But he took the soft hand in his, and proudly surveying the one ring it wore, went on with the air of an admiral aboard his flagship.

'The captain proposed waiting a spell; but I told him we weren't like to see any rougher weather than we'd pulled through together, and if we didn't know one another after such a year as this, we never should. I was sure I shouldn't be worth my pay without this hand on the wheel; so I had my way, and my brave little woman has shipped for the long voyage. God bless her!'

'Shall you really sail with him?' asked Daisy, admiring her courage, but shrinking with cat-like horror from the water.

'I'm not afraid,' answered Mary, with a loyal smile. 'I've proved my captain in fair weather and in foul, and if he is ever wrecked again, I'd rather be with him than waiting and watching ashore.'

'A true woman, and a born sailor's wife! You are a happy man, Emil, and I'm sure *this* trip will be a prosperous one,' cried Mrs Jo, delighted with the briny flavour of this courtship. 'Oh, my dear boy, I always felt you'd come back, and when everyone else despaired I never gave up, but insisted that you were clinging to the main-top jib somewhere on that dreadful sea;' and Mrs Jo illustrated her faith by grasping Emil with a truly Pillycoddian gesture.

'Of course I was!' answered Emil heartily; 'and my "main-top jib" in this case was the thought of what you and Uncle said to me. That kept me up; and among the million thoughts that came to me during those long nights none was clearer than the idea of the red strand, you remember – English navy, and all that. I liked the notion, and resolved that if a bit of my cable was left afloat, the red stripe should be there.'

'And it was, my dear, it was! Captain Hardy testifies to that, and here is your reward;' and Mrs Jo kissed Mary with a maternal tenderness which betrayed that she liked the English rose better than the blue-eyed German *Kornblumen*, sweet and modest though it was.

Emil surveyed the little ceremony with complacency, saying, as he looked about the room which he never thought to see again, 'Odd, isn't it, how clearly trifles come back to one in times of danger? As we floated there, half-starved, and in despair, I used to think I heard the bells ringing here, and Ted tramping downstairs, and you calling, "Boys, boys, it's time to get up!" I actually smelt the coffee we used to have, and one night I nearly cried when I woke from a dream of Asia's ginger cookies. I declare, it was one of the bitterest disappointments of my life to face hunger with that spicy smell in my nostrils. If you've got any, do give me one!'

A pitiful murmur broke from all the aunts and cousins, and Emil was at once borne away to feast on the desired cookies, a supply always being on hand. Mrs Jo and her sister joined the other group, glad to hear what Franz was saying about Nat.

'The minute I saw how thin and shabby he was, I knew that something was wrong; but he made light of it, and was so happy over our visit and news that I let him off with a brief confession, and went to Professor Baumgarten and Bergmann. From them I learned the whole story of his spending more money than he ought and trying to atone for it by unnecessary work and sacrifice. Baumgarten thought it would do him good, so kept his secret till I came. It did him good, and he's paid his debts and earned his bread by the sweat of his brow, like an honest fellow.'

'I like that much in Nat. It is, as I said, a lesson, and he learns it well. He proves himself a man, and has deserved the place Bergmann offers him,' said Mr Bhaer, looking well pleased as Franz added some facts already recorded.

'I told you, Meg, that he had good stuff in him, and love for Daisy would keep him straight. Dear lad, I wish I had him here this moment!' cried Mrs Jo, forgetting in delight the doubts and anxieties which had troubled her for months past.

'I am very glad, and suppose I shall give in as I always do, especially now that the epidemic rages so among us. You and Emil have set all their heads in a ferment, and Josie will be demanding a lover before I can turn round,' answered Mrs Meg, in a tone of despair.

But her sister saw that she was touched by Nat's trials, and hastened to add the triumphs, that the victory might be complete, for success is always charming.

'This offer of Herr Bergmann is a good one, isn't it?' she asked, though Mr Laurie had already satisfied her on that point when Nat's letter brought the news.

'Very fine in every way. Nat will get capital drill in Bachmeister's orchestra, see London in a delightful way, and if he suits come home with them, well started among the violins. No great honour, but a sure thing and a step up. I congratulated him, and he was very jolly over it, saying, like the true lover he is, "Tell Daisy; be sure and tell her all about it." I'll leave that to you, Aunt Meg, and you can also break it gently to her that the old boy had a fine blond beard. Very becoming; hides his weak mouth, and gives a noble air to his big eyes and "Mendelssohnian brow", as a gushing girl called it. Ludmilla has a photo of it for you.'

This amused them; and they listened to many other interesting bits of news which kind Franz, even in his own happiness, had not forgotten to remember for his friend's sake. He talked so well, and painted Nat's patient and pathetic shifts so vividly, that Mrs Meg was half won; though if she had learned of the Minna episode and the fiddling in beer gardens and streets, she might not have relented so soon. She stored up all she heard, however, and, womanlike, promised herself a delicious talk with Daisy, in which she would allow herself to melt by degrees, and perhaps change the doubtful 'We shall see' to a cordial 'He has done well; be happy, dear'.

In the midst of this agreeable chat the sudden striking of a clock recalled Mrs Jo from romance to reality, and she exclaimed, with a clutch at her crimping-pins, 'My blessed people, you must eat and rest; and I must dress, or receive in this disgraceful rig. Meg, will you take Ludmilla and Mary upstairs and see to them? Franz knows the way to the dining-room. Fritz, come with me and be made tidy, for what with heat and emotion, we are both perfect wrecks.'

CHAPTER 19

White Roses

While the travellers refreshed, and Mrs President struggled into her best gown, Josie ran into the garden to gather flowers for the brides. The sudden arrival of these interesting beings had quite enchanted the romantic girl, and her head was full of heroic rescues, tender admiration, dramatic situations, and feminine wonder as to whether the lovely creatures would wear their veils or not. She was standing before a great bush of white roses, culling the most perfect for the bouquets which she meant to tie with the ribbon festooned over her arm, and lay on the toilette tables of the new cousins, as a delicate attention. A step startled her, and looking up she saw her brother coming down the path with folded arms, bent head, and the absent air of one absorbed in deep thought.

'Sophy Wackles,' said the sharp child, with a superior smile, as she sucked her thumb just pricked by a too eager pull at the thorny branches.

'What are you at here, Mischief?' asked Demi, with an Irving-esque start, as he felt rather than saw a disturbing influence in his daydream.

'Getting flowers for "our brides". Don't you wish you had one?' answered Josie, to whom the word 'mischief' suggested her favourite amusement.

'A bride or a flower?' asked Demi calmly, though he eyed the blooming bush as if it had a sudden and unusual interest for him.

'Both; you get the one, and I'll give you the other.'

'Wish I could!' and Demi picked a little bud, with a sigh that went to Josie's warm heart.

'Why don't you, then? It's lovely to see people so happy. Now's a good time to do it if you ever mean to. She will be going away for ever soon.'

'Who?' and Demi pulled a half-opened bud, with a sudden colour in his own face; which sign of confusion delighted little Jo.

'Don't be a hypocrite. You know I mean Alice. Now, Jack, I'm fond of you, and want to help; it's so interesting – all these lovers and weddings and things, and we ought to have our share. So you take my advice and speak up like a man, and make sure of Alice before she goes.'

Demi laughed at the seriousness of the small girl's advice; but he liked it, and showed that it suited him by saying blandly, instead of snubbing her as usual, 'You are very kind, child. Since you are so wise, could you give me a hint how I'd better "speak up", as you elegantly express it?'

'Oh, well, there are various ways, you know. In plays the lovers go down on their knees; but that's awkward when they have long legs. Ted never does it well, though I drill him for hours. You could say, "Be mine, be mine!" like the old man who threw cucumbers over the wall to Mrs Nickleby, if you want to be gay and easy; or you could write a poetical pop. You've tried it, I dare say.'

'But seriously, Jo, I do love Alice, and I think she knows it. I want to tell her so; but I lose my head when I try, and don't care to make a fool of myself. Thought you might suggest some pretty way; you read so much poetry and are so romantic.'

Demi tried to express himself clearly, but forgot his dignity and his usual reserve in the sweet perplexity of his love, and asked his little sister to teach him how to put the question which a single word can answer. The arrival of his happy cousins had scattered all his wise plans and brave resolutions to wait still longer. The Christmas play had given him courage to hope, and the oration today had filled him with tender pride; but the sight of those blooming brides and beaming grooms was too much for him, and he panted to secure his Alice without an hour's delay. Daisy was his confidante in all things but this; a brotherly feeling of sympathy had kept him from telling her his hopes, because her own were forbidden. His mother was rather jealous of any girl he admired; but knowing that she liked Alice, he loved on and enjoyed his secret alone, meaning soon to tell her all about it.

Now suddenly Josie and the rose bush seemed to suggest a speedy end to his tender perplexities; and he was moved to accept her aid as the netted lion did that of the mouse.

'I think I'll write,' he was slowly beginning, after a pause during which both were trying to strike out a new and brilliant idea.

'I've got it! perfectly lovely! just suit her, and you too, being a poet!' cried Josie, with a skip.

'What is it? Don't be ridiculous, please,' begged the bashful lover, eager, but afraid of this sharp-tongued bit of womanhood.

'I read in one of Miss Edgeworth's stories about a man who offers three roses to his lady – a bud, a half-blown, and a full-blown rose. I don't remember which she took; but it's a pretty way; and Alice knows about it because she was there when we read it. Here are all kinds; you've got the two buds, pick the sweetest rose you can find, and I'll tie them up and put them in her room. She is coming to dress with Daisy, so I can do it nicely.'

Demi mused a moment with his eyes on the bridal bush, and a smile came over his face so unlike any it had ever worn before, that Josie was touched, and looked away as if she had no right to see the dawn of the great passion which, while it lasts, makes a young man as happy as a god.

'Do it,' was all he said, and gathered a full-blown rose to finish his floral love-message.

Charmed to have a finger in this romantic pie, Josie tied a graceful bow of ribbon about the stems, and finished her last nosegay with much content, while Demi wrote upon a card:

DEAR ALICE – You know what the flowers mean. Will you wear one or all tonight, and make me still prouder, fonder, and happier than I am?

Yours entirely,

JOHN

Offering this to his sister, he said in a tone that made her feel the deep importance of her mission, 'I trust you, Jo. This means everything to me. No jokes, dear, if you love me.'

Josie's answer was a kiss that promised all things; and then she ran away to do her 'gentle spiriting', like Ariel, leaving Demi to dream among the roses like Ferdinand.

Mary and Ludmilla were charmed with their bouquets; and the giver had the delight of putting some of the flowers into the dark hair and the light as she played maid at the toilettes of 'our brides', which consoled her for a disappointment in the matter of veils.

No one helped Alice dress; for Daisy was in the next room with her mother; and not even their loving eyes saw the welcome which the little posy received, nor the tears and smiles and blushes that came and went as she read the note and pondered what answer she should give. There was no doubt about the one she *wished* to give; but duty held her back; for at home there was an invalid mother and an old father. She was needed there, with all the help she could now bring by the acquirements four years of faithful study had given her. Love looked very sweet, and a home of her own with John a little heaven on earth; but not yet. And she slowly laid away the full-blown rose as she sat before the mirror, thinking over the great question of her life.

Was it wise and kind to ask him to wait, to bind him by any promise, or even to put into words the love and honour she felt for him? No; it would be more generous to make the sacrifice alone, and spare him the pain of hope deferred. He was young; he would forget; and she would do her duty better, perhaps, if no impatient lover waited for her. With eyes that saw but dimly, and a hand that lingered on the stem he had stripped of thorns, she laid the half-blown flower by the rose, and asked herself if even the little bud might be worn. It looked very poor and pale beside the others; yet being in the self-sacrificing mood which real love brings, she felt that even a small hope was too much to give, if she could not follow it up with more.

As she sat looking sadly down on the symbols of an affection that grew dearer every moment, she listened half unconsciously to the murmur of voices in the adjoining room. Open windows, thin partitions, and the stillness of summer twilight made it impossible to help hearing, and in a few moments more she could not refrain; for they were talking of John.

'So nice of Ludmilla to bring us all bottles of real German cologne! Just what we need after this tiring day! Be sure John has his! He likes it so!'

'Yes, Mother. Did you see him jump up when Alice ended her oration? He'd have gone to her if I hadn't held him back. I don't wonder he was pleased and proud. I spoilt my gloves clapping, and quite forgot my dislike of seeing women on platforms, she was so earnest and unconscious and sweet after the first moment.'

'Has he said anything to you, dear?'

'No; and I guess why. The kind boy thinks it would make me unhappy. It wouldn't. But I know his ways; so I wait, and hope all will go well with him.'

'It must. No girl in her senses would refuse our John, though he isn't rich, and never will be. Daisy, I've been longing to tell you what he did with his money. He told me last night, and I've had no time since to tell you. He sent poor young Barton to the hospital, and kept him there till his eyes were saved – a costly thing to do. But the man can work now and care for his old parents. He was in despair, sick and poor, and too proud to beg; and our dear boy found it out, and took every penny he had, and never told even his mother till she made him.'

Alice did not hear what Daisy answered, for she was busy with her own emotions – happy ones now, to judge from the smile that shone in her eyes and the decided gesture with which she put the little bud in her bosom, as if she said, 'He deserves some reward for that good deed, and he shall have it.'

Mrs Meg was speaking, and still of John, when she could hear again, 'Some people would call it unwise and reckless, when John has so little; but I think his first investment a safe and good one, for "he who giveth to the poor lendeth to the Lord"; and I was so pleased and proud, I wouldn't spoil it by offering him a penny.'

'It is his having nothing to offer that keeps him silent, I think. He is so honest, he won't ask till he has much to give. But he forgets that love is everything. I know he's rich in that; I see and feel it; and any woman should be glad to get it.'

'Right, dear. I felt just so, and was willing to work and wait with and for *my* John.'

'So she will be, and I hope they will find it out. But she is so dutiful and good, I'm afraid she won't let herself be happy. You would like it, Mother?'

'Heartily; for a better, nobler girl doesn't live. She is all I want for my son; and I don't mean to lose the dear, brave creature if I can help it. Her heart is big enough for both love and duty; and they can wait more happily if they do it together – for wait they must, of course.'

'I'm so glad *his* choice suits you, mother, and *he* is spared the saddest sort of disappointment.'

Daisy's voice broke there; and a sudden rustle, followed by a soft murmur, seemed to tell that she was in her mother's arms, seeking and finding comfort there.

Alice heard no more, and shut her window with a guilty feeling but a shining face; for the proverb about listeners failed here, and she had learned more than she dared to hope. Things seemed to change suddenly; she felt that her heart *was* large enough for both love and duty; she knew now that she would be welcomed by mother and sister; and the memory of Daisy's less happy fate, Nat's weary probation, the long delay, and possible separation for ever – all came before her so vividly that prudence seemed cruelty; self-sacrifice, sentimental folly; and anything but the whole truth, disloyalty to her lover. As she thought thus, the half-blown rose went to join the bud; and then, after a pause, she slowly kissed the perfect rose, and added it to the tell-tale group, saying to herself with a sort of sweet solemnity, as if the words were a vow, 'I'll love and work and wait with and for my John.'

It was well for her that Demi was absent when she stole down to join the guests who soon began to flow through the house in a steady stream. The new brightness which touched her usually thoughtful face was easily explained by the congratulations she received as orator, and the slight agitation observable, when a fresh batch of gentlemen approached soon passed, as none of them noticed the flowers she wore over a very happy heart. Demi meantime was escorting certain venerable personages about the college, and helping his grandfather entertain them with discussion of the Socratic method of instruction, Pythagoras, Pestalozzi, Froebel, and the rest, whom he devoutly wished at the bottom of the Red Sea, and no wonder, for his head and his heart were full of love and roses, hopes and fears. He piloted the 'potent, grave, and reverend seigniors' safely down to Plumfield at last, and landed them before his uncle and aunt Bhaer, who were receiving in state, the one full of genuine delight in all men and things, the other suffering martyrdom with a smile, as she stood shaking hand after hand, and affecting utter unconsciousness of the sad fact that ponderous Professor Plock had camped upon the train of her state and festival velvet gown.

With a long sigh of relief Demi glanced about him for the beloved girl. Most persons would have looked some time before any particular angel could be discovered among the white-robed throng in parlours, hall, and study; but his eye went – like the needle to the pole – to the corner where a smooth dark head, with its braided crown, rose like a queen's, he thought, above the crowd which surrounded her. Yes, she has a flower at her throat; one, two, oh, blessed sight! he saw it all across the room, and gave a rapturous sigh which caused Miss Perry's frizzled crop to wave with a sudden gust. He did *not* see the rose, for it was hidden by a fold of lace; and it was well, perhaps, that bliss came by instalments, or he might have electrified the assembled multitude by flying to his idol, there being no Daisy to clutch him by the coat-tail. A stout lady, thirsting for information, seized him at that thrilling moment, and he was forced to point out celebrities with a saintly patience which deserved a better reward than it received; for a certain absence of mind and incoherence of speech at times caused the ungrateful dowager to whisper to the first friend she met after he had escaped, 'I saw no wine at any of the spreads; but it is plain that young Brooke has had too much. Quite gentlemanly, but evidently a trifle intoxicated, my dear.'

Ah, so he was! but with a diviner wine than any that ever sparkled at a class-day lunch, though many collegians know the taste of it; and when the old lady was disposed of, he gladly turned to find the young one, bent on having a single word. He saw her standing by the piano now, idly turning over music as she talked with several gentlemen. Hiding his impatience under an air of scholastic repose, Demi hovered near, ready to advance when the happy moment came, wondering meantime why elderly persons persisted in absorbing young ones instead of sensibly sitting in corners with their contemporaries. The elderly persons in question retired at length, but only to be replaced by two impetuous youths who begged Miss Heath to accompany them to Parnassus and join the dance. Demi thirsted for their blood, but was appeased by hearing George and Dolly say, as they lingered a moment after her refusal, 'Really, you know, I'm quite converted to co-education and almost wish I'd remained here. It gives a grace to study, a sort of relish even to Greek to see charming girls at it,' said Stuffy, who found the feast of learning so dry, any sauce was welcome; and he felt as if he had discovered a new one.

'Yes, by Jove! we fellows will have to look out or you'll carry off all the honours. You were superb today, and held us all like magic, though it was so hot there, I really think I couldn't have stood it for anyone else,' added Dolly, labouring to be gallant and really offering a touching proof of devotion; for the heat melted his collar, took the curl out of his hair, and ruined his gloves.

'There is room for all; and if you will leave us the books, we will cheerfully yield the baseball, boating, dancing, and flirting, which seem to be the branches you prefer,' answered Alice sweetly.

'Ah, now you are too hard upon us! We can't grind all the time and you ladies don't seem to mind taking a turn at the two latter "branches" you mention,' returned Dolly, with a glance at George which plainly said, 'I had her there.'

'Some of us do in our first years. Later we give up childish things, you see. Don't let me keep you from Parnassus;' and a smiling nod dismissed them, smarting under the bitter consciousness of youth.

'You got it there, Doll. Better not try to fence with these superior girls. Sure to be routed, horse, foot, and dragoons,' said Stuffy, lumbering away, somewhat cross with too many spreads.

'So deuced sarcastic! Don't believe she's much older than we are. Girls grow up quicker, so she needn't put on airs and talk like a grandmother,' muttered Dolly, feeling that he had sacrificed his kids upon the altar of an ungrateful Pallas.

'Come along and let's find something to eat. I'm faint with so much talking. Old Plock cornered me and made my head spin with Kant and Hegel and that lot.'

'I promised Dora West I'd give her a turn. Must look her up; she's a jolly little thing, and doesn't bother about anything but keeping in step.'

And arm in arm the boys strolled away, leaving Alice to read music as diligently as if society had indeed no charms for her. As she bent to turn a page, the eager young man behind the piano saw the rose and was struck speechless with delight. A moment he gazed, then hastened to seize the coveted place before a new detachment of bores arrived.

'Alice, I can't believe it – did you understand – how shall I ever thank you?' murmured Demi, bending as if he, too, read the song, not a note or word of which did he see, however.

'Hush! not now. I understood – I don't deserve it – we are too young, we must wait, but – I'm very proud and happy, John!'

What would have happened after that tender whisper I tremble to think, if Tom Bangs had not come bustling up, with the cheerful remark, 'Music? just the thing. People are thinning out, and we all want a little refreshment. My brain fairly reels with the 'ologies and 'isms I've heard discussed tonight. Yes, give us this; sweet thing! Scotch songs are always charming.'

Demi glowered; but the obtuse boy never saw it, and Alice, feeling that this would be a safe vent for sundry unruly emotions, sat down at once, and sang the song which gave her answer better than she could have done:

BIDE A WEE

'The puir auld folk at home, ye mind,
    Are frail and failing sair;
And weel I ken they'd miss me, lad,
    Gin I come hamė nae mair.
The grist is out, the times are hard,
    The kine are only three;
I canna leave the auld folk now.
    We'd better bide a wee.

I fear me sair they're failing baith;
    For when I sit apart,
They talk o' Heaven so earnestly,
    It well nigh breaks my heart.

> So, laddie, dinna urge me now,
>> It surely winna be;
> I canna leave the auld folk yet.
>> We'd better bide a wee.'

The room was very still before the first verse ended; and Alice skipped the next, fearing she could not get through; for John's eyes were on her, showing that he knew she sang for him and let the plaintive little ballad tell what her reply must be. He took it as she meant it, and smiled at her so happily that her heart got the better of her voice, and she rose abruptly, saying something about the heat.

'Yes, you are tired; come out and rest, my dearest;' and with a masterful air Demi took her into the starlight, leaving Tom to stare after them winking as if a skyrocket had suddenly gone off under his nose.

'Bless my soul! the Deacon really meant business last summer and never told me. Won't Dora laugh?' And Tom departed in hot haste to impart and exult over his discovery.

What was said in the garden was never exactly known; but the Brooke family sat up very late that night, and any curious eye at the window would have seen Demi receiving the homage of his womankind as he told his little romance. Josie took great credit to herself in the matter, insisting that she had made the match; Daisy was full of the sweetest sympathy and joy, and Mrs Meg so happy that when Jo had gone to dream of bridal veils, and Demi sat in his room blissfully playing the air of 'Bide a Wee', she had her talk about Nat, ending with her arms round her dutiful daughter and these welcome words as her reward, 'Wait till Nat comes home, and then my good girl shall wear white roses too.'

CHAPTER 20

Life for Life

The summer days that followed were full of rest and pleasure for young and old, as they did the honours of Plumfield to their happy guests. While Franz and Emil were busy with the affairs of Uncle Hermann and Captain Hardy, Mary and Ludmilla made friends everywhere; for, though very unlike, both were excellent and charming girls. Mrs Meg and Daisy found the German bride a *Hausfrau* after their own hearts, and had delightful times learning new dishes, hearing about the semi-yearly washes and the splendid linen-room at Hamburg, or discussing domestic life in all its branches. Ludmilla not only taught, but learned, many things, and went home with many new and useful ideas in her blonde head.

Mary had seen so much of the world that she was unusually lively for an English girl; while her various accomplishments made her a most agreeable companion. Much good sense gave her ballast; and the late experiences of danger and happiness added a sweet gravity at times, which contrasted well with her natural gaiety. Mrs Jo was quite satisfied with Emil's choice, and felt sure this true and tender pilot would bring him safe to port through fair or stormy weather. She had feared that Franz would settle down into a comfortable, money-making burgher, and be content with that; but she soon saw that his love of music and his placid Ludmilla put much poetry into his busy life, and kept it from being too prosaic. So she felt at rest about these boys, and enjoyed their visit with real, maternal satisfaction; parting with them in September most regretfully, yet hopefully, as they sailed away to the new life that lay before them.

Demi's engagement was confided to the immediate family only, as both were pronounced too young to do anything but love and wait. They were so happy that time seemed to stand still for them, and after a blissful week they parted bravely – Alice to home duties, with a hope that sustained and cheered her through many trials; and John to his business, full of a new ardour which made all things possible when such a reward was offered.

Daisy rejoiced over them, and was never tired of hearing her brother's plans for the future. Her own hope soon made her what she used to be – a cheery, busy creature, with a smile, kind word, and helping hand for all; and as she went singing about the house again, her mother felt that the right remedy for past sadness had been found. The dear Pelican still had doubts and fears, but kept them wisely to herself, preparing sundry searching tests to be applied when Nat came home, and keeping a sharp eye on the letters from London; for some mysterious hint had flown across the sea, and Daisy's content seemed reflected in Nat's present cheerful state of mind.

Having passed through the Werther period, and tried a little Faust – of which experience he spoke to his Marguerite as if it had included an acquaintance with Mephistopheles, Blocksburg, and Auerbach's wine-cellar – he now felt that he was a Wilhelm Meister, serving his apprenticeship to the great masters of life. As she knew the truth of his small sins and honest repentance, Daisy only smiled at the mixture of love and philosophy he sent her, knowing that it was impossible for a young man to live in Germany without catching the German spirit.

'His heart is all right; and his head will soon grow clear when he gets out of the fog of tobacco, beer, and metaphysics he's been living in. England will wake up his common sense, and good salt air blow his little follies all away,' said Mrs Jo, much pleased with the good prospects of her violinist – whose return was delayed till spring, to his private regret, but professional advancement.

Josie had a month with Miss Cameron at the seaside, and threw herself so heartily into the lessons given her that her energy, promise, and patience laid the foundation of a friendship which was of infinite value to her in the busy, brilliant years to come; for little Jo's instincts were right; and the dramatic talent of the Marches was to blossom by and by into an actress, virtuous, and beloved.

Tom and his Dora were peacefully ambling altar-ward; for Bangs senior was so afraid his son would change his mind again and try a third profession, that he gladly consented to an early marriage, as a sort of anchor to hold the mercurial Thomas fast. Aforesaid Thomas could not complain of cold shoulders now; for Dora was a most devoted and adoring little mate, and made life so pleasant to him that his gift for getting into scrapes seemed lost, and he bade fair to become a thriving man, with undeniable talent for the business he had chosen.

'We shall be married in the autumn, and live with my father for a while. The governor is getting on, you know, and my wife and I must look after him. Later we shall have an establishment of our own,' was a favourite speech of his about this time, and usually received with smiles; for the idea of Tommy Bangs at the head of an 'establishment' was irresistibly funny to all who knew him.

Things were in this flourishing condition, and Mrs Jo was beginning to think her trials were over for that year, when a new excitement came. Several postal cards had arrived at long intervals from Dan, who gave them 'Care of M. Mason, etc.', as his address. By this means he was able to gratify his longing for home news, and to send brief messages to quiet their surprise at his delay in settling. The last one, which came in September, was dated 'Montana', and simply said,

> Here at last, trying mining again; but not going to stay long. All sorts of luck. Gave up the farm idea. Tell plans soon. Well, busy, and *very happy*.   D. K.

If they had known what the heavy dash under 'happy' meant, that postal would have been a very eloquent bit of pasteboard; for Dan was free, and had gone straight away to the liberty he panted for. Meeting an old friend by accident, he obliged him at a pinch by acting as overseer for a time, finding the society even of rough miners very sweet, and something in the muscular work wonderfully pleasant, after being cooped up in the brush-shop so long. He loved to take a pick and wrestle with rock and earth till he was weary – which was very soon; for that year of captivity had told upon his splendid physique. He longed to go home, but waited week after week to get the prison taint off him and the haggard look out of his face. Meanwhile he made friends of masters and men; and as no one knew his story, he took his place again in the world gratefully and gladly – with little pride now, and no plans but to do some good somewhere, and efface the past.

Mrs Jo was having a grand clearing-out of her desk one October day, while the rain poured outside, and peace reigned in her mansion. Coming across the postals, she pondered over them, and then put them carefully away in the drawer labelled 'Boys' Letters', saying to herself, as she bundled eleven requests for autographs into the wastepaper basket, 'It is quite time for another card, unless he is coming to tell his plans. I'm really curious to know what he has been about all this year, and how he's getting on now.'

That last wish was granted within an hour; for Ted came rushing in, with a newspaper in one hand, a collapsed umbrella in the other, and a face full of excitement, announcing, all in one breathless jumble, 'Mine caved in – twenty men shut up – no way out – wives crying – water rising – Dan knew the old shaft – risked his life – got 'em out – 'most killed – papers full of it – I knew he'd be a hero – hurray for old Dan!'

'What? Where? When? Who? Stop roaring, and let me read!' commanded his mother, entirely bewildered.

Relinquishing the paper, Ted allowed her to read for herself, with frequent interruptions from him – and Rob, who soon followed, eager for the tale. It was nothing new; but courage and devotion always stir generous hearts, and win admiration; so the account was both graphic and enthusiastic; and the name of Daniel Kean, the brave man who saved the lives of others at the risk of his own, was on many lips that day. Very proud were the faces of these friends as they read how their Dan was the only one who, in the first panic of the accident, remembered the old shaft that led into the mine – walled up, but the only hope of escape, if the men could be got out before the rising water drowned them; how he was lowered down alone, telling the others to keep back till he saw if it was safe; how he heard the poor fellows picking desperately for their lives on the other side, and by knocks and calls guided them to the right spot; then headed the rescue party, and working like a hero, got the men out in time. On being drawn up last of all, the worn rope broke, and he had a terrible fall, being much hurt, but was still alive. How the grateful women kissed his blackened face and bloody hands, as the men bore him away in triumph, and the owners of the mine promised a handsome reward, if he lived to receive it!

'He must live; he *shall*, and come home to be nursed as soon as he can stir, if I go and bring him myself! I always knew he'd do something fine and brave, if he didn't get shot or hung for some wild prank instead,' cried Mrs Jo, much excited.

'Do go, and take me with you, Mum. I ought to be the one, Dan's so fond of me and I of him,' began Ted, feeling that this would be an expedition after his own heart.

Before his mother could reply, Mr Laurie came in, with almost as much noise and flurry as Teddy the second, exclaiming as he waved the evening paper, 'Seen the news, Jo? What do you think? Shall I go off at once, and see after that brave boy?'

'I wish you would. But the thing may not be all true – rumour lies so. Perhaps a few hours will bring an entirely new version of the story.'

'I've telephoned to Demi for all he can find out; and if it's true, I'll go at once. Should like the trip. If he's able, I'll bring him home; if not, I'll stay and see to him. He'll pull through. Dan will never die of a fall on his head. He's got nine lives, and not lost half of them yet.'

'If you go, Uncle, mayn't I go with you? I'm just spoiling for a journey; and it would be such larks to go out there with you, and see the mines and Dan, and hear all about it, and help. I can nurse. Can't I, Rob?' cried Teddy, in his most wheedlesome tones.

'Pretty well. But if mother can't spare you, I'm ready if uncle needs anyone,' answered Rob, in his quiet way, looking much fitter for the trip than excitable Ted.

'I can't spare either of you. My boys get into trouble, unless I keep them close at home. I've no right to hold the others; but I won't let you out of my sight, or something will happen. Never saw such a year, with wrecks and weddings and floods and engagements, and every sort of catastrophe!' exclaimed Mrs Jo.

'If you deal in girls and boys, you must expect this sort of thing, ma'am. The worst is over, I hope, till these lads begin to go off. Then I'll stand by you; for you'll need every kind of support and comfort, specially if Ted bolts early,' laughed Mr Laurie, enjoying her lamentations.

'I don't think anything can surprise me now; but I am anxious about Dan, and feel that someone had better go to him. It's a rough place out there, and he may need careful nursing. Poor lad, he seems to get a good many hard knocks! But perhaps he needs them as "a mellerin' process", as Hannah used to say.'

Ted came rushing in, with a newspaper in one hand, a collapsed umbrella in the other, and a face full of excitement

'We shall hear from Demi before long, and then I'll be off.' With which cheerful promise Mr Laurie departed; and Ted, finding his mother firm, soon followed, to coax his uncle to take him.

Further enquiry confirmed and added interest to the news. Mr Laurie was off at once; and Ted went into town with him, still vainly imploring to be taken to his Dan. He was absent all day; but his mother said, calmly: 'Only a fit of the sulks because he is thwarted. He's safe with Tom or Demi, and will come home hungry and meek at night. I know him.'

But she soon found that she *could* still be surprised; for evening brought no Ted, and no one had seen him. Mr Bhaer was just setting off to find his lost son, when a telegram arrived, dated at one of the way-stations on Mr Laurie's route:

Found Ted in the cars. Take him along. Write tomorrow.

                                        T. LAURENCE

'Ted bolted sooner than you expected, Mother. Never mind – Uncle will take good care of him, and Dan be very glad to see him,' said Rob, as Mrs Jo sat, trying to realise that her youngest was actually on his way to the wild West.

'Disobedient boy! He shall be severely punished, if I ever get him again. Laurie winked at this prank; I know he did. Just like him. Won't the two rascals have a splendid time? Wish I was with them! Don't believe that crazy boy took even a nightgown with him, or an overcoat. Well, there will be two patients for us to nurse when they get back, if they ever do. Those reckless express trains always go down precipices, and burn up, or telescope. Oh! my Ted, my precious boy, how can I let him go so far away from me?'

And mother-like, Mrs Jo forgot the threatened chastisement in tender lamentations over the happy scapegrace, now whizzing across the continent in high feather at the success of his first revolt. Mr Laurie was much amused at his insisting that those words, 'when Ted bolts', put the idea into his head; and therefore the responsibility rested upon his shoulders. He assumed it kindly from the moment he came upon the runaway asleep in a car, with no visible luggage but a bottle of wine for Dan and a blacking-brush for himself; and as Mrs Jo suspected, the 'two rascals' did have a splendid time. Penitent letters arrived in due season, and the irate parents soon forgot to chide in their anxiety about Dan, who was very ill, and did not know his friends for several days. Then he began to mend; and everyone forgave the bad boy when he proudly reported that the first conscious words Dan said were, 'Hallo, Ted!' with a smile of pleasure at seeing a familiar face bent over him.

'Glad he went, and I won't scold any more. Now, what shall we put in the box for Dan?' And Mrs Jo worked off her impatience to get hold of the invalid by sending comforts enough for a hospital.

Cheering accounts soon began to come, and at length Dan was pronounced able to travel, but seemed in no haste to go home, though never tired of hearing his nurses talk of it.

'Dan is strangely altered,' wrote Laurie to Jo; 'not by this illness alone, but by something which has evidently gone before. I don't know what, and leave you to ask; but from his ravings when delirious I fear he has been in some serious trouble the past year. He seems ten years older, but improved, quieter, and so grateful to us. It is pathetic to see the hunger in his eyes as they rest on Ted, as if he couldn't see enough of him. He says Kansas was a failure, but can't talk much; so I bide my time. The people here love him very much, and he cares for that sort of thing now; used to scorn any show of emotion, you know; now he wants everyone to think well of him, and can't do enough to win affection and respect. I may be all wrong. You will soon find out. Ted is in clover, and the trip has done him a world of good. Let me take him to Europe when we go? Apron strings don't agree with him any better than they did with me when I proposed to run away to Washington with you some century ago. Aren't you sorry you didn't?'

This private letter set Mrs Jo's lively fancy in a ferment, and she imagined every known crime, affliction, and complication which could possibly have befallen Dan. He was too feeble to be worried with questions now, but she promised herself most interesting revelations when she got him safe at home; for the 'firebrand' was her most interesting boy. She begged him to come, and spent more time in composing a letter that should bring him, than she did over the most thrilling episodes in her 'works'.

No one but Dan saw the letter; but it did bring him, and one November day Mr Laurie helped a feeble man out of a carriage at the door of Plumfield, and Mother Bhaer received the wanderer like a recovered son; while Ted, in a disreputable-looking hat and an astonishing pair of boots, performed a sort of war-dance round the interesting group.

'Right upstairs and rest; I'm nurse now, and this ghost must eat before he talks to anyone,' commanded Mrs Jo, trying not to show how shocked she was at this shorn and shaven, gaunt and pallid shadow of the stalwart man she parted with.

He was quite content to obey, and lay on the long lounge in the room prepared for him, looking about as tranquilly as a sick child restored to its own nursery and mother's arms, while his new nurse fed and refreshed him, bravely controlling the questions that burned upon her tongue. Being weak and weary, he soon fell asleep; and then she stole away to enjoy the society of the 'rascals', whom she scolded and petted, pumped and praised, to her heart's content.

'Jo, I think Dan has committed some crime and suffered for it,' said Mr Laurie, when Ted had departed to show his boots and tell glowing tales of the dangers and delights of the miners' life to his mates. 'Some terrible experience has come to the lad, and broken his spirit. He was quite out of his head when we arrived, and I took the watching, so I heard more of those sad wanderings than anyone else. He talked of the "warden", some trail, a dead man, and Blair and Mason, and would keep offering me his hand, asking me if I would take it and forgive him. Once, when he was very wild, I held his arms, and he quieted in a moment, imploring me not to "put the handcuffs on". I declare, it was quite awful sometimes to hear him in the night talk of old Plum and you, and beg to be let out and go home to die.'

'He isn't going to die, but live to repent of anything he may have done; so don't harrow me up with these dark hints, Teddy. I don't care if he's broken the Ten Commandments, I'll stand by him, and so will you, and we'll set him on his feet and make a good man of him yet. I know he's not spoilt, by the look in his poor face. Don't say a word to anyone, and I'll have the truth before long,' answered Mrs Jo, still loyal to her bad boy, though much afflicted by what she had heard.

For some days Dan rested, and saw few people; then good care, cheerful surroundings, and the comfort of being at home began to tell, and he seemed more like himself, though still very silent as to his late experiences, pleading the doctor's orders not to talk much. Everyone wanted to see him; but he shrank from any but old friends, and 'wouldn't lionise worth a cent', Ted said, much disappointed that he could not show off his brave Dan.

'Wasn't a man there who wouldn't have done the same, so why make a row over me?' asked the hero, feeling more ashamed than proud of the broken arm, which looked so interesting in a sling.

'But isn't it pleasant to think that you saved twenty lives, Dan, and gave husbands, sons, and fathers back to the women who loved them?' asked Mrs Jo one evening as they were alone together after several callers had been sent away.

'Pleasant! it's all that kept me alive, I do believe; yes, I'd rather have done it than be made president or any other big bug in the world. No one knows what a comfort it is to think I've saved twenty men to more than pay for – ' There Dan stopped short, having evidently spoken out of some strong emotion to which his hearer had no key.

'I thought you'd feel so. It is a splendid thing to save life at the risk of one's own, as you did, and nearly lose it,' began Mrs Jo, wishing he had gone on with that impulsive speech which was so like his old manner.

' "He that loseth his life shall gain it",' muttered Dan, staring at the cheerful fire which lighted the room, and shone on his thin face with a ruddy glow.

Mrs Jo was so startled at hearing such words from his lips that she exclaimed joyfully, 'Then you *did* read the little book I gave you, and kept your promise?'

'I read it a good deal after a while. I don't know much yet, but I'm ready to learn; and that's something.'

'It's everything. Oh, my dear, tell me about it! I know something lies heavy on your heart; let me help you bear it, and so make the burden lighter.'

'I know it would; I want to tell; but some things even you couldn't forgive; and if *you* let go of me, I'm afraid I can't keep afloat.'

'Mothers can forgive a*nything*! Tell me all, and be sure that I will *never* let you go, though the whole world should turn from you.'

Mrs Jo took one of the big wasted hands in both of hers and held it fast, waiting silently till that sustaining touch warmed poor Dan's heart, and gave him courage to speak. Sitting in his old attitude, with his head in his hands, he slowly told it all, never once looking up till the last words left his lips.

'Now you know; can you forgive a murderer, and keep a jailbird in your house?'

Her only answer was to put her arms about him, and lay the shorn head on her breast, with eyes so full of tears they could but dimly see the hope and fear that made his own so tragical.

That was better than any words; and poor Dan clung to her in speechless gratitude, feeling the blessedness of mother love – that divine gift which comforts, purifies, and strengthens all who seek it. Two or three great, bitter drops were hidden in the little woollen shawl where Dan's cheek rested, and no one ever knew how soft and comfortable it felt to him after the hard pillows he had known so long. Suffering of both mind and body had broken will and pride, and the lifted burden brought such a sense of relief that he paused a moment to enjoy it in dumb delight.

'My poor boy, how you have suffered all this year, when we thought you free as air! Why didn't you tell us, Dan, and let us help you? Did you doubt your friends?' asked Mrs Jo, forgetting all other emotions in sympathy, as she lifted up the hidden face, and looked reproachfully into the great hollow eyes that met her own frankly now.

'I was ashamed. I tried to bear it alone rather than shock and disappoint you, as I know I have, though you try not to show it. Don't mind; I must get used to it'; and Dan's eyes dropped again as if they could not bear to see the trouble and dismay his confession painted on his best friend's face.

'I *am* shocked and disappointed by the sin, but I am also very glad and proud and grateful that my sinner has repented, atoned, and is ready to profit by the bitter lesson. No one but Fritz and Laurie need ever know the truth; we owe it to them, and they will feel as I do,' answered Mrs Jo, wisely thinking that entire frankness would be a better tonic than too much sympathy.

'No, they won't; men never forgive like women. But it's right. Please tell 'em for me, and get it over. Mr Laurence knows it, I guess. I blabbed when my wits were gone; but he was very kind all the same. I can bear their knowing; but oh, not Ted and the girls!' Dan clutched her arm with such an imploring face that she hastened to assure him no one should know except the two old friends, and he calmed down as if ashamed of his sudden panic.

'It wasn't murder, mind you, it was in self-defence; he drew first, and I had to hit him. Didn't mean to kill him; but it doesn't worry me as much as it ought, I'm afraid. I've more than paid for it, and such a rascal is better out of the world than in it, showing boys the way to hell. Yes, I know you think that's awful in me; but I can't help it. I hate a scamp as I do a skulking coyote, and always want to get a shot at 'em. Perhaps it would have been better if he had killed me; my life is spoilt.'

All the old prison gloom seemed to settle like a black cloud on Dan's face as he spoke, and Mrs Jo was frightened at the glimpse it gave her of the fire through which he had passed to come out alive, but scarred for life. Hoping to turn his mind to happier things, she said cheerfully, 'No, it isn't; you have learned to value it more and use it better for this trial. It is not a lost year, but one that may prove the most helpful of any you ever know. Try to think so, and begin again; we will help, and have all the more confidence in you for this failure. We all do the same and struggle on.'

'I never can be what I was. I feel about sixty, and don't care for anything now I've got here. Let me stay till I'm on my legs, then I'll clear out and never trouble you any more,' said Dan despondently.

'You are weak and low in your mind; that will pass, and by and by you will go to your missionary work among the Indians with all the old energy and the new patience, self-control, and knowledge you have gained. Tell me more about that good chaplain and Mary Mason and the lady whose chance word helped you so much. I want to know all about the trials of my poor boy.'

Won by her tender interest, Dan brightened up and talked on till he had poured out all the story of that bitter year, and felt better for the load he lifted off.

If he had known how it weighed upon his hearer's heart, he would have held his peace; but she hid her sorrow till she had sent him to bed, comforted and calm; then she cried her heart out, to the great dismay of Fritz and Laurie, till they heard the tale and could mourn with her; after which they all cheered up and took counsel together how best to help this worst of all the 'catastrophes' the year had brought them.

Aslauga's Knight

It was curious to see the change which came over Dan after that talk. A weight seemed off his mind; and though the old impetuous spirit flashed out at times, he seemed intent on trying to show his gratitude and love and honour to these true friends by a new humility and confidence very sweet to them, very helpful to him. After hearing the story from Mrs Jo, the Professor and Mr Laurie made no allusion to it beyond the hearty hand-grasp, the look of compassion, the brief word of good cheer in which men convey sympathy, and a redoubled kindness which left no doubt of pardon. Mr Laurie began at once to interest influential persons in Dan's mission, and set in motion the machinery which needs so much oiling before anything can be done where Government is concerned. Mr Bhaer, with the skill of a true teacher, gave Dan's hungry mind something to do, and helped him understand himself by carrying on the good chaplain's task so paternally that the poor fellow often said he felt as if he had found a father. The boys took him to drive, and amused him with their pranks and plans; while the women, old and young, nursed and petted him till he felt like a sultan with a crowd of devoted slaves, obedient to his lightest wish.

A very little of this was enough for Dan, who had a masculine horror of 'mollycoddling', and so brief an acquaintance with illness that he rebelled against the doctor's orders to keep quiet; and it took all Mrs Jo's authority and the girls' ingenuity to keep him from leaving his sofa long before strained back and wounded head were well. Daisy cooked for him; Nan attended to his medicines; Josie read aloud to while away the long hours of inaction that hung so heavily on his hands; while Bess brought all her pictures and casts to amuse him, and, at his special desire, set up a modelling-stand in his parlour and began to mould the buffalo head he gave her. Those afternoons seemed the pleasantest part of his day; and Mrs Jo, busy in her study close by, could see the friendly trio and enjoy the pretty pictures they made. The girls were much flattered by the success of their efforts, and exerted themselves to be very entertaining, consulting Dan's moods with the feminine tact most women creatures learn before they are out of pinafores. When he was gay, the room rang with laughter; when gloomy, they read or worked in respectful silence till their sweet patience cheered him up again; and when in pain they hovered over him like 'a couple of angels', as he said. He often called Josie 'little mother', but Bess was always 'Princess'; and his manner to the two cousins was quite different. Josie sometimes fretted him with her fussy ways, the long plays she liked to read, and the maternal scoldings she administered when he broke the rules; for having a lord of creation in her power was so delightful to her that she would have ruled him with a rod of iron if he had submitted. To Bess, in her gentler ministrations, he never showed either impatience or weariness, but obeyed her least word, exerted himself to seem well in her presence, and took such interest in her work that he lay looking at her with unwearied eyes; while Josie read to him in her best style unheeded.

Mrs Jo observed this, and called them 'Una and the Lion', which suited them very well, though the lion's mane was shorn, and Una never tried to bridle him. The elder ladies did their part in providing delicacies and supplying all his wants; but Mrs Meg was busy at home, Mrs Amy preparing for the trip to Europe in the spring, and Mrs Jo hovering on the brink of a 'vortex' – for the forthcoming book had been sadly delayed by the late domestic events. As she sat at her desk, settling papers or meditatively nibbling her pen while waiting for the divine afflatus to descend upon her, she often forgot her fictitious heroes and heroines in studying the live models before her, and thus by chance looks, words, and gestures discovered a little romance unsuspected by anyone else.

The *portière* between the rooms was usually drawn aside, giving a view of the group in the large bay-window – Bess at one side, in her grey blouse, busy with her tools; Josie at the other side with her book; and between, on the long couch, propped with many cushions, lay Dan in a many-hued eastern dressing-gown presented by Mr Laurie and worn to please the girls, though the invalid much preferred an old jacket 'with no confounded tail to bother over'. He faced Mrs Jo's room, but never seemed to see her, for his eyes were on the slender figure before him, with the pale winter sunshine touching her golden head, and the delicate hands that shaped the clay so deftly. Josie was just visible, rocking violently in a little chair at the head of the couch, and the steady murmur of her girlish voice was usually the only sound that broke the quiet of the room, unless a sudden discussion arose about the book or the buffalo.

Something in the big eyes, bigger and blacker than ever in the thin white face, fixed, so steadily on one object, had a sort of fascination for Mrs Jo after a time, and she watched the changes in them curiously; for Dan's mind was evidently not on the story, and he often forgot to laugh or exclaim at the comic or exciting crises. Sometimes they were soft and wistful, and the watcher was very glad that neither damsel caught that dangerous look for when they spoke it vanished; sometimes it was full of eager fire, and the colour came and went rebelliously, in spite of his attempt to hide it with an impatient gesture of hand or head; but oftenest it was dark, and sad, and stern, as if those gloomy eyes looked out of captivity at some forbidden light or joy. This expression came so often that it worried Mrs Jo, and she longed to go and ask him what bitter memory overshadowed those quiet hours. She knew that his crime and its punishment must lie heavy on his mind; but youth, and time, and new hopes would bring comfort, and help to wear away the first sharpness of the prison brand. It lifted at other times, and seemed almost forgotten when he joked with the boys, talked with old friends, or enjoyed the first snows as he drove out every fair day. Why should the shadow always fall so darkly on him in the society of these innocent and friendly girls? They never seemed to see it, and if either looked or spoke, a quick smile came like a sunburst through the clouds to answer them. So Mrs Jo went on watching, wondering, and discovering, till accident confirmed her fears.

Josie was called away one day, and Bess, tired of working, offered to take her place if he cared for more reading.

'I do; your reading suits me better than Jo's. She goes so fast my stupid head gets in a muddle and soon begins to ache. Don't tell her; she's a dear little soul, and so good to sit here with a bear like me.'

The smile was ready as Bess went to the table for a new book, the last story being finished.

'You are not a bear, but very good and patient, we think. It is always hard for a man to be shut up, mamma says, and must be terrible for you, who have always been so free.'

If Bess had not been reading titles she would have seen Dan shrink as if her last words hurt him. He made no answer; but other eyes saw and understood why he looked as if he would have liked to spring up and rush away for one of his long races up the hill, as he used to do when the longing for liberty grew uncontrollable. Moved by a sudden impulse, Mrs Jo caught up her work-basket and went to join her neighbours, feeling that a non-conductor might be needed; for Dan looked like a thunder-cloud full of electricity.

'What shall we read, Aunty? Dan doesn't seem to care. You know his taste; tell me something quiet and pleasant and short. Josie will be back soon,' said Bess, still turning over the books piled on the centre-table.

Before Mrs Jo could answer, Dan pulled a shabby little volume from under his pillow, and handing it to her said: 'Please read the third one; it's short and pretty – I'm fond of it.' The book opened at the right place, as if the third story had been often read, and Bess smiled as she saw the name.

'Why, Dan, I shouldn't think you'd care for this romantic German tale. There is fighting in it; but it is very sentimental, if I remember rightly.'

'I know it; but I've read so few stories, I like the simple ones best. Had nothing else to read sometimes; I guess I know it all by heart, and never seem to be tired of those fighting fellows, and the fiends and angels and lovely ladies. You read "Aslauga's Knight", and see if you don't like it. Edwald was rather too soft for my fancy; but Froda was first-rate and the spirit with the golden hair always reminded me of you.'

As Dan spoke Mrs Jo settled herself where she could watch him in the glass, and Bess took a large chair facing him, saying, as she put up her hands to retie the ribbon that held the cluster of thick, soft curls at the back of her head, 'I hope Aslauga's hair wasn't as troublesome as mine, for it's always tumbling down. I'll be ready in a minute.'

'Don't tie it up; please let it hang. I love to see it shine that way. It will rest your head, and be just right for the story, Goldilocks,' pleaded Dan, using the childish name and looking more like his boyish self than he had done for many a day.

Bess laughed, shook down her pretty hair, and began to read, glad to hide her face a little; for compliments made her shy, no matter who paid them. Dan listened intently on; and Mrs Jo, with eyes that went often from her needle to the glass, could see, without turning, how he enjoyed every word as if it had more meaning for him than for the other listeners. His face brightened wonderfully, and soon wore the look that came when anything brave or beautiful inspired and touched his better self. It was Fouqué's charming story of the knight Froda, and the fair daughter of Sigurd, who was a sort of spirit, appearing to her lover in hours of danger and trial, as well as triumph and joy, till she became his guide and guard, inspiring him with courage, nobleness, and truth, leading him to great deeds in the field, sacrifices for those he loved, and victories over himself by the gleaming of her golden hair, which shone on him in battle, dreams, and perils by day and night, till after death he finds the lovely spirit waiting to receive and to reward him.

Of all the stories in the book this was the last one would have supposed Dan would like best, and even Mrs Jo was surprised at his perceiving the moral of the tale through the delicate imagery and romantic language by which it was illustrated. But as she looked and listened she remembered the streak of sentiment and refinement which lay concealed in Dan like the gold vein in a rock, making him quick to feel and to enjoy fine colour in a flower, grace in an animal, sweetness in women, heroism in men, and all the tender ties that bind heart to heart; though he was slow to show it, having no words to express the tastes and instincts which he inherited from his mother. Suffering of soul and body had tamed his stronger passions, and the atmosphere of love and pity now surrounding him purified and warmed his heart till it began to hunger for the food neglected or denied so long. This was plainly written in his too expressive face, as, fancying it unseen, he let it tell the longing after beauty, peace, and happiness embodied for him in the innocent fair girl before him.

The conviction of this sad yet natural fact came to Mrs Jo with a pang, for she felt how utterly hopeless such a longing was; since light and darkness were not farther apart than snow-white Bess and sin-stained Dan. No dream of such a thing disturbed the young girl, as her entire unconsciousness plainly showed. But how long would it be before the eloquent eyes betrayed the truth? And then what disappointment for Dan, what dismay for Bess, who was as cool and high and pure as her own marbles, and shunned all thought of love with maidenly reserve.

'How hard everything is made for my poor boy! How can I spoil his little dream, and take away the spirit of good he is beginning to love and long for? When my own dear lads are safely settled I'll never try another, for these things are heart-breaking, and I can't manage any more,' thought Mrs Jo, as she put the lining into Teddy's coat-sleeve upside down, so perplexed and grieved was she at this new catastrophe.

The story was soon done, and as Bess shook back her hair, Dan asked as eagerly as a boy, 'Don't you like it?'

'Yes, it's very pretty, and I see the meaning of it; but Undine was always my favourite.'

'Of course, that's like you – lilies and pearls and souls and pure water. Sintram used to be mine; but I took a fancy to this when I was – ahem – rather down on my luck one time, and it did me good, it was so cheerful and sort of spiritual in its meaning, you know.'

Bess opened her blue eyes in wonder at this fancy of Dan's for anything 'spiritual'; but she only nodded, saying, 'Some of the little songs are sweet and might be set to music.'

Dan laughed; 'I used to sing the last one to a tune of my own sometimes at sunset,

> Listening to celestial lays,
> Bending thy unclouded gaze
> On the pure and living light,
> Thou art blest, Aslauga's Knight!

'And I was,' he added, under his breath, as he glanced towards the sunshine dancing on the wall.

'This one suits you better now;' and glad to please him by her interest, Bess read in her soft voice,

> 'Heal fast, heal fast, ye hero wounds;
> O knight, be quickly strong!

Beloved strife
For fame and life,
Oh, tarry not too long!'

'I'm no hero, never can be, and "fame and life" can't do much for me. Never mind, read me that paper, please. This knock on the head has made a regular fool of me.'

Dan's voice was gentle; but the light was gone out of his face now, and he moved restlessly as if the silken pillows were full of thorns. Seeing that his mood had changed, Bess quietly put down the book, took up the paper, and glanced along the columns for something to suit him.

'You don't care for the money market, I know, nor musical news. Here's a murder; you used to like those; shall I read it? One man kills another – '

'No!'

Only a word, but it gave Mrs Jo a thrill, and for a moment she dared not glance at the tell-tale mirror. When she did Dan lay motionless with one hand over his eyes, and Bess was happily reading the art news to ears that never heard a word. Feeling like a thief who has stolen something very precious, Mrs Jo slipped away to her study, and before long Bess followed to report that Dan was fast asleep.

Sending her home, with the firm resolve to keep her there as much as possible, Mother Bhaer had an hour of serious thought all alone in the red sunset; and when a sound in the next room led her there, she found that the feigned sleep had become real repose; for Dan lay breathing heavily, with a scarlet spot on either cheek, and one hand clinched on his broad breast. Yearning over him with a deeper pity than ever before, she sat in the little chair beside him, trying to see her way out of this tangle, till his hand slipped down, and in doing so snapped a cord he wore about his neck and let a small case drop to the floor.

Mrs Jo picked it up, and as he did not wake, sat looking at it, idly wondering what charm it held; for the case was of Indian workmanship and the broken cord, of closely woven grass, sweet scented and pale yellow.

'I won't pry into any more of the poor fellow's secrets. I'll mend and put it back, and never let him know I've seen his talisman.'

As she spoke she turned the little wallet to examine the fracture, and a card fell into her lap. It was a photograph, cut to fit its covering, and two words were written underneath the face, 'My Aslauga'. For an instant Mrs Jo fancied that it might be one of herself, for all the boys had them; but as the thin paper fell away, she saw the picture Demi took of Bess that happy summer day. There was no doubt now, and with a sigh she put it back, and was about to slip it into Dan's bosom so that not even a stitch should betray her knowledge, when as she leaned towards him, she saw that he was looking straight at her with an expression that surprised her more than any of the strange ones she had ever seen in that changeful face before.

'Your hand slipped down; it fell; I was putting it back,' explained Mrs Jo, feeling like a naughty child caught in mischief.

'You saw the picture?'

'Yes.'

'And know what a fool I am?'

'Yes, Dan, and am so grieved – '

'Don't worry about me. I'm all right – glad you know, though I never meant to tell you. Of course it is only a crazy fancy of mine, and nothing can ever come of it. Never thought there would. Good Lord! what could that little angel ever be to me but what she is – a sort of dream of all that's sweet and good?'

More afflicted by the quiet resignation of his look and tone than by the most passionate ardour, Mrs Jo could only say, with a face full of sympathy, 'It is very hard, dear, but there is no other way to look at it. You are wise and brave enough to see that, and to let the secret be ours alone.'

'I swear I will! not a word nor a look if I can help it. No one guesses, and if it troubles no one, is there any harm in my keeping this, and taking comfort in the pretty fancy that kept me sane in that cursed place?'

Dan's face was eager now, and he hid away the little worn case as if defying any hand to take it from him. Anxious to know every-thing before giving counsel or comfort, Mrs Jo said quietly, 'Keep it, and tell me all about the "fancy". Since I have stumbled on your secret, let me know how it came, and how I can help to make it lighter to bear.'

'You'll laugh; but I don't mind. You always did find out our secrets and give us a lift. Well, I never cared much for books, you know; but down yonder when the devil tormented me I had to do something or go stark mad, so I read both the books you gave me. One was beyond me, till that good old man showed me how to read it; but the other, this one, was a comfort, I tell you. It amused me, and was as pretty as poetry. I liked 'em all, and most wore out Sintram. See how used up he is! Then I came to this, and it sort of fitted that other happy part of my life, last summer – here.'

Dan stopped a moment as the words lingered on his lips; then, with a long breath, went on, as if it was hard to lay bare the foolish little romance he had woven about a girl, a picture, and a child's story there in the darkness of the place which was as terrible to him as Dante's Inferno, till he found his Beatrice.

'I couldn't sleep, and *had* to think about something, so I used to fancy I was Folko, and see the shining of Aslauga's hair in the sunset on the wall, the glim of the watchman's lamp, and the light that came in at dawn. My cell was high. I could see a bit of sky; sometimes there was a star in it, and that was most as good as a face. I set great store by that patch of blue, and when a white cloud went by, I thought it was the prettiest thing in all this world. I guess I was pretty near a fool; but those thoughts and things helped me through, so they are all solemn true to me, and I can't let them go. The dear shiny head, the white gown, the eyes like stars, and sweet, calm ways that set her as high above me as the moon in heaven. Don't take it away! it's only a fancy, but a man must love something, and I'd better love a spirit like her than any of the poor common girls who would care for me.'

The quiet despair in Dan's voice pierced Mrs Jo to the heart; but there was no hope and she gave none. Yet she felt that he was right, and that his hapless affection might do more to uplift and purify him than any other he might know. Few women would care to marry Dan now, except such as would hinder, not help, him in the struggle which life would always be to him; and it was better to go solitary to his grave than become what she suspected his father had been – a handsome, unprincipled, and dangerous man, with more than one broken heart to answer for.

'Yes, Dan, it *is* wise to keep this innocent fancy, if it helps and comforts you, till something more real and possible comes to make you happier. I wish I could give you any hope; but we both know that the dear child is the apple of her father's eye, the pride of her mother's heart, and that the most perfect lover they can find will hardly seem to them worthy of their precious daughter. Let her remain for you the high, bright star that leads you up and makes you believe in heaven.' Mrs Jo broke down there; it seemed so cruel to destroy the faint hope Dan's eyes betrayed, that she could not moralise when she thought of his hard life and lonely future. Perhaps it was the wisest thing she could have done, for in her hearty sympathy he found comfort for his own loss, and very soon was able to speak again in the manly tone of resignation to the inevitable that showed how honest was his effort to give up everything but the pale shadow of what, for another, might have been a happy possibility.

They talked long and earnestly in the twilight; and this second secret bound them closer than the first; for in it there was neither sin nor shame – only the tender pain and patience which has made saints and heroes of far worse men than our poor Dan. When at length they rose at the summons of a bell, all the sunset glory had departed, and in the wintry sky there hung one star, large, soft, and clear, above a snowy world. Pausing at the window before she dropped the curtains, Mrs Jo said cheerfully, 'Come and see how beautiful the evening star is, since you love it so.' And as he stood behind her, tall and pale, like the ghost of his former self, she added softly, 'And remember, dear, if the sweet girl is denied you, the old friend is always here – to love and trust and pray for you.'

This time she was not disappointed; and had she asked any reward for many anxieties and cares, she received it when Dan's strong arm came round her, as he said, in a voice which showed her that she had not laboured in vain to pluck her firebrand from the burning, 'I never can forget that; for she's helped to save my soul, and make me dare to look up there and say, "God bless her!" '

CHAPTER 22

Positively Last Appearance

'Upon my word, I feel as if I lived in a powder-magazine, and don't know which barrel will explode next, and send me flying,' said Mrs Jo to herself next day, as she trudged up to Parnassus to suggest to her sister that perhaps the most charming of the young nurses had better return to her marble gods before she unconsciously added another wound to those already won by the human hero. She told no secrets; but a hint was sufficient; for Mrs Amy guarded her daughter as a pearl of great price, and at once devised a very simple means of escape from danger. Mr Laurie was going to Washington on Dan's behalf, and was delighted to take his family with him when the idea was carelessly suggested. So the conspiracy succeeded finely; and Mrs Jo went home, feeling more like a traitor than ever. She expected an explosion; but Dan took the news so quietly, it was plain that he cherished no hope; and Mrs Amy was sure her romantic sister had been mistaken. If she had seen Dan's face when Bess went to say goodbye, her maternal eye would have discovered far more than the unconscious girl did. Mrs Jo trembled lest he should betray himself; but he had learned self-control in a stern school, and would have got through the hard moment bravely, only, when he took both hands, saying heartily, 'Goodbye, Princess. If we don't meet again, remember your old friend Dan sometimes,' she, touched by his late danger and the wistful look he wore, answered with unusual warmth, 'How can I help it, when you make us all so proud of you? God bless your mission, and bring you safely home to us again!'

As she looked up at him with a face full of frank affection and sweet regret, all that he was losing rose so vividly before him that Dan could not resist the impulse to take the 'dear goldy head' between his hands and kiss it, with a broken 'Goodbye'; then hurried back to his room, feeling as if it were the prison cell again, with no glimpse of heaven's blue to comfort him.

This abrupt caress and departure rather startled Bess; for she felt with a girl's quick instinct that there was something in that kiss unknown before, and looked after him with sudden colour in her cheeks and new trouble in her eyes. Mrs Jo saw it, and fearing a very natural question answered it before it was put.

'Forgive him, Bess. He has had a great trouble, and it makes him tender at parting with old friends; for you know he may never come back from the wild world he is going to.'

'You mean the fall and danger of death?' asked Bess, innocently.

'No, dear; a greater trouble than that. But I cannot tell you any more – except that he has come through it bravely; so you may trust and respect him, as I do.'

'He has lost someone he loved. Poor Dan! We must be very kind to him.'

Bess did not ask the question, but seemed content with her solution of the mystery – which was so true that Mrs Jo confirmed it by a nod, and let her go away believing that some tender loss and sorrow wrought the great change all saw in Dan, and made him so slow to speak concerning the past year.

But Ted was less easily satisfied, and this unusual reticence goaded him to desperation. His mother had warned him not to trouble Dan with questions till he was quite well; but this prospect of approaching departure made him resolve to have a full, clear, and satisfactory account of the adventures which he felt sure must have been thrilling, from stray words Dan let fall in his fever. So one day when the coast was clear, Master Ted volunteered to amuse the invalid, and did so in the following manner, 'Look here, old boy, if you don't want me to read, you've got to talk, and tell me all about Kansas, and the farms, and that part. The Montana business I know, but you seem to forget what went before. Brace up, and let's have it,' he began, with an abruptness which roused Dan from a brown study most effectually.

'No, I don't forget; it isn't interesting to anyone but myself. I didn't see any farms – gave it up,' he said slowly.

'Why?'

'Other things to do.'

'What?'

'Well, brush-making for one thing.'

'Don't chaff a fellow. Tell true.'

'I truly did.'

'What for?'

'To keep out of mischief, as much as anything.'

'Well, of all the queer things – and you've done a lot – that's the queerest,' cried Ted, taken aback at this disappointing discovery. But he didn't mean to give up yet, and began again.

'What mischief, Dan?'

'Never you mind. Boys shouldn't bother.'

'But I do want to know, awfully, because I'm your pal, and care for you no end. Always did. Come, now, tell me a good yarn. I love scrapes. I'll be mum as an oyster if you don't want it known.'

'Will you?' and Dan looked at him, wondering how the boyish face would change if the truth were suddenly told him.

'I'll swear it on locked fists, if you like. I know it was jolly, and I'm aching to hear.'

'You are as curious as a girl. More than some – Josie and – and Bess never asked a question.'

'They don't care about rows and things; they liked the mine business, heroes, and that sort. So do I, and I'm as proud as Punch over it; but I see by your eyes that there was something else before that, and I'm bound to find out who Blair and Mason are, and who was hit and who ran away, and all the rest of it.'

'What!' cried Dan, in a tone that made Ted jump.

'Well, you used to mutter about 'em in your sleep, and Uncle Laurie wondered. So did I; but don't mind, if you can't remember, or would rather not.'

'What else did I say? Queer, what stuff a man will talk when his wits are gone.'

'That's all I heard; but it seemed interesting, and I just mentioned it, thinking it might refresh your memory a bit,' said Teddy, very politely; for Dan's frown was heavy at that moment.

It cleared off at this reply, and after a look at the boy squirming with suppressed impatience in his chair, Dan made up his mind to amuse him with a game of cross-purposes and half-truths, hoping to quench his curiosity, and so get peace.

'Let me see; Blair was a lad I met in the cars, and Mason a poor fellow who was in a – well, a sort of hospital where I happened to be. Blair ran off to his brothers, and I suppose I might say Mason was hit, because he died there. Does that suit you?'

'No, it doesn't. Why did Blair run? and who hit the other fellow? I'm sure there was a fight somewhere, wasn't there?'

'Yes!

'I guess I know what it was about.'

'The devil, you do! Let's hear you guess. Must be amusing,' said Dan, affecting an ease he did not feel.

Charmed to be allowed to free his mind, Ted at once unfolded the boyish solution of the mystery which he had been cherishing, for he felt that there was one somewhere.

'You needn't say yes, if I guess right and you are under oath to keep silent. I shall know by your face, and never tell. Now see if I'm not right. Out there they have wild doings, and it's my belief you were in some of 'em. I don't mean robbing mails, and Ku-Kluxing, and that sort of thing; but defending the settlers, or hanging some scamp, or even shooting a few, as a fellow must sometimes, in self-defence. Ah, ha! I've hit it, I see. Needn't speak; I know the flash of your eye, and the clench of your fist.' And Ted pranced with satisfaction.

'Drive on, smart boy, and don't lose the trail,' said Dan, finding a curious sense of comfort in some of these random words, and longing, but not daring, to confirm the true ones. He might have confessed the crime, but not the punishment that followed, the sense of its disgrace was still so strong upon him.

'I knew I should get it; can't deceive me long,' began Ted, with such an air of pride Dan could not help a short laugh.

'It's a relief, isn't it, to have it off your mind? Now, just confide in me and it's all safe, unless you've sworn not to tell.'

'I have.'

'Oh, well, then don't;' and Ted's face fell, but he was himself again in a moment and said, with the air of a man of the world, 'It's all right – I understand – honour binds – silence to death, etc. Glad you stood by your mate in the hospital. How many did you kill?'

'Only one.'

'Bad lot, of course?'

'A damned rascal.'

'Well, don't look so fierce; I've no objection. Wouldn't mind popping at some of those bloodthirsty blackguards myself. Had to dodge and keep quiet after it, I suppose.'

'Pretty quiet for a long spell.'

'Got off all right in the end, and headed for your mines and did that jolly brave thing. Now, I call that decidedly interesting and capital. I'm glad to know it; but I won't blab.'

'Mind you don't. Look here. Ted, if you'd killed a man, would it trouble you – a bad one, I mean?'

The lad opened his mouth to say, 'Not a bit,' but checked that answer as if something in Dan's face made him change his mind. 'Well, if it was my duty in war or self-defence, I suppose I shouldn't; but if I'd pitched into him in a rage, I guess I should be very sorry. Shouldn't wonder if he sort of haunted me, and remorse gnawed me as it did Aram and those fellows. *You* don't mind, do you? It was a fair fight, wasn't it?'

'Yes, I was in the right; but I wish I'd been out of it. Women don't see it that way, and look horrified at such things. Makes it hard; but it don't matter.'

'Don't tell 'em; then they can't worry,' said Ted, with the nod of one versed in the management of the sex.

'Don't intend to. Mind you keep your notions to yourself, for some of 'em are wide of the mark. Now you may read if you like;' and there the talk ended; but Ted took great comfort in it, and looked as wise as an owl afterwards.

A few quiet weeks followed, during which Dan chafed at the delay; and when at length word came that his credentials were ready, he was eager to be off, to forget a vain love in hard work, and live for others, since he might not for himself.

So one wild March morning our Sintram rode away, with horse and hound, to face again the enemies who would have conquered him, but for Heaven's help and human pity.

'Ah, me! it does seem as if life was made of partings, and they get harder as we go on,' sighed Mrs Jo, a week later, as she sat in the long parlour at Parnassus one evening, whither the family had gone to welcome the travellers back.

'And meetings too, dear; for here we are, and Nat is on his way at last. Look for the silver lining, as Marmee used to say, and be comforted,' answered Mrs Amy, glad to be at home and find no wolves prowling near her sheepfold.

'I've been so worried lately, I can't help croaking. I wonder what Dan thought at not seeing you again? It was wise; but he would have enjoyed another look at home faces before he went into the wilderness,' said Mrs Jo regretfully.

'Much better so. We left notes and all we could think of that he might need, and slipped away before he came. Bess really seemed relieved; I'm sure I was;' and Mrs Amy smoothed an anxious line out of her white forehead, as she smiled at her daughter, laughing happily among her cousins.

Mrs Jo shook her head as if the silver lining of that cloud was hard to find; but she had no time to croak again, for just then Mr Laurie came in looking well pleased at something.

'A new picture has arrived; face towards the music-room, good people, and tell me how you like it. I call it "Only a fiddler", after Andersen's story. What name will you give it?'

As he spoke he threw open the wide doors, and just beyond they saw a young man standing, with a beaming face, and a violin in his hand. There was no doubt about the name to this picture, and with the cry 'Nat! Nat!' there was a general uprising. But Daisy reached him first, and seemed to have lost her usual composure somewhere on the way, for she clung to him, sobbing with the shock of a surprise and joy too great for her to bear quietly. Everything was settled by that tearful and tender embrace, for, though Mrs Meg speedily detached her daughter, it was only to take her place; while Demi shook Nat's hand with brotherly warmth, and Josie danced round them like Macbeth's three witches in one, chanting in her most tragic tones, 'Chirper thou wast; second violin thou art; first thou shalt be. Hail, all hail!'

This caused a laugh, and made things gay and comfortable at once. Then the usual fire of questions and answers began, to be kept up briskly while the boys admired Nat's blond beard and foreign clothes, the girls his improved appearance – for he was ruddy with good English beef and beer, and fresh with the sea-breezes which had blown him swiftly home – and the older folk rejoiced over his prospects. Of course all wanted to hear him play; and when tongues tired, he gladly did his best for them, surprising the most critical by his progress in music even more than by the energy and self-possession which made a new man of bashful Nat. By and by when the violin – that most human of all instruments – had sung to them the loveliest songs without words, he said, looking about him at these old friends with what Mr

Bhaer called a 'feeling-full' expression of happiness and content, 'Now let me play something that you will all remember though you won't love it as I do;' and standing in the attitude which Ole Bull has immortalised, he played the street melody he gave them the first night he came to Plumfield. They remembered it, and joined in the plaintive chorus, which fitly expressed his own emotions:

'Oh my heart is sad and weary
    Everywhere I roam,
Longing for the old plantation
    And for the old folks at home.'

'Now I feel better,' said Mrs Jo, as they all trooped down the hill soon after. 'Some of our boys are failures, but I think this one is going to be a success, and patient Daisy a happy girl at last. Nat is your work, Fritz, and I congratulate you heartily.'

'Ach, we can but sow the seed and trust that it falls on good ground. I planted, perhaps, but you watched that the fowls of the air did not devour it, and brother Laurie watered generously; so we will share the harvest among us, and be glad even for a small one, heart's-dearest.'

'I thought the seed had fallen on very stony ground with my poor Dan; but I shall not be surprised if he surpasses all the rest in the real success of life, since there is more rejoicing over one repentant sinner than many saints,' answered Mrs Jo, still clinging fast to her black sheep although a whole flock of white ones trotted happily before her.

It is a strong temptation to the weary historian to close the present tale with an earthquake which should engulf Plumfield and its environs so deeply in the bowels of the earth that no youthful Schliemann could ever find a vestige of it. But as that somewhat melodramatic conclusion might shock my gentle readers, I will refrain, and forestall the usual question, 'How did they end?' by briefly stating that all the marriages turned out well. The boys prospered in their various callings; so did the girls, for Bess and Josie won honours in their artistic careers, and in the course of time found worthy mates. Nan remained a busy, cheerful, in-dependent spinster, and dedicated her life to her suffering sisters and their children, in which true woman's work she found abiding happiness. Dan never married, but lived, bravely and usefully, among his chosen people till he was shot defending them, and at last lay quietly asleep in the green wilderness he loved so well, with a lock of golden hair upon his breast, and a smile on his face which seemed to say that Aslauga's Knight had fought his last fight and was at peace. Stuffy became an alderman, and died suddenly of apoplexy after a public dinner. Dolly was a society man of mark till he lost his money, when he found congenial employment in a fashionable tailoring establishment. Demi became a partner, and lived to see his name above the door, and Rob was a professor at Laurence College; but Teddy eclipsed them all by becoming an eloquent and famous clergyman, to the great delight of his astonished mother. And now, having endeavoured to suit everyone by many weddings, few deaths, and as much prosperity as the eternal fitness of things will permit, let the music stop, the lights die out, and the curtain fall for ever on the March family.